FOOTSTEPS IN THE DARK

AN M/M MYSTERY ROMANCE ANTHOLOGY

THE SNICK OF A LOCK.

THE SQUEAK OF DOOR HINGES.

THE CREAK OF A FLOORBOARD.

ARE THOSE APPROACHING STEPS THAT OF A LOVER...

OR AN ENEMY?

Entrée to Murder. After a steady diet of big city trouble, Chef Drew Allison moved to the island town of Orca's Slough to get a taste of life in the slow lane. But hometown hospitality goes stale when he finds a dead body in the basement of his own Eelgrass Café.

Twelve Seconds. A mysterious phone call, a missing executive, and an exploding rocket throw space reporter Justin Harris and Air Force Special Agent Greg Marcotte into an investigation that will change their lives...if it doesn't kill them first.

Reality Bites. Detective Cabot Decker is called to the set of hot-shot TV producer Jax Thornburn's reality-TV show after a contestant is mauled to death by a tiger. Is someone trying to ax Jax's career—or Jax himself?

Blind Man's Buff. A game of Capture the Flag turns deadly inside an abandoned shopping mall when Tommy and Jonah stumble into a homicidal maniac's hunting grounds.

A Country for Old Men. Inspector Calum Macleod has returned to the Western Isles of Scotland to bury a part of himself he can't accept. But the island has old secrets of its own. When a murderer strikes, Calum finds his past can't be so easily escaped.

Pepper the Crime Lab. When Lonnie Boudreaux's neighbor is murdered, he must foster the man's dog, befriend a mysterious former cop, and stop the killer—or else!

Lights, Camera, Murder. NY PI Rory Byrne must go undercover on the set of the ground-breaking historical drama *The Bowery* to recover a stolen script—a job complicated by Rory's unexpected attraction to handsome, talented, and out-and-proud actor Marion Roosevelt.

Stranger in the House. Miles Tuesday's memories of Montreal are happy ones, but now that he has inherited the mansion at 13 Place Braeside, everything feels different. Was Madame Martel's fatal fall really an accident?

Authors L.B. Gregg, Nicole Kimberling, Josh Lanyon, Dal Maclean, Z.A. Maxfield, Meg Perry, C.S. Poe, and S.C. Wynne join forces for *Footsteps in the Dark*, eight sexy and suspenseful novellas of Male/Male Mystery and Romance

FOOTSTEPS IN THE DARK

AN M/M MYSTERY ROMANCE ANTHOLOGY

VELLICHOR BOOKS

An imprint of JustJoshin Publishing, Inc.

FOOTSTEPS IN THE DARK: An M/M Mystery Romance Anthology

May 2019

Copyright (c) 2019 by Josh Lanyon

Cover by Reese Dante reesedante.com

Book design by Kevin Burton Smith

Edited by Keren Reed

Copyedited by Dianne Thies

All rights reserved

ISBN: 978-1-945802-84-3

Published in the United States of America

JustJoshin Publishing, Inc.

3053 Rancho Vista Blvd.

Suite 116

Palmdale, CA 93551

www.joshlanyon.com

This is a work of fiction. Any resemblance to persons living or dead is entirely coincidental.

FOOTSTEPS IN THE DARK

AN M/M MYSTERY ROMANCE ANTHOLOGY

INTRODUCTION

INTRODUCTION

Motive.

For me, the most interesting aspect of any mystery or crime story is the Why? What makes people do the things they do? Why are some people driven to commit crimes? Why are some people committed to solving them?

And why do we fall in love with the people we do?

It's the need to explore that element of unpredictability in human interaction that compels me to write—and guides my reading choices. My favorite M/M stories are those that blend mystery and romance in equal measures, and when I turn that last page I want to be convinced that our sleuth has the right man in handcuffs. On or off the job.

The eight stories in this anthology deliver on the promise to explore that why and wherefore with plenty of spine-tingling mystery and suspense as well as healthy dollops of sweet and spicy romance. But what I love even more about Footsteps in the Dark is the variety and unity of this collection.

Here you'll find private eyes, police detectives, and unlucky bystanders rubbing shoulders (and other body parts) with artists, actors, chefs, journalists, and other unlucky bystanders. You'll discover crimes of cold-blooded calculation and crimes of pure and unadulterated crazy. Three stories—Nicole Kimberling's clever culinary cozy "Entrée to Murder," S.C. Wynne's smart and sassy take on Hollywood vs. Real Life in "Reality Bites," and Meg Perry's adroit and original police procedural "Twelve Seconds"—kick off brand new series.

The authors gathered between these pages offer a variety of scenes and settings. Dal Maclean's haunting "A Country for Old Men" is set in the Outer Hebrides of Scotland. Montreal, Canada is the backdrop for my mysterious morsel "Stranger in the House." L.B. Gregg's heart-stopping "Blind Man's Buff" takes place in an abandoned mall in Anywhere USA.

We have old love and we have new. An ailing chef gets a second chance at love in Z.A. Maxfield's "Pepper the Crime Lab," and it's very nearly love at first sight for an idiosyncratic private detective in "Lights. Camera. Murder." by C.S. Poe.

In short, whatever your motive in picking up this anthology, I feel sure you'll find something here to amuse, entertain, and maybe even enlighten.

—Josh Lanyon

ENTRÉE TO MURDER

BY NICOLE KIMBERLING

After a steady diet of big city trouble, Chef Drew Allison moved to the island town of Orca's Slough to get a taste of life in the slow lane. But hometown hospitality goes stale when he finds a dead body in the basement of his own Eelgrass Café.

CHAPTER ONE

When I saw the crumpled tower of waxed corrugated boxes filled with sweating tomatoes and limp romaine slumped on the back stair at eleven a.m., I knew it would be another rough lunch service at the Eelgrass Bistro.

Doubtless, if I were to go around to the front of the building, I would find Evelyn, my favorite octogenarian, peering through the window, wondering what fate had befallen my business partner, Samantha, that would cause her to fail to open our restaurant.

That's the problem with being unreliable around older people—they're at a time in life when any failure to appear means the absentee is most likely deceased. Or if not actually dead, the no-show could be lying somewhere injured and alone.

I needed to get in there to make sure Evelyn didn't do anything rash. Already once this month she'd dialed 911 after she'd spied Sam slumped over in the kitchen. In reality, Sam had just spent the night partying and then fallen asleep on a sack of potatoes in the back.

I sidled past the abandoned produce order to let myself in the back door of the Eelgrass Bistro, only to find it had been unlocked all night. Again.

Perfect.

With the lights off, the restaurant became a long tunnel leading from the service entry where I stood to the ornate doors and large windows up front.

Our restaurant sat mid-block in a row of Victorian brick buildings in the historic heart of downtown Orca's Slough, a six-block town on Camas Island in the middle of Puget Sound. The building's sandstone facade formed an almost perfect square: twenty feet high and twenty feet wide and stretched back nearly one hundred feet from sidewalk to alley—though the turn-of-the-century basement stretched much farther underground.

I squinted through the gloom of the kitchen and dining room to see Evelyn pressing her cupped hands against the plate-glass window to peer inside. Despite being in her mid-eighties, her loose-fitting jeans and sweat-shirt lent her the look of a spindly kid. Her shock of short gray hair bristled atop her head like a raccoon skin cap. I hurried through the kitchen, flipped on the lights, and waved at her. I made it a big, theatrical, flagging-down-a-passing-ship motion so that she could see me through the haze of the cataracts she regularly claimed kept her from reading various CLOSED signs and KEEP OUT postings around town.

She waved back and went to stand in front of the door, waiting, like a cranky old cat, to be let inside and fed.

As I sidestepped the concrete stairs leading into the basement, my eyes adjusted to the gloom.

The Eelgrass was a wreck. Floors unswept, the steel prep tables in the kitchen strewn with debris. Dank, fetid water stood in the three-compartment sink. Empty, unwashed beer glasses on every surface. Party detritus.

I wondered if Sam had left any money in the till or if that too had fallen victim to poor impulse control.

I took a breath.

Getting angry would do me no good. First, there was no one here to be angry with, and second, mentally raging at Sam would only force a confrontation that would end in tears. Her remorseful tears. And I had no defense against that kind of emotional blackmail.

I could do nothing but give myself up to the ridiculousness of this day and try to enjoy it like some kind of tragicomedy I was watching from afar.

How much longer could my pride take it? I didn't know. For as long as I could turn my anger at her inward to fester as shame for consenting to enter this business venture at all? Six months, perhaps? Assuming I had enough nostalgia to sustain me.

Sam and I hadn't always been this way. Years ago I had adored her freewheeling spirit and sincerity. Back then, I and my then-boyfriend had hung out with her and her then-husband. Together we'd manned a high-end hipster restaurant in Seattle and spent three boozy years feeling impressed with ourselves and the newness of being adults.

But that had been before her husband started having his ongoing series of affairs and all of Sam's enthusiasm had devolved into personal makeovers and increasingly potent bouts of self-medication. My own private life had mirrored Sam's, with my boyfriend declaring that he needed the support of a less opinionated lover to truly feel appreciated. By that time, the restaurant started losing money, and my paychecks began to bounce like pinballs ricocheting off every possible overdraft fee imaginable.

So when Sam announced that she'd inherited a restaurant space from a distant cousin, I agreed to pull up stakes, empty what was left of my bank account, and venture into a partnership with her far from Seattle.

Well, not that far. Twenty-five miles and a ferry ride. But still: I'd left town. That was the important thing.

We'd been determined to put the bad times behind us.

Now the dining room at the Eelgrass looked like old times: the tables and chairs stood huddled together in one corner as though ordered to stand aside to make floor space for an impromptu after-hours dance party, which is most likely exactly what had happened.

Probably half the people in the local restaurant industry had been here getting loaded last night.

I walked behind the bar, hoping to find nothing alarming, and stopped dead in my tracks.

Lying prone and snoring on the floor was the seventeen-year-old dishwasher, Lionel.

He was half-Black and half-Korean and had yet to decide if he wanted to talk like a cartoon character or a member of N.W.A. Most of the time he just sounded like a dork. But he was a smart dork and a quick learner.

I nudged Lionel with my toe. "Time to wake up, kid."

Lionel lifted his face to squint at me. His cheek was marked with a hexagonal impression from the rubber fatigue mat he'd spent the night on. He had a slim build—more or less a replica of his Asian mother's. His skin was the color of dark mahogany. The combination ensured that no member of either race ever immediately recognized him as one of their own, which had caused Lionel to develop the bad habit of making gratuitously racist comments that, when challenged, allowed him to clarify his identity.

"Quit kicking me, chief," he mumbled.

"Quit sleeping on the job, and I will," I said. "Now get up and open the door. Evelyn wants her breakfast."

"Why can't you let her in?"

"'Cause I told *you* to. Why the hell are you sleeping here anyway?"

"Sam said I could sleep here since I had to open in four hours." He pushed himself up to all fours, then rose, hunched and wobbly as if this was his first-ever attempt at walking on two feet.

"You all were here till six a.m.?"

Lionel nodded.

"If you're going to puke, do it in the trash can. Not the sink," I advised.

"Jeez, chief, I'm sick—not an idiot."

It's weird how if someone calls you something enough, you can start acting like it's true. I suppose that's the magic of terms like *champ* or *Dad*. Once Lionel started calling me *chief*, I started feeling invested in his professional development. I began teaching him what I knew about being a cook. It also triggered in me a steady trickle of unsolicited guidance that made me sound and feel way older than thirty-one.

"You want to play with the grown-ups, you've got to get up and work like one," I said. Then, glancing at his hangdog expression, I added, "If you make yourself useful to me, I'll fix you an omelette."

"Okay." Lionel dragged himself to the front door, flipped the lock, and turned the sign to OPEN. Evelyn walked in immediately, heading toward her usual seat at the end of the bar.

I managed to find a towel and wipe down her place before she got onto the sleek steel barstool. She took her *Wall Street Journal* out of a plastic grocery bag and laid it out next to her place.

"I'm sorry to be opening late," I said. "Sam had an emergency."

"What was Lionel doing on the floor back there?" Evelyn asked.

"He was looking for something," I ad-libbed.

"He looks like he's drunk."

"I wouldn't know anything about that." I met her watery blue eyes. I knew she didn't believe me, but I wasn't prepared to admit to knowledge of any of the county statutes concerning alcohol that had been broken the previous night. "Anyway, coffee isn't brewing yet, but can I get you an espresso?"

Evelyn wrinkled her nose. "I don't need anything fancy."

"It'll take twenty minutes for the coffee pour-over to heat up."

"I can wait." Evelyn unfurled her paper and put on her reading glasses.

"The espresso would be on the house," I said.

"I said,"—she paused meaningfully and skewered me with a look—"that I can wait."

Behind her, I saw Lionel roll his eyes as he arranged the tables and chairs into their usual order.

"So what would you like for breakfast today?" I asked Evelyn. "One egg and one piece of toast?"

The Eelgrass didn't serve breakfast, but that didn't stop Evelyn from ordering it anyway.

"One piece of bacon today too. Crispy." She spoke without glancing up.

"Splurging on the cholesterol count, huh? Is it your birthday?"

"People my age don't celebrate birthdays anymore," Evelyn informed me. "I just feel like eating bacon."

"Can I tempt you into a slice of tomato? I can brûlée some sugar onto it." As far as I knew, Evelyn rarely ate any sort of vegetable except asparagus.

"I suppose." I saw a hint of a smile at the corner of her mouth. "So long as you don't charge me an arm and a leg for it."

Behind me, the coffeepot began to gurgle. I found some clean flatware for Evelyn and was just setting it down when I heard a colossal *bang* from the basement.

"What the hell—"

"Sounds like a pressure cooker exploding." Evelyn had worked in the restaurant industry for nearly fifty years and had apparently endured every possible form of catastrophe. "That happened once at a place I worked in New Orleans. Blew a hole right through the roof."

"I better check it out." I headed into the kitchen. To my surprise, Lionel followed me and cut me off right as I reached the concrete steps leading into the musty underground.

"I can go down there for you." His eyes darted from side to side, showing incipient panic. "Probably some junk way in the back just fell over."

It wasn't impossible that a cache of abandoned rubbish had collapsed somewhere in the basement. The space was cavernous and poorly lit. Dug in the mid-eighteen hundreds, it had once been a part of a much larger network that catacombed the entire downtown. Supposedly, gold miners and bootleggers had left a variety of mementos behind in the numerous tunnels beneath the city—though moldering rat traps and empty oilcans made up the bulk of what I'd encountered.

"Why don't you want me down here?" I took the steps down two at a time, ducking as I entered the low space. Something wasn't right about the air. A new tang seeped into the normally musty smell.

"It's nothing really bad—"

"Why does it smell like putrid garlic?"

I peered down into the darkness. A single bare bulb illuminated a few feet—enough for me to make out the five shelves of dry storage we used for Eelgrass. But beyond that, the light faded away. I knew from experience that after another ten feet, the poured concrete of the floor gave way to fine, silty dirt.

"You know how I was talking about how I wanted to reconnect with my Korean roots?" Lionel came hot on my heels, practically running into my back.

"Yes." I vaguely recollected that Lionel's grandmother had refused to teach him to cook because "his wife would take care of that for him," while his busy single mother possessed neither the time nor the inclination. While Lionel worked up the courage to tell me the rest of his story, I took a quick inventory of the dry goods on the shelves. Aside from a can of garbanzo beans standing among the canned tomatoes, all appeared in order.

"I decided to teach myself how to make traditional pickles," Lionel confessed. "And Dorian said the basement would be the perfect place to ferment them, so long as I didn't mess with any of the stuff he stashed down there."

The kind of "stuff" our sleazy, drug-dealing bartender Dorian might be hiding in my business alarmed me far more than any pickle Lionel could concoct or even the threat of a tunnel-collapse in the basement.

Just outside the circle of light, close to the edge of the concrete, a small red light blinked. And it seemed to me that the darkness around the blinking light was denser and more solid than the deep gloom surrounding it.

"And you think that noise was pickles?" I asked.

What was that blinking light anyway? I took a step closer. The pungent smell of garlic, fish, and fermentation gone foul did seem to be coming from the far wall.

"I think my kimchee blew up. I'll clean it up, I swear."

That would explain the bang and the stink. Fermentation in the wrong hands could produce all the wrong gasses and literally weaponize cabbage. That still didn't explain the blinking light, nor the dark shape behind it.

Sam kept a flashlight down here, but the batteries had run down around New Year. I pulled out my phone and approached by the harsh blue-white light of the flashlight app.

Lionel continued, "I used the space at the back of the cellar to mature my first batch. But I don't know... Maybe it got too warm?"

"Possibly." I knelt down. The blinking light turned out to be the message alert on an old slider-style cell phone. It lay in the dirt next to a hand. The hand emerged from the sleeve of a white-and-red hoodie that clothed the body of a man.

"What are you looking—" Lionel stopped speaking and froze.

I'm not sure what makes it so obvious at only a glance that a person is dead. There's the flat, unblinking eye, sure. But also the blood streaking from multiple stab wounds helps fix the idea that the man one is eyeballing has shuffled off this mortal coil.

For a second, I could not move or even breathe. Everything stopped, including my ability to feel—like someone flipped a giant toggle switch shutting down all nonessential functions.

Was this shock?

It occurred to me then that the hoodie wasn't red and white at all— just white and stained with red—and that it belonged to my least favorite employee: Dorian Gamble.

And the knife still jutting from his back belonged to me.

CHAPTER TWO

Orca's Slough boasted a sheriff and two deputies, all named Mackenzie. The deputy who arrived at the Eelgrass was a fit young bison known as Big Mac. Evelyn said he'd been given the nickname because he held the record for the biggest baby ever born on the island. Even among the Mackenzie clan (widely rumored to be half Bigfoot) Big Mac's brutal muscularity stood out. He had thighs like tree trunks (which he displayed year-round in shorts) and biceps big as grapefruits.

I worked out when I had the free time, but compared to Big Mac I felt scrawny and sallow. My blond hair probably looked stringy and unkempt; it was hard to care about manscaping while witnessing my business fall apart.

I was pleased to note that I was just slightly taller than him.

And, I suspected, a whole lot smarter. Big Mac spoke in a slow, quiet way that gave the impression he might have repeated third grade a couple of times.

He ate dinner at the Eelgrass every Wednesday, always ordering the special, no matter what. He had dark hair, heavy brows, and the kind of perma-stubble that indicated his capacity to grow a prize-winning beard if only the sheriff's department had allowed it.

During the tourist season, he often manned the police kiosk at the ferry terminal and, as far as I could tell, spent most of his on-duty hours giving driving directions to the island's three hot-springs resorts.

After he had a look at Dorian, he returned to the dining room and joined me at the bar. Lionel sat at a table in the corner, slumped over and mumbling into his phone, most likely to his mother, who worked as a nurse at the local medical center.

Evelyn had been exiled to the sidewalk but continued to lurk, monitoring the interactions inside with a fierce, stricken expression.

Big Mac seemed to make a point of learning the name of every single person living in Orca's Slough, so it didn't surprise me when he remembered mine.

"So, Mr. Allison, quite the smell down there."

"That's the kimchee, I think." At least I hoped so.

"And that was what made you look in the basement?" He glanced at his notebook, probably checking to make sure I'd kept my story straight.

"No, we heard a bang, which we think was the crock exploding," I said.

"Mr. Allison, can you tell me when was the last time you saw Mr. Gamble alive?"

"Just Drew is fine," I said.

"Okay, Drew, when did you last see Mr. Gamble?"

"I worked with him the day before yesterday—Wednesday. You would have seen him."

Big Mac nodded and looked slowly up from his cop notebook. What color were his eyes anyway? Blue? Green? It was hard to tell.

"You know, that steamer-clam special was so good. Where did you get the idea for it?"

"It's a classic dish. Moules marinière," I spluttered.

"But you made it original." Big Mac spoke as if savoring the clams once more in his memory. "Don't suppose you can tell me how, though. Secret recipe."

"Actually, legally I'm required to disclose all the ingredients in anything I serve. And I have to have all the processes vetted by the health department, so it's only the proportions of a recipe that could ever be secret."

"That I did not know," Big Mac said.

"I think the whole secret-recipe thing is an advertising ploy."

"Oh, I don't know. Evelyn out there has kept the recipes for her preserves secret since she won her first ribbon at the fair. And she's been the Island County Pickle Queen for as long as anybody can remember."

Despite the grim circumstances, the words *pickle queen* brought a smirk to my face. So sue me. I'm juvenile.

Big Mac smiled back—an action that dramatically improved the quality of his face. "So what's the secret to your clams, then?"

"Lemongrass-infused vodka," I said.

"See, I didn't even know that existed."

"It's house-made here by Dorian. He's very oriented toward signature cocktails. Or he was…"

"Did you speak with Mr. Gamble or see him between Wednesday and now?" Big Mac asked.

The swift return to the subject of murder startled me. How easily this cop had lulled me into complacency with his soft, complimentary voice.

"Dorian and I haven't really been on speaking terms for a while."

"Why is that?" Big Mac asked.

"I didn't think he was a good influence on Sam."

"Really? How so?"

Some lingering vestige of loyalty prevented me from mentioning that Dorian's alternative revenue stream was generated through sales of cocaine, largely to other members of the restaurant industry, so I just said, "He encouraged her to make poor financial decisions."

"Such as?"

Big Mac held my gaze for a long moment, and I fought not to look away before he did.

"Ordering too much of expensive ingredients he wanted for his infusions. A lot ended up going bad before he got around to making anything. And half of what he did make was pretentious and terrible. Nobody is going to pay eighteen dollars to drink salmon-infused vodka. Nobody."

Big Mac nodded.

"So to recap your previous statement, only Mr. Fogle was in the building when you arrived, and he was unconscious."

It took me a minute to register who he was talking about. "You mean Lionel? Yes."

"And can you think of any reason why Lionel—or anyone—would feel like they needed to kill Mr. Gamble?"

"I haven't heard of anyone specifically out to get him. Especially not Lionel. He was always asking Dorian for advice about women."

"I've heard that Mr. Gamble was quite the ladies' man and that he could be insistent."

I almost asked where he'd heard that, but Evelyn had frequently made her opinion of Dorian's womanizing known.

"I've never known him to be the kind of person you'd have to use lethal force to escape, if that's what you mean," I said, offended on Dorian's behalf. Then again, now that the kernel of doubt had been sown, I began to wonder.

It wasn't like Dorian led a blameless life in any respect. Had he tried to force himself on some girl at the party, and she or her boyfriend had decided to take him out?

It didn't seem his style, though. He dealt coke, and he was smarmy, but a lot of women seemed to find him attractive and charming. On a couple of occasions I'd even overheard him complain about so many female clients pulling him into their beds that he was "shooting dust." Clearly, he wasn't hurting for action.

"Do you know what Mr. Gamble was doing here last night?"

"I don't know, but obviously, there was a party."

"You didn't attend?"

"No, I wasn't invited." Saying that somehow stung even after discovering a body. "I was at my apartment all night."

"Were you with anyone?" Big Mac had an expression on his face that told me he already had his own theory on my relationship status, probably based on my argumentative personality.

"No one. I live alone."

Big Mac made a special note of this. I watched him underline the word *alone*.

"And besides you and your business partner, who has a key to the building?"

"I have no idea," I said, shrugging.

"What about Lionel?"

We both turned our attention to the dishwasher. Lionel looked up in wide-eyed alarm. I hoped that Big Mac hadn't immediately decided that Lionel was guilty because he'd been passed out in the same building. Or because he was Black.

"No. Lionel doesn't have a key, and he didn't do this."

"You know that for a fact?"

"Listen." I lowered my voice. "Lionel's the kind of kid who can't bring himself to lie about setting up a secret pickle crock. And even if he did somehow get caught up in something like this, he would have called me and his mom right away to ask what to do with the body."

Only after I'd spoken did I realize I shouldn't have even made the joke. Big Mac's lips moved, but I cut him off. "Plus Lionel didn't have any blood on him, which…he would have."

"And he didn't have a key." Big Mac paused to write something in his notebook. Belatedly I recalled that this had started with who had keys to the restaurant.

Sam and I.

"Who did or didn't have a key wouldn't matter," I said, "because the back door was unlocked when I arrived this morning."

Big Mac's smile faded, and he paused, seeming reluctant to continue before saying, "What can you tell me about the knife found in Mr. Gamble's body?"

"It's mine." There was no point in denying it. That would just make me look guilty. "But I don't know how it got downstairs. I keep it in my knife case, and I keep that locked in the office when I'm not here."

Big Mac made another note in his book, then asked, "Would you mind if I had a look at your hands?"

I did mind, but I silently held them out anyway, palms down. Big Mac reached out and caught hold of my fingers in a professional manner, firm yet gentle, like a doctor might. He took some time scrutinizing them, as if memorizing every scar, before turning them palm up.

"What's this here?" he pointed to a mark on my wrist.

"A grease burn." I squirmed a little, embarrassed to still be getting amateur injuries at my age.

Big Mac held my hands for about thirty seconds longer, then released me.

"I think that's all for now. Here's my card. Text me anytime." He stood and turned toward Lionel.

The thought of Lionel being interrogated scared me. I could easily picture him getting frustrated and saying something like, "Fine, okay, I did it. Will you just shut up now?" as if he were arguing about dirty laundry with his mom. But Big Mac only said that they would wait till Lionel's mother arrived to have their conversation.

I relaxed enough to take a paper cup of coffee out to Evelyn in lieu of breakfast.

As I stepped outside the front door, the ambulance (Orca's Slough only had one) was just pulling up.

Evelyn stopped eyeballing the interior proceedings long enough to ask, "Dorian...is he really dead?"

In a town so small, all locals knew each other. And I vaguely recalled a waitress remarking that Dorian and Evelyn were related.

"Yeah," I replied, at a loss.

We stood together watching the medics. Evelyn sniffed and then took a swig of her coffee. The town's second Deputy Mackenzie arrived: a sleepy, doughier version of Big Mac.

Clerks and patrons from the surrounding businesses gathered outside, staring at the scene. Two trim middle-aged women from the yoga studio across the street edged toward the restaurant. Then they caught sight of Troy Lindgren as he scowled from the doorway of his high-end sportswear shop.

Fit and fortyish, Troy was Sam's only non-deceased cousin and the owner of the beautifully restored historic building that abutted Eelgrass Bistro. Local fishermen called him a rich snob, but he exemplified the conservative taste that many yacht-owning tourists appreciated. I had never seen him without cuff links and a tie.

I missed most of what passed between the three of them, except the mention of Sam's name. Troy shook his head.

"Probably just another grease fire," he told them, then offered me a tight, forced smile before retreating into his shop.

"Prick," Evelyn muttered. She glanced to me. "Where is Samantha, anyway? She wasn't down there too?"

"No!" Just the suggestion rattled me. Frustrated as I was, I would never have wanted to see her like that. "She's probably just passed out somewhere. I'm going to try and find her."

Pacing the sidewalk, I tried Sam's number and got no reply.

The slanting autumn sun shone down on the fallen maple leaves that carpeted the sidewalk. I kicked at them, stirring them up as I went. The numb fog of shock began to wear thin enough that I started to feel. Not horror over seeing Dorian dead—that remained a void in my consciousness, still too terrible to be experienced—but worry about Sam's safety.

Her various social-media feeds showed no activity after she'd put up a bleary selfie captioned: "happy after a night with good friends" at four a.m. In the photo, she wore a silver spaghetti-strap tank top and a lot of red lipstick. She'd dyed her hair again and now sported a black bob with a bright-red streak. In the background I could see Lionel and Sam's plump, pink-haired friend Danielle trying to push their way into the frame.

So now I knew at least one other person who had been present, but a text to Danielle yielded no response either.

I sat down on the sky-blue powder-coat sidewalk bench across the street from the Eelgrass and stared hard at my phone. It had 213 contacts in it. I started going down the list, texting everyone I knew to see if anybody could tell me Sam's location.

Sixteen people replied with more or less the same story—they had been at the party but left before it was over.

Time passed. The sheriff arrived, spoke with the doughy deputy through the window of his police car, and then drove away. More onlookers gathered to gawk at the spectacle.

"Andrew, where is Samantha?" I glanced up to see Troy frowning down at me. "They're saying there's a dead body in her basement. Dorian Gamble."

"I don't know if I can talk about it," I replied. "You'll have to ask Big Mac."

Troy gave me a quizzical once-over.

"You look terrible," he said.

"Well, I'm having kind of a challenging day, Troy."

He didn't seem to know what to say to that and so made a little show of adjusting his jacket. At last he said, "I don't know who's going to eat there now."

Like I didn't have enough to worry about.

"You'll probably have to sell up," he continued.

I felt sure Troy would have gone on to give me some lowball offer, but thankfully the doughy Deputy Mackenzie called Troy over. Muttering his disbelief that any of this terrible mess could have anything to do with him, Troy left me.

Time to get provocative.

I texted Sam: I found Dorian's dead body in the cellar about an hour ago.

Within ten minutes the woman herself sat down on the bench next to me.

She smelled like men's soap, wore an oversize blue hoodie that didn't belong to her, and sported dark sunglasses despite the autumn day's gloom. Behind her stood a burly, handsome surfer-looking guy. Maybe Sam's pickup from the night before? He looked kind of young for her, but I had enough to worry about at this moment without also bothering to card Sam's one-night stand.

Leaning close to me, Sam whispered, "Is this for real?"

"Yes," I said. "For extra real."

Sam stared at me in total shock, mouth agape, color draining from her already pasty cheeks. Her lip quivered as she whispered, "What happened? Did he OD?"

Sam's date shrugged like he thought the question was addressed to him.

I shook my head, and seeing tears forming in her eyes, the icy grip of shock receded. My throat tightened. Dorian hadn't always been the best person, but we'd all worked together for nearly two years. It hadn't all been bad times.

"He was stabbed." I could barely voice my response.

"Oh Jesus." Sam threw her arms around me in a tight hug.

Out of reflex, I returned her embrace. This attracted the attention of Evelyn, who leaned in through the door of Eelgrass and called something to Big Mac.

Sam's date just stood there with his hands in his pockets, looking bored. Then he asked, "Are you guys all right?"

"Look, we're obviously not all right," I snapped. "Who are you anyway?"

"That's Freddy." Sam dragged the back of her hand across her nose.

"I prefer Alfred," the date said.

Sam rolled her eyes. "He's Danielle's brother."

I took a moment to process this, recollecting Danielle's jokes about her dorky kid brother and his recent high-school graduation. "You hooked up with Danielle's little brother?"

"Don't judge me," Sam mumbled.

"Never mind. Listen," I said. "The cops want to speak with you."

As if on cue, Big Mac emerged from the front door of the Eelgrass Bistro and jogged across the street calling, "Ms. Eider?"

"That's me." Sam pushed herself up to her feet and went to meet him.

I found myself sitting awkwardly alone with Alfred.

"It's crazy that Dorian is dead," Alfred finally said. "We were just partying together last night. I mean, we could have been still drinking when he was lying down there." Alfred's expression turned bleak and sick.

It occurred to me then that I didn't have to sit waiting for the cops to tell me what happened at the party. I could ask this guy and know. Or at least know his version.

"Why do you think he was down there bleeding when you were all still drinking?" I asked.

"Because me and Sam were the last people to leave. I mean, except for Lionel, but he was already passed out on the floor. I asked Sam if we should move him or bring him back with us, but she seemed to think he'd be okay." Alfred shrugged. "I didn't fight too hard because she was already touching me a lot, you know, so…"

"Gotcha. When was the last time you saw Dorian?"

Alfred paused, head and shoulders drawn back in suspicion. "Why are you asking this?"

"Because that's my restaurant too, and I want to know what happened in it," I said, flushing, unable now to keep the anger out of my voice.

"Oh, right." Alfred relaxed again and sat down next to me. "Well, I'll tell you what I can, but I was pretty drunk the whole time."

"That's okay; just do your best."

"I just came into town on the eight o'clock ferry. Danielle came to pick me up, and then we went to meet Sam and Dorian at the Anchor for drinks. At first it was just the four of us. Then some other girls joined us—about six of them, I can't remember all their names, but Dorian knew them. After that some guys from the kayak shop showed up."

"Naturally."

"And then there were maybe twenty of us, and the girls all decided they wanted to go dancing, except there was nowhere to dance 'cause it was Thursday."

"So the Eelgrass dining room was the next logical step," I said. "How did Lionel end up with you guys?"

"Sam saw him walking home alone and invited him." Alfred trailed off, staring into space.

"Anyway, after you got to the Eelgrass?"

"Right, right. Dorian went behind the bar to line up the drinks, and a couple of the girls from the fish-and-chips place went back to the kitchen to make something to eat. The girls came back to get Sam because they couldn't find any knives, and Sam went to the office and brought a couple out for them. Nice ones."

The surge of anger that burst red behind my eyes was only partially mitigated by the tiny pleasure of solving the mystery of how my knife got out of the office.

I must have flushed because Alfred again asked, "Are you all right, man? Your neck veins just popped up."

"I'm fine. I just don't like it when other people lend out my things."

"Oh, I hear that." Alfred gave a nod. "Sam loaned my lighter to Dorian, and that's the last I saw of it. It's a Zippo too, monogrammed. Did you see it there? When you found him?"

"It's not like I went through his pockets."

"Right. And there were a lot of people going in and out the back door to smoke, so I guess he could have loaned it to anybody."

"Why didn't you just smoke out front by the ashtray?"

"We couldn't. That big cop was sitting in his patrol car down the way. Speaking of smoking, though"—Alfred pulled a joint out of his pocket—"do you have a lighter I can borrow?"

CHAPTER THREE

Orca's Slough's lone diner, the Prospector, sat about four blocks from the Eelgrass physically but resided in another dimension temporally.

It wasn't old-fashioned so much as old. The late-seventies decor did not qualify as retro, as it had genuinely been installed forty years prior. Duct-tape repairs striped the vinyl booth seats silver and blue.

It served breakfast all day and hard liquor well into the night, and it was where Big Mac went after leaving the Eelgrass.

When I walked through the door, the waitress gave me a nervous, shifty look, which told me she knew who I was and what had happened.

"Excuse me, Deputy." I rushed up behind him before he sat down at the bar. "Can I speak with you?"

"Sure thing. But please, call me Mac." He turned from the bar with clear reluctance and gestured to a booth. He took off his mirror shades and his hat and raked his fingers through his hair, which improved his visual aesthetic. If I could somehow have removed the cop badge from my field of vision, he might have even been attractive.

The waitress automatically brought Mac coffee with cream and gave me an even shiftier look than before. I ordered two fried eggs and a Bloody Mary.

"Come here a lot?" I asked.

"Closest thing to a donut shop in town." He shrugged out of his jacket before taking a seat opposite me. Once again he'd defaulted to that deceptively quiet manner of talking. He took a drink of his coffee, stirred in a spoon of sugar, then tasted it again, all with agonizing slowness.

"Don't you want to know what I have to say?" I asked, unable to wait any longer.

Mac turned his full attention to me. A hint of a smile creased his cheek.

"I'm sorry. I was just getting comfortable. I've been on duty since six this morning. Please go ahead and tell me whatever it is." He retrieved his notebook from the pocket of his jacket. His pen looked small in his hand and somewhat awkward. The face of his watch also seemed like it had been owned by a smaller guy—his grandfather maybe?—and I could just see the tip of a thick scar protruding from his right shirtsleeve just above his elbow.

I related my conversation with Alfred. Mac listened, nodding occasionally and jotting down notes.

"Alfred Tomkins," Big Mac clarified.

"Yeah, Danielle Tomkins' brother."

"He specifically told you that Dorian had taken his monogrammed Zippo lighter?"

"He didn't go out of his way to tell me. Just mentioned it in passing." Mac must have found the lighter. Maybe he'd hoped it would be the clue that busted the case open. "When I found out he had been at the party, I asked him if he knew what had happened to Dorian."

"What time did this conversation take place?"

"Right after I finished talking to you. Two o'clock maybe."

"I'm curious why you waited until five p.m. to contact me."

"What do you mean?"

"You had my number, you could have easily texted me right then, and I could have spoken to Alfred myself." Mac sat back to allow the waitress to set a plate containing a pretty good-looking Rueben sandwich down in front of him. She delivered my food without making eye contact.

"You seemed busy with the investigation, and I didn't want to interrupt you. Plus I didn't want to seem weird." I slurped my Bloody Mary.

"Weird in what way?"

"Because I was asking people about the murder. Isn't that one of the giveaways of a guilty person—inserting yourself into the investigation?"

"That does sometimes occur, yes," Mac said. "If I were you, I would be more worried about my personal safety in questioning potential murderers than relating information to a member of law enforcement."

"Alfred is a suspect?"

"Everyone is a suspect," Mac intoned.

"And that includes you then, right? Because you were there too, sitting in a patrol car down the block."

Mac went quite still. "Did Alfred tell you that?"

"I'm not saying you killed Dorian." I put myself into full backpedal mode. "I mean, why would you?"

"Why would anybody?"

"Are you serious?" I leaned forward, lowering my voice to a whisper. "Who knows what he might have done to you? He's slept with practically every woman in this town. I mean, if you have a girlfriend, Dorian probably tried to bird-dog her at some point or other."

Mac also leaned forward, close enough for me to smell his aftershave.

"I don't have a girlfriend." He took his time having another drink of coffee before saying, "Drew, I'm going to ask you straight out: did you kill Dorian?"

"No," I spluttered, then childishly countered with, "Did *you* kill Dorian?"

Mac laughed then, a full, unexpectedly melodious laugh. "You really are quite a comedian."

"I'm not trying to be funny."

"That's what makes it perfect." Mac flipped his pocket notebook to an empty page. "I'd like you to do me a favor. Write down the names of all the women you know Mr. Gamble had intimate relations with in the last year."

"It's going to be more than one page," I said.

"Take as many as you need."

Mac engaged his sandwich while I tried to put Dorian's conquests into a timeline. But as I mentally scrolled through the women I'd seen sitting at the bar talking to him, I kept getting distracted by the fact that Big Mac hadn't actually ordered a sandwich but one arrived anyway. He must be such a regular here that the staff started making his food when they saw him walk in.

Normally, when a person is a regular like that, their order never changes. Those kind of customers like their food to be just so, resist variation, and complain bitterly when their plates are even the slightest bit different. But when he dined at the Eelgrass, Big Mac ordered the daily special, which was always different.

I set down the pen and asked, "How's the sandwich?"

"Good," he replied. "Slaw's a little soggy today, but still good."

"Oh yeah?"

"Yeah." Mac glanced back to the kitchen. "Juan must have the day off. He's usually here on Friday."

"You keep track of who's cooking at the places you eat?"

"Don't you?" He seemed genuinely surprised.

"Not unless I know them," I replied.

"Well, I eat out a lot," Mac said. "Actually, I don't cook at all. Except spaghetti."

"So what's best in this town?" I asked. "Is it the sandwich you're having now?" It did look quite well made, and it smelled great.

"It's the best thing they serve here. But I'd say the best food in town is whatever you're cooking Wednesday night."

I am not immune to flattery. Also fishing for compliments is a persistent vice. "Just Wednesday?"

"Your Friday and Saturday night specials are good, but not as unique as Wednesday." Mac took another bite of his Reuben. "Actually, I have no idea where I'm going to eat my Wednesday supper now..."

"Fish-and-chips place?"

"I'd rather get a burrito from the gas station hot case."

"Ouch." For a split second I almost offered to make him dinner, just for being a valued customer. Then I came to my senses. I did not want him to think I was coming on to him, get scared, question his sexuality, and beat me up to prove he was straight. I went back to eating my eggs.

Mac finished his sandwich, then folded his hands in front of him.

"Okay, so what you're saying is that there is a witness who saw both Sam and the fish-shop girls handling your knives on Thursday evening."

"Right."

"And you think that puts me closer to finding the killer because..."

"Because now we know how the knives got out of the office?" I felt lame even uttering that sentence. He was right. Just knowing how the knives got out of the office didn't prove any single person's guilt or innocence.

"Ms. Eider mentioned that you and Dorian had fought earlier in the week. Can you tell me what the argument was about?"

"Business."

"Ms. Eider said the argument was about cocaine."

I felt my eyes go wide. How could she put our personal business out there like that? I clenched my jaw and nodded.

"What exactly were you angry about?" Mac asked.

I hesitated, feeling like a snitch. But Dorian was dead and Sam had already exposed herself, so it hardly mattered now.

"I didn't want him using our place to make drug deals, and I didn't want him selling to Sam."

"You weren't one of his customers?"

"No. I came here to get away from that scene, and I've stayed away from it. So I can't tell you much about Dorian's sideline business. I'm more of a hard-liquor guy." I rattled my ice cubes at him. This finally attracted the attention of the waitress, who asked me if I'd like the same again.

I decided to go for coffee.

"Was there a reason why you didn't want him to procure drugs for Ms. Eider in particular?"

"Would you? You saw how she partied. Would you want a bunch of random moochers coming into your business after-hours to drink for free, disrespect your belongings, and fuck up your kitchen?" I felt my cheeks flushing.

He nodded, then said, "I couldn't help but notice when I looked up your particulars that you have a criminal record. Malicious mischief and obstructing a law-enforcement officer."

"I was drunk and fell into the window of a bar and broke it. It wasn't malicious or even mischief, just clumsiness. I spent the night in the drunk tank and paid a fine."

"What about the other charge?"

"I tried to keep the cops from coming into a house where we were having a drag party. There was some swearing, and I was perhaps somewhat rude."

"You've got a temper, in other words."

"People have said that, yes." I didn't cross my arms in front of my chest, but it took all my willpower not to.

"Did your argument with Mr. Gamble turn violent?"

"Not even a little bit. He never even stopped smiling. He was that kind of guy. He never took other people's feelings very seriously."

"You know, Drew, my problem is that I want to believe you—that you had nothing to do with this—because I want to have my Wednesday night dinner back. But you are currently the only person who is known to have had a significant conflict with Mr. Gamble. So I want you to think hard whether anybody could have seen you after you left work last night."

"I don't remember seeing anyone."

"Did you text or…or log in to any websites from your home computer or pass by any ATMs or places likely to have security cameras?"

"I don't think so. I went home and went to bed by myself."

Mac sighed. "In that case I'm afraid you can't be ruled out right away so…best not to leave the island for the time being."

"For how long?"

Mac shrugged. "I guess until we find out whether or not you did it." He stood and started to pull on his jacket. "Thank you for contacting me. I'll be in touch."

CHAPTER FOUR

Saturday morning started off well. Still half in my dreams, I fantasized about creating a scallop special for Wednesday. Something classic like angels on horseback but paired with avocado and heirloom tomato… Could it be a sandwich? Or should it be more of a main-course salad with bruschetta? Mac would be there for sure.

Then my phone buzzed, and I sat up, coming to full consciousness. It was Mac, telling me the Eelgrass would remain closed today. I forwarded his message to Sam.

Six o'clock. I fell back onto my dank pillowcase.

Because housing on Camas Island was scarce and expensive, I'd taken the first place I could get: an elderly mobile home about half a mile from town. Originally, Sam had lived in the second bedroom here, but she'd moved in with Danielle after she realized that her booming social life often left her too bleary to make the trip back to her bed without ending up in a ditch.

Wan yellow light glowed through my bedroom curtains, indicating sunny skies ahead. I lay there for some time, trying to figure out how I would occupy myself for an entire day without work.

Pathetic, I know. Better people would walk down to the beach, or take a hike, or binge-watch some TV show all day, but that's not the way I'm built. I needed to get up and move. And in addition to that, I had no food in the house.

I dressed and headed down to the Prospector. My route took me past the Eelgrass, where I spied Evelyn standing outside on the sidewalk, peering in.

"Hey, Evelyn, how's the peeping?"

Evelyn gave me a rather savage side-eye. "I'm monitoring, not peeping."

"Thanks for the clarification."

Inside, technicians in white paper bunny suits performed activities that I hoped involved getting the DNA of the killer and not just my and Lionel's genetic markers. I turned back to Evelyn.

"You're up early."

"I wanted to see what was going on here." Even cocooned inside her puffy jacket, Evelyn shivered. "Dorian and I didn't always agree about what was right, but he was still family. He shouldn't have died like that. He was my brother's grandson, you know."

I nodded. I hadn't liked Dorian, but not even at my angriest would I have thought that he deserved to be stabbed to death in a dank basement.

"He came to see me Thursday afternoon. He told me he was going to pay back some money he borrowed from me last year, which shocked me half to death."

So he must have had something going on? That he thought would get him...

Aloud I said, "How much money?"

"Ten grand."

"That's a chunk of change. Do the cops know?"

Evelyn shook her head. "I tend to keep my trap shut around the fuzz. Our sheriff is a sexist and a bigot."

"Then talk to Mac instead. He seems okay."

"Mac's good-hearted, I'll give you that," she said. "But there's something else that doesn't look good for me. I'm the beneficiary of Dorian's will."

"What? Why?"

"I made him write one when I loaned him the money, so that after he got killed doing whatever idiot thing he was planning to do, I could at least sell his car and recoup part of my losses after he was dead." Evelyn spoke matter-of-factly, as though this were a perfectly normal thing to demand.

"Damn. That's cold."

"You gotta be tough. Otherwise a charmer like Dorian will run all over you." Evelyn took a quick breath, and I realized she was trying not to cry. She sniffed and regained her normal cranky composure. "I thought drawing up a will would be one of those...what do you call them? Wake-up calls? Teachable moments? Make him consider how dangerous it was for him to get involved with married women and big-time gangsters." Evelyn shook her head. "He agreed just like that. We went to the bank to get it notarized and everything. He just smiled the whole time, joking, acting like I was some dingy old bat. Now the poor kid's dead as a doornail."

"I think the police really need to know this," I said. "I can text Mac directly and let him know you want to talk to him."

Evelyn arched a brow. "I didn't realize you were on such friendly terms with the law."

"Mac's a regular customer at the restaurant," I said, as if that explained it all.

"All right, then. Do it."

I tapped out the message quickly, fingers already stiffening from the cold wind blowing off the choppy sea. The clear day was giving me a much-needed infusion of sunshine and vitamin D, but without the insulating layer of cloud, the sharp wind cut straight through my jacket.

"I was just going to have some breakfast," I said. "Do you want to come with me?"

Evelyn cocked her head as if I'd done something incredibly strange and unexpected.

"At your place?" she asked.

"No, the diner." I gestured down the street at the Prospector.

"Oh, God no." She sniffed. "If you're hungry, come back to the Beehive with me."

"The what?"

"The Beehive—it's where I live. I'll cook you an omelette."

* * * * *

The Beehive was a women-only assisted-living facility situated in a long, green one-story building three blocks from the Eelgrass. As we walked through the door, I saw a comfortable-looking lounge with a television. An assortment of unmatched recliners, love seats, and sofas made the space seem snug. Several of these were occupied by old ladies. A couple of them worked crosswords. Another crocheted, while three others seemed glued to the TV screen.

All but one looked up as I entered.

"This is Andrew," Evelyn announced, waving her hand back as though I were some stray dog that had followed her home. "He's the chef at the murder restaurant."

To my surprise, only one of the old ladies seemed scandalized, and she appeared to be mainly irritated at Evelyn.

"I'm sure he doesn't want to be introduced like that." She used her cane to push herself to her feet and steady herself as she held out her hand. "I'm Julie."

She said the word *Julie* with a strong French accent, though the rest of her English sounded free of regional inflection. She wore stylish black slacks and a bold red blouse. Her white updo managed to be elegant without appearing stiff.

Julie's bones felt frail as a bird's and her skin fragile as paper. She certainly wasn't intimidated by Evelyn, though.

"It's nice to meet you," I said.

Evelyn headed to the side of the living area, where there was a small kitchen with regular residential appliances. I followed, trailed by Julie.

"Katie isn't going to like you in there," she said to Evelyn.

"Katie's not my mother." Evelyn found a skillet and some butter and eggs. "Only cheese here is Colby-Jack, I'm afraid."

"That's fine with me." At this point I was curious what she was going to do. Plus I don't have anything against Jack, or any other food when applied appropriately. "I'm more of a food nerd than a food snob."

Evelyn nodded as though this was the right answer. As she began to beat the eggs, Julie made it to the small table inside the kitchen alcove and sat down.

"Are you going to make me one too?" she asked Evelyn.

"You and me can split one," Evelyn said. This seemed to satisfy Julie.

My phone buzzed. Mac had replied with a text.

Drew, I strongly advise you to stop interviewing people about the murder.

I texted back: I'm not. I just ran into Evelyn, and she told me.

Mac wrote: You are not to question Evelyn further.

So I replied: I will not. I'm just sitting here at the Beehive, having breakfast. But if she happens to start talking about it, I'm not going to stop her. That would be rude.

Mac made no reply for so long that I thought he'd given up. Then finally, a message popped up.

You are impossible.

To which I sent a smiley face.

As Evelyn cooked, I found myself distracted by the deftness of her gestures. Though she was normally stiff, while she cooked her gestures became fluid and more or less perfect.

"That's a nice, classic omelette you're making here," I remarked.

"She's just trying to show off," Julie said. "Do you know that she cooked for Pierre Troisgros? Back in the day she worked in the best French restaurants."

"That I didn't know. I didn't think women were allowed back then."

"A few of us got in." Evelyn finished sliding the omelette onto a plate and set it before me. "But we had to be tenacious and willing to work twice as hard as any man."

"And it helped to be homosexual," Julie added. "You know, no family or children with birthdays to take off. No romantic interest in any of the men in the kitchen. No distracting boyfriends. Just work, work, work."

"Somehow they never noticed the distracting girlfriend." Evelyn started cracking eggs for the second omelette.

"They always thought I was dropping by to flirt with them." Julie laughed, and Evelyn grinned.

I tried to keep my eyes from popping at this revelation. It wasn't Evelyn being family that surprised me, so much as the notion that Evelyn had been such an adventurous person. She seemed like such a creature of habit now.

The doorbell rang, and Julie struggled up to look out the doorway.

"It's a flatfoot," she whispered toward Evelyn. "Big Mac."

"We've been texting since the murder," I said. "He eats at my place all the time."

I'm not sure why I felt the need to drop this information. Maybe I wanted to impress Julie with my inside track to the sheriff's department.

"Oh?" Julie hobbled back to the table, sat down, and leaned forward. "You know, I can't remember him ever having a girlfriend."

"You don't say." I tried to keep a neutral face.

"Not one. Ever," Julie reiterated.

"Here's breakfast." Evelyn brought the second omelette over. She had only one plate with two forks. As they began to eat, I listened to Mac talking with the old ladies, then to a younger-sounding woman, who I imagined must be the dreaded Katie. I couldn't make out any distinct words. Then came the sound of cop shoes disappearing down the hall.

I glanced up to Julie, and meeting her eyes, realized she'd been attempting to eavesdrop as well.

"I couldn't hear what they were saying," she whispered.

"Me neither," I said.

Julie gave a big smile. "Evelyn said you were interesting. I'm so glad you've finally come to visit, so I can look at you myself."

"You're welcome to come to the restaurant anytime," I offered.

"No, your place is where Evelyn goes to get away from me and read her paper," Julie said. "I'm a talker, you know."

"I didn't, but I'm gathering that now." I scraped up a forkful of my breakfast.

"So tell me about yourself, Drew. Where were you born?"

"Wyoming. But I moved to Washington State when I was a teenager."

"That must have been a huge change. I had a transition like that myself when I left Port-au-Persil," Julie said.

"In France?"

"Canada," Evelyn corrected. "Though Julie and I met in France."

"I went to study design." Julie spoke as though studying design was the single most provocative action a person could take, which I guessed it might have been at the time Julie did it.

I'll admit, I haven't spent a ton of time with elders—particularly not lesbians. But I didn't want to offend. Julie seemed nice.

"Did it work out?" I asked.

"Like it was my fate! Design led me to Paris, and there I met Evelyn. And we're married, aren't we? For two whole years now." Julie waved her ring finger under my nose. It sported an impressive rock. "Before, we've been living in sin for decades and decades. Now I can finally hold my head up when I'm pushing my little trolley through the supermarket."

"You haven't been to the supermarket for anything but a *Vogue* magazine in forty years," Evelyn commented.

"Because of the shame." Julie put the back of her hand to her head like the heroine in a black-and-white film.

I wasn't quite sure how to reply. I'd only just started to perceive Evelyn as a whole person. Interacting with her melodramatic other half challenged my social capacity. Fortunately, Julie seemed to notice my discomfort and reined it in.

"Do you like living in Orca's Slough?" she asked, introducing a non-sequitur so breezily that I could easily picture her at home in any sixties' Parisian soiree.

"It's all right," I replied. "I admit I didn't expect it to be so murder-intensive."

"These tiny island towns are like dormant volcanoes," Julie said. "They sleep and sleep and sleep, but there's always a molten mass of resentment and secrets roiling like magma beneath the surface. The pressure builds, then KABLOOEY! The place erupts, and everyone is incinerated. Then the scar heals over, and everybody forgets until…KABLOOEY!" Julie emphasized her point by waving her hands in the air. "You've heard about Charlie Lindgren's murder, I'm sure. Fishing with his brother and then gone into the sea never to be seen again."

"Wasn't that ruled an accident?" I asked. Sam had only mentioned her cousin's death in passing, but it had sounded like an open-and-shut case of too much alcohol and rough waters.

"The Lindgren brothers competed over everything." Julie said it like sibling rivalry was damning evidence. "They even fought over how much more each of them could leave to Samantha. That may have been the breaking point."

I started to suggest that fondness toward Samantha didn't sound like grounds for murder, but Julie wasn't done.

"And there's Sean Mackenzie—"

"Big Mac's father," Evelyn provided quickly. "He was a deputy fifteen or so years ago."

"He should have been sheriff, but instead he vanished and that brother of his took over," Julie announced. "Of course, his children were heartbroken. The big one—"

"Mac," Evelyn clarified, and Julie nodded.

"Yes. He's been stunted ever since."

"He looks robust enough to me," I remarked.

"Stunted inside." Julie clutched the front of her blouse. "In his heart."

"Well, I think I hear his big feet clomping back our way," Evelyn commented, deadpan.

Sure enough, Mac poked his head around the corner of the kitchen door. Dark shadows hung beneath his eyes, but otherwise he seemed as crisp and clean as normal.

He acknowledged Evelyn and Julie with a slightly wary, "Ladies," then turned his heavy cop-gaze on me. Steady, unblinking, and—unusual for Mac—unsmiling.

"Can I have a word with you outside, Drew?"

"Sure," I said. "Mac."

Somehow we both made the use of our own names sound awkward.

Mac's cruiser was parked across the street, and I padded toward it, careful to stay out of his arm's reach. I wasn't sure he didn't plan to just chuck me in the back. I glanced inside, and saw a sheaf of stapled papers on the passenger seat. The title page read: *Officer's Evidence Handbook*.

"Do you recall how you were worried that involving yourself in a police investigation of a murder wasn't a good idea?" Mac asked.

I suspected I knew where he was leading with that question, but it wasn't as if I was chasing down leads or conducting interviews. Not really.

"I do," I said. "It was right before you told me that I was a suspect and that I couldn't reopen my business until you worked out who killed Dorian. How's that going?"

"These things take time—"

"And information from the public. At least that's what the morning paper said." I planted my hands on my hips, feeling pleased at having put him on the defensive.

Mac offered me a silent, penetrating stare.

"You understand that whoever killed Dorian has already committed murder, right?" he asked. "If they ever felt any reluctance to take a human life, they're past that now. That's not the kind of person you want to corner."

I didn't want to think about that. Mac clearly read my discomfort because he offered me a sympathetic smile and his tone softened a little. "I suspect you don't like guys telling you what to do, but I'm not trying to do that at all."

"Yes, you are. You clearly are."

"No, I am requesting that you resist the urge to interfere. I am worried for you—"

"So you said, but that doesn't get me any closer to having my restaurant back."

Mac's expression darkened at my interruption.

"And I am also worried that you will wreck our case by doing something stupid," he finished.

"I'm not stupid," I said, bristling.

"No, you are ignorant. You don't know the rules of evidence or understand how admissible evidence can be outweighed by countervailing considerations."

"Countervailing… Did you just read that this morning?" I pointed to the manual on his seat.

"I did a little refresher. Let's say you actually hear some information or, God forbid, find a piece of physical evidence someplace: your ignorant actions could render that piece of information or evidence inadmissible, meaning that even if we had the right perpetrator, we couldn't use in court the evidence you tampered with. Is that what you want? What is your thought process here?"

"I want to be able to pay my bills! I want to open my restaurant!" The words came out with more force than I intended. "I want to make a scallop special. But can I? No. What's stopping me? We don't know who killed Dorian. What can I do, then? Find out who killed him so I can keep going with my own stupid life."

Mac cocked his head slightly and said, "Well, no one can say you're not proactive."

"You asked what I was thinking. I told you."

"What if I told you that you could go back to work tomorrow? Would you lay off the investigation then?"

"Can I?" Part of me thought this might be a setup. I leaned forward so we were eye to eye. "Will you let me back in?"

Mac said, "Yes. The basement will remain sealed, but you can resume business tomorrow."

Relief swept through me. "I am so happy."

"You're welcome." As Mac opened his car door, he turned back to me. "I'll be there for dinner."

CHAPTER FIVE

At seven o'clock Sunday morning I stuck a sign on the door announcing that the Eelgrass would open at five, and got to work.

It felt good to walk into the darkened space, turning on the lights as though I were some kind of wizard bringing the kitchen to life.

I unlocked the office and found my chef's coat but had to search to locate my apron. Eventually I found it in the bar. Undoubtedly it had been worn by Dorian, who frequently forgot his own gear. As I tied the strings, I felt through the pockets for any detritus Dorian might have left.

Sure enough, I removed two corkscrews and a couple of ballpoint pens with the Eelgrass logo on them. But I also found a small, clear sandwich bag containing a photograph. An actual picture, printed on paper. It looked old, with faded Kodachrome colors and one bent corner. It showed two men and two boys on a fishing boat, holding up the homely bulk of a delicious Pacific halibut. The final item was an Eelgrass bar napkin with Mac's phone number written on it.

I'm not in the habit of memorizing numbers, and I never added Mac to my official contacts, but I'd been seeing his digits pop up frequently over the last couple of days.

So before Dorian died, he had taken down Mac's number in addition to visiting Evelyn. What did I make of that? Had he feared for his life? Had someone threatened him? Did he ever get a chance to use this number? And why hadn't it been discovered when the police had searched the place? Wouldn't they have recognized Mac's personal number?

Then again, maybe not? Who actually memorized numbers these days?

Hardly anybody.

And a bartender having a phone number written on a napkin wasn't exactly an unusual occurrence. I knew I should call Mac and report it right away, but I didn't want the cops coming around again before I even had a chance to open. I slid the baggie into my back pocket.

I know it sounds selfish. And it was, but that's what I did.

I put the picture and number on the back burner of my mind and got to work prepping ingredients for my dinner service.

An emergency order phoned in to my purveyor the previous afternoon meant that one hour into my usual routine a grizzled old Native guy arrived at my door, holding a thirty-pound box of live, local scallops.

Being superstitious (and secretly softhearted), I muttered a quiet apology to the shellfish, then set about shucking them.

I found myself saddened by the waste of removing the coral and mantle from the adductor muscle. When I was twenty-one, I'd gone to Japan on a whim, and there eaten a scallop—gonads, gills, and all—and it had been delicious.

It had been a revelation to me, and I wondered if Mac would be game to try it, since I knew few others on the island would be so inclined to experiment.

I set aside three large scallops for him and went to work on the others, leaving intact the sac of vivid orange coral (a.k.a. gonads) curled around the familiar cylindrical white muscle. I wasn't sure anyone would come dine, really. But I felt like giving them a treat if they did—a reward for still believing in me.

Because that's how I like to reward loyalty: by providing surprise gonads.

I checked my messages. Sam hadn't answered yet. I wondered if she'd gone to the mainland. If she didn't show, I didn't know what I was going to do. There would be no front of house person—nobody to serve the food or pour drinks.

I texted Lionel to make sure he planned to come to work, and he replied with a jaunty, Yeah, chief, still gonna be in at 5 like I said.

It was around noon when Evelyn walked in through the open back door.

"You should get a lock put on that," she said. "Anybody could come in here anytime."

"Yeah, I know," I said. "Were you knocking in the front? I'm sorry if I didn't hear you."

"Doesn't matter. I could see you back here." Evelyn held a plastic grocery bag in one hand and a knife case in the other.

"What's up?" I turned my attention back to my parsley chiffonade.

"I came to help you."

I heard a rustling of plastic and saw that she'd pulled a white chef's coat out of the plastic bag and was buttoning it on. She tugged at the bottom and frowned.

"I think I must have shrunk," she said. "They say you shrink when you get old."

"Come on now, I can't expect you to come in here and do my work for me," I protested.

"I didn't think you did, or you wouldn't look so surprised," she said. "Give me something to do."

"I can't pay you," I said. "I can't even pay myself."

"Don't worry. You can trade me lunch credit." She glanced swiftly around the room and saw the piece of paper lying on the table behind me. "Is this your prep list?"

"Yeah."

"Looks small."

"I'm not expecting too many clients," I admitted.

"What's for dessert?" she asked.

"I don't know yet."

"Got apples?"

I told her I did. She then quizzed me on the availability of a few basic staples.

"I'll make tarte tatin, then," she finally announced. "It's easy, and people like the fancy name. Hopefully by the time I've finished that, you'll have found something else for me to do."

Evelyn set about peeling apples for the tarte tatin while I continued with my preparation.

"Julie wants to know if you're single." Evelyn started to place the sliced apples into the pan of bubbling caramel. "If you are, there's a physical therapist at the medical center, who she's been trying to set up for ages. Do you like massages?"

"Can we all get massages or just Drew?"

I glanced up to see that Sam had entered through the back door. She wore her usual work attire: black pencil skirt, spangled black sleeveless top, and patent leather clogs. The red streak in her black bob had turned purple, and her eyelids gleamed with crisp, freshly applied eyeliner.

I won't say I was astonished to see her turn up ready to work, but it definitely hadn't seemed like a sure thing. I decided to go for diplomacy and positive reinforcement.

"Sam," I said, "I'm so glad to see you."

Sam offered a tentative smile, though she frowned immediately when she saw Evelyn working over the stove.

"Evelyn's helping me out today," I said.

"I'm broke and need to work for my supper." Evelyn spoke without looking up from the pan full of apples.

Sam and I locked eyes. Her expression questioned my sanity. I answered with a helpless shrug. Sam went on her way.

We worked throughout the day, speaking occasionally. Sam had misplaced an invoice for an order of lettuce, something that normally wouldn't have fazed her at all, but I guess it showed how edgy we both were, because she couldn't seem to stop searching for it. Neither of us mentioned Dorian. Sam just tidied the bar herself. Evelyn took a couple of breaks, visibly fatigued but unwilling to admit it. I thought of cutting her loose, but the fact was I did need the help, and I sensed in her a need to help me—and also to dispense various criticisms of my technique. This rankled my pride, but I took it anyway because: elders. And because she was right.

Though I was glad Lionel wasn't present to hear Evelyn busting my balls all day.

Fifteen minutes before we were to open for dinner, Lionel himself arrived, cloaked entirely in the blue rain poncho he always wore in inclement weather. Beneath this he wore his usual uniform of baggy sweatpants and a T-shirt for a band I didn't recognize.

"Hey, chief, there's a whole line of people waiting outside to get in," he said in an excited rush.

"Really?" Glancing up, I saw that this was, inconceivably, the case. Though I felt a shadow of disappointment to see that Mac was not among them. "Damn."

"That's what I said." Lionel then saw Evelyn, and cocked his head theatrically before saying, "Hey, Granny."

"Hey, Fuzz Nuts," Evelyn replied. "Best get to work now. You're three minutes late."

"Yes ma'am," Lionel replied. But when he turned, he rolled his eyes so far, I thought he could use them to massage his brain.

Sam appeared at the food pass-through, looking happier than I'd seen her look in weeks.

"Did you see the line? Are you ready for me to unlock the doors?"

I made a point of surveying the kitchen in the manner of a king gazing out across his kingdom.

"Ready whenever you are."

* * * * *

The dinner service was so busy, I didn't notice when Mac arrived. The only thing that clued me in on it was Lionel returning from bussing a table in the dining room, singing "Fuck Tha Police" under his breath.

Mac sat in his usual place by the window, his back to the wall, where he could see everyone on the sidewalk and everyone in the dining room.

How strategic.

Again, that dissonance slithered through me. There was no denying I found him attractive. Obviously. I'd set aside special shellfish just for him.

And yet…a cop? Really? The personalities of the cops I'd met ranged from rule-obsessed wiener to fascist sociopath.

Had I somehow become masochistic during my tenure at the Eelgrass? Had entrepreneurship warped me so completely that I'd begun to find authority figures comforting?

For a second I nearly gave up my plan of making his "special-special," then went into heavy rationalization mode. Even if this guy was just as diametrically opposed to me as I suspected him to be, it couldn't hurt to suck up to him a little. If I got him to like me, it might make him think twice before finding a reason to convict me.

So I stuck to the plan. I removed only the black sac of guts from the scallops and placed them back into their shells. I added some butter and a little soy sauce and left them to grill while I made the pasta that would accompany them—lightly dressed that with mentaiko citrus cream sauce and added a fresh vitamin-C-laden tomato salad on the side so that Mac would not die of scurvy before being able to clear my name.

"Are we serving this?" Sam squinted at the plates with grave suspicion. "He ordered the special."

"Tell him I decided to substitute something else," I said. And when Sam looked as though she might refuse, I added, "If he doesn't want it, he can send it back."

"What's it called?"

"Hokkaido-style scallops, pasta with mentaiko yuzu cream, and grilled tomato with sesame and ginger."

"Oh my God, are you *into* him?" Sam raised her eyebrows in alarm.

"Please just take it before it gets cold."

I tried not to watch as Mac received my gift—not because I didn't want to know what he thought, but because I didn't want to be caught watching. I spied what I thought looked like an expression of stunned delight, which could have also been shock.

Sam returned immediately.

"He doesn't want it remade, but he wants to talk to you when you have a moment. I told him I'd comp it, but he refused."

I finished my last two tickets and took off my apron. I left my chef's coat on, wanting to counter his uniform with mine, even though he had dressed in plain clothes.

"How are you enjoying your meal, Deputy?" I asked.

"It is so, so good. I've never even seen anything like this." Mac gave me a bigger smile than I'd previously seen on him. It made him look younger. "Sit down and tell me all about it."

It's not that this has never happened to me before. At certain venues, it's actually pretty common to be summoned to explain the intricacies of your culinary creations. But in my experience, the guys—it was always guys—who demanded explanations just wanted to show off their influence over the kitchen staff. I'd never been invited to sit down and talk about how and why

I made a dish with a person who seemed so impressed with me or so deeply awed by what I'd created.

So I told him all about the ingredients—what they were and where they came from. Mac listened, nodding occasionally, but mostly eating.

It made me wonder whether dining with a companion was unusual for him. Come to think of it, I couldn't remember him ever being anything but alone. There were no new customers, so I stayed at the table, talking. I went on from the mechanics of the dishes to the first time I ate scallops prepared in this fashion—how I ordered them accidentally, then was too embarrassed to say so, but also confused about how to approach this weird food.

"It must be fun to travel," Mac remarked. He was almost at the end of his pasta.

"Yeah. I like it."

"Is that experience why you decided you wanted to be a chef?"

"Not exactly. I was the problem child. I got expelled in high school for fighting. So I went to work with my dad, doing construction. He had a job in the city doing renovations on this restaurant. Dad and I stayed with my oldest brother, who was in college, while we were doing the work on the restaurant. One day, the chef needed a dishwasher at his other restaurant, and the owner offered to pay me cash to fill in. I was sixteen years old. The rest is history. How about dessert? Evelyn made a fancy apple pie."

Mac brightened. "Absolutely."

I went back into the kitchen to plate the tarte tatin. I noticed that Evelyn hadn't dated the container—probably not that big of a thing in her day, but now an offense against the health-department gods. As I reached into my back pocket for a Sharpie, I touched the napkin and photo Dorian had left there.

I had to ask Mac about these, I thought. Yeah, it might ruin the mood, but I should still do it. I would just wait for the right time. Plus, I wanted a piece of this pie myself.

So I came back with two plates, reseated myself, and said, "But enough about me. What about you? How did you get into police work?"

At the change of subject, Mac shrank a little and shrugged. "I joined the sheriff's office to help my mom pay the bills after my dad wasn't around anymore."

Mac's change of demeanor when speaking about this didn't encourage me to continue along these conversation lines. But ultimately my curiosity won out.

"Did you not want to be a cop when you grew up?"

Mac paused, fork held in midair as he gazed out into the rainy autumn night—as if I'd asked a question too difficult to answer.

Maybe I had.

I gave him some space and kept eating my luscious slice of fancy pie. I was about to casually introduce a new subject when he continued.

"My dad was a really good guy and a great deputy. I guess I wanted to be like him, but I didn't necessarily want his job. Now I've been doing it for twelve years, though, so I don't know what else I'd do." Mac finally ate his bite of pie. "I can't imagine going to college now. I'd be so much older than everybody else."

I hadn't expected his answer to be so candid.

"Older people go back to college all the time."

"Yeah, but in this job I'm already halfway to retirement," Mac said. "I suppose I'll think about doing something crazy like going to school when I've finished out my twenty-five years."

I couldn't imagine doing anything for twenty-five years and said so. Mac just laughed.

"How long have you been cooking?"

"Fourteen years."

"See? You're more than halfway there." Mac gave a smile.

"Yeah, except there's no retirement…or really any other sort of benefits. The best thing you can hope for is to sell your place to somebody who invariably takes what you made and runs it into the ground."

"Wow. Outlook so bleak."

"Just realistic," I said.

"It might be precarious, but at least you get to live the life of an artist."

"Artist? Oh please, I spent an hour today making french fries."

"Fancy french fries."

"They're still fries. That's hardly artistic."

Mac gave a shrug. "I think you're an artist."

Normally, I'm a sucker for a good compliment, but Mac's, delivered with such sincerity, made me shy.

"Listen, I'm going to have to go back to the kitchen soon, but I found something." I handed him the napkin and photograph I'd found in my apron. "That's your phone number, right?"

The napkin didn't faze him, but when he saw the photograph he became transfixed, turning it over and scrutinizing every part of it.

"That's Dorian's handwriting on the napkin. I think he might have been wearing my apron. I don't know what the photograph is of," I said.

"It's all right. I do."

"What is it?"

"It's nothing to do with the case," Mac said.

"If it's nothing to do with the case, can I have it back?"

"I think I'll keep it."

"Are you kidding? This could be evidence."

"I told you it doesn't have anything to do with the case." Mac met my glare with stone-faced refusal.

"Is it the reason you were outside the restaurant that night?" I demanded.

Mac ran his finger along the edge of the photograph. After a few seconds, his easygoing demeanor returned.

"Okay, yes. It's none of your business, but I'll tell you. Dorian called me and said he had something for me. At the time I thought maybe he'd decided to become an informant rather than get caught in a big bust. He asked me to meet him outside, but he never showed up." Mac's eyes returned to the photo, and his expression seemed almost tender. "He must have found this picture of my dad while he was going through his grandma's old photo albums."

I took this information in and said, "Which one is your dad?" Though looking closely, I realized the answer was obvious. The brawny man sporting a shock of dark hair and giving the camera a charming grin closely resembled Mac.

"The guy on the left," Mac said. "Next to him is Bill Lindgren. The boys are the Lindgren twins, Charlie and Troy. I couldn't say which is which."

I stared at the two boys, trying to pick out Troy's features in either of their youthful smiles. In their pre-teen androgyny, they reminded me of Samantha more than anyone else.

"Your dad looks nice."

"He was," Mac said. "Bill was his best friend. They used to tell all us kids stories about the hidden smugglers' loot buried in the old tunnels beneath the buildings. Sometimes they'd even take us down there to dig around in the dirt for old beer cans. Made my mother hopping mad."

"'Cause they were condemned tunnels or because of the risk of tetanus?"

"Probably both. Listen, I have to thank you for the excellent meal, Drew. Your best so far." Mac smiled at me, and then his gaze slid toward the photo, preoccupied and slightly melancholy. I took this as my cue to go, and excused myself.

As I receded into the kitchen, I felt a cold draft flow over me as the door opened to admit a new table of customers. Except it wasn't customers—it was the other deputy, Mac's cousin Chaz. He was yawning in a dramatic fashion. Mac quickly pocketed the photo and napkin as Chaz approached. The two of them spoke only a few words, and then they both departed.

My disappointment at seeing him go was mitigated somewhat by Sam's announcement that he'd left without paying.

CHAPTER SIX

Sam locked the doors of the Eelgrass at nine p.m. and had her own work done by nine thirty—aside from never locating the elusive lettuce invoice. But that was probably long past recovering. We'd just have to trust our produce purveyor's monthly bill when it arrived.

Danielle's smiling face flashed up on Sam's phone, accompanied by a retro-disco ringtone. Sam spoke to her briefly, then glanced to me.

"You don't mind if I go, do you?" she asked.

This was a purely ritualistic interaction. I wouldn't say no, however much I could have used her help. I gave a nod.

"Me and Lionel will be another hour at least."

My statement elicited a groan from Lionel.

"See you tomorrow, then." Sam whisked herself out the back door.

"We're not really going to be here another hour, are we, chief?" Lionel tugged his yellow plastic gloves off.

"Why? You got somewhere to be?" I turned to start scraping char off the grill.

"Well…yeah. I was going to go with my friends to meet some girls."

"What girls?"

"The fish-and-chips girls." Lionel sounded exasperated. "You're as bad as my mom. Hey, speaking of my mom, though, I was going to show you this the other day but forgot."

Lionel crossed the kitchen and showed me a photograph on his phone: a white plate with a dark-brown cube on it. In the background I could see another crock like the one that had exploded in the Eelgrass's basement the morning we discovered Dorian's body.

"What's that supposed to be?"

"My mom made salmon. I cannot tell you how tiny and burnt it was." Lionel pocketed the phone. "So I'm done with the dishes. Are you really gonna make me stay, 'cause I will, but those girls…"

Honestly, I had no reason for keeping him, except for the company. Not a good enough reason for depriving Lionel of the opportunity to court females.

"Go." I waved him away. "Be safe."

After he left, I tried to bury myself in rote tasks—making the prep list for the next day, rotating stock in the refrigerator—all the while aware of the building's eerie emptiness and of the yellow police tape that still draped the back stairs.

Is it any wonder that my subconscious mind chose that moment to remind Mac, via text, that he had forgotten to pay?

The man himself arrived fifteen minutes later, ghosting through the back door and scaring the hell out of me when he seemed to materialize in the dry-goods storage area.

I did yell, yeah. And brandish a skillet.

Mac held up his hands in surrender.

"See, this is exactly why you should lock this back door," he remarked. "Anybody could come in here."

"Yeah, Evelyn already chewed me out about it." I dropped the skillet back on the range with a *clang*.

"Is this door always unlocked?"

"While somebody's here, yeah. Fire codes require it."

"It is very, very unsafe," Mac said. "I cannot tell you the number of times I've investigated crimes that could have been prevented by taking the preemptive step of locking the door."

"Is one of those crimes dine-'n-dash?"

Mac's cheeks colored, and he hung his head. "I'm sorry for that. The matter was urgent."

"Was it to do with Dorian's death?"

"I'm not at liberty to say." Mac pulled his wallet out of his pocket and started thumbing through the bills contained therein. He pulled out a fifty and handed it to me.

"That's about ten bucks more than you owe—even accounting for the tip."

"Call it an additional finance fee."

I pocketed the money. "Pleasure doing business with you."

"How long do you plan to stay here tonight?"

"I still have the fryer to break down. Then it's just mopping. But I thought I'd stay to do some deep cleaning."

"By yourself in the middle of the night?" Mac asked.

"You make it sound so creepy."

"Hey—you said it, not me." Mac observed the mop bucket Lionel had left behind. "I was planning on driving up to Top Hat Butte. It's so clear tonight, we should be able to see the Milky Way right across the sky."

"You've got a date?"

"I mean we in the general sense. We being the residents of Orca's Slough."

"The Milky Way, huh." I placed my hand on the side of the fryer. It was still too hot to drain the oil without damaging the machine. "I haven't seen that since I was a kid in Wyoming."

"You should come see it, then—get yourself out of this building."

"I just barely got back in here," I said. "I think I'll pass."

"You're really going to stay here alone?"

"It's not like there's someone else here to close down for me."

Mac stood there for a moment, taking in the kitchen and then studying me. At last he said, "How about I help you out?"

"Doing what?" I asked, to stop myself from thinking too much about why he might be willing to abandon gazing at the open beauty of the Milky Way to spend his evening cleaning a commercial kitchen.

"I can mop," Mac offered.

"Are you just worried that I'm going to violate the crime-scene tape and go downstairs?" I asked.

"To be honest, I'm worried that you won't lock the door after I leave." With that, Mac went to fetch the mop bucket. I stared after him, puzzled.

What was he playing at, anyway? If Mac hadn't been a cop, I'd have known exactly what was happening because nobody—*nobody*—hung around mopping a restaurant floor just to be matey. If Mac had been a normal guy, I would have instantly known he was trying to hook up. But Mac wasn't normal—even by cop standards. I supposed he could be trying to make friends. Or, was this some weird extension of being the "great cop" his dad had been?

I just couldn't figure out what he was going to do. Or what his motives were.

Because there he stood, dressed in his street clothes, churning up the greasy mop water as though it was what he'd expected to be doing this evening.

Mac glanced up at me.

Embarrassed to be caught staring, I said, "You don't have to do the dish room. Lionel's already done it."

"He has?"

"Yeah."

"Not very well," Mac remarked. "Your side isn't too much better."

"You're killing me here."

"My littlest sister mops like this." Mac tipped the old gray mop water out into the mop sink and started to refill. "She also used to hide her dirty dishes under her bed for no reason I could figure out. Once a week I'd go looking under there for all the little plates and bowls she squirreled away."

"How many sisters and brothers do you have?"

"There are six of us altogether. I'm the oldest." Satisfied with the new water, Mac went to work swabbing the deck in an efficient, fast manner. "A house can get filthy fast with six kids in it."

"Must be where you learned your sweet moves," I remarked.

"You can just call me Mop King," Mac said, then squinting into a dark corner, he added, "Lionel has a long way to go before he'll be challenging my title."

"Somehow I don't think that bothers him." I checked the fryer and decided that it had cooled enough to be cleaned. For the next fifteen minutes Mac and I worked in an oddly amiable quiet. He asked after my own family. I confessed to being the youngest of three sons. My mom often speculated that my defiant personality stemmed from constantly resisting my outgoing brothers. I didn't tell Mac that.

Mac paused in his mopping. "I guess I can tell you that Lionel's no longer a person of interest."

"No?"

"As you said, he would have been covered—absolutely covered—in blood if he'd assaulted Dorian, and there wasn't a drop on him. Photographs taken at the party show him wearing the exact same clothes he had on when we interviewed him the next morning, so lucky for him, he likes taking selfies with pretty girls."

"And what about the girls themselves?" I asked.

"The girls from the fish-and-chips shop? They all have alibis—and not just with each other," Mac said. "We're working on running down the whereabouts of a couple stragglers who went back to Seattle."

"That's good news, I guess. About Lionel at least." All at once I felt very light. Without being consciously aware, I'd been carrying that worry that Mac would arrest Lionel like an anvil lodged in my chest. But with the dissipation of that tension came a wave of fatigue. The idea of cleaning the restaurant all night no longer held that manic appeal.

"So how long will it take you to finish the floor?"

"Twenty minutes, maybe."

"I'll go get changed, then," I said. "Do you think you could give me a ride home?"

Mac smiled. "Absolutely."

* * * * *

Apart from the contents of his phone, is there any space more personal than a man's car? My second-hand station wagon, for example, spoke of a life spent hauling giant boxes of paper towels and engaging in drive-through dining. The perennial occupants of my passenger seat were my unopened mail and stacks of industry magazines I meant to read someday.

In contrast, Mac drove a twenty-year-old silver Ford F-150. Very clean blue seat covers concealed what I could feel was cracked vinyl. But both seat belts functioned, and when he cranked the engine, the vehicle chugged to life with only a tiny hiccup. At midnight, the town of Orca's Slough was mostly asleep. Here and there a couple of raccoons ambled along the sidewalk, their eyes flashing yellow-green as they watched us pass by.

"Business at your place seemed to be fine today," Mac remarked.

"I'm pretty sure it was morbid curiosity," I said. "Once that wears off, who knows. Maybe I'll set up an 'Orca's Slough Underground Ghost Tour' like they have in Seattle."

"You are quite the schemer, aren't you?" Mac said, giving a sideways smile.

"I like to call it the entrepreneurial mindset."

As we drove, I grew relaxed and for a few seconds slipped outside my day-to-day. What would it be like to live life like a normal guy? To make time to go up and look at stars I'd already seen hundreds of times, in a tiny town on a little island in the middle of a dark sea? I found myself manufacturing a different trajectory for myself. Could I ever be the one going to barbecues I was not catering, attending weddings as a guest instead of staff? Paying for a room at a bed-and-breakfast instead of being the guy making breakfast? Regular activities that people with regular jobs did?

What was that like? How did people know how to behave socially without a function to complete? I almost asked Mac, but then realized it wasn't as though Mac had a regular job either. Probably a fair number of people hated him just for being the law. And I knew he worked weekends and holidays just like me.

What had moved him to invite me on a stargazing trip, anyway?

He was probably lonely. He'd mentioned a couple of times that his brothers and sisters were all gone. Did he think of me as some little brother replacement? Or was he one of those guys who'd grown up and forgotten to make new friends?

One more turn in the road and then the trees on either side thinned, revealing the ratty trailer I called home.

"I guess this is me," I said. "I've got an early morning. You?"

"I'm off tomorrow."

"Yeah? Where will you be having dinner?"

"Not sure yet. What are you cooking?"

"Chicken Provençal—that's with wine and mushrooms," I said. "And butternut squash. Haven't figured out the details yet, though."

"Butternut squash, huh?"

"I promise that even though it's a vegetable, you have nothing to fear."

"Maybe I'll give it a try." Like a gentleman, Mac waited until I'd gotten fully inside to drive away.

It was only as I was watching his taillights recede that I realized I'd never told him my address.

But he would know that, wouldn't he?

I drank beer in the shower, then at the last second remembered tomorrow was trash day. I struggled into a pair of sweats and took out my measly bag, only to discover my trash can had been stolen.

CHAPTER SEVEN

Monday I had a busier than usual lunch—now certain I was getting the rubberneck assist, but whatever; I was happy to take it if it meant revenue coming in—then got right into ordering food for the next week. I figured I'd get a bump in sales during the time of the investigation, just because people love to associate themselves with any kind of infamy, so I decided to increase my meat order.

I walked out to the alley to get a breath of fresh air while I placed the call. As I disconnected I noticed Lionel arriving for work. He hunched in the passenger seat of his mother's green Subaru, looking miserable while she told him off in Korean. I stood gawking, impressed by the volume she managed to produce from her tiny body. She put to shame a couple of chefs I'd trained under.

When she noticed me watching, she changed her tone to chirpy English. "Okay, I love you, bye, bye!"

Lionel exited the car, dragging his feet like a condemned man. His mother sped off down the alley.

"What's up with your mom?" I asked casually.

"She's mad at me for blowing up Grandmother's kimchee crock. Mom says it's irreplaceable."

"You used a family heirloom to make your bootleg pickle?"

"I didn't realize it was an heirloom!" Lionel insisted, actually going so far as to stamp his foot. "How am I supposed to know that? Nobody tells me anything about cooking stuff except for you."

To be fair to Lionel's mom, she was a nurse, not a professional chef. But obviously, fermenting kimchee was another matter, especially if the crocks she used were heirlooms.

As I stood there, wondering if I was going to have to go find some Korean antiques dealer to repair my relationship with Lionel's mom, a cop car drove up.

I'm not saying my heart skipped a beat, because then I would be a nine-year-old girl. But I can't deny that a childish excitement lit within my chest as I walked over, expecting it to be Mac.

The man in the driver's seat was not Mac. He was an older, shorter, more heavily mustached iteration of the Mackenzie line: Sheriff Michael Mackenzie.

Though I'd never personally had a run-in with the guy, he was well known in Orca's Slough as a staunch supporter of the middle-class status quo. He liked to keep the town a peaceful event-free tourist haven, and if that meant rounding up the town's few bums and personally ferrying them to Seattle to set them free, that was what he would do.

Like Evelyn, Dorian had hated him. It seemed sadly ironic that Dorian's murder was being investigated by a man who, in life, Dorian had routinely referred to as the "laziest fucking cop in Washington State."

Sheriff Mackenzie's son, Chaz, rode shotgun, looking like he was going for gold in a mini-me contest. Not for the first time, I wondered if policing Orca's Slough was some kind of hereditary position or if the dominance of the Mackenzies was just another gross display of small-town nepotism.

"Mr. Allison, how are you today?" The sheriff's smile seemed genuine and warm. A dimple creased his cheek in exactly the spot Mac had his. And yet somehow on the sheriff the expression struck me as manufactured—a professional facade.

Chaz looked like he was about to fall asleep, which seemed to be his factory setting.

"I'm good," I said. "How are you?" Out of the corner of my eye I watched Lionel slink into the safety of the building.

"Very well, thank you. I was wondering if you'd be kind enough to come down to the station for a little conversation with us."

"We could talk now in my office," I suggested.

"I'd rather we speak in private at the station, if you don't mind." The sheriff nodded to Deputy Chaz, who got out and opened the back door of the police car.

Now, I wanted to be cooperative—I genuinely did. But there was no way in hell I was getting into the back of a police cruiser unless I was under arrest.

"Am I under arrest?"

"Not right now." The sheriff's smile faltered slightly.

"Then I'll meet you down at the station in ten minutes. I could use the walk anyway."

"Ten minutes, then." The sheriff motioned Chaz back into the vehicle, and the car glided away.

When I went back in to drop off my chef's coat, I found Lionel lurking right beside the door.

"So I guess you already know that I'm going down to talk to the cops."

Lionel nodded, his silence betraying his fear.

"I'm not under arrest," I assured him.

"That's what they say to get you down there, but once you're locked in that little room, there's no way to tell what they're going to do."

"Right. I get that, but I'm also not too worried." Somehow putting on a brave face for Lionel helped me shore up my own courage. "But just in case I don't come back by five, I'm going to give you Evelyn's number."

"Granny? Again?"

"Yes, again. She cooked professionally longer than you and I have been alive." I copied her number from my phone and handed the piece of paper to

Lionel. "If you don't piss her off, she could probably give you some real pro tips. She's even worked with Pierre Troisgros."

"Is he somebody famous?"

"He's the OG of French cooking. Serious, old-school, brigade-style cooking." I let that sink in with Lionel. After a moment he decided to be impressed, though I'm sure he had no idea what a brigade system really was. It probably sounded tough as hell to him, and in reality it was, especially back in Evelyn's time.

"She really was a pro?" Lionel asked.

"Yes, really. But don't call her unless I'm not back by five. I don't want to bother her for no reason. In the meantime, I need you to take over for me."

"By myself?"

"Yeah, you can handle it." I wasn't sure that was entirely true, but good enough for this situation. "Just finish the rest of the prep list and keep making orders till I get back. You'll be fine."

Lionel's chin lifted with pride, though the expression on his face remained dubious.

"Yeah, sure. No problem, chief."

Most of me did think Lionel could handle the slow afternoon business, maybe even the start of dinner service. And if he couldn't? Well, sink or swim—that's how the cooking life works. He might as well see how long he could dog paddle while it was still plausible for him to find a different calling in life.

As I walked down the street, I texted Evelyn to inform her that Lionel might be calling her to ask her to give him a hand at the restaurant. Which was my roundabout way of asking her for her assistance while avoiding actually stating why I wouldn't be there. Not that I fooled her.

She texted: Call if you need a lawyer or bail. I'll see what I can do to keep Eelgrass from burning down while you're in the slammer.

* * * * *

I sat in the locked interview room for three hours before the sheriff bothered to come in. During that time I memorized every part of it, from its industrial blue carpet to its conspicuous camera.

When he finally trundled in, trailed by his still-drowsy son, I was exhausted from anxiety for my business. Or at least that's what I told myself to avoid panic.

"I'm sorry for the wait. We had some urgent matters to attend to. I guess I'm just curious to know one thing." Sheriff Mackenzie sat down opposite me in a great jangling of keys and other cop utility-belt gear.

"Okay," I said. I tried not to show my anger or give him a reason to beat me up, but it was hard.

"Why did you kill Dorian Gamble, Andrew? Did he reject your advances?"

"What?!" I didn't mean to yell, but seriously?

"Last night officers discovered a set of bloody clothes in your trash can, and I feel confident that the blood on those clothes will prove to be Dorian Gamble's." The sheriff folded his hands together and gazed at me with an understanding expression. "So what was the last straw? Did he make fun of you? Insult your food?"

"I did not kill him." Even as I spoke, my mind raced backward. Last night? Was that why Mac had stayed late at the restaurant helping me? To distract me while his cousin stole my garbage?

Or worse yet—had he helped his cousin plant evidence when he'd been called away? Or had the cousin planted the evidence there while Mac had me in his truck, reevaluating my life like a chump?

"If you didn't kill him, why did we find blood-covered clothes in your trash can?" Chaz roused himself to ask.

"I don't know anything about any bloody clothes in the trash can. I didn't put them there," I answered. "I couldn't put anything in my garbage can because somebody stole it. Wait—was that you?"

"Where did you put the clothes you were wearing when you killed Mr. Gamble?" the sheriff asked.

I didn't fall into the trap, but just barely.

"Am I under arrest?"

"Should you be?" the sheriff asked.

I glanced from him to Deputy Chaz, who now stood rubbing his eyes like a tired child. What the hell was going on here?

The sudden sound of the door opening startled me almost out of my skin. Mac walked into the room in plain clothes.

Sensing the opportunity for escape, Deputy Chaz staggered out.

Mac didn't look at me.

To say I felt betrayed at this point would be like saying Luke Skywalker felt "disappointed" when Darth Vader chopped his hand off. Still, I wanted to believe he might somehow be on my side, if only because it gave me hope of rescue.

"Am I under arrest?" I asked Mac directly.

"May I please see your shoes, Mr. Allison?" Mac asked.

Yes, I did want to physically assault him, thank you for asking. But I didn't. Not taking my eyes off him or his shitty uncle, I unlaced my Converse, removed them, and handed them to Mac without another word.

Mac turned them over, studied the soles, then said, "I'm going to need to keep these for now."

"Fine. Am I under arrest?"

Mac glanced to his uncle and shook his head. "No, Mr. Allison, you're free to go."

I don't know if I imagined it, but I thought I caught the shadow of rage cross the sheriff's face.

Mac opened the door and held it for me as I walked through. He didn't follow me as I walked, shoeless, out of the police station.

* * * * *

I walked the few blocks to the Eelgrass in my socks, fuming with rage and humiliation. I wondered how Lionel had held out on his own. He was a good line cook but had a tendency to become overwhelmed when his emotions were running high, which they naturally would be for the entire time I was in the cop shop, so the dinner service would probably have been a disaster. Sam would be furious. But there was still time to help them clean up the carnage, at least.

As I drew closer I realized I shouldn't have worried. Sam sat out at one of the tables in front of the restaurant, smoking a cigarette. A CLOSED sign hung on the door.

Though it was only seven thirty, all the lights were off.

There had been no reputation-damaging business disaster because she had closed. Most likely as soon as she'd arrived at five. She looked down-trodden but also twitchy. I guessed she knew she shouldn't have closed the restaurant before even attempting to serve dinner, and maybe she was waiting there, half expecting me to storm up and tell her as much. But I didn't have it in me to feel angry or disappointed with her right now. After hours in a police station, facing claims of bloody clothes in my trash and having my shoes taken as evidence, the dark restaurant and the CLOSED sign seemed inevitable.

"Jesus, what happened to your shoes?" she said, by way of greeting.

"The cops took them—hopefully to eliminate me from the pool of suspects, but who knows? How did things go tonight?"

"I decided to cut our losses."

No big surprise. Despite my earlier thoughts, I found myself growing annoyed.

"If you never open, we won't have anything but losses," I muttered.

"Dorian's dead!" Sam rounded on me, eyes blazing with fury. "You were taken in by the cops. And you expect me to just go on recommending specials?"

"It's what I would have done. Or tried to do."

"We should sell this place," Sam said. "If I asked, Troy would buy it right now, and we could get the hell out of this rotten town."

"It's not like leaving town would make the cops less suspicious of me, you know," I said.

"Yeah, but it wouldn't have anything to do with me anymore."

Sometimes there is a silence that indicates the exact end of a relationship. During that silence it can feel like all the wind in the world blows between two people, eliminating the very last vestiges of amicability.

A breeze raised goose bumps across my arms.

Suddenly, Sam's expression turned horrified.

"Oh God, Drew, I didn't mean it like that! I just can't take any more stress. I was struggling even before Dorian was murdered..." She trailed off as her lip began to quiver.

I stared at her, fighting my reflex to comfort her and forestall her tears.

I currently faced trumped-up murder charges, and the only thing that concerned her was how much more stressed it made *her* feel. And before Dorian's murder, she'd been throwing parties in our business and snorting all our profits. How much of a struggle could that have been?

Sam stood trembling, tears streaming down her cheeks. Across the street I saw the old man from the souvenir shop watching us. Great. Now we were a spectacle, and I was the villain—making a woman cry.

"I know it's my fault," Sam gasped out between sobs. "None of this would have happened if it wasn't for me."

"You didn't kill Dorian," I told her but uncertainty rose in me. She could get pretty unbalanced when she was high. Dorian had joked about cutting her off on a couple of occasions—not that he would have, but still. Could Sam have murdered him? "I mean, you didn't kill him, right?"

Sam gave me a horrified stare, and her tears dried up at once. "No! Did you?"

"No," I said. "See? Neither of us is to blame."

"I was responsible for him being there. If I hadn't thrown the party, he might still be alive." Once again tears began to fill Sam's eyes. "And if I hadn't come back to Orca's Slough, you wouldn't have gotten mixed up in any of this. It's all my fault."

I wondered if she realized how self-centered this guilt of hers made her sound. Probably not.

"Listen, you're really tired—" I began.

"Don't patronize me." Sam wiped her face with the sleeve of her jacket. Her waterproof mascara didn't budge.

"I'm not patronizing you. I'm making a statement of fact." I rolled my eyes. "I'm tired too. That doesn't mean I want to throw our business away just because one bad thing happened."

"One bad thing?" Sam gaped at me. "Oh my God, how can you trivialize murder like that?"

"It's not trivializing—"

"Yes. Yes it is." Sam glared at me with glassy-eyed fury. "He was our friend, and you're not even sad that he's dead."

"Dorian was not my friend!" Now the roiling fury rose up in me. "And he wasn't your friend either. He was a lying, cheating, coke dealer."

Sam looked like she might argue, but then she seemed to deflate.

"At least he was fun to hang out with," Sam muttered. "Since we came to Orca's Slough, you've turned into some sort of dried-up old man who can't think about anything but money."

"That's not true," I said. "I also think about food. That's because I'm a chef. This restaurant is my whole life."

"But is that really a good thing?" Her tone turned from angry to weirdly sincere.

"It's not like I have anything else going on," I answered.

Sam nodded as though I'd spoken some great truth.

"But you should, Drew. You could do amazing things somewhere else." She reached out and squeezed my cold hand in her icy fingers. "If we sell Eelgrass now, nobody will think we failed. We had a personal tragedy and had to close the restaurant. That kind of thing happens. We could each start again someplace better. Please?" Her grip tightened, and she gazed up at me as if she couldn't fathom how our friendship had reached this all-time low. "Please, let's just sell."

I looked down at my socks, now filthy and wet.

"Okay. If Troy makes an offer, I'll consider it," I said.

I couldn't tell whether or not I was lying.

CHAPTER EIGHT

Tuesday morning I woke up in a different reality. I had agreed to consider closing the restaurant. I might be charged with murder. I didn't have a lawyer, and I wouldn't have a job for much longer.

I had never felt so alone. Nor had the island seemed so claustrophobic. I needed to get away, even for a day. Forget my life. Make some new friends. Get laid.

Fortunately, modern technology has created a cure for isolation and loneliness, and that cure is the hookup app.

I found a likely candidate in Seattle and immediately booked the next ferry to the mainland. During the ferry ride to Seattle I tried to put things together just for myself.

First, I had to face the fact that somebody was deliberately trying to set me up as Dorian's murderer. After working through the surge of fear and hurt at the notion that anyone hated me enough to want me to go to prison for something I didn't do, I tried to narrow the candidates to people who might hate me.

Sheriff Mackenzie hadn't seemed like a fan of mine, but it was hard to imagine him, much less his sleepy son, going to the trouble of planting evidence in my trash can when they could have just done it in the restaurant and saved themselves the drive out of town.

I wondered if Sam could have set me up. She felt like I judged her for being an addict—which, yeah, okay, I did—plus she could find a way to sell the Eelgrass without my consent if I was convicted. But even as bad as our relationship was, I didn't think she hated me. Sam was too spontaneous and emotional to frame anybody. She might stab me in a fit of rage one day—and regret it the very next second—but she wouldn't frame me.

That left me with no one else to consider. I had so few connections on the island. Which was unlike me. Back in Seattle I'd had plenty of rivals and inspired more than a few grudges. But here I'd been so preoccupied with just trying to keep Eelgrass afloat that I hadn't made many friends, much less enemies.

Lionel and Evelyn were the very closest I'd come to making friends. Maybe Big Mac—until yesterday when he'd taken my shoes.

I scowled at the gray water of the bay.

Maybe this wasn't personal, or even about me.

Because no matter how much being framed offended me personally, framing me could not have been the murderer's initial goal—just an added bonus on the way to eliminating the primary target: Dorian.

That led me back to the question of who would kill Dorian who also didn't care about what happened to me…which brought it back to a very wide group of angry husbands and drug associates. Not for the first time, I revisited the pics of the party. There had to have been at least twenty people there. Had they all been identified and dragged down to the station as well? If they had, no one was mentioning it.

And although I didn't realistically think Sheriff Mackenzie would trouble himself with framing me, I doubted he would bypass an easy opportunity to close the murder case. Thinking about that put me right back in the interrogation room. And unwillingly, I relived that feeling of hope and then disappointment I'd felt when Mac came in.

In the transitional space of the ferry, I could admit to myself that being pulled into the police station had terrified me. And because of it, maybe I'd been unnecessarily angry at Sam, who only wanted, essentially, to quit her job and escape the small town where she'd grown up.

I should apologize to her. I *would* apologize to her.

But maybe not right now. Both Sam and I needed time to cool off.

The grim October weather didn't help my descending mood. Gray skies merged with a gray sea. The shoreline bristled with dark conifers.

I was not in the greatest mindset for a date with a stranger and was considering calling it off and going back home when I noticed that, seated among the passengers, in plain clothes, was Mac. He wore jeans, a gray wool Henley, and a blue rain shell. His attention was directed downward at his phone.

Now there was a coincidence.

Or was it?

Surely if Mac was surveilling me, he'd make more of an effort to hide.

I considered ignoring him and going about my business, then decided waiting and worrying wasn't my style. And that glimmer of recognition I'd felt when he'd been mopping my floor… Though even if Mac was gay, that didn't mean he wasn't playing the long game on behalf of his uncle.

Only one way to find out, I decided.

When I sat down next to him, Mac did not seem surprised, which meant he'd already seen me.

"Hello, Drew."

"Hello, Officer. Going to Seattle?"

"Not sure yet," Mac replied.

"How do you mean?"

"I'm going wherever you're going," he replied amiably.

"So you're following me?" Even though I had suspected as much, the certain knowledge ignited an ember of fearful anger.

"That's right. Where are we headed?"

"What the hell gives you the right to ask?"

Mac blinked. Then he reached into his jacket pocked and silently withdrew his shield wallet. The badge inside glinted at me.

"Touché," I conceded.

Mac flipped the leather case closed. "You realize that fleeing the island after your interview seems extremely suspicious."

"I'm not fleeing. I'm going on a date."

"That's a long way to go for a date."

"I find the offerings on the island to be somewhat limited."

Mac nodded his agreement, then asked, "Where's this date taking you?"

"He's not *taking me* anywhere. We're meeting at the Boiler Room for dinner."

"Not my favorite," Mac said. "Dull menu."

"Of course, I forgot you are Western Washington's foremost restaurant critic." My acid tone sounded catty even to me, and Mac colored slightly. Feeling like an ass, I offered a conversational olive branch. "Where would you have *taken* me?"

Mac's mouth curved up in a private smile he suppressed to bland professional friendliness by the time his eyes met mine.

"If it were me, I'd have taken you to that conveyor-belt sushi place by the convention center. Or Vietnamese. Something we don't have on the island, anyway. Or a food truck."

While all those things did appeal to me, I wasn't ready to admit that.

"Well, it's not you, so you're going to have to settle for overpriced unimaginative appetizers and wood-fired pizza," I said. "Or you could just say you followed me, go get sushi, and meet me on the ferry back tomorrow morning."

"Can't do that, I'm afraid."

"Sure you can. Think of it as an undercover investigation you're performing on my behalf. Take some pictures. Bring me back a takeout menu."

Mac just shook his head and looked back down at his phone. I watched as he found the Boiler Room menu and started thumbing through his future dining options. The announcement came that the ferry would be docking shortly, and I stood to go. "I'm going to check in at my hotel. It's the Spencer on Second Avenue. I'll see you at the Boiler Room at eight."

* * * * *

Probably the only thing more demoralizing than being on a boring date is the knowledge that there is a cop watching you tread water.

The guy—Erik—was nice enough. He was a tall, sandy-haired California transplant, who worked in tech (shocker) and had a nice condo in Belltown only a couple of blocks away from the dark, trendy restaurant where we sat. He sipped bourbon and told me about being new to town while I drank Rainier and struggled to find his conversation even remotely interesting.

Why had I thought I needed this? Why had I thought I could be attentive to another human being after having been interrogated by the police? Why a date and not the simplicity of an anonymous grope in the back of some dark bar?

And glancing over Erik's shoulder to where Mac sat alone at a table, I felt a weird need to go there and relax. At least the guy knew what I was going through. Even if he was one of the people putting me through it. Was this how a person comes to welcome Stockholm Syndrome?

Mac pulled out his phone, texted something, and I felt a buzz in my pocket. Then another.

After the fourth alert, I finally excused myself to look.

This guy seems nice.

Kinda boring, though.

You work in tech? You don't say...

I think he's going to regret ordering the mahi-mahi tacos.

Struggling to suppress an unwanted smile, I typed: Maybe you could come over and arrest me, and then we can both get out of here.

Mac smiled when he got my text. Then, to my shock, he stood, walked over to our table, and said, "Drew! Wow, buddy, it's great to see you!"

I sat paralyzed for just one second before I stood and gave him a big, long-lost-friend hug. I meant it to be just for show, but when he wrapped his arms around me, I suddenly realized that this was what the child inside me wanted when I went searching online. I didn't want a date or dinner or even somebody down to fuck. I just wanted a hug.

Kinda pathetic, but that's what we monkeys are like. We get scared and need comfort even if it's wearing cop shoes.

Mac sat down uninvited, and without consulting Erik or me, directed the server to bring his duck prosciutto, chèvre, and fig pizza to our table.

Erik didn't last long once Mac started on a dull monologue of the least interesting aspects of island policing. He thanked me for my time, and I promised I'd text next time I was in town.

He left two of his three tacos uneaten on his plate.

Once Erik had gone, Mac said, "See? The mahi-mahi just didn't sound like a winner."

I laughed and finished my beer.

"I suppose being on duty means you can't have a drink," I remarked.

"Nah, it'll make it hard for me to keep tailing you."

"You really don't need to. I'm walking three blocks to my hotel room and spending the night in. Where are you going to be? Your truck?"

"I'm in an unmarked cop car," Mac said. "The seats recline pretty far."

"Now that's just ridiculous." I dismissed the idea with a wave of my hand. "Tell you what: I'm booked into a double room for tonight because it was the only one they had on short notice. Why don't we go to the convenience store, buy a six-pack, go back to my room, and watch something stupid together? You can even have the bed that's closest to the door, in case I try to creep out and murder somebody in the night. Unless you're scared of me. Then I guess you could sleep in your car."

"I don't think you're going to creep out and murder anybody." Mac sighed and folded his hands on the table. "All right, I'll come up. But you can't tell anybody I did this. I'm not even supposed to be talking to you."

"Fear not, I know how to keep my big gay mouth shut about who I've been in a hotel room with." I gave him a wink, which brought a little color to his cheeks.

Our walk to the hotel was mostly silent, punctuated with only perfunctory talk about who would pay for the beer. We got back to my room before ten.

I liked the Spencer Hotel because it reminded me of my first apartment—built around the turn of the century, heated by clanging radiators, and decorated in a shabby kind of hipster chic.

Mac sat down on the bed closest to the door, looking nervous, but also happy—like he'd been chosen by a television crew for a man-on-the-street interview.

"This hotel is my home away from home," I announced, spreading my arms out like I invented the place. "How do you like it?"

"It's nice. High ceilings."

"Right? I like to be able to stretch and not scrape my knuckles on the ceiling…or get whacked by some low-hanging fan."

We fell silent. The sludgy waves of awkwardness lapped at the shores of hospitality. What was I really doing here apart from wading into strange and murky waters? I needed to step back and think.

"I need a shower." I cracked a beer and handed it to Mac. "Please make yourself at home. Also feel free to search my overnight bag for any items you might need…or just to satisfy your curiosity. Whatever."

"I'm not going to search your bag, Drew."

"Just saying that *mi casa es su casa*."

With that, I took myself to the mostly hot shower. To be honest, I hadn't expected Mac to do something as inappropriate as agree to come to my hotel room. And now that he'd called my bluff and we both inhabited this neutral, rented space, I didn't really know what to do.

The way Mac vacillated between professional and those shy, private looks undid me in a way I found profoundly distressing. Mac was into me, certainly. Or was he setting me up? Or was he into me *and* setting me up? Or was he setting me up and not consciously acknowledging he was into me?

And above all, why had I invited him to my room?

I supposed I shouldn't have been so cavalier, but that's the story of my life. Low impulse control. I can't keep my mouth shut. I say something, make that joke, and then suddenly I'm bunking with the cop who's supposed to be following me.

I turned off the water and stepped out of the shower. Mac had turned the TV on, but I couldn't tell to which channel.

I pulled on my boxers and paused before putting on my jeans. I hadn't planned to need loungewear as I'd either be sleeping alone or having sex— and in either case I'd be naked.

I decided the jeans would go back on, but I could leave the shirt behind. I emerged from the bathroom still toweling my hair dry.

Mac had removed his shoes and socks and left them by the door. He sat propped up against the headboard, legs straight and ankles crossed in front of him. If he meant for this to be sexy, I couldn't understand how.

I realized that maybe all my obsessing on whether or not Mac was attracted to me might actually be me finding my way to the terrifying knowledge that I wanted *him*. A lot.

I sat down on my own bed, and taking in the salient points of the on-screen cooking competition, remarked, "That guy's really in the weeds. Can't take the pressure."

"Yeah, I think he's gonna get cut." Mac glanced over at me, looked me over. "Good shower?"

"Yes and no. The pressure's lackluster, but the nozzle's high enough. Did you search my stuff yet?"

Mac sighed. "I told you I'm not searching you."

"Why not?"

"What do you mean why not?"

"Well," I said, "I watch a fair number of those forensics shows, and it seems like you should be rifling through my bags for evidence that would eliminate me as a suspect."

"I don't have to. I've already eliminated you."

"Then why are you following me?"

"My uncle hasn't cleared you." Mac turned off the TV. "Look, I know those clothes were planted at your place, but until the experts come back with their findings, my uncle won't rule you out."

"But what makes you sure they're not mine?"

"The shoes we recovered are too small. You've got feet like water skis," Mac said.

"Thanks for that."

"Well, you do, and the shoe impressions will confirm it," Mac said. "I volunteered to tail you because you don't seem to realize you're not safe."

"I'm definitely in danger of being wrongfully convicted by your uncle," I conceded.

"That's honestly the last thing you have to worry about." Mac spoke with more urgency than I'd heard from him before. "The real danger to you is that there's a murderer out there whose attention you've attracted. Probably with all the questions you keep asking. Once it becomes obvious they can't get rid of you by pinning Dorian's death on you, they may take more extreme measures. And it's not like they haven't already solved one problem with homicide. You could be in serious danger, Drew."

After the sting of Truth with a capital *T* wore off, I managed, "First a food critic, then an arbiter of men's fashion, now a bodyguard. You are truly a man of many dimensions, aren't you?"

"Everybody has a hidden side," Mac said.

"Like the side of you that secretly wants to get down with me?" I teased. Then, understanding the confirmation in Mac's complete silence, I continued, "'Cause that's not hidden."

"Well," Mac said slowly. "I'm not trying to hide it from *you*."

And this is why banter is not always a good idea. Nonetheless, I am not one to shirk. He'd met my challenge, and now I would have to escalate. Because I'm competitive. And because I wanted another hug.

I crossed the room, pulled the stiff orange curtains closed, then sat on the edge of Mac's bed.

"Have you ever kissed a guy?"

Mac let out a laugh. "I'm thirty years old."

It wasn't really an answer, but I leaned forward and laid one on him anyway. Gently. His lips parted slightly. I felt his hand on my thigh. I pulled back far enough to look him in the eye and said, "I only need to know one thing."

"What's that?"

"Your first name," I replied.

"Cormac," he said. "Cormac Patrick Mackenzie. You can stick with Mac, though."

"Okay, then, Mac." I swung my leg over to straddle his lap. "Wow me."

Mac stared unblinking at me for so long, I thought I'd made a grave error in judgment. But then he laced his fingers behind his head and said, "You're apparently the expert. Why don't you show me how it's done?" Mac's quick concession made me pause, but then he gave a challenging smile and added, "No pressure."

"Oh, it's *on*." My hands went immediately to his belt.

Mac lifted his hips as I pulled his pants and boxers, and then my own, down and off.

I stared at his half-hard dick with something approaching awe.

There was a long silence, and Mac didn't try to fill it, which was unusual enough to make me drag my eyes away from possibly the finest cock I'd seen outside of porn, to his face. His confidence was vying with something that looked like embarrassment or maybe uncertainty, which is a normal reaction to having your dick assessed by a comparative stranger. But with a cock like that, it made no sense at all. He should have been waving it at passersby. Still, something in his expression made me want to reassure him.

"Well, you're, um…" I cleared my throat. "You're definitely in proportion."

Mac blinked and blushed. He had lovely eyelashes. I hadn't noticed that till then. Or how nice his skin was. Or that his stomach looked like a laundry washboard.

"So…" I said, with an attempt at flirty roguishness, "are you going to let me suck it?"

Mac drew a visibly deep breath, and his cock jerked against his muscular thigh as it filled to full erection.

That'd be a yes, then. It certainly wasn't a no.

I leaned down and licked the silky tip of the now-swollen head. Mac groaned in disbelief. I pressed my mouth against the rigid length of his dick and smiled. The sense of control I felt was unbelievable.

"You still haven't said," I murmured against hot, taut velvet skin. "Do you want me to?"

"Are you kidding?" It sounded desperate. Outraged.

"No, Deputy, I am not." I blew on the wet stripe, scratched my fingernails through thick, dark pubic curls, and peered up at him with a try at polite interest.

But beneath the frustration I thought I saw...he looked lost, as if he didn't understand or enjoy the sleazy etiquette of casual encounters. I felt a melancholy hook land in my shriveled, jaded heart.

"Why don't you put your hands on my head," I said, "and just push down when you're ready to signal your complete consent."

His eyes widened. He looked about twelve years old. So I leaned down, took the head of his dick in my mouth, and began to suckle very gently. Tormenting him with it.

It didn't take long before I felt his hands in my hair, fingers opening and closing helplessly on my skull, but instead of trying to hold me in place, he cradled my head and let me set the pace. Which was really just as well, given the size of that dick. I don't know what I'd have done if he'd decided to go triple X on my face.

This could have been Erik, I thought randomly, but it wasn't, so...lucky me.

And then it escalated too fast. I was starving for release, too long without touching another body, never mind an attractive one.

In no time I was holding Mac's hips, jaw aching, as he tried not to fuck too far into my throat, and I was humping the puffy hotel comforter like a horny mutt. Mac kept saying my name, as if it added to his high. It certainly added to mine.

I love giving head. The smell and sound of it—the obscene sucking squelch, the panting and whimpering as I take someone else apart with my mouth.

Our stamina was frankly pathetic, but we came pretty much together, which is more or less the desired endgame, isn't it? It'd never happened to me before anyway, and it was crazy it happened now. I just knew that Mac felt and smelled and tasted perfect, and I shot like a fire hose.

I had needed it, and I think, probably he did too.

When I'd finally caught my breath, I rose, turned out the lights, and lurched into my own bed. I didn't look at Mac. Somehow I couldn't bear to see his reaction to what we'd done, now that the clammy chill of reality settled over my damp skin. If he didn't regret it now, he probably would once the sun came up.

But I couldn't help saying, "You can come to my side if you want. It's dry over here."

Mac said nothing, but a few seconds later I felt him slide into bed beside me. And just before I fell asleep, I felt him pull the crisp white comforter up over my bare shoulder.

Like some kind of romantic dork.

CHAPTER NINE

The next morning I had texts to reply to. I started with the one from Lionel, asking if he was supposed to come to work at five or if the bistro would be closed because I was in jail.

I glanced over at Mac, still asleep, arm draped across my abdomen. I considered waking him up and asking whether he thought I'd be taken in for questioning, then decided to err on the side of optimism. I told Lionel to report to work at five as per usual. Even if we didn't open, I wanted to tell him in person that we were considering selling the Eelgrass.

My second text came from Sam, apologizing for losing her shit and asking if I wanted to open the bistro for dinner. I told her that I did. After a few moments, Sam agreed. Then she informed me that Troy wanted to meet with us both at the restaurant at three to discuss a possible offer.

I'll see you there, I wrote. I hit the Send icon before I could rethink the decision.

I lay there for a few moments, feeling adrift. I ran my hand over Mac's arm, admiring its foreign solidity and wondering if I'd ever cook for him again. If the restaurant closed, would we ever see each other again? Naked or any other way?

My phone buzzed again, and a flurry of messages scrolled up my phone screen. All of them from Evelyn.

"Mac?" I patted his arm—very gently. He didn't rouse. Or even shift. "Mac!"

"What?" His eyes popped open, then seeing me perfectly fine, drooped closed. "What the hell?"

"There's been a break-in at the Beehive. A guy tried to choke Julie."

That got Mac's attention.

"Is she hurt?" Mac reached for his phone.

"I don't think so. Evelyn says it's not too bad."

"Do they have the perp?"

"No. Evelyn texted me to warn me that the sheriff was coming around looking for me because apparently I'm his favorite suspect for all crime on the island now." I leaned closer to try and get a look at Mac's texts. "Any official messages about that?"

"You don't have to worry about being charged with that." Mac shifted to prop himself against the headboard, where I couldn't see his screen.

"I don't?"

"Obviously not." Mac patted my shoulder but kept his eyes on his screen. "You have a really solid alibi."

"But do I really?" I had hoped not to broach the subject of whether or not Mac would have my back—at least not so early in the morning—but needs must...

Mac twisted his fingers through my hair and gently tilted my head toward him. If I were to deny a thrill went through me, would you believe me?

He looked me in the eye. "I know you were in a hotel in Seattle. Though I would prefer if we didn't go into great detail about it, for the sake of my professional reputation."

"Sure. But if we have to..."

Did I believe that Mac's sole concern about being revealed to have slept with me was police-integrity related? No. Not for a second. But I also didn't want to argue about it. Call me lazy.

"You have an alibi." Mac released his grip. "Did Evelyn say if anything was taken?"

"No, but I can ask." I started to tap out the question.

"No need. My cousin's already telling me about it. He wants me to verify your whereabouts, which I am doing right now," Mac stated firmly.

"So what actually happened?" I asked. Not only were Evelyn's texts uninformative, but their disjointed nature worried me. She was old and probably wasn't all that familiar with texting, but still…

"I can't tell you." Mac continued his laser-tight focus on his concealed phone screen.

"Oh, come on!"

"She's okay, all right?" Mac said. "But I can't tell you anything more, not before the sheriff has decided what information to release. That's for your own protection, Drew. So that you don't appear to have information that only the police and the perpetrator would have."

"Oh. Right."

"That said, I can't stop you from going straight to the source. I bet Evelyn would love to tell you all about it. She isn't the type to say so, but I think it would reassure her to have you visit her."

"I will do that." I tapped out a query and shot it out into the ether.

Evelyn didn't immediately reply, so I started my morning routine. When I emerged from the bath, I saw that Mac had already gone. But he left a note that read: *Have to go talk with Seattle PD. Meet me on the ferry.*

* * * * *

The ride back to the island proved uneventful. We sat together, though once outside the hotel space, Mac reverted to his blandly friendly demeanor—his professional face.

It annoyed me more than I thought it would. But I couldn't stop myself from wanting to be near him, thirsty for his attention.

"What do you think the odds are of having a murder and an assault happen in the same week?" I asked.

"Good if they happened at the same place and time," Mac replied. "These were a few days apart. Still, the chances of them being related are better than average."

"Please, Mac, don't overstate it. I can't stand it when you're such a drama queen." Belatedly I noticed that more than a few of the ferry seats were occupied by familiar faces—not people I knew by name, but I'd seen them around town. I toned it down. "Are you going to go see Evelyn and Julie with me?"

"No, I'm going to the station before I pick up the investigation," Mac said. "What are your plans after that?"

"For the investigation? I'm not sure."

"Please be joking."

"I'm really not." I lowered my voice below the range of the gaggle of commuting snoops who surrounded us. "I need this thing solved, like, yesterday."

"I understand that. What you don't seem to get is that these things take time. And some crimes never get solved and you just have to live with that." Mac's deadpan delivery communicated more to me than mere words could. "A solution is not guaranteed, no matter how big a nuisance you make of yourself."

"That does nothing to reassure me that I'm not going to be wrongfully convicted, you realize," I informed Mac.

"I'm sorry I have to put it bluntly," Mac said, "but it's like you're not capable of perceiving that you're not a law-enforcement officer." Mac spoke without anger. More with incredulity at my arrogance. "Okay, let's say you do figure out who this murderer is. What do you think you're going to do?"

"Perform a citizen's arrest?"

"That's only for felonies committed in your presence. I'm assuming you weren't present for either of these felonies?"

"No." I felt a sulk coming on.

"Then you can't arrest anyone, okay? Just try to be patient. I'll find out more about it when we get back to the island."

"That won't help me, though, since you won't tell me about it."

"Just because I'm not telling you about it doesn't mean it's not ever going to help you," Mac said. "It just means you won't be in control of it, which is as it should be. You shouldn't be planning to confront a violent person. Ever."

"You can be surprisingly annoying," I said.

Mac shrugged as though his behavior was out of his hands.

The autumn morning was gray and foggy. Slate-gray seas and dove-gray sky. As we neared the shoreline, Camas Island seemed to coalesce into existence just in time for the ferry to dock. Deep-green conifers crowded the shoreline, punctuated by intermittent bursts of yellow leaves.

Finally, Mac broke the silence. "So from what Evelyn's texted you, what do you know?"

"Around three a.m., a man broke in and tried to smother Julie. Evelyn raised the alarm, and the guy escaped."

Mac nodded.

I continued, "My question is: why attack Julie? And even if you decided to do that, why would you think Evelyn would just lay there and watch you do it?"

Mac sighed. "Maybe the intruder didn't realize they'd be in the same bed. Neither of them is physically imposing. And in the dark it might be easy to miss that there are two old ladies instead of one."

Inspiration hit me like a flash.

"Which means we don't really know if Julie was the intended target. The guy could have been going for Evelyn, which makes more sense."

"How is that the next logical step?" Mac asked.

"Julie hardly ever leaves the Beehive, whereas Evelyn is always wandering around town, looking into people's windows and snooping. What if the murderer thinks Evelyn saw something on the night Dorian was killed? He'd think he needed to silence her. What—" I leaned closer to Mac. "What if she actually did see something?"

"If Evelyn had any information regarding this case, she'd have reported it," Mac said. "She may not be all that fond of the police department, but she's not the type to let anyone get away with murdering her family."

I had to agree with Mac on that point.

"So you really think the break-in and the murder aren't related?" I asked.

"I didn't say that," Mac replied. "I just don't believe that Evelyn would knowingly withhold information that could convict Dorian's killer."

"But unknowingly?" I suggested.

"Maybe," Mac allowed. "The reality is that it's too early to be leaping to conclusions. At this point we still don't know why Dorian was killed. Was the murder motivated by jealousy? Rage? Greed?"

"Probably not greed," I said. "Dorian burned through his cash way too fast to have some big, hidden stash of money. As long as I've known him, he hadn't owned much more than an old Subaru Outback."

And the man-purse he dealt coke out of.

I paused, allowing myself to listen to my thoughts.

"Oh my God! His bag. I just realized. That thing was hardly ever out of his possession, but it wasn't downstairs with him when I found the body."

I pulled out my phone and went to Lionel's social-media feed. I scrolled back through dozens of new, virtually indistinguishable selfies until I came to the pictures Lionel had taken at the party that Thursday night. I spotted Dorian's bag sitting on the back bar next to the espresso machine.

"See? Here it is on Thursday night. But the bag definitely wasn't on the bar when I went in and discovered Lionel sleeping on the floor the next morning." I continued swiping through the photos until I spotted the bag again.

"Here! It's here!" My heartbeat picked up as I studied the picture and realized I recognized the man wearing Dorian's bag slung over his shoulder. "This is Sam's fuck-buddy…what the hell is his name? Danielle's brother…"

"Alfred Tomkins," Mac supplied.

When I turned to look at Mac, he pinned me with a vexed stare and said, "It's kind of amazing that you will break off a conversation with me to actively research a case I literally just told you to stop researching."

"I'm not just researching it." I wiggled my phone in front of him enticingly. "I'm solving it. This is your guy."

"You think Alfred Tomkins—the vegetarian surfer—killed Dorian to steal his bag?" Mac studied the picture with an unconvinced expression.

"There's nothing that prohibits a vegetarian from committing murder; just from eating the body," I responded. "And he's got Dorian's bag in this photo."

"And after he stole the bag, he broke into Evelyn and Julie's place… why?"

My triumph deflated, but I clung to the fact that I had discovered something fresh. Alfred Tomkins had stolen Dorian's bag. Though that didn't make him a murderer and it didn't give him a motive to accost Julie or Evelyn.

"What if the person who killed Dorian and the person who attacked Julie are different people? What if when Alfred stole Dorian's gear, he set off a chain reaction?"

"Hold on." Mac held up his hand like he was directing traffic and I was doing forty in a school zone. "Tell me *exactly* what you think was in the carryall."

"Cocaine," I said. "And probably MDMA. At least that's what was in it the last time I saw him open it up."

Mac raised his brows. "You saw it. Right. So Dorian was in possession of a carryall full of drugs at the time of his murder. It would have been helpful to have this information earlier." I could hear the edge of annoyance in his voice. "Certainly points to one strong motive for killing him."

"Right, except like you said, it wouldn't make sense for the person who had the bag to bother with a break-in." I pondered the problem. "Unless someone else had the same idea—to rob Dorian. Maybe they went to the Eelgrass and killed Dorian, but then they couldn't find his bag?"

"Because Alfred had already stolen it," Mac finished.

"And then when they heard that Dorian had gone to see Evelyn before he went to Eelgrass, they broke into her place, looking—"

"Wait!" Mac cut me off again. "Dorian visited Evelyn directly before he was murdered? How was I not informed of this?"

My blood ran cold. In my rush to impress Mac, I'd blabbed Evelyn's previous confidence.

"Evelyn just mentioned it offhand…" I trailed off.

I could see the flush of frustrated anger rise in Mac's face. He glared past the railing at the green-gray water. Slowly the tension drained from his expression. He took in a deep breath, then released it very slowly and turned back to me.

"Is there anything *else* you've been holding back from me?" Mac asked.

"I wasn't purposefully omitting information. I just didn't know you then."

"But you do now?" The direct challenge in Mac's voice surprised me, but I held my nerve.

"I know you're more than a pair of cop shoes."

"That is true." Mac's voice warmed fractionally. "So now that you've gotten to know me with my shoes off, you're going to tell me everything, right? Because you can understand how knowing that Dorian had been to see Evelyn might have given us a heads-up. It might have helped us prevent the assault on Julie."

I hadn't thought of that, but hearing Mac say it, I realized why he'd been so angry.

"Yeah, I do now," I admitted. I hoped Evelyn would see it the same way.

I spent the remainder of the ferry ride detailing all I could remember of my conversation with her about Dorian. After the ferry docked, Mac didn't offer me a ride. I hadn't expected him to, but still felt disappointed anyway.

Because I'm an idiot.

CHAPTER TEN

For the first time since I'd stepped off this ferry two years earlier, I considered the nature of Camas Island. It had both real and conceptual borders and barriers. There were less than seven thousand residents on the whole rock, and Orca's Slough was home to half of them.

In this kind of close environment, people couldn't hide nearly as much from each other. Everyone knew everyone else's business—or thought they did. Gossip and grudges couldn't dissipate across vast distances. But people could also be close, in the best way. Nowhere else would I have found myself hanging out daily with an oldster like Evelyn and a kid like Lionel like some kind of three-generation advertisement for family of choice.

I needed to see Evelyn and Julie, if only to apologize for being off in Seattle the one night they needed help. And for taking the only trustworthy cop on the island with me.

When I stepped into Evelyn and Julie's room at the Beehive, the first thing I saw was a large cardboard square covering a basketball-sized hole in the room's one window. Autumn cold seeped around the makeshift patch. Next I laid eyes on Julie's battered face, and immediately and without reservation wanted to murder whoever did that to such a small, frail old woman. I couldn't stop myself from looking down at Evelyn's hands. Two of her nails were torn, and her knuckles were red and swollen.

"I'd say you should see the other guy, but I barely scratched him," Evelyn said glumly.

"You did your best. You're just not the bruiser you once were." Julie's voice was slurred.

"Did he give you a concussion?" I knelt down beside Julie's overstuffed red armchair.

"*No.*" Julie's exasperation with my question was obvious. "And I'm not having a stroke either. I sound funny because my lip is split. That's all."

"You really didn't see him at all?" I asked.

Evelyn patted my shoulder. "Drew, we can barely read the subtitles on the television, and it's sixty-five inches."

"I think this has to do with the murder," Julie said in a stage whisper.

The fact that the assailant hadn't knocked the theatricality out of her comforted me. And made me want to cry, and to strangle the guy who had hurt them. I hadn't expected to be such a mess. I had to pull myself together.

"I agree," I managed to say.

We both looked at Evelyn, who sighed.

"Yeah, that's what the Five-O said when he phoned and gave me business for not telling him that Dorian had visited me." Evelyn sighed again and then gave me a sidelong look. "I think I need you to give me a ride to the bank."

"What for?"

"On that day, Dorian asked to put some things in my safe-deposit box. Most of it was just junk he'd picked up and a couple photos of his grandma's. But he had a sealed envelope too. It's probably time I looked inside it," Evelyn said.

Julie nodded in vigorous agreement.

"Wait...what? You didn't tell this to Mac when he called just now?" I demanded.

"Look, this morning the sheriff trotted in here and started squealing at me about how I brought this on myself and how Dorian deserved what he got." Evelyn glared at the empty doorway as if she could still see the sheriff standing there.

"We're not used to having a friendly relationship with Sheriff Mackenzie," Julie explained. "And that envelope could contain absolutely anything."

"Dorian trusted me with it. I can't just hand it over to some pig before I know what's in it." Evelyn gazed down at her bruised hands. "Dorian had his faults, I know. But I can still remember what a sweet little boy he was. He used to make me laugh. And when he got older and realized about me and Julie, he didn't care. He was the only member of my family who didn't care."

I nearly responded that Dorian's open-mindedness probably resulted from having literally no morals, but stopped myself. Of course they cared about the one person who seemed to accept them as they were. And who knew? Maybe he had. What did I know about it?

Nothing. Nothing at all.

"I can give you a ride to the bank, but...what about this?" I gestured at the broken window. "Why isn't there someone here fixing it?"

"The handyman's on the other side of the island at the other facility. He says he can be here tomorrow." Evelyn crossed her arms over her chest.

"So what? They expect you to just stay here in this freezing, pre-broken-into room overnight? What if the assailant comes back? What if you get fucking hypothermia?"

"We've got electric blankets," Evelyn said.

"And we can snuggle close." Julie threw Evelyn the sort of playful, blatantly sexual look I was not used to seeing outside of a black-and-white movie. Though charming, it was not convincing.

"That's just not good enough. Who's in charge here? Katie the kitchen cop? They could at least put up some plywood instead of this." I flicked the cardboard with my finger.

"Don't be mean, Drew. Katie does her best," Julie said.

"Who is Katie's boss, then?" I pulled out my phone and started to search the Beehive's website.

"Drew, don't cause trouble," Evelyn said. Then Julie laid a hand on her arm.

"Go on. Let him. I like this new butch persona he's trying on," she said.

"I'm not trying on a new persona!" I returned to my regular tone. "I just don't want anybody to think they can push you around."

"Anymore," Evelyn added.

Never again, I promised them silently.

For the next forty-five minutes I harassed the management until they finally agreed to let me hire a handyman myself in Orca's Slough. Then I spent another hour finding a handyman willing to be hired by me on short notice, in the rain.

His name was Cliff, and his fee drained what was left of my savings, but by three that afternoon, the broken window at the Beehive had been secured and Julie was resting beneath an electric blanket cranked all the way up to nine.

With the arrangements around the window, I hadn't had time to worry about Mac. Now I wondered if I should tell him I was taking Evelyn to the bank. I decided that although I should, I wouldn't. The envelope could contain anything or nothing, and it was Evelyn's call whether we would, in her words, "involve the law."

The safe vault at the Orca's Slough branch of the Island Federal Bank was small, well lit, and exactly like every other bank vault I'd ever seen. After we retrieved the box, the bank manager escorted us to a private room. I looked away as Evelyn opened the box, feeling that the contents were none of my business. But then Evelyn just upended the thing, spilling out a dozen or more old photos as well as numerous corroded antique coins. A piece of tarnished silver skidded across the table and fell to the floor, and I snatched it up. It turned out to be a battered and dirty cuff link that looked like it had been buried for years.

"Dorian was always hoping he'd uncover some piece of treasure," Evelyn commented. "When he was a little boy, I used to tease him for being such a magpie. He'd grab anything shiny."

I remembered Alfred lamenting his lost lighter and nodded.

Many of the assorted pictures looked similar to the photo Dorian had intended to give to Mac. The Lindgren twins peered at me from most of them, no longer boys but now men. I recognized Troy by his dress shirts and suits. Charlie, who'd drowned before I even came to town, seemed tired and worn down despite his crisp white chef's coat.

"Why would Dorian have so many pictures of Troy and Charlie?" I wondered aloud.

"Those would have been his grandmother's. She was a Lindgren before she joined our family." Evelyn picked up a photo and considered the group of people gathered around a boat. Then she tossed the photo down. "She never once spoke to me."

Evelyn fished a white business envelope from the pile.

"Here is what we came for." Evelyn tore the sealed flap open and pulled out a yellow piece of paper. I recognized it at once as a produce invoice, the kind that pulls out of a three-part carbonless copy. It detailed the contents of a vegetable delivery that had been received a couple of days before Dorian was killed. "Recognize this?"

I nodded. "Sam tore up the whole office looking for this the other night. What's written on the back?"

"Don't know. Didn't bring my glasses." Evelyn handed it over to me. The writing was neat, feminine, and definitely not Dorian's jittery script.

"For and in consideration of the three-hundred dollars," I began to read aloud, "the receipt of which is hereby acknowledged, Samantha Eider does hereby sell and convey to Dorian Gamble all the assets, property rights, and interests of the Eelgrass Bistro—" I stopped speaking and skimmed to the end. "It's a bill of sale."

Evelyn's eyebrows shot up. "Is it signed?"

"Yes, by Sam and Dorian and witnessed by Lionel and some other guy I've never heard of—Adam Vukoja. So I guess...Sam had a reason to kill Dorian after all." At first my shock was so complete, I couldn't feel anything. I expected rage—hurt—but all I felt was a deep paroxysm of contempt curling like an anaconda through my guts. She had sold out. And for what amounted to pocket change. That couldn't be right, could it?

"Vukoja's one of Dorian's coworkers from his other line of business." Evelyn's disapproving expression spoke volumes. "Some Croatian person from Portland. Dorian's main supplier, I think. Do you think Sam was, you know, too high to remember?"

"The handwriting looks like she's sober. And why would she have been looking for a paper she couldn't remember? Once we get out of here, I'll call Lionel and ask him if he remembers signing this." As I glanced at my phone, I saw a text from Sam telling me I was half an hour late for our meeting with Troy.

"Damn it," I muttered.

It's not like me to forget a major commitment—even one I didn't want to meet. But since the murder, it was like my mind had come unwound and with it my ability to prioritize had gone. But when your life is all just pissing on one dumpster fire after another, that's what happens.

"Bad news?" Evelyn said.

"I forgot about an appointment. Sam and Troy are waiting for me at the restaurant. Sam was arranging for us to sell Eelgrass—"

"What?" Surprise bordering on loss showed in Evelyn's face. "Why would you do that now?"

"I don't want to," I said hastily. "And with this receipt, I'm not even sure that she can. But it's obvious that I need to talk to Sam and straighten this whole thing out."

"Seems pretty clear what she's doing: selling up. Twice. Doubling her money," Evelyn said.

"For three hundred bucks?" I shook my head. "Her share of Eelgrass is worth way more than that." I didn't want to speak ill of Dorian to Evelyn, knowing that she cared for him, but I was pretty certain of how this bill of sale came about.

"You know, this Vukoja guy may have coerced Sam into signing this." I turned to see Evelyn gazing at me with blatant skepticism. She probably realized Dorian would have had to be in on it as well. Neither of us wanted to say as much, though. I could see Evelyn weighing the possibility of just locking the receipt away again.

"You need to take this to the police," I told her. "It could be a big part of why someone—maybe Mr. Vukoja—murdered Dorian."

"On the way over here you said you thought he was killed for his supply," Evelyn said, but I could tell she wasn't putting up a real argument. She just didn't want the sheriff to be right about Dorian playing a part in his own murder.

"Maybe Vukoja wanted both, and Dorian refused to give him what he wanted," I said. "The thing is that if Vukoja did play any part in Dorian's murder, then this receipt is the only physical evidence pointing to his involvement. Mac needs to know about it. If he doesn't, then how is he gonna have any chance of getting justice for Dorian?"

"You think any of them in that flatfoot family care about Dorian?"

"I think Mac cares about justice and the law. And I think he cares about you, Evelyn."

"Yeah...maybe." Evelyn absently poked at the cuff link I'd picked up earlier.

"I tell you what. I'll text Mac directly to say you're bringing something important to him. I could ask him to meet you outside, or better yet, I'll ask him to come here and meet with you. That way you won't have to go to the police station or even look at Sheriff Mackenzie."

I held out the receipt and Evelyn took it, but she didn't look happy.

"You'll call him?" Evelyn asked. "Just him?"

"Yes. Just Mac."

"Okay, then," Evelyn decided. "Go on and phone the fuzz."

I pulled out my phone and nearly dropped it when it buzzed in my hand. Mac's now very familiar number flashed up as my ringtone of "Hey Good Lookin'" wondered what I had cookin'.

"Hey," I answered. "I was literally just about to call you."

I wasn't sure if the brief silence that followed was alarmed or dismayed, but I quickly realized the last thing Mac probably wanted was me calling him at work after we'd…gone on a date? Or was it a one-night stand? I didn't want it to be, but at the same time…

"I don't mean calling you personally," I said quickly. "I mean I was about to call the police, and you're the only one I know and also the only one Evelyn likes—"

"Mr. Allison, we'd like you to come in to the police station at your very soonest convenience. In fact, if you give me your present location, I can come and pick you up." Mac's formality made me feel certain that either his uncle or his cousin—maybe both—were listening to him.

"I'm with Evelyn at the bank. Why do you want me at the police station?" I had a terrible feeling I knew why.

"We have a few questions we're hoping you could answer. Routine questions."

"Routine questions that I can't answer now over the phone?"

Mac was silent for so long that I thought maybe we'd been disconnected. Then he whispered, "A witness is claiming he saw you break into the Beehive."

"What witness?"

"I'm not allowed to say," Mac replied. "And please don't go around town trying to hunt him down because—"

"I thought I had an alibi!" My voice echoed through the room.

"You do, but this is a very credible witness—"

"More credible than my alibi of being pinned naked next to you all night in Seattle?" I demanded.

Evelyn raised her brows at me.

"Look, Drew, you aren't being arrested." Mac sounded like he was trying to calm a rabid dog with soft tones and meaningless words. "But I would really like you to come in, for your own safety, if nothing else."

"But I'm not under arrest."

"No…"

The way his voice trailed off did not fill me with assurance. How shoddy of an alibi had he given me?

"Well, I was going to feel kind of shitty about not telling you what I was doing here at the bank with Evelyn, but now I hope it really pisses you off," I announced.

"What? Why would it—"

"We just opened up her safety-deposit box. It seems we forgot to tell you that the last time Dorian visited her, he asked her to put some things of his away."

"Forgot?" Mac muttered something else under his breath. "So you thought that instead of telling me, you needed to take it upon yourself to go check it out?"

"I would have hated to waste police time," I snapped. Next to me Evelyn chuckled.

"You know, it's for the police to decide whether our time is being wasted—" He cut himself off, and I heard his cousin's drowsy voice mumble something. Mac assured him that he had everything under control. His voice was again formal and clipped when he spoke to me. "So you believe you may have discovered something important?"

"Yes, and Evelyn is willing to share it with you. But she won't talk to the sheriff and she's not stepping foot in the police station."

"All right." Mac sounded resigned. "I will be there in a few minutes. We'll work this out—"

I hung up without telling him I wouldn't be there when he arrived.

* * * * *

I paused outside the bank to call Lionel and confirm that he had been the one to sign the bill of sale.

"Yeah, chief, I did sign something. I didn't read it, though. Am I in trouble?" he asked.

"No, not at all. I just wanted to know—was Sam sober when she signed it?"

"Oh yeah. Dead sober. And crying. I got out of there as fast as I could, for real," Lionel said. "Anyway, I'll see you at five, right?"

"Right." Even to me, my voice sounded strange.

"Do I still have a job?" His plaintive tone jabbed me right in the heart. "You haven't been arrested again, have you?"

"I haven't been arrested at all, and yes, you still have a job," I replied firmly. Who knew how long I'd retain my liberty or if Lionel would be working for me after today, but I tried to reassure myself that Troy wanted to keep the restaurant going. "I'll see you later," I said and disconnected.

When I came within sight of the Eelgrass, I stopped walking and took several breaths till my heart stopped racing. Better to go into the situation late but calm, than to race in shouting angry accusations in front of Troy.

I decided to let myself in the back door and walk through my kitchen, like I normally would have done. There was something relieving about the familiarity of stepping into the dark, quiet back room. It was my ritual moment of calm before I faced the challenges of a day filled with rush orders, sharp objects, and grease burns.

Through the dim shadows of the kitchen I saw Sam standing in the dining room. I guessed the dapper suit with his back to me was Troy.

They'd gone ahead and started arguing without me.

"I cannot take this!" Sam's shout echoed around the dining room. "I know you're trying to help me out. And I know I screwed everything up, but the place is worth more than that."

"I'm sorry, but I don't have that kind of money just lying around." Troy's lugubrious whine rolled back toward me with so much force that I practically had to sidestep it.

Sam crossed her arms over her chest and curled down as if in agony.

"Drew's not going to accept less than twenty thousand," she said. "That's what he put into this place. He deserves to get his money back."

"I can't pay what I don't have," Troy responded. "If you're worried about Drew, then maybe you could sell your half for less."

I'll admit, I was torn. After so long, it felt good to hear Sam arguing in my defense. But only a dick would have allowed her to accept less than a fair deal for her half of Eelgrass. Not after she'd already been intimidated into signing it over for a pittance once.

So I took that opportunity to flip on the kitchen lights and crank the radio. Sam jumped, and Troy spun around to glower at me.

I strolled up to them and then walked behind the bar toward the espresso machine.

"Hey, guys, sorry I'm late. The ferry was delayed."

"What ferry? Where did you go?" Sam's surprise turned to bewilderment.

"Seattle," I said. "I had a date. Do either of you want a coffee? I need about twenty shots, I think."

"I'm fine." Sam seated herself at the bar.

Troy took a seat next to Sam's. "I'll take a quad half-caff low-fat tall latte with extra foam."

It took all my strength of will, but I smiled instead of rolling my eyes.

"Sure." We didn't have decaf, but he'd be long gone by the time he realized that. "So you're no longer interested in entering our noble industry, Troy? I can't say I blame you."

"It's not that I'm not interested; I'm just not made of money. I don't know why you and Sam can't seem to understand that." Troy raked his fingers through his hair so dramatically that I could vividly imagine him spending hours perfecting the move in front of a mirror. "We all know this place isn't going to make me anything. When Charlie had a restaurant here, it was a complete failure, and now nobody's coming to this place either."

"Well, that's partially due to the fact that it hasn't been open." I shot Sam a meaningful glance, then returned to assembling Troy's ridiculous beverage. "But also it's not the tourist season. Your store hasn't exactly been rocking the customers. No business on the island is booming this time of year. But to my thinking, that would make this the perfect time for you to learn the ropes."

"What ropes?"

"Learning the recipes, for one thing. Or did you plan to hire a different chef?" As the espresso shots poured out, I pondered the correct vessel in which to build Troy's monstrous latte. I settled on a paper to-go model. That way he could have a mountain of foam and I could get rid of him without giving up one of my cups...at least while they were still mine.

"Well, I wasn't planning on using any of your recipes, Andrew." Troy pulled a wry smile at the notion. "If I do buy the business and building from you, I'll probably reopen it as something more commercial. Orca's Slough needs a place like a chain but better. A great burger and a fancy cocktail. The people in this town can't appreciate real cuisine. I told Charlie as much, years ago."

"Poor Charlie." Sam nodded and wrapped her arms around herself tighter as if feeling the chill of her cousin's ghost passing over her.

"I've found that the people here are generally excited about quality food that's prepared with real skill and care." I handed Troy his drink without touching his hand and then tamped down the grounds for my own shot of espresso. "And it's not like I don't have a great burger on the menu."

"Listen, I understand the position you two are in." Troy sipped his drink, and I wondered how he could possibly think we would believe he understood our situation. "You're obviously not going to last now that this horrible crime has occurred. No one is going to buy this business off you lock, stock, and barrel either, not with it sinking further and further into debt every day."

"Maybe it would be better to just tear this whole place down," Sam muttered.

"It's a historic building. We're not allowed to tear it down," I reminded her. "And we're not sinking further and further into debt. We've been closed, but when we did open, the customers came."

"That's true." Sam's expression lightened a little. She offered a warm smile to Troy, which I didn't feel he deserved. "We made good money. Drew's recipes are popular—"

"Maybe before he was dragged away by the police, but now..." Troy trailed off.

"Oh, right." Sam's expression sank further.

I kept my face turned away, focusing on the shiny espresso machine. I wondered if this had always been Troy's angle with other people. Feign interest in their well-being, using a front of concern, while constantly shooting down their every word.

What did Troy really plan to do with this space? He had no discernable interest in feeding the people of Orca's Slough. An expansion for his clothing store maybe? The building alone was worth a cool two million. Never mind the restaurant equipment.

"Thirty thousand," Troy said.

"Each?" Sam sounded painfully hopeful.

"Thirty total. That's all I can offer. Take it or leave it." Troy waved a dismissive hand.

"Then we're going to have to leave it." The words were out of my mouth before I even knew I was going to say them.

But I'd had enough. I turned to Sam, whose face showed a weird mix of alarm and amazement.

"Sam, things are rough right now, but we don't have to put up with your asshole cousin jerking us around." I glanced back to Troy, watching as his bland expression turned fully hateful. I drank it in, happy to have spited him. "No offence, Troy, but you're a fucking idiot if you think you can pressure me into jumping at some lowball offer."

"You won't find anyone in this town who'll give you better," Troy thundered, his true inner bully finally showing himself.

"Even if that were true—and I don't think for a second that it is—I'd rather let the bank seize this place and everything in it to sell at auction rather than sign it over to you. Now take your coffee and fuck off. I need to speak with Sam privately."

Troy's face went from red to purple. He picked up his coffee, and pointedly ignoring me, turned to Sam.

"You know I'm being incredibly generous offering you anything, Samantha." He pretended to straighten his cuffs and then turned and huffed across the empty dining room. With a sense of satisfaction, I watched the front door fall closed behind him.

It was then that the oddness of Troy's words struck me. Why would he feel that offering Sam any money for her share of the business was an act of generosity? Unless… Could he know Sam didn't actually own her share anymore?

I turned back to Sam, who just sank her head down to the bar in tears. And no wonder. With family like that, of course she wanted off the island. Had Troy been treating her like this her entire life?

"Come on, Sam, it's not as bad as that," I coaxed. "Yes, we are in a fucked-up situation right now, but we're not beaten. Eelgrass is still getting customers, right? We did amazing business Sunday. We'll be able to survive until a deal comes along that's worth taking."

"I just don't see how this can be fixed." She lifted her head, and I saw that her face was pale and streaked with red. Her eyes bloodshot. "I can't sleep. I can't eat. I've wrecked everything."

Did I agree with her? Mostly. But telling her that wouldn't do either of us any good. I took her hand.

"Sam, no one person can wreck everything. It takes a whole team to wreck a team."

"Oh yeah? What did you do to contribute to this disaster?" She waved her hand around the spotless dining room as though it were filled with the carnage of some massive battle, which is probably how she saw it in her mind.

"I could have tried to talk to you instead of just checking out." I said it offhandedly, but listening to my own words, I knew the truth in them. "I never even attempted to confront you about what was going on here, even though it enraged me. I was too passive."

"Nothing you said could have made me stop," Sam said.

"Maybe not, but at least I could have tried. I could have stepped up and stopped the business from becoming the main venue for Dorian's coke-dealing operation."

We were both silent for a few minutes after that. Thinking of Dorian made me angry and frustrated. Even dead, he was still causing people pain. Then I remembered the fondness in Evelyn's voice when she'd described Dorian as a child. I remembered how Julie had smiled because he had accepted her. It was strange how the impression left by a single person could be so fractured—bouncing between the twin poles of good and evil at the speed of light.

"I wish I could go back to the day I hired Dorian and stop myself." Sam turned toward the kitchen. "I don't think I can ever go into that cellar again. I don't see how you can be here alone."

"I'm not afraid of ghosts, I guess." I shrugged and took a drink of bitter espresso. "Listen, I know you signed over your part of the bistro to Dorian."

Sam froze, seemingly afraid to even look at me. "How do you know that?"

"I found the bill of sale. That lettuce invoice you couldn't find. Evelyn had it."

"I didn't want to do that, but I owed Dorian money. Then his friend came, and he—he's terrifying, Drew."

"Vukoja?" I asked.

Sam nodded. "They went away and talked and came back and said they wanted part of the business. I didn't want to be involved, so I just signed my part over so I could leave."

I nodded and thought it over.

"Whose idea was it to steal Dorian's stash?" I asked after another bracing drink of espresso. "Yours or Alfred's?"

"Freddy's. I was supposed to leave the island with him the next morning. We were going to sell the coke and use the money to go live in Bali. Just get away from everything we grew up with here on the island. But then…everything happened. I got stuck here. Freddy left without me. I haven't heard from him, and he isn't answering any of my texts."

"You don't think he…" I let the question hang as Sam nodded.

"Yeah, I think he must have killed Dorian. Not on purpose, but everyone was really drunk. Lionel had passed out, and Dorian had wandered down into the cellar to dig around for more junk like he always did."

"Okay." That directly contradicted her previous statements to everyone. "What then?"

"Freddy went to get his lighter back from Dorian while I tried to wake Lionel up. But it was so late, I figured I should just let him sleep. I knew you'd be coming in soon and you'd take care of Lionel." She dragged her hand across her eyes, wiping away tears. "Then Freddy came back up in a rush. He said Dorian must have already taken off because he couldn't find him down there... I didn't know until after I was talking to the cops. Figured out they must have gotten into a fight. Freddy was so mad at him..."

"Just over a lighter?" I asked, but of course it wasn't just a lighter. It would've probably been a lot of other small slights and frustrations that had built up over the years.

Hadn't that been how Julie had described Orca's Slough: a cauldron of resentments and secrets roiling like magma beneath the calm surface?

"The stupid thing is he didn't even take his dumb Zippo in the end." Sam stared past me at the bottles of infused vodkas Dorian had concocted. "God, why am I always so stupid about people? That Vukoja guy is probably going to come after me for Dorian's stash *and* my half of the restaurant now."

"If he tries, we'll call the cops on him," I said.

It gave me a feeling of bitter satisfaction to realize I'd been right, back on the ferry. Vukoja must have been the one who broke into the Beehive. He'd probably been after the bill of sale. Maybe he'd thought he could get it signed over to him? Maybe he'd forced Dorian to sign a will and then belatedly found out that Evelyn had too?

"That's what Troy said. He thought that if I sold to him, he'd be in a better legal position to fight Vukoja's claim. But then I guess he took a big loss in the stocks and couldn't afford to buy us out..." She shook her head, exposing remnants of red in her purple-streaked hair. "It feels like I'm cursed, like everyone I get close to just falls apart or goes crazy or gets killed or...or leaves me. You're the only one who's stuck it out with me. I'm sorry I've been such a shitty friend, Drew."

"It's okay." I said it out of reflex, but her apology did seem to wash away a lot of my resentment. "And I'm not sure who made you think that *everything* was your fault, Sam. But you aren't to blame for all of this. You definitely aren't responsible for Dorian's murder."

"I don't know," Sam said quietly. "I feel like he's haunting me. Like he knows he'd still be alive if I hadn't agreed to try and steal his stash. And he probably would be."

"No one is responsible for his death except the guy who killed him."

"Yeah, but Freddy's gone and that just leaves you and me here with Dorian's ghost," she said.

"I don't believe in ghosts," I said. Sam's gaze faltered. She didn't share my skepticism. "But if this is going to be a problem, then we can have the basement exorcized or cleansed or whatever you do to evict ghosts."

"I probably just need to tell him I'm sorry," Sam said. "And that I hope he can move on."

For a moment I wondered what Mac would think of all this.

I had to call him and tell him everything Sam had said to me, but I really didn't want to talk to him right now. Then again, if I could hand him the solution to Dorian's murder, well, I probably wouldn't have to talk to him or any other member of his family again.

"Sam, I need to make a call. But I'll come back here after, okay? We need a real plan if we're going to get this place running again."

* * * * *

Outside, the crisp autumn air felt bitingly cold. I was about to call Mac, but then stopped myself. If I called him directly, there would be a record of me contacting him. I wasn't certain that would be a good thing, especially with me having not come to the station as he'd requested. Plus I was still mad.

I texted Evelyn instead.

Is Big Mac still with you right now?

Yes, she wrote; then another text popped up from her: He's sorting through Dorian's collection. I told him it's all sentimental junk, but I guess he needs to feel useful.

A third text bubble: He wants to know if you're texting me right now. I told him he can't see my phone without a warrant.

I laughed.

Tell him Samantha admitted that right before they left, Alfred went down into the basement after Dorian to get his lighter. He claimed Dorian wasn't down there, but Sam's pretty sure Alfred and Dorian fought and that Alfred killed Dorian.

There was a long pause, then the response, Okay, I'll tell him.

A few seconds later a text from Mac popped up: WHERE ARE YOU?

It was petty, I know, but I didn't answer him. Instead I deleted his message and texted Evelyn.

Tell him I'm at Eelgrass, but we aren't open for business today. Sam and I have a lot to work out before we open up again.

You're not selling? A series of smile emojis and fireworks flashed up on my screen.

Nope. You're not getting rid of me that easy. I'll come by the Beehive later. If Katie will let me in.

Just as I pressed Send, Mac started blowing up my phone.

WE

NEED

TO

TALK

I deleted each single word bubble as it arrived. It gave me a childish pleasure, and maybe in some corner of my heart it did me good to know he was annoyed enough for all caps.

I KNOW YOURMAD ATME BUTYOUAREIN REALDANGER.YOU ARE NT A SUSPECT ANYMORE

My finger hovered over the reply arrow. Before I could inform him that I was perfectly fine and just hashing out things with Sam, another message from Mac popped up.

IM SERIOUS DREW DONTBE A FOOL

Deleting a text never felt so good.

My ringtone sounded, and Mac's number appeared on my screen. I declined the call, turned off my phone, and strode back into my restaurant with a renewed sense of purpose.

Inside, Sam had dimmed the dining-room lights and turned the music to the ChillWave station we both found relaxing. I peered around but couldn't pick her figure out of the gloom.

"Sam?" I called over the hazy melody drifting from the sound system.

"I'm down here." Sam's voice rose from the basement.

"What are you doing down there?" I tried not to sound alarmed. But what the hell was she doing in the basement? I peered down and saw the beam of a flashlight sweep up toward me. Sam stepped closer to the dry-goods shelf. The small overhead light made her hair look glossy as a raven's wing.

"I'm telling Dorian I'm sorry," Sam announced as if it were obvious. "I won't take long."

As much as I didn't want to descend into the basement, I recognized that Sam was genuinely trying to face not only her fear, but her past actions. I made myself walk down the concrete steps and pace into the deep, musty gloom to stand beside her.

Sam moved the beam of the flashlight across the cracked cement floor, revealing several scuff marks and a crumpled wad of police tape.

"Where was he found?" Sam whispered.

"Over to the right and farther back." I lowered my voice as well despite knowing that Dorian's immortal spirit wasn't lingering around our old cellar. He'd much prefer to haunt the liquor cabinet of some adventurous divorcee.

Sam linked her arm with mine and edged slowly farther into the darkness. I moved with her. Her hands shook. The white beam of the flashlight trembled as it exposed a dark bloodstain. A blue latex glove lay a few inches away.

A disturbing chill rolled out from the pitch-black depths ahead of us. It carried a humid, dank smell that instantly roused the thought of moldering old corpses. Realistically, I knew it was just the ghost of kimchee gone wrong.

Sam's fingers dug into my arm.

"Dorian," Sam whispered, "if you're here, I want you to know I'm sorry. I never wanted anything like that to happen to you, no matter what I ever said. I'm so sorry I didn't pay you the money I owed you and that I let Troy and Charlie call you white trash. I'm sorry I said your mom was a crack whore. And I'm sorry I left you here on the island when I ran off to Seattle." Her voice caught, and she shuddered.

I'd known she had grown up here and that she had some kind of history with Dorian, but until now it hadn't truly struck me that the two of them had shared so much of their childhood. No wonder Sam was such a mess.

I squeezed her shoulder, and she leaned against me.

"I guess that while we're clearing the air, Dorian," I addressed the darkness, "I might as well tell you that your yuzu-infused vodka was actually really good. And your black-walnut bitters were amazing."

"They were, weren't they?" Sam's voice lifted. "That charcoal-flavored ice-cream was terrible, though." She gave a laugh that sounded a little like a sob.

"Don't forget the gluten-free, salmon-infused Sea Breeze," I reminded her. This time Sam laughed out loud.

"You know, half the time he was just trying to impress you, Drew. You were the classiest person he'd ever met, and you didn't even have to try."

I took a moment to let the idea of that sink in. Part of me didn't want to think warmly of Dorian—not now when he was dead and it was too late for us to ever be friends. But at the same time it seemed pointless and petty to keep holding on to the idea of him as some one-dimensional dude. I might not have liked the side of him that I knew, but obviously I hadn't known all aspects of him.

"I'm sorry you're gone, Dorian," I said.

Sam hugged me, and I returned her embrace. The stale scent in the air seemed to lift, and I could have sworn a warm breeze wrapped around us.

"Did you feel that?" Sam whispered.

"I...did."

"I think Dorian's okay. I think he's moved on."

I nodded, but there was something about the heat and hint of air freshener that made me think this breeze had more to do with a draft blowing through the basement than it did with the gates of paradise opening up to admit our skanky, deceased bartender.

"We should go upstairs—" I began, but then a faint grating noise sounded from far back in the rough wall of the basement. Sam and I both jumped.

"Probably mice," Sam said.

Or rats, I thought, but mice sounded cuter.

Then a very metallic noise rose up and was followed by an earthy scrape. *Shhhhick. Thup. Shhhhick. Thup.* Over and over. Digging?

Sam's body went rigid.

"Oh no," Sam whispered. She pulled away from me and started after the noise.

"Wait, Sam, where are you going?"

Darkness closed in around me. I stumbled after her and the bouncing beam of her flashlight. The concrete floor broke off into packed dirt, and I nearly fell.

"I think Freddy has come back for the safe." Sam stilled for a moment as she shone her light on a rough section of the rocky basement wall. Shards of Lionel's kimchee crock littered the ground at her feet. Sam looked frantic as she scanned the random pieces of basalt protruding from the sandstone wall.

"What safe?"

"Uncle Bill's safe. Dorian thought it was buried in the floor, but it's actually back in the bootleggers' tunnel that Charlie and Troy's dad cleared out to connect his two properties. Like a fucking idiot, I told Freddy about it. Damn it, where is—"

More glints of jagged ceramics caught my attention. How probable was it that Lionel's crock had cracked apart on exactly the day Dorian was murdered? What if instead, someone using this tunnel had knocked it over and broken it while making a fast escape?

Suddenly Sam reached out and shoved her shoulder against one of the basalt stones. It sank back into the wall. What had appeared to be an outcropping of sandstone swung inward, revealing a narrow black seam. Warm, perfumed air gushed from the opening. I recognized the fragrance now. The swank "room cologne" that perfumed Troy's shop.

The digging noise grew louder.

Sam shoved the false stonework farther open.

"Sam, I really don't think we should go in after—"

"I let that fucker kill Dorian. I won't let him rob the family too!" Samantha darted through the crack. Her flashlight illuminated a low, uneven ceiling and a rocky dirt floor.

I knew I'd regret the decision, but I followed her. If she was going to confront the man who'd murdered Dorian, I wasn't going to let her do it alone. My shoulder smacked against a stone, and I felt cobwebs clinging to my head. The beam of Sam's flashlight ricocheted erratically off the clammy rock walls.

I dug my phone out of my pocket and prodded it blindly. The screen lit. A string of glaring text notifications rolled up. I squinted against the light as I turned my phone away and hit the flashlight function.

The blue-white beam illuminated what looked like a small rocky chamber and part of a roughhewn staircase. Ahead of me, Sam gave a startled shout. Then she dropped suddenly out of sight—like the ground just swallowed her whole.

I shone my light across the dirt floor as I rushed ahead. I sidestepped a mound of freshly dug soil, and a gaping hole came into view. Maybe five feet square but it looked much deeper.

"Sam, are you down there? Are you okay?" I knelt at the side of the hole. The blaze of Sam's flashlight swung up, burning into my eyes. I shifted my head to see Sam sprawled across disturbingly familiar shapes. An arm curled under matted, filthy hair. Legs tucked up in an almost fetal position, pale bones jutting out from a badly decayed suit.

"There's a body down here, Drew." Her voice came out in a hoarse whisper. Her eyes were wide with horror.

"Are you hurt?" I asked again.

"I don't think so."

I reached out to her. "Take my hand. I'll pull you—"

A shadow loomed over me. I tried to lurch aside, but a boot caught me hard in the back. My phone went flying as I crashed down into the grave with Sam and the corpse.

A pained whimper escaped Sam. I scrambled off her. My knee burned and my wrist throbbed, but nothing was going to stop me from bounding up and reaching for the edge of the grave. My heart pounded deafeningly as adrenaline raced through my body. I heaved myself up.

The beam of a headlamp flashed on, and the silhouette standing at the edge of the grave swung a shovel down. I jerked my hands back and fell just as the shovel slashed a deep gash into the soil. Gritty, damp dirt sprayed across my face.

"Stay down." Troy's voice floated from the dark figure standing above us.

"Troy? What are you doing?" Sam called out. "It's us! Sam and Drew!"

"I have eyes in my head, Sam," Troy snapped. "Goddamn it, Samantha, you just can't stop screwing things up, can you? What are you doing down here?"

He raised the shovel, and I thought he was pondering taking a swing at my head. I tensed. If I had the chance to yank that thing out of his hands, I would. But then Troy stepped to the right.

"If you'd taken the damn deal, we could have all gone on just fine. But you had to fuck it up." His headlamp shone across the mound of freshly turned dirt. He scooped up a shovelful.

"I'm sorry," Sam whispered. "I'm so sorry."

Troy hurled the dirt down onto us. A terrified gasp escaped Sam.

I spit out a mouthful of dust, scooped up a fistful of dirt, and hurled it back at Troy. No fucking way was I just going to let him bury us alive. I grabbed another handful of dirt, compacted it, and hurled it hard. This time the mass of damp grit slammed into Troy's head.

"You little motherfucker!" Troy hefted his shovel. "Do that again and I'll take the top of your head off."

"You don't have to do this!" Sam shouted. "Whatever happened here, Drew and I won't say anything about it. You can have Eelgrass. We'll just go."

"If it was just you, Sam, maybe I'd believe that." Troy scraped up another shovelful of earth. "But we all know Andrew is trouble."

"I'm trouble?" It was a minor slight, but at that moment it filled me with outrage. "You're attempting to bury us alive! And you have the gall to claim that *I'm* trouble? What? Because I wouldn't let you con Samantha out of her half of Eelgrass?"

"The restaurant isn't hers! It's mine!" Troy shouted as he hurled the dirt down onto me. "I was going to help her set it up and run it just how it should have been. But then YOU came along!"

The light of Troy's helmet burned into my eyes.

"Everyone loses their minds over you, because YOU'RE a hotshot Seattle chef. I was a chef! They just turned up their noses and kept stuffing greasy burgers and fries into their faces while I lost more and more money!"

Troy slammed his shovel into the heap of dirt and leaned against it. He struck me as agitated and exhausted at the same time. And what was he talking about? When had he ever been a chef?

"I was up to my neck in debt. The bank was foreclosing on my house," Troy went on, and I wondered why he was telling this to Sam and me. Then I realized. He was in the process of justifying killing us. He was explaining everything—as if we'd somehow concur with his reasoning and lie down and let him bury us. But the more he talked the more our chances improved because these slow shovelfuls of dirt would eventually provide me with enough ground to get out of this hole.

"That's the business," I replied. "It's tough."

"No one gave a damn. And Troy! Troy just laughed at me. Wouldn't give me a penny, but he offered to help me fake my death. What a brother, offering me a fucking penniless fresh start at forty-six. He deserved what he got."

Any time any guy speaks about himself in the third person, it's a sign of insanity, but Troy didn't seem crazy. Just furious. So if "Troy" deserved what he got, the man singing me a dirt nap lullaby must be…

"So you're Charlie." I stole an instinctive glance to the corpse at my feet. I thought I saw the glint of a cuff link. Probably a match to the one Dorian had locked away in the safe-deposit box. "After Troy kept his part of the deal and reported you dead, you lured him down here?"

"I didn't lure him. I was hiding down here in Dad's old man-cave, and he came to show me the blueprints of the improvements he'd make to my place. The joke was on him." Charlie gave a dry laugh. "I'm running his shop better than he ever did, and not a single goddamned one of the people in this town even noticed the switch."

"I did," Sam whispered.

"You did not," Charlie snapped.

"I did. I thought I was going crazy. At first Dorian teased me about how I kept confusing you with Charlie..." Sam bowed her head and then sank to the ground.

"And then he realized you were right," I finished.

"You should've kept you mouth shut, Sam." Charlie swung the shovel and hurled dirt across us, then swept up another mound and tossed that after quickly.

I watched Charlie closely, trying to sync up to the rhythm of his movements. If I could grab the shovel and give it a hard enough yank, I felt pretty certain I could pull him down. Or at least take the shovel from him.

Sam remained hunched with her head down, as if she'd withdrawn entirely into herself to await her fate. Then I saw light flickering beneath her hands. The whisper of tapping sounded just beneath the noise of Charlie scraping up more dirt.

Sam had my phone. And it looked like she was getting a signal—talking to someone. Most likely Mac. I put my plan to grab the shovel on hold and tried to do what I could to keep Charlie from noticing Sam.

"So I guess it was you who killed Dorian as well."

"I don't have to answer that."

"Why did you do it? Did he discover this grave? Who are we standing on? Your brother?" I asked.

"No, he did not discover the grave," Charlie corrected me. "He just found some junk that fell out of Troy's pockets three years ago when I was dragging his corpse back here. A cuff link. He took it to the sheriff. Mike and I had a good laugh over the whacked-out little kook's paranoid delusion."

Charlie tossed another mass of wet earth at me, but it fell short. He was getting tired and distracted. I edged a little nearer.

"But if the sheriff didn't take it seriously, then why did Dorian have to die?"

"Because he just would not give it up. He contacted Mike's nephew Big Mac." Charlie gave a frustrated, snarling noise. "He's dumb but persistent."

"Mac's not dumb," I spoke without thinking.

Charlie gave a derisive snort.

"What? Are you some kind of boy badge bunny? Dream on. He's a Mackenzie. They're not trash like your lousy employees. Fucking Dorian… The *one* time I come back just to make absolutely sure there's nothing left here that he could have used against me, what happens? All of you show up to have some idiot after-hours party. And he comes traipsing down the stairs with a chef's knife and starts laughing at me."

"That's when you took the knife away and killed him."

"Yeah. He looked pretty surprised by it too." Amusement sounded in Charlie's voice. "If he really thought I'd murdered Troy, what was he expecting me to do to him? He never did think things through."

"Chief?" Lionel's voice sounded far away.

Charlie switched off the headlamp immediately. "You call him for help and I swear to God, I'll take him out," Charlie hissed at Sam and me.

"Chief, you down here?" Lionel quieted, and I think we all strained to hear if he was coming any closer. For his sake, I prayed he wouldn't.

"I have a new crock of kimchee. This time my mom told me…" His voice trailed off in a curious way that made me feel certain he'd encountered the open door to the tunnel.

Charlie sighed. He hefted his shovel up.

I had to stop him from taking a swing at Lionel, I realized, even if it meant taking a blow from the edge of that shovel.

I bounded forward, caught the edge of the grave, and heaved my chest out of the hole. I swung one leg up and looped an arm around Charlie's leg to drag him down.

Charlie spun on me and kicked me off. I fell back into the grave with a heavy *thud*.

Then suddenly a huge dark mass burst up from behind Charlie and wrenched him back and off his feet.

"Mac?" Even through the dark I knew there was no one else that size on the island. But where had he come from? How long had he been here? Then behind him I glimpsed the light of the staircase that must have led up to Troy's shop.

Charlie swore and cursed as Mac slammed him into the dirt and mechanically Mirandized and cuffed him.

Then Mac pulled out his flashlight and shone the glaring beam on me.

"Are you hurt?" Mac demanded.

"No." I pulled myself up out of the grave and tried to brush the dust off.

"Ms. Eider?" Mac called.

"Present." Samantha stood up, shading her eyes from the flashlight's full force. I reached down and helped her climb up.

"Very quick thinking calling us, Sam. Maybe next time don't ask Lionel to provide distraction, though."

"He was on his way over anyway. There were like a million texts on Drew's phone." Sam handed me my phone. "You really should read these, Drew. Mac totally called Troy trying to murder us and told you to stay in plain view from the street until he got here."

"Nice." I brushed a glob of dirt off Mac's shoulder while Sam stepped gingerly around her prone cousin, heading for the staircase up. "But did you also figure out this asshole on the ground is really Charlie, the twin?"

"Yes, I did." Mac switched off the flashlight and pulled me into a crushing hug. His arms felt comforting, and his breath was warm against the side of my shoulder. He kissed me, and I kissed him back, my previous anger swept away by a rogue wave of relief.

Over Mac's shoulder I saw Lionel standing goggle-eyed, holding a celadon pickling crock in front of himself like a shield.

"Woah, chief," he said. "Get a room."

THE END

TWELVE SECONDS

BY MEG PERRY

A mysterious phone call, a missing executive, and an exploding rocket throw space reporter Justin Harris and Air Force Special Agent Greg Marcotte into an investigation that will change their lives...if it doesn't kill them first.

CHAPTER ONE

When his phone rang at 3:12 a.m., Justin answered half-asleep. "'Lo?"

He was resigned to being awakened by his phone. As a space reporter for the Hughes-Simmons news syndicate, parent of the *Orlando Tribune* and other major newspapers around the US, Justin Harris was expected to respond to space news regardless of the hour. If an air leak developed in the International Space Station, if a rocket failed on a launch pad in French Guiana or Kazakhstan, if Elon Musk tweeted *anything*, Justin needed to hear about it.

The voice was male, and low, as if the caller didn't want to be overheard. "Justin Harris?"

"Yes?"

"This is Roy Shaw with Skyose. I have a scoop for you."

Justin sat up in bed, shoving his hair out of his eyes, immediately alert. Roy Shaw was the chief operating officer of Skyose, a relatively new company, which was launching its first rocket in under twelve hours. Whatever scoop he had would be worth waking up for. "Okay, Mr. Shaw, what is it?"

"I can't explain it over the phone. This is something you need to see. Meet me at the Wawa on US 1 in Vero Beach at five."

Justin squeaked. "*Vero Beach?*" Even at this time of night, Vero was over an hour from Justin's house in Cocoa Beach.

"Yes. We can't be seen. You won't regret it." Shaw hung up.

Justin stared at his phone and said out loud, "What the *hell*?"

But he had no choice. Whatever this news was, it must be *huge*.

He switched on the bedside lamp and swung his legs out of bed. In so doing, he dislodged Elton and Bernie, his orange-and-white tabby cats, who turned baleful glares on him and meowed their displeasure. Justin meowed back, then thought, *Good God. I'm the guy who meows at his cats.* He said in English, "Get over it."

The cats curled up in the warm spot Justin had vacated. He showered and dressed, added food and water to the cats' automatic dispenser, and checked his messenger bag even though he knew it was packed perfectly. He'd readied it last night for the launch. When it came to his work, Justin left nothing to the last minute.

He wasn't quite so organized in the rest of his life.

At 3:45 a.m., Justin was in his car, heading west over the 520 Causeway toward I-95. At this time of night—morning, really—the only other drivers on the interstate were big rigs and older model cars with New York plates, traveling at precisely one mile per hour under the speed limit. Drug runners.

Justin stayed well clear of all of them. As he drove, he tried to imagine what Roy Shaw might possibly have to tell him this close to launch. The *SkyCatcher* was scheduled for liftoff at two that afternoon. Ten hours away.

Justin and his fellow reporters had placed their remote cameras at the launch site yesterday morning. They'd then attended a press conference, where officials from Skyose had answered questions for nearly two hours.

Shaw hadn't spoken at the conference; the discussion had been dominated by the Skyose engineers and the company's CEO.

Justin had already submitted his story on the press conference and had opened a file for the one he'd write after the launch. Which might be modified considerably depending on what Roy Shaw had to say.

* * * * *

There was a Wawa right at the I-95 interchange in Vero, but Shaw had specified the US 1 location. Justin turned east toward the Intracoastal, then south a couple of blocks when he reached US 1. Wawa stood like a glowing beacon in the otherwise sleeping town. Justin parked and went inside. There was one other customer, a young guy with a baby strapped to his chest, walking the aisles, drinking a soda, and crooning softly to the baby. The cashier, a burly guy in a muscle shirt, growled, "Welcome to Wawa."

"Thanks." Justin ordered a breakfast burrito and coffee and sat down to eat. He checked his watch. Shaw was due in two minutes. Justin scarfed down his burrito and dug his notepad and pen out of his messenger bag.

Twenty minutes later, Shaw still hadn't arrived. Justin was concerned. Sometimes a big crash on I-95 would close the highway for hours; maybe he was stuck behind a wreck.

But he could have called…

At 5:45, Justin was mad. The guy was a no-show and hadn't bothered to call. *He'd better have a fucking good reason if I see him at the post-launch news conference.* He called Shaw, ready to bawl him out over his excuses… but the call went straight to voice mail.

Justin muttered, "Shit," and didn't bother to leave a message. He sent a text to Tim Farmer, his coworker and the reporter responsible for the space-related video content of the Hughes-Simmons website, who'd recorded yesterday's press conference. Hey Tim, will you send me the link to your raw footage from yesterday? Want to review it. Then he bought a carton of milk and a donut, chastising himself for the junk calories as he did so, and headed home.

* * * * *

He started a load of laundry, then settled onto his sofa with his laptop and clicked on Tim's link. The pre-launch press conference at Skyose's Port Canaveral headquarters had been scheduled for an hour but had lasted almost two. Cabo Barnes, the CEO of Skyose, hadn't seemed to mind answering the same inane questions again and again.

Justin didn't remember hearing anything out of the ordinary, but then he hadn't been listening with Roy Shaw's phone call in mind. He clicked Play and attempted to listen between the lines of the mind-numbing repetition.

He rolled his eyes at the cliché as, on video, Cabo Barnes described his company's *SkyCatcher* rocket as "a giant leap in rocket technology." Barnes was yet another eccentric billionaire who wanted to fly to space, but he wasn't nearly as quotable as Musk, Bezos, or Branson. He'd made his fortune not by building companies, but by investing in them early and often. He'd bought Apple, Google, Microsoft, and Amazon stocks low and sold high. Rumor was he was an idiot savant when it came to investing and didn't know shit about anything else related to his business. The company was managed by the COO, Roy Shaw, and by the CFO, Lyle Briggs.

On Justin's screen, Shaw and Briggs were sitting to Barnes's left. Briggs, who had the misfortune to resemble an oversize hamster, was tapping on his phone, not bothering to hide his boredom. *Probably playing a game*, Justin thought. Shaw, a slender, intense guy, seemed nervous; Justin could see his left knee bouncing up and down under the table.

Hmm. He hadn't noticed Shaw's tension yesterday.

Two Skyose engineers were sitting to Barnes's right, along with two executives from a communications company called Ideodax, Sam Boone and Glenn Pietras. Ideodax was the manufacturer of the unidentified payload that was along for the ride on the *SkyCatcher*.

Reporters kept asking Boone and Pietras about the payload, and they kept responding, "No comment." Justin didn't understand the secrecy. He figured the cargo *must* be a communications satellite. Nothing else made sense.

As Barnes and the engineers droned on, Justin mentally reviewed what else he knew about Skyose. The company was the newest private rocket venture, hoping to divert business away from Elon Musk's SpaceX and Jeff

Bezos's Blue Origin. Their home base was in New Mexico, where they built their rockets in a sprawling factory southwest of Las Cruces, and rented space to test them from Sir Richard Branson's Spaceport America. Their Port Canaveral office building was vast and state-of-the-art, with a shimmering exterior that seemed to change color with the position of the sun. No expense spared.

So far, Skyose had struggled to get a rocket off the ground. They'd suffered several spectacular disasters during testing and had redesigned their engines over and over. But their latest iteration, the *SkyCatcher* rocket, had been relatively trouble-free. Its initial flight this afternoon would be the event of the year for the space journalism community.

Justin was starting to think he was wasting his time, when a question caught his ear. "Mr. Pietras, why aren't Ideodax's CEO or president here today?"

At the time Justin had thought that was a good question. But the answer had seemed plausible enough. On the recording, Pietras ran his hand through his red hair, avoiding eye contact with the reporters as he answered, "Alan Moroney had an emergency appendectomy on Thursday night and wasn't cleared to travel, and Preston Brickman had a family emergency that required him to be in Seattle. They wanted to be here, but it wasn't possible."

Cabo Barnes added, "We're thrilled that Ideodax has enough faith in us and *SkyCatcher* to entrust us with their first payload."

Someone else asked another question about rocket specs. Justin sighed. There didn't seem to be anything on the video that could hint at Roy Shaw's scoop. But the man *had* been anxious about something.

At eleven thirty, Justin closed his front door behind him and checked the sky. Cloudless blue, probably in the upper 80s, not a breath of breeze. Perfect launch weather.

He drove north on A1A to the Sands Space History Center, then parked on the grass and went inside, where he showed his driver's license to the officials. They checked his name off the list and handed him the sheet of printed paper that served as his pass. Once all the reporters were lined up, they activated the flashers on their cars and were escorted in a line through the South Gate of Cape Canaveral Air Force Station to the ITL Causeway, their designated viewing spot for Canaveral launches.

When everyone was out of their cars at the causeway, the other reporters began chattering among themselves. Christie Osborne, brand new to the space beat and the only female reporter in the group, called out to him. "Hey, Justin! Heard anything about the payload?"

"Nope. What about it?"

"That's what I'm wondering. We know it belongs to Ideodax, right? But *no* word has leaked out about what it might be."

Justin shrugged. "Ideodax has enough confidence in Skyose to send up a payload with 'em. That's the only story they want out there, apparently."

"Yeah, but if someone could find out... What a story, huh?"

"Yup." *What a story.* Could Roy Shaw have planned to tell him something about the payload?

Even so, it was moot now. And Justin wasn't inclined to tell the others about his missed appointment. That bit of information might prove valuable later.

The other reporters scurried around, taking selfies with the launch pad in the background and rehashing recent space news. Justin joined in the selfie parade but not the conversation. He felt unsettled, and he wasn't sure why. A combination of early awakening and aggravation at Roy Shaw's actions, he supposed.

And uncertainty about what he would write. So far, this launch was proceeding entirely to plan. Nominal, in the terminology of space flight.

The countdown reached sixty seconds. The reporters arranged themselves so that each had a clear view of the pad. Even though they all had cameras posted within 150 feet of the launch pad, they readied their phones on tripods to record video.

The Launch Vehicle Officer intoned, "Ten. Nine. Eight. Seven. Six. We have ignition. Four. Three. Two. One. And we have liftoff of the first *SkyCatcher* rocket."

Justin sucked in a breath as the sleek rocket climbed from its pad. The sight of a spacecraft lifting off never ceased to thrill him. He trusted his phone to capture the video, and watched as the rocket cleared the tower and soared ever faster into the sky...

Then disintegrated in a massive fireball.

CHAPTER TWO

Greg Marcotte baited his hook with a chunk of shrimp and cast his line into the Indian River toward an underwater clump of grass. In the bow of the boat, his friend and occasional fuck buddy, Ryan Utley, pulled his third Dos Equis from the cooler. "Dude. You're just *feedin'* the fish."

"Somebody's got to."

Ryan swatted at a mosquito, which was attempting to penetrate the layer of insect repellent on his skin. "How soon is this launch gonna happen?"

Greg picked up his phone and increased the volume of the launch director's loop. The Launch Vehicle Officer's voice stated, "*T* minus two minutes and counting."

A pair of Jet Skis screamed past, creating a wake that rocked the skiff. Greg's phone slid from the console, but he managed to catch it before it hit the deck. "Assholes."

"Want me to arrest 'em for you?"

Greg snorted. "Yeah, I can imagine the news report: 'A Lake County sheriff's deputy was charged with BUI this morning when he attempted to apprehend a pair of obnoxious Jet Skiers. The arrest was made when the deputy was found to be more intoxicated than the Jet Skiers.' Channel 6 would *love* that."

Ryan grinned. "You know how at the start of every episode of *Hill Street Blues,* the sarge would say, 'Be careful out there?' My sheriff says, 'Stay the fuck off the news.'"

"Excellent advice."

From Greg's phone, the LVO's voice said, "Thirty seconds and counting."

"Ooh, ooh." Ryan twisted in his seat so he was facing north. "Here we go."

"It's just an unmanned rocket, Utley."

"Unmanned rockets are all we've got these days. Besides, you never know when one of 'em is gonna blow."

The LVO said, "Twenty seconds and counting."

Greg threw a shrimp at Ryan. "You're like a fuckin' NASCAR fan. Just waiting for a wreck."

Ryan brushed the shrimp from his chest. "Hey! This is my *good* T-shirt."

Greg laughed. "You dressed up for me, huh?"

Ryan wiggled his eyebrows suggestively. "Maybe I'll *undress* for you later. If you're lucky."

"Ten. Nine. Eight. Seven. Six. We have ignition. Four. Three. Two. One. And we have liftoff of the first *SkyCatcher* rocket."

They watched as the rocket ignited and rose into the sky. The launch director said, "*SkyCatcher* is pitching downrange."

Then the rocket blew apart in an enormous ball of fire.

Ryan gasped. "*Shit!* I didn't *mean* it!"

Greg groaned. "Aw, *fuck* me…"

"You're fucked, all right. You've gotta go to work, I assume?"

"Yeah. *Dammit.* We'll be flagging debris for the next *week*…" Greg looked at his watch. "Wait for it."

"What?"

"When I say so, plug your ears."

"*Oh.* Right." Ryan held up his forefingers.

"*Now.*" Greg dropped the phone onto the console and wedged his fingers into his ear canals.

Even so, the roar from the explosion was nearly overwhelming. They crouched as the concussive blast rolled around and through them, rocking the boat. When it subsided, Ryan stared at Greg, his eyes wide. "*Whoa.*"

Greg's phone was lighting up with text messages. Most of them said the same thing.

HOLY SHIT, did you SEE THAT?

The only one he responded to, though, was his boss—Col. Ward Vernon, Detachment Commander, Air Force Office of Special Investigations, 45th Space Wing, Patrick Air Force Base.

Report to base.

AFOSI's Special Agent Greg Marcotte typed: Yes, sir. On my way.

* * * * *

An hour and a half later, Greg pulled his F-150 up to the South Gate at Patrick and showed his badge to the guard, who waved him through. He passed the golf course and the runways, entered the main complex of the base, and parked behind the nondescript building that housed the AFOSI offices. He swiped his ID, then pressed his thumb to the biometric lock and pulled the door open.

The rest of the team—Special Agents Zach Wells, Mindy Leonard, and Tom Santos—were arrayed around the conference-room table. From the head of the table, Vernon raised a sardonic eyebrow. "Glad you could make it, Special Agent Marcotte."

Zach and Mindy smirked. Tom, who had no discernible sense of humor, frowned.

Greg said, "Sorry, sir. I was north of Pineda Causeway in the boat when you texted."

Vernon shook his head slightly, but Greg knew he wasn't seriously peeved. "As I was saying, a two-mile perimeter has been established around SLC-14. Several brush fires were ignited, and fire crews are on scene. There are no reports of casualties on the ground. The 0083s are removing nonessential personnel from the area."

An 0083 was the federal equivalent of a beat cop. In the Army or Marines, they'd be called MPs. Cape Canaveral Air Force Station had its own 0083s, but the ones from Patrick would be called in for this search as well.

Vernon continued. "I don't have to tell you, this is a sensitive forensic operation. Our task is to make sure that every fragment in that debris field is flagged, mapped, and collected. The FAA investigators are already on the way." The Federal Aviation Administration was the investigative body for commercial space transportation mishaps.

"Debris will be taken to a hangar at Canaveral. Once the FAA is on site, the investigation of the explosion belongs to them. If they ask for assistance, we will provide it. Questions?"

The four agents spoke in unison. "No, sir."

"All right. Let's move."

Greg and Mindy hurried to the office they shared. Mindy said, "I already stocked our cases."

"Thanks." Greg retrieved a two-frequency GPS receiver from a desk drawer. "Where were you?"

"Playalinda." The beach, part of the Canaveral National Seashore, was just north of the Kennedy Space Center. "Can you *believe* it? The concussion blast nearly blew me off my feet."

"Tell me about it. We were a good twelve miles away, and the blast rocked the boat."

Mindy poked him in the shoulder. "*We?*"

"Ryan came over." Mindy was one of the few people in Greg's professional orbit who knew for certain he was gay. But he didn't particularly want to discuss Ryan with Mindy right now. "Why did they launch from 14?"

Space Launch Complex 14 was the pad from which John Glenn first flew into orbit. It had been decommissioned, then restored in the late 1990s, but hadn't been used for a launch since the 1960s.

Mindy shrugged. "It's been designated as Skyose's pad." The parent company of the *SkyCatcher* rocket, and one of the corporate entities they'd be dealing with. "Don't know why they picked it. Why are you taking extra ammo?"

Greg tucked two extra clips for his SIG SAUER into his bag. "Snakes? Gators? Wild boar? Panthers? Rabid seagulls? Y'all's critters down here are as crazy as your people."

Mindy snickered. Unlike Greg, she was a Florida native, entirely unfazed by its lethal flora and fauna. "I'm *sure* you had snakes in North Carolina."

"Yeah, and they knew their place." Greg grinned at her. "Let's go."

* * * * *

Greg and Mindy tossed their bags and boxes of equipment into the back of Greg's truck, then formed up in a convoy behind Col. Vernon in his car, and Zach and Tom in Zach's SUV. They exited Patrick onto A1A and turned north, passing base housing on the left and the ocean on their right. They maneuvered through Cocoa Beach—traffic was terrible, thanks to all the lookie-loos who'd gathered for the launch—then passed the Preacher Bar on the left. Mindy gazed at it longingly. "As soon as we're done…"

"Oh, *hell* yeah."

"Unless Ryan will be waiting for you at home."

Greg snorted. "He won't."

Mindy gave him a sideways look over the top of her sunglasses. "How is Ryan?"

"Just dandy. Right now he's at my house, sobering up while he hoses down the boat. He'll probably eat one of my steaks, then head back to Clermont."

"You need a *real* boyfriend."

"Uh-huh. I don't have *time* for a real boyfriend. What guy in his right mind would put up with the hours we keep?"

"Jack does."

Greg returned Mindy's sideways look. "Right. Will Jack be waiting for you at home?"

"Pfft. Hardly. He's working this weekend." Mindy's boyfriend, Jack Clauson, was a DEA agent in South Florida.

Mindy said, "I'll see Jack next weekend. When are you gonna see Ryan again?"

Greg sighed. "I don't know. Look, Ryan is not relationship material. He's still trying to convince himself he's bi, not gay. He'll end up marrying some poor girl just to keep the rednecks in the Lake County Sheriff's Department from speculating about him."

"But he'll still come fishing with his good buddy Greg, I bet."

"Maybe. Forget about Ryan, okay?"

Mindy grinned at him. "Sure. Whatever you say."

"Shut up."

She laughed.

Greg turned onto State Road 401, passed the Port Canaveral cruise terminals, and pulled up to the South Gate of Cape Canaveral Air Force Station behind Col. Vernon and Zach. He noted that the security presence at the gate was seriously enhanced. They were allowed through, and followed the others to the staging area, which was the infield of a running track at the edge of the cluster of buildings that constituted the operations of the station. In the distance Greg could see clumps of firefighters, still mopping up hotspots in the brush.

Vernon exited his car and began a conversation with a uniformed colonel, whom Greg recognized as the commander responsible for Canaveral. Greg and Mindy hauled their equipment from the truck and joined Zach and Tom at the edge of the gathered crowd of military law-enforcement personnel.

The commander handed Vernon a bullhorn, and he switched it on. "All right, people, we've divided the search area into four sectors." He outlined the boundaries. "Also, be aware that we have a report of a missing Skyose employee. He drove through South Gate at 5:15 a.m. today and never left, and is currently unaccounted for. Male, 5'10, dark hair, last seen wearing khaki slacks and a blue button-down shirt. Keep your eyes open for anything that might relate to his whereabouts."

Greg called his assigned team together and led them to the border of their quadrant, about 2000 feet from the buildings, and spoke as he handed out contamination suits and latex gloves. "All right, folks, we're going to walk our sector in a line behind the guys with the sniffers." The sniffer techs would be testing the air for toxic chemicals. "Suit up, then grab a bundle of marker flags. When you see something, plant the marker, take photos of the item in place, then record the GPS coordinates. If you have a question, get my attention. I'll walk in the center of the line." He arranged the mixture of 0083s and airmen in a long row. "Ready?"

"Yes, sir!"

A half hour later, there was a small forest of marker flags planted in Greg's sector. Greg was taking the coordinates of a large chunk of metal, when one of his search team waved at him. "Sir? Over here."

A circle of four, three men and a woman, were staring at a flagged item on the ground. At Greg's approach, they parted. The woman, an 0083 Greg recognized from Patrick, pointed. "Check it out, sir."

Greg stared at the object on the ground. "What. The. Fuck?"

Lying at his feet was what appeared to be the rearview mirror from an automobile.

The woman said, "Exactly, sir."

"Have you photographed and marked GPS?"

"Yes, sir."

He picked it up and turned it over. The mirror was oblong and looked old. The glass was cracked, but otherwise the mirror was in decent shape.

One of the others said, "It must have already been out here. Right, sir?"

"The problem with that theory, Airman, is that it's not rusted. So wherever it came from, it hasn't been here long." Greg set the mirror back beside its flag. "Keep your eyes peeled for anything else that shouldn't be out here."

"Yes, sir."

Greg had just reached his previous location when his phone rang. He glanced at the screen; it was Tom Santos.

"Hey, Tom."

"Um…Special Agent Marcotte? This is Airman First Class Fleshman. Sir."

"Hello, Airman Fleshman. Why are you using Agent Santos's phone?"

"He asked me to call you, sir."

"Okay…where is Agent Santos?"

Airman Fleshman's tone was buoyantly cheerful. "He's puking on the crime scene, sir."

"*Crime scene?*"

Greg's yelp attracted the attention of several people around him, who stopped and stared. Airman Fleshman said, "Yes, sir. It's… Agent Santos said you'd better come over here."

"All right. Send me your coordinates, and then do me a favor and call Col. Vernon on Agent Santos's phone. Tell him the same thing you told me."

"Yes, *sir.*"

Greg turned to the kid next to him, who looked like he was about twelve. Since Greg had turned forty last year, it suddenly seemed as if the United States Air Force was populated primarily with teenagers. "Staff Sergeant… Collins. You're an 0083, right?"

"Yes, sir."

"Outstanding. You're in charge. Keep the team moving. I'll be back. Possibly."

Collins grinned. "Yes, *sir.*"

Greg's phone beeped with the coordinates. He set his satnav and started walking.

A mile away, he located Tom Santos, who was pale and sweating. "Greg. Thanks for coming. I didn't know…" His voice faded, and he simply pointed.

Greg turned his gaze in the same direction the rest of Tom's team was staring and groaned. "Oh, for *fuck's sake.*"

About twenty yards away, on the riverbank, a massive gator crouched under a clump of palmettos. Greg figured it was at least nine feet long. And clenched in its jaws was what matched the description of the missing Skyose employee.

Tom said, "I've never…"

"Me either." Greg frowned at the offending gator, who didn't seem to be in a rush to go anywhere or do anything. "How close did you get?"

"Close enough. I nearly stepped on its tail."

"You're sure the guy's dead?"

Tom gulped and nodded. "I'm sure."

Airman Fleshman, who was eyeing Tom warily, asked, "Should we kill the gator, sir?"

Greg said, "Unless you know another way to convince it to abandon its lunch."

"Oh, God…" Tom turned and ran.

Airman Fleshman watched him go. "I thought you guys were cops. Sir."

"Most of us aren't that kind of cop. Do you know how to kill a gator, Airman? 'Cause that thing is armored like an M1."

Airman Fleshman spread his hands in a shrug. "I'm from Montana, sir. This is not exactly in my skill set."

Greg considered his options. "So the question is, do we kill it ourselves, or do we call a trapper?"

"Won't a trapper take a while to get here, sir? That thing could start eating…"

Greg clapped Fleshman on the shoulder. "This sort of decision, Airman, is why God invented colonels. And here comes mine now."

Ward Vernon strode up to them, scowling. "Where the hell is Santos?"

Greg said, "Throwing up, sir." He pointed to the gator.

Vernon's jaw dropped. "Jeeezus Hallelujah Christ!"

Airman Fleshman was biting his lip to keep from laughing. Greg said, "Should we call a trapper or kill it ourselves, sir?"

"A trapper could take a couple of hours to get here. The gator could drag the body into the river, and we'd be shit outta luck. Where is Agent Leonard? She used to work as a National Park cop in the Everglades. She should know how to handle this."

"I'll call her, sir." Greg tapped his phone. When Mindy answered, he said, "Hey, we need you in Tom's sector. We think we found the missing man, but a gator has him."

"What do you mean, a gator *has* him?"

"In its mouth. Carrying him around. This is a BFG. You know how to kill 'em, right?"

Mindy grunted. "Yeah, except it's illegal to kill a gator in Florida unless you have a license. Send me your coordinates."

Greg sent them. "She's on her way." He'd let her explain to Vernon that they weren't legally allowed to kill the gator.

Vernon said, "BFG?"

"Big fucking gator, sir."

Airman Fleshman was nearly biting through his lip. Tom reappeared, and grew even paler when he saw Vernon. "Sorry, sir."

Vernon brushed it off. "It's a unique situation, Agent Santos. I'm sure it won't happen again."

"No, sir." But Tom didn't look sure at all.

Mindy arrived a few minutes later and surveyed the situation, shaking her head. "*Damn.*"

Vernon said, "Indeed. What kind of gun do we need to kill this gator, Agent Leonard?"

"Our service weapons would work, sir. But it's illegal to kill a gator without a permit."

Vernon scowled. "We're the United States Air Force, dammit. We'll shoot whatever we like. I'll deal with the Department of Fish and Wildlife later. How do we do this?"

"Shoot it in the eye, sir." Mindy smirked. "If someone was to use a sniper rifle, for example, it would kill the gator but not damage the remains any further."

Vernon and Tom both turned expectantly to Greg, who sighed. "I'll fetch the rifle, sir."

CHAPTER THREE

The group of reporters responded to the explosion in unison. "*Oh, shit!*" Someone yelled, "*Run!*"

Justin snatched his phone and tripod and ran for his car. But he knew they didn't have time…

The roar of the explosion and the accompanying concussion blast reached them in fifteen seconds. Justin dropped to the ground, gasping. It felt like his brain, muscles, and other internal organs were all vibrating in sync.

It took him several seconds to regain his senses. He scrambled to his car, dumped his stuff in the back seat, and fumbled for the keys in his pocket.

They weren't in any danger, unless the wind shifted and blew the fumes from the explosion in their direction. But he'd noted earlier that the breeze was from the west. All the toxins should be carried out to sea.

He was easing out of his parking spot when two white Jeeps appeared at the west end of the causeway. A man in uniform climbed out of one Jeep and started waving the cars in his direction. The other Jeep waited until the cars were lining up behind it, then began leading them off the property. Once the reporters' cars were all moving, Justin glanced into his rearview mirror to see the first Jeep pull in behind them. Ensuring they all left ASAP.

The Jeeps guided them through Kennedy Space Center property until they were through the gate, then turned around and left them. Justin called Roy Shaw's number, not really expecting an answer. Shaw would be in the thick of corporate damage-control efforts.

Shaw didn't pick up. Justin gripped his steering wheel, still rattled.

Nothing a beer couldn't fix.

It was unspoken custom. After every launch, members of the press corps headed for the quirky Preacher Bar, just outside the Port Canaveral cruise ship terminals, at the northern tip of the small town of Cape Canaveral.

Inside the bar, Justin stood still for a second, allowing his eyes to adjust to the dark interior. He grabbed a table with Tim Farmer and his other fellow Hughes-Simmons reporter, still photographer Enrique Castro.

Tim and Enrique pounced on him as soon as he sat down. "Have you heard anything?"

"Nope." Justin poured himself a glass of Heineken from the pitcher on the table and checked his Twitter feed. "You know the drill. The military will maintain total silence until they get a handle on what happened."

Tim pulled out his phone and clicked on the video he'd shot of the launch. "Holy *shit*. What the hell happened here?"

Enrique had his phone out too. "Twelve seconds after *T* minus zero. Twelve *seconds*."

Justin shook his head, thinking about Roy Shaw and wondering if there was a connection. What had Roy wanted to show him? Had Roy discovered a design flaw? Or a shortcut taken somewhere in the rocket's construction?

Christie Osborne stopped at their table. "Can I sit with you guys?"

Tim shrugged, and Enrique said, "Sure."

She plopped down. "What *happened*?"

"Beats me." Tim ran the video again, in slow motion this time, and squinted at the screen. "Shit. I don't see anything."

Christie asked, "Why'd we have to leave through KSC?"

Justin and Enrique exchanged an amused glance. This new kid had a few things to learn. Tim explained patiently, "The road back through Canaveral is probably covered with flaming debris."

Christie's eyes widened. "*Oh.* Wow. When will we get our cameras back?"

Tim and Enrique both burst out laughing. Justin said, "We're not getting them back. Either they were destroyed, or they'll confiscate them for evidence."

"What? Can they *do* that? That's my property!"

Tim said, "Did you *read* those agreements you signed? Your camera, or what's left of it, belongs to the US Air Force now."

Christie tugged at her hair. "I can't *afford* another one."

Enrique said, "Five months till Christmas." He'd lost a camera too, but had another one with him. It was probably his photo that would grace the front page of the newspaper tomorrow.

Justin lost track of the conversation at that point. He was watching the two men who'd just entered—Sam Boone and Glenn Pietras, the Ideodax executives who'd been at the pre-launch press conference. Both men were slender and pale, with scruffy beards, and wore jeans and polo shirts. They didn't seem familiar with the bar; they scanned the room, then chose a pair of seats as far away from everyone else as possible.

Hmm. Justin waited until the pair had ordered, then said to his friends, "Be right back," and sidled up to the two men.

They fixed him with a morose stare. Pietras said, "Who the hell are you?"

"Justin Harris, *Orlando Tribune*." He sat down uninvited. "I haven't seen you in here before."

Boone said, "That's because we haven't been here before. And we're not talking to a reporter."

Justin said, "That's the beauty of the Preacher. Nothing said in here ever makes it into a news story."

Boone was skeptical. "That's hard to believe."

"But it's true. You're with Ideodax, right? I recognize you from the press conference yesterday."

"Right."

"Shit. Sorry about your loss."

Pietras snorted, which made Justin wonder why. Boone eyed Justin with interest. "Thanks."

"Once the investigation is underway, will you be able to release any information about the payload?"

"Doubtful."

"I'm sure you understand my curiosity. It's unusual for a corporate payload to be classified, and even more unusual that nothing leaked about it."

Boone asked, "What did you say your name was?"

"Justin Harris."

The guy offered his hand. "Sam Boone. My taciturn friend here is Glenn Pietras. Do you have a card?"

Justin dug in his pocket. "Here you go."

Boone smiled as he slipped Justin's card into his pocket. "It's reassuring to hear that no information leaked about the payload."

Justin shook his head. "If it had, I'd have heard. Thanks."

"You're welcome."

When Justin returned to his seat, Tim asked, "Aren't those guys from Ideodax?"

"Yup."

Tim, Enrique, and Christie said in unison, "*Sheeee-it.*"

Justin had to laugh.

CHAPTER FOUR

In his previous life, Greg had been a cop—*that* kind of cop, as Airman Fleshman would see it—with the Charlotte-Mecklenburg Police Department. In addition to his duties as a homicide detective, he'd served as a SWAT team sniper. After joining AFOSI, he'd qualified through the Air Force's Close Precision Engagement Course to maintain his sniper status.

Once a sniper, always a sniper. You never knew when it might come in handy.

Like today.

Greg kept his Remington 700 behind the seat of his truck. He scooped up a handful of rounds of ammo, hoping he'd only need one, and jogged back to the location.

The gator hadn't moved, fortunately. Vernon said, "We've established that the area behind the gator is clear."

"Yes, sir." Greg loaded the rifle, stretched out on the ground, and sighted, lining up the gator's right eye. *Easy-peasy*, he thought, and squeezed the trigger.

The gator bucked on impact, then collapsed onto the ground as its tiny gator soul ascended to gator heaven. Its jaws relaxed, and the dead man's body shifted forward. Greg stood and unloaded the remaining rounds from the rifle, then brushed himself off.

Mindy said, "Nice shot."

"Thanks."

Vernon took out his phone. "I'll contact OAFME." The Office of the Armed Forces Medical Examiner, who would be performing the autopsy. "Call Agent Wells over here, then secure the scene and start gathering evidence."

Greg, Mindy, and Tom said in unison, "Yes, sir."

* * * * *

The four agents gathered at a spot about ten yards from the gator and studied the scene. Tom asked, his voice quavering slightly, "Are you sure he's dead?"

Mindy smirked. "Oh yeah, he's dead. How shall we approach this, Detective Marcotte?"

Once again, the others turned to Greg expectantly. He sighed inwardly; he'd known this was coming. The others were outstanding investigators—they'd have never made it through training if they weren't—but they didn't have his experience.

Greg passed out clean latex gloves. "Let's work our way toward the body."

They approached gingerly, despite Mindy's confidence in the gator's demise. When they reached the scene, they relaxed. The back of the gator's skull was obliterated where Greg's round had exited. Zach aimed the camera and started snapping photos. Greg squatted a couple of feet from the body and studied it.

The dead man fit the description of the missing Skyose employee. It wasn't entirely clear—half of the torso was still in the gator's mouth—but it appeared to Greg as if the guy had been shot or stabbed in the chest. The front of his shirt was drenched in blood. The only other finding of note was that the guy's face and shirt were coated in sand.

Tom was still hesitant, standing back about a foot behind Greg. "Did the gator kill him?"

"I doubt it." Greg pointed to a set of punctures on the left arm. "The gator grabbed him there, but the bites didn't bleed. He was already dead."

Zach said, "I predict that when we pull him out of there, he'll have a big ol' hole in his chest."

"Sounds right to me." Greg stood. "Zach, why don't you let Tom handle the documentation?" If Tom was observing the scene from behind a camera, maybe it would provide enough distance for him to overcome his squeamishness.

Zach caught on immediately. "Sure." He handed the camera to Tom, who gladly accepted.

Mindy said, "He's wet."

"Yeah." Greg reached down and touched the guy's shirt. It was saturated. So were his pants and shoes. "He's been in the river at some point."

The Banana River wasn't really a river, but a lagoon, separating Cape Canaveral and KSC from Merritt Island. It was a refuge for manatees, but also provided a home for a healthy population of alligators.

Greg asked, "So did this fella find the dead guy in the water and decide to move him? Or did he drag the body into the water, then changed his mind?"

Mindy said, "My guess? He found the body in the water and was moving him to his den. Gators will store big prey underwater for a while before..." She noted the green tinge on Tom's face and stopped. "Sorry."

Greg said, "Mindy, wanna see if you can find drag marks? Follow them to their origin?"

"You bet." She readied her phone to record video and circled the gator. "Oh yeah. I've got a trail." She headed off to the south. Tom followed her, snapping photos.

Zach said, "Not much else we can do until the ME gets here, right? We can't move the body."

"No, but we can search the pockets we can reach."

Greg found the dead man's wallet in his left rear pants pocket. He handed it to Zach and reached into the left front pants pocket. "Bingo."

"What?"

"Phone." Greg extracted the phone and examined it. "It might be ruined."

"I've got SoChlor in the car. The granules will soak up the blood."

Greg took back the wallet and handed Zach the phone. "Good. Stick it in an evidence bag with some of that."

"You bet. I'll be back."

Greg opened the wallet just as his own phone buzzed in his back pocket. He pulled it out and found a text from Ryan. Boat's cleaner than the day you bought her. How's it going?

Greg smiled despite himself. Good man. It's complicated here. Found a body in the debris field.

WTF??

Exactly. You going home?

Nah. I'll wait.

It'll be late.

'S cool. :-P

Greg grinned. All righty, then. See ya.

Ryan replied with a thumbs-up.

Greg returned to his examination of the wallet. The interior had been mostly protected from the water and was only damp around the edges. Maybe the body hadn't been in the river that long. The driver's license identified the dead man as Roy Shaw, of Las Cruces, New Mexico. The slots were all filled with credit cards and photos, several of a couple of kids at various ages.

Shit.

He counted the cash; $157 in bills. Robbery wasn't part of the motive. Greg hadn't thought it would be.

He'd partially pulled the cash from its slot, so he tried to tuck it back in, only to realize there was something else in there. He peered into the opening and spotted a slip of paper.

It was a phone number with a 321 area code. Brevard County. A local.

Greg considered calling the number, then decided against it. He'd wait until he was back at the office.

He was bagging and tagging the wallet when Tom jogged up. "We think we found the crime scene. There's blood on the riverbank."

"Excellent." Greg showed Tom the wallet and phone number. "Our first lead."

"Good." Tom squinted at the bright blue sky. "Shouldn't we get a canopy over the body?"

"Yeah. Then we'll check out the river."

Tom went to the cars and returned with Zach and a canopy, which the three of them spread over the palmettos, then tied each corner to a nearby frond. Zach stayed to guard the body while Greg followed Tom to the river, where Mindy was looping crime-scene tape around a scrubby tree near the bank.

She pointed. "Blood's over there."

Greg studied the scene. Mindy finished taping and came to stand beside him. "Scenario?"

"Let's say he was shot from the front." Greg pointed to two shallow, scooped-out indentations in the sand, behind the blood pool. "The shooter has his right side to the river, the victim is opposite. Victim falls to his knees, then falls onto his face. The distance is about right. Then...these look like drag marks to you?"

"Yep. Straight from the blood to the water."

"It would explain the sand on his face and chest. The killer either thinks that the water will conceal the body longer, or that a gator will come along and dispose of the remains before they're found."

Mindy nodded. "Which said gator was in the process of doing when we came along and ruined his day. The gator drag marks start over here." She pointed a few feet to the north of the human-created drag marks.

Greg's phone rang; it was Vernon. "Greg, the medical examiner is en route, ETA about an hour. Zach told me what you've found. Collect samples for the ME. We'll meet you at the body when he arrives."

"Yes, sir."

Greg, Mindy, and Tom spent the next thirty minutes collecting soil and blood samples. After a discussion of angles and distances, they also found five 9mm casings in the spot they'd predicted. Mindy held one of them between her thumb and forefinger, frowning at it. "Five shots? Overkill?"

Tom said, "Not law enforcement or military." They'd all been taught shot placement: two to the chest, one to the head.

Greg agreed. "No. Maybe someone with a hair-trigger gun, who panicked and emptied the clip."

They recorded measurements of every angle and distance they could think of, then headed back to the body. The ME and his forensic team had arrived, as had a gator trapper, who would remove the beast once all evidence was collected. Greg, Mindy, and Tom turned over their blood and soil samples to the forensic techs, then watched as a couple of them removed the body from the gator's jaws. The techs began swabbing and lifting evidence from the victim's clothing and the gator's teeth, while the ME bent over the body. "Multiple shots to the chest and one to the shoulder."

Mindy said, "Yes, sir. We found five casings."

A Skyose employee ID on a lanyard was stuffed into the victim's right shirt pocket. The ME allowed Zach to bag and tag it, and listened to the agents' recitation of the events of the morning. Another half hour passed. Greg was trying to decide whether or not to pass out from hunger when the ME said, "All right, we're done here. Autopsy will be first thing tomorrow morning. Col. Vernon, we'll be in touch."

Vernon said, "Appreciate it."

* * * * *

Greg and the others drove back to Patrick and logged their evidence into its designated secure locker; then Vernon gathered them in his office. He plucked a rook from the chessboard he kept on his desk and rolled it between his hands as he spoke. "I've instructed everyone that we are maintaining *absolute silence* on this. We will not notify Skyose or Ideodax. The killer might have been one of the victim's colleagues. If asked, we're investigating the employee's disappearance. Understood?"

"Yes, sir," they replied in unison.

"All right. What's the plan going forward?"

Greg said, "The victim's phone needs to dry out. I'll request records in case it turns out to be unsalvageable. And I found a local phone number in the guy's wallet. I'll call it and see who it belongs to."

"All right. Zach, Mindy, dig into our victim's background, see what you find. Tom, I want an org chart on Skyose, all this fella's responsibilities, other jobs he's held within the company, all that. All of you, I want a list of suspects by the end of the day."

"Yes, sir."

Vernon nodded to them. "Get to work."

The agents scattered to their desks. Mindy, Tom, and Zach jumped to their computers and began the quest to uncover the intricacies of Roy Shaw's life. Greg shoveled a handful of peanuts into his mouth while he booted up his computer, then realized there wasn't much he could do. He didn't know what company the victim used for cell service, and probably wouldn't until Monday.

But he did have a phone number.

He'd made a note in his own phone of the number from the scrap of paper in the victim's wallet. He ate another fistful of peanuts, lifted the receiver on his desk phone, and dialed.

CHAPTER FIVE

Justin didn't linger at the Preacher. On the way home, he called Roy Shaw again. He didn't answer.

Justin was at home, stripping off his sweaty T-shirt, when his phone rang. He snatched it up, hoping someone had news. But when he checked the screen, he nearly dropped the phone. The middle three digits of the number displayed indicated that the call came from Patrick Air Force Base.

Who the hell would be calling him from *Patrick*?

He answered tentatively, "Hello?"

The voice was deep and...melodious almost, the accent markedly Southern. "This is Special Agent Greg Marcotte, AFOSI Patrick. Who am I speaking to?"

AFOSI? Not for the first time that day Justin thought, *Oh, shit.* "This is Justin Harris."

"Mr. Harris, I need to ask you some questions in connection with the failed Skyose launch today. Where do you live?"

"Er... Cocoa Beach. But—"

"Address?"

"732 Java Road. But—"

"Outstanding. I'll be there in thirty minutes." The agent hung up.

Justin found himself saying again, "But…" into dead air. He lowered his phone and pinched the bridge of his nose. Could this day get any weirder?

Best not to ask that, maybe.

He changed into a clean T-shirt and tossed the dirty shirt into the laundry basket, where it landed on top of Elton. Justin considered corralling the cats in the bathroom, then decided against it. Maybe Special Agent What's-his-face would turn out to be allergic and wouldn't stay long.

In the TV room, Justin cleared some clutter from the coffee table and straightened a couple of pillows, wondering while doing so why the hell he was bothering. Special Agent—what was his name? Greg something— wouldn't give a shit what his house looked like.

He took a bottle of water from the fridge and waited.

CHAPTER SIX

Greg parked in the driveway of the Harris house, behind a dusty Ford Focus with a *Challenger/Columbia* tag and a peeling "My other car is a TARDIS" sticker on the bumper. The house was typical for the area—a one-story concrete block with a St. Augustine grass lawn and a one-car garage.

Greg had Googled Justin Harris before he left the office, and discovered an active Twitter account and a sizable collection of newspaper articles on space-related topics, dating back about twelve years. Harris had sounded young on the phone, but his work history indicated he might not be that young.

Greg peered into the car windows. The press credential for today's launch was still lying on the dashboard. The back seat was a mess, with notebooks and papers slumped in a pile and empty fast-food wrappers and bottles of water scattered on the floor.

So Justin was probably single. Greg smirked, then chastised himself. After all, he was single too.

He rang the doorbell, noting the well-tended pots of geraniums on either side. When the door opened, Greg automatically offered his badge and ID, having temporarily lost the power of speech.

Justin Harris had the most beautiful eyes he'd ever seen.

Greg pulled himself together. Maybe this wasn't Justin. "Mr. Harris?"

"Yes. Special Agent..." Justin squinted at Greg's ID. "Marcotte. Come in."

"Thanks." Greg followed Justin into the house, observing the dated furnishings in the formal living room—such a waste of space—and the Formica countertops in the minuscule kitchen. Beyond the kitchen was the room where Greg supposed Justin spent most of his time. Newer leather sofa and matching recliner, flat-screen TV, and a coffee table sculpted from what looked like an oversize chunk of driftwood. It was a gorgeous piece of furniture. Greg said, "I like the coffee table."

"Thank you. My dad made it. Would you like a bottle of water or something?"

"No thanks, I'm good." Greg removed a pen and notepad from his pocket, and pretending not to, surveyed Justin more closely. He had a slightly crooked nose, which looked as if it had been broken at some point. His hair was dark blond and fine, too long to flatter his face, with a prominent widow's peak on the right side of his forehead. He had freckles, plenty of them, scattered over his nose and cheeks. And those *eyes*...long-lashed, the color of Scotch whisky.

Justin was a tad pudgy, probably a result of all those fast foods, but he was tall enough to carry it off. And he was tanned, not a pale-faced doughboy.

And he's 95% likely to be straight. So knock it off. He clicked his pen open. "Who do you work for, Mr. Harris?"

"Hughes-Simmons Newspapers. They own the Orlando and Tampa papers, among others."

"How long have you been with them?"

"Since 2009."

"Where did you work before that?"

Justin named a website Greg had never heard of. "And I freelanced too. That's how I got my current job."

It occurred to Greg that he could ask Justin almost anything and get away with it. "You live here by yourself?"

"Yeah." Justin flushed, like he was embarrassed. "I grew up in this house."

"Local boy."

"Yes." Justin tipped his head, studying Greg. "You're not."

"No. I'm not." Implying, *I'm here to ask questions, not answer them.*

Justin looked down at his hands. "Sorry."

Come on, Marcotte, don't be a dick. He could tell Justin was nervous.

But he was trying to be helpful. Greg could use that.

He decided to cut to the chase. He could run background and a credit check on Justin tomorrow. "How do you know Roy Shaw?"

CHAPTER SEVEN

Justin mentally added another *Oh, shit* to his growing stack. "Oh my *God. Did* something happen to him?"

Agent Marcotte raised an eyebrow. It was the only shift in expression Justin had seen in his face. So far, the guy was a walking stereotype of military law enforcement. Classically handsome, cropped blond hair, keen blue eyes, square jaw, broad shoulders, all business. Oozing confidence. He said, "So you *do* know him."

That voice… Justin had a fleeting notion of asking Marcotte to read yesterday's classified ads to him, just so he could listen to that voice. *Pay attention, Justin.* "No. I mean, I never met him. But I was supposed to." He related the conversation he'd had with Shaw in the wee hours.

Marcotte was taking notes. "He told you to meet him at five."

"Yes."

"And didn't give you any hints as to why."

Justin almost said, *I just TOLD you,* but held his tongue. "He said he had a scoop. He didn't offer any indication as to what it was about."

"And he said, 'We can't be seen'?"

"Right."

"You'd never met Shaw anywhere before?"

"No. I saw him from a distance at the pre-launch press conference yesterday, but I've never met him. I only recognized his name because I write about Skyose. I know who all their top executives are."

"What did you think, when he didn't show?"

"I was aggravated. Asking me to drive all the way to Vero, then ditching me… I called him to complain, but it went straight to voice mail."

That piqued Marcotte's interest. Justin could almost see his ears perk up. "What time did you call?"

"Um…it was about a quarter to six, I think." He picked up his phone from the coffee table and opened his call log. "Yeah, it was 5:46. Here." He handed the phone to Marcotte.

Marcotte made a note. "And here's his call to you at 3:12."

"Yeah. And I called him twice after the explosion, but he didn't answer."

Marcotte jotted down a few more details, then handed Justin's phone back. "If Shaw had a scoop of some sort, why would he call you? Why not another reporter?"

Justin shrugged. "I suppose he wanted his story in the major newspapers."

"Do you and the other reporters share information?"

"It depends on the information. If I have an exclusive, I'm not gonna tell anyone else about it until the story is filed."

"Did you tell anyone about your conversation with Shaw?"

"No."

"Why not?"

"I…don't know, really. I just had a feeling it might be important later."

Marcotte looked skeptical. Justin didn't blame him. Marcotte asked, "What time did you get home from Vero Beach?"

"About 7:15."

"What time did you check in to Canaveral?"

"At noon."

"And you went directly to the ITL Causeway?"

You must know this already, Justin thought. He was tired and getting cranky, and allowed it to seep into his voice. "Yes. We're not allowed to go anywhere else. So what the hell happened to Roy Shaw?"

Marcotte paused before he answered. "Pretend we're at the Preacher. You *must not* write about this. If I see this reported *anywhere*, I will toss your ass in jail faster than you can *blink*."

"I won't." Justin held up two fingers. "Scout's honor."

Special Agent Marcotte was not amused. "Shaw is missing, and an unidentified man was found dead inside the debris field after the explosion."

Justin's jaw dropped. *"Dead?* Do you think it's Shaw?"

"Unknown. We won't have positive identification until the autopsy is done."

"But whoever he is, he couldn't have been killed in the explosion; he wouldn't have been able to get close enough—"

"He wasn't killed in the explosion." Marcotte stood. "Thanks for your cooperation, Mr. Harris."

"Wait." Justin scrambled to his feet. "Is there *anything* you can tell me about what happened?"

"No, sorry." Marcotte didn't sound sorry. "I may have follow-up questions tomorrow."

Please, PLEASE, have follow-up questions tomorrow. "No problem. I'll be home all day."

Marcotte offered his hand to shake. Justin gripped it and felt a jolt of… not electricity, but *something*… "I'm glad to meet you, Agent Marcotte."

Marcotte was studying him, holding the handshake a second longer than expected. *Mentally fitting me for an orange jumpsuit, most likely.*

"Good to meet you too, Mr. Harris. Thanks again."

He walked Marcotte to the front stoop. The agent climbed into a pickup truck and drove away. Justin sagged against the front door. The guy *had* to be straight, right? Pickup truck, that steely gaze…those shoulders…that *voice*…

He said out loud, "I'm a fucking *idiot*."

He went inside, locked the door behind him, and stumbled over Bernie, who'd decided to make an appearance. "Bernie, your dad's a fucking idiot."

Bernie didn't disagree.

CHAPTER EIGHT

When he reached A1A, Greg hesitated for a moment, deciding whether to turn right or left. Mindy and Zach might be at the Preacher by now. But Ryan wouldn't wait all night. And he was tired. And, though he hated to admit it, he was completely rattled by Justin Harris. That handshake... What the hell had *that* been?

He mentally kicked himself for trusting Justin. He should *not* have told him that Shaw might be dead. But he'd meant what he said. If he saw it in the news or on social media, he'd throw Harris and his beautiful eyes in the brig.

God, he was exhausted. And *ravenous*. Maybe his reaction to Harris was due to low blood sugar. He texted Ryan. On my way. Throw a couple of steaks on the grill?

You bet. C U in a few.

He turned right and headed home.

Greg lived in Satellite Beach, the next town south of Patrick. It would have been handier to live on base. Tom and Zach both did. But when the workday was done, Greg wanted to put it behind him. So he'd bought the house, a five-minute walk from the beach, and had never regretted it.

When he pulled into the driveway, the aroma of grilling meat almost made his knees weak. He parked in the garage and entered the house through the kitchen door. The sliding glass door between the kitchen/great room and the back porch was open. He stepped through and found Ryan at the grill. "Hey, how long till medium rare?"

"About five minutes." Ryan looked him over. "You been wrestling gators or something?"

"No, but I had to shoot one. I'm gonna wash up."

"*What?*" Ryan's query followed him down the hallway.

When he returned, Ryan was forking the steaks onto a plate. Greg pulled utensils from a drawer while Ryan unwrapped the foil from two baked potatoes and sliced a tomato. Having the food groups covered, they sat on the back porch to eat.

As he stuffed food into his face, Greg related the highlights of his day, leaving out Roy Shaw's name. Technically, he wasn't supposed to discuss it with anyone, but he knew Ryan would maintain silence. When he got to the gator part, Ryan laughed. "Oh my *God*. You might be the first person ever to kill a gator with a *sniper rifle*."

"Yeah, it'll make a great anecdote for my memoirs." Greg scraped the last of the baked potato from inside the skin. "You're quite the chef, Utley."

"Nah. Just single-guy food. Speaking of…"

Greg glanced up from his plate. Ryan was studiously cutting a bite of steak, not looking at him.

"What?"

"Well… I've been texting with Connie today."

Greg raised an eyebrow. Connie was a dispatcher in Lake County, who'd had her eye on Ryan for months. "And?"

"And…we're going out Monday night. It's her night off."

Greg sighed and set his plate aside. "You're really gonna do this, Ryan?"

"Oh, you're *serious*. You called me by my *name*."

"Hell, *yes*, I'm serious. You're gonna fuck up your life like this? *Connie's* life? You're no more bi than I am."

"I'm thinking that Connie might be cool with it, actually. She's a quirky gal." Ryan scraped at his potato skin. "I'm not like you, Greg. I can't be satisfied with weekend jaunts to Orlando to find some action. I *can't* come out to the sheriff's department. And I want kids." He held up his hand as Greg began to speak. "I know. I can have 'em either way. But *not in Clermont*." He spread his hands in supplication. "You understand, don't you?"

Greg sighed heavily. "Yeah. I do. So after tonight, this is it?"

"Of *course* not." Ryan grinned. "I'm not gonna give up fishing, am I?"

"I reckon not."

But he knew better. This exact scenario had played out in his life once before. Ryan and Connie would settle down, they'd buy a house and have a kid or two, and Ryan would never be able to get away on the weekends. He'd do his fishing with his kids, closer to home, in the lakes of their eponymous county.

Ryan's face told Greg that he knew too, but he maintained the facade of bravado. "So. You ready for my goin'-away present?"

Greg shook his head, but he couldn't help smiling. "Did you wrap it for me?"

Ryan crossed the porch and pulled Greg to his feet and into the house, closing the door behind them. "Nope. But I'll *unwrap* it for you, *right now.*"

CHAPTER NINE

Justin woke the next morning with the sun streaming through his bedroom window. He'd forgotten to close the blinds last night. *Ugh.* He rolled over and realized he was alone. The cats were already up and about. Not an unusual occurrence when he overslept; their automatic feeder was set to seven o'clock, morning and evening. They were in the kitchen, crunching kibble.

It took him a moment to remember what day it was. Sunday. He didn't have to be anyplace; he had all day to chase the story of yesterday's rocket failure.

Besides, he'd told Agent Marcotte he'd be home today...

He mentally kicked himself. *Forget that guy. He's gotta be straight.* He'd had a crazy dream last night, where Marcotte had been the one who escorted the reporters to the ITL Causeway, and he'd invited Justin to ride in his truck with him. Justin had accepted, but then nothing else had happened.

He sighed and climbed out of bed.

In the kitchen, Elton and Bernie were sitting by their bowls as expected, washing their faces. Elton ignored him, but Bernie rubbed against his legs, purring. He reached down to scratch the cat's ears. "Hey, buddy. Time for breakfast for everyone, huh?"

He filled and started the coffeepot, poured a bowl of cereal, and checked Twitter while he ate. There was a ton of speculation about the explosion, but all official channels were maintaining silence. As they would.

And no one had mentioned Roy Shaw's name.

When the coffee was ready, he poured a mug and carried it to the driveway, where he retrieved the newspaper. He sat on the stoop, dumped the paper out of its plastic wrapper, and searched for his story. He'd filed it last night, just before the deadline.

Apparently it had been a slow news night elsewhere in the world. Enrique's photo of the explosion was front and center, above the fold, and Justin's story was right beside it.

He grinned. *Above the fold.* He scanned the story, noting the minimal edits with pleasure.

God, he loved his job.

He scanned the rest of the sections as he drank his coffee, then decided he'd mow the lawn before starting his research. It was beginning to look shaggy compared to the neighbors'.

He donned his steel-toed boots—his dad had always been adamant about wearing steel-toed boots to mow—then opened the garage door to extract the mower. He paused, gazing at the garage. His car wouldn't fit because all his dad's woodworking equipment was still in the back. Justin couldn't bring himself to get rid of it. He kept thinking he'd learn to use it someday…

But not today. Justin poured gasoline into the mower, fired it up, and headed for the backyard.

He cruised back and forth across the lawn, propelled by the earworm of Cher's "Believe," which was accompanied by fantasies of Agent Marcotte, despite Justin's efforts to quash them. Justin advised himself out loud— "*Forget* that guy, will ya?"—then tuned out Cher and turned his mind to the problem of Roy Shaw.

Marcotte had mentioned that the man they found didn't die in the explosion. And AFOSI certainly wouldn't be asking questions about a natural death. So he must have been murdered.

If the body was even Shaw's. But if Shaw was missing…it must be him.

He made a mental list. *First, investigate Skyose and see if I can ferret out Roy Shaw's scoop.* One of Justin's valuable contacts was a University of Central Florida librarian, Valerie DeSoto, who would do research for him when needed. He'd email Valerie, then dig into his own company's newspaper archives and see what he could find.

Who would have wanted Roy Shaw silenced? Justin thought that depended on what Roy's secret was. Find the scoop, find the killer.

He started daydreaming again. He'd help Agent Marcotte solve the case, and Marcotte would be so grateful that—

His thoughts were rudely interrupted by the sight of a car pulling into his driveway. An unfortunately familiar face was behind the wheel.

Clay Garrett, his ex.

Justin had met Clay Garrett at the University of Central Florida, in freshman English. It had been a good match for a while. But a couple of years after they'd graduated, while Clay was in law school, he'd joined the Log Cabin Republicans.

Justin had been aghast. Clay attempted to mollify him by claiming that his membership was solely for networking purposes. But as the years passed and Clay became more deeply involved in local politics, it grew more difficult for Justin to ignore the elephant in the room. On the night of the 2016 election, Clay's delight in the outcome had collided head on with Justin's horror. They'd had an epic shouting match. After eighteen years of gritting his teeth, Justin was over it. He packed that night and drove to his mom's empty house in Cocoa Beach.

Ever since, about once a week, Clay would text him:

Hey, babe, have a good day.

Hey, babe, happy birthday!

Hey, babe, just thinking about that time we went to Cedar Key for the weekend.

Justin never replied. Besides, he absolutely loathed the term *babe*. Yet he couldn't bring himself to block Clay. Justin hadn't dated much since the breakup. Between his crazy work schedule, his dumpy body and plain features, and the paucity of out gay people in conservative Brevard County, he hadn't connected with anyone. He'd tried online match sites, but had posted a realistic photo of himself, and no one had swiped right.

So he hadn't blocked Clay. And he despised himself for it...for the realization that someday he might just be that desperate.

He muttered, "*Fuck* my life," and stopped the mower. Clay bounced out of the driver's seat of the Prius—*that* was new—and ran toward Justin. "Oh my God, babe! I saw your article!" He threw his arms around Justin and tried to hold him. "How awful for you!"

Justin pushed him away. "Cut it out. It was just a rocket explosion. Now you've got grass stuck to you."

"I don't care." Clay brushed at the grass impatiently. "What *happened?* Do they know yet?"

"Of course not. It's way too soon. What the hell are you doing here?"

"I was worried about you. And I thought..." Clay waved his hand at the sky. "It's a gorgeous day. We can get Publix subs and go to the beach."

"*No.* I am not getting *anything* or going *anywhere* with you. In case you've forgotten, I *broke up* with you, and since then your fucking president has made life more dangerous than ever for us. And it's partly *your fault.*"

"I *know*, babe. That's what I came to *tell* you." Clay dug into his pocket and produced a voter registration card. "I've changed parties! See? I've *quit* the Log Cabin. I even bought a Prius! Now we can be together again!"

"Clay, that is not—" Justin stopped as his attention was drawn to another vehicle pulling up to his house. "Oh, *shit.*"

Agent Marcotte stepped from the cab of his truck and crossed the lawn to them. "Hi, Mr. Harris. Is this a bad time?"

"No. It's *perfect* timing. Clay was just leaving."

Clay bristled. "Who's this?"

"Special Agent Marcotte is with the Air Force. He's investigating the rocket explosion yesterday."

"Why does he need to talk to you?" Clay squared off to Marcotte. "I'm his attorney. He's not answering any questions."

Marcotte raised an eyebrow, and Justin groaned. "For fuck's sake, Clay, shut it." To Marcotte, he said, "He's *not* my attorney. He's a contract lawyer for Disney."

Marcotte seemed to be trying not to laugh, but Clay wouldn't quit. "Since when does the Air Force have special agents?"

Justin said, "He's the Air Force equivalent of NCIS. He's a *cop*, Clay, and I'm gonna ask him to arrest you for trespassing if you don't *leave*."

Clay turned back to him. "Justin, babe, I'm serious. I've had enough. I've seen the light, and I'm a changed man. There's no barrier to us being together now."

Justin gritted his teeth against the hated *babe*. "The barrier is that I don't want to be with you anymore." He pointed to the voter registration card. "You're a Democrat now. You can do a lot better than me. Please just go and have a nice life before I have to get a restraining order."

Clay pointed at him, high points of red on his cheeks. "You'll be sorry. You'll never find *anyone* like me. You'll never find *anyone* living in this backwater town, hanging out with the other sad-sack space nerds. And when you change your mind and come crawling back to me, it'll be *too late*."

"It'll be too late for *all* of us, because that'll be the day hell freezes over. *Goodbye*, Clay."

Clay stomped to his car, slammed the door, and peeled out...to the extent that a Prius could peel out.

Justin said, "Agent Marcotte, I'm really sorry you had to hear any of that. Why don't we go inside?"

"Okay." Marcotte trailed Justin into the house.

Justin grabbed a cold bottle of water and downed half of it. "Would you like something to drink?"

"Sure, I'll take a bottle of water. So that's your ex?"

"It's been nearly *two years*." Justin thumped the water bottle onto the counter and rubbed his eyes. "I couldn't be with someone who supported right-wing policies. Some things are too important to compromise on. Sorry, I know you're probably one of them."

"A right-wing nut? No. I'm not."

"Really?" Justin mentally kicked himself. "Of course really. Why would you say that otherwise?" He pointed his water bottle toward the front door. "I'm sorry. Clay showing up here has fried my last nerve. And it was shaping up to be *such* a lovely day."

Marcotte's expression was impossible to read. "I could help you file for a restraining order."

"Oh, thank you, but it's not necessary. He won't be back. Halfway back to Orlando, he'll realize I'm right. He *can* do better than me. *Anyway.*" Justin sighed. "I'm sorry. What can I do for you, Agent Marcotte?"

"You can call me Greg. You can stop apologizing, and you can explain to me why you think that clown will ever do any better than *you.*"

CHAPTER TEN

Earlier that morning, after updates from the rest of the team, Greg had run background and credit checks on Justin Harris and found a thirty-eight-year-old man who owned his own home, paid his bills on time, had never been married, and earned a bachelor's degree in physics and a master's in technical communications from UCF.

Time for another visit.

He found him in his front yard, arguing with a preppily dressed guy, who turned out to be Justin's ex. So Justin *was* gay. Greg was surprised at his own relief. The ex was an asshole, and to top it all, also a *lawyer.* Once Justin convinced the guy to leave, he spent the next five minutes apologizing with one breath and running himself down with the next. When he finally came up for air, he said, "I'm sorry. What can I do for you, Agent Marcotte?"

Greg threw caution to the wind...although a tiny piece of his brain wondered if he had totally lost his mind or was only sleep-deprived. "You can call me Greg. You can stop apologizing, and you can explain to me why you think that clown will ever do any better than *you.*"

Justin's jaw dropped. To his credit, he recovered quickly. "Pfft. You *saw* him. He's a catch."

"What I *saw* was an obnoxious jackass who doesn't deserve a decent guy like you. And your verbal jousting with him was impressive."

Justin blushed, which Greg found endearing. "I'm a writer. I use my words. And how do you know I'm a decent guy?"

"I've met a lot of indecent guys. I know a decent one when I find him."

Justin seemed nonplussed by that. "Huh. Well. Thanks. Um…"

"I didn't mean to make you uncomfortable."

Justin grinned. "Now who's apologizing?"

Greg laughed. "Yeah, okay. I don't suppose you've remembered anything else about your conversation with Roy Shaw."

"No. I told you everything. Have you learned anything else about him?"

"Not much. Just that he acted as the payload liaison for Skyose."

"No kidding." Justin scratched his nose. "That's odd."

"How so? Did Shaw mention it to you?"

"No, not at all. Some of the other reporters were talking about it before the launch, just saying it's atypical that *nothing* leaked about a non-military payload. Usually there's at least a rumor. Not this time."

"Wouldn't that only indicate that Skyose is better than most at stifling leaks?"

"I suppose. Then there were those two Ideodax guys at the Preacher."

Greg sat up straighter. "Who?"

"Sam Boone and Glenn Pietras."

"What did they say?"

"I asked whether they'd release the payload information after the investigation was complete. They said probably not. They asked me if I'd heard anything about the payload, and they were happy when I said no. Boone asked for my card. He said he'd call me first if the information was ever released."

"Do you know anything about Ideodax?"

"Very little. This was their first space venture. They're a communications company, so the assumption would be that they were sending up a communications satellite." Justin shrugged. "Shouldn't be any big secret about that. Unless they're a military contractor in disguise."

"Not to my knowledge, but we'll check to make sure." Greg drained his water. "Can I ask a personal question?"

"Sure."

"How did you get interested in space?"

"My dad was an engineer with the Shuttle program. Thirty-five years, from beginning to end." Justin smiled, as if remembering. "He was busy during launches, but he took me to every landing. He said it was a miracle, every time the shuttle landed safely."

Greg said, "It almost always did."

"Yeah." Justin winced. "I was at KSC with my dad, waiting for *Columbia*. Such a horrible day."

"Are your parents still living?"

"My mom is." Justin traced the pattern of the Formica with his finger. "When the Shuttle program ended, my dad was kinda lost. He built that coffee table and a few other pieces, but he didn't really know what else to do with himself. Then just over a year later he dropped dead of a heart attack."

"Oh no. I'm sorry."

"Thanks. Anyway, Mom remarried a couple of years later and moved to The Villages."

"Ugh."

"Right? Now can I ask you a personal question?"

"Turnabout, huh? Okay."

"Where are you from?"

"Swannanoa, North Carolina. Just east of Asheville."

"Oooh. I bet that's gorgeous."

"Sure is."

"How'd you end up at Patrick?"

"With the military, you go where they tell you. I applied for Kirtland and Holloman, wanting to go west and live near mountains. So they sent me to the beach."

Justin laughed. "It's not that bad, is it?"

"Nah. It's grown on me."

"Are you in the Air Force?"

"Nope, I'm a civilian. About half of us are."

"Why AFOSI?"

"I thought it was the best gig when I decided to go federal."

"Oh, what did you do first?"

"I was a cop in Charlotte. A homicide detective."

Justin made an *O* with his mouth.

"Yeah. I was sick of arresting fifteen-year-olds for killing each other over shoes and girlfriends." Greg rolled the empty water bottle between his hands. He had no idea why he was spilling his guts to Justin, but it felt right. "Listen, I need to get back to base. But…would you like to get dinner later? Unless you have other plans."

Justin narrowed his eyes. "You're not just feeling sorry for me because of Clay, are you?"

"*What?* God, no. Trust me, if I didn't want to have dinner with you, I wouldn't have asked."

Justin's smile was tentative. "Yeah. I'd like that. We could get takeout and eat here, if you'd rather. Since I'm a witness in your case, maybe we shouldn't be seen together in town."

Greg grinned. "I like the way you think, Mr. Harris."

Justin grinned back. "Text me when you're free, Agent Marcotte."

CHAPTER ELEVEN

After Greg left, Justin nearly had a panic attack. A gorgeous federal agent had asked him to *dinner*! And he'd *agreed*! What the *fuck*!

And they were having dinner *here*! Justin zipped from room to room, all the flaws of his house now glaringly obvious. The dated living room, the worn carpet, the harvest gold flooring in the kitchen, the dirty spots where Elton and Bernie rubbed against walls…

Justin stopped, took a deep breath, and attempted to calm himself. He needed a plan.

First thing on the list was to finish mowing the lawn. He zipped outside and practically ran behind the mower, then completed the edge trimming in record time. He dragged the pressure washer out of the garage and power cleaned the driveway, sidewalk, front stoop, and backyard patio. He washed his car, remembering the gleaming white of Greg's truck. He ran inside, dusted and vacuumed the entire house, scrubbed the kitchen and bathrooms, and even washed out the cat box and filled it with fresh litter. He collected cat toys from all over the house and corralled them in his office. He scoured the dirty spots from the walls.

Then he stopped.

He walked through the house, scanning for anything he'd missed. He tweaked a throw pillow here, a book on a shelf there, but short of painting the walls, he'd done everything he could.

He wolfed down a peanut butter and jelly sandwich, then took a long shower and shaved. He started to put on aftershave but then hesitated. Greg might be allergic. Some people were.

He studied his face in the mirror, shaking his head as he always did. He needed a haircut, but his barber was closed on Sundays. There wasn't anything he could do about all those freckles. He touched the angle in his nose, wincing involuntarily as he remembered the volleyball slamming into his face.

It was in middle school. Brandon Everett had spiked the ball at him on purpose. But when the teacher asked, Justin hadn't ratted on Brandon. Someone else had, though. Naturally Brandon thought it was Justin, so when Justin returned to school two days later, Brandon and two of his pals had beaten Justin up. Brandon and his thugs had been expelled then.

Years later, Justin had spotted Brandon at a gay club in Orlando. He'd deliberately made eye contact; Brandon had turned eighteen shades of red and run out of the club.

He should get his nose fixed. At the time, his face was so swollen, his parents hadn't realized his nose would heal crooked until it was too late. Clay had always bugged him to have the surgery—it would have to be broken again—but Justin had never been able to take the time from work. Even if his health insurance would cover it, which it probably wouldn't.

He sighed. It was too late for any of that now. He comforted himself with what Greg had said. *"If I didn't want to have dinner with you, I wouldn't have asked."*

The memory made him smile.

* * * * *

At three in the afternoon, with a few hours to go before dinner, he decided to attend to the action plan he'd created while mowing, before Clay showed up. He was more curious than ever, now that he knew Roy Shaw was Skyose's liaison to Ideodax.

Something was going on there.

He called a friend who worked for NASA, to see if she'd heard anything yet. She hadn't. He composed an email to Valerie DeSoto, his friendly librarian at UCF, requesting any background information she could provide on both companies. Then he logged in to the Hughes-Simmons news archives and began searching.

He already knew most of what was written about Skyose; he'd been covering them himself almost since the company was created. He downloaded for review their history of rocket failures, thinking he could use that as the basis for his next story.

Fortunately, the newspaper in Las Cruces, home of Skyose's headquarters, was part of the Hughes-Simmons syndicate. Justin had an online acquaintance with Gretchen Holt, the woman who covered their air and space news; she was also the business reporter for her paper. He wondered if Gretchen had heard of Roy Shaw's disappearance yet. If so, she hadn't tweeted or written about it.

Once he'd satisfied himself that he'd gleaned everything relevant about Skyose, he turned to Ideodax. The company was based in Sunnyvale, California, in the heart of Silicon Valley. A pair of software engineers named Moroney and Brickman founded it in 2016. They'd taken the company public in 2017.

Huh. Two years of existence, and they were sending a satellite into orbit? That was *awfully* quick. The average time from design to completion for a satellite was four to seven years. He opened a separate tab for the company's website and found their mission statement: *to provide free connectivity to the world.*

Pretty ambitious, to his thinking. Not to mention, a questionable business model. But it explained why they were in a hurry to get a satellite up.

Assuming the payload had been a satellite. But what else could it have been?

CHAPTER TWELVE

Greg was grinning as he drove away from Justin's house. He'd been delighted to learn that Justin was gay and single. And *witty*. He chuckled at the memory of Justin's words to that doofus ex-boyfriend. *"It'll be too late for all of us, because that'll be the day hell freezes over."* But somewhere along the line, Justin had bought into a negative self-image, and Greg would bet that ol' Clay had something to do with that.

If he ever saw that Prius again, he'd pull it over. Just on general principle.

He drove back to base, where he found Zach and Mindy in his and Mindy's office. He asked, "Learned anything?"

Mindy said, "I talked to Cabo Barnes. He said Shaw was a stellar employee, no problems. He gave me a couple of names that Shaw would have been working with at Ideodax. Sam Boone and Glenn Pietras. We've added them to the list of suspects."

Greg's ears perked up. "No shit. Harris—the reporter—told me he met those two at the Preacher yesterday. Said they were extremely pleased to hear that no word of the payload had leaked out."

Mindy leaned back in her chair and propped her feet on the edge of her desk. "Why would they care? It had to be a communications satellite, right?"

Zach said, "Call 'em. Put them on speaker."

Greg dialed Glenn Pietras first. No answer. He left a voice mail: "Mr. Pietras, this is Special Agent Marcotte, AFOSI. It's imperative that I speak with you within the next twenty-four hours. Otherwise you will be charged with obstruction of justice in a federal investigation. I expect to hear from you soon." He ended the call.

Mindy laughed. "Go get 'em, cowboy."

Greg stuck out his tongue at her as he called Sam Boone. No answer. He left the same message.

Zach said, "Maybe they're traveling. If they were in town yesterday, they might be en route back to California."

"Maybe. That's why they have twenty-four hours."

Mindy said, "You're in a generous mood."

"Don't get used to it. Who else is on our suspect list?"

"Everyone from either company that was in town for the launch. Cabo Barnes, Lyle Briggs, Sam Boone, Glenn Pietras, and two Skyose engineers."

Zach said, "You need to call Mrs. Shaw."

Greg spluttered. "Why me? I *always* have to call the families."

Mindy said, "Because you've got the *skills*. You're a kind person, and it comes through. You can ask questions without making it sound like the Spanish Inquisition."

"Gee, thanks."

"You know I'm right."

Greg sighed. "Yeah. I do."

"So you're saying I'm *not* kind?"

"Argh! I can't win with you."

Zach laughed. "Use my office."

"Thanks." Greg went across the hall and closed the door, took a deep breath, and called Mrs. Shaw from Zach's desk phone.

A woman's heavy, tentative voice answered. "Hello?"

She sounded too old to be married to Shaw. Greg said hello and introduced himself. "I'm investigating the disappearance of Mr. Roy Shaw. Are you Mrs. Shaw?"

"Yes, but I'm his mother."

"Would it be possible to speak with the other Mrs. Shaw?"

"I think so. Hold on."

Greg waited for a full minute before a younger woman's voice said, "Hello?"

He introduced himself again. "I'm sorry, Mrs. Shaw. We're trying to locate your husband."

Young Mrs. Shaw sounded angry. "I'm glad someone is. Those fuckers at Skyose won't tell me anything."

Greg bit back a smile. "What *did* they tell you?"

"That he disappeared before the rocket blew up. What the hell does *that* mean? How does someone just disappear from an *Air Force base*? How dare they keep information from me!"

Greg winced, thinking of the information *he* was keeping from her. "Mrs. Shaw, do you have any idea where Roy might have gone? Or why?"

"Not specifically, but I know it must be related to the launch. And there wasn't a soul at that fucking company he could trust, especially that moron Cabo Barnes—"

"That he could trust with what, ma'am?"

"I don't know." Mrs. Shaw sighed. "A week ago last Thursday he came home from work highly agitated. He'd uncovered something off with the launch. I don't know what; he wouldn't tell me. But whatever it was had him up pacing the floors at all hours of the night."

"Did he specifically say it was something to do with the launch?"

"Yes. So Skyose must know about it, right? But Barnes won't tell me shit."

Greg was growing to like Mrs. Shaw quite a bit. "Does the name Ideodax mean anything to you?"

"No. What's that?"

"It's the company whose payload was on the failed rocket. Mr. Shaw never mentioned that name?"

"No. An odd name like that, I'd remember."

"Does Mr. Shaw talk much about his work?"

"Only in general terms. I know there's a lot he can't be specific about. When he comes home for the day, he wants to leave it behind, you know? Have dinner, watch a movie, help the kids with their homework..." Her breath caught in a sob.

"How old are your children, Mrs. Shaw?"

"Fourteen and twelve. They're frantic." She started to cry.

"Mrs. Shaw, I'm going to find your husband. Let me give you the direct line to my office. You can call me at any time."

She snuffled. "Okay. I need something to write with..." He heard muffled conversation. "Go ahead."

Greg recited his number. "If I'm not in, leave a message, and I'll return your call as soon as I can."

"Thank you, Agent Marcotte. You're very kind."

Yeah, I'm the kind one... "You're welcome, Mrs. Shaw. I'll speak with you soon."

He crossed the hall to his own office and told Zach and Mindy about his conversation. "We need to talk to Cabo Barnes again."

"That's on my list." Mindy lifted the receiver of her phone. She dialed, waited, then mouthed, *"Voice mail,"* to Zach and Greg. She left a message—"It's urgent that I speak with you"—then hung up. "So no one's returning our calls. Think we can convince Vernon to spring for a jaunt to New Mexico?"

Greg sighed. "I wish."

* * * * *

By the time Col. Vernon arrived, Zach, Mindy, and Greg had completed their assigned tasks and learned nothing new. Vernon called them together for a report; when he heard of their unsuccessful phone calls, he scowled. "I'll call Barnes right now. Any of you have that number handy?"

Zach found it on one of Tom's spreadsheets. Vernon called, but his experience matched the others'. He left a clipped voice mail, then said, "All right. You three, write up your reports, then take the evening off. If no one has responded to any of us by tomorrow morning, we'll ask our colleagues at Holloman and Travis to visit Skyose and Ideodax. Up close and personal."

Mindy said, "Aw, Colonel, we were hoping for a road trip."

Vernon snorted. "Not this time, Agent Leonard."

It took about an hour for the three of them to complete their reports. Mindy said, "We didn't get to the Preacher yesterday. How about it? Maybe we'll find all of our missing executives there."

Zach agreed enthusiastically, but Greg said, "You two go on. I need a *nap.*"

Mindy threw an eraser at him. "Hot date tonight?"

"Ha-ha. Text me if there's actually anyone there worth seeing."

Zach said, "We will. Come on, Min."

Greg said goodbye to the others and drove home. He set his alarm for 5:30 p.m., kicked his shoes off, and fell into bed and a dreamless slumber.

It felt like he'd been asleep for only twelve seconds when his alarm went off. He sat up to get his bearings, then texted Justin.

Dinner at 6:30? Any requests?

Sounds great. I'll eat anything.

Siam Orchid?

Perfect!

OK. C U at 6:30.

Justin returned a thumbs-up. Smiling to himself, Greg stripped off his clothes and headed for the shower.

CHAPTER THIRTEEN

That afternoon, at around four thirty, Justin had texted Gretchen Holt, the reporter in Las Cruces. Hi, Gretchen, call me when you get a chance. I have a couple of questions re: Skyose. She didn't respond immediately. Since it was Sunday, Justin figured she might be out having fun somewhere.

He'd spent the next hour writing a story about Skyose's history of rocket failures and the testing record of the *SkyCatcher* rocket that had exploded yesterday. He'd just submitted the article to his editor when he received a text from Greg. Dinner at 6:30? Any requests?

Justin's heart skipped a couple of beats. He took a deep breath and replied: Sounds great. I'll eat anything.

Siam Orchid?

Perfect! Justin loved Thai food. Clay had hated it.

OK. C U at 6:30.

Justin returned a thumbs-up, then—he couldn't help it—did a little happy dance.

Then he chastised himself. He was getting too excited about possibilities that didn't yet exist.

He had an hour left. He checked Twitter again and found nothing useful. The companies involved were still silent, and everyone else was still in speculation mode. He was waking up his computer when his phone rang. Gretchen Holt, returning his call.

"Hi, Gretchen, thanks for calling. I didn't really expect to hear from you today."

"Hey, it's no problem. We're working on the same story, I think. I've been out, trying to track down Skyose people all day. It's like they're all in hiding. No one's returning my calls or texts, no one's tweeted *anything.*"

"I haven't even seen an official statement."

"They haven't released one. It's been over twenty-four hours, for God's sake. I guess you were there when it blew?"

"Yup. It was impressive."

"I'm sure. So what did you want to know?"

"Is there anything you know of that could account for this secrecy?"

"Nothing solid. But there's a rumor that there was something squirrelly with the financing for the payload."

Justin told Gretchen about his encounter with the Ideodax employees. "I just don't understand the secrecy."

"Neither do I. Anyway, I'm working on the financing angle. I'll let you know."

"Super, thanks." Justin said goodbye, then realized Gretchen hadn't mentioned Roy Shaw. Maybe she didn't know. In which case, Justin was glad he hadn't raised the subject. Roy Shaw was going to be *his* story.

He busied himself in the kitchen, setting out plates, moving beverages to the front of the fridge, waiting for six thirty to arrive.

Despite his anticipation, when the doorbell finally rang, he jumped. Elton and Bernie, who'd been curling around his ankles in hopes that he'd produce food, shot down the hall to the bedroom. Justin went to the door, took a deep breath, and opened it.

Greg looked even better than he had before. He grinned, and Justin nearly melted into the floor. He held up two full bags of takeout cartons. "Hope you're hungry."

"Ravenous. Come on in." Justin closed the door behind Greg and followed him to the kitchen, admiring his cute ass and legs. Greg was wearing shorts, and his legs were toned and tanned. Perfect. Justin was drooling, and it wasn't all about the food.

They spent a few minutes plating up various dishes. Justin noted with pleasure that Greg had brought pineapple curry, Thai basil fried rice, drunken noodles…all his favorites. Justin unwrapped his chopsticks and was poised to dig in when Greg said, "Um, do you have a fork?"

"Oh, shoot, I'm sorry. Of course." Justin leaped to his feet and got a fork for Greg.

"Thanks. I never learned to use 'em." Greg pointed with his fork at the second set of chopsticks. "Every time I tried, it took way too long to eat, so I gave up."

"My mom taught me." Justin snared a chunk of pineapple. "I suppose that unless you're gonna travel in the Far East, it's not a crucial skill."

"If I ever get transferred to Japan or Korea, I guess I'll learn."

No... "How likely is that?"

"Not very. Don't worry."

"Who, me?"

They ate in silence for a moment, and then Justin asked, "Are you from a law-enforcement family?"

"No. My parents and siblings are all college professors."

"Whoa. What did they think of you being a cop?"

Greg shrugged. "It wasn't what my parents would have chosen for me, but they're okay with it. They're *more* okay with it now than when I was with Charlotte PD."

"So they're progressives?"

"Oh yeah." Greg chuckled. "The day after I came out to them, my mom cooked my favorite dinner and baked a cake. It was better than a birthday."

"That's amazing."

"It is. I know I'm lucky." Greg paused for a moment. "What about your family?"

"My mom is supportive. She doesn't want to know much detail, though. I think she doesn't understand how two men would relate to each other without one being 'the woman.' I've told her that isn't how it works, and she accepts that, but she doesn't have another concept map to use."

"Your dad?"

"He wasn't thrilled. He didn't give me a hard time about it, but he *really* didn't want to know anything about it. And he couldn't stand Clay. As you can probably imagine."

Greg laughed. "Yeah, I can imagine. Did you and Clay live together?"

"Yes, in Orlando. When my mom remarried in 2015, Clay and I used this house for weekend getaways until we broke up. My mom's new husband wanted to rent the house, but Mom transferred the house to me with a quit-claim deed. The house was paid off, and she didn't need the money for it."

"What about the new husband?"

"Pure, unadulterated asshole. We don't have any contact."

"What's your mom see in him?"

"He treats her wonderfully, and they share a lot of the same hobbies." Justin shrugged. "As long as my name isn't mentioned, all is well."

"Hm." Greg's expression was studiedly neutral.

"What?"

"Well… I guess I wish your mom would stand up for you to him."

Justin sighed. "It's too much to ask of her. I'm used to it. But thank you."

The scent of seafood—the drunken noodles contained shrimp—had drawn the cats out of hiding. Bernie wound around Greg's ankles, meowing loudly. Greg grinned. "Who's this?"

"That's Bernie. His brother is Elton."

Bernie stood on his back legs and rested his paws on Greg's thigh, scrutinizing the food on his plate. Greg rubbed Bernie's head. "Hey, big fella. I don't reckon you're allowed to have people food."

"No, he's not. But it doesn't stop him from begging."

The cats' feeder released their seven o'clock dinner, and both felines trotted to their dishes. Greg smiled, watching them. "They must be good company."

"They are. You don't have pets?"

"Nah. I'm hardly ever home. It doesn't seem fair."

"Cats don't mind much, as long as they get fed on time."

Greg opened his mouth to respond, but his phone chimed with a text. "Crap. Sorry."

Nooooo. "Do you have to leave?"

"No." Greg read the text, frowning. "Let me just answer this… There." He set the phone aside.

"Anything to do with Roy Shaw?"

"My boss spoke with Cabo Barnes about what Shaw had told you. Barnes says he has no idea what might have concerned Shaw and suggests it must be related to Ideodax, not Skyose."

"I guess that's possible."

"Sure. You said Shaw was at the press conference, right? How did he seem?"

"Nervous. His legs were jiggling under the table the entire time."

"Did he answer any questions?"

"Nope." Justin told Greg about his call to Gretchen Holt in Las Cruces. "If she uncovers anything, I'll tell her to call you."

"Good. Thanks." Greg smiled. "Let's forget about Roy Shaw for a while."

Justin grinned. "Agreed."

CHAPTER FOURTEEN

Greg hadn't had any preconceptions of how the evening would go, although he'd been guardedly optimistic. He was delighted to find he was enjoying himself far more than he'd anticipated.

It occurred to him—talking to Justin, watching him, looking at his house—that Justin could use a positive influence in his life. Maybe he could fill that role.

Whoa. Slow down. Move too fast, and you might frighten him off.

Although, unless he was mistaken, Justin was enjoying himself as much as Greg was.

They talked for another hour, until they'd eaten all they could and the leftovers were getting cold. Justin got to his feet. "Let me get this in the fridge."

"I'll help."

Justin waved him off. "As you can see, this kitchen only has room for one operator at a time. Do you want a beer?"

"Sure." Greg made his choice from the selection Justin had—of which he approved—then watched as Justin busied himself with locating and filling storage containers.

Justin said, "You should take the leftovers when you go. I mean, I don't *want* you to go. I mean…"

He was getting flustered, so Greg said, "I know what you mean. And it's fine; you can keep the food. I don't know how much I'll be home to eat it this week, anyway."

"Is your schedule usually irregular?"

"No. Maybe one evening a week, I'll have to be out on an investigation. Sometimes a weekend. But we don't have many death investigations. This is an atypical circumstance. How about you? What fills your time when you're not covering a launch?"

"Oh, I don't just cover launches. I'm *the* space reporter. So when there's news about one of the Mars landers, or one of the space telescopes, or a new astronomy finding—anything—it's mine to write about. I usually file a story every day."

"You work from home?"

"Mostly. Sometimes I'll get bored of looking at my lawn and go to Starbucks." Justin snapped the lid onto the last container and stowed it in the fridge. "Want to see if there's a breeze out back?"

They carried their beer bottles to the back patio, where there were two plastic Adirondack chairs with a matching table between them. Greg was pleased to see that the backyard was surrounded by privacy fencing. "Hey, there is a breeze. How far are you from the water?"

Justin pointed. "A cut in from the Banana River is about four houses in that direction."

"Nice. Do you have a boat?"

"No." Justin scrunched his face. "We had one, but my mom took it with her when she married Gil."

"That's a shame." Greg considered, then decided to make the leap. "I have a fishing boat. Maybe we could go out sometime."

Justin beamed. "I'd love that."

They talked for two more hours, drinking another beer apiece, covering every topic from politics to their college days to favorite TV shows growing up. Justin talked a bit more about Clay, and Greg told him about his own ex, Scott Alexander, whom he'd met in the criminal justice program at Western Carolina University. Scott had become a cop in Hickory, North Carolina, and like Ryan Utley, felt that he couldn't possibly be out because of where he lived and worked. Their tentative relationship had finally ended four years ago, when Greg had moved to Florida.

As he spoke, Greg realized that his history with Scott and Ryan wasn't bothering him nearly as much as it had just yesterday.

Eventually the two of them found themselves swatting at mosquitoes and were forced inside. Greg rinsed their beer bottles and propped them in the drainer, then turned to Justin. "Thank you for this evening. I have thoroughly enjoyed myself."

Justin stammered a bit. "Thank *you* for dinner. I've had... This has been wonderful."

Greg reached for him, rested a finger under Justin's chin, and kissed him lightly, lingering for just a moment. "I have to be at work early. But I'll call you tomorrow."

Justin's beautiful eyes were wide and dark. "Will you?"

"Yes. I will." Greg smiled. "Count on it."

CHAPTER FIFTEEN

Justin couldn't possibly sleep. After that kiss, his head wouldn't stop spinning. He brushed his teeth, made a circuit of the house to check doors and windows, then decided to strip his bed and change the sheets. Once the washer was running, he sat down at his computer and peered into Greg's previous life. It felt a tad stalkerish, but Justin had never been to North Carolina. He wanted to check it out.

He visited Western Carolina University's website, then opened Google Earth and zoomed in on Swannanoa. He tried to imagine growing up in the mountains, in a place with seasons and snow, and couldn't.

Maybe he'd have the chance to visit someday.

On that happy thought, he fell asleep where he was, on the sofa.

He woke to the sound of kibble falling into bowls and the surprisingly loud crunching sounds Elton and Bernie made when they ate. He scrubbed at his face and checked his phone—he hadn't missed anything overnight—then went outside for the paper. His article about Skyose's history of failure, accompanied by another of Enrique's photos, was below the fold, but still front page.

Justin grinned. He hoped that in the next day or two he'd have yet another front-page story, this time about Roy Shaw.

But at the moment, the most productive thing he could do was go for a run.

He'd never been athletic. When Justin lived in Orlando, Clay had insisted that they belong to a gym—another networking opportunity. Justin had been bored by it all, and had jogged on the treadmill, watching TV, while Clay "networked." As much as he'd despised it, though, it had kept him in shape. Except for walks on the beach, he hadn't exercised much in two years. The evidence of his sloth had accumulated around his waist.

Those days are over. He feared that Greg wouldn't tolerate sloth for long. He dug his newest sneakers out of the closet, laced them up, and headed out.

He made it around his block three times. By the fourth circuit, he was gasping, and slowed to a walk. He could feel the tightness in his calves. *I'll be sore tomorrow, but it will be worth it.*

He showered and dressed, went to his office, and sat at his computer. A potential twelve-mile-wide lake had just been discovered below the south pole of Mars; that subject would serve as his article of the day. Justin downloaded the paper on the topic that had been published in *Science* and got to work.

He was finished by noon. He emailed the article to his editor and was about to choose which of the Thai leftovers to heat up for lunch when his phone rang.

He snatched it up and checked the screen. When he saw Greg's name, he whooped, "Yes!" then took a deep breath and answered. "Hi."

"Hey. Whatcha doing?"

The sound of that *voice*... "I just finished writing an article about Mars. How's your day so far?"

"Running into dead ends, mostly. I'll tell you about it. Are you free for lunch?"

"Sure."

"How about Taco City?"

"Sounds great." Taco City was a terrific, inexpensive Mexican restaurant near the tip of Patrick AFB. Equidistant from the two of them. "When?"

"How about at one? The lunch rush will be over."

"Perfect. I'll see you there."

Greg chuckled. "Yes, you will."

They said goodbye. Justin did a happy dance around the kitchen, startling Elton, who'd been snoozing on top of a barstool. Elton meowed, that chirpy sound made by orange cats that almost sounded like he was asking, *What?*

Justin scooped him up and squeezed him, which provoked Elton to bop Justin on the head with his paw. Justin didn't care. "Two dates in two days, Elton! Life is good!"

Elton was unmoved.

CHAPTER SIXTEEN

The previous evening, on the drive home from Justin's, past Patrick on his right and the blackness of the ocean on his left, Greg had replayed their date, searching for any indication that he shouldn't flat-out pursue a relationship with Justin Harris. He couldn't find one. Justin shared his enthusiasm for fishing, reading, travel, and classic rock. Greg didn't know much about another of Justin's passions—sci-fi literature and TV shows—but he could certainly learn.

Once home, he'd hit the remote and eased the truck into the left bay of the two-car garage, then lowered the door and entered his house. It was cool, dark, and quiet, the humming of air-conditioning and fridge the only sounds.

It would be wonderful to have someone waiting when he came home.

With that thought, he collided with the same issue Ryan had presented. It was problematic to be comfortably out in this community, much less out and openly partnered. Orlando was a different matter; it was a fairly progressive city, and most there wouldn't care. But Brevard County was far more conservative.

But they'd figure something out.

When his alarm sounded the next morning, he bounced out of bed, feeling invigorated. He went for a long run, then showered, gobbled a bowl of cereal, and drove to work. Short-term goal: solve the Roy Shaw case.

He got to the office at 7:45. His phone's message light was on; he punched the Playback button as he booted his computer, and listened.

"Agent Marcotte, this is Officer Derrick Rose, Florida Fish and Wildlife. We received a report from one of our licensed trappers about the shooting of an alligator in the Banana River Lagoon on Saturday. He named you as the perpetrator. Please call me to discuss this matter."

Greg said, "For fuck's sake. *Perpetrator?*" just as Ward Vernon entered his office.

Vernon raised an eyebrow. "Problem?"

"Yes, sir." Greg replayed the message.

Vernon huffed an exasperated breath, reached for Greg's phone, and placed the call. "Officer Rose, this is Col. Ward Vernon, 45th Space Wing, Patrick Air Force Base. I'm Special Agent Greg Marcotte's commanding officer, and he shot the alligator in question on my authority. No, the animal was on US Air Force property, not in the water, and its death was necessary to recovering human remains." He listened for a moment. "No, Officer Rose, here's what's going to happen. My commanding officer, Brigadier General

Loren Watson, will call your commanding officer, whoever that may be, and they will determine the outcome of this incident. No, I will not allow you to speak to Special Agent Marcotte. I'd recommend you inform your superior. Goodbye."

Greg grinned. "Thank you, sir."

"Absurd. How many damn alligators are there in this state, anyway?" Vernon rapped the top of Greg's desk with his knuckles. "I'm going to speak to General Watson right now." He strode from the room, nearly bowling over Mindy as she came in. "Excuse me, Agent Leonard."

"Yes, sir." Mindy watched Vernon march down the hall. "What's on his mind?"

"A Fish and Wildlife officer called me this morning. Vernon returned the call."

"Damn, wish I'd been here for that." Mindy turned on her computer. "Any news?"

"Nope. No one's called me back yet. Shouldn't we have autopsy results today?"

"Yes, but what's that gonna tell us?"

"You never know with autopsies. Sometimes there's a surprise." Greg opened his email. "Hey, here's the ballistics report."

"Anything?"

"The murder weapon isn't in NIBIN." The national ballistics database managed by the Bureau of Alcohol, Tobacco, and Firearms.

"Huh. Guess that's not surprising. Our shooter probably never committed a gun-related crime before."

Zach arrived, stuck his head in the door to say hello, then went to his desk.

Greg scanned his email; it contained nothing useful. "You know what our problem is, Mindy?"

"We don't have enough evidence?"

"Yup. We're gonna need a break to solve this. Someone needs to panic and do something stupid."

Mindy laughed. "Shouldn't be a long wait. What's your instinct telling you?"

Greg counted on his fingers. "One: the killer had to be someone with access to the base for the launch. Chances are it's someone from either Skyose or Ideodax."

"Unless Shaw had a NASA or Air Force connection we don't know about."

"Nothing's turned up in his background so far. Two: it had to be someone Shaw would agree to meet with, which makes me believe that the killer is either Shaw's near-equal or superior in one of those companies."

"That narrows it down. We're looking at either our Ideodax guys, or Cabo Barnes, or the other executive staff at Skyose."

"Of which there are…" Greg checked Tom's org chart. "Five. Chief financial officer, chief information officer, chief R&D officer, chief compliance officer, chief engineering officer. Were they all here for the launch?"

"I'm sure they were. I'll find out." Mindy picked up her phone and dialed. "Hi, Sharon, this is Agent Mindy Leonard with AFOSI. I'm great, how are you? Nice! That's cool. Listen, do you have a list of all the Skyose and Ideodax personnel that were in town for the launch? Awesome. Sure, that makes sense. Could you scan and email me a copy of that? Super. Thanks, Sharon. You bet." She hung up.

Greg said, "Who's Sharon?"

"The receptionist at the Skyose building. She had to make hotel reservations for all the executives, other than Cabo Barnes, who owns a condo on the beach. So she has the list." Mindy grinned. "Always endear yourself to the underlings, Greg. They're the ones who know shit."

Ward Vernon strode into the office with as much determination as he'd stridden out. "Alligator problem will be dealt with, Agent Marcotte."

"Thanks, sir."

"You're welcome. Skype conference with the medical examiner in fifteen."

Greg and Mindy said in unison, "Yes, sir."

* * * * *

The medical examiner appeared on the screen in the conference room, larger than life. "We confirmed that the victim is Roy Shaw. Nothing unexpected on the autopsy. Two of the shots to the chest would have been instantly fatal. One transected the aorta and the other took out the left ventricle. Did you receive the ballistics report?"

Vernon said, "Yes. It's an unknown weapon."

The ME grunted in sympathy. "Sorry I can't help be of more help. Mr. Shaw's murder occurred exactly as it appeared to have."

"Thanks, Doctor."

"No problem." The ME signed off.

Mindy's phone dinged with an email notification. "Here's the list of Skyose and Ideodax personnel who were in town for the launch."

"Outstanding. Bring them in for questioning. If they've left already, track them down."

"Yes, sir."

Greg heard his office phone ringing and ran across the hall to grab it. "Special Agent Marcotte."

"Special Agent Marcotte, this is Sam Boone with Ideodax. I understand you've been trying to reach me."

"Yes, Mr. Boone. We have questions about your relationship with Roy Shaw of Skyose. Are you still in Florida?"

"No, I'm back in California. I don't know what I can tell you about Roy. I did hear that he was missing."

Did you now. Greg said, "We'd like to interview you on Skype, if possible."

"Of course. Is it possible to do so now? I have meetings for the rest of the day."

"Yes, it is. What's your username?"

"Sam Boone Ideodax."

"All right. We'll be in contact shortly." Greg said goodbye and hurried back to the conference room. "We have Sam Boone. He's in California, but I have his Skype information."

Vernon said, "Perfect. Get him on the screen."

Greg made the connection. Boone was a pleasantly nerdy-looking guy with glasses and dark hair. "Hello, Agent Marcotte."

"Mr. Boone." Greg introduced the other agents. "When did you arrive in Florida?"

"Last Wednesday evening."

"Who did you travel with?"

"My coworker, Glenn Pietras."

"Who else from Ideodax attended the launch?"

"We were the only ones."

That was odd. Mindy asked the question. "Why didn't the CEO or any of the other executives come?"

"The only other executives besides Glenn and myself are Alan Moroney and Preston Brickman, the company founders. Alan had an emergency appendectomy on Thursday night and wasn't cleared to travel, and Preston had a family emergency that required him to be in Seattle."

Easy enough to check, Greg thought, and yet the answers sounded rehearsed to him. He said, "Tell us about your relationship with Roy Shaw."

"Roy is our liaison with Skyose. All our communications with that company pass through him."

Tom asked, "Why did you choose Skyose for your first launch? Why not SpaceX or another company with a proven rocket?"

"Obviously, in retrospect, we wish we had. At the time, we wanted to be supportive of another company on their maiden voyage. And Skyose's requirements were far more favorable than those of other companies."

Zach asked, "When was the last time you saw Mr. Shaw?"

"Glenn and I had dinner with Roy, Cabo Barnes, and Lyle Briggs on Thursday evening."

"How did his demeanor seem to you?"

Boone shrugged. "Quiet, tired, jet-lagged. I believe he'd only arrived from New Mexico that afternoon. He certainly didn't say anything that would indicate any intention on his part to disappear."

Greg asked, "How long have you known Mr. Shaw?"

"About a year. But we only met in person three times."

Greg decided to lead Boone down the missing-person path. "Is there anything you know or suspect about Mr. Shaw's personal life that would explain a disappearance?"

Boone shook his head. "I didn't know him that well. We never discussed anything other than business."

Mindy asked, "Where do you think Mr. Shaw is?"

That seemed to throw Boone. Greg thought, *He didn't plan for that question.*

"Er...I have no idea. I'd assume someone at Skyose might be able to answer that question."

Vernon said, "Mr. Boone, how did you hear that Mr. Shaw was missing?"

"I saw it myself. He was missing from the observation room at launch. I hadn't heard that he'd been located, so I assumed he was still missing."

The agents exchanged glances. Greg said, "All right, Mr. Boone. Thanks for your cooperation. When you see Mr. Pietras, please ask him to contact us."

"I will."

Tom broke the connection, and Vernon said, "Thoughts?"

Zach said, "Sounded rehearsed to me."

Greg agreed. "Me too. And the appendectomy and family emergency stories were awfully convenient in terms of timing."

Vernon agreed. "Check on the details of those."

All four of them said, "Yes, sir."

* * * * *

Tom emailed Alan Moroney and Preston Brickman, the Ideodax founders whose emergencies precluded their attendance at the launch.

Moroney responded promptly, assuring Tom that yes, he had suffered an emergency appendectomy, and attached his hospital discharge instructions. Brickman didn't answer.

Mindy determined that the only Skyose execs in town were Cabo Barnes and Lyle Briggs. She called and left voice mails, and then she and Zach went out to locate them. Greg, tired of playing games with corporate executives, placed a call to the AFOSI detachment at Holloman AFB in New Mexico.

The voice on the other end of the line stated, "Special Agent McCarthy. How can I help you?"

"Hi, Special Agent McCarthy, this is Special Agent Greg Marcotte at Patrick."

The no-nonsense tone of the other agent's voice warmed considerably. "Hi there, Special Agent Greg. This is Russell McCarthy. What can I do for you?"

Greg explained. "So we'd deeply appreciate it if y'all could visit Skyose for us and see if they'll allow you to search Mr. Shaw's office, and also ask whoever's there if they know where Mr. Shaw might be. If they act squirrely about that, lean on 'em."

"You mean, if they act like they might know *exactly* where he is?"

Greg laughed. "*Exactly.*"

"You bet. Sounds fun. Maybe they thought they could hide from AFOSI in New Mexico, huh?"

"Ha! Show 'em different, Special Agent McCarthy."

"With pleasure. I'll let you know."

"Thanks." Greg signed off, then considered. There wasn't much else he could do until Zach and Mindy returned or he heard from Russell McCarthy.

Time for lunch. He smiled to himself and called Justin.

CHAPTER SEVENTEEN

When Justin got to Taco City, Greg was already there, waiting by the door. Justin didn't think he was imagining the way Greg's eyes lit up when he spotted Justin. He was pretty confident that his own eyes were equally lit. Greg lifted a fist to bump in greeting, and Justin grinned and bumped fists. "Dead ends, huh?"

"Oh God. Let's order, and I'll tell you about it."

They placed their orders and sat, their knees brushing slightly under the table. The sensation shot up Justin's leg straight to his groin. He shifted to give his dick a bit of room. "No progress at all?"

Greg glanced around the restaurant casually. "See anyone here you recognize?"

"Nope."

"Good. I wouldn't say no progress. We talked to Sam Boone, who's back in California now. He wasn't able to explain to my satisfaction why his company chose an untested rocket to ferry their first payload to orbit."

"What have they found in the debris so far?"

Greg tipped his head quizzically. "Good question. We turned everything over to the FAA, and they haven't contacted us since. But there was that one thing…"

"What thing?"

"We found a car's rearview mirror in my sector of the debris field."

Justin froze, his drink halfway to his mouth. "What?"

"I suppose it was already there. Odd, though."

"No shit. Where's the debris?"

"In a hangar at Canaveral. I'll drive up there after lunch."

"Don't talk to the Skyose engineers. Only talk to the FAA."

Greg raised an eyebrow. "Tellin' me how to do my job?"

Justin flushed. "No. Shit. I'm sorry…"

"Aw, I'm just teasing you." Greg winked at him. "Guess I'll have to be careful about that."

"No, you don't. I mean…we're still getting to know each other, right? I'm not always sure how to interpret you yet."

Greg smiled. "Well, then, I'll have to see that you get more practice."

Their food was ready, and they dug in. Greg asked Justin about the Mars article and listened attentively while Justin expounded on the ramifications of finding water on the planet. At one point, when Justin stopped for breath, Greg said, "You love this stuff."

"I do. If you want me to shut up about it, just say so."

"Not at all. I always liked science in school. Keep talking."

"I guess you have to know some forensic science, huh?"

"Quite a bit, yeah. I don't use it as much in this job as I did in the police department."

Justin tucked the last bite of taco into his mouth, then drained his iced tea. "Do you have to work tonight?"

"Probably through dinner, unfortunately."

"But not *all* night?"

Greg lowered his voice. "What are you suggesting, Mr. Harris?"

"Well, if you wanted to…if you had time…maybe you could stop by for a while? I know it's in the wrong direction from your house, so if you don't want to…" Justin mentally kicked himself for the stammering. Why was he acting like a high schooler asking for a prom date?

Greg held up his hand. "I *do* want to. Very much. And it's only a few miles. I figure, if we're gonna pursue this, we'll both spend some time familiarizing ourselves with that particular stretch of A1A."

Justin relaxed. A bit. "I want to pursue this."

"So do I." Greg wadded his napkin and tossed it onto his plate. "I'll text you later when I have a better idea of what time I might get loose."

"Works for me."

As they walked to the parking lot, Justin was hyperaware of his position relative to Greg. *Not too close. Just a couple of pals meeting for lunch.* He sighed.

Greg glanced at him. "What?"

"Sometimes I wish I lived somewhere else."

Greg nodded. "I hear that… See ya later."

"Yup." Justin climbed into his own car, then watched as Greg pulled onto A1A and headed north.

He wants to pursue this. Don't fuck it up.

CHAPTER EIGHTEEN

Greg smiled as he drove, remembering Justin's enthusiasm when explaining the Mars lake to him. He began to daydream. Maybe he could get transferred to Vandenburg. Justin could still do his job from there. Or they could move to California… Except that Justin probably wouldn't want to leave his mom.

And…he was rushing it again.

Dammit, I'm forty years old. I know what I want.

And what he wanted was Justin Harris.

He pulled himself back to reality with a sigh.

At Canaveral's South Gate, he presented his credentials and then continued north to the hangar where the debris from the explosion had been taken. He texted Vernon, Zach, Mindy, and Tom: At CCAFS looking at debris. He swiped his badge at the entrance and pushed through to the vast space, where a gaggle of workers in white coveralls was sorting the debris into sections. One of the workers spotted him and approached. "Virgil Yates, FAA. Can I help you?"

Greg introduced himself. "We're investigating the disappearance of a Skyose employee on the day of the launch."

"Ah, right, I heard about that."

"Are any of the Skyose people here?"

"Not at the moment. They've been hovering this morning, but they went to lunch a while ago and haven't come back."

"Who's been hovering?"

"Barnes. And the other guy, I don't know his name. Looks like a hamster."

Greg laughed. "Where's the stuff that's non-rocket?"

"You mean the supposed payload?"

"What do you mean, *supposed*?"

Yates smirked. "You gotta see this."

He led Greg to a locked door, which opened to a smaller room tucked into a corner, where chunks of metal, rubber, and plastic were laid out carefully in a grid. Greg asked, "Why is it locked up?"

"I didn't want Skyose to see it until we confirmed what it was. This is messed *up*."

Greg squatted down to get a closer look. *Huh.* "Does this look like a busted-up satellite to you, Virgil?"

"Nope."

Greg's phone dinged with a text from Mindy. We found Cabo Barnes in his office. Gonna question him in a few. No sign of Lyle Briggs.

He asked Virgil for gloves, then picked up a piece of rubber from the nearest grid. "Am I crazy, or is this a chunk of tire tread?"

"You're not crazy. Check this out." Virgil reached into another grid and picked up another chunk of rubber. "What's that look like to you?"

Greg barked a laugh, amazed by what he was seeing. "That's half of a *brake pedal*."

"Yup. You know what I think this is? When we were kids, my brother and I tore down and rebuilt a couple of VW Bugs. The old ones, you know. I spent a lotta time pounding out fenders and hoods and such on those cars. I couldn't say for sure, but these chunks of metal look awfully automotive to me."

Greg pointed. "My team found that rearview mirror. Is it the only bit that's intact?"

"Yes. And it's consistent with a 1960s Bug."

"And that car would be about the right size to pass as a satellite."

"Yup."

"Have the Skyose guys not even asked about this yet?"

"Nope. They're looking for it, but they're acting too cool. I think they're wondering where the car debris is."

"Perfect." Greg pulled out his phone. "I know Cabo Barnes won't be back today, because we have him in custody, but if The Hamster shows up, don't let him in here, and call me."

"You bet."

Virgil locked the door of the small room, then returned to his work. Greg texted Mindy as he left the building. Payload appears to have been a VW Bug.

WTF???

You still talking to Barnes?

Yup.

Don't ask him about it until I get there. On my way.

She returned a thumbs-up. Greg pocketed his phone and headed back to Patrick.

* * * * *

At the office, the rest of the team was in the conference room, waiting. Vernon pounced first. "A *Volkswagen*?"

"Seems to be, sir. In addition to the rearview mirror from my sector, there are chunks of tire tread, part of a brake pedal... It's *not* a satellite."

"Agent Santos, what's the probable scenario here?"

"It could be simple. Skyose and Ideodax would have agreed at least a year ago for Skyose to carry Ideodax's payload. I checked the stock prices for each of the companies, and both soared after the announcement that Ideodax had contracted with Skyose."

Zach said, "Then Ideodax couldn't fulfill the contract?"

Tom nodded. "That's my guess. And I'd bet that Ideodax only informed Skyose about this a few weeks ago, at which point Skyose had a decision to make. They'd scheduled time on the launch pad already, and it would cost them too much to delay. The only option that wouldn't adversely affect their stock value was for them to continue as if nothing was amiss. Ideodax also wouldn't want it known that they'd missed the deadline, so they were happy to join the charade. Someone at Skyose probably said to someone at Ideodax, 'Give us something to launch; we don't care what it is.' Enter the VW."

Mindy said, "But because of the explosion, Skyose's stock must have tanked anyway on Monday when the markets opened."

"It did. But Ideodax's didn't."

Vernon asked, "Which means what?"

Tom shrugged. "As long as the nature of the payload remains secret, Ideodax isn't any worse off than they were before the launch. Eventually they'll build a satellite, send it up on a *Falcon 9*, and live happily ever after."

Greg said, "So if Roy Shaw had revealed the subterfuge, it would have hurt both companies. There's our motive."

Mindy said, "Yeah, but it doesn't narrow down our suspects list."

Vernon stood. "Greg, why don't you speak with Mr. Barnes now? See if you can shorten that list."

Greg grinned. "Yes, *sir*."

* * * * *

Cabo Barnes was the picture of calm centeredness when Greg entered the room. He smiled. "Ah, another member of the Air Force constabulary."

Greg sat. "Mr. Barnes, I'm Special Agent Marcotte. I've just had a look at the debris from the explosion. Anything you want to tell me about the payload on your rocket?"

Barnes shrugged, all innocence. "Shouldn't you be asking Ideodax about that?"

"We will. Right now, I'm asking you."

Barnes sighed deeply and held out his hands, wrists together. "You got me, Officer. Lock me up and toss the key."

Greg gave Barnes a deadpan stare. "Funny guy. Whose idea was it?"

"Preston Brickman's. He had an old VW sitting in a storage shed."

"Brickman is the CEO of Ideodax?"

"No, he's the president. Alan Moroney is the CEO. Not that it matters."

"Who was at the meeting?"

"Preston, Alan, Lyle, and myself."

"Not Roy Shaw?"

"*No.*" Barnes was emphatic. "Roy *did not know.*"

"We think he did."

"If so, he did *not* hear it from me or Lyle. One of the Ideodax guys must have let it slip."

Greg crossed his arms and rocked back in his seat. "Wouldn't be healthy for your bottom line if the word spread, would it?"

"It would be equally unhealthy for Ideodax."

"Where's Lyle Briggs?"

"I haven't seen him since noon, when we left Canaveral together. I went to my office, where your agents found me. Lyle didn't say where he was headed."

Greg's phone beeped with a text. Hi, it's Russell McCarthy at Holloman. Skyose told us to get a search warrant. Want to?

Greg typed back: Yes, please, thx.

On it.

Greg pocketed his phone. "Where's Mr. Shaw?"

Barnes shook his head vigorously. "I *do not know.* What I *know* is that he'd better show himself soon, or there'll be hell to pay. We have a major disaster on our hands that needs to be managed, and I need my executive staff to *manage* it. Roy is my right hand. The other guys will mill around with their thumbs up their asses until he tells them what needs to be done."

Greg believed him. "All right, Mr. Barnes, one more thing."

"What's that?"

"Find Lyle Briggs for us."

Barnes picked up his phone and called. He rolled his eyes and mouthed, *"Voice mail,"* then said, "Lyle. I'm with the Air Force investigators. They found the VW, and now they're searching for Roy. You need to contact them *now.*" He clicked off. "Satisfied?"

"That'll do. You're free to go, but we'd prefer that you stay in town."

"That's fine. I'm not leaving until Roy turns up."

Greg stood and escorted Barnes to the door. "Thanks, Mr. Barnes. We'll be in touch."

CHAPTER NINETEEN

After lunch, Justin spent an hour in his driveway, cleaning out and vacuuming his car. Then he went inside to spend some quality time on Twitter.

He saw that Skyose had released an official statement about the rocket explosion, but didn't mention Roy Shaw. He wondered if Gretchen Holt had learned anything, and sent her a text. He noted with a smile that his Mars article had been retweeted 172 times. He checked his email and was pleased to see a response from Valerie DeSoto, the librarian at UCF.

Hi Justin,

Good to hear from you again! We felt the explosion all the way over here. Skyose doesn't have any secrets that I could find.

Next time you're in Orlando, stop in!

Valerie

Justin responded: Thanks! Next time I'm in Orlando, I'll take you to lunch. Then he forwarded the email to Greg.

* * * * *

He spent the rest of the day puttering around the house. He found a half-can of white semi-gloss paint in the garage and painted the interior doorframes. He was rinsing the brush out in the backyard when Greg texted.

I should be finishing work at about 6:30, and then I have a couple of errands to run. Okay if I come over around 7:15?

Perfect. Do you want dinner?

Nah, still full from lunch. See you in a bit.

Justin returned a thumbs-up and a smiley face. Then he hustled to jump in the shower.

At 7:13, the doorbell rang. Greg was standing on the porch, holding a six-pack and a bunch of flowers. He held them out. "I come bearing gifts."

"And you're not Greek, so it's okay." Justin took the flowers and breathed in the scent. "*Thank* you. These are lovely. No one's ever bought me flowers before."

Greg smiled. A bit shyly, Justin thought.

"I've never bought flowers for anyone before."

"Really? Then these are super-special." Justin inwardly winced at his choice of words, but he didn't seem capable of sophisticated banter at the moment. "I'll put these in water."

Greg followed him into the kitchen, where Justin fished a vase from under the sink, rinsed it, and added the small packet of preservative that came with the flowers. "How was the rest of your day?" he asked Greg.

"Fascinating. I found out what the payload was."

Justin nearly dropped the vase. He set it carefully on the kitchen bar, then said, "I was starting to wonder if there *was* one."

"There was. It was an early 1960s Volkswagen Beetle."

Justin stared. "Okay... Not as weird as a wheel of cheese, but what the *hell*?"

Greg stared back, his thought processes seeming momentarily derailed. "A wheel of *cheese*?"

"The payload on the first launch of the *Dragon* capsule in 2010."

"*Seriously?*"

Justin tutted in exasperation. "Google it. Why did they launch a VW Bug?"

"Ideodax didn't have a satellite ready by the deadline. Their guys are already back in California, so we're sending agents from Travis to question them."

Justin frowned. "I need a beer."

"Me too."

They uncapped their bottles and clinked them together. Justin took a drink, then asked, "Is this what Shaw knew?"

"It makes sense. Either Shaw's killer found out somehow that he was about to spill his guts to you, or Shaw decided to give whoever it was one more chance to come clean on his own, or else he'd tell you. Either way, Shaw and the killer must have met out there on base and had a confrontation."

"Why would Ideodax go along with that? Why wouldn't they just say, *We don't have a satellite ready, launch without us?*"

"It boils down to money, as it almost always does. Both companies would have lost significant stock value if they'd made that announcement." Greg set his bottle aside. "I'd rather not think about business for the rest of the evening."

"Agreed."

Greg reached for him, and Justin moved into his arms. They kissed, tentatively at first. The tentativeness didn't last long. Greg was a marvelous kisser. He tasted like peanuts and beer.

Take me out to the ball game... Justin almost giggled.

Greg's lips smiled against his own. "What?"

"Tell you later." Justin opened his mouth to Greg's tongue, and they kissed deeply for a few minutes. Justin's dick was straining against the fly of his shorts, and he could feel that Greg was in the same predicament. He reached for Greg's belt buckle, and Greg groaned as Justin unzipped his fly and freed his dick, wrapping his fingers around it.

"*God*, Justin..."

"Mm-hm." Justin dropped to his knees. There wasn't anything on earth he wanted more at that moment than to have Greg Marcotte's dick in his mouth.

He kissed and nibbled his way up Greg's dick while caressing his balls. Greg had both hands wound into Justin's hair, but he wasn't pulling. Or pushing. Justin arrived at the head of Greg's dick, where he lingered for a moment, then took him in.

Greg moaned. "Jeeeezus *God*, Justin, don't fuckin' stop."

Justin chuckled around Greg's dick, which caused Greg to grip Justin's hair more tightly.

He had no intention of stopping. He took himself in hand, attempting—unsuccessfully—to match the rhythm of his hand to that of his mouth. *So good...*

When Greg came, Justin swallowed it down and nearly came himself. It had been so long—two years—since he'd tasted another man. He lost his stroking rhythm entirely and fumbled briefly as Greg's dick slipped from his mouth.

Greg dropped to the floor, whispered, "Allow me," pushed Justin to his feet, and sucked him down nearly to the base of his dick. Justin cried out, mumbling incoherently—if asked to repeat the words under oath, he wouldn't remember—and thirty seconds later he was coming so hard, his eyes rolled back in his head.

They stayed like that for a long minute, panting. Then Greg pulled Justin down to him and kissed him, and Justin kissed him back. Eventually Greg drew back, brushing Justin's hair back from his widow's peak. "You want to know the first thing I thought when I saw you?"

"Hm?"

"That you had the most beautiful eyes I'd ever seen." Greg kept stroking his hair. "It's even truer close up. Your eyes are amazing."

"Thank you. I didn't have much to do with that."

Greg smiled. "Who do you look like?"

"My mom, mostly. You know what I noticed first about you?"

Greg shook his head.

Justin tapped his shoulder. "Broad shoulders. I love broad shoulders. And I thought anyone within a half mile could pick you out as a cop."

"Yeah, I'd be lousy undercover." Greg shifted. "Maybe we should get off the floor."

Justin allowed Greg to pull him to his feet. He had to laugh at the sight of both of them—dicks hanging out of pants, a hint of razor burn. "The aftermath of great sex isn't very sexy."

Greg grinned. "The clothes are the problem. Maybe we should shed 'em."

Justin grinned back. "I like the way you think, Very Special Agent Marcotte."

CHAPTER TWENTY

A couple of hours later, Greg was in Justin's bed, entirely spent. One thing about being forty…his recovery time was not what it used to be. Especially after two rounds of the best sex he'd had in years. Maybe ever.

Both of them were lying on their backs, shoulder to shoulder and hip to hip, enjoying the breeze from the ceiling fan on their bodies. They were talking about movies—specifically the merits of the various *Matrix* films—when he noticed that Justin was gingerly stretching his calf muscles.

"What are you doing with your legs?"

"Hm? Oh. My calves are kinda sore. I went for a run this morning, and it had been a while."

"You're a runner?"

Justin grabbed at his waist, pulling out a fistful of skin. "That would be *no*, as these love handles demonstrate. I used to, but I quit when I moved here."

"Love handles?" Greg rolled up on his side to face Justin, frowning. "You're not overweight."

Justin snorted. "It's kind of you to say so. But I've been sitting on my ass eating junk food for two years. I'm overweight."

"Does it bother you?"

Justin thought about that for a moment. "I suppose so. If it didn't, I wouldn't have gone running this morning. But I want to be healthier." He turned his head to look at Greg. "You're in great shape. I want to be able to keep up with you."

"Listen. Don't think that you have to lose weight for me. If you want to get in better shape for your health, that's awesome. I'll support you one hundred percent. But I'll take you exactly as you are."

Justin's smile was tentative. "Really?"

"Yes." Greg brushed the hair out of Justin's eyes. "You're smart, beautiful, funny, a terrific conversationalist, and an adventurous eater. And you give an out-of-this-world blowjob. What else could a guy ask for?"

Justin's smile widened. "Naw. Now you're just makin' shit up."

"I am *not*. Do you honestly think I'd be lying here right now if I didn't want to be? If I didn't mean everything I just said?"

Justin regarded him. "No. I don't think you'd be here. I don't think you ever do anything you don't want to do."

"Not when I can help it. Sometimes the job requires it...but not in my personal life." Greg continued to stroke Justin's hair. "One thing you learn working homicide: life can be short. One moment you're walking down the sidewalk, not a care in the world. Twelve seconds later, you're laid out, dying, with someone doing CPR on you, because someone mistook you for someone else. Or because you got caught in the middle of a gang shootout. Or some idiot drove up on a sidewalk. You never know."

Justin stroked Greg's chest with the backs of his fingers. "And that's why you left."

"That was a big part of it." Greg sighed. "The randomness. Dead kids, for no reason other than stupidity. We're a few steps removed from that on the federal level."

"But you love law enforcement. I can tell."

"Yeah, I do." Greg rolled onto his back. "I love righting wrongs. I love solving puzzles. And I love weeding bad actors out of the US Air Force."

"Do you have many of those?"

"Not nearly as many as the Army. But we still have a few who don't respect their uniform enough. Who think they can get away with shit on the taxpayers' dime." He snorted. "Not on my watch."

Justin laughed. "Go get 'em, Agent Marcotte."

"You bet."

One of the cats—Greg wasn't sure which—leaped with a *thump* onto the bed, then walked into the narrow gap between Greg and Justin, delicately stepped onto Greg's chest, and stared at him, his amber eyes barely visible around the ring of wide pupil in the darkened room. Greg said, "Hey, cat."

The cat meowed at him. Greg scratched it under the chin. "Which one is this?"

"That's Elton. Bernie has a narrow white stripe down the center of his forehead."

"Pleased to meet you, Elton."

Elton lowered himself onto Greg's chest and started purring, the vibration warming Greg. He chuckled. "I could get used to this."

"Elton's picky. You've passed his test, whatever that is."

"How old are they?"

"Four. They're littermates."

"I figured. Where did you get them?"

"A neighbor in Orlando trapped ferals. She didn't get to these guys' mama in time."

Greg stroked Elton, whose purr intensified. "The contract lawyer didn't mind you taking them when you split up?"

Justin snorted. "Nope. The cats never took to Clay."

"Smart cats." Greg turned his head to look at Justin. "You two were together for a long time."

"If you count from the time we met, eighteen years. So yeah. Too long."

"Why so long?"

Justin sighed. "Inertia. The guaranteed availability of sex. Someone to go to the movies with. And Clay is a terrific cook."

Greg laughed. "Yeah, okay, I've known of marriages built on less."

"And...fear of the unknown."

Greg thought of Ryan. "I know what that's like."

Justin changed the subject. "Do you hate cop shows? I bet most of them are completely unrealistic."

"Oh God. The *worst*. NCIS, I mean...holy *shit*. That is *not* the way it works."

Justin grinned. "You don't have a Goth chick in the basement, running all your lab work for you?"

"*No.* Although, I have to say, it's made it a lot easier to explain to people what I do. 'The NCIS of the Air Force.' Everyone gets it."

Justin smiled. "What do you do when you're not solving murders?"

"Most of what we do falls under two headings. Drug enforcement on base and threat assessment to the space program. My partner Mindy is the drugs expert, and my partner Zach is the threat-assessment guy."

Justin poked Greg in the shoulder. "And you're what? The muscle?"

Greg laughed. "That's right." He rolled onto his side, dislodging Elton, and pulled Justin into his arms. "Say good night, Elton."

Elton meowed and curled up against Greg's back.

Greg fell asleep thinking, *I could* really *get used to this.*

CHAPTER TWENTY-ONE

Justin had been jolted awake at five thirty in the morning by Greg's phone alarm. As an apology, Greg had cooked breakfast—huevos rancheros—then kissed Justin on his way out the door, promising to call that afternoon. Justin had spent the morning writing about SpaceX's next launch, then outlining a story on Roy Shaw. He figured it wouldn't take Greg much longer to solve the case.

He fixed a sandwich for lunch and cleaned the kitchen, then settled on the sofa to read. An hour later, when his phone rang, he picked it up with a smile, anticipating it would be Greg. He stopped short when he saw the blocked number.

Rats. But maybe it was a news item of some sort. "Hello?"

"Mr. Harris, this is Roy Shaw."

Justin sat straight up. Had he gasped? He hoped not. Who the hell *was* this? His mind was racing. He couldn't let on that he knew Shaw was dead. He said, "Mr. Shaw. You stood me up on Saturday morning."

"Yes, I'm sorry about that. An unavoidable conflict presented itself. But I want to meet with you now. In thirty minutes. Same place as before."

He doesn't know where Shaw wanted to meet, or he'd know I can't get there in thirty minutes. Justin said, "Tables Beach? At the covered tables?"

"Yes. Thirty minutes." The caller hung up.

Justin stared at his phone in shock for a moment. Then he called Greg.

Greg sounded surprised but pleased to hear from him. "Hey, what's up?"

Justin poured out what the caller had said. "Whoever it is knows that Shaw was going to meet with me, but he doesn't know where. It must be the killer, right?"

"Or someone who's involved… Okay. You did good, meeting at Tables Beach. We'll head up there right now."

"What if he sees you all?"

"He won't. He clearly doesn't know that *you* know Shaw's dead. Keep up the pretense as long as you can."

"Okay. I'm scared *shitless.*"

"I'd be worried if you weren't. Pretend you're still mad at him for standing you up that morning. That'll help cover your nervousness."

"Okay."

"My whole team will be there. We'll see you soon."

"Okay." Justin said goodbye and spent the next fifteen minutes pacing in an attempt to forestall a panic attack.

Then he picked up his keys and wallet and headed out.

He hoped it wasn't the last time he'd see his house.

CHAPTER TWENTY-TWO

Greg had spent the morning coordinating with local law enforcement in an attempt to locate Lyle Briggs. He hadn't returned to his hotel room or the Skyose offices, and hadn't contacted Cabo Barnes. His open-ended return ticket to New Mexico hadn't been used yet, and there wasn't a record of him having taken another flight. Greg supposed that Briggs could have rented a car, intending to drive to New Mexico. It didn't matter. He'd be found soon.

He'd spoken to Russell McCarthy at Holloman, who'd executed the search warrant on Roy Shaw's office and had come up empty. He'd also received the forensics report on Shaw's car. They'd found no one else's prints and no evidence of anyone else having been in the vehicle. Another dead end.

When Justin called, Greg had just ended a phone conversation with Roy Shaw's wife, updating her on the "search" for her husband. It pissed him off to have to deceive her. He wasn't sure how she'd react when she learned that Roy was dead, and he was glad it wouldn't be his job to tell her. That news would be delivered in person.

After the emotional conversation with Mrs. Shaw, he was delighted to see Justin's name on his caller ID. "Hey, what's up?"

Justin's words chilled him. He tried to sound calm and reassuring, but he was as scared shitless as Justin was. He said, "My whole team will be there. We'll see you soon," then said goodbye and ran to Vernon's office. "Sir! A man claiming to be Roy Shaw has arranged a meeting with the reporter Shaw initially contacted."

Vernon didn't hesitate. He stepped into the hallway and shouted. "Everyone! In the hallway, now!"

Mindy, Zach, Tom, and four 0083s scurried into the hallway. Vernon outlined the situation. "First, get everyone else out of the area. Mindy, Zach, you'll be near the volleyball net."

Zach said, "I've got a Frisbee in my truck."

"Perfect. Abbott, Kaminski, you'll be at a picnic table. Pretend to be on your phones. Tom, you and I will be at another table, playing chess. Greg, take your rifle and find a spot to hide yourself with a line of sight to the impostor."

"Yes, sir."

Vernon clapped his hands. "Let's move."

The agents scattered. Vernon packed his chess set. Zach and Mindy changed into shorts and T-shirts. The others untucked shirts and pulled them over their waistbands, hiding their sidearms.

Greg hustled to his truck. He'd cleaned the rifle after firing it at the gator, so it was ready. He loaded it automatically, the motions second nature, with only one thought in his head.

If the bastard moves on Justin, I'll kill him.

He sped to Tables Beach, parked, and scrambled across the dunes. He found a concealing spot among the sea grape and dune grass, wriggled on his belly to the top of the dune, and poked the barrel of the rifle through the vegetation.

He was ready.

CHAPTER TWENTY-THREE

When Justin pulled into the parking lot at Tables Beach, it was about a quarter full. Scanty for a midsummer's day. He got out and looked around. He didn't see anyone that was obviously law enforcement, but Greg's truck was one of the vehicles in the lot.

AFOSI was here. He breathed a deep sigh of relief.

He approached the tables, which were partially occupied. At one, two men were playing chess. At another, a young couple in shorts and T-shirts were on their phones, ignoring each other. There was another couple nearby on the grass, tossing a Frisbee back and forth.

And at the farthest table from the parking lot, there was a man in a baseball cap with a fish on the front, wearing a polo shirt and jeans. Justin approached tentatively. "Mr. Shaw?"

The man looked up, and Justin tried not to react.

It was Preston Brickman, the president of Ideodax.

Justin thanked the gods that Brickman hadn't attended the pre-launch press conference. He obviously hadn't considered that Justin might have been there and would therefore recognize Shaw.

So Brickman wasn't thinking very clearly. That could work in Justin's favor.

Or not.

Brickman said, "Yes. Have a seat, Mr. Harris."

Justin sat. "I didn't appreciate being stood up in the middle of the night on Saturday."

"I know, and I apologize again. My conflict was truly unavoidable."

Justin removed the notepad and pen from his pocket. "Better late than never, I guess. What is this story you have for me?"

"Thanks to the explosion, there *is* no story. *That's* what I wanted to tell you this time. There's no point in you or any of your colleagues pursuing information about the payload on this rocket anymore. The explosion made all that moot."

"Made all of *what* moot? What were you going to tell me on Saturday morning?"

Brickman sighed. "Mr. Harris. You'll have to trust me on this. It's in everyone's best interests, including yours, to forget about this."

"In my best interests? That sounds kind of threatening, Mr. Shaw."

Brickman held his hands up, placating. "It's not meant to be. But I'm certain your employers wouldn't long support any efforts by you, or Ms. Holt in Las Cruces, to pursue a story that doesn't exist. There's plenty of fascinating space stuff to write about. You should move on."

He knows that Gretchen has been asking questions. Justin said, "Honestly, Mr. Shaw, I'd like to believe you. But your insistence, and all this cloak-and-dagger business, makes me curious. Give me a solid reason to drop my investigation, and I'll comply."

Brickman stared at Justin. Justin returned his gaze, pressing his heels into the ground beneath the table in order to keep his knees from shaking. Finally Brickman said, "Your solid reason is that you will never uncover anything. You will be wasting your time."

"Wouldn't be the first time."

Brickman's eyes narrowed. "Continue to pursue this line of questioning, and it may be the last investigative reporting you ever do."

Justin saw movement out of the corner of his eye. "Mr. Shaw, I don't take well to—"

The young couple dropped their cell phones and pulled guns from beneath their T-shirts. The chess players grabbed Brickman's arms, one on each side, and lifted him out of his seat. Brickman yelped, "Hey! What the hell!"

The older of the chess players snapped handcuffs on Brickman. The younger one said, "Special Agent Tom Santos, Air Force Office of Special Investigations. You're under arrest for the murder of Roy Shaw."

The older chess player patted Brickman down and pulled a gun from his waistband, then handed it to the male Frisbee player, who, with his partner, had jogged up to them. The woman Frisbee player said, "Justin Harris?"

"Yeah?"

"I'm Special Agent Mindy Leonard, Greg Marcotte's partner. You okay?"

"Yeah. I'm…" Justin sucked in a deep breath. "Yeah. Can I stand up?"

"Sure. Can you identify this guy?"

"Preston Brickman. He's the president of Ideodax."

Brickman spat. "Son of a *bitch*. You *played* me."

Justin opened his mouth, but Mindy held up a finger, and he closed it. The other agents hauled Brickman away. Mindy said, "Sorry. Best if you don't say anything to the suspect."

"Of course." Justin hugged himself. Now that the experience was over, he was shaking even more violently. "Sorry. Where's Gr—er—Agent Marcotte?"

Mindy pointed in the direction of the sand dunes. "Hiding over there with his sniper rifle. He'll be along in a moment. Then you can ride back to base with me, and we'll take your statement."

Justin turned to see Greg on the boardwalk from the dunes, jogging toward them, carrying a truly impressive rifle. His knees sagged in relief, and Mindy touched his elbow to steady him. "Okay?"

"Yeah. Thanks." Justin tried to control his facial expressions. If he outed Greg to his coworkers, even by a glance, he'd never forgive himself.

* * * * *

Justin had never been on the grounds of Patrick AFB, although he'd driven past it on A1A plenty of times. As Air Force bases went, Patrick was small, but it made Canaveral look positively dinky.

Mindy entered the base through the East Gate. She pulled into a parking lot behind a nondescript building, swiped an ID card, and pressed her thumb to a pad, then held the door for him. "Come on in."

This is Greg's workplace, Justin thought, trying not to gawk, but also trying to take in as much detail as possible as he passed open doors. Mindy led him to a conference room. "Make yourself comfortable. Can I get you a soda?"

"Um, sure. Coke, if you have it."

"You bet." Mindy disappeared.

Justin took in the room. Just another boring conference room, with a computer, projector, and whiteboard. Nothing to distinguish it in any way as belonging to law enforcement. He was mildly disappointed.

Mindy returned and set a bottle of Coke in front of him. "There you go. We'll record your interview, if you don't mind."

"Not at all."

She nodded, and spoke into the air. Justin figured the recording equipment was probably being monitored in a separate room. "Special Agent Melinda Leonard interviewing Mr. Justin Harris in the Roy Shaw case." She leaned back in her chair and crossed her arms. "Please tell me what happened today, beginning with the phone call."

Justin repeated the events of the day, ending with the moment of Brickman's arrest. Mindy asked for clarification on a couple of points. "You have a memory for detail."

"I'm a reporter. It's my job."

"I suppose so. Anything else you want to add?"

"No, I think that's it."

"All right. End interview." She slapped the table in front of her and stood. "I'll find Greg, and he can take you back to your car."

"*Oh*. Okay." With trepidation, Justin watched her leave the room. Did she *know*? How could she?

A few seconds later, Greg popped his head into the room. "Ready to go?"

"*Yes*." Justin scrambled to his feet.

Once they were safely out of the building and in Greg's truck, Justin blurted, "I think she knows."

"Who, Mindy? Knows what?"

"About *us*."

"Nah. She might suspect, but she doesn't know anything. At least not yet."

"Does she know..."

"That I'm gay? Yeah. Everyone else doesn't ask, and I don't tell."

Justin frowned. "I thought those days were behind us."

"Not entirely." Greg pulled through the main gate and turned left onto A1A. "I suppose the others have a pretty good idea about me, but we don't discuss it."

"Are you and Mindy friends away from work?"

"Yeah." Greg's expression was fond. "She's like my little sister."

"She seems nice. But feisty."

"Ha! That's a perfect description." Greg glanced at him. "Are you really okay?"

"Yeah. I think so, anyway. But I still need a drink."

They arrived at the Tables Beach parking lot, and Greg pulled up next to Justin's car. "Are you going home?"

"I guess." Justin stopped, his hand on the door handle. "You'll have to work late, huh?"

Greg grimaced. "It's hard to say how long it'll take to process Brickman."

Justin smiled ruefully. "I'll have to get used to late evenings."

"Like I'll have to get used to middle-of-the-night launches, huh?"

Justin's smile widened into a grin. "I can handle it if you can."

"Oh yeah. I can handle it. See you later tonight."

Justin opened the door. "Promise?"

"Promise."

Buoyed by the warmth of that, Justin drove home.

* * * * *

It was close to nine in the evening by the time Greg pulled into Justin's driveway. Justin met him at the door and nearly dragged him inside. "Did he confess?"

Greg laughed tiredly. "Hello to you too."

"Sorry." Justin kissed Greg. "Want a beer?"

"God, yes."

They went to the kitchen and perched on barstools. Greg took a long drink, then said, "No confession. Brickman lawyered up. But if the ballistics on that gun he was carrying match, we've got him."

"Even without witnesses?"

"I think so. We also collected Brickman's clothing, which didn't appear to have been laundered. We may be able to get gunshot residue from some of it. And we'll get Shaw's phone records eventually, which should reveal contact between him and Brickman on the morning of the murder. *And* Cabo Barnes and Lyle Briggs will testify against him."

"You found Briggs?"

"Yeah. He was searching for Brickman, as it turned out. I'm not sure what he was gonna do if he'd found him, but Briggs told us that Brickman spoke to him about shutting Shaw up."

"Do you think the other Ideodax guys knew what Brickman was up to? Boone and Pietras?"

Greg sighed. "I don't know. My guess would be yes. We have agents from Travis Air Force Base questioning them and the CEO."

"Has Shaw's family been notified?"

"Yeah." That unfortunate job had fallen to Russell McCarthy from Holloman, accompanied by an officer from the Las Cruces Police Department.

Greg had called Mrs. Shaw to apologize for deceiving her; she'd hung up on him.

"Can I write my story now?"

Greg spluttered. "*Now?* I was hoping you'd rather do something *else* first."

Justin laughed. "I *would* rather, but this will just take a sec. Except for the ending, the story is written. I've referred to you as 'a source close to the investigation.' Do you want to read it?"

"I suppose I'd better."

Justin retrieved his laptop, added the final details to the story, and turned the screen toward Greg. "For your approval."

Greg read, nodding a couple of times, then handed the laptop back. "The truth and nothing but. My boss can't object to that."

"Perfect. Just let me do this…" Justin sent the story to his editor, then texted him—Exclusive on Roy Shaw's murder at Canaveral, check your email—to ensure he would read it. "Done. Now. What were you saying? You had some other activity in mind?"

Greg grinned and reached for him.

CHAPTER TWENTY-FOUR

Six weeks later

Greg pulled the F-150 up to the gate at Jetty Park and leaned out his window. "Hey, Arnie."

Arnie, rumpled and dozy, grunted. "Hey, Agent Marcotte." He pushed a button in the guardhouse, which raised the striped arm. "You can let yourself out."

"You bet. Thanks, Arnie."

"No problem." Arnie waved Greg onward. The park was closed at this hour—three in the morning—but Greg had called in a favor to gain admittance. SpaceX was launching a *Falcon 9* in about an hour, and Jetty Park was an ideal spot from which to watch. Greg wanted to provide Justin with an exclusive show.

As they jostled over a speed bump, Justin mumbled. He'd fallen asleep against the passenger door almost as soon as Greg had picked him up.

Greg grinned as he pulled into a parking spot and cut the engine, then nudged Justin. "Wake up, sleepy. It's showtime."

"Mmph." Justin rubbed his eyes. "We're there?"

"Yup." Greg opened the truck door and climbed out, then lowered the tailgate. "Come on."

They carried lawn chairs and a mini-cooler to the end of the pier and settled in. Greg opened the cooler and popped the top of a can of Coke. "What's the payload on this rocket?"

"It's a *Dragon* capsule with cargo for the International Space Station."

"No VW Beetles this time? Or wheels of cheese?"

"Ha! Not as far as I know."

Justin checked his email and got the dial-in information for the launch director's loop. Over the feed, the voice said, "Launch auto has started."

They chatted about odds and ends. Justin verbally sketched out the story he'd submit for this launch. Thanks to Greg, he'd just published an exclusive on the preliminary report from the *SkyCatcher* rocket explosion; it appeared that a valve in a fuel line had failed. There was no evidence so far for sabotage.

Greg asked, "Are your pals over on the ITL Causeway?"

"Yup."

"Do they know where you are?"

"Kind of."

"They're not gonna request special treatment, are they?"

"Nah. After Skyose, they're still kinda shy about getting too close to a launch."

"We're farther away than they are. No worries."

"Oh, I know. But this *feels* closer. And frankly, it's delightful not to have everyone else yammering at each other the whole time we're down there."

They waited quietly. The sound of the LVO's voice on the loop and the waves lapping at the sand were soothing. Greg almost fell asleep himself.

Then the countdown began. "Ten, nine, eight…"

Greg reached over and took Justin's hand. Justin smiled and entwined his fingers with Greg's.

"Liftoff of the *Falcon 9*."

The rocket soared into the sky on its column of flame.

The LVO's voice intoned, "*Falcon 9* is pitching downrange."

Greg found himself counting. When he reached twelve, he let out a breath he hadn't realized he'd been holding. Beside him, Justin chuckled. "We're past twelve seconds."

"I guess we'll all be holding our breaths until twelve seconds for a while."

"Yeah. Sorta like after *Challenger*. When the shuttle started flying again, when *Discovery* got to 'go with throttle up,' the entire Space Coast was holding its breath."

They continued to watch as the *Falcon 9* flew, then as the first and second stages separated; the second stage ignited to take the *Dragon* to orbit and to the International Space Station, and the first stage flipped around and performed its boostback, entry, and landing burns. The sonic boom reverberated through their bodies, and then twelve seconds later the first stage settled gracefully onto its landing pad.

Justin laughed with delight. "This is so *awesome. Thank* you. I could get used to this."

Greg squeezed his hand. "That's the idea." He leaned over and kissed Justin, and Justin kissed him back.

"How about we make this a tradition?"

Greg grinned. "Works for me."

THE END

REALITY BITES

BY S.C. WYNNE

Detective Cabot Decker is called to the set of hotshot TV producer Jax Thornburn's reality-TV show after a contestant is mauled to death by a tiger. Is someone trying to ax Jax's career—or Jax himself?

CHAPTER ONE

The first things that struck me were the pungent smell of urine and the enormous tiger pacing back and forth in a steel enclosure. I'd never seen a tiger up close, and this animal was easily three hundred pounds. Its black stripes glistened against its sleek orange fur as the agitated animal chuffed and growled, its giant head hung low. My stomach clenched when my gaze settled on the tarp-covered body lying outside the enclosure.

My cell buzzed, and when I answered, my lieutenant's annoyed voice came over the line. "Are you there yet, Decker?"

I must have squeezed my paper cup of coffee too hard because the lid popped off, and it spilled down the front of my shirt. "Shit," I hissed, wincing as the hot liquid soaked through the material down to my skin.

"Did I get you at a bad time?"

"Not at all," I said through gritted teeth while wiping at the spreading stain to no avail. "I was just taking a bath in my coffee."

"What?"

"Never mind."

"Are you at the studio yet?"

"I'm here." I glanced uneasily toward the body. "Who's the dead guy?"

"Dale Larson. He was a contestant on *Don't Die*."

"*Don't Die*?" I grimaced.

"You've never seen it?"

"I don't have a lot of time to watch TV."

"The show is huge. The producer, Jax Thornburn, is a big deal at Zecker Studios right now. I want you to hold his hand and treat him nice."

"I'm still not clear about why I'm here. Shouldn't this be handled by Animal Control? What am I supposed to do, arrest the tiger?"

"Very funny."

"I'm partly serious. I don't get how an animal attack is Robbery-Homicide's problem."

"Mr. Thornburn thinks there might have been foul play."

Foul play?

I gave a short laugh. "Did he seriously use that term?"

"Decker, don't be a dick. Keep an open mind and talk to Thornburn. See if his suspicions have any merit." There were muffled voices in the background. "Look, I have to go. Treat the guy with respect."

"Of course," I said wryly. "What else would I do?" I hung up.

"He's a magnificent beast, isn't he?" A woman with a large felt hat approached. "He's very intelligent. He knows he's in trouble."

I showed her my badge. "I'm Hollywood Homicide Detective Cabot Decker." I studied her as I tucked away my ID. She was a cross between a librarian and the Mad Hatter. Her hat was wide and crooked, and strands of auburn hair hung messily around her shoulders. "Mind if I ask who you are?"

"Sorry. Lucinda Pinwheel." She held out her hand. "I'm Benji's handler." Up close, the deep lines around her eyes and forehead were obvious. With her long hair and slender build, she'd looked much younger from a distance. "Benji wouldn't hurt a fly...usually."

I glanced at the covered corpse. "Maybe he was having a bad day." I pulled on gloves and moved to the body. Lifting the tarp slowly, I held my gag reflex in check as I studied the bloody, torn mess in front of me. There were obvious teeth marks around the throat, and the head was almost severed from the neck. The smell of blood made my stomach roll, but I kept examining the corpse, looking for anything that might be inconsistent with an animal attack.

"Hey, Decker." Officer Eugene approached, looking a little queasy. "This is some grisly shit."

"Yeah." I dropped the tarp back over the body and pulled out my notepad and pen. "What can you tell me?"

He put his hands on his hips. "That some people will do anything for money?" He shook his head. "How desperate would a man have to be to spend the night in a cage with a wild animal? Jesus."

"I didn't mean I needed you to get philosophical. What do you know about what happened here?"

"It's pretty cut-and-dried. The guy was in the cage, and the tiger went after him."

"Was he alone?"

"You mean other than the tiger?"

I sighed. "I mean were there any witnesses?"

Officer Eugene pursed his lips. "He was alone when it happened. There's supposed to always be a cameraman with the contestants. But apparently the guy assigned to our victim had severe intestinal issues and was on the toilet when the attack occurred."

"I'll need to talk to the cameraman ASAP."

"He's at the hospital."

I frowned. "Why?"

"Dehydration and hysteria. He found the body."

"Got it."

"There was also a fill-in trainer, Levi Benson. Lucinda had a family function she needed to go to, and Levi took her spot for the night. Unfortunately, he was in desperate need of caffeine and was at the commissary grabbing a cup of coffee when Dale was killed."

Lucinda added, "Usually I'd never leave this to an underling, but it was my son's eighteenth birthday and I couldn't miss it."

"I see." I studied her. "Where's Levi now?"

Officer Eugene said, "He's outside. He's a bit freaked out and needed some fresh air."

"I can imagine." I made a mental note to hunt down Levi and talk to him.

Lucinda shifted uneasily. "I still can't believe this happened. It doesn't make any sense. I've worked with Benji for ten years, and we've never once had an incident. He's never even looked weird at a human before."

"Something triggered him," I murmured.

I noticed a guy standing a few feet away, his phone glued to his ear. He seemed to be in his early thirties, and he was tall, with broad shoulders and jet-black hair. He emanated an air of self-assurance, which combined with his expensive suit, told me he might be in charge. He hung up, lifted his chin, and strode toward me, holding out his hand.

"I'm Jax Thornburn." His grip was firm, and his palm felt smooth against my callouses. His cologne was spicy, masculine, and probably way out of my budget.

"Detective Decker." The intensity of his gray stare was unsettling. I didn't get unsettled easily, but he radiated power and confidence like a convection oven. When his gaze dropped to the dark stain on my shirt, heat filled my cheeks. "I had a run-in with a cup of coffee."

"Looks like the beverage won." His voice was deep, his gaze enigmatic.

I cleared my throat. "I'm not really familiar with the concept of your show. Could you fill me in? Why was a man inside the cage with a tiger to begin with?"

He exhaled roughly. "Dale was one of ten contestants. Each week one of them is randomly assigned an animal, and then they either spend the night in the cage or they decline and leave the show." His gaze flicked to the corpse. "Dale didn't decline."

"Why would he do something so crazy?"

"Money. If they spend the whole night, they get lots of money."

"How much money?"

"A million dollars."

"Wow." I wiped distractedly at the coffee stain on my shirt. "I think I'd rather be poor and alive."

Jax smirked. "Looks like things are working out for you, then, Detective."

Smart-ass.

I narrowed my gaze. "So why'd the animal attack him?"

Lucinda said brusquely, "Benji must have been provoked."

Jax turned to her with a grim look. "I hope you're not suggesting me or any of the crew did that sort of thing?"

She sniffed. "All I know is ratings are everything to you people."

His dark brows pulled together. "Having one of my contestants eaten by a wild animal isn't good for ratings. Besides, ratings are already through the roof."

"I'm happy for you and all, but why call for Homicide?"

Jax glanced at Lucinda. "Would you mind if I spoke to Detective Decker alone?"

She shrugged. "No problem." She pressed her big hat firmly on her head and wandered over to the cage, where Benji still paced.

Jax turned to me, looking uneasy. "The premise of *Don't Die* is people take a huge risk, and if they pull it off, they get a lot of money. But the risk is exaggerated."

"Obviously not."

"What I mean is, we take great care in picking animals that are gentle and have never been involved in anything violent." He swallowed. "We take precautions, such as making sure the creatures are well fed and exercised."

"I'm no expert in animal attacks, but it's pretty clear the tiger didn't just maul the victim. He ate parts of him."

Jax blanched. "But why would he? We feed the cats constantly to keep them sated."

"Obviously this cat wanted seconds."

"Listen, I don't want to be dramatic, but as I told your lieutenant, something seems off lately."

"Off how?"

"I don't know. Things keep happening."

"Could you elaborate?" I couldn't decide if Jax was truly concerned, or just loving the attention that dragging Hollywood Homicide down here gave him.

"One of the Burmese pythons got out of its cage last week and almost strangled a camera tech. The snake's cage has a double lock. How would he get out?"

"My pet iguana got out when I was ten. Shit happens."

His lips twisted. "I want to believe this is an accident. I really do. But I have a bad feeling."

"Well, just because you have indigestion, I can't open an investigation for murder. This could easily be a tragic animal attack."

"I understand you don't want to waste your time. I don't want to waste your time either, and I wouldn't if I didn't truly feel something was wrong." He hesitated. "I didn't mention it to your lieutenant, but I got a letter a week ago."

I perked up. "What kind of letter?"

"You have to understand I get mail from kooks all the time."

"What did the letter say?"

"That we needed to stop using animals for greedy profit, or there would be consequences."

"Where's the letter?" A mysterious threatening letter was something I could sink my teeth into.

"Well…"

"Tell me you still have the letter." Even I could hear my frustration.

"I'm afraid not." He looked embarrassed. "People say shit they don't mean to a man in my position all the time. If I paid attention to every threatening phone call and letter, I'd never get anything done."

"Damn." I exhaled. "Do me a favor; if you get another note, hang on to it."

"I will."

I looked around. "Are there other cameras besides the one the cameraman was using?"

"Yes. We have four cameras always rolling."

"That's great." I straightened. "I'll need to see that footage."

"Of course." His brow wrinkled as he held my gaze. He was close enough that I could see the dark ring around his slate-colored eyes and how thick and long his lashes were. "One thing keeps bothering me…"

"What?"

"Why didn't Dale go to his pod?"

I cocked my head. "His what?"

He sighed. "The rules of the show are, you spend twenty-four hours in the enclosure with the wild animal assigned to you. You must be in the area with the animal for at least twelve of those hours. But if you ever feel unsafe, each person has a protected cubicle they can retreat to." He ushered me toward the tiger's enclosure. "See behind that screen? There's a safe room if they actually think their life is in danger."

I squinted through the steel mesh. "I'd have been in there in a flash." Hell, I'd have never done the show.

A line formed on his smooth forehead. "That's what I'm saying. The second he felt threatened, he should have retreated to his safe spot."

"But he didn't."

He glanced toward the corpse. "Apparently not." He seemed to mentally shake himself. "I don't know. Maybe I'm being paranoid and this really is just a horrible accident."

I looked at the panting tiger. "You say you feed the animals well, but I have to be honest, Benji looks a little gaunt."

"He does?" He peered closer. "Huh. Maybe you're right."

"Shouldn't his handler have noticed that?"

"You would think so. She's paid well enough," he grumbled.

"I'm guessing starving a wild animal would definitely change its disposition."

"If the tiger's hungry, someone needs to explain how the hell that happened. The show pays through the nose for high-quality meat for Benji."

"Who's actually in charge of feeding the tiger?"

"Lucinda. The animal is owned by Hollywood Cats, but Lucinda is in charge of Benji when he's working."

"Interesting… Listen, I'll take a look at the footage, and depending on what I find, we may or may not proceed with an investigation. I need something more concrete indicating Dale might have been murdered and this wasn't a random animal attack." I glanced over at Lucinda, who was cooing to Benji through the cage. "You think she has it in her to be a cold-blooded killer?"

"Not sure. But in your line of work, how often does the bad guy waltz up to you holding the murder weapon and screaming how much he enjoys killing people?"

My lips twitched. "Not often enough."

"There you go." He stared at Lucinda with a blank expression. "Perhaps beneath Lucinda's cool exterior lies the heart of a cold-blooded maniac."

"If it was murder, it could be anyone who had access to this space. It could just as easily be you."

His eyes widened, and his lips parted. "I beg your pardon?"

It was hard not to laugh at how nonplussed he looked. "It's not unusual for the real bad guy to try and 'help.'"

"You think I'd call the cops if I were behind this?" His mouth was a straight, angry line.

I pulled a stick of gum from my pocket, unwrapped it, and pushed it in my mouth. I hadn't really meant any offense, but he was so touchy, it was kind of amusing. "Maybe you're just tossing out a bunch of red herrings. You know...to throw me off the scent."

He opened his mouth as if he was about to defend his honor, then snapped it shut. He narrowed his eyes. "You're an absolute riot, Detective Decker."

I laughed outright at his snippy tone. It wouldn't have surprised me if he didn't like me. Uptight suit types and I didn't usually get along; even when I didn't accuse them of being psychopaths. "Ah, come on. Lighten up, Hollywood."

"Right. Because there's nothing more hilarious than a man being eaten by a tiger."

"I meant no disrespect to the dead. I take every case seriously." I popped my gum. "I'm a professional."

"I can tell." His gaze dropped to my stained shirt.

His snooty expression annoyed me, but I tried not to show it. "I'll need a copy of the surveillance footage, including before and after Dale entered the tiger enclosure. Also, a list of absolutely everyone with access to this set. That includes the biggest big shot and the gofer who picks up donuts for the crew. I want everybody on that list."

"Whatever you say."

I glanced at the tiger and met his amber gaze; he watched us silently. "What's gonna happen to Benji?"

"I'm not sure," he murmured.

"It'd be a shame to put him down. He's a beautiful animal." I marveled at how huge he was. I couldn't imagine anything that would entice me to spend the night in a cage with a wild animal.

"I wish I'd never dreamed up this damn show." His voice was raspy.

"Well, at least you've gotten famous off the idea."

"You think that makes it worth this?"

I shrugged.

His cool gaze slid to mine. "Do you resent men like me, Detective Decker?"

"Why would I?"

"Just a feeling I get off you." He started to walk away, then stopped. "I'm not shallow, if that's what you think."

My face warmed. I wasn't sure how to respond. To be honest, I assumed he was mostly just worried about how this tragedy would affect his career.

His smile was tight. "I guess your silence is my answer."

"Who cares what I think?"

His jaw hardened. "Good point." He strode away, his head held high.

CHAPTER TWO

Watching twenty-four hours of surveillance footage was as exciting as it sounded.

Even speeding it up was as dull as watching paint dry. But I wanted to see every minute of the time that preceded Dale's brutal death. As I watched the video, I balanced a large pepperoni pizza on my stomach and rested my feet on my desk. Most of the tape was Dale sitting still as a mouse in the corner of the big cage, and anytime Benji seemed interested in him, he'd scramble toward his safe room. This was titillating TV?

Jax came on-screen and had Dale leave the cage. Jax had explained that there would be periodic timed breaks for Dale to eat and use the restroom. Once Dale was out, Levi Benson herded the big cat into a smaller enclosure while technicians cleaned up the animal's waste and tidied Dale's quarters. While the crew worked, Jax wandered around outside the cage. It looked like he was talking to the big cat as he leaned down near the animal. That made me smile for some reason. Maybe because everything about the guy screamed cool sophistication, not sappy animal lover.

Dale returned to the cage, and everyone cleared out of the hangar but the cameraman. About an hour before Dale's approximate time of death, the camera guy left the room. As time passed, the cat became agitated, pacing back and forth and coming nearer to Dale than he'd done previously. Then the tiger crouched and scooted closer to his human roommate as if stalking him. Dale, looking alarmed, got up quickly and headed to his safety cubicle. When he reached its door, he appeared to struggle with opening it as he punched at the keypad. The cat crept closer, and Dale's movements became more panicked.

I spit out my food and watched in horror as the cat pounced on Dale and dragged him away from the still-closed door. The attack was brutal, and I stood and looked away through most of it. Pressing a hand to my roiling stomach, I forced myself to watch until the cameraman with the intestinal issues returned. If the guy was faking his shock at finding Dale mauled to death, he was a good actor. He actually vomited several times after calling 911.

Feeling shaken, I grabbed my phone and called one of my main investigators, Detective Andy Wilson, who had forensic experience. He'd been on scene with me the day before. "Andy?" I asked breathlessly.

"Jesus, Decker, it's two in the morning." I heard a female voice in the background. "I'll be right back, baby." There was a lot of rustling and the sound of a door closing. "Okay. What's so important?"

"Did you check the lock on the door?"

"What?" He sounded confused.

"I mean the lock on the cage where the guy got killed by that tiger."

He exhaled. "Which door? There are several."

"The safe-room door. The keypad. Did you check if it was functioning?" I raked a hand through my hair as I paced back and forth.

"No."

"Why the hell not?"

"The door was open when I got there," he growled. "No one told me to look at the keypad."

I sucked in a deep breath and reminded myself he was still young, still green. Plus, he was right; the door had been open when I got there too. Until I'd seen the footage of Dale struggling to get into his cubicle, I hadn't thought about the keypad either. I'd just assumed the tiger had surprised

Dale somehow, and he hadn't been quick enough to get to safety. "I need you to do that first thing in the morning. I need to know if there's something wrong with the lock or if it looks like it was tampered with."

"You got it."

"We also need to figure out if somebody had a grudge against Dale. So far all I keep hearing is what an awesome guy he was."

"I've been hearing the same thing."

"Maybe he pissed off one of the other contestants. Maybe someone was jealous. We need to figure out if this was an attack against Dale or the show."

"I agree."

"Well, I'll let you go. Sorry about waking you up."

He snorted. "I'd believe you if it didn't happen so often."

I hung up and sat there, feeling agitated. A major rule when conducting an investigation was not jumping to conclusions. I'd definitely done that at the scene the day before. I'd assumed Jax was wrong, that this had been a simple yet tragic animal attack. And maybe it was. But the image of Dale frantically trying to open that door was burned in my mind. I glanced at the pizza splattered on the floor and grimaced. I didn't want to ever see a pepperoni pizza again.

I turned back to the video and leaned closer to the monitor. "Okay, so who opened the door?" I muttered. I watched the chaotic scene that followed the discovery of Dale's body. Levi seemed horrified, and for a brief time even borderline afraid of the big cat. Jax arrived on the scene about a half hour after Dale was discovered. I felt oddly uncomfortable watching him clutch his head and run toward Dale's mangled body; as if I were intruding on a very personal moment. He knelt over Dale and stayed there for a long while. Eventually, he rose slowly, shoulders bowed, and moved to talk to Levi.

Nobody went near the safe-room door, at least not until the cops arrived. A tall, thin guy I didn't recognize led one of the officers into the cage and to the closed door. They were there for a few minutes, and then I saw them in Dale's actual room. I froze the DVR there and made a note of the time. Whoever that skinny guy was, he'd managed to get the door open. I rubbed my burning eyes and rewound the video to the part where Dale was given a break. The safe-room door was open the entire time the crew cleaned the cage. Then one of the workers returned to the door and shut it firmly before leaving the area. He didn't look anything like the guy who'd opened the door after Dale's murder. He was shorter and rounder.

I rewatched those two events over and over until my head ached and my eyeballs felt like they were about to pop out of my head. I decided to call it a night and head home. I would visit Jax in the morning so he could identify the two men for me. I grabbed my jacket and took the elevator to the parking garage. As I slid behind the wheel, my phone buzzed in my pocket. I frowned, wondering who would call me at three-thirty in the morning.

I answered, and before I could even say hello, someone started speaking in a panicked voice.

"I've run off the road at Clifton Avenue, about a half mile south of Bradbury." The alarmed voice rattled on. "Somebody just shot at me and drove me off the road. Can you please hurry?"

"Mr. Thornburn?" I asked, feeling confused as I recognized his voice.

There was a pause, and then, "Detective Decker?" He cursed under his breath. "I… I meant to call 911."

"What's wrong?" I immediately started my car and headed out of the parking garage.

He sucked in a long breath. "It doesn't matter. I'll call the real cops."

I scowled. "I am a real cop." I turned in the direction of Clifton Avenue and punched it. The streets were mostly deserted at this time of the morning. "Are you hurt?"

"No. I don't think so."

"I'm three minutes away, tops. Sit tight."

"Okay." His voice wobbled.

"Is the person who shot at you anywhere around?"

There was an uneasy silence. "Not that I can see." He seemed breathless. "The road's empty."

"That's the best-case scenario." I made sure I sounded calm and like he had nothing to worry about. I wasn't sure that was true, but I didn't need him freaking out. I sped down the deserted roads and tried to keep him talking. "Did you get a look at anyone?"

"It happened so fast." He grunted. "God, that's such a cliché."

"So no glimpse of hair color or ethnicity?"

"No."

"That's okay. I'm sure it was a stressful situation."

"Yeah. Just a little."

"You're doing fine. Just breathe."

"I see headlights," he said, anxiety plain in his voice.

"That should be me." I slowed as I neared a sleek, white BMW half in a ditch on the side of the road. He poked his head above the roof of the car, and I relaxed slightly. I hung up and parked in front of his vehicle. As I left the car, he moved around the hood and met me halfway.

"I'm sorry. I told Siri to call the police, and she called you." He had a gash on his smooth forehead, and blood had trickled down to his eyebrow. He looked pale in the light from the street lamp.

"It's not a problem. I was nearby." I took his arm and led him to my passenger seat. I had a feeling he should sit because he looked about five seconds from passing out.

He slid into my car, keeping his feet on the ground, and I knelt in front of him. "Tell me what happened."

"I don't know. I was driving home, and this red car came tearing around my left side." He licked his lips. "I thought it was some asshole wanting to race. That happens a lot along this area because it's such a wide-open stretch. But then something hit the glass next to my head, and the window splintered but stayed put. It shocked me so much, I drove off the road."

"Why do you think it wasn't just a BB or a rock?"

"I'm pretty sure I saw a handgun."

"Any chance you got the license plate?" I knew he probably hadn't. People rarely did.

Wincing, he said, "No. Sorry."

"Okay." I stood. "Give me a minute while I call this in." I did just that and then checked out his driver's-side window. When I returned to him, his eyes were closed. "Are you dizzy?"

He startled and opened his eyes. "Not really."

"How did you hurt your head?"

He frowned and touched his forehead. Then he stared at the glistening blood on his fingers as if it did not compute. "Steering wheel maybe?"

"It doesn't look too bad. The paramedics will check you over just to be sure."

He glanced toward his car. "Maybe I'm overreacting. I mean, everything that's happened with Dale has me spooked. It might have just been some punk shooting a pellet gun at me."

"That's still dangerous as hell."

"Well, yeah. But it's less ominous than someone pulling a fucking gun on me."

"True."

"It was probably just random, though, right?"

I shrugged.

"You don't think it was?"

"I have no idea."

He sighed. "You're not giving me much."

"I don't like jumping to conclusions."

He clasped his hands between his knees. "Right. Sorry. You're a cop and you deal in facts. I'm a reality TV producer and I deal in drama and what-ifs."

I cleared my throat. "Do you have any enemies?"

"Do I have any *enemies*?" His eyes bugged out. "Why?"

"It's just a routine question."

"You know I do. Remember the letter I got?"

"Yes, but I mean anyone you personally know who would want to hurt you. Any psycho stalker ex-girlfriends we should know about?"

He hesitated. "No."

"Okay."

"It would be ex-boyfriends, by the way." His gaze was unflinching.

The fact that he was gay intrigued and pleased me for a split second, until I remembered that I wasn't exactly like catnip to sexy, rich, Hollywood producer types.

Dream on, idiot.

He pinched the skin between his eyes. "Maybe all my exes don't love me, but I certainly can't think of anyone who's mad enough at me to shoot BBs at the window of my car."

"I, uh...looked at the window. It wasn't a BB."

He stilled. "What makes you say that?"

"Experience."

"Then I was right? I did see a gun?"

"I believe you did. The size of the hole in your window indicates something larger than a BB. Also, the projectile passed through the glass on the driver's side *and* the passenger side. A BB most likely would have hit the safety glass on the first window and stayed there."

"Fuck."

"It's okay. Breathe."

His eyes were wide. "How is it okay?"

"It could be a simple case of road rage."

"Even after what happened to Dale?"

I kept my gaze steady. "We have zero proof that event was connected to this."

"Do you really believe that, or are you just trying to keep me calm?" His cheeks were flushed, and his eyes glittered in the car's dome light. "Because I prefer facts to being placated. I don't need you to pat me on the head and tell me I'm a good boy."

"I would never do that," I deadpanned. "I'd hate to mess up your perfect hair, and I have no idea if you're a good boy or not."

"Very funny, Decker."

We were interrupted when the paramedics and forensics showed up. The medical technicians examined Jax while I walked the road with my flashlight, looking for shell casings. I didn't find anything. The bullet had passed clean through the car and was long gone, and the odds of finding any physical evidence pinpointing the shooter were infinitesimal.

I stayed on scene another hour, talking to the team as they scoured the wrecked car. Eventually I let the tow truck drag the damaged vehicle from the ditch, and I returned to my car, where Jax waited. I was surprised to find him asleep. I got behind the wheel and studied him as he dozed. His face was relaxed, and he looked younger, maybe even vulnerable. His pretty, full lips were parted and tempting, and I swallowed against the raw attraction bubbling in my gut.

When he moved, I jerked away. He opened his eyes, sat up, and rubbed his face roughly. "Shit. I fell asleep?"

"Ah, Sleeping Beauty awakes." My voice was purposely sardonic as I started the engine. I was embarrassed I'd allowed myself to ogle him while he slept.

"Sorry. Wow. I never do that." He yawned.

"It's no big deal. Which direction?"

"Oh." He touched the door handle. "You don't have to drive me home."

"Which way?"

"I'm serious. I can call my personal assistant to come get me."

He started to open the door, but I grabbed his arm. "It's no problem giving you a ride."

"I've been enough trouble."

I sighed. "You're overthinking this. I'd drive anyone in your situation home."

"You're probably just saying that."

"No. Listen, you look exhausted. I'm exhausted. But if you stay here to wait for your PA, I'm going to have to stay here too."

His brows pulled together. "Why?"

"Because otherwise I'll worry."

"About me?" He laughed. "I find that hard to believe."

I frowned. "You do?"

"Definitely."

I pressed my hand to my chest dramatically. "I'm hurt."

His lips twitched. *"Riiight."*

"I have feelings."

"A hardened detective like you?"

"Of course. I even cry at movies." I smirked. "I'm a downright softie, depending on the subject matter."

"Sure you are."

I lifted one brow. "I'll have you know I cried during *The Revenant*."

He snorted. "What scene?"

"The one where he's telling his dead son he won't leave him." I fake-sniffed and wiped at my eyes. "It hit me deep, man."

His laugh was throaty and sincere. "Fine. You can drive me home."

I grinned. "Pasadena, right?"

"Yeah."

I pulled onto the highway. "I didn't think the movie thing was going to work. I thought for a second I would have to share my love of little kittens too."

"I had no idea this person was inside you."

"Well, you know, I have a tough-cop image to maintain."

"You do have that down."

"And you have slick Hollywood movie mogul down."

He exhaled and stared out the window. "I do reality TV. I'm not exactly Steven Spielberg."

We drove for a while in silence. "Do you actually enjoy what you do?" I asked.

"For the most part... Take a left at the red light. Then a couple miles down and turn right on Yellow Briar."

"You got it."

He fiddled with the air vent and then glanced over at me. "This thing with Dale has dampened my enjoyment of the job in a big way."

"I can imagine. I watched the footage last night."

His breath caught. "And…?"

"There are a couple of people I need you to help me identify."

"Of course." His voice was tense. "Did anything stand out to you? Anything that makes you think what happened to Dale was more than a random animal attack?"

I didn't respond right away. I couldn't tell him about the jammed door. From the video, it was obvious Jax hadn't gone anywhere near Dale's safe room. But that didn't mean he couldn't have had someone else do something to the keypad for him. Maybe this was all about a big insurance payout. "I need to rewatch it to make sure I'm not missing anything."

"You wouldn't tell me if you stumbled on something, would you?"

I glanced over and found him watching me. I still needed Andy to check the pad near the door. If it was an electronic failure, that was one thing, but if Andy discovered someone had tampered with the keypad, that was a whole other can of worms. I needed to know that important detail before I decided whether or not to classify this as a homicide. And if it was a murder case, I needed to remember everybody was a suspect, including Jax Thornburn. "I know it's frustrating."

"Yeah, it is."

"Don't worry. We'll get this sorted out."

He grunted. "It's not like I've lost my luggage. A man died."

"And I'm looking into things. You need to be patient."

"Your empathy is overwhelming."

"Look. I know this is hard for you—"

"Do you?" he snapped. "Because I feel like you don't quite get how horrible this is. *I'm* the reason Dale was in that cage. I need answers, or I'm going to lose my mind."

I held my tongue.

I turned on Yellow Briar as instructed, and parked in front of the sprawling mansion he called home. "I'm just following procedure. You're taking this personally, and that's a mistake."

"You know what? This *is* personal. I liked Dale. He was a good guy. He didn't deserve to die the way he did. He had a wife and a five-year-old daughter. I've gotta live with that." His voice quieted. "Maybe you're used to this kind of depressing tragedy. But I'm not. I make stupid, feel-good reality TV shows for a living. So yeah, excuse me if this all feels *really* fucking personal to me." He opened the door and got out, slamming it behind him.

My eyes followed him as he strode up the long flagstone walkway to his fancy house. After spending hours with him, I had to admit he wasn't exactly who I thought he'd be. He was obviously upset by what had happened to Dale, and my instincts said it wasn't because he was the killer.

But my instincts had bitten me in the ass before.

CHAPTER THREE

"Dale's passcode was deleted." Andy held out a folder to me and Jax.

"Andy—" My voice came out strangled. Even though we were in Jax's office on the movie lot, I hadn't expected Andy to simply blurt out his findings. I grabbed the file and gave Jax a wary look. "This isn't for everybody's eyes."

Jax's face turned red. "You can't still suspect me? I just want you to catch whoever killed Dale."

I gave Andy a stern look. "Our investigation is most effective when we play our cards close to our chest."

"Sorry," Andy said.

I ignored my coworker and addressed Jax, schooling my face into a more pleasant expression. "This is simply regular procedure. We keep certain details to ourselves; things only the killer might know. We can't go blabbing our initial findings all over town, or we lose our advantage."

Andy winced.

"Who would have the ability to change Dale's code?" I asked Jax.

His mouth was a hard line, and for a minute I thought he wasn't going to answer me. "Three people have that knowledge."

"Are you one of them?"

He scowled. "No."

"I need their names." I turned to Andy. "When was Dale's code deleted?"

He glanced toward Jax as if afraid to answer.

I sighed. "Mr. Thornburn already knows the most important part, and we have his alibi. He can't change that, so the time is what it is."

Andy shrugged. "I thought maybe it was a test."

"Still waiting," I said testily.

"Saturday." He squinted as if trying to remember some elusive detail. "I believe it was right after Dale's break, so that would make it around four a.m." He pointed toward the file I held. "It's all in there."

"Friday was the run-through and everything went fine?" I addressed Jax.

"Yeah, everything went like clockwork. As far as I could tell, there was no issue with Dale getting into his pod during the run-through."

"Okay."

"If I'm officially a suspect, does that mean you've decided to rule Dale's death a homicide?" Jax met my gaze, looking at me expectantly.

"That's exactly what it means," I grumbled. "According to the coroner's report, Dale was killed by the tiger. Dale tried to get into his safe room, but he couldn't get the door open. The fact that he tried and failed is what had me suspicious. Of course, *now* we know why he couldn't get in." I'd called my lieutenant that morning to let him know I wanted to move forward. Between the animal attack and Jax getting shot at, I felt there was enough for me to peek into things further. Now with this new information about Dale's code being erased, I was glad I'd decided to proceed. Something weird was happening, and it seemed connected to Jax.

"I'm relieved you opened an investigation. If someone hurt Dale on purpose, I want them found."

"Can I ask why the show didn't just use a basic slide lock on Dale's room? Seems like a keypad would complicate things."

"The network felt it made everything more suspenseful if Dale had to punch in a code to get to safety." Jax sighed. "I made sure his code was just two numbers, so there was nothing complicated about remembering it. But…I guess remembering the code wasn't the problem after all."

"Aren't keypads more susceptible to humidity and things like that?" I asked.

"We're filming inside a climate-controlled hangar. Didn't seem like an issue."

"I see."

"Also, let's not forget, the danger was supposed to be exaggerated. As far as we all knew, Benji wasn't an actual threat to Dale or anyone."

"Right." I opened my laptop and pulled up the surveillance video. "Jax, can you identify these two men?" Jax stood and came around the desk to lean over me. His masculine cologne hit my nostrils, and my pulse twittered annoyingly. "That guy who's with the cop." I pointed to my screen. "He got the door open somehow."

Jax put his hand on the back of my chair, and his chest brushed my back. "That's Lee Price. He's my head set designer."

"Any bad blood between you and him?"

"Not at all. I just went to his kid's birthday party a week ago." He glanced down at me, his gray eyes sincere.

"Hmm." I searched the video until I found the guy who'd shut the door after cleaning the cage. "What about this guy?"

The heat of his body returned as he leaned in. "Ben Willoughby. He works maintenance. I don't know him that well. He's kind of quiet, and he just does his job."

"Does the studio do background checks on employees?"

"Yes." Jax straightened.

"You don't have to have a record to commit a crime." Andy crossed his legs and bobbed his foot up and down.

"Very true." I pointed at Andy. "When you get back to the office, check to see if either Ben or Lee are affiliated with animal rights groups. In fact, check if anyone on the crew is tied to animal rights groups." I closed my laptop.

"Will do." Andy stood. "Some of those animal lovers can get pretty militant."

"Well, in all fairness, animals can't exactly speak up for themselves, now can they?" Jax interjected.

I smirked. "Spoken like a true animal fanatic."

"Stating the obvious doesn't make me a fanatic." Jax's gaze was challenging. "Besides, I thought you loved little fuzzy kittens."

Andy guffawed. "Since when?"

My face felt hot, and I avoided looking either of them in the eye. I cleared my throat and put on my serious face as I addressed Jax. "You said three people knew how to program the keypad."

"Yeah, Lee, from the video." He chewed the inside of his cheek. "And I'm pretty sure Tim Sloan could as well. But Tim went out on disability a few days ago. He had back surgery."

I frowned. "You sure that's legit?"

"He posted a photo from his hospital bed a day ago. I don't think he could fake that, right?" Jax wrinkled his brow.

"Probably not. We'll check it out to be sure he's where he's supposed to be. Who's the third person?"

"Trevor Quinton. He's my PA." Jax lifted his chin. "He wouldn't hurt me."

"How can you be so sure?"

"He loves me. We've been friends for years."

I narrowed my gaze. "Does he *love*, love you?" Jilted lovers were notoriously common suspects.

Jax's cheeks pinkened. "We had a thing in college, but it didn't last. We're better as friends."

"And you both agree on that?" I took in his uneasy demeanor. "Sometimes one person wants to pull the plug and the other still wants more."

Jax arched his brows. "Speaking from experience, Detective Decker? Are you a serial heartbreaker?"

His sardonic tone irked me. Maybe men like him didn't fall all over themselves to be with guys like me, but I definitely did okay in the romance department when I bothered to put myself out there. "We're talking about you and Trevor."

"There were some hurt feelings, and then he was fine."

The line of his jaw was tight, making me suspect he felt guilty about what happened with Trevor. That and his reticence to talk about it. "I think I'd like to speak with him all the same."

He shrugged. "I assumed you'd talk to everyone. I'm sure he's expecting it."

"I'll need the video from the Friday night run-through, so I can see if we have someone on camera fiddling with the keypad."

"Almost every person working on the show was there. The set was packed."

"That's fine. I'll focus on the keypad and the time the code changed."

"Okay. I'll have the footage delivered to you in an hour. You're hanging out at the studio, right?"

"Yeah." I still needed to interview people, and it was easier staying on the lot during work hours than fighting traffic back and forth.

Jax's phone rang on his desk, and he jumped. Laughing sheepishly, he said, "I'm a little tense these days."

"That's understandable." I stood.

Jax took the call, and I headed toward the door. As I reached for the knob, the door opened abruptly, and a guy walked in talking on his cell. When he saw me, he stopped in his tracks and told the person on the phone he had to go. He smoothed a hand over his immaculate blond hair as his gaze traveled over my wrinkled suit jacket. "You must be Detective Decker. I'm Trevor Quinton."

I held out my hand, and we shook. His grip was damp. "You're just the man I wanted to see."

"I figured you'd come gunning for me eventually." His voice was stiff.

"I have to talk to everybody."

"Of course." His cell rang, and he looked apologetic. "I'm a little busy at the moment. Do you think we could do this later today? The other contestants are freaking out about what happened to Dale, and I'm trying to keep them calm."

"That can't be easy," Andy volunteered.

Trevor sighed. "No. It isn't."

"You'd be surprised at the crazies that have come out of the woodwork," Jax said from behind us.

I turned and met his disgusted gaze. "Meaning what?"

His lip curled. "We've been flooded with calls from nut-jobs who are even more excited to be on the show now that someone died."

"So then Dale's death *has* been good for ratings."

"It would seem so," Jax bit out.

"Everything Jax touches turns to gold." Trevor put his arm around Jax's shoulders. "Even when tragedy strikes, Jax comes out on top."

Jax shook off Trevor's arm. "If you think you're being funny, you're not."

Trevor reddened. "It was a compliment."

A muscle worked in Jax's cheek. "You can use my office to interview Trevor. What time is good for you, Detective?"

Trevor shifted uneasily, perhaps irritated that he wasn't being consulted.

"Three?" I threw out a random time that allowed me to have lunch and get some work done.

"Great. I'll let him off his leash around then so you two can have a chat." Jax turned to Trevor, his tone cool. "Sound good?"

Trevor smiled agreeably, although a hint of irritation flashed through his gaze. "Perfect."

I studied them carefully. Regardless of Jax claiming the two of them were good with one another, there was obvious friction. Maybe it was just work tension and had nothing to do with them being romantically involved in the past. It was hard to say what was bubbling under the surface. But one thing was certain: they had issues.

"I'll see you at three." I left the office, Andy tagging along.

When we reached the lot below, Andy grabbed my elbow. "I'm sorry about earlier."

I gave him a chiding look. "You know better."

"He's the one who called us in. I wasn't thinking he was on our list of suspects."

"How many cases have we worked together where the person being stalked was actually setting it all up?" I shook my head. "My gut says it isn't Jax. But I have to get a few more things figured out before he's off the list."

"Fair enough." He sighed. "It won't happen again."

Andy left, and I made my way to the cafeteria, passing a clown, a knight in shining armor, and a cowboy riding a horse. Movie lots were interesting... Once I reached the cantina, I grabbed the biggest cup of coffee they sold and texted Jax: I'm at the cafeteria. Send the footage over when ready.

A courier eventually arrived. My hands shook as I inserted the flash drive. I scanned through the recording until I found the approximate time Dale's code was deleted. Heart pounding, I watched as people milled around the cage and adjoining area. When four a.m. came and went and nobody approached the keypad, I frowned and rewatched several times. Had Andy got the time wrong? No one was anywhere near the safe room at four a.m. How had the code been changed if nobody was there?

I texted Andy: Are you sure the code was changed at four a.m.?

Absolutely.

Could the keypad clock have been different from the security camera?

Nope. I double-checked. The keypad clock was the same as the security camera time. Dale's code was definitely erased a few minutes before four.

Frustrated, I kept staring at the recording, when my phone buzzed with a text from Jax: Hey, change of plans, Detective. I need you to come and talk to Trevor now because I have something I need him to do for me later.

Scowling, I stood and closed my laptop. Typical pampered suit type, thinking I had nothing better to do than rearrange my schedule to fit his.

I made my way across the studio lot toward Jax's office. It was lunchtime, and Jax's office suite seemed quieter than usual. Jax's receptionist, Tressa, wasn't at her desk, so I knocked on Jax's door. When no sound came from inside, I opened the door tentatively.

"Hello? Jax? Trevor?" I walked slowly into the empty room. "Seriously? You're not even here?"

Silence.

I shook my head in disgust. "Thanks for wasting my time, guys."

I was about to leave when I heard a groan. I froze, then turned and scanned the office. Frowning, I moved cautiously toward Jax's executive chair. As I rounded the corner of his big mahogany desk, I was shocked to find Jax lying on the carpet, apparently unconscious. I hurried to his side and knelt next to him. "Jax?" I patted his cheek, but he didn't move. I checked his pulse, which seemed fine, and he stirred slightly. "Jax, what happened?"

He mumbled something incoherent.

A loud *bang* near the entrance made me stand up quickly. I watched in disbelief as smoke began to seep from under the closed door. *What the hell is going on?* I moved to the door and felt the wood. It was warm but not hot. I decided to chance opening it to see how bad the situation was. But when I attempted to open the door, it seemed stuck. I yanked on the handle, but it did no good. Coughing, I stood back and kicked at the door hard. It didn't budge. It was as if someone had wedged something against the handle. I tried again with the same result. *Shit.*

Plan *B.*

I pulled my cell from my pocket and called 911. I told the nice lady on the phone where I was and what was going on. The operator told me to remain calm and to hang on the line, but I hung up. I wasn't in need of her platitudes; what I needed was to get Jax and me out of this burning building as soon as possible.

Unfortunately, since Jax was a big deal at the studio, he occupied a prime space on the eighth floor. There were no fire escapes on this building, so going out the window wasn't an option. The smoke was getting thicker, and the various fire alarms screeched in warning. I pulled off my jacket and stuffed it at the base of the door, hoping to keep some of the smoke out. I returned to Jax and patted his cheek again. It would be so much better if he was awake. The idea of trying to carry him if the opportunity of escape presented itself didn't appeal. He was a tall guy, and while I was in good shape, I was no he-man type.

He groaned and opened his eyes. He wrinkled his brow, looking thoroughly confused. "What's going on?" He managed to sit up unsteadily and pressed his hand to his temple. "Why am I on the floor?"

"I don't know."

He looked around and sniffed. "Smoke. Do I smell smoke?" His voice rose with alarm.

"Yep. I called 911. We're just gonna sit tight for now."

Apparently he didn't agree because he tried to stumble to his feet. He got about halfway up before bumping back down on his ass. "What the fuck. What's wrong with me?"

"Don't know." I tugged at his arm. "Lean over. Let me see if you have a bump on your head." He did as instructed, and I smoothed my hand through his silky hair. The feel of his scalp under my fingers and the clean scent of his shampoo did strange things to me. It was an odd thing to be slightly turned on by touching him, considering we were trapped in a burning building. There were no lumps on his head, so I cleared my throat and played it cool. "All clear. Did you drink anything?"

"Just my coffee." He looked over at the spilled cup next to him. "Decker, what the hell is happening?"

"I'm not sure. I can't get the door open." I pressed my lips together, hoping I looked calm.

He coughed and covered his mouth and nose. "Are we gonna die?" His voice was muffled, his eyes worried. He was trying to be brave, but I could see through him.

"No. We're going to be fine." I had no real plan to save us. I didn't have a cape or superpowers. I'd called 911, and the smart thing was to wait for help.

"Okay," he said softly.

Something about the way he held my gaze told me he trusted me. He thought I had this handled. I had no idea why he thought that, but I could see he did. Maybe it was because he worked in an industry that made films where hero cops saved the day and always came out on top.

I liked his world better than mine. Mine had wives who poisoned their husbands with antifreeze, and husbands who murdered their wives so they could upgrade to a younger model. My world was riddled with people killed by those they trusted most.

I definitely preferred Jax's fairy-tale world to mine. Unfortunately, we were trapped in this ugly reality at the moment. Someone seemed to really, really want Jax Thornburn dead, and unless I came up with something quickly, they were about to get their wish.

CHAPTER FOUR

"What are you doing?" Jax's voice had a borderline hysterical quality.

I'd just pushed open the widow of his eighth-floor office, and I too felt a bit flustered. The wind whipped my tie around my face, and I noticed a small crowd gathered below. Unfortunately, there were no fire trucks yet.

"Decker?" Jax demanded, inching toward me. "What are you up to?"

"I don't think we can just wait." I gave the door an uneasy glance. My jacket wasn't doing a very good job of keeping the smoke out, and the air in the office was becoming increasingly toxic. I grabbed the sides of the window and put my foot on the windowsill.

"Wait. You're climbing out the window?" His voice was no longer borderline hysterical—it was full-blown panic-stricken.

I didn't answer, too busy trying not to hyperventilate. I didn't like heights. I'd never liked them, and staring down at the ground now, I still didn't like them. I pulled myself up until I was balanced on the wide sill. I clenched my jaw, trying to overcome the instinct roaring through me, telling me to get my ass down off the ledge *immediately*.

Jax grabbed the back of my shirt. "No way. You're going to die."

"We both might die if I don't do something," I muttered, inching farther out of the window.

"Crazy son of a bitch. You're out of your mind." His voice wobbled.

I didn't actually disagree with him, but I didn't respond to his comment. Instead, I said, "There's no smoke coming from the lower floors. That's a good thing."

"It is?"

"Yes. I'm hoping that means the fire is only on our floor." A gust of wind smacked me, and I dug my fingers into the aluminum windowsill.

What the hell am I doing?

Jax still had his death grip on my shirt, and I was kind of glad he did. "What's your plan? You must know you can't survive a drop to the ground."

"That isn't the plan."

"What *is* the plan?"

"I'm going to drop down to the balcony below."

"There's a balcony? Since when?"

"Balcony might be a stretch. It has enough room for flower pots." I prayed the small overhang was strong enough to hold the weight of a man. City inspectors could be a pain in the ass sometimes, but this was one time I hoped they'd been anal about their job.

Behind me, Jax coughed roughly, obviously feeling the effects of the smoke filling his office. My throat burned, and I wheezed loudly, accepting the fact that I didn't really have any choice. I had to try and save us. The fire trucks weren't even here yet, and at this rate, we'd probably both be dead from smoke inhalation by the time they did pull up.

"This is a horrible idea," muttered Jax, still holding my shirt.

"Hey, do you have a better one?"

"No."

I crouched on the sill. "You need to let go of me."

He blew out an impatient breath. "I'm not sure I agree."

Fighting the panic in my gut, I spoke calmly. "Jax, let go of me. I have to turn to face you, so that I can try and drop down onto the balcony. I can't do that if you're holding on to my shirt."

He hesitated, then let go. It took every ounce of willpower I had to stay out on the ledge. Everything in me screamed to seek safety. But the hard fact was, at the moment, Jax's office was just as dangerous as the ledge I stood on.

"Just for the record, I think you're out of your fucking mind," he muttered. "But…thank you for trying."

From the grim tone of his voice, I knew he thought I was going to die. Panic jolted through me, but I gritted my teeth and stamped it down. I had no choice. I needed to remember that. "If I…don't succeed…" I swallowed hard. "Stay put. I'm sure the fire department will be here soon."

He didn't respond. We both knew if that were true, my sorry ass wouldn't be hanging out over the ledge of this building.

I sucked in a raspy breath and twisted slowly, scraping my feet along the windowsill. Sweat gathered on my face, and my muscles trembled as adrenaline and terror flooded through me. I heard people below yelling. I had no idea what they were saying, and I tried to tune them out so I could concentrate on not slipping. My movements were slow and clumsy, but eventually I faced Jax, and the smoke-filled room. The haze was so thick, I couldn't even see the door anymore. Jax was pressed up to the windowsill, his eyes bright with fear. I could tell he was trying to control himself, but no sane person could be emotionless in the situation we were in. I really hoped he wouldn't panic and try to follow me out the window. At least, not until he knew if I'd succeeded. If I fell, he could make his own decision about how he died.

I dropped one leg over the ledge, my heart pounding so loudly, I couldn't hear anything else. I didn't want to lower my other leg. I really, really didn't want to. My muscles shook, and panic gripped me as I forced myself to drop my second leg. With my legs dangling, I held tight to the metal windowsill.

My fingers and arm sockets ached as they supported my full weight. When my arm muscles began to twitch with exhaustion, I wished I'd been better about my upper-body workouts.

Dear God, please let the windowsill hold.

I met Jax's gaze. He gave me a weak smile, and tears ran down his smoke-streaked cheeks. I had no illusions he was crying for me; his eyes were no doubt burning from the smoke. He did look disappointed. I wasn't sure if that emotion was for me, or for the predicament he found himself in.

"Good luck," he whispered, his Adam's apple bobbing in his tanned throat.

I gave a sharp nod and twisted my head to try and see below me. I could just make out the flower ledge. It looked a lot farther now that I was hanging by my fingertips. I slowly began to rock my legs back and forth. I had to move gently because of my precarious grip on the windowsill. Back and forth, back and forth, nausea built in my stomach as the moment of truth approached. If I let go too soon, or too late, I'd die. There was no room for error. None.

Jax surprised me when he covered one of my hands with his. When I looked up, he looked sick to his stomach. His jaw was clenched tight, and black smoke poured out of the window around his head. I wasn't sure why he'd touched me. Perhaps he just needed to feel connected to another human as death nipped at him? Or maybe it was genuine concern for me. I couldn't tell. But the resigned look on his pale face gave me a renewed sense of urgency.

"I'll be back in just a sec," I muttered, holding his gaze.

"Can't wait."

I pulled my gaze from his and swung my legs as hard as I could toward the lower balcony, at the same time releasing my death grip on the windowsill…and I was falling. Fear like I'd never known roared through me as my stomach seemed to rise up into my throat. With a loud crash, I smashed onto the flower pots below, crushing them beneath me. The wind was knocked out of me, and I couldn't move for a few moments.

Feeling lightheaded, I stared at cracks in the stucco and a fluttering spider web an inch from my face. Was this real? Had I actually made it onto the ledge alive? With a groan, I managed to suck air back into my lungs. I started coughing. The air was pure and it felt amazing to breathe it in, but I didn't have time to sit there smelling the literal roses. Jax was still in danger. I sat up, broken pottery and flowers stuck to my hands. I was bleeding from my palms, but none of my bones seemed broken.

Scrambling to my knees, I made a point of not looking down. I tried to push open the windows, but the good citizen whose office it was had locked them. Cursing under my breath, I grabbed one of the unbroken flower pots and slammed it repeatedly against the window. There wasn't a lot of space for me to maneuver, and the hair stiffened on the back of my neck at the thought of slipping off my precarious perch. One of the windows finally cracked; I said a prayer and started banging the glass even harder. Jax was counting on me.

When the window gave way, I could have cried with relief. I tumbled through the broken window, hissing when I sliced my arm on a jagged edge. I clambered to my feet and sprinted across the deserted office. I thought I heard sirens in the distance, but I just kept going. It would take the firemen a while to get upstairs; I felt I was Jax's best hope. I threw open the office doors and raced down the empty halls to the stairs, then up the steps, taking them two at a time.

My heart banged my ribs as I reached Jax's floor in the stairwell. I felt the door, finding it cool to the touch. I inched it open to find the hallway filled with smoke. I didn't see or hear flames, so I shoved open the stairway door and bolted toward Jax's private office.

When I reached the reception area, it was almost fully engulfed. I pulled off my shirt and held it to my face as I moved to his door. Anger mixed with panic when I found a cane wedged in the handles.

This wasn't an accident.

It was so hot, my skin hurt, but I couldn't give up on Jax now. Not when I was so close to rescuing him. Using my shirt to protect my hands, I yanked the cane loose and tossed it on the ground, then threw open the door to Jax's office.

The smoke was so heavy, I couldn't see anything, but I heard Jax coughing. Relief rolled through me, and I stumbled into the room. "Jax?" I yelled, trying to see through the smoke. My lungs burned, and I couldn't stop coughing. "Jax, come toward my voice," I growled.

Jax stumbled out of the smoke, his face red, his eyes wide and searching. I grabbed his arm and dragged him after me, gagging on the thick smoke. Once out of the reception area, the air was slightly better, and we were able to gulp in some oxygen. We lurched down the stairwell, stumbling and bumping into the walls. I kept my arm around Jax because he seemed like he was having trouble walking.

When we reached the third floor, we ran into a group of firemen storming up the stairs. One of them stopped and grabbed hold of my arm. "Is there anybody else up there?" he demanded.

"I don't know," I wheezed, wishing he'd let us get the hell out of the building.

He scowled, but he let go of my arm and continued on his way up. I pulled Jax after me, and eventually we reached the bottom floor. The lobby was deserted except for the fire crew, and they shuffled us out the front door to a paramedic truck. There were three fire engines, and firemen scurried around, pulling hoses and running lines to the building.

I pulled on my crumpled shirt and sat beside Jax on the back end of the paramedic truck. They gave us oxygen and tended to the cuts on my arm and my hands. I didn't want to think too deeply about what I'd done to get us out of the building. Every time I remembered hanging from the windowsill, my stomach rolled.

Jax gave me a grateful look. "Thanks," he whispered hoarsely.

I nodded, unsure what to say. I'd wanted to save my ass as much as his. I had felt protective of him, though. I couldn't deny that. I assumed that was just my cop instincts kicking in; protect and serve, right? Or maybe my need to rescue him had been spurred on by the resigned look he'd had when I'd dropped off the ledge. Clearly, he hadn't had any faith that either of us was going to make it.

Trevor rushed up to us at one point, looking flustered. He grabbed Jax in a hug, and I stood and walked away to give them privacy. I still wasn't sure what the exact nature of their relationship was, but Trevor seemed distraught.

I approached the Fire Captain, explaining I was positive it was arson. He promised as soon as the flames were out, he'd make sure the scene was preserved for the arson team. I called Andy, and he showed up, looking rattled.

"What the hell happened?" he asked, raking a hand through his hair.

"Someone set Jax's office on fire." I pressed my lips tight, suppressing a shiver. We'd had a close call. There was no way around that. Whoever had set that fire hadn't cared that a cop was in the room with Jax. In fact, they'd purposely lured me to the scene of their crime. Why? If the goal was to kill Jax, it wasn't logical to have me there. Why had this person texted me? Having me arrive on the scene seemed counterproductive to killing Jax.

"Why were you with him? I thought you weren't meeting that Trevor guy until three."

"I got a text telling me to come sooner."

"What the hell?"

I met his confused gaze. "I know. It's not making a lot of sense."

"Do you think they were just trying to scare you guys?" Even Andy didn't look like he believed that. "I mean, only an idiot tries to kill a cop, right?"

"I don't think this person was playing around."

"Wow, that's pretty nervy to go after Jax when you were with him."

"I agree." I glanced around at the gathered crowd. It wouldn't have surprised me if the arsonist was in the group of onlookers. Arsonists often returned to the scene of the fire. One guy stood out to me; he was chubby and short—Ben Willoughby.

Without thinking I moved toward the guy. His round face tensed as I neared, but he didn't try and run.

"You work on the set of *Don't Die*, right? Ben Willoughby?"

He frowned, then nodded. "Yes. Me and a bunch of other people."

"Any idea how this fire started?"

He blinked at me. "No. I saw the smoke and came over." He glanced around. "Just like everyone else."

"Did you see anyone run out of the building?"

"No."

I noticed a small black pin on his shirt: Animal Liberation Front. From what I remembered, the group liked to cause financial loss to "animal exploiters" through damage and destruction of property.

"Do you agree with using animals on the show the way they do?"

His hand moved to cover the pin. "What I do in my private time is my business."

"That's true. But I have to wonder why a guy with your beliefs works on that show."

He scowled. "I have to eat and pay rent like anyone else."

"Maybe you could come down to the station tomorrow for a longer chat?" I forced a smile. "I'm talking to everyone."

He swallowed. "Sure."

"How about three?"

"Okay," he said softly. He turned and walked away quickly, not looking back.

* * * * *

It didn't take long for the fire to be put out. Even though what I really wanted was to go to the commissary for a stiff drink, I shook off my jitters and made myself talk to the firemen who exited the building. There was no doubt in anyone's mind that the fire was set deliberately, and the cane wedged in the door handles cinched that thought.

At one point Jax made his way toward me, looking uncharacteristically bedraggled. Normally, he didn't have a hair out of place, but at the moment his suit was crumpled and his face streaked with sweat and soot.

"Is it okay if I go home? I gave my statement to one of your guys."

"I guess it's fine if you leave." I frowned. "But I'd appreciate it if you could put some thought into who the heck would want to hurt you."

"I've tried. There are lots of people who could resent me, but I can't think of anyone that would actually want me dead."

"Well, someone is after you." I blew out a tired breath. "Why don't you have a bodyguard? Big shots like you always seem to have a security detail."

"Big shots like me?"

"Yeah, you know, higher-ups."

He still looked annoyed. "I had a guy for a while. I found it awkward to have him around all the time. It just felt strange."

"You need to get someone again. Whether it's uncomfortable or not."

"I'll think about it." His jaw had a stubborn jut to it.

"You were lucky I was there today." My tone was grim. "You must know that."

"I can take care of myself."

I gave a gruff laugh. "Why are you being so stubborn?"

"I like my privacy."

"You're being foolish."

Lifting his brows, he said, "I prefer being alone once I'm home. Besides, I have an alarm system at my place."

"Cops don't respond to regular burglar alarms anymore in Los Angeles, unless a guard from your alarm company verifies there's a break-in."

"Seriously?"

"Yep. The police chief put that into effect April 2019."

"Why?"

"Because over 90% of the calls are false alarms."

He shrugged. "Well, if someone breaks in, I'll call 911."

"You're willing to take that risk simply because you like your privacy?"

He shifted uneasily. "Maybe."

"Suit yourself." I couldn't force him to get security, but I thought he was being stupid. "I noticed cameras in the halls around your office. I'd like my guys to look at that footage ASAP."

He looked pained. "They painted my floor this week."

"And?"

He sighed. "They're putting in new cameras. Those existing cameras aren't plugged in."

"You've got to be kidding." I scowled. "Who else would know the cameras aren't working?"

"Trevor. Tressa. Lots of people. It wasn't a secret."

"Hmmm…"

"Sorry." He gave the building an uneasy glance. "It's not like I knew anyone was going to come after me."

He was right, but that didn't make me any less annoyed that our arsonist wouldn't have been caught on camera. "What about the cameras in the stairwells?"

"Those should be working. But how is that helpful? Lots of people use the stairs."

"Between the stairwell cameras and the elevator ones, we can narrow down who got off on your floor around the time the fire started."

"Oh."

"The more we narrow it down, the better."

"Right. Makes sense. I'll see to it you get that footage right away."

"Thanks."

He shifted as if he was about to leave.

"Before you go, can I ask if anyone visited you right before you passed out?"

"No. Tressa asked if she could go to lunch. Then I made some calls, and started feeling woozy."

"Did you eat or drink anything other than your coffee?"

"Nope. I didn't have time for lunch."

"Do you fix your own coffee?"

He smirked. "You think a big shot like me has time for that? Tressa usually brings me a cup."

I ignored his snide comment. "Did she do that today?"

"I think so. My coffee was waiting for me on my desk after I got back from a meeting."

"Hmmm." I needed to talk to Tressa. I'd met her once, and she hadn't struck me as a criminal mastermind, but looks could be deceiving. "How long has Tressa worked for you?"

His eyes narrowed. "There's no way Tressa drugged my coffee and set fire to the office. There's just no damn way."

"You need to stop second-guessing everything I say and do, Jax."

"Tressa is a sweetheart. She can't even kill a fly. She has to ask someone else to do it."

"We have to look at *everyone*."

"Some people are just not the criminal type."

I squelched my irritation. "While I have no doubt you're an expert, I'll still need to talk to Tressa."

He pressed his lips tight, an angry glint in his eyes. "Of course. You know best."

"Yeah, I actually do."

He shook his head. "Can I take off now?"

"Sure." I hesitated. "Maybe instead of going home, you should think about going to a friend's house."

"What?" He looked confused.

"Well, you won't hire a bodyguard, and it's obvious someone isn't happy with you. It might be best if you didn't go home for a few days. Could you maybe stay with a friend?"

"The only person I know well enough to crash at their place is Trevor. I'm not staying at Trevor's place. That would be...awkward."

"I thought you two were fine just being friends?"

His cheeks tinted pink. "I can't stay with Trevor."

"Okay. Someone else, then? Any family in town?"

"My family is in Nebraska." He looked uneasy. "I don't really have any close friends. I have a lot of acquaintances, but not anyone I'd be comfortable imposing on."

"Then maybe you should stay in a hotel for a while. Just until we figure out who doesn't like you."

"Lots of people don't like me."

"I mean enough to try and end you."

He flinched at my blunt statement, looking lost. "I can't believe this is happening."

I had that familiar twinge of empathy; he looked so forlorn. "I'd feel better if you didn't go home for a couple of nights. Pick a hotel, and I'll make sure you get there safely."

He frowned. "How?"

"I'll follow you there."

"You'd do that?"

Not usually.

"Sure? Why not?" I did my best to sound nonchalant, but even I was confused by my impulse to babysit Jax.

He looked warily at the firemen and cops buzzing around us. "Seems like you probably have work to do here."

"I can't directly investigate the fire because it involves me. I have to wait for the arson investigator and my team to bring me info."

"Oh."

"Besides, I'm allowed a break. I'm in dire need of coffee and food." I studied him more closely, noticing tired lines under his eyes. "You could probably use a meal yourself. We should grab a bite."

Grab a bite? Why would he grab a bite with me?

"You're actually hungry?"

"Yes." While I didn't usually climb out of burning buildings, the stress of the job was a constant in my life. I barely noticed anymore, and certainly didn't let it interrupt my food and caffeine intake. "I haven't eaten all day."

He took in my wrinkled shirt with a distracted look. "Yeah, uh…I don't think I could eat right now."

I wasn't exactly surprised he hadn't jumped at the offer to have a meal with me. Even if I hadn't been disheveled, guys like him probably wouldn't set foot in the kinds of places I usually frequented. He was a fine-dining kind of guy, while I was a shove-food-in-my-face-fast-and-get-back-to-work kind of guy.

"What do you say? Pick a hotel, and I'll see you get there in one piece?"

His gray eyes softened. "I appreciate you doing that for me."

Shrugging, I said, "No problem."

"I need to grab some things from my place first." He shoved his hands into his pockets. "Is that okay?"

"Sure."

"Promise this isn't an imposition?"

Of course it was, but I avoided his question. "It's best you break up your usual pattern. Staying in a hotel will help with that."

"Okay." He met my gaze. "I'll go get my car. I'm in Lot *B*."

"I'll wait for you near the front entrance."

I told Andy and the others where I was going, then headed for my car to escort Jax to his house. I felt a bit silly jumping through hoops for the guy, but I also knew I'd rest easier knowing he was tucked away somewhere safe.

It only took him about ten minutes to pull up to the entrance, and from there we drove past the news vans that had gathered outside the studio gates. Dale's death was titillating news, so it wasn't surprising those vultures were circling.

On the way to Jax's house we passed the Grauman's Chinese Theatre with its pagodas and Chinese Heaven Dog statues, then the Hollywood Wax Museum. Tourist traps held no appeal for me. I couldn't grasp why people flocked to see celebrities' handprints in the cement, but I was in the minority. Even my parents fell for the Hollywood allure and insisted on visiting the Hollywood Walk of Fame each time during their annual visit from Wyoming.

Once we reached Jax's home, I'd planned on waiting in the car, but he tapped on my window and mouthed for me to come inside. Walking up the stone path to his palatial home, I felt out of place. Everything was impeccable, from the neatly trimmed roses to the bright yellow and purple petunias perfectly spaced along the walkway. As I neared the glass front door, my reflection reminded me I was anything but impeccable. I looked like a used-cars salesman, while Jax, even unkempt, looked like a menswear model.

I stayed alert as we entered Jax's home. The foyer was marble with an elaborate chandelier overhead. His alarm system beeped reassuringly, and he punched in his code to turn it off. The floor plan was wide open, with lots of windows, and the temperature was cool. I followed him into the living room, where he stood in the center, looking unsure.

"Would you like a drink?" He pointed to a bar on the far end of the room. "I have everything."

My mouth watered at the idea of whiskey, but I shook my head. "No thanks."

He pulled off his jacket, and my gaze was unwillingly drawn to the firm, tanned skin of his stomach peeking from his untucked shirt. I didn't want to be attracted to him, but it was hard not to be. He was perfect. I couldn't help but wonder what it would be like to be with a guy as flawless as he seemed. Would he be more vulnerable in bed? Maybe he'd be controlling because he was used to being in charge.

I pulled my thoughts back to reality. I wasn't ever likely to find out what Jax was like in bed. He hadn't even been willing to grab a meal with me; last thing he'd do was drag me to his bed. The thought of Jax trying to seduce me almost made me laugh, so I turned away and sat on the blue-velvet sectional.

"I'll go throw some things in a bag," he said softly. "Won't be long."

"No problem." I leaned back and closed my eyes. His house was quiet. The street I lived on was busy and noisy, and my two-bedroom home wasn't very well insulated. But Jax's house was as silent as a library. Since his alarm had been armed when we arrived, I felt relaxed. Odds were no evildoers lurked inside his closet.

He took a little longer than expected, and I must have drifted off because the next thing I knew Jax was waking me up. I jerked upright, feeling embarrassed. "Crap. Sorry." I raked a hand through my hair, my face hot.

"My hero, fast asleep." He sounded amused.

"Yeah, I'd be a lot of help, right?" I stood, still feeling groggy and self-conscious. His hair was damp, and he'd changed into different clothes. His cologne smelled crisp and clean.

He studied me. "I'm sure your work is exhausting. You don't need to be embarrassed."

I cleared my throat. "Um...yeah. So, are you ready to go?"

"Yes. But I was thinking...before we head to the hotel, maybe I could make us something to eat here."

"Why?"

"Oh, well, as a thank-you for going to all this trouble for me."

"I thought you weren't hungry."

"I'm a little hungry now." He shrugged. "It was just a thought."

Maybe he'd been hungry all along but had been too embarrassed to be seen with me in public. He probably had to be careful about his rep. After all, he was trying to climb the Hollywood ladder. Perhaps the paparazzi kept track of who he dined with, and the last thing he wanted was to have a photo of us dining together plastered all over the entertainment rags.

"Can you cook?"

He laughed. "Yes."

"What kind of stuff can you make?" I asked suspiciously. "I don't tend to eat fancy food."

"What's fancy to you?"

"Escargot. Stinky cheeses. Avocado toast. You know, a rich person's food."

He grinned. "Avocado toast isn't a rich person's food. And it's delicious for breakfast."

"I'm more of a steak-and-eggs kind of guy."

He smirked. "Of course you are."

I gave a grudging smile. "You don't have to cook for me. I'd do this for anyone in your predicament." That wasn't entirely true, but he didn't need to know that.

His smile faded. "I know. It's just...once I get to the hotel, I'll be alone with my dreary thoughts." His eyes glittered with uncertainty.

"I thought you liked being alone."

"I like being alone at home. A hotel isn't home." He sighed. "I'd like to just pretend none of this is happening."

That strange urge to comfort him returned, but I shook it off. "Being paranoid is probably a good thing right now."

He groaned. "God, don't say that." He dropped onto the couch near me.

His palpable fear got to me, and I softened my voice. "I just think you need to be alert. Pretending this isn't happening won't help anything."

"I know."

I sat down again, careful not to sit too close to him. "We can eat here if you want."

His expression brightened. "You sure?"

"Yeah. I'm pretty beat. I planned on going back to the studio, but I don't think I will. I can go in earlier tomorrow to make up for knocking off early this afternoon. I'll call my lieutenant and let him know." His pleased smile made my stomach clench. Jesus, what was going on with me? Since when did I care about pleasing some guy I barely knew?

"I have steaks in the freezer. We can barbecue out by the pool." His face seemed less tense. "Maybe we can even swim."

I frowned. "The point of this little trip was to get you checked into a hotel, remember?"

"We can do that after." He stood, looking much happier. "I have swim trunks you can borrow."

"Jax... I... I can't go swimming with you."

His dark brows pulled together. "Why not? Aren't you off the clock now?"

I was. But it still felt odd to hang out with him when I was investigating who was trying to hurt him. I no longer considered him a suspect, but it still seemed strange to socialize with him. "It's not good to get too close to people connected to the investigation."

"Why?"

"Well..." I struggled to find an answer. "It just isn't."

"That's not really an answer. Tell me what's wrong with getting to know me?"

"It's best if I see things impersonally."

"You can't do your job if you know me better?"

"I can. It's just best not to muddy the waters."

"Seems silly." He sighed. "But if you don't want to swim, that's fine. However, I'm still cooking you dinner. I mean, you climbed out of a burning building for me."

"I was saving my own ass too."

He nodded with a knowing expression. "Okay. You can play the uncaring tough guy role if that makes you feel better."

"This isn't a role."

"Whatever you say, Decker." He moved toward the doorway. "I guess I'll just have to win you over by dazzling you with my culinary skills."

My lips twitched. "I don't dazzle easily."

He snorted a laugh. "Of that I have little doubt."

CHAPTER FIVE

I ended up swapping out caffeine for a glass of whiskey. My nerves needed something to help calm the uneasiness nestled in my gut. Jax opted for wine, and as he defrosted the steaks he talked about coming to Los Angeles years ago from Nebraska.

"My parents thought I was nuts." He laughed, but pain fluttered through his gaze. "They wanted me to be an accountant."

"God. Really?"

"Yeah." He shrugged. "My dad's an accountant. It's very stable work."

"Sure. And also incredibly boring." I sipped my drink, enjoying the warmth spreading through my chest.

"Stability is a big thing in my family. My sister is a nurse, and my mom was a home-economics teacher."

"Is that where you learned to cook?"

"No. I took a few cooking classes when I got to Los Angeles." He smirked. "All the cool kids were doing it."

"Got it. I usually avoid all things cool."

His eyes widened. "Shocker."

"Hey, now." I frowned.

He smiled. "I thought being able to cook would come in handy when I became rich and famous. I saw myself throwing elaborate dinner parties and cooking for all my friends."

"That didn't happen?"

He rolled his eyes. "Hell no. Everybody hires caterers from their favorite restaurants so they can brag they know the chef personally."

"God, your world sounds exhausting." I took a long pull of whiskey.

"And murder isn't?"

"It is. It's also depressing. Or it can be."

"Do you always get your man?" His voice was slightly flirtatious.

My pulse tingled a bit at his husky tone, but I figured I was probably reading into things. "Usually."

He glanced up and batted his eyelashes. "I usually get mine too."

Okay, maybe I wasn't reading into anything after all.

Feeling out of my depth, I decided to change the subject. "I'll have to reschedule my interview with Trevor."

He blinked at me. "Oh...yeah. That's true."

"Maybe Trevor set the fire so he wouldn't need to answer my questions."

"No. I keep telling you Trevor wouldn't hurt me."

"You'd be surprised how many times I hear that from people, and they're wrong." I swirled my whiskey, watching different emotions roll across his handsome features.

"There is no way Trevor tried to murder us. If you knew the guy, you'd realize how silly that theory is." He took the steaks from the microwave and moved to the glass door.

I jumped up and opened it for him, and he gave me a curt nod. "Thanks."

I followed him outside, and had to stop myself from gasping at the size of his backyard. There was a big pool, an elaborate grilling area with under-the-counter refrigerators, lounge chairs, and a yard big enough to play football in.

He gave me a knowing glance. "Yeah. The yard is one of my favorite features of the house."

"Wow. This is nice." I stood on the edge of the brick patio, surveying the grounds. "It must take a week for your gardener to mow this yard."

He just smiled and fired up the grill.

I inhaled the scent of jasmine, and let out a long sigh. "You could rope steer back here."

He chuckled. "I'll take that under consideration."

"But seriously, what do you do with all this space?"

"Mostly I like it because it creates distance between me and the neighbors." He shrugged. "I don't get to enjoy the backyard as much as I'd like, to be honest."

"No. I wouldn't think so. Too busy taking Hollywood by storm."

He gave me an annoyed glance. "Maybe you shouldn't work the Hollywood division. You seem to have a chip on your shoulder."

"Nah. I'm just teasing."

"I'm not so sure. Did an actor break your heart or something?" He placed the steaks on the grill, and they sizzled loudly.

"I don't have a heart."

"That would probably come in handy in your line of work."

"That's the truth." I turned to watch him since he seemed distracted by tending to the meat. His hands were slender, with long, tanned fingers and perfectly buffed nails. I glanced down at my calloused hands, and it occurred to me I was still wearing the same smoky clothes. "I just realized I sat on your couch in these filthy clothes."

He looked over. "Oh, that's okay. I'm sure the couch is fine." He frowned. "Damn, I should have given you some clean clothes. Would you like to change?"

The idea of wearing his clothes was strangely sensual, and yet it also felt wrong. Not to mention my shoulders were broader than his; I wasn't sure I'd even fit into his clothes. But I hated smelling like a chimney. "Well…"

"You didn't expect to still be stuck in those clothes, I'm sure. You'd have probably gone home to shower and change if you weren't trying to look out for me." He wrinkled his brow. "Come on, let me get you some clean clothes."

Maybe it was the whiskey, or maybe I was too exhausted to argue, but I found myself nodding. "If it's not too much trouble."

He smiled. "Not at all." He eyed me, and my pulse sped up as he ran his gaze over my body. "You're more muscular than me. I have a few shirts that are too large for me. Come with me, and you can change upstairs."

I set my empty whiskey glass on a table and followed him into the house. He led me up a curved staircase to his master bedroom. I was embarrassed that my heart rate sped up as we entered his master suite. I wasn't someone who usually had trouble focusing, but something about Jax made staying aloof difficult. I made sure not to look at his king-size bed, and kept my gaze glued on him.

"Would you like to take a shower?"

I thought longingly of soap and warm water. "Maybe."

"Yeah. You should. Let me grab you some clean clothes for after your shower."

He went into a huge walk-in closet and returned with two shirts, one red and one blue. They both still had the tags on them, and they were a lot more money than I usually spent on shirts. He held up the red one and looked at me with narrowed eyes. "With your blond hair and blue eyes, you'd look good in either color."

"It's not a fashion show," I muttered, feeling self-conscious. "I just don't want to stink of smoke."

He didn't react to my grumpy tone. "I think the blue one." He held the shirt out to me. "Take off your dirty shirt and pants, and I'll have them cleaned at the hotel."

"What? I'm not stripping down in front of you."

He laughed. "So bashful. Who knew macho Detective Decker was shy about his body."

"I'm not shy about my body. I just don't feel it's appropriate to strip in front of a stranger."

He lifted one brow. "A stranger? We faced death together. We aren't *strangers*."

I made no move to take off my shirt.

"The steaks are going to burn if you keep being stubborn." He dropped his gaze to my slacks. "I think I have some jeans that will fit you." He went back into the closet, returning a few moments later with a pair of jeans. "Here. Shower and change, and I'll go check on the meat. Leave your dirty clothes on the floor. I'll grab them later."

"You don't have to clean my clothes. If you have a plastic bag, I'll take them home in that."

"I don't mind. You climbed out of a burning building for me; the least I can do is wash your clothes."

"I keep telling you that was mostly self-preservation on my part."

"And I don't believe you," he said softly.

I couldn't help but laugh. "Suit yourself. But I'm no hero."

He smirked, lifting his face. "You're my hero, Decker."

His full lips were tempting, and if I'd been braver, maybe I'd have leaned closer and kissed him. He almost looked like he expected me to. Instead, I took the jeans from him and moved away. I was no blushing virgin, and I certainly enjoyed one-night stands, but I didn't want to take advantage of Jax simply because he was feeling vulnerable and I happened to be here.

He hesitated, but then moved to the door. I couldn't tell if he was disappointed I'd moved away, or if he hadn't even noticed. Maybe this chemistry between us was all in my head.

"I'll be down in a minute," I said gruffly.

He left the room without a word, and I headed into the large master bath. I stripped and climbed in the shower quickly. The heated water rolled down my tired body, washing away the soot and sweat of my earlier adventure. My pulse was still beating swiftly, and my hands shook slightly. It had been so long since anyone really turned me on, I felt a little like a teenager. I needed to focus on this case and stop fantasizing about seducing the rich Hollywood producer. What was wrong with me? Why had I even allowed myself to entertain that thought?

Once I'd dried off and dressed, I made my way back outside. Jax was standing beside the pool, staring off into space. He startled when I approached.

He ran his gaze over me. "Not bad. It's nice seeing you in casual clothes."

"Yeah, I'm sure it's the highlight of your day."

He smiled. "You look less intimidating in baby blue."

I wasn't sure what to say, so I said nothing.

He went back to staring across the yard. "I keep thinking…if I'd never come to Los Angeles, Dale would still be alive."

"Maybe it was just his time."

He glanced over. "Do you really believe in fate?"

"Thinking we have no influence on when we die makes accepting death easier."

"True, but do you actually believe that?"

"No."

He sighed, his shoulders drooping. "Me neither."

"But I also think Dale was a grown man, and it was his choice to get in a cage with a tiger."

"I… I know logically it was his decision, but if I hadn't come up with this fucking show, he might still be alive." He clenched his jaw. "His wife and kid must hate me."

"No point in worrying about that."

He glanced over. "Does the job ever get to you? You obviously see a lot of death."

"Things with kids get to me. Other than that, it's just my job." I was exaggerating my objectivity a bit, but mostly I was able to keep a distance from my cases. That was one reason my protective urges toward Jax were so perplexing to me.

"I could never do what you do." He finished off his wine and moved to the grill.

"It's not that I'm heartless." I was almost shocked to hear myself say that. Why was I explaining myself to him? Who cared if he thought I was a cold asshole?

"I didn't say you were."

"It's best for the victims if I am objective. That's how they get justice."

"Right." He pulled the steaks from the grill and put them on plates. "I get what you're saying." He set the plates on a glass table with an umbrella. "I made a salad. I'll go grab it."

I watched him go back in the house, his shoulders stiff, his head down. He wasn't anything like I'd expected, and that almost annoyed me. If he'd been some vapid, shallow guy, I wouldn't have thought twice about him. But he wasn't. He was intelligent, empathetic, and for whatever reason, that was affecting me.

I sat down at the table and waited for him to return. He came outside, carrying a big bowl of salad and a plate of garlic toast, which he set on the table. His expression was pleasant, but I sensed an underlying current of tension. "I figured the steak wouldn't be enough food for you."

"Thanks." I was still puzzled as to how I'd ended up sharing a meal with Jax at his home. I should have refused his offer of food, and gone home to sleep. Instead, here I was, worrying about whether or not Jax Thornburn thought I was a cold, heartless asshole.

He sat, and our legs brushed slightly beneath the table. My pulse bumped up at the warm press of his leg, but then he moved it away. I focused on the food, helping myself to a big serving of salad and a piece of garlic bread. The steak was perfect, slightly pink in the center but not bloody. The garlic toast was crunchy on the outside but chewy too, and even the salad was delicious.

"Did you want another drink?" he asked, cutting carefully into his steak.

"No. I'm good." Seeing him slice delicately into his steak reminded me to at least pretend I was civilized. I'd practically pounced on my food, and I forced myself to slow down. I rarely shared meals with anyone, and I'd gotten into the bad habit of eating like a lion that had just taken down a zebra. I cleared my throat. "Everything is great."

He glanced up, looking pleased. "It was nice cooking again. I should do it more often."

"You probably work long hours."

"I do. I guess firing up the barbecue at two in the morning doesn't appeal to me like it should." He laughed. "I like to think eventually I'll have more time to have a real life again."

"You came here seeking fame. Looks like you got your wish."

"Reality TV wasn't really what I wanted to do. But in my business you take the jobs that come your way, hoping they lead to something bigger. This one did."

"I guess there are worse problems to have." I gestured to the house and big backyard. "People would kill to have your life."

He winced at my choice of words.

"In fact, people do kill to have your kind of life. Money is one of the biggest motives for most of my cases. That and jealousy."

"I get what you're saying, but I'm not sure how killing Dale would accomplish anything useful for anyone."

I took the last bite of my steak and sat back in my chair. "Maybe someone wants to ruin you."

"Jesus." His lips pulled tight.

"I know it's not a very pleasant idea, but that's people for you."

He set his fork down with a clatter. "If they just wanted to ruin me, why drive me off the road or burn my office? Both times I could have died."

"Not all murderers are bright."

"I can't believe I'm in this situation. It's like a nightmare."

"I'm sure." I hesitated. "Whoever this person is, they seem impatient."

"What does that mean?"

"Well, they're not letting much time pass between attempts. Can you think of any reason they'd feel they have to hurry?"

"No."

"Any life-insurance policy about to expire? Are you up for some big award and one of your competitors would like to get rid of you so they can have a better chance at winning?"

"I can't think of anything like that."

"The one good thing about them being this reckless is there's a big chance they'll make mistakes. That will make catching them easier."

He blew out a shaky breath. "Let's hope that's before they succeed in killing me."

"I think you'll be fine."

His expression was pained. "Such overwhelming confidence."

I laughed gruffly. "I *assume* you'll be fine."

"Better, but still not hugely reassuring." He glanced down at his mostly untouched food.

"You should eat more."

"Why? So I'll have the strength to fight off the next attack?"

"I didn't mean that." He looked so demoralized, it made my gut hurt. "Just keep your eyes open. Be alert. Don't drink or eat anything you don't fix yourself."

"How's that work if I'm at a fucking hotel?" he snapped. He immediately looked repentant, saying softly, "Sorry."

"I get it. You're scared."

"Yeah. I am. This feels...*insane*. Never in a million years did I picture someone trying to kill me."

"I understand." I exhaled roughly. "I'm frustrated I lost ground today. I didn't expect this person to be as brazen as they are. I'm pissed I didn't see today's attack coming. But tomorrow I'll get back to it. Once I start talking to people, I'll get this asshole. People let things slip. People fuck up. That's how we get them."

"Okay."

"But, Jax, you need to listen to what I'm about to say."

He looked uneasy. "All right."

"I'm not trying to scare you, but it's important that you don't trust anyone right now. Even people you think you can trust."

"You mean like Trevor and Tressa?"

"I mean anyone."

"Jesus, how do I do that?"

I felt for him. He looked lost. "It won't be easy. I'll get this guy. I will. But you have to stay alert. I'd feel a lot better if you'd reconsider hiring a bodyguard temporarily."

He nodded, looking pale and worried. "Okay."

"Yeah?" Relief washed through me. "You'll hire someone?"

"Well, the only time I feel safe is when you're with me." He looked embarrassed. "I just mean because you seem like you can handle any situation."

I was flattered, but I played it cool. "Not every situation."

"I can't think of anything you couldn't deal with," he said softly.

His intense gaze made me squirm. "Do you have a security company you trust? The sooner you get someone, the better."

"I do." He gave a crooked smile. "Unless you want the job?"

"Tempting, but I'm a little busy trying to catch the person who killed Dale."

His smile faded. "Yeah. Of course."

"If you're done eating, we should be heading out."

"Oh, sure." He rose, grabbing the plates. "I'll just rinse these, and we can go."

"Sounds good." I followed him into the house. "Tomorrow I'll talk to Trevor and the people who could have erased Dale's passcode."

"Okay." He rinsed the plates and put them in the dishwasher. Then he faced me as he dried his hands with a paper towel. "I'll grab my bag and meet you by the front door."

I glanced down at the clothes I wore. "I can change into my dirty clothes if you want."

"No. I'm sure I'll see you tomorrow. I'll have the hotel wash your clothes, and we can swap then."

"You sure? I'm perfectly capable of washing my own clothes."

"I know. But I want to do this for you." He studied me. "You've been so kind to me today. I... I didn't think you were a compassionate person when I first met you."

"I'm really not."

"But you have been to me," he said quietly. "You've been great."

I could have said it was just my job, or some other thing to make him stop staring at me the way he was. I knew it wouldn't take much to spoil his nice opinion of me. We'd probably get there soon enough without even trying. But I kind of liked the way he was looking at me; it was heady, flattering, like I was someone he believed in. Like I was his hero. I knew it was foolish to let him in even a little, but I didn't have it in me at the moment to stomp on his feelings.

"You must bring out my better side."

He looked pleased. "Yeah?"

I cleared my throat, forcing myself to focus. "We should go."

"I'll go get my bag."

"Meet me out front."

I left him and headed to the door. I was no doubt overthinking things with Jax. I didn't need to worry about him getting too attached. He felt vulnerable today, and I represented security. By tomorrow, things would probably return to normal. After all, I was known for being a good detective, not for my charming personality.

CHAPTER SIX

Lee Price didn't seem at all bothered by having to sit down with me at the station to talk about his movements the night of Dale's death, and the attempts on Jax's life. He seemed concerned and willing to help.

"I've never had anybody bad-mouth Jax to me." He met my gaze. "Maybe they know I'd rip them a new one if they did."

"So you and Jax are close?" I studied him for any flicker of hesitation but saw nothing.

"I love the guy. I'm pushing sixty, and a lot of the younger producers won't hire me. But Jax did, and I'll always be grateful for that."

"You know how to program the keypad on the tiger enclosure, is that right?"

"Yeah. I haven't done it in a while, but I'm sure I could fumble my way through if I had to."

"Who else is able to do that?"

"I'm not sure exactly. For security reasons, I wouldn't think it's a lot of people."

"No. It's a short list."

He leaned toward me. "Good. It should be."

"I noticed you were able to get into Dale's safe area after the attack. How did you do that?"

"My code overrides everything. It's like a janitor's master key."

"Ahhh. I see."

He gave a tense laugh. "Does the keypad have something to do with what happened to Dale?" For the first time, he looked uneasy.

"Possibly."

"Is that yes in cop speak?"

"We're looking at why Dale didn't go into his safety pod."

"Yeah, I've kind of wondered the same thing myself." He hesitated. "Was he not able to get in?" When I kept my expression blank, the color seemed to drain from his face. "Are you fucking kidding me? Some son of a bitch tampered with the keypad?"

"Like I said, we're just looking for reasons why Dale didn't get to safety in time."

"Oh my God," he whispered, looking nauseated. "Why would anyone do that? Dale was a great guy. Jesus, what sick fucker would do that to another person?"

His anger and revulsion seemed sincere, not that people couldn't put on a show when necessary. But Lee seemed genuinely upset.

"How well do you know Trevor Quinton?"

He looked a little thrown by the change of subject. "He...he seems like a nice guy. I don't hang out with him or anything, but he seems fine."

"So you wouldn't say you're friends?"

"No. He mostly sticks close to Jax and the contestants. His sister, Robin, is easier to talk to."

"He has a sister?"

"Yeah. She's a Location Assistant. Hard worker too."

"I'd like to talk to her. I didn't realize Trevor had family on set."

"She doesn't like anyone knowing she's related to Trevor. She's prideful. Wants to make it on her own with no hint of nepotism."

"Didn't she get the job because of Jax's relationship with Trevor?"

He laughed. "Oh, God no. If anything, she got Trevor the job. She'd be pissed to hear you think Trevor got her hired."

"Huh."

He gave a stiff smile. "I can't see Robin hurting anybody."

"Sure. Sure. But we're talking to everybody. In fact, I'm interviewing Trevor later today." I tried to sound pleasant and non-threatening. "I'm leaving no stone unturned."

"Right. I guess you need to do that."

"What do you know about Lucinda Pinwheel?"

Again, he looked thrown by the change of topic. "Um, nice lady. Treats her animals like they're her children."

"I'm curious why she didn't seem to notice the tiger was losing weight."

"Oh, she did notice. She thought Benji had a parasite. She was treating him for that, but he just wouldn't put on weight. She said she was going to call a vet if he didn't improve soon."

"So then it probably wasn't a parasite?"

"Doesn't sound like it."

"She didn't mention anything about Benji possibly having parasites when I spoke to her the day of the attack."

"Odds are she was in a panic. She knows people are going to want to have Benji put down."

"Are they going to do that?"

"I'm not sure. Lucinda can't use him anymore, that's for sure. No one in their right mind will work with that tiger now."

I shuddered inwardly, remembering the chewed corpse. "No. I wouldn't think so."

"Lucinda said there's an animal rescue in Nevada that might take Benji. They've taken other show animals that turn bad."

"I wonder why the cat was still losing weight."

He shrugged. "I don't know. Maybe he was stressed out from all the lights and people."

"Perhaps." I nodded. "What's your opinion of Ben Willoughby?"

He raised his brows. "Ben? Very quiet. Doesn't socialize with anyone on the crew."

"Is that unusual?"

"Yeah. It is. Most of us are pretty buddy-buddy. Even when people don't like each other, we all socialize." He laughed. "But Ben rarely joins in."

"Ever see him lose his temper?"

"No. Nothing like that. Just keeps to himself."

"Okay, well, I appreciate your coming in to answer my questions." I handed him one of my business cards. "If you think of anything else that might be helpful, please don't hesitate to call."

He stood, looking thoughtful. "Okay."

He left the small room, and I headed to the break area for some horrible coffee. I had Ben coming in next and then Trevor. While I waited for Ben to arrive, I killed some time talking with my fellow detectives, and when one of the officers alerted me Ben was in an interview room, I went to meet him.

Ben didn't look thrilled to see me. His expression was guarded, and he had sweat stains under his armpits.

I sat across from him, and he avoided my gaze. "Thanks for coming in, Ben."

"Sure."

"You work mostly maintenance, is that right?"

"Yes."

"Do you like your job?"

"Yes."

If he was going to just give me one-word answers, this interview would prove fruitless. "You seem like a quiet and private guy. I'm curious why you'd belong to an organization that believes in violence."

His face flushed. "You mean the ALF?"

"Yeah."

"They're not like that."

I narrowed my eyes. "They encourage damage and destruction of property."

"They're protecting innocent animals."

"So anything is okay, then?"

He flicked his brown eyes to mine. "I just send them money. I don't actually do anything with them."

"You've never carried out any acts of violence to save an animal?"

"No." His mouth drooped. "I should do something."

"I don't agree, Ben. You'd risk arrest and lose your job."

He scowled. "Well, sometimes you have to do things that are bad to make something good happen."

"Is that right?" He really didn't look like a vicious type, but people could fool you sometimes.

His gaze glittered. "Yeah. The American Revolution was violent. The Civil Rights Movement was violent. Sometimes violence is all anybody will understand."

"Have you ever wanted to be violent against Jax Thornburn?"

He stilled and dropped his gaze. "No."

"Why not? He's the one who created *Don't Die*. Shouldn't he be held responsible for exploiting those animals?"

"Probably."

I leaned toward him. "Did you send a threatening letter to Jax?"

His color deepened. "No."

"We have the letter, Ben. We can check it for your fingerprints," I lied. He would have no way of knowing Jax had destroyed the letter.

He crossed his arms. "I want a lawyer."

I laughed. "We're just talking, Ben. I haven't arrested you. Would you like me to arrest you so you can have a lawyer?"

"I didn't do anything violent. I swear."

He was hiding something, of that I was sure. Maybe he was just embarrassed about sending a harassing letter to his boss. I continued asking him questions, but he seemed to shut down. After ten minutes of one-word responses, I decided to let him go and bring him back another time. I wanted more details about where he was when Jax was attacked.

"I'll need to talk to you again when I have more information. Will you be willing to do that, Ben?"

He clenched his jaw. "Can I say no?"

"Not really."

"Then I guess it's fine," he muttered.

I stood. "Why don't we leave it there for now?"

He got up, moved to the door, and hesitated. He gave me a grumpy glance over his shoulder and then left the room.

I wrote down my thoughts on Ben's and Lee's interviews, then went to meet Trevor in the other interview room.

Trevor looked nervous. He had a bottle of water in front of him, and I could see he'd scraped the label off with his nail while he waited. I had to wonder why he seemed so worried. I realized being interviewed by the police made a lot of people uneasy, but Trevor looked sweaty, pale, and downright guilty.

I shook his hand, registering his weak grip. I settled across from him, shuffling through a folder and giving him time to compose himself. When I finally looked up, he still looked wary. "Thanks for coming in."

"Of course." His expression wasn't nearly as gracious as his tone.

"After what happened to Dale, I'm sure you have a lot of uneasy contestants on your hands."

He nodded. "I've been on the phone nonstop."

"I can imagine." I leaned back in my chair, taking in his flawless appearance. Not counting the sweat, he was handsome perfection.

He and Jax probably made a beautiful couple.

I was surprised by how annoying I found that thought.

"You've known Jax for a long time?"

He avoided my gaze. "Since college."

"You're Jax's personal assistant?"

"Yes."

I narrowed my eyes. "Just how personal are you two?"

His face tinted pink. "It's not like that."

"But you were more than just friends in college, right?"

He glanced up, looking surprised. "You know about that?"

"Jax told me."

"Oh."

"Was there some reason you wanted to hide that info?"

He shook his head. "Not exactly. I simply wasn't sure if Jax wanted that to be common knowledge."

"Trevor, you need to tell me the truth, not what you think other people want you to tell me."

"Sorry."

"This is a murder investigation. If you keep secrets, you're liable to end up in jail."

His eyes widened. "I'm not a murderer."

"Then don't hide stuff." My voice was firm. "Dale is dead, and someone is trying to hurt Jax. I need you to be completely honest with me so we can catch this person."

He rubbed his face roughly. "Yeah. Okay. Shit, I just don't understand what's happening. I mean Dale was just a normal, nice guy. He was the kind of person who'd offer a ride to the airport if you needed it. He was kind. Goodhearted. There was no reason to kill him."

"What about Jax?"

He glanced up. "What about Jax?"

"Is there a reason to kill him?"

"No. Of course not."

"You sure?"

"Are you actually insinuating I'd want to kill Jax because we used to date?"

"I'm simply trying to figure out if there are lingering resentments because he broke up with you."

His lips thinned. "How do you know I didn't break up with him?"

"Did you?"

"It was *mutual*," he snapped.

Sure it was.

"Still, it must be awkward to be around Jax if he's seeing other guys."

"No. I see other people too." He dropped his gaze to the table. "We're both grown-ups."

"Hmmm."

He glanced up, anger glinting in his eyes. "I would never hurt Jax. I love him. He's one of the best guys I know, and I'd never, *ever* harm him."

His passion was so intense, I had to work hard not to flinch. He definitely sounded and looked sincere. The veins bulged in his forehead as he stared at me, and his voice was raw with emotion.

"Take it easy. No need to get upset," I said quietly.

"Well, it makes me sick to think you could suspect me of trying to kill Jax." He exhaled and sat back in his chair. "I worship the guy."

Spurned lover or not, I was inclined to believe him. Trevor seemed more like he'd take a bullet for Jax rather than harm him. "I have to ask everyone hard questions, not just you."

"I guess," he muttered. He was still scowling, but he seemed calmer.

I cleared my throat. "Is your sister fond of Jax too?"

He wrinkled his brow. "Robin?"

"Yeah. Does she like Jax?"

"She doesn't *dislike* him."

"If I ask her, will I get the same answer?"

"Look, she's protective of me, but Robin's no murderer."

"Anyone you can think of who would want to hurt Jax?" I clasped my hands on the table. "Anyone he had a falling-out with?"

He scrunched his face. "Jax has to fire people sometimes. I guess maybe someone he let go could hold a grudge."

"Can you think of anyone he fired recently who maybe threatened him?"

He shook his head. "Not really. We have a good crew."

"Perhaps he had to cut a contestant?"

"Nope. We have all the original people." He sighed. "Of course, we may have to cancel the show now."

I was surprised to hear that wasn't a given. "Wait. You mean the show might still continue?"

"The network is trying to argue Dale's death is no different than when a race-car driver dies. Plenty of drivers have died, and it's not like the Indy 500 has stopped being a thing."

"Well, Dale's death wasn't accidental."

"Hey, I get what you're saying. But the money guys don't seem to agree."

I shook my head. "I don't get you Hollywood types."

"If it were up to me, I'd cancel the show for sure. So would Jax. He just got the call today, and he's pissed they might try and start up again."

I was glad to hear that. The idea that Jax would have been fine continuing the show would have made him pretty coldhearted. "I see."

"But it's not our call."

"I suppose not." I rifled through some papers. "I think someone told me you know how to program the keypad in the tiger enclosure?"

"Yeah. So?"

"Have you done that recently?"

"No."

I studied him, searching for any sign he was lying. "Did you see anyone else fiddling with the keypad?"

Rubbing his jaw, he said, "Not that I can recall. Did it malfunction or something?"

Or something.

"Were you on set the morning Dale died?"

"No."

"How about the previous night during the run-through?"

"I was working in Jax's office, but not on the actual set."

He was telling the truth about not being on set that night. "So you, Lee Price, and Tim Sloan are the only ones who know how to program the keypad?"

"I think so." He frowned. "You're awfully interested in the keypad."

"I'm interested in everything."

He nodded, but he didn't look like he believed me. "Lee Price is the nicest guy you'll ever meet, and Tim was having back surgery." He bit his lip. "And I'm a chickenshit, so no way I'd murder Dale."

I was getting frustrated because it seemed as if the three people who could have messed with the keypad hadn't had the opportunity or motive. Plus, by all accounts, Dale had been a great guy. I couldn't seem to grasp why he'd been killed or how it tied to the attempts on Jax.

"Do you think Robin would be willing to talk to me?"

He raised his brows. "Of course."

"Okay. Can I get her number?" I pushed my pen and folder toward him. "Just write her number on here."

He did as I asked, looking confused. "Have you ever considered this is all being done by someone who isn't on our crew?"

"Yes."

"But you don't buy that?"

"It's possible, but usually in cases like this it's someone closer to the victim or victims."

"Okay, but random shit does happen."

"Yep." I smiled pleasantly.

He scooted the folder back toward me. "I can't believe this person is anyone I know."

"I understand."

He studied me, looking like he wanted to say something. Eventually, he said, "Thanks for saving Jax's ass yesterday."

His comment took me by surprise. "Oh, well, of course. But I was looking after my own ass too."

"Yeah, Jax said you keep saying that." His smile was melancholy. "He couldn't stand you at first, but now he seems to think you're some kind of superhero."

My face warmed. "Hardly."

He smirked. "That's what I told him."

"Trust me, the more Jax gets to know me, the faster that idea will disappear."

"Good."

I narrowed my eyes. "I thought you were fine with him seeing other people?"

"I am."

"Sure about that?"

"I'm not jealous, if that's what you're trying to imply."

"What, then?"

He shrugged. "You're all wrong for him." His tone was dismissive. "You wouldn't fit into his world."

I stamped down my irritation. I had no desire to fit into Jax's world, but something about Trevor's judgmental expression pissed me off. "He wouldn't fit into mine either."

"I'm glad we agree."

I clenched my jaw and stood, scraping back my chair. "I appreciate your coming in to talk to me." I forced a smile. "You've been very helpful."

He stood too. "No problem. Anything to help Jax." He left the interview room, and I went in the other direction.

When I got to my desk I was still feeling irritable, but when I saw that Jax had sent over the security footage of the stairwells and elevators for his floor, I cheered up. I spent the next six hours watching people walk up and down stairs and get on and off the elevator. While there were lots of people who came and went, no one was carrying a cane or anything that looked like an incendiary device. It was surprising how many people used the stairs instead of the elevator. Maybe it was because so many people in the movie business were fitness freaks and worried about having perfect bodies. I scowled when Trevor's snooty comments about me not fitting into Jax's world came back to me.

Fuck him.

He knew nothing about me. Regardless of what he said, he was plenty jealous of Jax. I didn't think he'd hurt Jax, but he was definitely still territorial about his ex. I shook off thoughts of Trevor and continued watching the surveillance footage. As evening rolled around, my eyes were getting blurry and I had a headache coming on. There were certainly more enjoyable ways to spend my day than watching hours of people wandering in stairwells.

I didn't see anyone I recognized near Jax's office around the time of the fire. His receptionist, Tressa, left for lunch just as Jax said, and no one else showed up until I arrived. It was weird watching myself on the camera when I reappeared to help Jax out of his office. The memory of climbing out of the window and fighting the smoke and heat to return to Jax made my heart pound. Once the footage was just firemen fighting the fire, I paused the film and leaned back in my chair.

When my cell rang, I jumped. Pressing my hand to my chest, I glanced around sheepishly, hoping none of my coworkers had noticed me flinch. "Hello?"

"Hey, Decker, it's me, Jax." He sounded confident but a little breathless.

Surprised it was him on the line, I hesitated. "Everything okay?" I'd been busy interviewing people most of the day, and hadn't gone to the studio. I assumed Jax was fine or I'd have probably heard about it, but I couldn't deny it was nice to hear his voice.

"Uh, yeah. Everything is fine. I was wondering if you'd be willing to do me a favor tonight?"

"What kind of favor?"

"Well, I have your clothes…"

I had his too, in a bag tucked in my trunk. "Right. I can drop yours off at the studio if you want?" I glanced at my watch, noticing it was almost six.

"I'm not at the studio. I'm at my hotel. I left a little early because I have this thing tonight."

"Oh, well, I can just drop them off tomorrow, then."

"Yeah." He gave a short laugh. "Actually, I wasn't really calling about the clothes."

"No?" Something about his tone made my pulse spike. "Why did you call?"

"I have to go to this party tonight."

I frowned but didn't speak.

He gave another breathy laugh. "I was wondering if maybe you'd want to go with me?"

I was shocked at the invitation, and it took me a second to regain my composure. "You're inviting me to a party?"

"I thought it might be a good way for you to meet and talk to some of the people I work with, without being so obviously questioning them."

"I see." I was surprised that I felt a bit let down at his reason for asking me out. Not that that made any sense. I had no expectation of anything from him, and after my conversation with Trevor earlier, I still felt a little touchy.

"You could get a feel for what they're like without them even knowing you're a cop."

"Ummm…." I glanced down at my cheap suit jacket. "I'm not really sure I'd fit in."

Just ask Trevor.

"Why not?"

"I'm not a Hollywood type."

"What does that even mean?" He sounded puzzled.

"Come on, you must know I'd stand out like a sore thumb. The minute I walked in, they'd know I'm a cop."

"I guess." There was disappointment in his voice. "Well, even if they did figure that out, I think they'd still be loose-lipped with booze in them."

"I had no idea you were this devious."

"I want to find the asshole that has made my life hell." His voice wobbled with anger.

"That's not your job. That's my job."

"Which is why I'm inviting you to join me," he said smoothly.

My lips twitched. "Socializing might not be a great idea."

"With me or with my friends?"

"Either."

He sighed. "I don't want to show up at that damn party alone."

"How flattering."

He chuckled. "Come on, Decker, we both know that if I say I actually want to see you, you'll run screaming."

"Probably."

"You're allowed to do what you want on your own time, right?" His voice was coaxing.

"Yes."

"So why not come with me?"

"How old are you?"

"Thirty-five. Why?"

"I'm forty-two."

"So?"

"You must have better options than me." I leaned back in my chair, feeling less grumpy than earlier. Even my headache seemed to be better.

He hesitated. "Of course I have options, but I called you."

My gut fluttered oddly. I knew I should decline. He was way too appealing, and getting involved with him when he was at the center of my case was really, really dumb. Could I spend time with him socially and not get even more attracted? I wasn't sure. "I don't know about this."

"I'll be safer if you're with me."

I scowled. "Haven't you hired a bodyguard yet?"

"No, I did. But I'm not bringing him to the party."

"Why not?"

"Because having Harry around would be a constant reminder of the shit I'm dealing with. I'd rather enjoy myself and not think about all this crap for one night."

"I'm not a reminder?"

"Well, I guess you are, but you can get something out of being there. I'm telling you, these people like to drink. Once they start talking, it's impossible to get them to stop."

I laughed gruffly. "Who will be there?"

"Most of the crew."

"Hmmm." I was tempted. It would be nice to talk to people when they were less guarded. But would I be able to get anything out of them without seeming like I was interrogating them? I wasn't sure I possessed those skills. I wasn't known for my subtlety.

"Come on, Decker. Be my date," he said softly.

My pulse picked up again. "This is probably a really bad idea."

"Most of my bad ideas turn into something great."

"Is that right?"

"Moving here from Nebraska was something everyone told me was a terrible plan. But now look at me; I'm filthy rich." There was a smile in his voice.

"Just so you know, most of my bad ideas just turn out bad."

He laughed. "What do you say?"

"I don't own a tux."

"No one will be wearing a tux. This is a jeans-and-nice-shirt kind of party. Everyone will spend hours getting ready so that they can look like they just threw on any old thing." He snorted a laugh. "Wear the blue shirt you borrowed and skinny jeans."

I recoiled. "I don't own skinny jeans."

"Oh, well, then just wear the tightest jeans you have."

I raked a hand through my hair, feeling anxious, but also kind of excited at the idea of spending some time with Jax. Jesus, this was such a dumb, dumb, *dumb* idea. We were not a good match. We were like vinegar and water. This was like the Queen bringing her gardener as her date. "I'm still not sure about this."

"I'll make sure you have fun."

"I don't want to have fun."

"Then I'll make sure you have a horrible evening."

"I can do that all by myself."

"I'll pick you up at eight." He sounded as if the matter was settled. "Oh, and text me your address."

"You're awfully pushy."

"If you have cowboy boots, wear them. Everybody in Hollywood loves cowboy boots."

"I haven't said yes." I stood and shut down my computer. I caught my reflection in my laptop screen and realized I was grinning. There was just something about Jax that got to me, and I didn't seem able to keep him at arm's length like I knew I should.

"Don't worry about eating first. There will be tons of food."

"I hope I don't regret this."

"I'll see you at eight, Decker."

I sighed. "See you at eight."

CHAPTER SEVEN

The party was at the house of Jax's agent, Sidney Steinberg. Nestled on a quiet cul-de-sac in the hills, the home was dazzling with post-and-beam design and wall-to-wall windows.

I'd never have guessed Jax didn't like these people very much. He smiled and chatted with the party guests as if they were his best friends. I also couldn't tell if anyone in the room didn't like Jax. Everyone seemed to adore him.

I, on the other hand, got a lot of funny looks.

Trevor was there before us, and he looked less than thrilled to see me. Lee Price was also there, and though he was surprised to see me, he greeted me warmly. But then Trevor looked unhappy enough for everyone.

Even wearing my best jeans and the shirt Jax had loaned me, I felt conspicuous among the beautiful people. There was just something about their skin that seemed to glow like the sun. I had little doubt they got 24K colloidal gold facials, dermaplaning, and acid peels on a regular basis. The fact that I even knew what those things were probably meant I'd worked in Hollywood too long already. I felt like an old oak tree next to Jax. But he didn't seem to notice the looks I got, didn't seem embarrassed to be with me. He stuck next to me, his shoulder brushing mine, smiling into my eyes often.

"That's Robin," Jax whispered into my ear, his warm breath wafting over my skin.

I kept my face expressionless as a pleasurable shiver rolled through me. "The blonde girl?" I eyed a petite girl across the room. She looked a lot like her brother, although she seemed softer, whereas Trevor had more of an edge.

"Yes."

I sipped my whiskey, trying not to be too obvious as I studied Robin. I recognized her from the stairwell footage. She'd visited Jax's office about three hours before the fire, but hadn't been anywhere around after that. She was with a tall dark-haired guy who seemed as out of place as me. "Who's the guy with her?"

"Paul. That's her husband."

"Is he in the business?"

"No. He used to work for a cable company, but he's unemployed at the moment. They've had some problems in their marriage, but they seem to be trying to work it out."

I accidentally met Trevor's surly gaze. "Your boyfriend isn't very happy to see me."

Jax gave me an irritable look. "He's not my boyfriend. Why do you keep implying he is? If I didn't know better, I'd say you're jealous of Trevor."

"Yeah, I'm dying of jealousy about a guy I hardly know." My face was warm in spite of my bravado. I knew it was childish to needle Jax about his past romantic relationship with Trevor, but I was tired of the resentful glances Trevor kept throwing me.

"I guess you really didn't want to have fun."

"Then it looks like I came to the right place."

Jax shook his head and asked in a tight voice, "Do you want me to introduce you to Robin?"

I shrugged. "Sure."

I followed him over to Robin and Paul. Trevor saw us coming and thankfully wandered away. As we neared the couple, Robin gave me a tentative smile. Her eyes were big and blue, and her skin a golden honey color.

"Robin, this is Cabot Decker," Jax said.

She lifted one light brow. "Oh, you're the cop."

So much for flying under the radar.

Since she knew who I was, I didn't see the point of not just going with it. "I was going to call you and set up an interview."

Her eyes widened. "Me? Why would you want to talk to me?"

"I have to talk to everybody who works with Jax."

"Oh." She looked relieved.

Paul spoke a little too loudly. "I guess you won't have to interview me because I don't work with Jax. Hell, I don't work anywhere." He gave Robin an uneasy look. "My lovely wife brings home the bacon."

Robin's laugh was brittle, and she didn't look at him. "What did you need to ask me, Detective?"

"Nothing too deep. Where you were when Jax was attacked, and whether or not you get along with your boss."

Paul grimaced. "If that's not deep, I can't imagine what is."

She wrinkled her brow. "I get along with Jax just fine."

"Your brother used to date him. Any anger about how things ended?" I tried not to sound accusatory, but she still tensed.

"Their relationship was none of my business."

"But you're family. It's hard not to get involved sometimes." I watched her color deepen.

She flicked her gaze to Jax. "Yeah, I was mad at first. Jax knows that. He broke Trevor's heart, and I felt protective."

Jax flinched. "Our breakup was mutual, Robin."

She studied him. "I know you want to believe that, but it's just not accurate. You know Trevor still has feelings for you."

"I don't think that's true."

She rolled her eyes. "Whatever you say, Jax."

He didn't respond.

"Sounds like maybe you're still mad at Jax."

She sighed and touched Jax's arm. "No. I'm really not."

"I hope not," Jax said quietly. "You and Trevor are like family."

She smiled at him. "Water under the bridge."

"Good." Jax nodded.

Robin glanced toward her brother and lowered her voice. "If my brother is stupid enough to still sleep with you knowing it's not going anywhere, that's his business. He's a big boy."

Jax stiffened but stayed quiet.

I ignored the bizarre churning in my gut at her implication that Jax and Trevor still slept together. That definitely wasn't any of my business. "You went to Jax's office yesterday. Mind telling me why?"

"I needed to discuss some logistical issues."

"But you didn't actually talk to him. Why is that?"

"He was busy. Tressa said he was on the phone. Since it wasn't anything that couldn't wait, I took off."

"I see."

"Hey, man, is this an interrogation or a party?" Paul put his arm around Robin.

She didn't say anything, but her expression was annoyed. Whether she was miffed at Paul or my questions, I couldn't be sure.

"I guess I take my job seriously." I smiled, hoping I'd come off less intimidating that way. "It's hard to turn it off sometimes."

Paul's laugh was strained. "I can imagine."

Jax met my gaze. "I, for one, am glad you take your job seriously."

Robin watched us closely. "I suppose you want to know where I was the night Dale was killed?"

"I need to know everyone's whereabouts. But I don't want to ruin your evening. You can just come to the station and give your statement." I actually hoped she would just tell me now, but I wanted her to feel like it was her idea.

She shrugged. "I don't mind telling you now." She glanced at her husband. "I was with Paul. It was our anniversary."

"Yep. She was with me." Paul's grin seemed forced. "Ten years. If you can believe it, she's put up with me for a whole decade."

"Congrats," I said, noticing Robin looked annoyed yet again. I had to wonder if these two had another decade of wedded bliss in them. Paul couldn't seem to open his mouth without Robin scowling.

"Thanks." She bit her lower lip. "Have you talked to the whole crew yet?"

"Most of them. I still need to see Tim Sloan. I guess he was having surgery." I met Jax's gaze for confirmation.

"Yep. I think he's home now, though."

Robin nodded. "Obviously he couldn't have done anything."

"I'm still going to have to question him."

She laughed. "What could he have done from his hospital bed?"

"You'd be surprised. Murder for hire is popular."

"Tim wouldn't hurt anybody." Robin wrinkled her brow. "He's a great guy."

Paul shifted uneasily and dropped his arm from her shoulders. Robin gave him a funny look, and he straightened. "I think I'm going to get another beer? Anyone else want anything?"

I declined since I'd decided to only have one drink. I needed to be sharp so I could remember the information they gave me tonight. Pulling out a pen and notepad and scribbling down everything they said probably wouldn't have gone over too well. I watched Paul cross the room toward the bar, noticing Robin watched him too. It seemed as if the mention of Tim had bothered Paul. I had to wonder what that was all about.

The conversation drifted to less serious topics, and I didn't bother trying to drag it back to the case. As far as I could tell, I'd gotten all I could from Robin. It was obvious she and Paul had marital issues, but other than that, I didn't get any diabolical vibe off her.

Jax drank a bit more than me. I couldn't blame him; he'd been under a lot of stress. But when it came time to go home, I took the keys from him.

He frowned. "What are you doing?"

"You shouldn't drive."

He looked like he wanted to argue, but then just shrugged. "I'll call an Uber."

"No. I'll drive." I smiled. "I've never driven a BMW before."

He fake-gasped. "How horrible for you."

"I know. I've suffered terribly."

"It's just a rental, though."

"Yes. You rented a BMW while your other BMW is in the shop. Poor baby."

He laughed. "This one doesn't have heated seats. The struggle is real."

"Good Lord." I rolled my eyes.

Once Jax said goodbye to everyone, I led the way toward the front door. From the stares we got, it seemed everyone at the party shared Trevor's opinion that Jax and I were an odd pair. It was a little annoying to be honest. You'd have thought Jax was driving home with a unicorn.

Once outside, I opened the passenger-side door for Jax, and he slid in with a giggle. I'd never seen him so relaxed. I couldn't help but smile at his silly grin. I got in behind the wheel and started the engine. It purred to life, and I drove down the long driveway to the highway.

"Crap." He glanced over at me. "I picked you up. How will you get home if you take me to the hotel?"

"I'll take a cab from your hotel."

"I'll reimburse you." He shifted toward me. "I probably could have driven."

I scowled. "You had three glasses of wine."

"Did I have three? I thought I had two."

"Nope. Three."

"I guess I was feeling a little tense." He sighed, and his gaze settled on me.

I felt self-conscious but tried not to show it. I focused instead on how nice it was to drive his luxury car. My car was fine, but his was like floating on clouds, and it took the corners like a dream. The house we'd gone to for the party was up in the hills above Los Angeles, and the city lights below resembled shimmering fireflies. We rode in silence for a while, but as we neared the city, he finally spoke, his voice soft.

"Thanks for coming out with me tonight."

I gave him a quick glance. His features were mostly in shadow, but my pulse quickened at the interest in his gaze. I still didn't understand why he seemed attracted to me. Maybe he was intrigued by the idea of bedding someone so different from him. My body flushed at the thought of giving him what he seemed to want, but my brain told me no.

"I'm glad I came. It was useful talking to everyone."

He gave a little laugh. "All business again."

"Yep."

"Do you ever think about anything other than work?"

Feeling breathless, I said, "Of course." I turned into the parking lot of the hotel and pulled into a space near the building. I turned off the engine and swiveled to face him. "Home, safe and sound."

"Home." He eyed the hotel. "Hardly."

"Hey, it beats Motel 6, right?"

"Of course. But I'd still rather be at my own place."

"This is just temporary."

"I know."

"I'll get your shirt and jeans back to you tomorrow." I ran my hands over the soft material. "I don't really want to go home without a shirt on."

"Oh, that's right. I have your stuff up in my room." He hesitated. "Want to come up and get it?"

The look he gave me made my heart beat faster. "I can just get it tomorrow."

"You need to call a cab still. You should come up and wait." He gave me a playful smile. "You don't want to loiter in the lobby like a creeper."

I knew I should tell him no. I knew I should just say good night, call my cab, and go home. But something drew me to him. "You're trouble," I said quietly.

"Why?" He sounded surprised.

I shrugged.

"Come on, Decker," he said breathlessly. "Come upstairs."

I tried to fight my desire for him. "You're at the center of my case."

"You don't think I'm a suspect anymore, though, right?"

"No."

"Then what does it matter if we get…to know each other?" He touched my arm, and the heat of his fingers burned into my skin. "Come up to my room."

My cock warmed as my brain seemed to shut off. "I must be out of my mind."

He smiled and opened his door. "Come on."

Against all reason, I did as he said. I got out of the car and followed him into the hotel. He walked ahead of me, and I seemed unable to pull my gaze from his narrow hips and firm ass. I wasn't impulsive. I didn't do stupid shit like this. What was wrong with me? As those thoughts swirled in my head, I stepped into the elevator with him.

There were other people in the elevator, and Jax made no move to touch me. But he held my gaze as sexual energy buzzed between us. I clenched my jaw, wishing I had the self-control to get off the elevator. I didn't. I just didn't have it in me to go home when this beautiful man was looking at me like he wanted to eat me whole. I respected him. Liked him. He was the full package; brains and looks. It was intoxicating to be wanted by someone like him.

The elevator dinged, and Jax stepped out. I followed him, our shoes soundless on the plush carpet of the hotel hallway. My heart pounded with every step, but I didn't turn around.

Jax stopped at a room and used his key card to open the door. The door next to his room opened, and a burly guy with a shaved head poked his face out.

"You're back." The guy's voice was emotionless as he sized me up. If he had an opinion about Jax bringing me to his room, he didn't show it.

"Good evening, Harry," Jax addressed the guy. "This is Decker."

Harry gave me a curious look. "Hey, Decker."

I gave a nod, but my face was warm. I felt uneasy and way, way out of my comfort zone. I took a step back, half thinking I should just go before it was too late. Maybe Jax sensed something because he put his hand on my back.

"See you tomorrow," Jax said to Harry.

"Okay, boss." Harry closed his door.

I met Jax's gaze, and he smirked, pulling me into the room. "You're not going anywhere." His voice was gruff, and as the door slammed behind us, he pushed me against the wall. My hands were at my sides as he leaned into me. "Touch me," he whispered.

I hesitated, my cock aching as it pressed against my zipper, but then I put my hands on his hips. His warm body beneath my palms seemed to calm me. He lowered his head, and his heated mouth covered mine. I groaned and opened wider, letting his seeking tongue inside. It felt so good yet so wrong, but I tightened my arms, feeling out of control.

He smiled against my lips, and deepening the kiss, rocked his hips into me. His arousal was obvious, and I had little doubt he was aware of my need too. I was usually the more aggressive person during sex, but I felt like putty in Jax's hands. Was this how Trevor felt? Did he hate himself for giving in to Jax? Did he feel weak and used? Was Jax just using me? Toying with me? Probably. This sure as hell wasn't love. I frowned, not wanting to think about anything but how sweet Jax's mouth tasted and the trembling warmth of his tongue against mine.

He slid his hands down my shoulders, to my hips, then pulled his mouth away. "Bedroom," he panted.

I nodded and let him tug me after him. We fell onto the big soft bed, and he laughed. I didn't feel like laughing. Feeling feverish with need, I rolled on top of him, trying to reclaim some control. He just grinned up at me, looking relaxed and happy. My heart squeezed at his trusting expression, and some tension left me. He wasn't evil or manipulative; he was just a guy who wanted to fuck. I needed to stop thinking this was anything other than what it was— two horny guys needing to get off.

I pulled my shirt off and tossed it on the end of the bed, then got rid of my pants and underwear. He wiggled out of his clothes, his cock full against his abs. His body was flawless. No fat, just sinewy muscle and smooth, tanned skin. I had a momentary flash of insecurity, but I tried to push it away. Maybe I wasn't perfect, but I had a nice enough body and was in good shape. I was a little pale compared to him, but my life wasn't about sunning by the pool.

He frowned. "Stop thinking so much."

I hesitated. "What?"

Smiling, he said, "You look like you're studying for a math test."

I gave a grudging laugh. "I do?"

"Yeah. Relax." He slid his fingers up my thighs. "Lube and condoms are in the drawer next to the bed."

I flicked my gaze to the bedside table. We hadn't discussed who was pitching and who was receiving. I rarely bottomed, and I had no idea what he expected. He must have seen something in my expression because he gave another husky laugh. "Pfft. I wouldn't dream of asking you to take it up the ass, Decker."

"Good." I leaned over and grabbed what we needed from the drawer. Now that I knew my role, I felt better. I set the rubber and lube next us on the comforter. I straddled him again and smoothed my hands up his taut abs, exploring every inch of him, fluttering softly over his flat nipples. They beaded under my palms, and he sighed and rolled his hips.

He opened his legs, stroking his cock, his slate-colored eyes pinned on me. I'd never really admired a man for his beauty before, but Jax was stunning. A lock of onyx hair fell over his forehead, and his plump lips parted in anticipation. He looked like a Renaissance painting, only he was warm and alive under my hands.

I grabbed the lube and squirted the cool gel onto my fingers. I leaned down and kissed the ruddy head of his cock, and he moaned. I took him into my mouth, tasting his tangy precum on my tongue. Sliding down his length, I took him deep into my throat, and he hissed and bucked his hips. I buried my face in his soft bush, inhaling his soapy scent while sucking him. I caressed my slick fingertips over his puckered hole, and he tangled his hands in my hair, whispering words I couldn't quite make out. His cock swelled in my mouth, and I pulled off when his groans got louder. I didn't want him coming until I was inside him.

He tugged at my hips, his fingers digging into my skin. "Fuck me," he pleaded.

I liked this vulnerable side of him. I loved having him quivering and needy beneath me. I no longer felt intimidated. Maybe he was a rich, powerful guy, but in bed we were both just men who wanted the same thing.

Nudging his thighs wider, I tore open the condom and slid it on. I pressed one lubed finger into him, and he groaned. He was so hot and tight, I couldn't wait to be inside him. But I wanted this to be good for him too, so I held back my impatience and took the time to ready him. I teased and stroked as he writhed on the bed, grasping handfuls of the comforter. He arched his back, his hips undulating to the rhythm of my moving fingers.

"You like that?" I whispered, stroking that perfect little pucker, loving how he tightened those delicate muscles on my fingers.

"Yeah. I want *more*."

"Good. 'Cuz I'm gonna give you a lot more."

He whimpered and pulled his knees to his chest, letting me see him fully. My mouth watered as I settled over him, bumping my cock to his hole. Our eyes met, and his expression was serious, all laughter replaced by want. I pushed in slowly, and he cried out and threw his head back.

The tight squeeze of him was almost too much, but then his muscles loosened and opened, and I was seated fully inside, my cock cradled in the heated perfection of his body. I'd fantasized about a moment like this since meeting him, never really believing it would happen. I'd imagined how good it would feel to bury myself inside him. Taking what I wanted, watching him shudder beneath me, begging for more.

"Shit, Decker." The muscles of his neck bulged as he took me deeper.

I started to thrust, grateful he'd been willing to submit to me. I'd have been too self-conscious to bottom for him. If Jax had insisted on topping, I'd have felt too exposed. Too vulnerable. I appreciated that he'd intuitively known that about me. We were very different men, and yet he seemed to understand me.

"So good," I panted.

He moaned, his pupils blown with lust, lips parted, fingers digging into my back.

My heart thundered, and my thigh muscles burned as I pumped into him. The room was silent other than our raspy breaths and grunts of pleasure. The friction of sliding in and out of him was delicious, and my balls throbbed and buzzed as my climax approached.

"Oh God. Please," he whimpered.

His husky voice sent a thrill through me. "What do you need?" I started thrusting slower and deeper. "You want to come, Jax?" I craved hearing how much he wanted me to fuck him.

"Yes," he whispered, his eyes glittering. "Need it."

"You want to come with me inside you?"

"*Please. Please.*"

I felt powerful with this perfect man under me, begging me to let him come. My insecurities were washed away by lust and the obvious hunger in his eyes. I kissed him, and he opened his mouth greedily. When I lifted my head I was hanging onto my control by a thread. I was going to come any second, but I wanted him to come first. I knew he was right there, and when I gave two hard thrusts, his eyes widened and he trembled. "Yeah, let go," I whispered.

With a hiss, he arched his back, and the hot spill of his release washed between us. His body convulsed, and his muscles squeezed my cock, sending me over the edge too.

I clenched my teeth, trying to bite back my cry of pleasure. But it was impossible, and I groaned as my cock jerked inside him. It had been a while since I'd really felt connected to a sexual partner. But because Jax was so willing to be vulnerable with me, it made things easier. I held him tight as our bodies trembled and quaked, finally quieting as our orgasms ebbed away.

Eventually, he stirred and lifted his head. His hair stood up in messy tufts. "Holy fuck." He grinned.

I felt sweaty and exhausted, but I managed a gruff laugh. I pulled out of him and collapsed beside him. "I'm beginning to think you didn't really invite me up here to get my clothes."

He snorted. "You really are a detective."

I smirked, stretched, every muscle in my body warm and relaxed. It had been way too long since I'd allowed myself to enjoy another man. I hadn't really even been tempted in a long while. Not until Jax. I didn't want to examine too closely why a guy who I basically had nothing in common with was the one I found irresistible.

He grabbed tissues from the nightstand and wiped off his stomach. I did the same and tugged off the condom, tossing it into the small trash can next to the bed.

"Now, I'm sure this could make things awkward if we let it." His tone was good-natured. "I say we don't let it."

I chewed the inside of my cheek as I studied him. "We're just letting off steam."

"Absolutely."

"Harry knows you brought me up here."

"So?"

"He's not a gossip, right?"

"Harry is nothing if not discreet. Besides, it's nobody's business who we sleep with. It has nothing to do with the case."

"I agree. It's just that my coworkers can be assholes sometimes. Going to a party together is one thing, but I'd rather nobody knew we slept together."

He made a zipping motion in front of his lips.

I was relieved we seemed to be on the same page. I smiled and moved to get off the bed. I got dressed quickly, called for a cab, and then I sat back on the bed to slip on my shoes.

"Can't get out of here fast enough, can you?" His expression was agreeable, but there was a slight edge to his voice.

I frowned. "Is that a problem?"

"No."

"You sure?" I rubbed a hand over the back of my neck. I hadn't expected to sleep over, and I couldn't imagine he'd wanted that either.

"Actually this is a refreshing change."

"Meaning what?"

"You're not asking for anything."

I squinted at him. "Why would I?"

He laughed dryly. "Let's just say it's not unheard of for a guy to hand me a script after we fuck."

"You're kidding."

"I wish. This business is filled with users."

I studied him. "I slept with you because I'm attracted to you."

"Good."

I smirked. "Although, now that you mention it, I have secretly been working on a tough-guy-detective screenplay for years."

"Is that right?"

"Oh yeah."

"It sounds intriguing; maybe we can set up a meeting." His tone was flippant, but I got the feeling he wasn't as unaffected as he pretended.

"Believe me, you're not the only one who gets used. I've had people I barely talked to in college call, hoping I can fix tickets for them."

"Really?"

"Yeah."

"That's nervy." He laughed.

"I agree. Sometimes I say I'll help, but I don't. Serves them right if they get a warrant."

"Whoa. Remind me not to piss you off."

I grinned and stood. "Well, this was fun."

"Yeah. It was." He got off the bed and slipped on his underwear, and then we moved into the front room. "You can wait here until your cab arrives."

I hesitated but moved to the door. "Nah. They said it would only be about five minutes."

"Suit yourself."

"Thank you again for a fun evening."

"My pleasure."

I didn't bother to say I'd call. I wasn't sure I would call, and it wasn't like he was asking me to. "Well, I'm sure I'll see you around."

"No doubt." His expression was soft and sleepy.

I opened the door, and on impulse, I leaned in and kissed him. He responded warmly, and when I lifted my head, his smile made my chest tight. "Lock the door."

"You got it."

I left his room, closing the door softly behind me.

It wasn't until the cab dropped me off in front of my house that I realized I'd never actually gotten my clothes from Jax.

CHAPTER EIGHT

I arranged to meet Tim Sloan at his home because he was still recovering from back surgery. He was younger than I'd pictured. He also wasn't as happy to see me as I'd hoped. When his wife, Tammy, led me into the living room, he was lying on the couch, watching TV. He turned the volume down, but he seemed edgy and had trouble meeting my eyes.

"Would you like anything to drink?" Tammy asked. She was a timid woman, with hair so limp, her ears stuck out through the strands.

"No thank you."

She gave a nervous laugh. "Okay. Well, just call me if you need me." She left the room.

I turned to address Tim. "I appreciate your taking time to meet with me, Tim. I'm sure you're not feeling great." I smiled and sat on a chair near him.

He shrugged. "I can't very well say no, can I?"

"Did you want to say no?"

His face tensed. "I just don't know how I can be of any help. I wasn't even on the set when Dale died."

"It still helps to talk to anyone who works on the crew. You might have seen or heard something and not even realized it." I gave what I hoped was a pleasant smile. In truth, his attitude raised red flags. Someone he knew had been murdered. Most people—innocent people—tended to want to talk to the cops.

"I guess," he muttered.

"Do you know of any reason why anyone would want to hurt Dale?"

He shook his head, then gritted his teeth for a few seconds as if in pain. "Dale was a nice person."

"That's what everyone keeps saying."

"I heard about the attacks on Jax."

"Yeah." I studied him. "Any idea who would want to hurt Jax?"

"Nope." He stared at his clasped hands. "I told you I wouldn't be any help."

I ignored his surly comment. "You're one of three people who know how to program the keypad in the tiger's cage. Right?"

He stiffened. "So what?"

"Have there ever been any issues with the keypads and codes? Anybody's code get erased without their knowledge?"

"Not that I know of. Why?"

"We think maybe someone tampered with it and erased Dale's code." I watched him closely.

He wrinkled his brow. "Seriously?"

"Yeah."

"Well, you know it wasn't me. I couldn't possibly have done that since I wasn't anywhere near the cage."

"I don't know that that would matter in this instance."

"How do you figure?" he asked warily.

"The manufacturer of the keypad says the pad is programmable from a distance. You could be in another country and still mess with things. You just need passwords, a laptop, and some technical knowledge." He didn't look surprised, which piqued my interest. "Jax says you have a degree in electronics."

His eyes narrowed, his face flushed. "Hey…just what exactly are you trying to say?"

"I'm just asking questions."

"No. You're implying I somehow fucked with the keypad and got Dale killed." He sounded breathless. "I ain't no murderer."

"I'm not saying you are."

"You're definitely hinting." He scowled. "I suppose you think I got off the operating table and drove Jax off the road? Hell, maybe I started the fire in Jax's office with my magic wand." He gestured toward his prone body. "Going after Jax would be quite a feat, seeing as I can barely get to the bathroom to take a piss without my wife helping me."

He seemed truly offended, but that didn't mean he was innocent. He could have had an accomplice who handled the physical stuff while he reprogrammed the keypad from home. The fact that he had experience with electronics put him high on my list of people to watch. Now if only I had a motive for why he'd want to hurt Dale or Jax. "Do you get along with Jax?"

He blinked at me. "Yeah."

"No run-ins at all?"

"Why would I have a problem with him? He hired me. I owe him big-time."

"I find it interesting that everybody seems to love Jax, and yet two attempts have been made on his life. Obviously not everyone thinks he's a great guy." I leaned toward him. "Someone has a grudge against him. That someone has access to the studio and knows his movements."

Eyes bugging out, Tim said, "It's not me. I swear."

He seemed sincere, but I couldn't shake the feeling he was hiding something. "If not you, then who?"

"No idea."

"If this person succeeds in hurting Jax, and you know something but don't tell me, you'll be an accessory."

"There are a lot of people who work on that show. I don't get why you're giving me such a hard time."

"You have experience with electronics."

"It's not impossible for anyone to have figured out how to program that thing. It's probably on the Internet."

"Okay, give me the name of someone you think would be able to do that."

"No way. I'm not accusing anyone." He dropped his gaze. "Besides, I can't picture any of the people I work with doing anything violent. They're all good people."

"Obviously not all of them are good because Dale is dead."

He swallowed hard. "I'm sorry about that, but it has nothing to do with me."

"I really hope you're not hiding something from me, Tim. Whoever this person is, they're dangerous."

His gaze flickered, but he didn't speak.

I exhaled and stood, feeling frustrated. I wasn't sure if he was protecting someone, or if he really had no idea who the murderer could be. I handed him my card. "If you decide you want to talk, call me."

He grudgingly took the card. "I keep telling you I don't know anything."

"I'm not sure I believe you."

"Why not?"

I shrugged. "Instinct."

He licked his lips nervously. "Well, your instincts are all wrong."

I moved toward the door. "I hope for your sake that's true."

Tammy appeared, looking uneasy. "Everything okay?" She twisted a dish towel in her hands, giving a nervous glance toward her husband.

"Everything is fine. Just show the detective out, please," Tim snapped.

"Oh, sure." She gave me an apologetic look and led me to the foyer by the front door.

I hesitated before leaving. "Did you know Dale?"

She shook her head. "I never meet the contestants. I don't even know most of the production crew. Tim doesn't like to bring me around them."

"Why not?"

"Well, I got a little drunk at one of the cast parties, and he's embarrassed by me now."

"We've all had a bit too much to drink one time or another."

She gave me a grateful smile. "That's what I said…but he still doesn't take me to the set anymore." She bit her lip, a line between her brows. "I think it's because Robin doesn't like me."

"Robin? You mean Trevor's sister?"

She nodded, her expression disgruntled. "Robin and Tim used to date in high school," she whispered.

Surprise rolled through me. "Really?"

"Yes." She looked like she had a bad taste in her mouth. "She broke up with him and went with Paul instead. That didn't work out so great."

"That's why she doesn't like you?"

"Well, when I got tipsy that one time, I may have told her to keep her hands off my husband." She sniffed and tucked a strand of hair behind her ear. "She had her chance."

"I see." Tim hadn't exactly struck me as a chick-magnet type. He was okay-looking, but not really the kind of guy I'd have thought women fought over. I remembered how Paul had looked annoyed when Robin mentioned Tim being a great guy. Made me wonder if Paul had a current reason to feel territorial about Robin where Tim was concerned.

Tammy shot a nervous glance toward the living room and opened the front door. "Sorry if Tim seemed grumpy. He's usually much nicer."

I stepped out onto the porch. "Don't worry about me. I have a thick skin."

"I guess you'd have to. Everybody hates cops," she announced breezily, closing the door in my face.

I grimaced, but then my phone buzzed in my pocket, distracting me. When I saw the caller ID, my pulse picked up because it was Jax. I headed to my car and answered. "Decker here."

"You know what I was thinking?" His voice was confident. "There aren't nearly enough gritty detective reality shows."

I laughed, surprisingly pleased to hear from him. It had been two days since we'd slept together, and I'd been so busy interviewing people, I hadn't had time to really think about our night together. Well, that wasn't quite true; I'd thought about it plenty, but I hadn't had time to go by the studio and talk to Jax. "I already sold my show to another famous producer."

"Is that right? Who?" He sounded amused.

Racking my brain for any reality TV person I could think of, I said, "Oh, um…you know…the guy who does *Survivor*."

"Jeff Probst?"

"Uh…sure, let's go with that."

"You sold your show, but you don't know the name of the person you sold it to?" He was outright laughing now. "You're a heck of a business man."

"Thank you." I got in my car, started the engine, and turned on the air full blast. "If you need me to negotiate any of your deals, just let me know."

"I will."

We fell silent, and he cleared his throat. "You forgot to get your clothes the other night."

"I know. I still have your clothes too."

"Maybe you should come to my hotel, and we can do the exchange."

I smiled. "Or maybe we should just keep the clothes we have. I'm starting to really like that blue shirt."

"Sure. Keep it. But come over anyway."

Excitement ramped in my gut. "I don't know if I should."

He groaned. "Enough with the playing hard to get, Decker. Come on. We're grown-ups. We're just having fun. Is fun not allowed in your world?"

"I try to keep it to a minimum so I don't get used to it."

"Please. I had a rough day, and I'd love to hang out with my favorite Robbery-Homicide detective."

"I'm the only detective you know, right?"

"So insecure."

I smirked as I pulled out into traffic, heading toward the station. "I still have some stuff to finish up."

"That's fine. I just got back to the hotel. Would you want to eat dinner here? I can order room service."

"Harry is still guarding your ass, right?"

He sighed. "Yes. My shadow is still parked next door."

"Will he be joining us for dinner?"

"Uh, no."

I found it hard to stop smiling. The idea of spending time with Jax had me feeling downright giddy, and I didn't really do giddy. Of course, while this was fun, I was realistic enough to realize that whatever this was between us, it had a limited shelf life.

"What time?" I found myself asking.

"Seven?"

"Sounds good." We hung up.

I had a few more interviews lined up with the film crew. My interview with Tim had me intrigued. I couldn't shake the feeling he knew a lot more than he was saying. I got that feeling from Robin and Paul too. Maybe the couple had an alibi for Dale's murder, but where were they when those two attempts were made on Jax?

When I arrived at the precinct, Andy met me at my desk. "Just got off the phone with the arson investigator." He waved a paper under my nose. "There was an incendiary device set up near the door to Jax's office."

"I figured because I heard a loud *bang* right before the fire started." I frowned. "If it was well hidden, that's going to make it harder to pinpoint who dropped it off. Someone could have put it there anytime during the day, and we don't have the camera footage for that floor. Just the stairs and elevators."

"Yeah. But we know who visited Jax during the day." He rubbed his chin. "Robin was there during the day."

"Her and twenty other people. Plus, she works for Jax. There's nothing weird about her talking with him."

"True." He bit his lip. "There were no prints on the device, which sucks."

"I doubted there would be. Probably wore gloves."

"Wouldn't that have flagged the receptionist's attention? It would be unusual for someone to just walk around with gloves."

"I've been in Jax's office when it's busy. There are so many people coming and going, and the phone rings constantly. My guess is Tressa would have been pretty distracted."

"Damn." He scowled. "By the way, other than Ben Willoughby, Lucinda Pinwheel is the only person who has obvious ties to animal rights groups. But she has no record, and as far as I can tell she's not an extremist."

"Okay." I nodded. "Do we know yet where Robin and Paul were when those attempts were made on Jax?"

"I have it in my notes." He frowned. "I'm drawing a blank. I'll check and get back to you."

"Sounds good."

I spent the next few hours interviewing some of the crew, including the camera guy who'd been in the bathroom during the attack on Dale. If he was our guy, he deserved an Academy Award. The guy was still a wreck and started crying at least four times during the interview.

Andy came back by my desk in the late afternoon. "The night of the drive-by shooting, Paul and Robin were supposedly home all night together."

"How convenient."

"They ordered a pizza and rented a movie. I saw the receipts for both."

"Okay. What about the day of the fire?"

"Paul was in San Diego for a job interview, which I verified. Robin was at a tanning salon about ten minutes away. I spoke to the girl who runs the place, and she said Robin is a regular about three times a week. She remembers Robin coming in that day."

"Well, hell."

"I know. Every time I think maybe we're getting somewhere, it falls flat. Everybody appears to have verifiable alibis."

"Someone has to be lying."

"That Tim guy seemed pretty sketchy from what you said, but he was having surgery."

"Exactly." I tapped my pen on the desktop. "I still don't see how Dale's death connects to the stuff happening to Jax."

"Maybe Dale's death really was an accident. Could the keypad have malfunctioned and erased Dale's code on its own?"

"Not according to the manufacturer."

"Like they'd admit anything."

"True." I glanced at my watch, noticing it was six. I'd wanted to swing by my place and shower before going to Jax's hotel.

Andy noticed me looking at my timepiece. "You got a date or something?"

My face warmed, and I avoided his gaze. "No."

"You've checked your watch, like, five times." He laughed.

"The battery is dying." I shook my wrist to make my lie more believable.

Andy narrowed his eyes, looking unconvinced. "You're allowed to have a personal life."

"Obviously."

"No obviously about it. I can't even remember the last time you went out on a date."

I scowled. "It's not like I'd announce it to you when I do."

"No, but I can tell when your love life is going well. You're less grouchy. You've been grouchy for at least six months."

"Save your detecting skills for the case, okay?"

He shrugged. "Fine by me. It's not like I want the details of who you're dating. I got enough trouble keeping track of my own love life."

"You probably need an Excel spread sheet to keep all your women straight."

He chuckled. "That's a great idea."

I stood. "I'm gonna take off. See you tomorrow." I pulled on my jacket, and he grinned. "What's so funny?"

"Just that you're trying to play it so cool."

"You're nuts."

"Decker, we've worked together for five years. I know you." He smirked. "It's hurtful that you won't confide in me."

"Bullshit." I laughed, heading for the elevators.

"Have fun on your date," he called after me.

Luckily, the traffic wasn't bad. I was able to get home, shower, and still get to Jax's hotel by seven. My hands felt a little sweaty and my pulse was zipping as I knocked on his hotel door.

Harry poked his head out of the adjoining room. "Oh, hey, Decker."

I gave a curt nod. "Harry." I didn't love that he knew I was seeing Jax, but since it had been my idea for Jax to have a bodyguard, I couldn't exactly complain now.

Jax opened his door. "You're five minutes early. You must have actually wanted to see me."

"Or my watch is fast."

Jax rolled his eyes. "Ignore him, Harry. He just doesn't like to show his feelings."

Harry simply nodded and closed his door.

Jax stepped aside to let me in. He smelled like coconut sun tan oil, and his hair was wet as if he'd just showered. He closed the door and gave me a happy smile.

"You look nice." He ran his gaze over my body.

I pressed my lips tight, resisting the urge to kiss him. "I thought about bringing a bottle of wine because I know you like wine. But then I figured you probably wouldn't even drink the swill I call wine."

He frowned. "You act like I eat pearls and drink from golden goblets."

"No. I just know you have more expensive tastes than me."

"I've had plenty of average vino in my time."

"Yeah, before you were rich."

He sighed. "Decker, stop." He moved closer, and his gray eyes were warm. "Don't fixate on my money. I certainly don't."

I pushed my tongue into my cheek, struggling with annoying insecurities that always seemed to pop up when I was around Jax. I'd never dated anyone who made a lot more money than me. I'd dated guys who made a little more than me, and guys who made less, but Jax was in a completely different tax bracket. I enjoyed seeing him, but his wealth did make me uncomfortable.

"Relax," he whispered as he put his arms around my neck, pressing close. I groaned when he kissed me, my hunger flaring the minute I tasted him. He pulled my shirt out of my waistband and pushed his hands up under the soft material. His palms were smooth as silk as they glided over my chest.

"I planned on us eating at seven thirty, but right now all I can think about is you inside me," he whispered against my mouth.

My cock seemed to swell at the sound of his voice, and I wrapped my arms around his narrow waist. I'd expected the evening to start a little slower too, but the minute he kissed me, all I wanted was to fuck him. Dinner could wait. I had other appetites that needed satiating.

"Should I call room service and reschedule dinner for eight thirty?" He was breathless as he kissed a trail up my neck and along my jaw.

"Whatever you think is best." I took his lips roughly, and he moaned into my mouth. I unzipped his jeans and slipped my hand into his underwear, palming his dick.

He groaned. "I don't think I remember how to use the phone."

"What's a phone?"

Grinning, he pulled back, raking a hand through his hair. "God, my heart is pounding."

I liked hearing how much I affected him. "Let's definitely eat later."

"Okay." He moved toward the hotel phone on the desk.

When my cell buzzed, we both groaned.

"Shit," I muttered.

"Can't you just ignore it?" he asked hopefully.

"Depends." I tugged my phone from my back pocket. "Damn. It's Andy. I have to take this."

Jax looked disappointed, but shrugged and went into the bedroom.

Feeling annoyed at the interruption, I answered the phone curtly. "Decker."

"Hey, sorry to bother you." Andy sounded uneasy.

"What's up?" I asked, feeling exasperated. Apparently, I actually wasn't allowed to have a personal life.

"I've got some bad news."

"What?"

"Well…Tim Sloan just blew his brains out." Andy's voice wobbled.

A chill went through me. *What?*

"We just got the call. His wife went shopping, and when she came back, he was dead."

"What the fuck?" Nothing about Tim had made me think he was a man about to end his life. "I just saw him earlier today."

"I know."

"Can we verify his wife was actually shopping?"

"I requested the grocery store's video."

"Could it have been accidental?"

"Doesn't look like it."

"Shit." I met Jax's gaze when he came out of the bedroom. He didn't speak, just came closer and watched me, his expression serious. "I'll be there as soon as I can."

"Sorry about ruining your evening." Andy sounded sincere.

"Can't be helped." I hung up and met Jax's gaze.

"Something bad happened?"

"Uh, yeah." I swallowed hard. "Tim Sloan is dead."

His eyes widened. "What?" He stepped back, the color draining from his face. "How?"

"Possible suicide."

His mouth moved, but no sound came out.

"I have to go."

He seemed to gather himself. "Of course."

"I think Harry should be in this room. Next door isn't good enough."

"Does that mean you don't think it was suicide?"

"I don't know yet. All I know is Tim is dead from a gunshot wound. But I saw him earlier today, and he didn't strike me as suicidal."

He grunted and turned his back to me. "What the hell is happening? I don't understand."

I moved close to him and pulled him against me. He didn't resist, and I wrapped my arms around him from behind. Pressing my face to the nape of his neck, it was impossible not to feel protective of him. I could feel fear trembling through him, and it bothered me more than I'd have expected.

"That's two people dead." His voice wobbled. "I'm afraid I'm next."

"No." I tightened my hold on him. "I'm not going to let that happen."

"You can't be with me all the time."

He was right. But I wasn't about to feed his fear. "This could easily be suicide. But just in case, stick close to Harry."

"If someone murdered Tim, this person must be crazy, right?" He swiveled in my arms, his gaze meeting mine. "They're so erratic. Do most murderers behave like this?"

I shrugged. "They're all different." I was worried too about how unpredictable this person was. I had no idea what they would try next, or who they'd go after. If this wasn't suicide, I had to assume Tim must have known something, and the killer had gone after him to shut him up. But I didn't know that for sure. Maybe this person was just nuts and simply killed when they had the opportunity.

I felt awful leaving Jax, but the best way to keep him safe was to find the killer. I sucked in a breath and forced myself to let go of him. "I have to go. I'm sorry."

He nodded, clenching his jaw. "Right."

"Remember what I said about not trusting people right now."

"How could I forget?" His smile was tight.

I tucked in my shirt and headed to the door. I opened it and knocked on Harry's door. He opened it quickly, looking alert. "What's up?"

"Something happened, and I have to take off." I glanced toward Jax's room. "You need to stay with Jax in his room."

"Sure. Whatever he wants."

"Okay, good." I shifted uneasily. "Be super careful, Harry. It's possible the person after Jax just killed someone else."

"No problem." He patted his hip. "I'm ready."

I nodded, feeling slightly reassured.

Jax came to the door. "I guess we're roommates now, Harry."

Harry nodded. "Just let me grab my stuff." He closed his door.

I faced Jax. "If anything seems off to you, call me."

"Okay."

The night had started so promising. Now Jax looked scared, and I felt like a dick abandoning him, even though I knew I had to. I wanted to kiss him, but I didn't. It might be too hard to let go.

"I'll call you later to check on you."

"You don't have to." He leaned on the doorjamb.

"Maybe I want to."

"Jesus, you must really think I'm in danger if you're being this nice to me."

I studied him, searching for words of comfort. But I couldn't think of anything that wouldn't be a lie. I wasn't prone to coddling people, and I didn't want to reassure him too much in case he let his guard down. "I'll call you."

He looked a little let down by my response. "Hey, if I'm still alive, I'll answer."

Before I could speak, Harry opened his door, and I stepped back. I nodded to them both, then headed down the hallway toward the elevators.

CHAPTER NINE

Tim's body was being removed as I arrived. I parked haphazardly, pulled on gloves, and hurried to the coroner's van to take a look at the body.

"Give me a minute, guys." I pulled back the covering. I winced at the sight of the bloody corpse as I examined the single shot to the temple. I couldn't help wishing he'd been more forthcoming when I interviewed him. If he'd had secrets, they were going to the grave with him. "Was there any sign of a struggle?"

One of the technicians replied, "Not that I noticed."

Andy walked up as I was examining Tim's arms for bruising. "Hey, boss."

I met his gaze. "Did he leave a suicide note?"

"We haven't found one."

"How about a cell?"

Andy frowned. "Maybe forensics already bagged it."

"Could you please find out?"

"Sure." He wandered toward the house.

I examined Tim a bit longer, then pulled the cover back over him. I'd need to wait for the ME to tell me if the evidence proved it was suicide, or staged to look like that. I moved toward the house. Even from outside I could hear Tammy Sloan wailing. When I entered the small home, she was at the kitchen table, sobbing into a paper towel.

She looked up, her eyes puffy and red. "If this was a suicide, why did your people check my hands for gun residue? Do you really think I could kill my own husband?"

"We'd have to check anyone in your situation, Tammy."

"Well, I'd never hurt Tim. I loved him." She waved her hand. "I didn't even know we had a gun in the house."

"I know this is very difficult for you, and I'm truly sorry for your loss."

"Thank you," she said softly.

I sat across from her, and my gaze fell on a bright yellow plaque on the wall over the stove that read: *Destination Happiness*. Ouch. "Did Tim seem depressed when you left to go to the store?"

"No. He seemed a little agitated after your visit, but not depressed." She started sobbing again.

"Had Tim ever suffered from suicidal thoughts?"

"No." She wiped at her eyes, giving little hiccups. "We were going to go to Hawaii as soon as his back was better." She sniffed. "I can't understand why he'd do this."

"Was he in a lot of pain?"

"Not horrible. I mean, he was taking Vicodin, and it seemed to work just fine."

"Did you maybe have a fight?"

"N-No." She leaned her elbows on the table. "We were getting along great. I mean, he was kind of crabby after the surgery. But we were doing great."

"Any visitors today?"

"Just you." She wiped at her face with the paper towel. "That I know of."

"How long were you at the store?" I got up and grabbed her a dry paper towel.

She took the towel gratefully, smiling weakly. "Thanks." She dabbed at her eyes. "I was gone about an hour and a half. I hadn't shopped in a while, so the list was kind of long." She started crying again. "Now I have all this food, and it's just me."

I noticed two bags of canned goods and other grocery items spilled on the kitchen floor. I assumed Tammy had dropped them when she came in the house and found Tim dead. She seemed truly distraught, but this was Hollywood.

Andy came into the kitchen, holding an evidence bag with a cell phone. "Found it. It was under the couch."

I took the bag from him. "I'd love to know who Tim talked to last."

Tammy looked up, her tearstained face pale. "I just remembered something." She sniffed and pointed to the house phone on the wall. "Somebody called and left a threatening message today."

"Threatening to whom?"

"Tim."

"Do you know who it was?"

"I can't be sure, but the guy sounded just like Paul Hernandez."

"Robin's husband?" I moved to the wall phone. "Is the message still on here?"

"No. Tim made me erase it. He was pissed."

Crap.

I glanced at the cell phone Andy held. "If we're lucky, Paul also called Tim's cell. Maybe forensics can recover the message."

"I was thinking the same thing." Andy nodded, examining the cell through the plastic.

"We'll need to dump that phone ASAP."

"I'll see to it."

Tammy clenched her jaw. "I don't know why Paul would be mad at Tim. Robin was the one always circling my husband, not the other way around." She scowled. "Why couldn't she just leave Tim and me in peace?"

"Is it possible they were having an affair?" I asked softly.

She shook her head vigorously, her eyes filling with tears again. "No way. I don't believe Tim would do that to me."

Hopefully Tim's cell phone would give us some clarity about what he'd been up to. "Now, Tammy, I don't want you to overreact, but I'm going to have one of my officers take you to the station while we sort out what happened to Tim."

Her eyes bugged out. "What?"

"It's just so you can answer some more questions."

"You mean so you can check out my story." Her face was red.

"If it were just my call, I wouldn't put you through this. But we don't know exactly how Tim died, and I have to bring you in while we figure that out." I leaned toward her. "I don't think you'd hurt Tim. I want you to know that. But I have an obligation to fulfill."

She sniffed. "Fine. But you'll see I was at the store just like I said."

I patted her hand. "I'm sure that's true." I turned to a female officer hovering near the door. "Officer Thomas will escort you to the station."

Officer Thomas approached and smiled at Tammy.

Tammy stood, looking lost. "I can't believe this is happening." She followed Officer Thomas out of the house.

Once outside, Andy turned to me. "Do you think she could have done it?"

"I don't think so. But we'll see what the GSR evidence says. I could be wrong."

"She seems a bit meek to cold-bloodedly blow her husband's brains out. Plus, it's a little suspicious that Paul left a threatening phone message and then Tim suddenly turns up dead the same day. Maybe we should pay Paul a little visit?" Andy asked.

"You read my mind."

We got the address from my notes and drove to Robin and Paul's house. They lived on a quiet palm-tree-lined street with a view of the Hollywood sign. The house was a rustic Spanish Revival-style bungalow with a white-washed exterior and a red-tile roof. There was only one car in the driveway, and I hoped it was Paul's.

When Paul answered the door, he looked like we'd woken him from an evening nap. He was shirtless, wearing only jean shorts.

"Well, this is a surprise." He ran a hand over his dark curls. "Robin's not home right now."

"We came to talk to you," Andy said in an agreeable tone.

"Me?" He frowned. "Okay. Well, let's sit, I guess." He led the way inside, gestured to a brown suede couch.

Once we were seated, I said, "How's your job hunting going?"

He shrugged. "Not great."

"That must mean you have a lot of free time on your hands," Andy said.

"Yes and no. I spend a lot of time driving to interviews."

"Maybe you don't really want to find a job." Andy laughed. "Must be nice to stay home during the day."

Paul shook his head. "No way. I definitely want a job. Robin has been riding me hard about that."

"Is that right?" I lifted one brow.

"Yep. She wants to buy a bigger house, and her income won't quite cut it. Not around this area." He hesitated. "But something tells me you didn't come here to talk about my job-hunting woes."

"Nope. Not really. We wanted to know why you left a threatening message for Tim Sloan." I watched as color rose from his neck to his face.

"Did he tell you that?"

"His wife did."

He squirmed. "Well, why did she think it was me?"

"Didn't you leave your name?"

"No, I— It wasn't me." He avoided my gaze.

I leaned toward him. "You don't want to lie to us, Paul."

His jaw had a stubborn jut to it. "I have the right to protect what's mine."

"Meaning what?" Andy asked.

"Meaning that asshole has been calling Robin for months. I'm tired of it. She's my wife, and he's not weaseling his way back into her life. Not if I can help it."

"So then you did leave a threatening message?" I asked.

He rolled his eyes. "Fine. Yeah, I left the guy a few messages. So what?"

"It's not nice to threaten people," Andy said softly.

Paul's laugh was spiteful. "I hope that little pussy peed his pants when he heard it."

"Leaving menacing messages is harassment, Paul. It's against the law." I watched him closely.

He frowned. "Seriously?"

"Yep."

"Oh, for God's sake. I can't believe that wimp complained to the cops." He shook his head. "What a dick."

Right. He's the dick.

"Did you threaten his life?" Andy asked.

"What? No. Is that what he said? He's a liar. I said I'd kick his ass if he didn't stop sniffing around my wife."

"That's it?" I watched for tells indicating he was lying.

He pushed his face toward me belligerently. "Yeah. That's it. He's full of shit if he said anything different."

I met Andy's astute gaze, and he shrugged as if he believed Paul. I was getting the same feeling. Paul struck me as a bully, not a murderer.

"We have a little problem Paul," I said quietly.

"What kind of problem?"

"Well, it tends to catch our attention when someone threatens another person, and then that person ends up dead."

"What?" Paul's brows drew together as if he was confused.

"Tim is dead," I said.

He went perfectly still. "Wh... What?"

"He died of a gunshot wound to the head this afternoon," Andy said.

Paul's mouth fell open. "No." He shook his head. "No way."

"Judging by how angry you were toward him, we can't help but wonder if maybe you had something to do with his death."

He stood, his face white. "No way. I... I just left a few messages." He licked his lips. "I swear to God. It was all just talk."

"Considering the circumstances, we can't just take your word for it." Andy stood.

Paul looked horrified. "Guys, you have this all wrong."

"Have you been alone all evening, Paul? Is there anyone who can vouch for your whereabouts?" I rose and moved toward him.

He held out his hands. "This is nuts. I'm not a murderer."

"We're not saying you are. But it would be helpful if you'd come down to the station."

He raked a hand through his hair, mumbling, "I'm not taking the fall for this. No fucking way." He looked toward the door.

"Don't try to run, Paul. That will only make things worse," I growled, bracing myself in case he bolted.

His eyes were wild. "Do you swear to God Tim is dead?"

"Yes," I said.

"Jesus fucking Christ. She's lost it. She must be off the rails."

I frowned. "Who?"

He licked his lips and didn't answer.

"What do you know, Paul?" My voice was hard. "If you don't start talking, you're going to be the one in trouble."

"That's not fair." He looked nauseated. "I didn't have anything to do with any of them. It's all her."

"Who do you mean?" Andy rasped.

"Are you talking about Robin?" I asked, uneasiness creeping through me.

He met my gaze and swallowed hard.

"Did Robin hurt Tim?" I inched toward him.

He didn't say yes, but his expression was telling.

"If you know something you need to tell us," I urged.

Paul gritted his teeth. "I kept hoping she'd calm down, but she's getting worse. I mean, am I next? Jesus, is she going to kill me because I know too much?"

My heart started pounding. "What exactly do you know?"

"Everything. I know *everything* she's done."

A feeling of dread rippled through me. "Where's Robin now?"

His eyes bugged out. "How the hell would I know? I had no idea she was going to hurt Tim."

"Why would she go after Tim?" Andy asked, looking puzzled. "I thought she liked Tim."

"She did! But she's so fucking paranoid." He blew out a shaky breath. "She was scared he'd tell you guys that he showed her how to reprogram the keypad remotely. I kept telling her Tim wouldn't rat her out, but if he's dead, obviously she didn't listen."

"So she's the one trying to hurt Jax?" I found it hard to believe that Robin could be behind the attacks. She'd seemed pretty normal. Tense, but not homicidal.

He gave me a wary glance. "I can't just throw her under the bus. She's my wife."

"She's a lunatic," Andy said, looking disgusted. "Why would you protect her? Two seconds ago you were freaking out about her coming after you."

He blinked at us. "I... I don't think she'd really hurt me."

"I'll bet Tim thought that too," I muttered. "Look where that got him."

"Maybe it was an accident." Paul didn't even look like he believed his own words.

"Do you really buy that?" I asked.

He wouldn't meet my eyes.

"Look, if you cooperate, there's a chance you won't spend the rest of your life in prison for something Robin did."

His mouth gaped. "Wait, why would I go to prison? I didn't kill anybody. I was just trying to keep my marriage together."

"That's not how the law sees it, buddy," Andy hissed. "You're an accessory to murder."

He looked shocked. "No. I'm innocent. I didn't do anything wrong. In fact, I was trying to help."

"How so?" I asked.

"The fire. When Robin set the fire, I texted you so you could come and help Jax." He licked his lips. "That must count for something, right?"

"You texted me?" I frowned.

"Yes. I figured Jax had a better chance if you were trapped with him. It worked too. You both got out alive."

"Yeah, no thanks to you," Andy grumbled.

"Tell us everything you know, and maybe we can put in a good word for you with the DA." I was trying to stay calm, but I was now certain that Robin had murdered Tim. If she'd gone after someone she liked, I had a horrible feeling she'd snapped. That meant she might be even more desperate, and hell bent on getting to Jax.

"I knew she hated Jax, but I had no idea what she was going to do to Dale. You have to believe me."

"I find it hard to believe you didn't have an inkling," Andy said.

"You're wrong." He started pacing back and forth. "When I found out what she'd done to Dale, I thought about leaving her. But she begged me to stay. She fucking begged me." He groaned and covered his face. "Why did I go along with that crazy bitch? Why?"

"Why did she go after Dale in the first place?" I asked.

He slumped. "She wanted Jax to be disgraced. She thought if his show blew up in his face, he'd be ruined."

I squinted at him. "She murdered a man just to destroy Jax's career?"

"She hates him."

"Why? Because of her brother?"

"She blames him for Trevor's stalled career. She thinks he's tried to keep Trevor under his thumb all these years."

"How would Jax manage that? Trevor's a grown man." Andy chuffed.

"She thinks Jax toys with Trevor. I guess he was almost suicidal after Jax broke up with him. She's crazy protective of Trevor."

"Emphasis on crazy," mumbled Andy.

"Is Trevor in on this?" I pinned Paul with my angry gaze.

"No. He has no idea about any of this."

I nodded. "Okay."

"Robin really thought she could destroy Jax by killing Dale." Paul groaned. "But Dale's death didn't ruin Jax. Jesus, if anything, he got even more popular. That sent her into a frenzy. I kept telling her to just let it go, but she wouldn't." He moved toward me, looking desperate. "I'm not a murderer. You have to believe me."

"If you know where she is, you need to tell us immediately." I had a really bad feeling in my gut.

"She went to tan. At least, that's what she said." He looked uneasy.

"Shit." I grabbed my cell, and my fingers shook as I dialed Jax's number. "Andy call the tanning salon and verify she's actually there."

"Okay." He pulled out his phone.

Since *Don't Die* wasn't currently filming, there was a good chance Jax was at the hotel right now. I gave Paul a searching look. "Does Robin know where Jax is staying?"

He looked sheepish. "Yes. She knows he's at the Jeremy. She followed him home one night."

I grunted, frustrated I hadn't warned Jax to be more careful about that. But Harry should have known to watch for a tail.

Andy hung up, his expression grim. "The receptionist said Robin wasn't in the tanning bed when she checked just now."

I scowled when my call went straight to Jax's voice mail. "Andy, call for a black-and-white to pick up Paul, and stay with him until they arrive. I'm heading over to Jax's hotel."

"No problem." Andy's expression was tense. "I'll meet you there after."

I redialed Jax's number and bolted out of the house. *Jax is fine. He has Harry with him.* Harry had seemed competent enough, although he had screwed up on the tail thing. My biggest worry was that Robin wouldn't seem threatening to Harry, and that Jax's instinct would be to trust her. If Jax trusted Robin, there was a good chance Harry would too. Even though I'd warned Jax not to trust anyone, he would. By his own admission, Robin and Trevor were like family to him.

As I raced across town toward Jax's hotel, adrenaline pumped through my body like a tsunami. I kept telling myself that odds were Jax was perfectly safe. But I couldn't shake the foreboding that something was wrong.

The hotel was only about ten minutes away on La Cienega and West Sunset Blvd, but the drive felt endless. When I finally screeched up in front of the hotel, I jumped out of my car, flashed my badge to the alarmed-looking valet, and bolted through the front doors. Ignoring startled looks from guests and the front desk, I took the elevator to Jax's floor.

I trotted down the hallway, and when I reached Jax's room my stomach clenched. The door was ajar, and there was a smear of blood on the doorjamb. I pulled my SIG P228 and took a deep breath. Peering through the cracked door, I saw someone on the ground near the door. All I could see were boots and jeans. Leaning in, I heard voices. Relief washed through me when I recognized Jax's voice, but it was short-lived because Robin started yelling.

From the hysterical timbre of her voice, it didn't seem like waiting for backup would have a happy ending for anyone in that room. I slowly pushed the door open…and cringed when it squeaked. *Shit.* I was positive Robin heard the squeak, so I pushed through fast and raised my weapon.

I found Robin standing with a gun against Jax's temple, Harry lying on the ground by the door, and Trevor looking distraught. I trained my gun on Robin, and her frantic gaze met mine. She looked like something out of a horror movie, with dark streaks of mascara running down her cheeks.

"Don't come any closer or I'll kill him," she shrieked.

"Robin, Jesus, please stop." Trevor's voice wobbled.

I did my best to speak calmly. "Robin, put your gun down. Let's talk."

She gave a high-pitched laugh, although she wasn't smiling. "Right. Let's talk. That's a good one."

When Jax's gaze met mine, I gave sharp nod. Jax was pale, but he seemed calm. Maybe resigned was a better word. He didn't look like he had any expectations of surviving, which made me mad.

"If you shoot Jax, I'll shoot you. Is that how you want this to end?"

"So long as he dies, I don't really care," she hissed.

"Why are you doing this?" Trevor's voice shook. "You love Jax."

She sneered. "I don't love him. I hate him."

Jax winced, but he didn't speak.

"Why would you hate Jax?" Trevor looked truly bewildered.

"*Why?*" she screeched. "Why do I hate Jax?" Her eyes widened. "Because he's an asshole, Trevor. How do you not see that? He's used you all these years, and you just keep running back to him like a fucking pathetic puppy."

Trevor swallowed. "That's not true."

"You both came up with *Don't Die*, but he took all the credit. And you just let him. You just let him use you and you don't even care."

Trevor shook his head. "You're wrong, Robin. Jax came up with the idea for *Don't Die*. We talked about other projects, not that one. You're getting confused."

"You're confused. Not me," she growled. "You can't even think straight, you're so obsessed with Jax. He treats you like shit. He won't let you have a career of your own."

Jax scowled. "Bullshit. I've given two of Trevor's scripts to friends of mine."

She pushed her face closer to his. "Then why is he still picking up your fucking dry-cleaning and running all your errands? Huh? You don't want him to succeed."

"You're wrong, Robin," Jax said quietly.

"Oh, is that right? Well, if the great Jax Thornburn says I'm wrong, then I must be wrong. Jax knows everything. Everything Jax touches turns to gold because he's so fucking *perfect*," she spat out.

Jax frowned. "Robin—"

"Be quiet!" she snarled. "God, I can't even stand the sound of your voice!"

"So you killed Dale just to hurt Jax's career?" I asked quickly, wanting to distract her from Jax. The more she fixated on him, the more likely she was to pull the trigger.

She blinked at me. "I… I didn't have anything against Dale, but it had to be done. One of the contestants needed to die so that the network would cancel Jax's show."

"Benji wasn't aggressive naturally, though. How did you know he'd attack Dale?"

"I made a point of being on set when Lucinda fed Benji. She had a little routine she never deviated from. Whenever she would feed him, she'd go straight to the cantina for coffee after. I'd just pull his food tray back out of his cage and toss the remaining food in the dumpster behind the hangar. So long as I remembered to slide the empty tray back in the cage, that old bat was clueless." She sighed. "I felt kind of bad starving the poor thing, but I needed him to be mad and hungry so he'd attack Dale."

"Then you erased Dale's code so he couldn't get to safety?"

She nodded. "Tim showed me how to reprogram the keypad remotely, so it was a piece of cake to erase Dale's code. I wasn't anywhere near the set, so I figured no one would suspect me."

"But it didn't work." If I could keep her talking, I might be able to get close enough to grab the gun from her, or at least knock it away from Jax's head. If I shot her, her gun might go off. With the weapon so close to Jax's head, that didn't bode well for his chances of survival. "They didn't cancel the show."

"No. It didn't work. Jax is so very *special*, his bosses can't bear to lose him." Her voice was mocking. "Well, I guess they'll need to find a new golden boy once I splatter his brains all over the room. Not going to recover from that, are you Jax?"

Jax's jaw clenched, and he closed his eyes.

"Maybe Trevor will finally get noticed," she mumbled. "Maybe they'll even give Trevor Jax's job."

"That's not gonna happen," Trevor said.

"You don't know that. Without Jax around to take all the credit, you'll finally get the attention you deserve, Trev."

"I wouldn't want it, not like this. Robin, I'm begging you to put the gun down," Trevor whispered. "You're going to get yourself killed."

"I don't care!" she yelled, pressing the gun harder against Jax's temple.

"Robin," Trevor whimpered. "Don't hurt Jax."

She curled her lip in disgust. "Are you so stupid you think Jax will come back to you, Trevor? Because he won't. He's a player. He uses people and moves on. That's what he does. How can you not see that?" She scowled toward me. "You know he's fucking that cop, right?"

Trevor gave me a strained glance. "I figured."

"And you still think he wants you?" Her laugh was harsh. "Wake up, brother, he's not into you. Been there done that, right, Jax?"

"Why'd you kill Tim?" I interjected. "Wasn't he your friend, Robin?"

"Wait. What?" Trevor's eyes widened. "You killed *Tim*?"

"She shot him in the head."

She swallowed, giving her brother an uneasy look. "He knew about me being able to reprogram the keypad, remember?"

"You killed Tim?" Trevor raked a shaky hand through his hair. "I can't believe you'd hurt Tim. Jesus, Robin."

"It had to be done." Her mouth was a grim line. "Things will turn around for you, just you watch, Trevor."

Trevor took a step toward her, looking angry. "Really? How's that work, sis? You don't think maybe having a psychopath for a sister might hurt my career just a little?"

She frowned. "No one will blame you."

"Of course they will. No one will want anything to do with me. Jesus, Robin, how could you not know that?"

I inched closer still. "Why did you bother killing Tim if you were just going to come here and murder Jax anyway?"

"I didn't plan on doing this today. But after killing Tim... I...I was rattled and came straight home. I should have gone back to the salon, but I was upset. Tim was different from the others. I've never killed anyone I cared about before, and it was harder than I thought it would be. But then I saw you talking to Paul"—she sneered—"I knew it was now or never. Paul never could keep his mouth shut."

"You must realize it's over now. There's no point in killing Jax," I said softly.

"You're so wrong about that," she hissed. "I didn't go to all this trouble for Jax to walk out of this smelling like roses as usual."

"Someone will have heard you shoot Harry," Trevor said. "The police will be here any minute."

"Yeah, Robin. Put the gun down before anyone else gets hurt." I tried to sound coaxing.

Robin gave a cold smile. "They won't get here in time to stop me."

Jax met my gaze, and he gave a sad smile, as if saying, *Thanks for trying*. It made me sick to know he thought he was going to die. I was angry and disappointed as I raised my SIG higher. Angry that this stupid bitch was about to try and kill the only guy I'd been interested in for ages, and disappointed that I hadn't been able to get here sooner. I aimed the gun at her shoulder, hoping the impact would spin her away from Jax. I tightened my finger on the trigger, and just as my gun fired, Jax dropped to the ground.

My round hit Robin, and a spray of blood splattered across the white carpet. She screamed and stumbled sideways, her gun going off with a loud *bang*. For one heart-stopping moment I was afraid she'd still managed to hit Jax, but he appeared unharmed as he crouched on the ground. Trevor ran to his sister and wrestled the gun from her.

"No. No!" Robin was screaming and sobbing. She clutched her shoulder as blood ran over her fingers.

"Jax, call 911," I barked, moving to take the gun from Trevor.

Trevor fell to his knees beside his sister, and I moved to Harry. He had a gunshot wound in his back, and his pulse was weak, but he was alive.

Jax sat on the edge of the bed and made the call. He was pale, and the hand that held his cell trembled. I squeezed his shoulder, wanting to comfort him more, but I couldn't. I still needed to secure the scene and make sure Robin was no longer a threat.

Trevor sat next to his sister, tears running freely down his cheeks as he applied pressure to her wound. I felt bad for him. He'd done his best to talk her out of hurting Jax, but there had been no reasoning with her. It was obvious he loved her. Crazy or not, she was still his sister, and as twisted as her logic had been, she'd done it all for him.

Andy arrived the same time as the regular cops. The paramedics stabilized Harry and Robin before transporting them to Cedars-Sinai Hospital. I wasn't able to talk to Jax because Andy pulled him aside to take his statement. From what I overheard, apparently Trevor had dropped some papers off at Jax's hotel room, and they'd both been surprised when Robin showed up. No one, including Harry, had been ready when Robin pulled out her gun. She'd shot Harry from behind and then gone after Jax.

I was busy talking to my lieutenant when Jax left. I watched him go, noticing he was still visibly shaken. He made no attempt to say goodbye, which seemed odd. I wouldn't say it hurt my feelings exactly, but I did wonder why he'd just left without a word. Maybe now that his stalker had been apprehended, he didn't really see the point in having a personal connection with the lead detective. Or maybe I thought that because some of Robin's accusations about Jax using people had crept in.

I went back to the precinct and finished filing my paperwork. Since I'd discharged my weapon, that meant even more forms and interviews. It was after midnight by the time I was able to go home. Once there, I had two glasses of whiskey and a mini frozen pizza. After the whiskey, I felt brave enough to try calling Jax. He'd been rattled, and I thought maybe he could use someone to talk to. Unfortunately, all I got was his voice mail. I left a message and hung up, feeling vaguely depressed. I knew my dissatisfaction came from the lack of communication with Jax.

He didn't owe me anything. I'd have taken that shot whether it was Jax I was protecting or anyone else. But it had definitely felt more personal because it was him. I was relieved he'd had the brains to duck when I'd fired. Good instincts had probably saved his life.

I washed up and crawled into bed, Jax still on my mind. It bothered me that he hadn't returned my call. Probably because now that the case was about to wrap up, I wasn't confident he'd have any interest in hearing from me. Jax wasn't shy. If he'd wanted to talk to me, he'd have called me back. It was probably best if I took the hint and let the credits roll on whatever it was I'd had with Jax Thornburn.

CHAPTER TEN

I spent most of the next two days wrapping up loose ends in the case against Robin. She'd given her statement to Andy in the hospital during the night, admitting everything. When I saw Andy next, he seemed disturbed by the level of hatred Robin still expressed toward Jax. She'd shown zero remorse, and there was little doubt in Andy's mind that if she could, she'd still try and kill Jax.

It turned out Paul wasn't as innocent as he'd made out. Yes, he had texted me and tried to stop Robin from burning Jax to death, but mostly he'd gone along with whatever Robin told him to do. He did have an interview in San Diego the day of the fire, but he'd gotten back hours earlier than he'd told the police. He'd also driven the car the night Robin shot at Jax and drove him off the road. While Paul clearly wasn't the brains of the operation, or a homicidal maniac like his wife, he'd definitely been an active participant, and he'd have to pay for that.

Another day had passed without a word from Jax. He'd never returned my call, and I was disappointed at how things had ended. One second the taste of him on my tongue had held such promise, and then everything had exploded into madness. While I told myself I hadn't expected things to last, I couldn't deny I'd hoped they'd go on a little longer.

I left work that evening feeling beat. I slid behind the wheel, and when I looked up, I saw Jax walking toward my car. I felt breathless as I watched him approach. His stride was relaxed yet confident. He looked really good in jeans and a pink fitted shirt that hugged his lean torso. I climbed out of the car, and he stopped in front of me. It was so nice to see him, and I had to resist the urge to reach out to touch him.

His smile was hesitant. "Hey."

"Hey, yourself." I really hoped he couldn't see how much he affected me. I had no idea why he was here, and I didn't want to seem pathetic. "How are you?"

"I'm okay."

"I heard through the grapevine you rejected the network's offer to continue the show." Andy had run into Trevor, who'd told him the news.

He bit his bottom lip. "Yeah. They offered me an obscene amount of money to continue, but I just couldn't do it."

"So you'll be on the breadline soon?"

He smirked. "Nah. I pitched them another reality show, and they took it."

"I guess you really are the golden boy."

"They're using my notoriety to make more money, that's all."

"Well, after all you went through, I'm glad you landed on your feet."

He dropped his gaze, a line between his brows. "I guess."

A group of detectives came out of the building, laughing as they passed us. I felt self-conscious as they cast us curious glances, but I forced myself to focus on Jax. "I heard Harry is doing well."

"Yeah, he is. I'm glad. I don't think I could handle anyone else dying because of me."

"None of this was your fault, Jax."

He scrunched his face. "Feels like it was." He cleared his throat. "I didn't get a chance to thank you for saving my life. Yet again."

I shrugged. "Just—"

"Doing your job?" he interrupted, his smile strained.

I considered him for a moment. "Maybe it was a little more personal than that."

He looked surprised. "Yeah?"

"I kind of hoped we'd have a chance to talk after everything went down, but you took off, and then you didn't return my call."

"Yeah. I was feeling a little...raw."

"Understandable, considering the circumstances."

He dropped his gaze. "I wanted to call you back, but I was too depressed." He glanced up, his gray eyes pained. "It's hard to swallow that a girl I loved like a sister hated my guts so much, she wanted to murder me."

"Robin is nuts."

"Sure. But still." He sighed. "I considered her family."

"If it makes you feel any better, it's not that unusual for family members to try and kill each other."

"No. That doesn't actually make me feel better." He glanced around. "Actually, I came here to talk about something else."

"Okay… What did you want to talk about?"

"Us."

I clenched my jaw, not wanting to give into the excitement that shot through me. "Is there an us?"

His gaze was intent. "Maybe that sounds too serious. What I'm trying to say is… I'd still like to see you."

"We're really different people."

"Yeah. We are. So what?"

I crossed my arms. "It doesn't bother you at all that your Hollywood friends probably think you're nuts for seeing me?"

He grinned. "I told you before my bad ideas usually turn out great."

"Yeah, you did say that."

"I'm willing to put up with my friends being jerks if you are." There was a hint of uncertainty in his gaze.

I couldn't deny the happiness I felt that he was still interested in me. "You're probably just trying to get your blue shirt back."

He laughed. "Nah, it looked better on you anyway." He surprised me when he moved forward and put his arms around my neck.

His crisp cologne filled my nostrils, bringing back a flood of nice memories. I put my hands on his narrow hips, tugging him closer. It felt so *good* to touch him again. "I still think you're trouble."

"Come on, Decker, don't be a chickenshit. Let's see where this takes us."

"I can't wine and dine you like you're probably used to."

He lifted one shoulder. "I'm more interested in quiet nights skinny dipping in my pool with this cantankerous detective I know."

"Hmmm. Sounds promising." I kissed him, turning him so he was pinned against my car. He smiled against my lips, molding to my body perfectly.

I felt happy. Relieved. I didn't know what it was about Jax that got to me, but I wasn't ready to stop trying to figure it out. Maybe we were too different. Hell, maybe we were perfect for each other. I wasn't sure. I only knew I wanted to see what Act II would be like.

THE END

BLIND MAN'S BUFF

BY L.B. GREGG

A game of Capture the Flag turns deadly inside an abandoned shopping mall when Tommy and Jonah stumble into a homicidal maniac's hunting grounds.

ENTER

We waited, the six of us, at a service entrance behind Parkway Mall as Dougie pried the effing door open with a crowbar.

The process of entering usually took mere seconds—bing, bang, done—but precious minutes had ticked by since he'd started, and anyone else would have read this as an omen.

Not me.

I focused on the positive. We were completely hidden by shadow. The rain had stopped, leaving a checkerboard of shallow puddles across the torn asphalt, and on the far side of the barren parking lot, well out of sight from both the access road and the old highway, not a single vehicle had driven by.

Most importantly, Jonah Theroux, friend, coworker, crush, had arrived for this evening's adventure wearing actual aftershave.

He never wore aftershave.

I aimed for casual, but between the thrill of his presence, the peppery scent of his cologne, and the prospect of a night game in an abandoned shopping mall, I rocked on my toes, childishly striking that balance of attentive, cheerful, and way, way too eager. Currently living up to my moniker Tommy instead of Tom.

I sneaked a peek at the object of my desire.

Hood up, hands stuffed in the front pocket of a drab sweatshirt, Jonah was decked in the unofficial uniform of the urban ninja. We all were. Mud-colored, camo athletic wear—which blended into the shadows far better than black—and worn running shoes. He stared pointedly at the door, watching Dougie. "You think we might get in sometime tonight, Chief?"

Vinnie swung his backpack by the strap. "I second that question." He held the first-aid kit and, knowing Vinnie, he also had some kind of horrible fruit-scented juice for vaping and a delicious snack to parcel for everyone later. My money was on Pop-Tarts, for both. Humor laced his voice, and he grinned at me. "If no, I vote for tacos. Taco Tuesday."

I reminded him, "It's Friday, Vin."

"Taco Friday, then. Taco any day. Taco every day."

Litter-strewn and damply lit, the ramshackle cement path circled an island of decay and neglect—better known as Parkway Mall. Tonight marked our very first foray inside, but the volume of paint-ball stains covering the exterior said plenty of others had come before us.

As a dead mall, some people thought Parkway was haunted, or unlucky, or cursed. Some said it held a history of murder, meth labs, and hobos, but people say a lot of things, about a variety of topics, and I'm fairly certain urban legends exist just to keep private property private.

Fact was, the place was empty. And had been for a long time because Parkway had never thrived. Not even when the shiny, unblemished doors first opened in the '70s, and not for the three decades it managed to hang on after that. From what I remembered, when the mall finally croaked, no amount of money changing hands could have pumped life into its bloated corpse.

What remained? Boarded glass and padlocked doors and not a soul to be found except for us. So if there had been a credible haunting—and I scoffed simply stringing that sentence together—the lot would be crawling with people determined to prove the existence of paranormal activity. It wasn't.

Parkway had been yet another victim of the statewide retail apocalypse.

Water dripped from broken downspouts. Towering weeds reclaimed the cracked pavement, creeping along walls plastered with NO TRESPASSING warnings, KEEP OUT signs, assorted graffiti, and, just in case you missed one, about a thousand FOR SALE or LEASE posters.

Lonely. Bleak. Isolated. Earthy. Empty. And fucking *perfect*.

I cast another sideward glance at Jonah, and this time, I caught him watching me. He smiled and swiftly looked away.

Okay.

He'd asked me twice today if I was coming. As if I, boy gamer, would miss. First, he texted this morning when we were technically in class and theoretically teaching—completely off-book for Mr. Theroux. And later, he swung by the computer lab at 2:35, as the last bell rang, knocking on my door and smiling cautiously. The students cut him a wide berth as they passed because Jonah ran a tight ship over on the academic hallway, and things were a little more loosey-goosey on our wing. It was a real surprise to see him.

But when I arrived tonight, he'd been stone quiet as he relieved me of my cell phone, locking mine with all the others in the trunk of his Jetta. We'd left our cars hidden in the desolate parking garage to the west of the mall. He'd given me a weird, terse, unreadable nod, and a tight-lipped smile that fell somewhere between nervous and cautiously optimistic and nothing like the eager smile he'd worn earlier.

He smelled damn good, though, and I fumbled my hello, wishing I could be smooth and confident in this arena of my life, but I was plain awkward. I don't know why. It wasn't like we weren't friends. Just lately, he seemed more everything to me, and finally, when natural charm counted, I'd turned into a tongue-tied dork.

Fortunately, Piper dove into a thick conversation about Fortnite and salvaged the moment.

Vinnie waged his campaign for El Toro. "Nachos and tequila. Just up the road."

"Not to mention dysentery and regret," I added cheerfully, and a smatter of chuckling followed. "Let's give him a minute."

Dougie strained, leveraging the way inside. "All. Most. There." The door yielded a teeny, tiny metallic moan and about a millimeter of give before snapping closed. "Tight bitch. Maybe the hinge broke. It's definitely rusted. Although, I snipped the chain earlier and had zero problems getting inside."

"Hey, man. No judgment here," Vinnie lied. "Uh…couldn't you remove the pin?"

"Negative. This is a secure door."

The youngest of our group, baby-faced Chris, piped in expertly, "What you need is WD-40."

Dougie countered, "Maybe, as Tommy suggested, you could give me a sec?"

Not to mention, no one had any. We were empty-handed—first-aid kit notwithstanding—packed light, and ready to run. Everything I personally carried fit into one pocket and could be categorized as essential nonessentials. I had ChapStick, because supple lips seemed important for some reason, and a key fob that included a Nano Light and a titanium whistle, a weenie pocketknife, and a mini Bic lighter.

Carrying more seemed like cheating, and that held no thrill. Challenge, however, did. I knew everyone else agreed.

Dougie smacked the doorframe. "Jesus Christ. Maybe it locked behind me when I left."

"That's sort of weird, right?" Chris fretted. "Like why? Could someone have locked it? On purpose?"

"No."

Piper pointed to a foreboding line of padlocks and sealed service doors. "Maybe we try another door?"

She rested against the stucco wall, knee cocked, a pair of carnival-colored braids poking from a brown Carhartt cap. A short, compact girl, admired for speed, agility, and strength, and now the much-appreciated splash of color in our group, she sported camouflage Vans instead of running shoes.

Jonah used his best teacher voice on Piper. "Try patience. It's a virtue."

She flipped him off.

I tried for patience. Despite the uncomfortable excitement of this thing I felt for him, I itched to get inside and do what I loved most. Playing a game.

Dougie had made us sign waivers, which I took to mean we had some form of permission to enter the premises, and that someone had a key or had opened the door. Apparently not. So on top of other pressing tensions, I wondered if our Chief was messing with us, you know, the way friends do.

Also, I hoped this prolonged standing around didn't make anyone sloppy later. People could get hurt. "Maybe we should find another location. Not that I want to, but—"

Dougie sighed. "But nothing, Tommy. We're almost in."

A lone truck rolled along Highway 21, headed toward the crimson aura of the old 76.

Chris frowned. "I thought you came to check everything earlier? You sure we're not going to get arrested?"

Jonah chuckled. "I think we can outrun a mall cop. I know I can."

Dougie answered Chris. "I did come earlier, and you're not going to get arrested. Look. The door sticks. Half the mall is rusted or broken or rotted or dead. Maybe I accidentally locked myself out." Not likely. "Doesn't matter. We're going inside. I set up all those fucking lights, which was incredibly difficult, super fucking creepy, they're on timers, and you're going in there, and you're going to play this game, and you're going to like it."

Vinnie saluted. "Aye, aye, Chief."

Dougie ignored him. "Lights go on in about eight minutes, so shut up and let me work."

Chris, worrier extraordinaire, stared wishfully down the walkway. "And you're sure this is the correct door?"

"Being the only door here without a padlock, yes, I am." Dougie poked again with the crowbar. "Having second thoughts?"

"No. I just don't want to stand here anymore. Makes me nervous. I keep thinking about the chicken factory. You know? The one that caught fire and was filled with illegals and they couldn't get out because the exits were padlocked from the outside or blocked by—"

Dougie hacked away, the noise awfully loud. "This mall isn't going to catch fire."

Vinnie exhaled a no-frills cloud of fruit-scented vapor. "Famous last words."

Chris glared between them. "How is that remotely reassuring?"

Dougie finally got a full grip on the edge of the door, clawing with both hands, and the crowbar clattered onto the cement. "A little help before I lose all my fucking fingers. And someone grab that. Might be handy later."

As Vinnie stood closest, he pocketed his vape pen and moved to assist.

Jonah snagged the crowbar and handed it to Chris. "Here. You're in charge of this. Don't lose it. And fire safety is *my* thing, remember. I'm not concerned. So we're good."

"Fine." You could tell he wasn't fine.

Vinnie muttered, "Fuck, this door is really heavy."

Chris stressed on. "If we can't contact each other once we split up, what if the door jams again and we can't leave? What if someone gets hurt? We should carry our phones."

I was about to say something upbeat and positive to redirect him, but Jonah ruffled Chris's hair. I was surprised Chris didn't bean Jonah with the crowbar. "I'm sure we can survive an hour without Instagram."

"Speak for yourself." I compulsively checked for my own phone, which was, as stated, locked in his trunk. Good thing too. When we first started exploring vacant places last year, we'd do the whole GoPro thing, which proved a huge distraction for low return. That's when people really got sloppy. And sloppy people get hurt. I changed the subject for everyone. "Where's the rendezvous?"

Dougie perked up, a twinkle in his eye. "The carousel."

The door yielded.

A shaft of light from the parking lot beamed inside, revealing a dank, cavernous void. Cold and silent.

Naturally, adrenaline lit my bloodstream, overpowering any problematic misgivings I might have had. Fuck that noise. Game on.

I sent Jonah a happy smile, and he, unexpectedly, grinned back, his face framed by a dirt-colored hoodie, his brown eyes bright.

Hell to the yeah.

Our leader waved us in. "Single file. One at a time. Take care. Watch for debris."

Jonah entered first. "Hey, Chief, if the teaching gig doesn't work out, you could always start a new career as a flight attendant." He immediately stumbled and caught himself. "Whoa. Sorry. You're not kidding."

Chris trailed Jonah. He palmed a small flashlight and revealed a field of debris.

Jonah stopped in his tracks. "What are we looking at?"

Dougie said, "Ceiling tiles. They're everywhere. Garbage. Broken glass. Electrical wire. The worst is on the second level, so stay alert. There's no power, so you're not in danger of electrocution, but there's plenty of tripping hazards. And watch for standing water. It's murder. This level clears pretty quick. The bathrooms are off-limits. Don't even try." A surprisingly long list of what-to-look-fors. "Piss anywhere else. And avoid the elevators. The shafts are full of bat shit and ready to implode."

That gave me pause because now we risked contracting rabies.

Piper tucked her braids under the cap and bounced on her toes. "I love imploding buildings. As long as I'm not inside one. Not so much the bats. Anything else?"

"Nope. Other than those minor details, the place is safe-ish. Use your head."

"Roger that."

Piper ducked in, Vinnie next. "If this place is so safe, why'd you make us sign something?"

"Ish, I said. Safe-ish." Dougie checked his watch. "And so you bozos don't sue my ass if you do something dumb. Now move, Tommy. Lights are coming on in five fucking minutes."

I followed Vinnie, entering a vast room that funneled quickly into inky nothingness. My heart skipped with excitement.

We met every week, playing Capture the Flag often enough, on all sorts of terrain. Our game more like tag, if tag was an Olympic sport. We played stuff online too—because of course we did—and sometimes we met for airsoft or paintball or laser tag. We mixed it up with Cards Against Humanity, Catan, any game except the ones with sport balls. Those were not our forte.

I'd met Dougie when I first came back to Hanover five years ago. He'd introduced me to his friends, a group of buttoned-up teachers, who by weekday were overworked and underpaid, but who let loose on weekends with gaming and beer and good times.

Tonight's good time was Capture the Flag, beer to follow.

Dougie masterminded the whole evening. He's that *D&D* kid you knew in junior high, who gave up a promising career in tech to teach history to high-school students and participates in Model UN for *fun*. He's also as socially equipped as a hockey puck outside of our friends group.

Apparently, he'd spent the afternoon systematically positioning small LEDs throughout the property and had more or less prepped a mazelike course for us, which gave him a slight advantage, yes, but he'd stay put, guarding his team's flag and territory.

This particular iteration would spread over two stories of pure Parkour excellence. We'd played in a three-level shoe factory once, and that night had been epic, chaotic, and I'd permanently altered Chris's worldview and vocal range when I kneed his nuts jumping from a balcony. An accident. I swear.

So yeah, we were friends. Long-standing. Chief Doug, Vinnie, Crybaby Chris, Hot Jonah, Piper, and me—Tommy. Never Tom. By day, Mr. Cline, computer-science teacher.

Note: I could outrun any of these lard-asses, and they'd never caught me yet.

What made tonight slightly extra? Jonah. Who, for the record, did not have a lard ass. At all. No.

If anything, he was a hard-ass. At least, his students thought so. Assume Jonah is the most thorough, list-laden, fact-based, nerdiest science nerd you ever met. And yeah, I called him a nerd twice. For Jonah, fitness was just another factor in an equation for optimal physical health. He had an A+ in that. And he gamed to maintain good mental health. I respected that.

Jonah slipped farther inside the building, blending perfectly into the background, until Chris's flashlight cut a swath through the darkness and I tracked him instinctively.

Chris propped the crowbar against the interior wall, and Dougie coaxed the door shut, which protested vehemently.

And we were in. Good times ahead.

The place reeked of mold.

Dougie led us across a thin, shallow space, which I imagined was maybe an old record store.

"Okay," he said, and something crunched underfoot. "Vinnie and Chris, you're with me on Red."

Which left Jonah, Piper, and me on Blue. Almost as if I'd told Dougie point-blank earlier that's how we would roll. I wanted to spend time alone with Jonah, working together toward a goal, maybe engaging in some flirting, not chasing after him in the dark. I'd done enough chasing already.

I'd just have to shake Piper.

Chris fist-pumped. I wouldn't take his reaction personally, because he was a total infant and thus a liability. He crowed, "Excellent. And you know where all the exits are in case of disaster."

"Nope." Dougie killed the assumption for all of us. "Listen up. This is the only exit. Don't forget where we are. Hopefully you reviewed the map."

He handed me our flag, a 12x12 inch square of blue fabric, which I passed to Piper. Problem solved. Why guard the base alone when I could run around the mall with Hot Jonah?

Dougie continued, "Lights coming on soon, so spread out. We start at"—he checked his watch—"seven thirty. You have ten minutes to locate a base, so boogie. Since I know the area better, we have the far end near Belks. Anchors are inaccessible. Mall center is the neutral zone—you can't capture anyone there, no bullshit. First one back to their home base with their opponent's flag and blows the whistle wins."

Vinnie shouldered his pack, taking on his appropriately appointed role as medic. "I have the first-aid kit. If you need me, blow twice. Three times—rendezvous. Once to check in. No fucking around, Tommy."

I'm not sure why he singled me out. There'd only been the one time I'd jumped the gun on the rendezvous.

Dougie nodded. "Blue, when you exit here, turn left. Give us a few. When we're clear, watch for obstacles."

He gestured "let's go" to his team, and they took off in formation at a fair clip. Chris's light bobbed. Sneakers crunched on rubble. And they were gone.

I'd studied Dougie's crappy map earlier, and although I hadn't been to this mall since I was seven, I knew where to find the basics. Escalators, stairs, food court, the carousel, the bathrooms. Like any mall, the building housed a rabbit warren of shops, corridors, offices, food vendors, kiosks, anchor stores, and open space. Some passages led to the parking lot and some to mysterious hallways and other stores. There were two sunken seating areas and a large fountain. All the exits, as stated, were locked and impassable. I supposed if I had an ax, I could chop through one. Or a chainsaw.

Truthfully, Dougie could have missed something, given the sheer magnitude of the place. He was probably scaring us so we would stay within boundaries.

I did know for a fact that the vacuous megastores weren't only off-limits—the roofs were collapsing.

Grinning happily in the dark, I waited as we let our eyes adjust for roughly two minutes, and then, using the narrow beam of my mini flashlight, we picked our way forward.

Moist silence filled the building. The pervasive odor of poop indicated animals had made homes here, coming in through unsealed pipes and ductwork or just the open sky above. Nothing moved. Not a *peep* or *chirp* or *scurry* or a *flutter*.

We exited the small shop, entering a side corridor near a cluster of second-string stores. Overhead, massive windows roofed a long mezzanine, letting in enough light that I pocketed mine. Overturned kiosks were everywhere, offering an inspired obstacle course. While the Red Team had bustled right through this space, we halted as one.

An odor accosted me, and not the usual musk of mold, dust, must, age, poop, and neglect.

Piper's voice sounded muffled, "What the what?" She'd stretched her shirt over her nose. "That's disgusting."

I gasped, "Assume dead rats."

"Dead something," she gulped. "Dougie could have warned us."

"Now where's the fun in that?"

Jonah swallowed thickly and nudged me. "Come on. Keep moving."

One second we were halfway along the murky corridor, picking a path around a mound of decrepit insulation, and the next? A gentle, luminous pathway kindled, beckoning us to the very heart of the mall.

Orbs of light were hidden everywhere—in the belly of some stores, or perched birdlike on railings, or crammed beneath piles of rubble. Dougie had carefully crafted a surreal, postapocalyptic landscape with glowing LEDs. A course lay before us of gloomy light and contrasting, tricky shadow. We could easily obscure or reveal ourselves at any moment.

We were players in a live video game. Although some of my friends were NPCs at best.

I whistled. "Wow. He totally outdid himself. Good job, Dougie."

Jonah nodded, a smile creasing his eyes. "Agreed. Holy shit. This is amazing."

A few real stars twinkled through some missing panels in the atrium, and from a distance, water dripped.

We wasted a few more precious moments enjoying the view. We could at last see shards of glistening broken glass on the tile and the rusted garage doors shuttering many of the shops. Our voices seemed less intrusive here, a false sense of security in the presence of light. Jonah spoke at a comfortable, if hushed, volume. "Okay. How do we want to do this?"

Piper stuffed our blue flag in her back pocket. "I know you want to get rid of me so you can make—"

"We can split up," I cut in.

"—out." Piper blinked innocently at me, and I glared.

What the hell, Piper? I mean, other than texting her that exact message earlier—that I wanted five seconds alone with Jonah to make a move, because if I'd misread him and things turned uncomfortable, at least we could keep playing and salvage the moment. Act like it never happened, she coached me. Works for me all the time.

Seriously. Piper had zero chill.

She offered her plan. "Look. I think we should just pass the flag between us and not use the base at all. We can take turns scouting, hunting, and running interference." She added with unnecessary drama, "Let's carry the prize with us. I'll take the mezzanine."

Jonah rolled his eyes but kept mum. Either he didn't have an opinion about our strategy, or he was letting me decide. That was kind of nice.

This wasn't our team's first rodeo, and spending the evening running circles around each other would take mental energy away from my plan to lure Jonah into a private niche and, as Piper said less delicately, see what was what. "We've tried the carry-it-with-you approach before. Not a successful strategy, in my opinion. We have to have a base to return to."

"Don't be so predictable, Tommy," she said. "Maybe it didn't work in a warehouse or strip mall or your apartment complex or whatever, but this place is enormous. Roll the dice. We can do it. I'll be the base. A moving target."

"Sounds good to me." Jonah nodded his consent, maybe because we'd been waiting around so long earlier, he was tired of it, or he didn't have a better idea, so I guess I agreed too.

"Fine."

We had a plan. A bad one, but it was ours and we'd stick to it.

Mission decided, we were off. Jonah led, with me close, and Piper as sweep.

We took about twenty focused, game-faced steps when something skittered on the second floor directly above us. A stone or pebble or more likely a fragment of glass. A real noise, though, so when it faded, the quiet rang hollow.

I craned to detect movement on the mezzanine while still keeping from sight. Possibly, Team Red had crossed back to our side. It felt like not enough time had passed for them to get all the way across the mall and back, so maybe someone had lingered. Maybe they'd sent a spy. Or maybe they'd adopted the same strategy—i.e., the bad plan—we had.

Could be a rat. Or a bat.

Whichever, we carried on.

Jonah chose our path, weaving through patches of deep-purple shadow and skirting islands of unnaturally white light.

He was a tall guy, slightly taller than me—a fact I rather preferred. Sure-footed and graceful for his height, he leaped a low brick wall near a former sunken seating area, his sneakers finding purchase with ease, and we followed him, up and over. A trio of gazelles.

My mind wandered, and I allowed myself the luxury of scoping him out. I didn't mean to cross the line taking note, but he had a world-class ass, and I knew this was probably a disastrous attraction.

We were friends, best friends in a lot of ways. Only, recently, my interest in him had turned, well, *carnal*. One day he'd been Jonah. Someone I gamed with and had beer with and sat with at lunch. Then, a few weeks ago, the blinders had come off.

There'd been a scuffle in the hallway as a couple of testosterone-fueled boys did what they do—swung at each other and called each other useless names. A bunch of students snapped them, and Jonah stepped in, snagged those dumbasses by the scruffs of their necks, got all the phones put away, and somehow talked the kids down. He had them shake hands without threatening punishment, or breaking any laws, or getting roasted on Twitter for disobeying school policy, or having any parents show up.

I'm not sure I could have managed the situation at all, let alone as well. The kids liked me, sure, I'm cool, but they didn't respect me like they did Jonah. Most of us who worked for the school system were reluctant to respond. Not because we didn't care, we absolutely did, but because we were afraid.

Seriously. The incident had been an eye-opener for me in more ways than one.

So an hour later, into the teachers' lounge strolled Jonah, looking to me like a snack, bearing an actual snack—a bag of Taco Bell. The clouds parted. The sun came out. I was hydrated and refreshed by an illuminated Jonah. Not the friend, or the teacher, but the man. The available, attractive, smart, funny, hard-working, athletic, tough as nails, take no shit, hard as a rock, capital *M* for man.

Woof.

So yeah, I took note of the burrito-bearing hot teacher, and now when he spoke, I really tuned in. He told a joke, I laughed a little too hard. He texted, I sent a fucking smiley-face emoji. *Kill me.* I'd officially become a thirsty seventh grader.

Did he feel the same way? I thought so. I mean, I really did, no kidding. I paid attention lately, and I noticed small things. Even so, hooking up with a random dude who swiped right on an empty Thursday night was one thing, and far too easy; hooking up with your closest friend had long-term consequences, and usually life sucked when the thing ended.

I tried not to overthink. Meaning, I wasted precious moments reflecting on bullshit I couldn't change, or do anything about, or had answers for, when I should have been paying attention to my surroundings. The *he likes me, he likes me not* solved nothing.

I splashed through a puddle, following the herd, and despite all that worried thinking, I appreciated the hindquarters of a certain, well-muscled buck. Point of fact, I couldn't change how I felt. I liked him. I was an idiot.

Probably, I missed something vital along the way as we loped ahead.

Since the weakest link is usually the first to be eliminated, I dragged my attention back to the game. Losing is not hot. Plus, my feet were starting to get soaked.

The corridor opened to the main hallway.

Hallway? More like a major thoroughfare, bisected with a series of fat, long, low-walled planters and cluttered with more toppled kiosks.

However, an indoor forest benefited from Dougie's well-spaced lights. Mall trees thrived inside Parkway, despite the conditions. Full and leafy, they were lit from below, so long, thick, shadowy branches stretched armlike toward the skylights. A line of hands reaching for freedom.

Roots snaked over container walls to a shallow, life-giving pond.

Our progress grew slick, our shoes squelching as we avoided as much water as possible.

We slipped along, bearing to the left at the T. There were probably a billion mosquitoes inside the mall during summer. Dengue. Malaria. Zika. Yellow fever. Fortunately, the water was ice-cold in early May.

Fewer LEDs shone from the second level as we closed in on the neutral zone. I wondered if Dougie meant to encourage or discourage players from climbing to the top, but those haunted shadows were a temptation. No getting around it. One of us would need to scout.

I knew exactly who.

We halted at the juncture, and I motioned for Piper to take the upper deck, not to get rid of her, not really. Jonah gave her an encouraging nod and thumbs-up, and I fought to maintain an innocent expression.

She rolled her eyes, made an obscene gesture with her fingers, and scampered soundlessly to the decrepit escalator, climbing with our flag— again, a stupid gamble.

Damn, that player moved fast, and I trusted her. Piper possessed rare athletic skills and laser-like focus after spending her childhood as an elite gymnast. She loved our games now because she'd never been permitted to play them as a kid, and she was easily as good as yours truly.

When she vanished from view, Jonah grinned boyishly at me for a full second, and I was a little nonplussed. His hoodie fell back, revealing shorn, dark hair and the strong planes of his handsome, devilish face. Brown eyes, square jaw, straight nose, butter-soft lips, slightly pointy ears.

Call me a goner.

With no warning, he snagged my hand. Just flipping reached out and took hold of me as if he wanted to lead me somewhere, and for the life of me, I couldn't remember if he'd ever actually touched me before. Like, skin to skin.

But that touch thrilled me, which sounds dorky and juvenile and queer, but I am all those things, so what do you know? I lit up. Like a fucking Christmas tree. I mean, he instantly charged my entire body with jolting electricity, his touch that powerful. That sexual. That intense.

Shocking and exciting and unlike anything I'd felt before. As if an actual electrical current zapped my central nervous system, hot-wiring me. From his hand to mine, up to my neck, down to my chest, and coursing way, way lower. Jonah ignited areas of my person not generally activated for gaming. Everything woke up, and at the same time, he fried all relevant thoughts from my mind.

I blinked at our joined hands, and his fingers curled tight, sealing our palms.

Oh, man. I thought I'd be the aggressor. Nope. No.

My gaze met his, and his smile turned sexy, bold, and mischievous.

I was fucking hypnotized. *What game? Where? Who? Huh?* Although for a second I did ask myself why had I taken so long to even notice him.

Clearly, he'd noticed me.

Go Tommy.

Jonah tugged me under a wide gap beneath the escalator. A nook. A fucking make-out nook right there, nestled within Dougie's fancy light show, in the crud-filled Parkway Mall. I didn't want to be too eager, but my dick homed in on Jonah, hard and reaching and absolutely inappropriate.

Heart hammering, mouth dry, zero resistance as he palmed my neck, whispering against the shell of my ear, "You ready, Tommy? I've been waiting forever for this."

Oh my Jesus, yes, holy shit beans.

"Forever?"

"You have no idea. Took you long enough." He nibbled my neck, and I groaned. No kidding. I hoped Piper couldn't hear me, and wasn't watching, and fuck it, who cared? His lips fluttered softly, and he murmured, "Open your mouth."

I did, and he pressed, tender and sweet, and totally removing any questions I had about my own intentions for later—yes, fuck yes. We were *so* doing it.

I kissed him, full tilt. No holding back, my palm snaking to grip him, and I took charge, pushing until his back met the wall, hard. I tipped his jaw and dipped my tongue deep. Licking into him. He was the one moaning now. Right freaking on. I lapped into his mouth, tongues swirling, and a noise rang from somewhere above and beyond our nook. A voice echoed around the bend, and Jonah and I jolted apart, dicks hard, breath ragged, stunned.

He grinned sheepishly at me, and I'm sure my expression mirrored his. We were blinking and listening and smiling and shuffling our feet, and I had to sort of tuck a certain overeager appendage back into a less obvious position. All said, at the very onset of our evening, I was smiling like a fucking clown and way ahead of schedule. Booyah.

Jonah turned, ready to go. "You think they have Piper?"

I nearly asked, Piper who? Honestly. "Maybe, but I don't think they'd nab her this fast." She was too sly and way too athletic for Chris and Vinnie— although Vinnie had a long reach, and his ability to climb outmatched most of us. Not me, of course.

I followed Jonah from under the escalator, skirting branches and checking doorways and tiptoeing around broken glass and skating puddles, grinning foolishly the entire time. My heart pumped as we came to the widest open area in the mall. Man. What a time to be alive. I flipping sparked with joy and hope and this crazy blossoming feeling for Jonah.

He'd kissed me.

We stopped under the mezzanine and assessed the route ahead.

A crumbling, stucco fountain marked the epicenter of Parkway Mall, a light burning within its topmost basin. This one cast a different sort of shadow, making everything flicker. A trick of the wide, voluminous space and the three-story, vaulted ceiling, perhaps. Or they weren't the same lights. Dougie may have gotten crafty.

A tumbled retaining wall ringed the dry fountain, and far to the right, near the old arcade, a ghostly carousel marked the bend to the food court. The rendezvous.

To the left of the fountain stood an information desk, currently lacking any authority, and next to that, one of those freestanding mall directory stations. Together, they perfectly blocked the sightline, and beyond them lay an inaccessible main entrance. The other less formal entrances were locked within the anchor stores.

Stars twinkled from the naked sky, the clouds having blown past. From every direction came the soft, arbitrary *ploink, ploink, ploink* of water dripping into puddles. The air felt cooler, but the view no less magical.

I scanned the mezzanine briefly; still no sign of anyone. The bad smell tickled my nose again, not as strong as when we first entered, yet lingering, its origin unclear. Jonah must have caught a whiff as well because his nose crinkled.

Making him even more attractive.

Jonah pointed to Red Territory ahead. An elevator hid their hallway. No hint where to find those a-holes, which meant they'd split up (which was appropriate) and had probably secured the base for their flag on the second level, near a balcony. That's what Dougie would do. Tighter control, better vantage point, easier to defend, textbook gaming. When a strategy proved successful, he didn't deviate.

I assumed someone would show his or her face soon enough, most likely along the open, multilevel staircase, or they'd drop down from above, all *Mission Impossible*-like and cool. Intervals of wide gaps were visible in the balcony railing, the ruined remains of twisted metal littering the tile around me.

Piper surely watched from up top, where at least one enemy lurked. Because Chris had a history of impulsive behavior, I assumed he had called out, moving the game along, or just being overly excited. I didn't see him either. No one.

Jonah turned and smiled. He tugged his hood back up, and presto chango, he turned into an ambiguous ninja. He gestured toward the elevator, obviously jacked for crossing the center of the mall and scaling that decrepit tower. He winked, my heart raced childishly, and he darted ahead, target locked. He moved with real beauty at a beastly clip, smoothly broad-jumping a pile of mall flotsam and landing deep in a stabilizing, athletic squat.

I remained under the lip of the mezzanine, hidden from view, waiting my turn. I checked again for Piper—

And a whirly gray blur fell fast and furiously, knocking me flat on my back and nailing me to the floor.

RUN

My skull cracked on the floor, stars exploded behind my eyeballs, and a wicked, resonant clanging hollowed my head and loosened my fillings. In that split second, right before the world ended, I figured either the light flashing before me was a massive overhead fixture coming to life, flooding the building, and falling smack on my head, or the welcoming glow of the afterlife greeting me. Or both.

Either way, I was fucked.

I woke up, cold, blinking as the night sky twinkled through a broken skylight, and struggling to remember what the hell. Mall. Parkway. Game. Jonah.

One second I'd crouched confidently like a dope-ass, Parkour ninja ready to hoist myself catlike to the balcony and impress the fuck out of Jonah, and the next? I'd been knocked stupid, that spectacular starburst inside my head actually a billion brain cells incinerating.

Things appeared more threatening and less of a good time from my new position, particularly in that section of broken balcony where shadows prickled with movement.

Assessment. Pressure on my chest and a probable, mild concussion.

Maybe. I didn't know. Hard to evaluate oneself after being knocked stupid and having virtually no medical training. I mean, yes, I could get by in a pinch, but I wasn't the EMT. That shit fell under Vinnie and Jonah's jurisdiction. I could treat shin splits, sprained ankles, and save someone from choking on a hotdog, or overdosing on narcotics, or staunch the bleeding in the case of gunshot. That was about all the first-aid training our school system could afford.

But something heavy definitely pinned me like a bug to the ground. Draped over my upper chest and shoulders like a—

Jesus.

Like a body.

Like an adult human *body.*

My world tilted, and I shimmied to free myself, not sure if I was dealing with someone dead or unconscious or something else. Was there something else? He didn't move, at all, and I couldn't sense him breathing.

I assumed dead.

And because my arms were trapped and I was out-to-freaking-lunch, I didn't gain any immediate ground. I didn't utter a sound either, because I'd had plenty of practice keeping silent when all hell broke loose. We were trained for that at work.

Shit. Where was Jonah?

The dude twitched back to life—and yes, a dude because I recognize a man when one is lying on top of me. Please.

He arched, and I completely, albeit *silently*, lost my caca.

Why did it matter more to me that he moved? I don't know. I wasn't rational. I'd blacked out. So yeah, I was relieved he wasn't dead, but oh my God, the situation became a little too real as he shimmied and bucked and humped on top of me, kneeing me in the ribs and elbowing my jaw and suddenly *quite* fucking alive, thank you very much—except, here's the weird thing: he remained silent too. Ghoulishly quiet. The only sound I heard was his breath sawing as he tried to roll over my hips.

Where the eff *was* Jonah? I couldn't see him anywhere. Maybe he'd been clobbered too. Maybe there were bodies dropping from the ceiling all around us, squishing people and nailing them to the floor, and we were all going to die under a terrible pile of rotting corpses and become fodder for the zombie apocalypse.

That would certainly explain the smell.

The thought propelled me into action and clarity. I was Tommy fucking Cline, and I worked out. I was strong and capable and was, at last, completely coherent. I shoved the shit out of that blue-sweatshirt-clad dude, launching him into the air, off and up and away from me, and Jonah materialized— *where the hell had he been?*—as I jettisoned to my feet and the guy landed with a splat.

Holy motherfucking shit. Holy shit.

I tried to process everything at once, but nothing made sense. None of us said anything. Not me. Not Jonah, who had a trickle of blood on his cheek and stared at the ground, wearing the same look of confusion as me. And not the dude, who inch-wormed toward the elevator, hands bound behind his back with a cable tie, ankles duct-taped together, head covered in a black sack.

Not a grunt or a whimper or a moan. I mean, *come on.* Obviously, he'd been someone's prisoner. A runaway prisoner. What other explanation could there be?

Unless another, simultaneous game was running inside the mall, and this guy was a player. But if that were the case, they were super fucked up. What was he supposed to do? Houdini himself to safety? Writhe across a finish line?

I realized that technically, we weren't in the mall legally either, sure, but we also weren't looking for trouble. We weren't vandals or delinquents or criminals or meth cooks or fucking weirdos, trespassing aside. We were legit playing a harmless game. Just a group of friends blowing off steam.

So Jonah gaped at the guy, and I gaped at Jonah, who must have been halfway up the elevator shaft before he realized I hadn't followed him. That's why he'd taken so long to assist me.

One of us should have said something. *Man down. Help. Are you okay? Run. What the fuck? Oh my God.* Something.

Instead, the moment elongated, and other than the sound of droplets splashing into puddles, there was a peculiar nothingness inside the building. The air around us thinned with expectation, the silence amplified by the simple noise of our breathing. I didn't dare speak. The wrong ears might hear.

The stranger quit inch-worming and slumped, chest to the ground, knees tucked under his hips, forehead to the floor. With his elbows bent and his hands fastened at his back, he presented a chillingly accurate impersonation of a man ready for execution.

He wasn't one of us. Not by a long shot. Not only would no one have had the time to truss one of our friends and send him on his way in the last twenty minutes, and Jesus, *why would anyone*? This guy wore light-gray joggers, the short kind with the elastic ankle thing—indicating he wanted to be Drake or someone—and a Hofstra sweatshirt in that particular shade of blue, although his was splattered with black across the left shoulder. He also sported the cleanest, whitest Adidas I'd ever seen. Worn to be seen and not to actually use in real life. Inside shoes.

What was a tidy little poser like him doing inside this dead mall? Not to mention, trussed and blindfolded.

Jonah mouthed, *"What the fuck?"* and I shrugged, not in an asshole or dismissive way, but because I had no fuck to what.

And where were our people? Why hadn't we seen anyone? We should be hearing Chris laugh, or Piper check in, or footsteps running on the tile. We should be chasing each other and calling each other names. Vaulting over railings and scaling walls. Engaging.

Adrenaline usually got the better of Chris because he's a third grader, and he'd taunt us from afar. I would swear that had been his *woot* of excitement earlier.

Someone must have heard the guy land on me. That couldn't have been quiet. It definitely rang my bell. Piper would have come to investigate. We weren't playing hide-and-seek, for crap's sake. So where were they?

I scanned the second floor and, no surprise, nothing.

While I wasted precious time pondering the same questions and flipping out and accomplishing nothing—blame the probable concussion for my lack of dynamic, decisive, masculine action and for the general standing around with my thumb up my ass—Jonah motioned to the mezzanine. He was asking about Piper. Had I seen her?

A bit late on that. I shook my head, which hurt, and shrugged again, pointing insistently to my cheek. Blood trickled from a spot where he'd been clocked by something. Hopefully, he was up-to-date on his tetanus.

Tight-lipped, Jonah swiped at his wound, leaving a smudge of red. He cleaned his hand on his pants, action-hero style, and went to assist the new guy. That was the correct, adult response, and I was damn grateful someone followed protocol.

The bound guy must have sensed Jonah coming because his knees straightened and he flung himself to his feet, landing smartly. It took a nanosecond for him to regain his balance. I mean, Russian acrobats had nothing on that guy.

With the element of surprise on his side, he was poised to…what? Face danger head-on and upright? All right, I could respect that. But what could he actually do to us? How could he possibly protect himself? Headbutt us?

Jonah observed from a safe distance, his expression inscrutable.

This new guy turned out to be fairly short, built no larger than Piper, and more reedy than compact. He hesitated, I guess to see if he was fucked or not, as a tight circle of cloth disappeared inside his mouth when he inhaled and bubbled on his exhale.

I checked the second floor again, where lights lent their eerie glow and shadows felt taller, more foreboding. Somewhere—and presumably within the mall—someone would come looking for this guy, and soon.

When whoever didn't find him exactly where they'd left him, bad things would happen. Prisoner situations never turn into happily ever afters.

We should head back, I motioned to Jonah, and he shook his head. He pointed again to the second floor. Did he want to investigate? See where the guy had come from? Or find Piper? Those options seemed irrationally dangerous, and since Jonah was neither, I realized he wanted to corral the group. Game over. Blow the whistle and get the fuck out of Dodge.

Drip, drip, drip, dripdripdrip, drip.

But Jonah didn't move. He didn't untie the guy. And he didn't blow his whistle. Instead, he appeared thoughtful.

It was officially my turn to take action. I went to uncover the guy's face, and again, he sensed movement and ducked. Seriously. Folded in half at the waist as I reached to help him, the guy moving like Obi-Wan flipping Kenobi.

Or he could see through the hood. There was that second possibility, which explained why he'd been hopping hopefully around on the upper deck, blindfolded. He wasn't completely blind.

He stilled and sort of acquiesced, leaning in, so it took barely a moment to remove the thin polyester bag someone had loosely tied at his throat. A pale, goat-bearded kid with razor-shorn, white-blond hair emerged, squinting warily.

A teenager. No kidding. A fey twerp with a fat neck tat—*XANAX*—in gothic style that shrieked: *tries too hard, middle-class white kid.*

He'd have been less obviously lame with *thug life* tattooed across his forehead. He looked exactly like the kind of weasel who regularly got roughed up and left for dead, and I briefly wondered if he'd done something to deserve his circumstances.

Which smacked of victim blaming, and I knew better. Knew better and still, I struggled.

I pocketed the hood, maybe to be used as evidence or something later, and he assessed us. What he made of two adult strangers in matching mud-colored hoodies saving his ass, I didn't know. I didn't care. I had his number, and this kid was trouble.

Unfair? Not really. I spent my days working with teenagers. I may act like one half the time, but I'm not one, and sadly, I knew this kid. He'd probably been in and out of juvie already, and his mother cried herself to sleep every single night while hiding her purse and locking the medicine cabinet and asking herself what she could have done differently.

Xanax. He was a walking cliché.

No doubt he'd caught himself up in something foul, and we'd accidentally stepped in it.

Drug-connect being my first, Mac-Miller-influenced guess. Mob hit ran a close Netflix-inspired second. Maybe he'd pissed off a gangbanger. Maybe he was meeting his Oxy dealer. Maybe he was his own Jesse Pinkman and had been double-crossed cooking meth or stealing cars or turning tricks. I didn't know. Maybe I spent too much time watching Amazon Prime.

I knew this: I didn't need to get involved with this kid or know his personal backstory to help him right now. Knowledge wouldn't change my impulse to flee this place tout suite and drag his skinny ass with me to safety, because it's my job to protect kids, even the ones I didn't particularly like. I didn't have to be his life coach after setting him free. I just needed to be an adult he could count on.

I could be that.

Something flickered behind the elevator shaft, high on the second floor. A shadow or trick of light or maybe a ghost after all, and then it instantly dissipated.

The need to find cover choked me. I motioned to Jonah, but he watched the teenager, whose gaze swept the opposite mezzanine. The kid's nostrils were crusted with blood, and he sported a juicy, puffy lip and a terrified look.

Again, I was struck by all the normal things he hadn't done. Asked for help, warned us of impending danger, thanked us, grunted, encouraged us to run and hide. Spoken a single word.

Jonah tapped my arm and signaled we should leave, his fingers fleeing rapidly on air before he pointed back toward the entrance. I gave him a thumbs-up. Right on. Aye, aye, Captain. Yes, sir. Let's go.

As soon as we untied the kid.

Christ on a fucking cracker, the kid *hopped* to Jonah, his super-sweet kicks crunching debris, louder than someone eating potato chips inside a vacuum, and we all cringed. I snagged him by his sweatshirt, spun him, and he wriggled his wrists at me. I just needed my pocketknife to slice through—

Jonah snicked the bindings; cable tie first, and then bent to saw through the duct tape, the going less quick, the sound reverberating to the atrium. He moved efficiently, but we were making hella noise, and the guy placed a finger to his lips, eyes round and darting all over the place. What could we do? We couldn't carry him, and we couldn't move any faster. We just had to practice patience.

I pinched the bridge of my nose and took a breath, keeping watch on both the upper deck and the lower as Jonah took what seemed like for-fuck-ing-ever. When he finished and straightened from his task, his questioning gaze landed on me. He mouthed, *"You—"*

A *crack* cut the air.

Pebbles sprayed from the defunct fountain, raining into the lower basin, and pinged onto the tile.

I knocked the kid down and ducked, arms shielding my head.

Some motherfucker had *shot* at us.

Actual *bullets.*

I play enough video games and watch enough media to recognize live ammo being fired at me. Also, a shell hit the ground, and the sound was unmistakable in real life, real time. I didn't turn to look. I grabbed that kid by the scruff of his sweatshirt and sprang toward cover.

Another *crack*, a zipping sound, Jesus fucking Christ, another shell clinking to the tile, and I circumvented the information counter, breaking every track record in the state. Jonah shoved me to the right with a palm to my shoulder, and I careened out of the line of fire.

Zigzag. You twit. That's what they'd taught us. Our new friend—the Xani kid—had obviously read the same pamphlet and attended an equally informative active-shooter drill. Of course he had. He zagged with us, his shiny new sneakers squeaking with effort.

Another shot, this one life alteringly close, and my heart ricocheted into my ribs, fear propelling me into light speed.

The time with Jonah had officially morphed from weird to fun to sexy to weird again, and now to a flat-out disaster in less than an hour.

I had no plan for anyone to die tonight, myself included, so I leaped an overturned kiosk, and the three of us raced into a side corridor, one Dougie had specifically marked off-limits. This hallway was polar opposite to where we wanted to be, and half the goddamn shops were barred, the metal gates drawn, or the storefronts were blocked with debris. Or worse, they were wide open, having no doors at all, and looked like giant animal pens, *or* they were chosen by Dougie specifically for ambiance and provided no refuge.

We lacked options as we churned through a thin lake of water, splashing like fucking hippos. I nearly took all of us down pivoting to tail Jonah, who headed for a cluttered but passable gate. He shouldered noisily through, shimmying between bent sections of twisted metal, causing them to warp and whine in protest. The noise echoed along the empty corridor. *Womp, womp, womp, screech.*

He scissored inside, and if he could fit, so could we. I was at his back, trying and failing to keep the racket to a minimum, the kid on my heels as we advertised our location with the volume set at eleven.

We entered a jewelry store. Maybe. Could have been a Claire's or a knock-off knickknack shop, or a Hallmark store, or a fancy beauty boutique. Who knew? The signage was gone, and there was no merch left, and I didn't actually give a fuck.

Murky light revealed a square of ruined display cases in the center of the narrow room. Twisted fixtures vomited wire and debris from the ceiling, and more glass cases lined the shop. Wall-to-wall, a carpet of diamond-like shards waited.

It was like *American Ninja Warrior*, only the course could cut you to ribbons.

Jonah Jackie-Chan-ed over a display case, fearless, and crouched for cover.

Too bad there was none to be had.

A noise. Another *clang* from somewhere, followed by a *pop* of gunfire. This shot farther away, and I wondered why the gunfire was spaced so far apart. Saving ammunition? Reloading? Sounded like a Glock or a semiautomatic of its equal, so probably the user was taking his time to line up shots from the second story, down toward us. Thank God he appeared to have shit aim.

We weren't being followed as far as I could tell, which was good news because there was no question where we were hiding. Panic underpinned any relief I might have felt. I kept moving, gingerly dodging another stalactite made from electrical wire and rancid insulation. The kid whipped by me, sprinting into a pitch-black rectangle halfway along the back wall, mindless of the glass under his feet. He didn't slow, just fled point-blank into the hidey-hole.

Maybe he'd found a storeroom or back office or a walk-in safe—a notion I found nauseatingly final. Getting locked inside a safe was a fear straight out of my worst nightmare, and again, I watch way too many movies.

One second I saw the kid, the next a shadow swallowed him. With all the shit hanging from the ceiling, at least the hiding spot wasn't visible from the entrance. Our best and only option was to join the kid. So I did, entering a small, unfurnished, boxlike room, which, I'm relieved to tell you, wasn't a safe, but felt like a coffin nonetheless.

I caught my breath, mind reeling, head sore, heart exploding, and Jonah sailed in behind me, taking every bit of air from the room. He gripped the doorway, tense and focused, game face on. Only, this wasn't a game. And his cheek was marked with blood.

Holy shit. Someone had shot at us.

Okay, yes. Not new information. Check. I was used to paintball and airsoft, not live ammo directed at me, and believe me, I am well versed in the games friends play where they can safely shoot each other, and the ones they play when they can't. My dad had been big on guns, real guns, and I knew how to break down a weapon and fire one safely. I'd learned from him that real bullets were no fucking joke, and you don't ever point a weapon at a person unless it's in self-defense. Or you're knocking over a liquor store.

That last part was a really poor attempt at breaking the tension because, man, I was tense.

My dad had been dead serious about firearms, and both my sister and I had been taught to shoot. These shots were well spaced, and the popping sound muted. Whoever fired at us had used a suppressor, maybe homemade, which didn't actually silence a shot, only, you know, suppressed it. Otherwise the sound of firecrackers would have echoed through the entire mall.

Who the hell uses a silencer anyway? Quentin fucking Tarantino? Why would anyone need one when there wasn't a person or a car for half a mile as the crow flies? We were deep inside a building. Okay, the skylights had partially caved in and sound did carry on the wind or whatever, but there was nothing out here along Highway 21. No one.

It stood to reason that someone wanted to terrify the kid. A silencer is a fear tactic. That's why you see them in movies. They're used for dramatic effect. You see one and you know someone's about to get iced. Execution style. And that someone is probably going to be you.

Great.

I motioned to Jonah, whose eyes shimmered intensely as he kept watch. Thank God some small light reached us in the back room. His gaze moved from the gloomy shop entrance to me. We stood inches apart, and when his hand brushed mine, our fingers touched, then laced. *"You okay?"* he mouthed, searching my face, and I nodded. *"Yeah. You?"*

The usual terse nod from him, and I admit I rather liked that about him, and he did look fine to me. His cheek had stopped bleeding. He squeezed my hand, I squeezed back—we were boyfriends now—and he let go, attention pinned on the door again. He had rules to follow, and keeping watch for danger ranked high on the list.

I felt slightly more settled. Although I had a million questions for the Xani kid.

And, I was pretty sure Jonah had saved my life when he'd heroically shoved me to safety in a scene taken straight from a Bruce Willis film. Be still my heart. I wanted to dwell on that. I opted to chill for a second and enjoy the miracle of breathing and being upright and uninjured and together. I let calm, positive thoughts prevail and took an appreciative breath.

He was fucking hot. No lie.

In the absence of direct gunfire, I listed our advantages.

First, as stated, no one had been shot. Go team. At least, no one in our coffin room had. I couldn't speak for the safety of Piper, Dougie, Vinnie, or Chris, which did worry me. They'd definitely heard the shots, unless they were far away in a forbidden anchor store, which they weren't because none of us cheats.

Second, there was a door against my back, the handle digging into my spine. We had an exit should we need one, a fact both useful and problematic.

What I could remember from Dougie's Pinterest map was that a group of midsized and micro stores in the central area of the mall accessed a long, skinny service hallway. The door behind me should lead to management and security offices. I couldn't quite recall. I was fairly certain the hall eventually filtered into a delivery area on one end and back to a corridor near restrooms and the food court on the other. Or it dumped us into a dead end. Which would be bad.

The file Dougie sent showed Parkway's basic floor plan, not an evacuation route, so the majority of exits weren't even labeled. Those were locked, boarded up, barred with gates, and impassable anyway. No new information.

I knew the only open exit from the mall to the parking lot was the one we'd entered earlier, through the sticky door requiring a crowbar, and that was far away. We'd either have to backtrack and cross the line of fire, or risk the pitch-black hallway. No way would Dougie have wasted lights back there. Those hallways were out of play, I bet because he'd blown his lighting budget to hell.

We could go through the roof.

I put that idea on the back burner because opportunity would have to present itself.

While my mind raced and I rode the roller coaster of both clearheaded and irrational thought, we waited for the next catastrophe to unveil itself. We were obviously straining to hear the telltale sound of oncoming danger. The kid breathed heavily beside me, huffing and puffing through his mouth. He smelled sweetly of sweat and fear, and either that cloying David Beckham cologne, or Axe Body Spray, or piss. Maybe all three. He hadn't moved, just stared venomously at Jonah, like he considered Jonah a threat.

We couldn't stay. We were sitting ducks, and no one would look for us for a long, long time. Eventually, someone would track our group's phones hidden in the parking garage and decide to search the mall, but not until tomorrow at the earliest. Or Sunday. Or Monday when none of us showed for work.

My mind careened out of control, but one thing stuck. Chris had been one hundred percent correct, and we should have bent a little and agreed to carry our phones. Why didn't we listen?

I leaned close to the new guy, spoke softly, and even so, the words hung large inside our tiny hiding hole. "Okay. Very quietly. Everyone okay?"

Jonah nodded. The kid nodded. "Good. I have zero skills in first aid."

I ventured another hushed question to the kid. "What the hell is going on?"

Thin and edged, he whispered back, "I can't tell if you arrived at the best or worst possible time, dude."

"That's not helpful." Jesus. *Dude.* We were being shot at, and he called me dude and answered cryptically. "Who's shooting at us?" *Who* seemed the most relevant question. At least, I thought so. Also, not so much as a thanks.

"He's a fucking psycho, who do you think?"

"I mean, do you know him? Is he the guy who tied you up? Did he hurt you?" Maybe this kid was a missing person, or a runaway. He'd been bound, so a kidnapping for sure. That didn't necessarily mean the perpetrator was a stranger. I kept my tone open, friendly. "We want to help. Who are you?"

"Me? Who the fuck are you guys? How do I know you're not part of his thing? What are you even doing here?"

I answered honestly. "We're a group of friends who came here to play a game."

"What the hell? You're cops or something, right?" I realized he assumed this of Jonah, with the buzzed haircut, the bloody cheek, the silent stare, and the broad shoulders, not me. I didn't take offense. Teenagers usually lumped me in with the cool teachers. They rarely confused me with an authority figure. I assumed he'd ask for help. Instead? "I haven't done nothin'."

My teeth clicked together. Unlike Jonah's students, mine chose to be in my class and we had a repartee. They liked me. So I had limited patience for attitude when I wasn't on the clock. Especially now, when bullets were flying and lives were at stake.

Jonah swiftly took up the gauntlet. "Do we look like cops?"

To this guy? Good cop/bad cop. I bit my tongue.

Jonah continued, "Tommy told you. We're here playing a game with friends."

As the information seeped into his brain, I stayed vigilant. No sight or sound of the shooter coming from the mall's center, only the torturous *drip, drip, drip, drip* of water and the soft glow of LEDs spilling through the gate.

On the positive side, no hint of violence. On the negative? No sign of life either.

A couple of seconds passed, and the goat-bearded boy scrubbed at his crusty face with the back of his hand. "What kind of game? I don't really like games anymore."

Jonah explained, "Capture the Flag. There are six of us. We have absolutely no idea what's going on here. We're not part of whatever you're involved in. Our friends are in danger. It would help if we knew who we're dealing with. So we can get everyone out."

"Wait. What? Like that game they played at camp?" His tone implied his feelings; his words defined his privilege. Yes, we were definitely lame, but despite his situation, he was acting a bit like a shithead. Maybe that was okay and he'd earned it, but the devil eye he'd previously sent Jonah turned into a massive eye roll.

"Aren't you guys a little old for kid stuff? Just text your friends. Why don't you just text them? Call 911. That fucking psycho smashed my phone with a hammer. Like an actual hammer. And then he chucked my cell somewhere. I can't do anything. I have nothing. I just want to get out of here and go home. Get me out of here."

I had to tell him, "None of us has a phone. And that's the pla—"

"What do you mean none of you?" The kid cocked his head as if I'd spoken in tongues.

Man, apologizing to Chris would take a lifetime. A long, long lifetime. "Exactly what I said. We left our phones in the car. Who brought you here?"

"Who leaves their phone in the car? I don't know who he is!"

"Shh. Shh. Calm down," Jonah soothed. "Let's help each other. If we wanted to hurt you, we have the opportunity right now, and we don't want to hurt you. We need to work together. We're on the same team."

The kid's panting eased; he nodded, and his lips unzipped. "Okay. You're right. I'm Carl." His eyes squeezed shut for a brief second. "I don't even know how this happened. My friend Ricky hit me up, I guess yesterday. Did I want to go with him to the 76 and pick up a package—something, but I didn't ask—and bring it back to his friend's house? No trouble and there's some money involved and it'll take a couple hours. Everything's cool, just ride along. So we go out there, and we smoke with this guy, and vibes are good, we're all mellow, and that fat fucker doesn't give us anything. No."

Drug deal. Great. Just what I expected. I freaking hated to be right.

Carl swallowed. "So Ricky's like, 'Hey, man, you have something for me, right? We've been in your car a while and thanks for the weed, but we need to get back.' And this fucking guy..." Carl winced. "This dead-eyed motherfucker says, yeah, he has something for Ricky, and takes out a piece and shoots. Just caps him. Like right next to me, and Ricky falls over and I have blood on my clothes. One minute he's asking about the thing, where's the stuff, nice guy, and the next he's dead."

Through the telling, the kid kept his volume low.

"I freak. Try to get out of the car, clawing at the handle, but the door's locked and there's blood and he has the gun on me. I thought he'd kill me, but no. He snags my phone and forces me into the trunk of this shitty fucking Neon, and then he drives. Not far. You'd think he would hide or go to another state or cross a border or something because he just offed a kid, but we went like a couple miles. I tried to get out, but he had the trunk rigged tight."

I would have asked a question, or said something, but Carl's story had spun into terrifying new territory. The situation much worse than I suspected. Although, what had I thought was happening?

Jonah tapped into words the kid needed to hear. "Hey. We're really sorry about your friend. That's rough."

The kid swiped at his nose again. "I didn't even know where I was. Or where Ricky is. Like, where that guy put him. Or his car. The seat was covered in—" He grimaced and shut his eyes.

How Carl kept his act together as long as he did, I didn't know. I curbed my opinion of him because he showed grit.

Jonah prodded, "What day did this happen?"

"Wednesday. No clue how long I've been here. Must be a full day, because it was after dark when he took me here."

I didn't have the heart to correct him. He'd been inside two full days. Wasn't anyone looking for him? And how had Dougie missed this?

How had the guy not seen Dougie?

Carl rested against the wall, and his guard dropped. "I didn't know where I was until you took that bag off my head. Parkway Mall, right?" He shuddered. "He made me climb through a bunch of stuff and go up some stairs. I think he's here a lot. And like…he takes people here. Like, I'm definitely not the first. He carried me partway. He's set up. He had a place for me to piss. He didn't try to kill me. He whacked me around to get me into a room, and he locked me in. He gave me water and a sandwich. He gave me some kind of drug, left me tied up in the dark, and was gone a long time. When he came back, he said we're gonna have some fun, play a game, and I thought I was going to throw up. But then we heard people out in the mall, and he got super excited. He put that bag over my head and bolted. I tried to get out. I knew it was my only chance."

The shooter must have heard Team Red innocently crossing the neutral zone to hide their ridiculous flag. Laughing and planning and scrambling over obstacles just for the fun of it.

I imagined the gun with the silencer, a rabbit warren of shops and corridors, dead ends and collapsed ceilings, and a psychopath on the loose. He could be a vagrant who lived here full time and flew under the radar. I bet he knew the layout of the mall better than any of us.

Carl said faintly, "I called out, but no one answered, and then I was pretty sure he would come back for me because he probably heard me. That was stupid of me."

"No," I said. "You did what you had to do."

So the voice I had hoped was Chris had actually been Carl.

Since disappearing into the dark when we first arrived—thirty-five, forty minutes ago—not one of our friends had made a *peep*. Not one. That was a long time.

I met Jonah's worried stare as he read my mind. "They're here, and we'll find them."

I nodded, and the kid's gaze seesawed between us. "Find? What do you mean? We need to leave, right? You're getting me out of here." That last a statement, not a request.

Jonah didn't sugarcoat anything. Just stated the facts. "We can't leave our friends."

A light winked out in the corridor, and shadows crept closer.

Something clattered on the tile, like a top wobbling, or a hub cab spinning, or a portable LED light rolling to a stop as it died.

Time froze.

We leveled up.

HIDE

Like everyone else in America, I'm familiar with active-shooter scenarios and not simply from my news feed and Twitter. My work practiced how to respond. Every school ran drills with students and staff and for parents and other caregivers.

There was "preparedness training" at my parents' church, and the local community offered programs at the park and in the supermarket and at the town hall. I mean, we lived under the weight of an unpalatable reality, and because we were human, we thought we could be ready.

Well, nothing prepared a person for the worst. Not during and not after. We have tough choices to make, and we don't know which way we'll go until the time comes.

The gist of what we were taught, and the best Homeland Security had to offer? *Run, hide, fight.* Specifically in that order.

That's just instinct. And we all know that self-defense is the last option, unless you're playing a game.

We weren't in a true, modern, horrifying mass-shooter situation, and thank God. And this wasn't a game. This was a drug deal gone wrong—or possibly gone exactly as any law-abiding citizen would expect—with a side of kidnapping and an added helping of fucking freak-show reject set on torturing a dumb teenager.

Basically stated, a goat fuck. Still, the run-hide-fight rule applied. I'd passed the required course on *what to do*, made my list of who to save, Jonah and I both, plus I had plenty of gaming experience under my belt.

With the sweat-soaked Carl kid hyperventilating passively next to me, and my date's eagle eye pinned on the door, I knew we needed a real strategy to get the hell out of the mall, with all our friends, and with no injuries or worse.

Then they could burn this deathtrap to the ground for all I cared.

That was where my mind lived as shapes formed and dissolved in the low light in front of the shop, and we waited. It became harder and harder to differentiate between what was real and what was illusion as minute after minute schlepped past in strained silence. A dreadful anticipation filled the air, and my mind ticked through a list of very limited possibilities.

Truth: I didn't like standing around, especially with my back to the wall and my head much clearer. I was programmed to be proactive, not wait for the inevitable.

When the *squeak* finally came, it was almost a relief to think of something else.

Almost.

Shoes tapped in the corridor, heading undeniably closer, the sound wholly audible, and not because there was no other noise to contend with. This person didn't bother to hide their approach. I guess they felt they didn't have to.

A *splish-splash* hit the small lake we'd crossed, and the loose shapes at the front of the store transformed into a hulking, Alfred Hitchcock-esque silhouette. He halted at the gate, a fraction of a foot from the crack we'd recently slithered through, and our options were clear. Hunker down and barricade ourselves in with…absolutely no materials to do so because the only thing inside these four close walls were three soft people and whatever we had in our pockets…or, I don't know, collect loose shit from the store to lob, which amounted to a lot of broken glass, a heap of rotted insulation, and a jungle of wires. And we'd expose ourselves to potential gunfire if we left the security of the coffin-shaped room.

Zero-sum game.

The door handle dug into my spine, reminding me we had another, and better, alternative. We would run, again. But we couldn't move. Not yet.

As stated previously, I had in my possession the bag from the kid's head, a key fob with a Nano Light, a titanium whistle, the world's smallest Leatherman, ChapStick, and a mini Bic lighter. Essential nonessentials.

The figure hovered near the rift in the gate, muttering unintelligibly.

Carl began to shake, poor bastard.

I shoved fear to the back of my mind and took a page from Jonah's book.

Think clearly. Logically. Stay cool and calm.

The shooter's size worked to our advantage. He was ungainly, and we had physical strength and endurance on our side. Of course, his firearm, his persistence, his knowledge of the mall, and his sheer crazy outmatched us. I was spitballing about that knowledge-of-the-mall part, yet the rest made sense.

A light flared—sharp and thin—and the three of us plastered ourselves against the wall, thankful a tangle of wires and insulation partially obscured the doorway. Nobody moved. We hardly breathed. A razor beam crisscrossed the inner reaches of the store, illuminating a sea of faux diamonds.

"Where's my little mouse?" a high voice crooned, sticky with sap, making my skin crawl. "Did you find a hole to hide in?"

Christ. I wanted to grip Carl's shoulder or something to steady him, the only thing holding me back being concern I'd startle the kid and he'd give us away.

The shooter probed for secrets with his flashlight and found the most important one: the narrow break in the gate, which he immediately wedged a shoulder into.

Fate smiled on us because the guy was a dozen tacos too wide to fit. He tried, believe me; he tried as the gate shook and creaked and protested.

He slammed full body into the metal, and the noise rang through the empty store. Then that fucker hacked the bent bars with the heavy end of his flashlight, hammering to widen the gap, humming jauntily. *Humming.*

We pressed the back wall like taunted, caged animals.

Eventually, he'd remember he had a weapon and start blasting at us. Maybe he'd blown through his ammo—that would be awesome—or maybe he was smart enough to conserve bullets for a better shot. I didn't know. I couldn't begin to guess. He had his own agenda.

He sang, "Come out, come out, wherever you are," and honestly, he was an asshole. Like, okay, yes, you're a fucking psycho killer with a gun, and we're scared and hiding and you have the upper hand, but in real life, you're also just an asshole. Which could explain why he was a killer.

His light had toyed with the dark, coming a hairbreadth away from us, then sweeping the glass carpet and the falling ceiling and the stalactite, but never touching our hidey-hole. There was a slim chance he intended to scare us into panicked action. Smoking us from our hole, as it were.

I chanced another look at Jonah. Stock-still and poised to spring. Confident and capable. That's what I saw in him. Duty-bound. He possessed the noble ability to fend for himself, protect others under his care, and never shy away from the hard task ahead. Teacher, EMT, athlete, role model—the action hero everyone hoped to be.

He'd saved my life.

A high-pitched whistle pierced the air, puncturing the tension holding us. One hundred and ten decibels, and the sound brought Jonah's gaze to mine, a hint of relief in his face.

Poor Carl's head whipped against the wall.

The flashlight cut, and from deep within the mall's catacombs, a Nitecore NWS10—the team's go-to—piped two more, short, clean, beautiful notes. *Tooooot. Toooooot.*

Rendezvous.

One of our friends called us to gather. They must have believed the area was safe enough to enter, despite the shooting. Or, they were creating a diversion because they knew we were cornered. Or they had no clue about our circumstance and were still playing the game.

Whichever, the whistle worked magic, and the shooter called into the store again, not quite so carefree. "Don't you go anywhere, Slim Shady."

That asshole trotted hulkingly back the way he'd come, slapping through water as we waited, and when the sound of his tip-tappy shoes faded, Carl wilted next to me, a *whoosh* of air escaping him. "Shit."

Here's some useless trivia. Our villain wore dress shoes. Not sneakers or loafers. Hard-soled shoes. Damn dapper of him, considering the water. Also, his reference seemed dated.

Carl appeared sickly and ready to vomit, but we couldn't waste time nursing him. We needed him quiet, moving in the same direction, and close, otherwise he would be a liability, or worse, he could be lost forever.

I'd checked in with Jonah about his health, so I figured we needed to do the same with Carl. "Did you get hit?"

He shook his head, muttering, "Only with a hammer."

I blinked. "What?"

"Jesus," Jonah swore under his breath. "Where? Show me."

The kid swallowed and touched his left thigh. "I'm okay. He hit me with a fucking hammer when he smashed my phone. Hurt so bad. He has tools. Like for building shit. Straight out of *Saw* or…something. I don't watch those. And I don't think he wanted to break anything, or he would have. I'm okay. I can run."

I said, "I guess so. You ran faster than me, and that's something." The kid must have had a bruise the size of a dinner plate. "You good to move now? Because we need to."

"Yeah. I'm good. Let's go."

Jonah led the way, opening the door, which swung in instead of out, making our exit awkward. No shock, as the place had to be almost four decades behind code, and clearly nothing would be easy.

Case in point, when Jonah shut the door behind us, it latched, locking us onto our new path—and absolute darkness. No choice other than to move forward.

Fine. Good riddance to the coffin room. I squared my shoulders and located my flashlight. The handy gadget had power and didn't bleed much, so a tight, narrow, direct beam illuminated the corridor.

Jonah spoke from beside me. "I'm starting to believe this place is cursed."

"That's fair." Seriously. "I can buy cursed, but is it haunted?"

"We're about to find out."

Carl's soft voice lanced the banter. "Yeah. I spent the night here. It's definitely haunted. I'd always heard things about this place—about people going missing and crazy stuff—but after last night, I think it's all true."

I wouldn't correct him. His very presence added truth to the legend.

My flashlight found a merry red lacquer and green plastic upholstered Santa sleigh. "Well, there's nothing scary here."

No shit. Ho ho ho. Not the expected dangerous or disgusting obstacle introducing us to the service hallway. Only the ghost of Christmas past. The sleigh sported gilded runners and a nest of faux Christmas holly that were in jolly good shape.

We found more holiday decor and, chock between a forest of artificial Christmas trees, a jumbo pumpkin, and about a hundred pastel basketball-sized Easter eggs were rolling office chairs, paper litter, and a long series of doors.

Cool.

We'd entered at the far end of a corridor housing the mall offices and security and whatnot. The thick must of mold spores scented everything. I would have put money on cold air killing mold, but again, all bad things were possible in Parkway Mall, and my sinuses agreed.

Following the hall would circle us back to the arcade, the food court, and the center of the mall. We were either stuck crossing the neutral zone again to find our OG entrance, or we could simply try the exit door directly next to me.

I pushed experimentally on the bar and received a *squawk* of protest. Of course it wouldn't budge. Chained from the outside. Locked. Barred. Boarded up. Impassable. Witchcraft or black magic or bad luck or destiny, whichever, all the signs read the same thing: *You Shall Not Pass.*

If only we had a wizard.

Or an ax.

Or just a goddamn cell phone to call for help.

We hadn't taken a step, and I turned to Jonah. "You know what? We need to listen to Chris more. Really."

He poked at a sprig of holly, which crackled with age. "I was thinking the same exact thing. We can take turns mea culpa-ing."

Carl breathed in my ear, "Who's Chris? What are you guys talking about?"

"Chris is our friend. And we're talking about pride," Jonah answered.

"Spot on." I mean, why didn't we ever listen to him? He was such a senior citizen about safety, true, but maybe we needed someone to state the obvious and hold us accountable. Maybe we could lower ourselves enough to take a few basic precautions. We spent all our hours on the job hemmed in by rules and lesson plans and procedures and guidelines and the school board and laws and, oh God, *parents*. Among our group were *two* emergency responders. Yet come Friday, we shucked off responsibility and acted as if we were invincible.

With thirty staring me in the eye, I needed to act more like an adult. I could get hurt. We all could. I owed Chris a thousand apologies.

First, I'd have to find him.

Jonah nudged me. "Hey, you with the light. Time to roll."

"Right." Woolgathering must be a symptom of concussion or stress.

We navigated the field of Easter eggs and Christmas trees, checking a small, suffocating, windowless room. No exits within, only a jumble of broken equipment. A fax machine. An ancient desktop chopped into pieces. Overturned file boxes and about a million paperclips. Graffiti, paintball, rodent turds. That's what room number one contained. The empty husk of a snack machine slept on its side, blocking the door.

The fire extinguisher, hose, and ax were unaccounted for in their emergency receptacle.

What a bleak place the hall must have been to work in, with no natural light, and white tile on white walls with mottled white ceiling tiles and white fluorescent fixtures. No-frills. The remaining furniture had once been solid white molded plastic. Of course, now everything was coated in graffiti, and dots of black mold plastered the drop ceiling. The fungus ombreyed everything.

Jonah grilled Carl as we crept along. Volume low, he used the teacher voice, firm and clear and authoritative. You'd think I wouldn't be into that particular tone. You'd be wrong. "Any info you have would be helpful to us. Is he operating alone? What kind of weapons does he have? What does he want? Anything you can tell us."

Carl breathed, "He's got a heap of shit in a store, right near where I fell, but it doesn't matter. We just need to get out of here. One of the doors has to be unlocked, or we wouldn't be inside in the first place. We could break a window maybe. Or climb to the roof."

I avoided an overturned office chair, Carl practically burrowed inside my pocket. "The window count in this hallway so far is nil. And if you find one not boarded over or covered in bars, then great, we'll try it. *After* we find our friends. How are you at climbing?"

"I can outclimb you old fucks."

"Maybe." I conceded he was small and agile, but he struck me as impulsive. Call me crazy. "How much do you weigh? Most of the roof is spent, and the skylights are hanging by a wire at best or gone completely. You look pretty light, though."

Jonah added, "Someone petite could get up there. Like Piper."

Exactly. She weighed about a hundred pounds and could Spiderman her way to an atrium window. Upper-body strength, flexibility, and leg power the hallmark of her athleticism. "Maybe she's outside already."

"Hold on to that hope."

We passed an empty janitor's closet. Not even a mop left.

Out of the blue, Carl threw, "I think I remember you. You're teachers, right? At Hanover? You had my sister a couple years ago. Sam Halpern."

Halpern. *Halpern.* "No. Sorry. Doesn't ring a bell." Another door, another disgusting mess.

"I was talking to him." Carl nodded toward Jonah. "The science guy."

I snorted and aimed my light toward Jonah, who squinted thoughtfully. If we were in a normal situation, I'd have thought he was cute. Truth? I thought he was cute anyway. "Blonde. Glasses. Short. Eighty-seven average. Good student. Looked like you."

Holy…he pulled her right out of his hat. Was he bullshitting? I could hardly remember the names of the students in my current classes. He caught my impressed expression, saying humbly, "I have a good memory."

"Damn. I guess so."

Carl said, "You're like a fucking robot."

Jonah's smile dissolved, and we soldiered on.

There were obstacles everywhere and the going slow. Jonah had a light in his pocket, I knew, but two lights would be overkill. Yes, the area felt safe, and we were in a sealed corridor. Even the perpetual dripping lay beyond this space. But silence didn't mean our light wouldn't create a soft glow and alert the hard-soled guy holding the gun. So we picked our way with the one light.

Mold clung to the ceiling fixtures, every fluorescent tube black. I wouldn't whine, though my head throbbed as we searched for an exit. Whether from the abundance of spores or from whacking my skull or from listening to Carl unravel, I didn't know.

As he grew more undone, suggestions fell like prayers. "This is a good place to hide. I think we can fit under that desk. That's what they say to do. Let's stop. Where are we going? We should hide here."

A bit of mental fortitude on my part and careful footwork for all of us, and we neared the bend. Creeping, tall shadows painted the walls.

Jonah stopped at the doorway to the canteen.

"Wait," he said and fished in his pocket. He produced his mini light, so I cut mine. "Let me check this out."

He straddled a pile of kindling which, in a former life, had been a ping-pong table. His flashlight swept the short, squat room, finding discarded packages of long-eaten food on the floor, probably devoured by animals and humans alike. And on a shelf, a lone can of SpaghettiOs sat spoiling.

Carl hovered. "What're you doing? Can't we barricade ourselves in here with the food and wait for help? I haven't eaten since that sandwich."

"The food here will kill you. So that's a no."

"Oh my God. Why are you guys being so stupid? We need to hide."

As if our evening wasn't hellish enough, Carl reverted to what I suspected was his default mode: sour teen.

Jonah unearthed a narrow box from the pile of debris. "We can hide and hope—that's what it's called—but your guy knows where we are. He's—"

"He's not my guy," Carl snapped. "He killed Ricky. He pretended he was going to shoot me half a dozen times. He hit me with a hammer, and he put a gun to my fucking forehead while I ate cheese. He called me a mouse. He's a psycho."

Mouse.

Shit. *Right.* Not a sour teen. A traumatized person who needed my help.

Jonah opened the box. "Yes. He is your guy. He's looking specifically for you."

"No. He's *our* guy now." Carl stuffed his hands in his sweatshirt pocket and hunched into himself. "And if he knows where we are like you say, then he's going to find us."

As he attempted to make himself into the tiniest target in the hallway, which was smart, Jonah—out of freaking Mars—Jonah asked him, "What do you know about ping-pong balls?"

There are some obscene answers to that question, so I zipped my trap and hoped for the best.

Carl's gaze flicked to Jonah. "What. The— What?"

Jonah continued mildly, "Ping-pong balls." His light fell on the box. "They're made from a composite material containing nitrocellulose, which is...?"

Jonah paused expectantly, and Carl's expression turned murderous. "You gotta be fucking kidding me."

I could have defused the situation before Carl launched Jonah into orbit or vice versa, but Carl surprised us both. "It's an explosive. They ignite fast. Firefighters use them to control burns."

Jonah sent him a gold-star smile. "That's right. Plastic explosives are made from nitrocellulose." Science class with Mr. Theroux could have been better timed, but he'd redirected Carl—and we discovered Carl was smarter than he looked. Both were a plus. Jonah shook the box of ping-pong balls, and, to be honest, I expected an explosion. "We may be able to use these."

"*Or we can hide,*" Carl countered. "Hiding sounds good."

"Nope." Jonah moved deeper into the room, treading through rubble. He did a quick search of the kitchenette drawers.

I strained to hear any hint of movement from around the bend, and a rush of profound urgency hit me hard. We'd been taking too long, searching, chatting, flashing our light, and beyond us the mall remained supremely, unnaturally, deathly quiet. Not a *peep* except our hushed conversation. If the shooter knew the mall as well as I suspected, we were fucked. "Find anything?" I asked Jonah.

"Unless we can fence our way to freedom with plastic knives and coffee stirrers, we're out of luck."

Carl sweated beside me, his head barely reaching my shoulder, and were it not for his shaggy goat beard and tragic tattoo, I would have pegged him for thirteen or fourteen tops.

He'd been through an ordeal, he had toughed things out, and he was only a kid. I refused to be a dick. I said for his benefit as well as mine, "We need to do the right thing and help our friends."

Carl clenched his fists, and then surprised me by shoving his sleeve to his elbow. There wasn't much light, just enough to see an unexpected, grotesque bruise covering his wrist and forearm. "He did this to me. I got away once. He's not going to give me a second chance."

"I won't let anything happen to you." I hoped I sounded more confident than I felt.

"Sure. Right." He slumped and wiped his nose again. His lip protruded. "Goddamn it," he choked. "We're walking dead."

"No. We're not. And we can't stay here, because this is a trap."

"You're both mental. You can't make me go with you."

"Sure we can," Jonah said, gingerly opening the last paint-splattered cupboard and exposing a few Styrofoam cups and a jar of non-dairy creamer. He shook the container, then tossed it to me. "There are three jars in the teachers' lounge that have been there since before I started." Jesus, he was chatty. "My grandmother had the same container for as long as I can remember. She gave it to people she didn't like. Save that."

I tucked the creamer into the bag—Carl's former head sack—and the kid balked. "What the hell? My actual blood is on there, and who knows who else's."

It did feel crusty. "Hey. We need to use what we have."

"This is insane. You guys want to meet your people, and I get it. I do. I mean, if we were dealing with a drug dealer or whatever, he'd have bounced by now and we could go on our way and have fucking tea with the Queen and your friends. He wouldn't like, *linger*. Or, he'd have a second with him and I'd be dead already." His words spilled together. "But he's-not a drug dealer. He's-not connected. He's-not even a normal criminal." Like himself, he didn't have to add. "I told Ricky the guy's cruising and he's-a fucking nutjob. I said so. I said, hard pass. And Ricky called me a whiny little bitch, so I got in the car."

Ricky should have listened to his friend.

Pot, kettle. I was in league to receive my own Darwin Award for not taking the sage advice of a cautious friend.

Jonah searched the last cupboard, the one under the sink. "What's your point, Carl?"

"My point? Do I even need one? Oh my God. That dude isn't normal. He planned something nasty for me. And not sex stuff, because he would have done that shit already. He's like living here. He had clothes. He was set up."

"Where you fell?"

Carl nodded. "Right up there. I didn't get far. I could see a little. It doesn't matter, though. I'm not going back. We need to run or hide until help arrives. That's what you fucking teach us in school. You know this. And, I told you, I'm not the first person he's brought here. He said as much. But I'm going to be the first to leave."

In the dull light, despite the cool air, Carl's face shone with sweat. On top of everything else he'd experienced, he'd been two days without drugs. I wasn't sure which flavor he self-medicated with, but something.

"Well, we can't leave our friends." Maybe if I repeated it a thousand times, he'd hear me. "And we're not leaving you."

So the shooter wasn't a random kidnapping psycho. He was a possible serial killer. Great. He was still an asshole.

He spat, "Fuck your friends. They're probably gone already."

"No. They're here. I didn't imagine the whistle."

Jonah had had enough. "We heard what you have to offer. Now shut up, Carl."

Bam. A+. From under the sink, Jonah had uncovered a rusted steel pad, a broken plastic bowl, and a can of WD-40, the last of which he tossed to me. "Give this to the big baby when we see him."

"Will do." The WD-40 went inside the bag, *clank-clank.* "Now may we go?"

He wiped his hands on the seat of his pants, smiling. "Yes. Now we may go."

"You guys are fucked up. Don't hurry or anything." Carl had rubbed his nose raw, and it bled a tiny trickle. "FYI. That guy is going to kill us."

"Not if I have anything to say about it." Jonah relieved me of the bag, shoved the box he'd found earlier inside, and tied the drawstring. Commandeering the supplies indicated he had a plan.

We placed Carl between us. Unwatched, pretty clear he'd bolt. Either crawl into the drop ceiling, or turn and run blindly, or barricade himself into a closet.

At the end of the corridor, where the first glimmer of LEDs eased the darkness, Jonah pocketed his light.

We crept forward, caution the watchword, moving as a unit, until we were flanked by the restrooms Dougie had warned us of earlier. He'd failed to describe the raw *immediacy* of the odor emanating from those simple, tiled portals.

In a perfect world, we would have halted at the mouth of that corridor, considered our options, planned a route to cross unseen and unheard, and then proceeded with due caution because danger lurked around every corner.

Reality inside Parkway Mall once again proved anything but accommodating and, no exaggeration, stink overpowered reason.

I grabbed Carl by his collar and sprinted for fresh air, gagging compulsively, dodging zigzaggedly at full speed, his sneakers squeaking madly, and we headed for the black husk of the empty arcade.

I dragged that dumb kid behind me, faster than any seventeen-year-old on the run, worried we would encounter a roll-down, garage-styled gate shuttering the entrance—that's just how they did back in the day—but no. We lucked out. The arcade was fully accessible.

A bit too accessible.

Point of fact, the enclosure was a glorified fishbowl, saturated in graffiti and empty of furnishings, a hip-high barrier the only thing left standing of the original entry. No glass, no drywall, no brick, no front wall to speak of, but no boards or bars or locks either. Just a heap of rubble in front. Booyah.

They must have swept the interior clean of games and goods before the mall shut down, leaving a shallow, wide, blackened room, reminding me of a laser-tag zone, devoid of obstacles, with the exception of a lone mop bucket.

I jumped the wall in a single bound and jerked the kid over and down beside me, heart in my throat. We gulped the clean, cool air.

Jonah sailed in silently and squatted low on the dry-ish ground, clutching the supplies to his chest. We were shoulder-to-shoulder, hip-to-hip, ducked low, my ears once again tuned for anything other than our labored breathing and the *drip-drip-dripping* of water from the atrium.

The spot offered limited cover at best.

If I could have acquired some real superpowers, I'd have gone with invisibility and ultrasonic hearing because the entire evening had turned into an exercise in both hide-and-seek and auditory processing.

The carrion smell hadn't followed us, and we were together—okay, the Jonah thing was turning out to be a sure bet—but you know what? For the first time all evening, I blanked on more positive thinking, and my skin prickled.

I didn't want to think about what might be inside those restrooms. Some unspeakable thing. Earlier, I'd imagined bodies falling from the ceiling and the zombie apocalypse. Had that been the blow to the head, or a heretofore unknown prescient ability?

Since I didn't believe in that Jenny of Oldstones crap, not in real life anyway, and because freaking out about what lived—or died—inside the mall solved nothing, I shoved fear aside. We had shit to do.

We held for long minutes. With no immediate threat outside the arcade, I pulled my hoodie up and ventured a peek over the ledge.

My head cleared the wall, making me easy pickings. At nine o'clock, the skeletal outline of the double-decked carousel rose toward heaven, or in this case, a narrow, sagging skylight. A LED illuminated the remaining, neglected, prancing animals fused to the platform. Wide gaps indicated missing pieces. That made sense given the general state of everything. Looked like all the light bulbs were busted. A few seats and the short staircase to the second level were intact. Ironically, the Parkway Mall sign perched solidly at the tip-top.

Jonah tugged my arm and pointed toward a purple shape—the hulking fountain where Carl had clobbered me a lifetime ago.

"What?" I mouthed, having no idea what he wanted me to see.

He pointed stiff, vee'd fingers at his eyes, and then back to the fountain. *Look*, he motioned vehemently. *Look.*

I looked, for crap's sake, and I didn't see anything.

Understanding dawned. I didn't see anything because the fountain lay shrouded in darkness. As I took in the big picture of the neutral zone, there were fewer LEDs all around, and beyond the mall center, the darkness deepened, the shadows thickened. The enchanting, twinkly forest we'd happily traipsed through earlier had become an opaque, unwelcome black.

Well, hell. A ton of lights were dead.

I didn't know why, maybe smashed or turned off, or maybe Dougie had programmed them to extinguish intermittently to increase our difficulty, but that was highly doubtful. His were simple, cheap, straightforward-timed LEDs from the hardware store. Multifunctional, fancy upgrades weren't available at our price point. Conclusion? The shooter extinguished the lights because he didn't want us to leave. Or he was making it damn hard to do so.

Or worse, he intended to corner us there.

Okay.

Jonah and I should have hunkered down, seeking shelter behind the wall. We didn't. We were in a pit of shadow, and unless a direct light found us, we were fairly invisible for now.

Turns out, my actual superpowers were vigilance, practicality, positivity, and of course, my stunning good looks.

His hand brushed against me. Honestly. Right there in front of people, his warm fingers interlocked with mine, and I didn't hesitate. He'd initiated three times, normalizing the intimacy, and it sounded lame, but my heart eased as we gazed on the nearly impossible course laid before us. We had hard work yet to do, with Carl, but shoulder-to-shoulder with Jonah, protecting a kid, we brought our best selves to the crucible—as a team.

It felt more right than anything I could remember. Ever.

Maybe a mild concussion made one delusional.

Jonah squeezed and leaned close, whispering, "Every adventure story ever written puts us in the role of protagonists. Hold that thought."

I held.

A shape detached from the murky edge of the neutral zone. Small, agile, moving rodent-like and swift, and heading straight for us. I squeezed Jonah's hand, leaned close, vocal cords constricted. "Holy crap. It's Piper."

"I see her."

A flurry of muted *pops* exploded from the floor above, and I dropped behind the wall, yanking Jonah with me as Carl pancaked to the ground.

"*Try again, you sick motherfucker!*" The atrium rang loud, defiant, and one hundred percent Dougie. A door slammed, and something clanged and rattled.

Piper summersaulted over the ledge, kicking me smack in my already bruised head with her miniature-sized Vans. She landed square between Jonah and me, crouching deep. Orange and pink braids had slipped from her cap. "I could see you two a mile away. You guys stink at hiding."

The urge to hug her overwhelmed me, so I went with my gut.

"Stop mauling me, Tommy. I don't like you that way." She hugged me back, her strong arms tight, her voice a hush, her clothes damp and musty.

All good. "Glad to see you too. I'll maul you if I want." I let her go. "Where'd you come from? Where is everyone?"

"TGI Friday's."

"The hell?"

"Yeah, I know. It's safe enough. We tried to get into Belks, but no go. I saw you guys run in here. Dougie trapped the shooter in a stairwell, otherwise you'd be toast right now. Maybe. He can't shoot for shit, but I still worried he'd already gotten you guys. We've been waiting a while. Don't do that again. You should have blown the whistle."

She hugged Jonah too, even as he shushed her and said, "We couldn't."

"It's okay," she assured him. "Dougie and I fixed all the doors, so the shooter is stuck inside a service stairwell for a minute. Dougie used the crowbar on the upstairs door, and I found some wire for the one down here. We should have just bashed that guy's brains in and tied him up." A grim dimple creased her cheek, and her eyes glittered. "Once he climbs those stairs a few times, he'll probably have a heart attack."

We should be so lucky.

Jonah said, "He'll try to shoot his way out."

She nodded. "Yeah. He's trying. Seriously, he'd have more luck blindfolded and firing from behind his back on horseback in a blizzard. I keep hoping he'll shoot himself."

"Eventually he'll run out of bullets." I lived in hope.

She didn't miss a beat. "He's like a fucking Pez dispenser. I don't know where he keeps his ammo—although he hasn't actually shot much. Just enough." She glanced around the arcade. "We need to get out of here."

"Best we could do. We passed the restrooms and—"

"Roger that. I puked. Left a puddle on the ground." She toed a silent Carl with her sneaker. "You okay, kid?" She smiled. "You've got something on your chin."

Carl hadn't budged. I thought maybe he'd suffered a fear-induced stroke when Piper jockeyed over the wall, carnival braids flying. He blinked a few times and his hand snaked up to cover his beard. He looked tired as he nodded.

She squinted. "He's looking for Carl. That's you?"

Carl grimaced. "Yeah."

"I don't know what the story is, but we need to hide you. I've heard things about this mall forever. About people living inside and the usual boogeyman folklore. I never believed it."

Carl's fat-lipped pout returned. "I told them. Nobody listens to me."

"I'm sorry, really I am, and I get it. But if Mr. Cline and Mr. Theroux tell you to jump, you ask how high. They have their reasons."

He nodded glumly. "Yeah, I know. Badass teachers. Can we leave now?"

Piper shook her head. "Wish it was that easy. I was scouting when the shooting started. I went all the way back to the door we used to get in, and it's blocked from the outside now." *Impossible.* Before I could formulate the word, Piper held up a hand. "I know. I have no clue how he managed it. Obviously he has some secret passage. Our door is a no."

Of course it was. "He wanted to corner us."

"Yeah. Pretty much. Hang on." She dug into her pocket and retrieved her own Nitecore NWS10. "Cover your ears." We did as instructed while she blew one quick note into the air.

She pocketed the whistle.

Jonah had been deep in thought, his attention fixed on the mop bucket. "What about the carousel?"

"What about it? Fine for a meeting point when we weren't in mortal danger, but we have a more secure spot now."

He clarified, "I meant, can the carousel be climbed?"

"Anything can be climbed," I said, and yes, I can be cocky.

The three adults jackrabbited up to assess the former rendezvous point, and popped directly back down. Carl didn't budge.

The carousel preceded the food court, right where the roof slanted toward a set of exit doors. Structurally, the ride appeared rickety as fuck, but stars glimmered buoyantly through the missing skylight. Best guess, roughly the height of a full-grown adult separated the top of the carousel's canopy from the roof.

Jonah gave me a crafty once-over. "Could it hold you?"

"Are you suggesting I'm too heavy?"

"Hardly. I'm just thinking if you can climb to the top, we only need one person to go through to the roof, retrieve a phone, and call for help. One very fast, very small, very light, very confident person you could toss through an opening and would stick a landing. A gymnast, let's say..."

Our gymnastics coach said, "Subtle. I'll do it. We just have to—"

Another whistle blast pierced the air, short, sharp, and far away.

Piper forgot whatever she'd been about to say. "We should head out." She spoke to Carl directly. "Stay close, keep low, and stick to the shadows. Don't muck around."

He sat up and nodded. Pale and sickly looking, the kid had proved he could still run. "It's not like I have a choice."

"Nope."

Jonah checked over the wall. No changes. His pep talk to Carl? "Do not fuck around."

"I said okay. *God.*"

He'd come this far, so I trusted he'd stay the course. I asked Piper, "Was that Dougie?"

"Vinnie—he's behind the escalator where we split earlier. But guys, before we go, I need to tell you something." She hesitated and took a breath. "First, he's okay. Totally fine. Just so you know. Chris got hit."

"Hit? With what? You mean with a bullet?" At her nod, guilt swamped me. "How? That guy can't hit anything."

"Except with a hammer," Carl added.

"Hey," Piper said. "You rain enough shit down on people, and someone eventually gets wet. Right in the shoulder. In a soft spot. He was lucky. Vinnie's taking care of him."

Gunshot wounds were something Vinnie had experience with. Shoulders were tricky, and again, I had virtually zero experience re: medical stuff, but Chris would need medical care. Stat. That was a given.

Tension eased from Jonah. He must have been mix-and-matching worst-case-scenario bullet wounds with his own knowledge of human anatomy. "He's alert?"

"Yeah. And saying I told you so, which isn't annoying at all. He's not bleeding. And he can sort of make a fist. I think Vinnie gave him a massive dose of CBD."

Jonah actually snorted. "Sounds like Vinnie. How long ago?"

"Second round of shots. That guy was firing in every direction. Just sort of walked into the zone and started spinning around in a circle, blasting his handgun."

He'd almost hit me and Carl. I went back to thinking our shooter had fired willy-nilly to elicit a specific response from us. As if he knew exactly what he was doing.

The whistle blew again. One short, sharp *toot*, and Piper gripped the edge of the wall, her gaze on the fountain. "Jesus Christ, we sound like pied pipers."

Jonah asked her, "Is that Vinnie or Dougie?"

"Hell if I know."

Carl rolled to his feet, still supple, though he winced. His sweatshirt, I realized, was the exact shade of blue as his eyes. Lose the goat beard and the neck tat, and he really did look twelve.

"You okay?" I already knew the answer. No. Not okay.

A curt nod. "Yeah. Stiff. Hungry. Sick. I'm ready."

I squeezed his shoulder gently. "I trust you'll do the right thing."

"Yeah, Mr. Cline. I'm here, right? But doesn't anyone have a cell phone?"

Piper beamed at him. "Yes, of course we do. We're just fucking with you."

The unlikely tinkle of shattering glass came from above. I was shocked any glass remained inside the mall to break. "So what's the plan?"

Piper shrugged. "Don't look at me. I'm just the messenger."

Jonah surprised me by grabbing the front of my sweatshirt and yanking me tight to his chest. "The plan is not to get hurt," he said against my ear. He squeezed tight, and I slanted to kiss him. I wasn't sure if that's what he meant to do, but it's what I meant to do.

Piper sighed. She either approved of this development, or thought we should speed things along.

Whatever. If things went south—and despite the whole protagonist pep talk, things probably would—this was *the* moment to express something. I sure as hell wasn't going to talk. Not with an audience. And words were overrated anyway.

Our kiss was swift and sweet, scented of pepper, tasting of mint, scraped by five o'clock shadow, and for a handful of seconds, spoke exactly what I needed to say.

Don't get hurt. I care about you. Why did we wait so long? Let's pick this up later.

He stepped away first.

Terror might rattle in the stairwell above, but I felt pretty confident about hooking up later tonight; i.e., something to live for.

Of course, Jonah morphed back into his robot self and scoped the carousel with a critical eye. "Are you thinking what I'm thinking?"

I had a feeling whatever he was thinking involved me personally doing something stupidly risky and unnecessarily dramatic. "Probably not. But I'm in."

FIGHT

Jonah spoiled everything. "Let's split up."

"Wh-what?" I blinked at him.

We were poised to leave, right? Together. Committed to the moment, stoked for our fool's mission to... Okay, we had no true plan other than getting Piper outside. Still. "Say again?"

Jonah gestured toward that wreck of a children's ride. "You, Piper, and the kid get to the carousel." For someone who'd been rather laissez-faire about what to do with our team earlier in the evening, he'd become astonishingly decisive. "I was at the top of the elevator shaft when Carl fell on you. It's not much of a technical climb, just a slippery one, so I'll join Dougie upstairs, and we'll go—"

"Nope."

His jaw snapped shut, and his eyes narrowed.

"That's not what I was thinking at all." My gaze bounced between point *a*, *b*, and *c*—round deathtrap, towering deathtrap, and sacrificial lamb. "We should stick together, get her out, and—"

"I want to go too," Carl said.

"—meet the others."

Carl added, "Seriously, yo. I'm going with her."

Jonah ignored him. "It's time to think tactically. The goal is safety. We need to divide."

For once his teacher tone didn't turn me on, and I ground my teeth. "Splitting up strikes me as problematic and unsafe." I turned to Piper, who could act as tiebreaker. "What do you think?"

"I think you never like anyone else's ideas—"

"Patently untrue," I said to her, and wow, that stung.

"Getting on the roof and calling for help is something I can do."

"And I said I'm onboard."

She jabbed a finger in the direction of the carousel. "We need cover so we don't get trapped there or picked off. Look at it. We'll be totally exposed on top. And we don't have much to work with. We need someone to cover us. Just in case he gets out."

Jonah tied the supply bag to his belt loop, which looked like a third leg and would knock him in the balls if he wasn't careful. "If anyone has a better plan"—he didn't say *Tommy*, but I heard my name plainly in his pause—"now's the time to share. I'm open."

I'd imagined Jonah and I embarking on a dashing, daring, heroic mission as a team. United. Along with Piper and…well, not Carl, who watched us in his silent, sweaty, pale, deer-in-the-headlights, I-want-to-hide kind of way, but we'd valiantly drag him behind us. Jonah and I would save our friends, the kid, and the day.

No guts, no glory.

My teammates waited for me to say something as water dripped like a metronome in the distance. And, maybe a trick of the light, I could swear a lick of fog swirled below the mezzanine.

Here's the adult learning curve in life—or mine, anyway. Adulting is about facing hard tasks, difficult decisions, and unpleasant realities. Stepping up to the plate even when you don't want to, because you have to. But sometimes adult life requires you to stand down, listen to others, and find the grace to compromise respectfully.

Therefore I admitted, "As far as actual, physical plans go, I have nothing. Carry on."

Jonah nodded as if he'd suspected as much. Obviously. "My gut says we rely on our individual strengths for the betterment of all."

Carl piped in, "I'm sure Beyoncé has an anthem for that."

"Shut up, Carl." Piper turned to Jonah. "You were saying?"

"You guys don't act like teachers."

Piper shrugged. "We're off the clock."

I said, "And she teaches gym."

Jonah stuck to the script. "Tommy runs faster, climbs higher, lifts heavier—" I *was* sort of the OG Parkour Geek Strongman Ninja of our group. I worked out a little. "So he's the brawn, and I'll be the brains."

"Wow, harsh." Carl gave me look. "Weren't you just sucking his face? He called you stupid."

"Shut up, Carl," I said. "He means well, even if his delivery needs improvement." A crash rang from across the neutral zone. Not a gunshot. Metal hitting metal. "Okay, Brainiac, you're on. Quickly. What do we do?"

Time ticked onward. And I hadn't imagined the fog. A rope of white hugged the floor near the fountain. Tendrils reached from the far corridor where we'd run, curling against the wall. The temperature had dropped.

Jonah conferred with Piper, "Where's Dougie?"

"Up top. Said to meet in fifteen—which is now, man. He's in an old card store behind the elevator. We're to gather everyone at Friday's and decide the next move."

"We need to keep the guy—" Jonah stopped and asked Carl, "Does your kidnapper have a name?"

"Ricky called him Herb. I thought he meant like, herb, you know? Kush." We knew. "But his name is legit Herb. Says so on his shirt."

Another curious detail. What kind of killer wore a freaking name tag?

Hello My Name Is: Your Worst Nightmare.

Piper frowned thoughtfully. "Wait a sec. There aren't a lot of Herbs, right? Not around here. Big guy. Red hair. Do you think he's Herbert the Pervert? The dude who hangs around the 76?"

How the hell? "How do you know that?"

"Our team bus used to fuel at the truck stop. Coach was like, that's Herbert the Pervert, do not engage."

Carl hunched his shoulders. "I don't know. He didn't molest me, so maybe not? But yeah. Probably. His hair's fire-engine red."

"Please stay on task." Jonah snapped his fingers, the sound alarmingly loud for the occasion, and was immediately followed by another *clang* from above us. He seemed psyched, bouncing on his toes, and ready. I knew I was. My shoulders were stiff with the need to move. My fists knotted. "I'll keep"—Jonah glanced between Carl and Piper and rolled his eyes—"*Herbert* occupied."

Hey, if he wanted to sacrifice himself on a suicide mission, who was I to stop him?

My brain complied. My mouth? Not so much. "With what? A few ping-pong balls and some creamer? Are you nuts?"

"Probably." He grinned. No shit. Mr. Robot had officially left the building. "You'll know it when you see it."

"So basically, you're going to wing it."

"Don't worry about me. Your task is to be a human catapult." He dug into his front pocket and exhumed a key fob, which he placed with care in Piper's outstretched palm. "And you get to the phones. Don't lose this."

The fob vanished inside her shirt. "Roger that."

Another shot dinged from the stairwell, and then an encore from someone's whistle. Once. Twice. Three times. Rapid and to the point. *Toot-toot-toot.*

Jonah held my gaze. "I'll go first. See you at TGI Friday's." Like we had a date or something. He instructed Piper, "Tell them where we are. I calculate it'll take twenty minutes from the time you call, so make every second count."

Piper nodded soberly. "Got it."

I touched his arm. "Just don't do anything more stupid than this already pretty stupid plan. Okay? Meet me."

"Confirmed." He spoiled this promise by yanking the mud-colored hoodie over his head and chucking it to Carl. "Swap with me."

Shit. His plan continued to spiral. At least he wore a long-sleeved undershirt, which would keep him warm while he waited for the ambulance to cart his ass to the hospital.

I didn't utter a damn word.

Carl removed the Hofstra sweatshirt, revealing a mosaic of purple and black tattoos across his chest and stomach. Only they weren't tattoos. They were bruises. And the kid wore a mesh tank top. That's all. He shivered as he covered himself.

Piper hissed watching him. "Oh man, kid. Go easy."

She shot me a look. What could any of us do for him other than stay the course and get him home?

Once Jonah had Carl's teen-sized sweatshirt donned, he yanked the hood up, winked roguishly at me, and scurried away, taking my heart. He retraced Piper's path. Confident. Capable. Brave. Busting at the seams. And barking fucking mad. I felt ill watching him run toward certain death.

Fog swallowed him.

Welp. That was that. Time to rally Team Carousel. "Carl"—I decided—"you're going with Piper."

He drooped. "Thank fucking God, man."

"You're welcome." I just hoped he didn't trip on the sleeves of Jonah's sweatshirt. "You up for it?"

"I am."

Piper nodded to me. "Solid move, Tom."

"Just don't lose him. He's quicker than he looks. And he needs to stay with you and speak with the police."

"Roger, dodger."

Carl sighed, grim-faced. "I guess I have to."

"Yes. You do. Okay. Let's go."

We were off. Vaulting, one, two, three in a row, over the barrier, we crouched low, hugged the gloom, and Carl's shoes called to every dog in town. *Squeak, squeak, squeak.*

No more questions or bitching, no endless yakking or terrible odors. The echo of Herbert clattering inside the stairwell hastened us along. Possibly he was constructing a weapon of mass destruction. Maybe a battering ram.

Carl trailed Piper. Closer to him in age, and while not exactly nicer than me, she was slightly prettier. They were nearly the same size too. If only the rest of his clothing didn't gleam like a signal fire in the dark. White shoes. Light-gray pants. White hair. He stood out.

We were going to die.

"Carl. Blend, man. Pull your hood up. Wipe some dirt on your pants. Something."

Herbert blasted at the wall or the stairwell door or the ceiling. He must be smugly assured we were trapped in his mall-sized maze. Probably having the best night ever. I bet he'd secured our special exit door as Jonah and

I were innocently making out under the escalator, just after we heard the sound of glass pinging. I wondered if he'd watched us.

Scratch that thought.

We rested against a column, judging the distance to the carousel. A patch of open space separated us, and two of Dougie's LEDs still burned, so not far, but no cover.

Piper pulled my sleeve. "Tommy. Do you hear that?"

"I don't hear anything."

"Exactly."

Herb must have completed his craft project. Or, if we were lucky, he'd gone into cardiac arrest.

Piper bit her lip, looking impossibly young, and responsibility for her safety bore down on me. "We need to go, champ. Seriously."

"Yeah. I know." Fog shrouded parts of the neutral zone, obliterating obstacles I knew for a fact littered the floor. Once I freed Piper and Carl, I would soon be cold, alone, damp, and tripping over debris as I fled, but so would Herbert. "Ready?"

Pale Carl gave me a flat look. Plainly, he'd been ready for two days.

I bolted, swift and silent, aiming for a tall, ebony-colored pony. My ride. When my foot hit the decking, I discovered a slick patch. Nothing felt stable either, and I slid, but plastered myself to the pony, one arm hugging its neck, the other gripping its gilded bridle.

A decade of rain from the open skylight had encouraged rot to settle in and make itself comfy. Unanticipated, debris from the roof covered everything. Given our luck, it contained asbestos. If the gunman didn't kill me, cancer might.

Dammit. We were alive. We were dry. We had half a plan. We were closer to an exit than we'd been in a lifetime, and if needed, I could slither through the fog and escape Herb the Perv like that snake Voldemort milked in *Harry Potter*.

Oh, plus, it wasn't raining. Five stars.

The next step seemed straightforward and well within my wheelhouse. Climb. As the carousel was two-tiered, and the second tier was shuttered by a wooden roof and thus, fuck that thing, I'd have to leap for a handhold closer to the outer edge.

No biggie.

One foot in the stirrup, then onto the pony's back, a hand to the inner spoke, let muscle memory take over from there. I could leap, grab a support pole, flip to the whatever it's called, and once on top, I'd scale the framework, my sneakers finding purchase on what I imagined were long, painted wooden arms jutting from the center pole. I'd find a perch and toss those two turkeys to freedom. Done.

The rest to be sorted later.

I checked above my head for signs of sharp edges, rotted wood, bats, broken bulbs, and asbestos. No bats, so things were looking up.

Because I'm six one, I snagged the top of my pony's pole—the crank gadget—and the carousel instantly became a wobbling mass of jell-oh my God.

The bony remains of the carousel were terrifyingly flimsy. And people used to pay to stick their kids on that thing for three minutes of peaceful entertainment at the end of a hellish shopping day. What the actual eff? Questionable parenting, in my humble opinion, and I was shocked a lawsuit hadn't hastened the closing of the mall, but also the carousel was in total alignment with Parkway's overall theme: Fucking Deathtrap.

In review, beyond the second tier, there was nothing to grip overhead except thin, rusted cables, some narrow metal slats likely covered in tetanus spores, and round steel poles. I could flip over the decorative edging—whatever *that* was called—and frankly, my carousel vocabulary could use some work. The painted wooden spectacle of frolicking ponies concealing the ugly interior framework—a facing? Yes, well, the *facing* was speckled with smashed light bulbs and spots of mold, but I could do it. I could climb anything. And, the facing offered a shield while we figured out how the hell to get to the top.

Check.

The climb tested more than my physically ability. There was physics to consider, momentum, trajectory, yes, and broken glass, and slippery mold, sure, but I struggled under the weight of causing Piper any harm.

Through the spokes, streaky clouds blurred the stars above us, and if I didn't move posthaste, rain would make escape impossible.

Piper scurried close, pressing against me, her expression stark as she eyeballed the structure up close. "Woof," she said under her breath.

"I know."

"Come on, Tommy. Challenge accepted. I'm good. Quit twiddling your thumbs and throw me through the skylight. I'll stick the landing. I'm trained for this."

Just toss her to the ledge, right? Mario Bros this crap. Leap, climb, save the princess. I could chuck that fucking kid into outer space—no problem— and still a notably bad idea. The evening had been chock-full of increasing difficulties, so why hesitate now? Level the fuck up.

Also, all things considered, our trio had the less onerous task.

I took a deep breath. "Okay, kiddies. Time to fly."

I scrambled onto my pony's chipped back. The floor rocked ever so slightly beneath us, and my number-twelve sneaker cracked right through the seat of the horse. Seriously. My shoe sank two inches deep in shattered circus plastic. Not the majestic move I anticipated. I caught myself one handed on the gilded pole.

I hated everything and everyone at that exact moment, and still pulled my act together, my sneaker free, and utilizing my excellent wingspan, launched off the pony's back. I snagged a support pipe, monkey-barred until I dangled from the outer lip of the carousel—again two-stories high—then flipped seamlessly onto the swaying fucking disaster above us.

Cables creaked. Debris sprinkled onto the platform. And the goddamn carousel moved. Spun slowly on its axis, wheeling a foot or so counterclock-wise, and not merrily. Carl and Piper were out of sight below me. Sure, they were fine, but now we faced the arcade, closer to being exposed to the neutral zone.

Carefully laid plans are bullshit, and since we didn't have one of those anyway, I let go.

Fortune favors the bold.

I dropped upside down, knees hooked over a pipe, feet tucked under a cable, and partially hidden by the facing. With a wish and a prayer, I grabbed those little fucking lightweights, and they climbed me like a ladder. Another kick to the head by random sneakers. How many times now?

Our ascent wasn't pretty, but we weren't being sponsored by REI. We scrabbled for purchase as the carousel groaned in agony. We were up, flattening ourselves from view.

The carousel gaily spun another few feet, making hella racket.

Not part of the plan.

If a soundtrack existed in some cosmic version of my life on film, our little ride would be underscored by a circus calliope poop-pooping us toward certain doom.

We teetered to a stop, and held. Hardly breathing, eye level with the second floor, we had the center pole yet to reach. Once there, I'd have to balance on a dime, overhead-press Piper, toss her a good seven feet into the air, and previously unforeseen, spin in slow-mo.

Oh, and then I'd have to repeat the process. Dos Amigos.

On the plus side, Piper and Carl weren't deadweight. They were fit and able and had adrenaline working in their favor, and nothing makes the impossible possible like the threat of imminent death.

I could do this. My gym sessions involved flipping truck tires up a hill four days a week and carrying sacks of grain on my shoulders and all the happy, Spartan-inspired good stuff. I'd spent most of the last decade working to become more like Thor because the weak, geek, queer motif hadn't paid off for me, personally.

Another plus? We had an unobstructed view of the neutral zone through a series of cutout charioteers racing along the facing.

Across the mall, where darkness intertwined with smoky curls of mist, danger arrived at the top of the floating staircase in the form of an oversize, pasty-faced ginger.

Herbert. The Pervert. Man. What took him so long?

An excellent opportunity for Dougie and Jonah to offer the you'll-know-it-when-you-see-it ping–pong-ball diversion.

Carl stiffened. "Mr. Cline. Get me out of here."

"Working on it."

Time spent in the stairwell had done a number on Herb's attitude. He looked tense, even from a distance and in the dark. Gone was the humming, carefree, confident serial killer of thirty minutes ago.

Puffy fingers and jowly cheeks, and very, very red hair, he muttered unintelligibly. The sound carried across the mall as slimy gobbledygook. I pegged him for under forty. He was clothed in black pants and what appeared to be a white button-down shirt. Like a waiter. Not exactly the avatar I envisioned for a crazed killer.

Guy must go through a ton of stain remover.

Herbert could have passed for middle management at, say, a used-car dealership. He possessed the failure-to-launch vibe one acquires from living in their mom's basement and blowing holes in juvenile delinquents for sport.

He crept down the stairs, and forget middle management, think door-to-door Bible salesman. You know. The kind who lures junkies into his car with the promise of a fifteen-dollar blowjob.

Man, I'm a judgmental jerk. I know it. I own it. But when I'm right, I'm right.

Possibly—and here the cogs in my brain squealed to a halt—he'd been a mall cop.

As I squinted at Herbert plodding stiffly down each step, he really did resemble a mall cop. And maybe the shirt and pants were part of a uniform.

Paul Blart, only sans tie and Segway, completely crackers, and wearing a holster and a gun.

Herbert paused on the landing, a dark bag in his left hand, gripping the railing with his right. He surveyed the area.

We barely breathed.

His existence at Parkway Mall made a sick sort of sense to me now. He'd have every square inch of the massive structure, inside out and backward, memorized. He probably still had a working set of keys.

Since Parkway had been closed for a decade—my mind went from dead stop to leap-frogging all over the place—had he been here the whole time? Hiding? Living in a store? Dressed in his old uniform? Eating SpaghettiOs? Using those toilets? Snatching wayward boys from the 76 and playing unspeakable games with them?

Impossible. No way. Someone would have noticed. Someone would have searched for a missing child. Teenagers don't just disappear—

Who was I kidding? Yes. They do. Unwanted teenagers disappear every single day, and often from places exactly like a truck stop, or a dead mall.

Who would look for a Ricky? Or a Carl, although I suspected Carl had family who cared, and a sister he cared about. Maybe I'd turned soft. Maybe I decided I liked him.

Liking him didn't matter. Every kid deserved to be cared about. To have someone to look for them. Someone to save them when they were in danger. Someone responsible for their welfare.

As I took a serious, assessing look at Herbert the Pervert, he continued his painful descent in those hard-soled shoes. Walking in the wide open as if he was bulletproof, which I supposed he was since none of us had a gun.

Kidnapper. Killer. Asshole.

"Carl"—a voice as pleasant as a coffin full of worms—"I see you brought some new friends to play with. I have a present for you. My way of saying thanks."

He hefted the sack, weighty and damp, and I didn't want to know, not ever, what was inside that bag. No.

What an excellent moment for an explosion, *Jonah*. Chop-flipping-chop.

We waited. Piper behind me. Carl panting faintly beside me. His expression telegraphed exactly what I was thinking.

Where are they?

Jonah should have finished his Rube Goldberg Saves The Day Cremora in a Jar Machine. What would that take? Five minutes? And Dougie would be…doing something else.

Herb crept along, at last reaching the first floor, and fog parted as he headed toward the Red Zone. The elevator blocked our view to the hallway beyond, but something clearly caught his attention.

Piper touched my arm, signaling toward the roof. *Let's go. Now.* She didn't speak. She didn't need to.

We crawled with care toward the center pole. Words that don't begin to do justice to the reality of traversing a four-inch-wide bendy, slippery, metal slat.

Hand over hand, we climbed hunched over, dead quiet, and in slow motion. My thighs screamed. My back screamed. My sneakers slid. White-knuckling metal until I thought my fingers would bleed, but we were focused, and God bless us, unseen.

I arrived first. Carl probably wanted me to lead in case Herb took note and aimed for the largest target. Understandable. Piper wanted me ahead because I was the base of our human pyramid. And I chose to be first because I wanted to get the job over with.

A wide hub held the spokes on what had to be a giant turn shaft. Above which, a solid banner was bolted to the center pole. Written in Papyrus: *Parkway Mall.* Roughly a couple of feet tall and maybe six feet long. I straddled that banner and braced my legs.

Good thing none of us was afraid of heights, because we were fairly high in the air. And we weren't exactly hidden. I held my breath as Herbert idled in the neutral zone, his lower legs lost in a puff of mist. A single glance in our direction and the jig would be up.

My heart galloped as I consulted the stars, and then I checked across to the elevator, where shadows seemed fixed and sleepy. Gray below, and maybe a flicker of something blue—

The atrium rang with the sound of metal striking metal. The suddenness almost knocked me from my perch. I didn't take my eyes off Herb, who armed himself and proceeded at the same knuckle-dragging pace toward the elevator.

Was this the thing I was supposed to know when I saw it? Because I didn't see a goddamn thing.

Piper hauled me into the present. She tapped her chest, right where she'd stowed Jonah's car keys. *"Now,"* she mouthed.

I lifted her. Damn, she weighed nothing, and I squatted as she settled her feet on my thighs. She faced outward—the prow of our very own ship—and as I straightened and tossed her into the air, she launched off my legs. Her arms flung forward, adding momentum, and she super-girl'd herself to the ledge. Holy hell, that Piper. She snagged the lip of the skylight, sure and true, and hopefully, not sliced to ribbons.

I almost toppled backward as I kept my eye on her, but Carl grabbed me, shouldering my weight, his face set. No hesitation, the spindly kid shored me up until I regained my balance.

Piper strong-armed herself to the edge of the window—Sarah Connor had nothing on her—and I watched for any sign or sound of pain or weakness. Hardly. Once her hips were parallel with the roof, she swung through the skylight.

A shot sounded, and I almost lost my perch again.

Herb wasn't shooting at us. He aimed at the elevator, then charged the tower. *"Don't you go anywhere."*

Luckily, he faced the opposite direction from us, and Carl prodded, "Mr. Cline. I'm good to go now."

Piper's face appeared in the skylight, her braids dangling. "Like, right now."

So I tossed that scrappy survivor like a bale of summer hay, and Piper latched on to his bruised, angry wrists. She unceremoniously hauled Carl to the roof. A quick salute from Piper and *poof,* they vanished.

Fly like the wind.

Another hail of gunshot, and I finally lost my balance for real and fell ass-first into the darkness.

EXIT

You know at the end of an action film when the actors are surrounded by emergency vehicles, and a helicopter arrives, and there's a cacophony of crazy energy, but invariably, the lead is sitting half inside the police cruiser, wearing a space blanket and drinking black coffee from a Styrofoam cup and being chatted up by the smoking-hot action hero?

That's the moment I longed for as I hit a few uncomfortable items on my journey into a pit of darkness.

A pipe...some cable...a slat maybe? I felt them all. Something clanked. The aforementioned calliope? Before I could be impaled by an embarrassingly pedestrian piece of bullshit, I landed without ceremony in a heap on the floor.

I groaned, loudly. Fuck keeping silent. That hurt.

The inner workings of a carousel aren't soft, FYI, and I'd been lashed to hell. The immediacy of my throbbing ankle was an alarming new development, but I was alive and breathing, I hadn't blacked out, not so far as I could tell, and I was free of skewers despite falling through the center housing— basically a well of sharp, pointy mechanical things that could have killed me.

A miracle.

I retrieved my mini light, and one glance at the blood splattering my hands had me cutting the light. Okay, then. I put my assessment on pause. Nothing to see here, folks. Just Tommy, hemmed in by a ton of debris and lying alone in the dark. Bleeding. A little.

As I'd done my part to set the kid free and send Piper for help, I shut my eyes for a sec or two. Maybe three. Rebooting.

A womanly wail cut short my siesta.

Definitely Herbert. Maybe we'd reached the critical moment when I would know/ hear/see Jonah's inspired diversion. I didn't have a clue. Technically, I'd been the one creating a diversion for them instead of the other way around. *You're welcome.* And yeah, my fall lacked subtlety, but I definitely distracted the hell out of Herbert and everyone else.

The scream subsided into a wail. *"Help me. Help me."*

Was he fucking kidding me? For the first time all evening, my blood boiled. Did he actually think— No. I would not help him. I couldn't help myself, and I was one of the good guys.

Whatever was happening out there, it wasn't my turn to take charge. I trusted Jonah and Dougie to be on top of the situation, because to think differently would land me in an even darker place. They were fine. They had things under control. So. Chin up. Trust your friends.

I no sooner thought those words when a small explosion rocked the mall and nipped Herbert's pleading dead short. Something massive crashed to the floor, and the sound stretched for multiple heartbeats as the ground shuddered under my butt. Earthquake? Not likely.

The carousel squealed, and another handful of sharp things rained down. I covered my head, which would help nothing if the giant gear engaged and mangled me.

Long seconds later, the noise ended. A few *bangs* and *clatters* and *thuds* followed, and then the earth settled. The carousel stood. And I was done.

Seriously. GAME OVER.

I flicked my light. A flurry of dust sifted from above like carcinogenic snow.

Something major had occurred in the neutral zone. Something large had collapsed or fallen. The roof?

No way. I refused to believe the combined weight of Piper and Carl had brought the building down. Impossible.

Maybe something had exploded, something more impressive than Jonah's box of ping-pong balls. Or, maybe the elevator had followed through on Dougie's earlier prediction and imploded. Did elevators implode? The lift itself could have fallen. It seemed destined to do so. Plus, the guys hadn't had a whole lot to work with to set up a diversion of such magnitude, and what Jonah did have seemed laughably inadequate.

Thoughts scattered. Anyone could have been inside the elevator. In or above on the roof.

I should investigate. Find my way free of the mess and open a door. Things sounded safer and less horror-movie soundtrack outside my cozy metal nest, but silence had proved to be misleading all evening, so I pocketed my light and waited. Eyes closed, breathing through the pain in my leg, until a Nitecore tooted super close to me. More notes followed from farther away.

And then, from a long distance, Piper's whistle. So thready, I could have imagined it.

Before I could join their call—I was probably the only one of us who hadn't blown their whistle—a panel opened in the wall and a light beamed in my face. I was too tired to shade my eyes, so I blinked weakly and offered a peace sign. "Hey, yo, what up."

"Hey yourself. You okay?" The first thing I saw other than blinding white light was the blue sweatshirt.

Jonah.

No. I was not okay. Not at all. The mere thought of standing upright made me want to lie down, meaning perhaps I'd snapped my ankle after bruising every other part of myself.

Naturally, I nodded. "Yeah. I'm good."

"You don't look good, you liar."

"I could use a beer."

A white nimbus outlined Jonah as Dougie materialized with a LED in his hand, illuminating the deathtrap where I lounged.

Dougie frowned. "Tommy. You didn't blow your whistle."

"I didn't capture your flag, Chief."

Detritus choked the space. Poles, wire, metal sprockets, broken mirrors. Jonah picked a path, coming the few scant feet to assist me. His face and hair were gray with dust. I'm sure I looked the same, or worse. At least he wasn't bloody. "I think I broke the carousel for good."

Dougie winced, and flakes of cement fell from his hair. "I think you broke yourself too. That wasn't part of the plan."

"Plans are overrated." Took me a sec, but I palmed a bald spot on the wall and attempted to haul myself to my fee…foot. Whoa. My right ankle was a firm no. Also, standing felt akin to work, and work on a Friday night was something to be avoided. "Are we good? Did you— What'd you do?"

Jonah slung an arm around me. He felt warm and smelled good as he wedged his shoulder under my arm. "I'm not proud of this, but I didn't do much. The elevator collapsed on top of him. Herbert must have shot something free near the roof, right before Dougie and I trapped him inside. We planned to wait for help, until he saw me and went bananas."

"I'm sure you let him see you."

Jonah shrugged. "Maybe."

Dougie kicked something free from the doorway. "Where else are you hurt?"

"Is everywhere an option?"

"Looks that way."

They helped me through a garishly painted door. "Hard to believe Herb hadn't stuffed anyone inside here."

"Thank God for small favors," Jonah said and half carried me down the first step.

Man. Everything hurt, and not the workout-related hurt where you know you're going to be ripped and mean. No. This was the I-require-medical-assistance kind of pain. "So what's next?"

Dougie said, "Next? You sit here for a hot minute while I retrieve Vinnie and Chris. Then we'll wait together for the police." He squinted across the neutral zone. "So. You guys okay here?"

I wasn't sure if he was asking if we were physically able to wait, or mentally equipped. I'd only fallen two stories. Chris had been shot. We could do nothing about the rest. "I thought the plan was to meet them."

"Chris can walk; you can't. Simple math. So. Sit tight."

Good to know Chris could walk. Galling to admit I couldn't. "Hey, Chief. Those lights were A+. Really awesome. Let's not do this one again."

Dougie smiled, and chalk-white lines feathered around his eyes. "At least not until you can walk without aid. There's a farm upstate I'm looking into for a paintball weekend." Dougie balanced the LED on top of a pony's saddle, and shadows galloped across the carousel. "Could be fun. Think it over."

He strode from the decking, things jangled and shook, and he headed into Blue Territory to find our friends, dust and cement falling from his clothing like dandruff. I parked my ass on a step as he faded into the mist.

"You need to elevate your foot." Jonah settled next to me, and when I turned to accommodate him, he hooked my right leg over his lap. Nice. Except the throbbing in my foot intensified.

We were tall guys, and a tight fit for a children's ride, so I leaned against the ornate railing. Jonah took my hands gently, turning them over. He used Carl's sweatshirt to swipe at tiny lacerations. My blood stained the fabric, joining Carl's and Ricky's. "You're a fucking mess, Cline."

"Yeah. I feel pretty good, all things considered."

"You usually do." He ran a palm over my shin and not in a sexy way. He inched casually toward my distressed appendage as if he hoped I wouldn't notice.

No thanks. "Would you mind if we take a rain check on exploring that? Wait for a doctor? And a sedative?"

"Yes. I mind. Tough it out."

"Fuck. Fine. Tell me what happened." My shoe became ten sizes too small as Jonah touched my ankle cautiously. I hissed, shut my eyes, and counted. One. Two. Three—

"Herb's dead, obviously. Crushed under the elevator."

Gross. But good riddance, and he deserved worse. "You saw him?"

"Affirmative. His feet stuck out like the Witch of the East." Jonah picked free the laces of my sneaker and gradually, professionally, slid my foot free. Instant relief. I actually sighed until he tried to place the shoe in my hand. "You'll want to hang on to this."

"Will I?" I still had my eyes closed. "Between the asbestos, the mold, the blood, the shit, and the smell, my current plan is to chuck everything

I'm wearing. Or set it on fire. Too soon to tell. You still have the ping-pong balls?"

"I do. Excellent call." His hand tenderly explored my ankle. He distracted me by adding, "I'm just relieved the elevator didn't collapse when I scaled it earlier."

"Oh my God. I totally forgot that. For the record, yours was a stupid plan."

"So you've told me."

A siren sounded, far off, the noise wafting from the hole in the sky. I finally looked at Jonah, wondering if he'd noticed help was on the way. He stared in distressed silence at the rubble. His face set and serious. I followed his gaze, and out there, hard to tell where the dust ended and the fog began. The entire area was shrouded in gossamer gray.

He kept quiet, and still, except for his thumb absently stroking my shin.

"Did you see anything else, Jonah?"

A short nod. "Yeah. Carl called it. Herb lived here. There's a porta potty and a camp stove—and there were other things. We searched for more weapons, but he must have stored them somewhere else, or he only had the one. All we found were clothes, photos, wallets, a few broken cell phones, some jewelry. A couple of toys."

Oh, man. "Like…what? Souvenirs?"

"Or trophies. They were arranged that way. He used a fitting room in the back as a holding cell, Dougie told me. I didn't venture as far inside. Carl's damn lucky."

"That poor kid."

I thought about Carl suffering two days with Herbert. The kid was okay. Strong. A fighter. If we could only do something about his neck tat…

"I saw you throw him through the window." Jonah grinned at me. "I wondered if you were helping him or yourself."

"Pain in my ass, but he's actually all right."

The low wail of a siren floated closer, louder now, and a light rain began to fall.

"You did good." Jonah took a deep breath. "I don't want you to think less of me, but I can't be present when the cops come inside here. When they find what they'll find. It's not in my wheelhouse. I know we can't avoid the facts—we're part of this thing now—but just not tonight. I can't—"

"Think less of you? Are you nuts? How in hell could I ever?" I gripped Jonah's hand and stared him square in the eyes. "You were a fucking rock star. A leader. Okay, the plan was not your usual thing, but you never hesitated, and I respect you for that. You make things happen, and because you do, we're safe. You saved my life. You saved that kid's life. So yeah, man, I got you. I have you. Whatever you want. We'll talk to the police, briefly, and then you will be my date to the hospital. No problem. You're fucking awesome."

"Back at you." He choked for the barest second and squeezed my hand. "You were unbelievable. Until you fell. That was terrifying. You were on top of the world, like a superhero tossing people to safety, and then I blinked and you just vanished." He brushed my knee, which actually made my foot throb harder; still, his intentions were nice.

"Me? I didn't do much. I'm the muscle."

"You were good to that kid. I was ready to throttle him."

"No way."

"Way. I… You're just a solid human, Tom. I should have followed through a while ago and asked you to do something. I'm not particularly adroit at this."

"A—what?"

He snorted. "Adroit, you fucker." His thumb stroked the back of my hand. "Truth? The thought of going to my car skeeves me out."

"Yeah. Me too. Maybe we can chuck those as well."

Beyond the neutral zone, people were on the move. A light flared, then another, and growing noises carried from the parking lot.

Jonah leaned into me. "You want to have dinner tomorrow?"

"Not really," I said. "I'd rather have breakfast."

"Done."

* * * * *

A good-looking EMT in a crisp uniform covered me with a blanket after strapping me to a gurney. Red, white, and blue lights streaked the sky above, and as Thor is my witness, not the way I envisioned my evening ending. Not really my best self at that moment. Especially when Vinnie appeared and harassed the EMT. "Hey, man, can you give us a sec?"

The EMT looked at him incredulously. "What? No. I can't."

"We've been through an ordeal, dude. Seriously. Step off. He's not dying, and I need a minute with my brother. Our mom is going to be so worried." Vinnie wore his I'm-ex-military face—the I-would-never-ever-lie-because-I'm-a-Vet face—and as soon as the EMT, narrow-eyed, stomped away, Vin leaned close and whispered, "You want some CBD, Tommy? Take the edge off? It's been a shit night for all of us, and it's a proper dose. It'll help."

How was Vinnie completely unscathed? Not a drop of blood or a speck of ash on him. I bet he hadn't even broken a sweat. He did have crumbs on his chest, and they looked suspiciously like flakes of pastry. Or Pop-Tarts.

"I hate you."

"Nah. You love me. But you're sure?"

"No. I'm not sure. Maybe. I don't know. Will it show in a piss test?"

"No way. I do this all the time. Scout's honor."

"You were never a scout." I believed him about the piss test, plus I no longer cared. My ankle had swelled so big, it needed its own zip code. "Sure. I bet Carl could use some too."

"Who the fuck is Carl?"

* * * * *

Parkway Mall was resurrected. A rainbow of multicolored lights bathed the building, and law-enforcement types marched industriously about, every one of them with distinct and important purposes. There were cars, and trucks, and reporters—and coroners.

Rain sizzled on the pavement, and I could swear I heard a helicopter in the distance. My friends gathered around me. Chris relaxed on the end of a gurney with an ice pack on his shoulder and an IV dripping from a bag Piper held in the air. She'd lost her cap.

"That was fun," she said.

Everyone murmured their agreement.

We'd freed a kid, killed a serial killer, I'd made out with the guy I had a thing for, and while I lay there with a foam stabilizer encasing my foot, Jonah and I held hands for the fifth time.

Life was good.

Across from us, Carl sat sideways in the back seat of a police cruiser, wrapped in a silver blanket, drinking from a Styrofoam cup, and speaking with a very attractive police officer.

That's the picture forever burned into my mind from our night. Not the bad shit. Just a kid. Alive and safe. Drinking coffee. And smiling.

We'd done that. The six of us. Carl had my phone number in his pocket, and I had his sincere thanks in return.

Not bad for a Friday.

Piper swung the saline bag. "So next week? Same time?"

"Yeah, I think I can do Friday," Chris said. "I'll have to check my phone, you fucking idiots."

Dougie waved to the EMT, who stalked over to cart me on my way. "I was telling Tommy there's this farm upstate…"

And I drifted away, the CBD doing its thing, and Jonah holding my hand.

THE END

A COUNTRY FOR OLDMEN

BY DAL MACLEAN

Inspector Calum Macleod has returned to the Western Isles of Scotland to bury a part of himself he can't accept. But the island has old secrets of its own. When a murderer strikes, Calum finds his past can't be so easily escaped.

CHAPTER ONE

It was all about discretion. Making the effort not to be noticed. It was about not letting anyone down.

A sharp midmorning summer breeze blew away the sounds of Calum's heavy car door clunking shut and the tailgate opening and closing to let out his father's ecstatic dog. Then, after a shifty look around, Calum set off with long-legged strides toward the beach, the dog trotting at his heels.

He'd parked his Subaru 4x4 off the main road at the Braighe, two bays separated by a narrow strip of land, where the Minch chewed into the eastern peninsula of Point from both sides.

When Calum was a child, he'd always hoped they'd drive up the road one day and find the sea had won; that they'd be living suddenly on another island, all of their own. But twenty-odd years on, the road was still there, and the medieval Ui chapel, and Aignish cemetery nestled next to it, all still defying the ruthless grey water.

The cemetery was the reason for Calum's stealth. His father and mother were at church, attending the funeral service of the graveyard's next occupant, a *bodach*—an old man—called Murchadh Toddy, and Calum's mother had made it very clear she didn't want the mourners to see her son jogging happily along the beach in the background.

So Calum had negotiated the kind of compromise he'd become used to since he'd come home. He did some of the things he wanted, but he made sure to hide them. A step-change from his time on the mainland, if he thought about it, when he'd felt safer conforming on everything. Now that he was back on the island, these little, pointless, harmless rebellions seemed to help.

Calum clambered down over the spew of big rocks at the end of the path, the dog mincing gracefully ahead of him, until they both jumped down onto the sands of Broad Bay. The sun climbed behind broken clouds, forcing thick poles of light down through the grey gaps, not sunshine in the accepted mainland sense of golden warmth and happiness, thinner and colder than that. But still...better than nothing.

The beach was long, pale gold, empty, as beaches in the Outer Hebrides tended to be, and the tide was advancing, breakers ten-deep, cresting far out from the shore, then rolling in, in foaming, frozen perfection.

The wind felt even sharper so close to the Minch, laced with salt and ozone; perfectly, inhumanly fresh. There was no pollution, no smoke or stench, just the pure, clean, hungry sea. It was so easy to imagine Viking longboats hitting the shore there, as they once had, or reaching the land clearly visible on the far side of the bay, at Back.

Calum began to run, fast and hard, earbuds in but no music playing yet to cover the sound of his trainers thudding on the compacted sand; his deepening breath. He had the morning off, he was running in absolute freedom, and he could convince himself that he'd been totally right to move back home.

The dog—Shep—raced joyously alongside him. Little imagination was wasted on the islands for something as trivial as naming a dog. But Shep was a personality in himself, a clever, cowed collie who'd been raised with strictness and absent, occasional affection by Calum's parents. To them, he was a working dog, a kind of organic tool.

Taking Shep for a walk or a run was a mainland conceit—he got more than enough exercise on Calum's parents' croft. But Calum had returned from his years away with his modified view of dogs as pets deserving attention, and Shep could hardly believe his luck. Calum's mother said he was ruining the dog. His father, as usual, said nothing.

Calum glanced up at the high ground on his left as he belted past it—a long grassy hill shored up by an elderly stone-and-cement wall.

The church service would be over by now, and the funeral procession would have begun, the coffin carried from the nave on a bier on the shoulders of relatives and village men, and out onto the road. Everyone who wanted to would take their turn, for up to a mile of slow, marching farewell, before sliding the casket into the hearse and breaking for their cars to begin the snaking trail to Aignish.

His parents, like many people on the Island of Lewis, were unflinchingly, morbidly serene about death, with all the confidence of the deeply religious. And even before he left at eighteen, Calum had seen too many funerals, taken along as a matter of course. He'd helped carry the coffins of numerous neighbors and his own grandparents, and stood looking down into their graves on the bleak mound of the cemetery, blown by the sea gales on both sides.

The last funeral he'd been to had been his grandfather's, on a glorious July day, hot and clear and rare, just before he left for university.

He could remember as if it had been branded into him, a phrase from a Gaelic psalm that had been sung...precented...in the church, before they set off with *Seanair*—grandfather—on their shoulders, all matched for height so that the coffin and the body inside didn't slip or slide. If he closed his eyes,

Calum could still feel the oppressive weight of the oak, and the symbolism of it—the boy carrying his father's father to his grave.

That phrase had stuck with him...the description of where Seanair was going...*an talamh trom*...the heavy earth. And taking his own handful of it, the heavy earth, and his turn to throw it onto the coffin, before he took up a spade with the other men and began to shovel banks of clay soil back into the hole, on top of Seanair, as the sun shone in a Mediterranean-blue sky and the sea stretched and waited.

He'd decided then and there, that was going to be his last funeral, though it was a hopeless hope. But at least he could resist funerals as social occasions. His mother, on the other hand, had become steadily more religious, so anything church-related—funerals, Worships, communions, services—had her full attention.

Shep, now soaking wet, grinned his thrilled doggy grin as he danced ahead of Calum with a poor excuse for a stick gripped in his jaws. But even with the whole expanse of sea and shore stretching for miles in front of him, all his, Calum found he wasn't in the mood for a chase.

Maybe the first euphoria of moving back for good—making that final decision and leaping into it—had started to pass.

Maybe it had been the grinding familiarity of watching his mother that week in her dark-blue hat and coat, and sensible, thick, flesh-colored tights, setting off, Bible in hand, for every night of the pre-funeral Worship at Murchadh Toddy's house.

Maybe it was the claustrophobia of the feeling that he'd never really left; never absorbed anything solid enough to distinguish him from his culture.

Maybe it was that all his experiences away from here were starting to feel like someone else's life.

Or maybe it was the knowledge that he'd walled himself in by choice, willingly mortared in each brick, watching dangerous freedom slowly disappearing out of view through the gap.

He jerked to a halt and turned around sharply, furious with his own melodrama, then started back along the beach, full tilt, eating up the distance toward the point he'd clambered down.

He was panting, but he got his breath back quickly as he and Shep climbed back up over the rocks.

Running was something else his parents side-eyed as pointless, but he was determined to keep his peak fitness through that, and his visits to a gym in Stornoway. Maybe it was vanity; maybe it was survival.

The short drive back to his parents' house in Shulibost was accomplished before the funeral procession could reach the village. But as he was about to turn into the lane up to the house, an elderly woman waved him down; raincoat on, handbag on shoulder, newly disembarked from the Stornoway bus.

Chrissie *Goirt* Macdonald had been a fixture of Calum's childhood. She'd be in her seventies now, white-haired, bespectacled and still full of relentless energy. She lived with her awkward husband, Angus, and their awkward middle-aged son, Norman—*Tormod* in Gaelic—bizarrely nicknamed Lucky. And theirs was the same dynamic as Calum's family: a lively, dominant, charismatic woman and quiet men bobbing in her wake. As a child, Calum had believed every family was like that.

He wound down the driver's window.

"Is that you wasting energy running nowhere again, *a' Chalum*?" Chrissie teased as she crossed the narrow road to his car. "You can do my floors if you want."

Calum laughed. He couldn't help but love Chrissie. She was less religious than his mum, more accepting of new ideas. She, for example, hadn't gone to Murchadh Toddy's funeral.

"You're like a tourist with those runs and walks. That dog must be bewildered."

After ten years away Calum heard the Lewis accent almost like an outsider would hear it—a kind of flat, exaggerated singsong, like nothing else. Maybe he was more of a mimic than he'd thought, because he'd been told by locals that he now sounded like an Englishman.

"I must have been infected on the mainland," he said.

"You must." Then, slyly, "Your mam was telling me you went out with a girl from the town." Chrissie grinned as if what she was saying was terribly risqué. But it explained why she'd stopped him. "That's the spirit. The only way to deal with a broken heart is just get over it."

The whole brisk, stiff-upper-lip island psyche was there—*just get over it*. If only Calum knew what it was he was getting over.

"It's a shame your old girlfriend couldn't come with you. But…once the *cianalas* takes hold, *a' bhròinean*, no Gael can help coming home. Your mam and dad are happy you're back, though. And you have such a good job!"

Calum made a noncommittal noise and held his smile. Invasive personal remarks and ignoring privacy were so much part of his experience growing up, that his own defensiveness startled him. Everyone knew your business here. Or thought they did.

"Your mam said your new girl's related to the Eoripe Morrisons," Chrissie swept on. "The Reverend Alexander Morrison?"

She sounded genuinely impressed by the church connection, which was why Calum's mother had told her, he supposed. That, and his mum's desperate eagerness for Calum to settle down and give her grandchildren.

"We've only been out once, Chrissie," Calum said. He knew he had to nip this in the bud before news of an imminent engagement spread, the way his last desultory relationship had attained a gossip-status of Tragic Romance. "I might end up an old bachelor."

"Oh, *mo chreach*, you can't let that happen! A handsome fellow like yourself. What was it they called you at school? Orlando Bloom!"

Calum glowered. "I look nothing like Orlando Bloom."

Chrissie peered down at him assessingly as he clenched his jaw, then relaxed it at once. Because, okay, perhaps he had a sharp jawline. And yes, maybe, he had large brown eyes. And his hair was… Okay, it was dark brown. And a bit wavy. But that didn't mean he looked like Orlando bloody Bloom.

Chrissie didn't usually get vibes, but she seemed to decide not to push the point.

"Well, in any case, *a' gràidh, tha u glè snog.*" Calum shook his head in despair. *Snog* meant pretty. "All we used to get from our Julia was Legolas this and Calum that. And you wouldn't go out with anyone!" Julia was Chrissie's only grandchild, the offspring of her daughter *Seonag*—Joan.

Chrissie shrugged. "*Co dhiù*, she got over it. And I'd better get on. *Tioraidh*, a' gràidh!"

She didn't wait for his mumbled goodbyes, but strode back across the main road and up the hilly side-road toward her own house, her stocky figure radiating energy and imperturbable good humor.

Calum looked after her, feeling as if he'd just been slapped around the head; then he put the car in gear and drove up the lane to park outside the house.

The sun had given up the struggle for the day; the sky was grey, and the air was full of the chatter of the starlings sitting on the roof of the weaving shed and lining the telephone wires.

Orlando Bloom. Calum had the name attached to him now as if it had been branded on his forehead.

In the islands, over the centuries, because people had tended—until recent generations rebelled—to be named after their parents and close relatives, and with a limited number of choices, most had nicknames, to tell one John Morrison or Murdo Maclean from another.

People inherited their family nickname, like Calum's father and grandfather—both Donnie *Maiseach*, from the first man in the family dubbed 'maiseach,' Calum's great-grandfather. Though the fact that *maiseach* meant beautiful, lovely, or handsome hadn't made Calum's life any easier at school.

Chrissie, on the other hand, had married into her nickname. *Goirt* meant 'sore,' since Angus's father had been viewed as a hypochondriac.

But there were also unfortunates like Calum, landed with their own, personal nickname on top, attached randomly and ruthlessly for any small peccadillo, and unshakable to the grave. He, Calum Maiseach, would also be known as Orlando Bloom until he was an old bodach with no hair. Though, he supposed, gloomily, Orlando would get there before he did.

Calum let himself and Shep in through the back door of the house, heeling off his trainers in the modest porch.

They lived in a 1980s bungalow, built on the family croft near the Old House, the now-empty shell his grandparents and their parents had lived and died in. The New House, as the family still called it, had been extended over the years, and it was relatively comfortable and warm, but far from beautiful. Aesthetics came near the bottom of the list of local priorities.

Now Calum could see clearly how dated the furniture was, how twee the ornaments and little religious plaques on the walls. But, it was home. Childhood. Safety. Certainty. A removal of temptation. And…his parents were getting older. He was their only child, and they were incredibly close, the three of them. They'd need the help soon enough.

The fire in the lounge was banked as usual, a black, smoldering slope of coal slack, because even in summer, the weather rarely got warm.

Calum headed straight for his iMac by the window. He wasn't sure he wanted to admit to himself how eager he was to get online, to get a window back into the world outside.

He sat down at the computer table, pulling his phone from his tracksuit trousers, and he thought about what Chrissie had said. *Cianalas.* That was why most people came home to the islands after experiencing other things. It was a word that meant more than *homesickness.* It was a kind of…implacable longing. But the stone weight in Calum's belly was telling him he'd come back for less positive reasons.

He stared out the picture window at the view: moorland scarred by old peat banks; the grey strip of road cutting through it; houses scattered around like little Monopoly buildings, an estate of them on the horizon; Broad Bay to the right, and over it all like a lid, the heavy pewter sky.

It was the view he'd seen every day for eighteen years before he left, and it would be the view he'd most likely see until the day he died.

Panic skittered in his belly—*trapped*—and he clicked his mail icon to distract himself. Desperate for it.

He sped through the usual spam, deleting as he went without opening, but there were also personal emails—one from Julia with an attachment about an Arts Centre exhibition in Stornoway. A couple from friends and ex-colleagues in Glasgow. Some from work. And one with two small, grey exclamation marks. High Priority. "For Calum."

He pulled it up cautiously in a side window without opening it, but there wasn't an attachment, just an empty space and then some text at the very bottom in a different font, apparently copied and pasted in.

He raised his eyebrows at the email address: còthaseo@gmail.com.

Cò tha seo? 'Who is this?'

Someone who knew how to use the accent keys, for a start. Someone, presumably, familiar with Gaelic, and computer literate.

He looked more closely at the text.

The first line was: "Translated from the Gàidhlig."

"I can't believe it's over, because isn't Hell…"

He clicked it open.

I can't believe it's over because isn't Hell meant to last forever? Though I don't think Reverend John Gillies had a clue Hell was in France. Or on the Atlantic.

I keep telling everyone I'm fine, but they treat me like one of those bone-china cups my mother keeps for the Communions and Worships. Of course I have nightmares, but we all do. It makes me shiver to think that soon, soon, I'll know yours.

I saw someone has published a poem about the battle that sent me home. Arras. It's one of those English public schoolboy efforts, bitter like we all are. But what's the point? You're right. We should try to forget, think of what we've won and what we have ahead.

I just realized today, it's been thirteen months since I was shipped back to Blighty, as they jolly well call it. Three months in a hospital, then ten in Kent, and finally home.

I thought being here would make it better. But it hasn't, because I see you everywhere I turn, and I've spent every day frightened the Lord might take you from me.

But we survived, my darling. Both of us. That's not tempting fate anymore. John Gillies's God is angry and vengeful, but my God is merciful and loving, and He has proved it by bringing you home to me.

It's been so long since I've heard your voice, or looked into your sea-grey eyes, or tasted your skin. I remember every heartbeat of that first night, after the minister told us we had to report for duty, that there was a war now. The hotel in London, that first leave, and the times after. And when you came to see me at the hospital in Kent. I remember every touch. Every word you said.

I'm writing this because I just saw your mother, and she told me you may have squeezed a place on the Iolaire, to get you home for New Year's Day. And I thought, if you get a berth, you'll be lying in my arms when you read this. If not, well, we can wait a week more.

I signed the lease on the croft yesterday, so we'll have land to work. No one will care about two bachelors, two friends forgetting the horrors of war. Even my mother says she understands we want to be left in peace. The truth won't trouble them, because to them, our truth doesn't exist. But if there were justice, I'd be singing from the hilltops how beautiful you are, the miracle of finding you beside me and having you love me in return.

Darling of my heart, I didn't know it was possible to feel such excitement and joy. The Lord has seen that we've suffered, and granted us His mercy.

I will shake your hand at the pier when I greet you, like a proper gentleman. Until we can be alone, my one true love.

Calum pushed violently away from the table as if he'd touched a bare, live wire, the wheels of his chair shooting back on the carpet to jam against an unnecessary rug. His wide eyes locked on the computer screen as though the words on there would melt away if he willed it hard enough, like a bad dream.

An old letter? Some sort of...historical fiction? Who the fuck knew? Who cared? The email was addressed to him by name.

"No one's going to care about two bachelors..."

Maybe the writer meant two friends, he thought desperately. But not even he could make himself believe that.

A gay relationship. And someone had sent him…*that*…anonymously.

Blackmail? A warning? *You're being watched?*

His heart pounded like a trip-hammer in his chest, though he tried to reason himself down. This was just…gut fear. Irrational, preprogrammed guilt. He had nothing to hide.

But someone who knew Gaelic had sent him that email.

Someone who'd known him at university? Who'd been there when he and…and Adam were? But…how had they known? And why wait till now, all these years on?

Because he'd come home. Because they were disgusted that a man in his position could have once…

But it *wasn't* who he was.

Nothing wrong with it—he truly believed that—but for *other* people. People who lived in—who'd been formed by—another world. Not for him. Not coming from this island. This family. This father and mother.

The sound of the back doorbell nearly sent him through the roof.

Immediately Shep began to bark with joyous indignation, and the sheer volume, mixed with more impatient bell ringing, was enough of a cacophony to douse Calum's stupid panic in the mundanity of the moment.

He hushed the dog and headed through the kitchen to the back door, still in his stockinged feet.

An old man—a bodach—stood on the doorstep, clad in the crofter's uniform of blue boilersuit tucked into gumboots, with a tweed flat cap on his head. It took Calum a second to recognize him, because he looked so generic. But then he realized it was Angus Goirt—and he was panting. And the expression on his face was all wrong.

Calum had seen it too often in Glasgow. But it didn't belong here.

"Angus?" Sharply.

"Please," the old man's voice quavered. His watery eyes focused somewhere behind Calum, seeing something else. But he'd remembered to speak English because Calum's Gaelic wasn't very good. "Please come. Please come. Please come."

"*Angus?* What's wrong?"

But Calum didn't wait for a reply. He was already jamming his trainers on his feet, heart racketing hard again, adrenaline surging. Fight or flight, twice in a few minutes.

He darted into the lounge for his phone, then back to the kitchen, out to the porch, urging Shep back inside, snatching his car keys from the small table near the back door. He could easily run the few hundred yards to Angus's house, but Angus appeared to be on his last legs.

"Please come," Angus said, a clockwork man, almost run down.

Calum hurried him to the car, helped him into the front seat, then shot off along the lane to the main road, seat-belt warning beeping, ignored. He barely stopped to check for oncoming traffic, and then the car was across, and racing up the side road to Angus's old croft house. Calum didn't wait for Angus to get out too; he ran through the gate, up the concrete path, and around to the faded, peeling back door.

The door was ajar and opened directly into the kitchen.

The first thing Calum saw was red. Red all over the worn, yellow linoleum floor. All over Chrissie as she sat collapsed on it, eyes blank, glasses askew, rocking her son.

And Calum flashed stupidly on a line from his Standard Grade Shakespeare: "*Who would have thought the old man would have so much blood in him.*"

Red all over him. Drenching dark on his blue boilersuit, on his chest, trickling from the gaping slash in his neck.

But Tormod's face was white, and his wide, dead eyes were afraid.

CHAPTER TWO

Violence was Calum's job.

Had been his job.

It shouldn't have paralyzed him.

Yet he stood in the open doorway, his knees weakened, his vision glaring, buzzing…as stunned and horrified as if he were some naive civilian who'd never seen blood and death before. As if he were just Chrissie and Angus's innocent neighbor.

But this was *home.* Where things like this didn't happen.

A long, ululating moan of grief sounded behind him, at his shoulder.

Angus—who'd forced himself back up the path to reenter his own personal hell.

Fuck! Get a fucking grip, *man!*

"Angus!" Calum had to raise his voice to be heard. "Don't. We have to…" He forced himself on. "We don't know if this is a crime scene yet."

What would be worse for the old man? That someone had done this to Tormod, or that Tormod had done it to himself? And left it for his mother to find.

Angus's eyes had fixed on his wife and son, and Calum didn't think he'd understood a word. But he stopped wailing as if a switch had been pulled, and stood obediently still in the open doorway, waiting to be told what to do to make things better.

Calum purposely slowed his breathing, making himself take in the details of the scene in front of him. Making himself strategize.

This isn't Kansas anymore, Toto.

Not Glasgow either.

Calum was a Detective Inspector in the Western Isles Police Force now, and that was a totally different ballgame.

There had been a total of two murders on Lewis in the course of the previous fifty years. There was no murder squad. There wasn't a specialist forensic unit. It was Friday lunchtime, and before anyone could begin the process of requesting the services of a CSI team, or a murder team, or a forensic pathologist from Inverness or Glasgow, they'd have to try to establish if Tormod's death was more likely murder or suicide.

Calum blew out a steadying breath, lifted his phone, and called the station in Stornoway.

To their credit, it took less than twenty-five minutes for an ambulance and two police cars to arrive, in a frenzy of flashing blue lights. Calum was well aware everyone in Shulibost would be at their windows. But there was no playing this down.

Still dressed in his running gear, he began to bark orders the moment his officers emerged. To don the forensic suits and overshoes he'd told them to bring, still sealed in their polythene bags. To string up scene-of-crime tape. To take scene-of-crime photographs but keep to the very edges of the room. To find and seize any electronic devices…phones, computers. To contact the next of kin… *Shit! Julia!* To keep everyone away if they tried to come near.

And then, when the police surgeon—a local GP—arrived, he and Calum pulled on forensic suits and overshoes, and together began the process of trying to extract Chrissie without destroying the scene.

At first, they feared they'd have to lift her out, but as they began to pull her upright, she seemed to break out of her fugue state, take in the men hovering over her, clad to the top of their heads in alien white suits, and she clutched Tormod still tighter and began to scream.

The doctor, an unfamiliar balding middle-aged man with a strong Stornoway accent, managed to administer a sedative, and eventually they got her out and into the waiting ambulance. The same ambulance that was also going to have to take Tormod to the hospital morgue.

Calum watched her being laid onto a narrow ambulance bed as if she were dead herself. Then he went back to the house, to the doctor examining the body with grim focus, though Calum knew he'd hardly have much experience analyzing suspicious deaths.

"I don't suppose you have any idea of time of—"

"He hasn't been dead long," the doctor said briskly. "Less than an hour." He looked up. "Graham Tavistock. English father." As if the surname paired with the accent required automatic explanation. His eyes were very blue.

Calum tried a smile. "Inspector Calum—"

"I know," Tavistock said. "You were a hotshot detective in the murder squad in Glasgow, but you came home to catch drunk drivers and small-time drug runners instead." He took in Calum's surprise. "It was in the *Stornoway*

Gazette," he said. "Along with your inside leg measurement and your auntie's postcode." They exchanged a wry glance; then they both looked down at Tormod's dead face as if they'd agreed it. "He was my patient."

Calum glanced up and caught a spasm of emotion crossing the doctor's weathered features before it vanished into professional calm.

"So…" Calum began, tone carefully delicate. "Would you say…?"

"That he was suicidal?" Tavistock's tone was dry as dust. "You know better than that, Inspector. I can't tell you anything without the approval of his next of kin." Calum grimaced. It had been worth a try. "But," Tavistock went on as he gently tipped back Tormod's head, "at this point I suspect the angle of the wound might show that he was sitting there"—he pointed behind him to a wooden chair with a worn cushion on its seat, pulled away from the table—"and *someone* cut his throat from behind and above. He fell forward onto the floor as he fought for…the final moments of his life."

"Right," Calum said. His tone was as neutral as he could make it. But he'd been used to infuriating caution about causes of death from Scenes of Crime pathologists. They never wanted to commit themselves to anything until the postmortem. And this guy was a GP, not an expert. Tavistock probably watched too much TV, with too many sexy, involved pathologists.

Tavistock read his mind again. "The weapon." He pointed to a large kitchen knife lying about twelve inches from Tormod's right hand, its wooden handle and blade stained with blood, as if it had dropped from Tormod's fingertips when Chrissie embraced him. Calum had spotted it from the door, after the first wave of shock passed. "If he'd cut his own throat," Tavistock went on, "it'd be more likely to be…over there. Beside the chair. That's where the blood splatter suggests the wound was inflicted. Even if a cut throat is self-administered, the reflex is to drop the weapon as the victim fights for air." He met Calum's surprised stare with a thin smile. "I took extra training before accepting a role as a police surgeon."

Calum opened his mouth, then closed it again. He'd done what too many officers from bigger forces tended to do when they came in to work with smaller ones. Assumed the locals were out of their depth.

But Calum *came* from here. He had no excuse.

He cleared his throat and picked up the knife with blue-gloved fingers, then dropped it into an evidence bag. But as he did, something else caught his eye.

"What's that?"

Tavistock glanced at the crumpled plastic bag lying near Tormod's legs. "I'd say it was beside, or caught underneath the body when it fell."

It was a Tesco carrier bag, its familiar white, red, and blue stained with drying blood. Calum had an officer take a photo of it in situ before he picked it up. He could feel something relatively bulky under the rustling, prickly plastic—a lump, light and solid. Carefully, he eased it out and put the Tesco carrier into one evidence bag, and the newspaper-covered object inside, into another.

"*O a' Thighearna!*" A wail of primitive agony. A cry to God. "*Mo bhalach!* Mo bhalach!" *'My boy!'*

Somehow, Calum had forgotten about Angus, who'd walked away from the young female PC who'd been trying to talk to him outside, and stood again now in the doorway, viewing the ruins of his life.

There was nowhere nearby to take him, to try to get the details a policeman should get. Nowhere humane.

But this wasn't the city, Calum thought with sudden purpose. And procedure could fuck itself. Not to mention he was currently the senior officer on the island.

"My parents' house is a couple of hundred yards away," he told the doctor as he levered himself to his feet. "I'm going to take him there."

Tavistock nodded with approval. "I'll get this finished and get the body to the hospital. I'll send you my report."

They both took it for granted that it was Calum's case for as long as he could hold on to it. Until the big boys arrived.

Angus was docile as Calum led him past the ambulance, where Chrissie now slept, back to the car. And he was just as biddable as he followed Calum into his house, ignoring Shep's joy, through the kitchen, and into the lounge, where Calum sat him down on the overstuffed sofa in front of the fire.

Angus's Wellington boots left bloody footprints on the pristine kitchen floor and echoes on the lounge carpet, but Calum was not going to ask him to take them off.

"Angus?" Calum dropped the three evidence bags he'd filled onto the low wooden coffee table in front of the sofa, and went to his desk for a notebook and pen. "Can you tell me what you remember?" Angus stared at the slope of barely smoking coal in the fire. "Angus? Please. Try."

Perhaps it was ingrained politeness that made Angus obey. He made a visible effort to force his attention to Calum, but his eyes caught and held on the evidence bags.

"We were at the bottom of the field," he said, slow and dazed. "Replacing the fence. We'd been working on it…for a couple of days. Tormod…" His breathing shook. His face twisted. "He always has a *strupag* at half past twelve." *A fly cup. A quick cup of tea.* "Where did you get that?" he asked. His traumatized gaze remained fixed on the bags lying on the table; the knife that had killed his son.

"It was on the floor by the…beside him," Calum said. "Angus, did Tormod have any enemies or…?"

He stopped as Angus reached across and touched a bag. But not the one that held the knife. The one with the lump of newspaper.

Angus made a sound like a sob. *"Obair an diabhail."* *The work of the devil.*

Angus snatched back his hand and began to rub his palms compulsively up and down his thighs—horrible to watch his agitation and distress—rumpling up the thick dark-blue fabric of his boilersuit.

"It's not my secret," he said. "It's not my secret to tell. *She* should decide. But *you* have it. You have it. And my boy is dead."

"Angus…?"

There was a noise, a clatter and bang beyond the thin, hollow, modern door into the kitchen, but Shep didn't bark. Calum's parents' voices sounded clearly through the plywood.

Calum closed his eyes against a rush of furious impatience, but it was his own fault. He'd gambled on his parents staying out longer for the funeral tea.

He stood, but before he could intercept them, the lounge door opened and Calum's black-clad mother and father spilled in, his mother speaking first as usual, bright and cheerful and overwhelming.

"Mo chreach-sa a thàinig, a' Chalum! What have you tramped into the kitchen? The dog's licking all over the floor!" She was a good-looking woman still—though she allowed no personal vanity—with even features, big blue eyes, and short, wavy, brown hair. *"Bha me a chreid gu robh... Aonghas!"* Angus shrank in on himself, but Calum's mother's response to the surprise guest in her lounge was ingrained. She immediately behaved as if Angus had done them all an enormous honor by coming to sit in her lounge. "Calum, did you not get Aonghas a strupag?"

The sheer horror in her tone at his huge hospitality failure made Calum want to snap to it, even then. Angus's eyes fixed again on the safety of the banked fire.

So Calum explained to his parents why Angus was there, in the shortest, most diplomatic terms possible. But it still sounded brutal. Literally, unbelievable.

In a daze, Calum's mother sank down onto the sofa beside the old man and embraced him, talking softly in Gaelic all the while. *"The Lord tests us. How the Lord tests us."*

Angus remained absolutely silent, still staring at the fire, so she bustled out into the kitchen to prepare tea, whether Angus wanted it or not.

Calum's father sat down with them then, shy and awkward in his stiff suit. He was tall, strong, and dark-haired like Calum, handsome, but his face and hands were lean and weathered. He was a Free Church elder, and he looked the part. Ascetic, like a saint or a martyr.

"Tha me cho duilich, Aonghas," he said to Angus, in his rich, deep voice. *I'm so sorry.*

Angus, at last, looked at him. His face twisted. "I've known you since you were a boy, Donnie." His voice shook. "Letting Tormod play with you, though you were older."

"Until he followed me onto the roof," Calum's father said with a sad smile, and Angus made a sound between amusement and a sob.

The door was shouldered open, and Calum's mother pushed through with a laden tray which she set down on the coffee table beside the evidence bags. She didn't seem to register the gory knife, shining through clear plastic.

"I trust you," Angus said with sudden desperation. "And I trust Ishbel." He looked at Calum then, frowning and intense, all fierce, grey brows like an angry eagle. "And I trust *you*, because you're your daddy's son as much as you're a policeman." He sniffed hard and rubbed a flat palm back and forth across his mouth. "Take it out of the bag."

Calum frowned, but he had no doubt which 'it' Angus meant. He rose to rummage in the desk for a fresh pair of forensic gloves, then extracted the lump of newspaper from its plastic covering. It was tied with a piece of fraying blue plastic string, and there were a lot of pages wrapped around whatever was inside—all from the *Stornoway Gazette*, Calum noted. He undid the string and loosened page after page of paper; whatever was in there had been protected, as if it was extremely fragile. So when the object at the centre finally rolled out into his hand, he was almost shocked by the extent of the anticlimax.

It was nothing fragile. Just a bog-standard piece from probably the most copied chess set in the world. A Lewis chessman; instantly recognizable. Even kids knew them, from *Harry Potter*.

The piece was a queen in familiar pose, sitting on her throne, with her left arm across her lap and her hand supporting her right elbow, cheek resting in her right hand. The figures never ceased to impress Calum, not least because, despite their naive style, they were all their own individual characters, ready to live. The queen he held was leaning forward, as if watching a conflict or a show, her expression perplexed, verging on grumpy.

Calum looked up at Angus.

He could see white stubble on his anxious, devastated face, and his old, dark eyes looked reddened and rheumy. He appeared, truthfully, on the point of death himself.

Calum looked down again.

It was good quality, not plastic like some he'd seen; from the weight, probably from a museum-shop set. Maybe resin, he thought, to best mimic the original walrus tusk or whale tooth. Maybe five inches tall. Bigger than the originals he'd seen in the British Museum, or the National Museum in Edinburgh, or any of the six pieces kept at Museum nan Eilean—the Museum of the Islands—in Stornoway, but he knew they made replicas in different sizes for sale.

He studied the piece in the palm of his hand, and unwanted memories gushed out like water through cracks in a flood wall.

"Why is this important?" he asked.

Angus looked stunned. "Because it's a chess piece," he said, as if it were obvious.

Calum blinked, beginning to understand. An acid burn of pity churned in his gut. He had no idea how to be tactful about it, on top of everything.

"Chrissie's father passed it on to her earlier this year," Angus added, as if that were irrefutable proof to back up what he was implying.

"Chrissie's father," Calum repeated. This was getting away from him. A pointless waste of valuable time. Angus was about seventy, like Chrissie, so his father-in-law... "How old is Chrissie's father?"

"The bodach? He's ninety-six."

Ninety-six.

"So...this old..." *Senile.* "...man has a copy of the Lewis chess set, and he thinks this piece is original?"

Angus, distressed as he was, clearly caught Calum's tone. His expression slid to betrayal. But Calum didn't have the time to indulge pretence. He had a deadline. Forty-eight hours. A wall for effective murder investigations.

"Chrissie believes him?" he asked. "You believe him?" Then, "Did *Tormod* believe him?" God. Had he actually tried to sell it as genuine?

Angus flinched as if Calum had spat on him.

"Chrissie told Tormod about it when it was passed to her," he said with dignity. "Though she'd known about it for long before that. She shouldn't have told me, but she trusted me. And now, in these times, I'm trusting you."

Calum glanced again at the piece. The queen's expression seemed somehow more impatient and imperious than he remembered any of the queens to look, and when he turned it, he could see the back of her carved throne was stained pale red, as if someone had painted it, then tried to rub the paint off.

Most importantly and tellingly, though, it was a queen.

Calum sighed and reached for a piece of newspaper, ready to wrap it again. There might be some forensic evidence on it, though he doubted it. But beyond that, could Chrissie's father's delusions, passed on to his credulous family, have any bearing on what happened to Tormod?

"Is the bodach still in Uig?" Donnie asked. Calum had almost forgotten he was there, which tended to happen a lot around his father. "In Mealista?"

Angus sighed. "He's never moved all his life. Chrissie's trying to make *me* move there now too, because *he* says we have to. Says his time is almost up." He made a harsh, surprised sound, as if he'd just prodded an open wound he'd forgotten was there.

Calum studied the queen again, the quirky, ivory face; then the red staining her white, rippled hair and her intricate throne.

"Did he or Chrissie try to paint it?" he asked. He wasn't sure why, but his pulse had started to pick up again. Instinct.

Stupid animal instinct, and those two things. Uig. Red.

Angus frowned. He seemed on the verge of tears. "Why would they? They both treat it like it's holy."

"Well…" Donnie put in, "the chessmen *were* found in Uig, and some are still missing. You should ask your friend, Calum."

Calum's throat tightened, and he thought vainly, *Please, no.*

"He only did a final-year thesis on the chessmen, Dad," he managed. "Someone in Stornoway'd have a better idea. Or in Edinburgh. Or at the British Museum."

"But he's *at* the British Museum," Calum's mother said. "And he wrote a whole book about the chessmen. It was in the *Scotsman* and the *Gazette*. I've got it on my Kindle! Your father and I both read it."

Calum hadn't known about the job or that the book existed, far less that his parents had bought it. He felt ambushed. His chest was tight. His ribs had transmuted into iron bands.

"I don't have his contact details anymore," he said firmly. And it was true. He didn't have Adam's number because he'd deleted it from his phone. He didn't have his email address or his parents' details because he'd wiped them. He'd removed Adam root and branch from his life. His father had asked him only once how Adam was, and Calum had said he was fine. Not because he knew, but because Adam had to be.

"Hold on." Ishbel stood and went into the kitchen, returning with her black handbag. "I'm sure I kept the number from when he was home with you from university." She extracted her phone and began to peck at it with her forefinger as Calum stared at her, appalled by her innocent doggedness.

He should be used to his parents' close interest in his life, to his mother's well-meaning bulldozer personality. But given that so many of his decisions had been made trying not to disappoint them, it felt stupidly like betrayal.

"Can Calum ask his friend about it, Aonghas?" Donnie asked. "His friend's an expert."

Angus rubbed his mouth again, visibly at war with himself, until finally, he nodded.

"Right, then," Calum's mother said briskly and began to tap at the phone. "I'll try him."

Calum fought to keep his panic below the surface. "He won't still be on that number," he said with desperate certainty.

"Hello!" she said into the phone. "Adam?"

Calum's heart stopped. He heard someone say something faintly on the other end of the line. "Yes, it is! You have a good memory!" A few more words from the almost inaudible, tinny voice. Adam? That was *Adam*? "Oh, I'm fine! Still waiting for grandchildren!" Calum drew a sharp breath.

"Listen, *a' ghràidh*, I don't want to keep you. Calum just needs a word." Calum stared at the phone in his mother's outstretched hand, then at her wide, encouraging eyes. "*Siuthad!*" she urged. *Go on!*

And Calum had no option but to take the phone. He wasn't going to display any of his stunned turmoil. He couldn't, with his parents watching. He was a man talking to his old friend.

"Adam!" he said. He tried for reassuringly hearty. "How are you?"

There was a pointed silence. Then, "I'm fine," Adam said, and with rote politeness but no interest, "And you?"

Calum had forgotten the exact tone of Adam's voice. He hadn't realized that, until he heard the smooth, deep tones, the posh English vowels. The distance in it. Like a stranger.

He cleared his throat. "Oh, I'm fine too. Look, I'm…sorry…to bother you." Stumbling. "I'm a policeman now. It's about a piece of evidence in a case. It's… It involves your main expertise. Or what *was* your—"

Adam cut in. "The chessmen."

Calum paused to gather himself. He sounded like a bumbling kid. His voice firmed. "It's one item. I'll send some photographs, if you could possibly take a look at them for us?"

"No need," Adam said. "I'm actually in Stornoway."

It felt like a whack in the solar plexus. A sucker punch from nowhere.

"In town?" Calum breathed.

"Yes," Adam said with curt economy. "So I can examine it in person. *If* that's what you want."

Calum couldn't understand how quickly, how totally, everything had disintegrated; the ground cut out from under him, just like that. All he'd deliberately turned his back on and worked to deny. Returned to his life, without warning, or permission, or choice.

"Yes," he lied. "That's what I want."

CHAPTER THREE

Calum showered with brisk efficiency, then donned his uniform.

He'd had to get used to that too, as well as everything else, after years in plain clothes as a detective in Glasgow. But at least the day-to-day Police Scotland uniform didn't demand a tie.

A black zip-necked, short-sleeved T-shirt made of wicking, with his two Inspector's pips on epaulettes on the shoulders. Plain black trousers. A black police microfleece to go on top. A traditional, stiff peaked cap with a checkered band and badge.

He refused to acknowledge his relief today that it suited him so well.

Adam was going to meet him at the station, to take a look at the chess piece.

Calum was tying his shoelaces when his phone rang. The name on the screen made him grimace.

"Sir…" he began.

"So were you going to mention we have a potential homicide? Or just wait for me to read it in the papers?"

Chief Inspector Kenneth Martin was area commander for the islands, a Lewis man twenty-six years older than Calum, content with his role, and in full control of his brief. Though his brief hadn't, until now, included murder.

Calum launched into as concise an explanation as he could: how he'd found the body, that he'd had two grief-stricken parents there and his priority had to be containing the potential crime scene. How he'd tried to use his relationship with the father of the victim to get a picture of why the victim might possibly have been murdered. That he hadn't been sure of time differences, so he'd just pressed on and taken charge on the spot, without calling his boss, on holiday in Seattle. But once officers in Stornoway entered the incident into the Police National Computer system, Calum had known it was just a matter of time.

"Inverness called me," Martin said. "Funnily enough *they* weren't bothered about my beauty sleep. They wanted to know why no one called *them*."

"With respect, sir," Calum said. "This is our patch. I know we have to call them in, but we needed to secure the scene. I have what could be the murder weapon bagged up."

He didn't mention it was on his parents' coffee table.

Or the chess piece. He didn't mention the chess piece either. He was withholding information that could be pertinent, that should already be entered into the PNC. But something silenced him. Angus's stated trust perhaps. And his own conviction that the chess piece was a ludicrous red herring anyway.

Then why not hand it straight in to the evidence locker? Why are you pursuing it?

Martin sighed. "Well…I suppose you've put your past experience to good use. At least we'll have a sealed crime scene when the Inverness murder team comes in."

Calum asked tightly. "When do they arrive?"

"They intended to be helicoptered in on Sunday, but there's some complication. So they're taking the ferry on Monday morning with the pathologist. Tavistock entered his initial opinion that it was an unlawful killing. That's what set the hares running."

"Sir, I'd like to keep going on this until the Inverness team arrives. You know about the forty-eight-hour rule in murder cases."

"Yes, Calum. I went to police college too."

"So the more information we can gather in that period…when it's fresh…"

The pause at the other end of the line sounded contemplative. "Well, I suppose it'd be no bad thing to show them what we can do." Calum had heard more than one rant from Martin about the treatment of island officers as "maws from the sticks."

But something made Calum say, "I should declare an interest, sir. I know the victim's family very well. It's my village. It could be seen as improper."

Martin snorted. "*Improper*, is it? Everyone knows everyone's family there, Calum. If we let that get in the way, we wouldn't leave the station."

"Sir."

"*But*. It isn't Glasgow. You're not a SIO with a murder unit behind you anymore. We're not set up for a high-powered investigation, so don't try to run one. You can use CID, though, and commandeer the department. *Just* until the Inverness lot come. Then you have to let them take over."

It was more than Calum had expected. It gave him a Detective Sergeant and a few Detective Constables.

When the call ended, Calum headed back into the lounge and fired up the iMac to send a fast email, ordering the team to set up an incident room and attempt an examination of any seized computer equipment.

Behind him he could hear the rattle of crockery as his mother poured more tea, his father's low, soothing voice talking to Angus.

But as the email whooshed off into the ether, his eye fell on the threatening email he'd opened just before Angus came to get him. còthaseo@gmail.com.

It had seemed wildly sinister then—a prod to unwanted memory. But that was before his past had arrived on his doorstep.

It took him a couple of seconds to recognize that it wasn't the same email. It was a new one. "For Calum 2." His parents' voices murmured on behind him. He opened it.

I thought I knew the face of God. But John Gillies was right. There's no forgiveness. No mercy or pity. Vengeance and destruction are the face of God.

Two hundred and seven men. And you, allowed to survive the carnage of Jutland, the terror of the Atlantic, to have you drown yards from the shores of home. Some people are saying the crew just made a mistake; others say they were drinking in the New Year, that they forgot the Beasts of Holm, until they crashed the ship onto them. But who can blame them, even if they were? They were just agents of John Gillies's God.

There were decorations up for you, bunting, men and women and children waiting on the pier to welcome you home, and instead we watched you die. I almost died too, did you know? Wading into the boiling water, into the gale. I dragged some of them out. But not you. Not you, my love.

Dead men washed onto Sandwick shore like so many carcasses. When the sun rose, I crawled among them, among the screams and the wails and the sorrow. I looked into every dead, grey face. They can say I was shell-shocked when I found you and lay down on top of you, all of my body on yours. When I kissed your cold, soft mouth and put my hands in your sodden hair. The villages of Lewis are like places of the dead. The homes of the island are full of lamentation, grief that cannot be comforted. They can say I didn't know what I was doing when I screamed for you, when I cursed God. But I can't say. I can't tell them what I've lost. They don't know I would lie on your grave forever.

Calum closed the email the instant he finished reading it, but even through his furious resentment, he could acknowledge the wild power and sadness of it. He'd been too horrified by the implications of the first message to register the name of the ship. But HMY *Iolaire* was a name like a trigger on Lewis—the worst peacetime disaster involving a British ship since the *Titanic*.

Every graveyard on the island held identical headstones with a chain and anchor. Sailors who'd survived the terror of the Great War in the Atlantic, drowned in front of their families waiting to welcome them home. A thousand out of six thousand Lewis men who'd gone to war had already died. And then, *after*, when it was meant to be all over—that. There was a theory the *Iolaire* disaster had changed the Lewis character forever, like the Passover in the Old Testament.

The emails read almost like poetry, though Gaelic translated to English often did. But poetry written from the mind of a man in love with another man.

If they were real—original to 1919, when the *Iolaire* sank—they wouldn't have been preserved.

Someone would have burned them and washed their hands afterward.

Fiction, then, sent to try to freak him out.

But who knew about his old mistakes? Was it some sort of sick joke? Blackmail? Now, of all times?

Who could have known Adam would be here? That Calum would be forced to acknowledge him again, because of a murder?

Adam himself? Fuck, no. It had to be a coincidence.

He glared at the dead screen, then stood and gathered his car keys.

He really needed to stop pissing about.

* * * * *

Stornoway police station was an unprepossessing two-story building of black brick and cream harling, set on Church Street, looking down to the masts of the boats in the harbor. To its advantage, Church Street also housed Indian, Thai, and Chinese restaurants, along with the chip shop Calum had gone to for the odd school lunch. No one at the station was ever short of a takeaway.

Calum drove his Subaru into the small car park at the side of the building, with Angus in the passenger seat beside him—a stubborn, broken old man who'd refused to allow the chess piece out of his sight. Calum had tried to argue it was police evidence and Angus would be better going to the hospital to see Chrissie. But Angus spat, "It's Chrissie's birthright!" And Calum had seen that the need to protect it was all that was keeping the old man going.

Ishbel had been worried enough about Angus to insist on going along too, to support him, and Calum hadn't bothered to argue. Angus should have someone with him, even if it was the current SIO's mother.

Calum led them both around to the front of the building and up the wheelchair ramp into reception, but none of them were expecting the woman they found sitting there.

Julia sprang to her feet the moment they entered. *"Shen!" Grandad.*

Calum watched as she embraced Angus, knowing instinctively that he wouldn't respond. Hugs weren't a big part of island life.

But Julia had always belonged somewhere else. Somewhere demonstrative, and fun, and glittering.

Calum had known her on a vague basis all his life. When they both went to Glasgow, though—Calum studying Maths and History at Glasgow University; Julia a rising star, doing Drama at the Royal Conservatoire—they'd met on level ground, like expats abroad. They'd had a few wild nights together as lovers, but they worked best as friends.

Then, one rain-lashed night, a lorry had slammed into Julia's parents' car—her father had been killed, her mother confined to a wheelchair, in need of constant care, and Julia had come back to Lewis. With unemployment levels as they were, she'd been lucky to find work as a care assistant at a home for the elderly, while she tried to support herself and the wholly dependent Seonag. And when Calum had finally followed her back to Lewis eight years later, Julia had grabbed on to him like a lifeline, though she could never comprehend why he'd actively chosen to return. They met up for coffee every week at a café in the Castle grounds.

Julia hugged Ishbel, then Calum, and he hugged her back hard, ignoring the interested receptionist behind her glass screen.

"I don't understand, Orly," Julia said. She never had lost her fondness for Orlando; never lost the habit of calling Calum that. "Uncle Tormod wouldn't harm a fly." Her cheeks were blotched with dried tears, her big hazel eyes reddened and swollen, but somehow she still radiated intrinsic glamour. She wore her mahogany-gloss hair in a chignon, showing off a long, slender neck and delicate jaw. Her mouth was full and pouting, and in her care-assistant coveralls, she looked like a major star inappropriately cast to play the role on TV.

Angus seemed less than happy to have Julia there, but Calum led all three of them into the inner station and on to his bland, overheated office. There, he shed his fleece and cap and organized tea for them; then he headed for CID, gratified to find a whiteboard already set up, with crime-scene photographs attached, along with the names of interviewees and an initial list of tasks.

CID on Lewis dealt mainly with the effort to stem the flow of illegal drugs onto the island, antisocial behaviour, and sudden deaths, caused most often by alcohol, drugs, or suicide. But, as the urgent purpose of a major investigation began to buzz in his blood, Calum was having to acknowledge that challenging detective work was something he'd missed like an addict would miss a drug high.

Detective Sergeant Willie John Mackay was on him immediately. Willie John was an imperturbable man of medium height, in his early forties; a *Niseach*, from Ness at the far north of the island. His hair was prematurely grey and preternaturally neat, and though Willie John could wear what he liked in CID, Calum had never once seen him without a suit, a buttoned collar, and a neatly knotted tie. He'd done his CID training in Inverness and Edinburgh, but he'd made the same trade-off as Calum had, to come back home. Neither of them mentioned boredom or understimulation when they reminisced together about their old cases. There was no point.

"We got access to the victim's PC, sir," Willie John announced. "His password was *password*." Calum wasn't surprised. Guile wasn't a virtue here. "His emails are interesting. He received a series of threats."

Calum's breath stilled. "Go on."

"He seems to have borrowed money. Money he wasn't paying back. He replied to one message, claiming he didn't know what they were talking about. But that made the threats worse."

Bingo.

"Who?"

"Trying to trace the IP, sir," Willie John said, very obviously enjoying himself. But Calum could hardly throw any stones on that score. "The email mentions Glasgow. His documents show he did take a trip there last December, for an operation on his knee. Maybe he borrowed the money then."

Calum sighed. "Why not ask a bloody bank?"

"Not many banks are keen on handing out money to crofters with no other income." The Lewis accent added a soft *sh* to the *r* sound in English. *Croftersh.* "We haven't got into his bank account yet, but we can't find any indications of another job or any income stream. Or any sign of the borrowed money. He seemed to be getting an agricultural grant, but that's peanuts."

"Anything else?"

"Very few emails from friends or family. And, uh…he was very focused on…um." Willie John suddenly looked as uncomfortable as he ever got.

"Jennifer Aniston." Calum's mouth opened and closed again. "You know... from *Friends*." Calum nodded dumbly. "He was on message boards. Fan groups, and the like. He even had a username. *Celticstud67.*"

Why did it all sound so much more ludicrous in a Lewis accent?

Back out in the empty corridor, Calum stood and took stock.

One of the first things he'd learned as a murder detective was that death uncovered surprises. That the cliché was true—no one really *did* know anyone else.

But Tormod had been a background fixture of Calum's life. Quiet, stolid, uninterested in anything but sheep and the croft and church. A stereotype of Calum's blueprint for Lewis men of his father's generation.

And all along, underneath that facade, a useless passion for...Jennifer Aniston? It made Tormod both more human and more alien, and Calum wasn't sure he knew what to do with that.

He checked his watch, and his insides immediately completed a full roll. Less than ten minutes left. He stood in place, trying to control his nausea, then gave up and headed for the gents'.

You're fucking ridiculous, he thought as he glowered at himself in the wall mirror. But still, he checked his appearance as compulsively as a bride about to walk down the aisle, except he didn't have the benefit of a veil.

The black uniform T-shirt clung to his broad shoulders, his pecs and biceps, his narrow waist. The trousers showed off his muscular thighs and his high, tight arse. He studied his reflection for a moment longer, then guiltily unzipped the neck of the T-shirt to expose his throat, emphasize the length of his strong neck. Because something in him needed Adam to see him at his best; show that he may have run away, but he hadn't gone to seed.

Adam, who'd once thought him beautiful. Adam, who'd loved him.

Hell, perhaps Adam had lost his hair and gained thirty pounds. It had been...what? Six years... And Calum knew he'd romanticized Adam in some perverse way, by deliberately forgetting him. Frozen him as a perfect boy and buried him beneath his memory.

Maybe he prayed that fat, bald man of his imagination was what Adam had become. Maybe that would finally purge the last of his old obsession.

* * * * *

"It's not up to me to say anything," Angus said the moment Calum walked back into his office. "It's up to Chrissie." His tone held a querulous appeal. *Sort it out for me.*

It took Calum a second or two to understand: Julia didn't know about the supposed family heirloom or what her grandparents believed about it. Chrissie had deliberately only told Tormod and Angus.

Julia looked between them with bafflement, but Angus folded his arms and turned away, the image of mulish old age.

So Calum gestured with his head, and Julia followed him out of the room. He led her back toward reception.

"What's he talking about?" she asked as they walked. "I should sit with him if he's being interviewed." Her Lewis accent had been ruthlessly expunged in her couple of years of drama school. She spoke now with perfect Received Pronunciation, like a stage actor. "He looks destroyed."

"He wants to talk in private, Jools," Calum said. "It's up to him."

"But it's okay to have your mum in?" she protested. "Is it something… personal about Uncle Tormod? I know more than he thinks! Uncle Tormod and I were close."

Calum frowned as he pushed open the door to the small waiting area. "He can choose who he wants to have with him. But if you don't mind waiting, I'll organize for someone to come and talk to you about Tormod? For background detail."

"How did he die?" she asked suddenly.

"I don't think it's a good idea," Calum said.

Her expression firmed. "I see death every day at work, Orly."

Calum blew out a heavy breath. Okay. "His throat was cut." Julia's face lost what was left of its color. Perhaps he should have made sure she was sitting down first. "Shit…I'm sorry. I'll get someone to take you to the interview room…get you some more tea."

She subsided with a *thump* onto one of Reception's red-plastic chairs, her pallor alarming. But Calum didn't have time left to do anything more than tell a passing PC to get Willie John to collect her.

The whole thing was turning into a farce, he thought savagely as he strode back to his office and took his seat behind his desk.

Why was he going along with Angus's insane cloak-and-dagger secrecy over a family delusion? No secrets were kept in a murder investigation. No one could afford to be gentle. The chess piece was potential evidence, no more, no less.

His landline rang. Calum answered, ready and yet not ready at all.

"Mr. Patterson at reception for you, sir. He says he has an appointment."

"Right," Calum said and replaced the receiver. He stood. "I'm just going to get...Adam." His voice sounded far away in his own head. There was a spiky lump of panic in his chest.

Hard to believe this was actually happening; reality, and not a bad dream.

The wall between reception and the inner station was made of toughened glass panels, and as Calum approached, he could see a male figure in a dark suit, sitting on the far side of Julia. They were talking, heads together. Of course—Julia and Adam knew each other from their time in Glasgow, when they'd all been so full of hope. Calum had introduced them, in fact.

He clenched his jaw, pulled open the door, and strode into reception.

Adam glanced up and rose slowly to his feet.

The shock was visceral.

Adam hadn't been kind enough to get fat. Or bald.

He was as tall and fit and lovely as when Calum had left him, except that his light-brown hair was longer and layered, parted in the middle, off his brow. His suit was a narrow cut black pinstripe, and he wore a white V-necked T-shirt under it. Calum's uniform suddenly felt stiff and ugly.

Adam's tanned skin was still smooth, his narrow jaw strong and sharp. Perhaps he had a few more lines around his eyes, but those eyes were a hooded, vivid light grey, taking in and assessing Calum in turn.

"...your sea-grey eyes..."

The treacherous echo of Calum's threatening emails slammed him back to reality.

Adam raised an eyebrow. He'd always had a tendency to act the super-cilious bastard when he didn't like someone. Now, that someone was Calum.

Calum made himself hold out a hand. He felt sick. Adam waited a moment too long before taking it.

"It's been a while," Calum said with what he hoped was an easy smile. "I appreciate your coming by."

"Not at all," Adam said. That smooth, whisky voice that used to weaken Calum's knees, when Adam whispered all he wanted to do to him. "I was just telling Julia I had to make the effort, after five years."

"Six," Calum said. *Shit.* His heart was galloping. *Ridiculous.* But at least Adam had somehow known to be discreet about why he was there.

"Julia just told me the terrible news about her uncle," Adam went on. "That you're investigating it. I can come back later if you..."

He was playing it beautifully. A friendly visit which had been arranged before the investigation had begun.

"No," Calum said. "It's fine. Come on through for a few minutes." He met Julia's innocent, anxious eyes. "Willie John'll take you in for a chat, okay?"

Julia nodded miserably. "I want to talk to *you*, though."

"Willie John'll take all the details." Calum gave a reassuring smile. "I'll come along if I can."

"*Fuck,*" he muttered, the moment the door closed behind himself and Adam. Cloak-and-dagger was not his strength.

"She doesn't know," Adam observed coolly. "I gathered that her uncle had to be your victim. And since she didn't mention the chess piece..."

"Thank you," Calum said, because he didn't know what else to say.

Sorry you despise me? How could he, when he wouldn't mean it? Their destruction had been a necessity.

Calum led the way, totally aware of how his uniform trousers fitted around his backside. Wondering if Adam was noticing. Furious and dis-gusted by his own thoughts.

But it was all instantly there again. Proof of why he couldn't be near Adam.

Around him, he'd had no self-control.

And incredibly, as attractive as Adam was, Calum had once had power over him too. Long ago.

Calum's name and title were on his office door. He was conscious of Adam taking them in, and then they were inside, and Ishbel rose to greet Adam like a long-lost member of the family.

Adam had stayed at Calum's parents' house for a few weeks in their final year at university, while he did some research at Uig for his thesis on the chessmen and Viking influence on Lewis. Every day, Calum had driven him over there, and helped him measure things and take photographs and interview people and dig. And every evening they'd come back to the house, and Calum's mum fed them far too much, and they'd watched TV, and gone to their separate rooms.

Friends. That holiday had been pure. Because they were on Lewis, and Calum could not stand to even consider the remote possibility that someone might see them touching or kissing. Adam had respected it and hadn't tried to sneak even a handhold, though Calum thought he saw it as regressive. Victorian.

But it had changed things, that holiday. It had reminded Calum graphically that he was living a fantasy. That there could be no future in what he was doing. It reminded him who he really was, and what he owed, and what was expected, and how stupid and self-destructive and unfair he was being.

Lewis was a place where religion mattered so much that ordinary people in congregations still fell out and had schisms and formed new churches over matters of theology and religious politics.

Just a few years before, the largest Church of Scotland congregation in the islands had split because the mainland church was willing to accept "practicing homosexuals" as ministers. The anti-gay dissenters had been welcomed into the Free Church—Calum's parents' church. His parents were kind and compassionate people, but the concept of homosexuality touching their own lives would be incredible and devastating for them. In a strange way, they were innocents.

Lewis had more than its share of alcohol abuse and illegal drugs and underage sex and unplanned pregnancies. They'd been around for a long time. But even in a community with such a close personal relationship with religion, you could be easily forgiven for those sins. You could even decide not to bother with the church at all.

But you couldn't be gay.

There was no overt unpleasantness or open homophobia, but that was the unspoken rule everyone understood. If you came from Lewis and you weren't straight, if you were *other*, no one should know. It was never talked about. There had been a gay pride march the previous year—the first ever—mainly outsiders and LGBTQ allies. But as many people in his parents' church alone prayed to stop it, as turned up to march.

"You're at the British Museum now," Calum's mother was saying. "You've done so well! Our Calum could have gone to London too. He got offered this big fancy job in the Met, but he wanted to come home instead. To be with his mam," she teased.

"Who can blame him?" Adam said. Calum could only see the back of his head. His beautifully cut, sun-streaked hair brushed his collar.

Ishbel regarded Adam with huge affection. "You're looking lovely, a' ghràidh. Are you married yet?"

"Not yet," Adam said. He sounded indulgent.

"The girls in London must be blind." She twinkled at him roguishly.

Calum looked down at his desk, moved papers aimlessly on the surface. In fact, he thought, if Adam had actually announced he was gay, his mother would probably have managed to accept it, after a period of adjustment. But that was because Adam was from "away," and these things went on *away*, with other people. Just not here.

"Donnie and I loved your book. We were very proud. I kept telling everyone, 'He sat at that table and ate my scones!'"

Adam laughed. "I'd have sent you a complimentary copy if I'd known."

But the way Calum had ended things had left no room for trailing friendships.

"Shall we look at the piece?" Calum asked. It had sounded too abrupt, like a headmaster calling an Assembly to order and crushing the fun.

Adam gave him a cool look, as if he'd just remembered he was there. "By all means."

It took a couple of minutes for Calum and Adam to glove up, and for Calum to extract the wrapped object from the evidence bag, then the chess piece itself from its paper layers. Finally, he handed it to Adam.

Adam lifted the piece to the light, frowning as he turned it round and round, scrutinizing it. It seemed to take an age.

Say it's a fake, Calum urged desperately in his head. *Please, let it be a bloody fake.*

When Adam lowered the piece, they were all hanging on his reaction. Even Angus, who seemed to have retreated into his own world since he'd seen off Julia, watched him as if he held all the answers.

"Right," Adam said, "I imagine you all know we have seventy-eight chessmen from the hoard of artifacts found by a local man on Uig Beach in 1831. Enough for four incomplete chess sets. And we suspect the missing pieces are out there somewhere, in private collections. There are four missing warders—now called rooks or castles—a missing knight, and forty-five missing pawns." He held up the piece and looked at it again almost regretfully. "What *isn't* missing, is a queen."

Every tense muscle in Calum's body relaxed.

That was the exact reason he'd known to resist Angus's evangelical faith in the chess piece. If it had been a knight or a pawn, then yes, it could just possibly have come from the lost part of the hoard.

But not a queen.

"Right," Calum said. "So now it's confirmed, hopefully to everyone's satisfaction…" He looked at Angus, then at Adam. "It's not an original piece."

Adam's glance flipped up to meet Calum's. Dark lashes and brows set off clear grey irises that looked lighter than ever in his tanned face.

"Actually," Adam said. "I think it's genuine. Which means there's potentially a whole other chess set out there. And that could be well worth killing for."

CHAPTER FOUR

No one spoke.

Then Adam said calmly, into the shocked silence, "Is it all right to ask where you found it?"

"It belongs…to Angus's wife," Calum managed. "It's a…a family heirloom. And it was at the murder scene."

Adam gave a thoughtful nod. "Something else you may want to know then. I'm not here by coincidence."

Calum stared at him. "Not by…coincidence," he repeated stupidly.

"I got an email at the museum with some images attached. Of this piece. The sender had read my book and wanted to discuss the value, with a view to putting it up for sale. Obviously, I thought it was highly unlikely to be genuine, but it intrigued me because the maker hadn't attempted a copy—it's… just a little different from the queen pieces we have. *And*…the red staining on the back. We're pretty sure one half of each set was originally red, but all the pieces we have are white, because the paint's worn off. That touch of red was…subtle for a copy." It had pricked Calum's instincts too, though he'd discounted it. "So…I came up to Lewis as the sender requested, and we scheduled a meeting for this afternoon. But they didn't show."

Because *they* were dead, Calum thought. But he couldn't say it in front of Angus.

Whatever Tormod had been dabbling in, he'd needed money urgently. So when Chrissie showed him the family inheritance, why wouldn't he try to hawk it off?

Adam pulled out his phone and scrolled through it before handing it across the desk to Calum.

The email was as he'd said. Two grainy shots of the queen piece were attached, taken in low light, but good enough to show important detail. And an email address that was all too familiar: celticstud67@yahoo.com.

God, had Tormod no instinct at all to cover his own tracks?

"He was trying to sell it," Angus said at last. He sounded destroyed. "He was going to betray his mam."

Ishbel grimaced and put a comforting hand on his arm.

"Angus…" Calum began, but what could he say? *We don't know that?* When they really probably did?

But Angus took no time to wallow. "Do other people have to find out about the piece? It's no one else's business."

Calum should call Martin right now and spew it all out. All about the new priceless chess piece and the possibility of a whole new chess set, maybe more than one. And Tormod's desperation for money, which had brought disaster down on his own head.

But the SIO from Inverness wouldn't wait to find out if the chess piece actually had anything to do with the killing. He or his bosses would most likely hold a press conference and announce the career-boosting details to the world. The piece, peripheral as it seemed to be to the murder, would be all the press and the authorities would be able to see. That, and the possibility of more out there. Chrissie and Angus, Seonag and Julia, and the bodach in Uig—they'd be overrun. As if they hadn't enough grief to contend with.

When it came down to it, why would any killer—especially if, as seemed likely, the murder had to do with Tormod's loan-shark debt—leave the chess piece behind?

Surely, only if they hadn't known about it.

Calum had an explanation now for why the piece was at the crime scene. Tormod had shoved it into a Tesco carrier bag, ready for his meeting with Adam.

So—if the piece wasn't a factor in the murder, was it any of Calum's business if Chrissie and Angus had it?

Angus's fierce dark eyes bore into him, and it occurred to Calum that this was the reason police officers were removed from cases if there could be a conflict of interest.

But Calum was the only experienced SIO there. And he had to keep going before the trail went any colder. He had until Monday.

"I can't guarantee anything," he said, though he knew it to be a kind of surrender.

"Actually," Adam said, "there are laws of treasure trove." Calum glared at him in disbelief. Just what Angus needed to hear, to boost his faith in the authorities. "In Scotland that means if the piece was found relatively recently, it belongs to the Crown," Adam went on regardless. "Now it's out there, your family probably has to hand it over, Angus, because it'd be state property."

Angus turned straight to Calum. "Come with me to see the bodach," he urged. "I'll call him. He'll know what to do."

"I can't spend that much time in a car, Angus," Calum protested. "There's an inquiry ongoing and—"

"If the chess piece has anything to do with this, the bodach will tell you things I don't know. We can take the Englishman. An *expert*." It sounded like an insult. "If Uilleam understands how close he is to losing that thing… maybe he can tell you something to help. He has a right to a say."

The surprising truth of that struck Calum squarely. He sighed. "All right." He looked at Adam, who gave a slow doubtful nod of acquiescence.

Angus sagged in his seat. All at once, he looked diminished, like a toy that had lost its stuffing. "That's it, then. That's all I can do."

Calum eyed him with concern.

"I'll get a car for you both," he told his mother. "Angus should rest."

"Angus is staying with *us*," Ishbel said with her usual certainty. "And *a' Thighearna, a' Chalum*, we're not going home in a police car. Can you imagine? We'll get a taxi."

"I've got a hire car," Adam said, unfolding from his chair. "I can take you."

"It's really not…" Calum began.

"Oh, *Adam*," Ishbel gushed. "That's very kind of you. You're *such* a good boy."

Calum didn't want to contemplate the thought of Adam, more or less alone under his mother's relentless interrogation, but she and Adam were already gathering up Angus and heading for the office door.

It's only twenty minutes, he told himself. And what was Adam going to say to her anyway?

So he led them out into reception without another word of protest, and it was as if he and Adam had never met before that day.

He'd seen Adam again, and the sky hadn't fallen in.

It was going to be fine.

* * * * *

Willie John was waiting outside the interview room when Calum got there, clutching his notebook.

"Have you finished with her already?" Calum found he felt far more relieved than guilty. He wanted to be able to sink into the investigation like any cop—detached, unaffected, uninvolved. "Anything interesting?"

Willie John grimaced. "I'm afraid Miss Morrison will only talk to you, sir. Alone. She's quite agitated."

Calum blew out a long breath. So much for that.

He was sailing so close to the wind.

But he said, "Okay, Willie John. Can you set up for a briefing after this? Maybe in twenty minutes?"

When he entered the interview room, Julia was sitting with her elbows on the table, mug of tea untouched beside her, face hidden in the palms of her hands. She looked up, and Calum could see she'd been crying again. The sorrow he felt for her worried him anew.

"Jools, it'd be better…"

"I know." She gave a watery sniff. "I wanted to talk to you because… I can't stand… They'll laugh."

Calum sat down and opened his notebook. He sighed. "No one's going to laugh."

Julia nodded, clearly unconvinced. Neither of them spoke for a second.

"He wasn't what anyone thought," she burst out, then looked almost startled by her own words. But she pressed on, "He was so much more, Orly."

Calum frowned. "Go on."

"He wasn't just some…small-minded middle-aged man who couldn't see past the croft. He was… He wanted…" She swallowed.

Calum looked up from his notebook. "What?"

"More," she said. "And *this* is where everyone'll smirk and *sneer*. Because he could spend all his days obsessed with the things they're obsessed with. Sheep and gossip and football and…*church*. But he couldn't care about *different* things."

"Different things?" Calum repeated as the light began to dawn. "You mean…Jennifer Aniston?"

Julia scowled. "So you've been into his computer. And *now* we get to it. It's okay to fall in love with a celebrity if you're a teenage girl, or a woman, but not if you're a middle-aged man."

Calum blinked. "No. That's not…"

"When I came home, Uncle Tormod was the *only* one who listened to me. Who didn't see me as just one more…exile who'd seen the light. Everyone else told me to 'just get over it.' But Uncle Tormod knew I needed time to accept. And he was fascinated by the business."

"By…show business?"

Julia sniffed and nodded.

"So…" Calum went on carefully. "We've established you were close. Did he ever mention borrowing money for the croft?"

Julia's large, damp eyes met his. "It wasn't for the croft."

Breakthrough, Calum thought with a rush of surprised relief.

"He wanted to see Hollywood," Julia blurted. Calum gaped at her. She rushed on impatiently. "To *be* there, not…view everything through a screen. But there was no way he could afford it. He was barely keeping the bills paid."

"You're saying…Tormod borrowed the money for a trip to California?" Calum's tone was pure incredulity.

"Yes!" Julia snapped. "*God*, Orly, *you* should understand what it's like when the whole *world* is out there and you can't reach it!" They stared at each other for fraught seconds.

"I came home because I wanted to," Calum said.

Julia's eyes searched his face. "Did you?" Her shoulders slumped. "Then at least you got to choose. Tormod was just *expected* to take over the croft, like his father and *his* father and... He wasn't encouraged to think of anything but...*here*. And being browbeaten into finding a wife and *having kids* by that stubborn old man in Uig."

"Your great-grandfather you mean?"

Julia's mouth twisted. "*Yes*. He's just...overwhelming. Like some sort of *patriarch*. We all try to please him. But the more time Tormod spent online, the more he realized how small and grey his own world was. And the clock was ticking, and he'd never done *anything* he wanted to do. So." She grimaced. "When he was in Glasgow, he borrowed some money, and he went to a casino. He said he needed to double it at least."

And Calum thought, *Could it really be that pitiful? That...small?*

"He lost it," he said.

"Yes."

"Why would he do something that *stupid*? He'd have no idea how casinos work."

"Because he used to play poker," Julia said. "He played with his friends when he was young, and he always won. Always. That's why he was called—"

"Lucky," Calum said on a breath. "*Shit*." It was fucking farcical. And tragic. And human. "So the people he borrowed from...?"

"I don't know who they are, but Tormod said they kept piling interest on it and sending him threats with more and more to pay back. Then he suddenly said he'd found a way to pay them *and* get his trip to LA and take me with him. He was so excited. I'd never seen him excited before."

Nor did anyone, Calum thought.

"It was kind of beautiful." Julia sounded wistful. "To see him come alive."

* * * * *

Calum left the station and drove home not long after half past eight.

In Glasgow, the forty-eight-hour window would have meant an all-nighter probably, but here, they were following leads for a murder that just possibly may not even be a murder, with a murder weapon that may just possibly not be the murder weapon. A murderer may well have left DNA and prints all over Tormod's house, and *maybe* they could match a perfect suspect on the PNC. But they didn't know.

They didn't know anything until they had conclusive forensics and a postmortem, and by the time that happened, Calum would have had to hand over the case to a new SIO.

But the closeness to the victim's family that had worried him, had inevitably become protectiveness. He didn't want anyone to laugh at Tormod either.

No nosy neighbor had seen anyone or anything suspicious at Tormod's house in the time frame they were working with—between Tormod leaving Angus, and Chrissie's arrival home. Chrissie was still under sedation in hospital.

So Calum set the small team the task of acquiring and checking incoming and outgoing ferry and plane passenger lists over the past couple of days, for anyone with a record that might incur police interest. He asked Willie John to check Tormod's email account for messages sent to Adam's address, and then he told him he was going to be following up a lead in Uig the next day.

Calum was still worrying compulsively at the nuances of the case as he turned the Subaru up the lane toward the New House. But the number of cars he found parked there told him, with a sinking certainty, what was going on inside.

Calum's parents must have organized a Worship for Tormod in their house.

If Calum had anywhere to go, after the day he'd had, he'd have accelerated away. Instead he parked in the space that had been politely left for him, and trudged inside.

Normally, when someone died, the coffin was in their home when people came to pay their respects: to pray and sing psalms; to talk about the Bible and reminisce about the deceased. But Tormod was in the mortuary until his postmortem was done, and Chrissie was in hospital. So, it seemed Calum's mother had inevitably taken over.

As Calum opened the back door to an ecstatic, wriggling greeting from Shep, he could hear his father's strong voice precenting a line of a Gaelic psalm from beyond the closed lounge door. Then, when Donnie's voice stopped, the sound of others in the room, men and women together, singing back the line in an eerie communal wail. The mournful power of it could still raise the hairs on the back of Calum's neck.

The empty kitchen bore signs of extensive preparations: plates with scones and pancakes covered with crowdie, the local soft cheese. Mountains of sandwiches and shop-bought cakes. Neighbors and visitors brought things to eat to help out at a Worship, and Calum's mother had obviously been busy filling the gaps.

Calum looked with longing at the second doorway from the kitchen into the hall, but he knew everyone would have heard his car arrive. There was no escape.

He tucked his police hat under his arm, and opened the door into the lounge.

The scene inside was as expected. People from the village and beyond, mainly older and dressed predominantly in black, were packed onto every seat that could be squeezed into the room. The minister sat in a place of honor by the fire; Angus, boilersuit removed, shrunken and far away, was beside him.

A respectful hush fell as everyone looked at the new arrival, and Calum raised a smile in response to the room-wide murmur of greeting. The village very much approved of his profession. But as his mother rose to embrace him, he realized that everything wasn't as expected, after all.

Adam was sitting in the far corner of the room, on one of the old-fashioned beige velour armchairs that made up Ishbel's three-piece suite. One of her best bone-china cups, balancing on a matching saucer, rested, with ludicrous fragility, in his hand. His expression, as he met Calum's eyes over her head, was uninterested.

In his suit and T-shirt, with his expensive haircut and tanned, chiselled face, he looked young and glossy and glamorous, somehow both comically out of place and perfectly at home in the middle of a Free Church wake. But Adam's savoir faire had always been unmatched.

Observing the customs of the native tribes, Calum thought savagely.

"I'll get you some tea, *m'eudail*," his mother said as she pulled back with a final comforting squeeze. Her voice was hushed and solemn, in keeping with the room.

Calum muttered, "Let me get changed first." Though he hadn't intended to. But he needed to regroup; to process the sight of Adam in his house again. To calm his anger that Adam would do this. Invade his life like this.

When he reached the safety of his bedroom, he stripped off his uniform and donned a black Aran jumper and black trousers.

He didn't want to go back out there.

He didn't want to have to interact with Adam as Calum again, rather than Inspector Macleod. It had been a miscalculation to change out of his uniform, but it was too late now.

He sat on the side of his bed, trying to prepare himself. But he found himself instead picking up his phone and going to his personal email, and he could even accept that he was using the threatening emails to stiffen his own backbone.

Another one was waiting, as he'd expected. "For Calum 3." He opened it with a mixture of determination and dread.

It's been a long time since I wrote to you, my darling. I've been trying to force myself to understand that this is all I will ever have. But it's fitting it should be today. The Catholic priest at Arras used to say that guilt and shame require expiation. So here is my confession: I'm getting married today. Please, please don't be disappointed in me. So many men died in the war... So few babies now. I have a responsibility, so I'm told. No choice but to betray you, since I must live on. And I must. John Gillies says self-murder is the ultimate sin. And I dare not sin again, or I won't find you when this ordeal is finally over. All I have left is the hope of a shred of mercy from Gillies's God. Gillies is conducting the ceremony, of course. It's right that he gets to turn the key. The girl is Mairi a' Bhragan, though I don't suppose you're interested. I'm not interested myself. But today I'll promise to spend the rest of my life with her, on our croft. Yours and mine. She doesn't see me. I know that. No one will ever see me clearly again.

Calum rubbed his eyes and closed the email. He should be focusing on why he was getting these messages. On who was sending them and what the sender wanted him to do. It was pretty obvious what they wanted him *not* to do.

But despite everything, Calum found himself reluctantly identifying with the writer's unending isolation. Pitying the fate of the woman the man was about to marry, with no concept of the destruction inside him.

The minister was talking in soft tones when Calum reentered the lounge, and the first thing he saw was the chair his mother had put out for him beside Adam, with a cup of tea and a plate of sandwich quarters on a small table in front of them. He could see why she'd thought it was a good idea—two old friends, both unequipped to do more than observe. But it felt like punishment. He didn't look at Adam as he walked to the chair and sat down.

He picked up his delicate cup and saucer. His stomach was too knotted to eat.

The people in the room were talking in English, he noticed only then, presumably so Adam could understand, though Calum was almost in the same boat. They wouldn't have made that allowance for him, but for a visitor…

"Angus had a bit of a breakdown on the way here," Adam murmured. Calum's teacup stilled at his mouth. "Your mother asked me to stay after we calmed him down."

A spontaneous hush fell over the room before Calum could formulate a reply. It lasted for minutes, with the occasional muttered vocalization of a response to a private thought.

"Aye, aye."

"It's like that."

"It's as the Lord wills."

Otherwise, an intense, introspective quiet, in keeping with a faith that reflected constantly on the impermanence of life, and its inevitable end. Calum wondered, with unwilling defensiveness, what Adam was making of it.

Then the minister spoke, and the evening wore on in singing and talking and praying, until the first people stood to go, a few at a time, all moving to clasp Angus's hands in silent support before they left.

Adam waited until close to the end to stand—before the minister went, but not so soon that he seemed to be grabbing the first chance to escape. He didn't speak to Calum, but went to Angus, hunkering down to say something to him; then he stood to talk to Ishbel, who listened to him with an innocent affection that hurt Calum's heart. And when she glanced expectantly at Calum, he had no choice but to see his friend to the door.

In the shadowy quiet of the kitchen, the only sound was the dull *thump* of Shep's hopeful tail as he lay in his bed. Calum's mouth tasted sour, his gut lumpen with nerves. But he was going to spend hours in a car with Adam the next day. He had to calm down. He had to normalize this.

Except, he didn't know how to handle it. How to be polite, but not encouraging.

Just in case…Adam still felt anything for him.

"Thanks for staying," Calum said as they reached the back door. It sounded too stiff. "It was kind of you."

Adam looked up from his phone, which he'd switched on as he walked. "The kindness was your mother's, for asking me." There was something disdainful in his tone, but not for the Worship. "It was very moving. Spiritual belief's so much a part of their everyday lives that it brings them genuine serenity."

Calum opened his mouth, but he realized he had no idea what to say.

Adam had seen what he saw—the beauty of a community fuelled by spirituality. And yet, how could he, from his urbane, liberal, cosmopolitan background, understand the flip side of that? To Adam, Lewis must seem like a quaint anthropological expedition. It was easy to patronize from that position.

Calum opened the back door, and as he did, Adam's phone came online and began to ping, message after message notification in fast succession. Calum stared at it wide-eyed until finally it fell silent.

When he looked up, Adam grimaced with chagrin, the least controlled expression he'd shown since Calum had first seen him in reception at the police station.

"Museum emergency?" he asked.

Adam huffed a reluctant laugh, then seemed to regret it. "My partner. I didn't get the chance to explain my phone would be off."

Partner. Well, of course he'd have someone. Someone clingy and paranoid. Or just, in love.

The confirmation brought a gush of feeling. Relief. Safety. Some stab of wild panic he stamped down.

He didn't know what made him ask, "Do they...work at the museum?" He sounded as tentative and naive as a little boy, he thought with disgust.

Adam's eyes were brilliant in the dim light, taking in everything about him and finding him wanting.

"*He's* an actor," Adam said.

Challenge and condemnation in one uncompromising little pronoun.

Calum raised his chin. Well. He could deal with Adam's contempt better than his love.

"Is an eight forty-five pickup okay?" he asked. "Where are you staying?"

"The Suilven," Adam said. One of the less modern hotels in town. "I'll be outside at a quarter to nine."

He stepped onto the path and disappeared into the pitch darkness. A few seconds later Calum heard a car engine start at the front of the house. And he stood there, listening, until it faded into the stillness of the night.

CHAPTER FIVE

Calum slept poorly, his mind buzzing with too many worries, too many images.

Chrissie cheerful; Chrissie destroyed.

Tormod's blood and his open eyes; Tormod's unknown inner life.

Adam. How he looked through Calum as if he were nothing to him. How Calum wanted it that way.

The gorgeous, grown-up Adam in Calum's twee lounge. In the kitchen. Watching his parents' pure faith. Adam, who'd reinserted himself into Calum's new life as he'd once unknowingly haunted the old.

Everything seemed to be conspiring in some sort of perfect storm. The murder, forcing Adam into Calum's orbit. His parents' unsuspecting lionising of him. Those bloody emails, showing Calum a full Technicolor imagining of the misery of a man from Lewis, who'd fallen in love with a man. Blackmail, or a well-meant reminder of where sin could lead?

He finally slept at around three and was up at seven thirty, showering before donning a fresh uniform.

He checked his email on his phone as he stood by the closed door of his bedroom, and as he'd expected, it was there.

"For Calum 4."

He stared at it for long seconds, telling himself to file it unread and wait for the bastard to show his hand.

But he opened it.

We've had a son. I should care, but I can't. It's a duty done. Except, if they'd let me name him after you...perhaps. But that isn't tradition. He must be called after me, and my father before me, and what does it matter anyway? It never gets better. Three years and it never gets better. I get so angry, and afraid, knowing that for the rest of my life, every day, I must be this pretense of a man. Never happy or honest again, as long as I live. I rage at God, and I rage at myself for enduring this punishment. But I have to swallow all that rage. And at least, I suppose, it's a feeling. I might as well feel something, to remind me I'm still above ground.

Angus, who'd stayed the night in Calum's parents' spare room, was sitting at the table when Calum came into the kitchen, for all he still appeared on the brink of collapse. He looked unfamiliar in a thick grey sweater and grey trousers, oddly naked without the ubiquitous flat cap. His mother had, of course, risen even earlier to cook a full breakfast before they left. Calum had rarely felt less like eating, but he did, to please her.

They picked up Adam outside his hotel, exactly on time. He'd dressed in blue jeans, a tweed jacket, and a collared shirt with a thin jumper, what Calum would call a university-lecturer look, as if Adam had calculated that an older man might respond to more formal clothing. Except, he looked as sexy as all hell in it.

Calum thought maybe he should text Donna, the girl Chrissie had teased him about the day before. Though it felt like months. Years. His mother had been thrilled by Donna.

They all exchanged a terse good morning, Adam climbed into the back seat, and then Calum pulled the car onto Bayhead, heading out of town onto the Barvas road. Uig was on the west coast, and the drive would take an hour from Stornoway, which, on the island, was a long journey.

The road was flanked by flat, bleak, relentless moorland dotted with the scars of peat banks, the odd shabby wooden hut, wandering blackface sheep, and every so often, a small village to break the scenic monotony, before more empty moor under the huge sky. But as they headed west, the landscape became prettier, with the mountains of Harris in the distance, and multiple small lochs scattered around the moor, gleaming like burnished metal in the ever-changing patterns of light. The weather was brisk again, sweeping unimpeded across the island from the Atlantic, and Calum barely noticed anymore how the sky turned from grey to blue, rain to sunshine, in a matter of seconds.

Every so often, though, they passed evidence that some things were changing—attempts at growing fields of trees as a crop, in defiance of that tyrannical wind. Calum still remembered his gaping astonishment at the size of sycamores on the mainland. The only one he'd ever known until then, in a village farther down Point, had been barely ten feet tall, though it was over a hundred years old. The wind wouldn't permit anything more.

It took close to thirty minutes, but eventually, on edge as Calum was, the absence of interaction in the car and the hypnotic purr of the engine became so oppressive that he blurted, "What kind of state's the old man in, Angus?"

He felt as if he'd rudely jolted the others from a trance.

Angus's eyes fixed on him. "State? He's ninety-six."

Adam gave a snort of amusement in the back seat.

"I know, but is he...um...?"

"Gaga?" Angus finished with typical island bluntness. "No. But he has a care assistant going in to get him up and put him to bed. He should be in Dun Eisdean." Dun Eisdean was one of Lewis's four care homes, the one where Julia worked, viewed by independent old people around the island less as a chance of an easier life, than an admission of senility and surrender. "He says he'll be carried out feet first, though. He was cutting and stacking peats just last summer. Shooting geese. But he went downhill."

"Shooting?" Calum repeated incredulously. "At ninety-six?"

"He was ninety-five," Angus said, unperturbed. "He did game-keeping for the estate." The west coast of Lewis was dotted with sporting estates, owned mainly by rich absentees. And vigorous physical activity into the nineties wasn't that unusual on the islands. But possession of a firearm was.

"I don't know very much about the chessmen," Angus volunteered suddenly. "Just that they were found at Ardroil. On the beach."

"Actually, we don't even know that for sure," Adam said. Calum's hands tightened on the wheel. "Those are just local stories. But we *are* sure the pieces are of Viking origin and they were carved in the twelfth century. At that time Lewis was actually part of the kingdom of Norway, not Scotland, and we think there may have been some important settlements along the west coast of the island. They'd be on the route between Norway and Ireland."

"But there's nothing important in Uig," Angus protested.

"Not now," Adam replied. "*Now* we rely on roads. But then, the sea was the easy way to travel long distances, so...that made the west coast important. Anyway, there are two theories about where the chessmen came from, but the main one's Trondheim in Norway, commissioned by the archbishop."

"So..." Angus pursed his mouth. "Why were they in Lewis?"

"Well, most investigators believe they were buried on the beach because of some crisis mid-journey. But a few think there may have been a major settlement a bit farther south of Ardroil, at Mealista, and they might have belonged to someone important there. That they were really found at Mealista, not on Uig beach."

"What a stupid thing to care so much about," Angus said tiredly.

"It's great art," Adam said. "Art and culture. And history. People'll pay any amount for that."

"*People* will pay for all sorts of things," Angus returned. "And they'll kill for them. But in the end, they'll have to stand before their Maker and explain what they did on earth, for *things*."

* * * * *

The bodach's house stood alone, an inhabited version of the Old House Calum saw every day. By the look of it, it had also been built at the turn of the twentieth century to replace a black house—the thatched stone dwellings that had once made up Mealista.

All that was left was the village's footprint—a floor plan laid out in rows of stone. If it had once been an important medieval settlement, it was a ghost now, looking out to sea. It had been cleared of people like many others in Uig in the nineteenth century, to make way for the landlord's sheep and shepherds, but the symmetrical lines of *feannagan*—lazy beds for crops—were still visible on the slopes around the ruins, hacked out by villagers over the years in the endless struggle to survive. A visual memory, an eternal reproach.

The old man's house, though, stood defiant, isolated in the bleak land-scape a few hundred yards from the old village, yet with the trappings of modern life attached. A satellite dish on the smoking chimney. PVC win-dows. A dusty, black Ford Fiesta outside. And as they walked around to the back door in the sharp, blousy wind, something more timeless: a peat stack, expertly built. Now central heating was the thing, fewer people cut and dried peat, even as free fuel. Calum missed the smell, one of the most evocative he could think of.

And this was the bodach's last stack; his last, long-held independence.

A man in his early thirties waited for them at the open back door; medium height and muscle-bound, with mid-brown, close-cropped hair and a well-trimmed beard. He eyed Calum's uniform with obvious surprise, but he identified himself, in a lowlands accent, as Kevin Reid, the old man's care assistant. He had the over-cheerful demeanor Calum associated with people who worked with the elderly and children, and which Julia refused to adopt as a matter of principle.

Kevin led them up a narrow hallway and in through a door on the right of the passageway.

The room they entered was large, but gloomy and muggy. Two small windows let in what light there was, and the walls were lined with painted tongue-and-groove wood. The whole room was yellow-brown, once-white walls and ceiling plaster stained by decades of tobacco and peat smoke. A small fire glowed meanly in an open hearth, and against one wall, toward the far corner, the door of a shotgun cabinet sat just ajar, like a provocation.

"How is he?" Angus asked.

"Quiet," Kevin said. "Not that he's usually chatty, but..." He shrugged and threw another curious glance at Calum. He didn't seem to know about the old man's loss. "It's good he has visitors."

The man sitting by the fire showed no indication he heard himself being discussed. And Calum barely heard it either.

The image was like a punch to his memory. Déjà vu, though he knew it was a trick of the mind.

The man wore a flat tweed cap, and beside him, a pipe sat smoking in a big glass ashtray. His face was seamed with age, but he sat stiffly upright, just like the man Calum saw in his mind's eye.

Calum had just been five when his great-grandfather died. His memory was of the old man sitting in the same chair in his grandparents' kitchen in the Old House every single day, stern and straight like this, with a pipe always in his mouth or by his hand, and his flat cap on his head. He'd been in his nineties too, and Calum had been terrified of him. But one day, when his grandparents were looking after him, Calum had contracted a stomach bug. His granny had given him lime cordial, and he'd associated the smell of it with sickness ever since. But his great-grandfather had risen from his chair and sat beside him, and Calum still had the sense memory of a hand, gnarled with age, stroking his hair. And the sound of his deep voice: *"Tha thu ceart gu leòr, a' Chalum."* *You're all right...*

When he snapped back to himself, Angus had seated himself on a smaller chair beside his father-in-law, talking to him in rapid Gaelic. Calum caught the word *poileas. Police.* And then, "*Tha fios agam air a phàrantan.*" *I know his parents.*

He clenched his jaw in annoyance. "In English, Angus. Please."

Both old men stilled and looked up at him. He took off his police hat and tucked it under his arm.

"Mr. Macaulay, I'm Inspector Calum Macleod of Western Isles Police Force," he said. "And this"—he gestured with his head at Adam, standing just behind his shoulder—"is Adam Patterson from the British Museum. He's an expert on the chessmen."

The bodach's gaze shot to Adam and stayed there.

"You need to talk to them, Uilleam." Angus sounded and looked exhausted. "They're saying the chess piece belongs to…to the country. Or the Crown. Not to the person who found it."

"How's Chrissie?" Uilleam asked, as if Angus hadn't spoken.

Angus hung his head. "The doctor says…she's not responding when they talk to her."

Uilleam patted his shoulder.

"Even if the piece was passed down," Adam said as he moved farther into the room, "I'm afraid there isn't a time limit on treasure trove in Scotland."

"Is that so?" Uilleam said. His gaze rose from Angus's bent grey head to fix again on Adam. His eyes looked almost white in the dim light, as if they had no irises, but Calum realized they were a sharp, pale blue. The words Julia had used sprang to his mind. *Overwhelming. Stubborn.* And he'd bullied Tormod.

Adam said mildly, "It's the law. Aimed to keep objects of cultural significance in the country."

Uilleam's lip curled. "What *country?*" His tone was so contemptuous, he may as well have spat on the floor. "I have no interest in any country, and they do not belong to any Crown."

They.

Fuck.

Calum's chest tightened with new tension. "The law is the law, sir, and if you have any information..."

"Spoken like a poileas," Uilleam said. It wasn't a compliment. "What my family has, is a trust which is unbroken. We have *found* nothing."

"It's your duty to tell us how you came to have that chess piece," Calum countered. "Which is now evidence in a possible murder case."

"That piece belongs with our family."

"It makes no difference who found it," Calum repeated. "It *belongs* to the Crown."

Adam put in quickly, "Is that the only piece you found?"

Uilleam regarded them both like rude children.

"We thought the worst had come and gone with my great-grandfather. I should have known...when I did not have a son." He scowled. "They were *given* by God, not found."

He is *gaga*, Calum thought with weary certainty. But he said, with all the patience he could muster, "Would you like to explain?"

"No, I would *not* like to," Uilleam snapped. "But it seems I must." He let out a deep breath. It sounded like resignation. "The piece has been in the protection of our family since it came to the island."

Adam threw Calum a quick, speaking glance, then looked away. "That was...most probably in the twelfth century," he pointed out.

"Yes," Uilleam said.

There was an uncertain silence. Calum had to fight not to roll his eyes, impatience rising in his chest like dread.

Calum's grandmother had taken to seeing fairies everywhere, and accusing his mother of stealing her underwear. This was just more elaborate. Uilleam must have been a well-read man in his prime to weave all this in his head now, but Calum had no time to indulge him.

"*Chan eil e air a bhith air a h-innse a-riamh roimhe ann am Beurla,*" Uilleam said suddenly. It sounded like a formal declaration, and it defeated Calum's basic Gaelic.

"Angus?" he gritted. *Fuck*, but it had been a huge misjudgment to come.

"He said, 'It has never been told before in English,'" Angus replied, then muttered something in Gaelic to Uilleam, who snorted with disdain.

"Listen, then," Uilleam said. "My forefather was on a great ship bound for Norway. A thrall and son of thralls, taken from Ireland to meet his fate. The pieces had been brought from Iceland to the court of a Norse lord." Adam made a sound, but the old man ignored him. "He was taking them and his household back to his first home. But the ship foundered in a huge storm, and the lord and all on board perished. All except the Macaulay. He pulled himself onto the top of...of a table, which bore a chest. He did not know what it held, but inside it were the pieces. He washed ashore at Mealista beach."

It sounded like a recitation. An oral legend learned and repeated, with the poetic formality of translated Gaelic.

"He was found close to death by a holy woman. One of the *Cailleachan Dubha*."

"Old...black women?" Calum could translate that much.

"Nuns," Adam said softly.

"Just that," Uilleam agreed. "At the time there was a terrible plague in the land, and many were being cared for in their last hours by the woman and her fellows. But when the Macaulay was borne into their house with his treasure, the people began to heal. When the women and the Macaulay opened the chest, they found carvings of men bearing the mark of God. The holiest woman understood that they had been sent to the island with the Macaulay for a purpose, and here they must stay or pain and suffering would surely return. So the Macaulay remained. And for three centuries, his sons and their sons served the women, and the pieces were kept in a place of honor."

A cheery knock broke the moment and Kevin pushed in, carrying a tatty tray covered with painted, varnished flowers and bearing four mugs and a plate of biscuits. He put it down on the table and straightened with a smile. Then he seemed to register the atmosphere.

"So," he said uncertainly, "I'll just... I'll be off, then, William. Sorry again."

Uilleam nodded. "That's all right, Kevin. We'll see you tomorrow."

Kevin gave a wave of farewell. The door closed after him, to silence.

"He was a few minutes late," Uilleam explained to Angus. "You'll have to help yourselves."

No one made a move to the tray. Uilleam gave a majestic nod and continued.

"The time came when the women's house was overthrown. Their kind of religion cast to the winds."

"The Reformation," Adam said.

"They told the Macaulay to hide the carvings," Uilleam went on. "To make sure they remained on this island, for the salvation of the people. And so it has been ever since. Eldest son to eldest son. Sgàire to Sgàire."

"Sgàire?" Calum repeated. "There's an old song isn't there? 'Calum Sgàire'?"

"It's a song," Uilleam said dismissively. "Sgàire is the name we all bear in memory. The name of the Macaulay. In English it has been made 'Zachariah.' But that's not it."

Zachariah was certainly not an island name.

Adam said, "But many of the pieces *have* been found."

"When the holy women were cast out," Uilleam said darkly, "the hoard was split into two smaller ones—easier to hide, and if the worst came, all would not be lost. And the worst did come. A Pennyroyal man found one hiding place…and then it was just as the holy woman had prophesied: the pieces were sent from the island, coveted and pawed and sold for coin, some lost to the four winds. And tragedy followed. The people were driven from the land. Mealista, and Pennyroyal, and villages like them, emptied of every soul. The very man who found and sold the pieces was exiled with the rest of his kin, never to see the shores of home. My great-grandfather watched it all, helpless, but he hid in the hills, starving and freezing, refusing to abandon his charge until it was safe to return, though all his people had gone. And here I am, in his wake. But…" His voice wavered, and for the first time, he sounded like an old man. "Now the next Macaulay is dead, and he had no sons."

The room fell into thick silence. When Calum darted a look at Adam, he was staring at the bodach as if he'd turned to gold. Angus was crying.

Calum's frustration burst into fury. *That* was the reason the old man mourned his grandson? That sad fairy tale? Julia had been absolutely right about him.

Stubborn. Implacable. Irrational.

The next Macaulay is dead.

"Your grandson was a Macdonald," Calum pointed out.

Uilleam's pale, watery eyes fixed on him. Grief hardened to contempt.

"You think I do not know how he was named, *poileas*? *Tormod Sgàire Mhic Amhlaigh Mhic Dhomhaill.*" *Norman Zachariah Macaulay Macdonald.* "He would have been next. But you say my boy betrayed his line."

Angus made a sound of distress.

Calum clenched his teeth on the words that wanted to spew forth.

"So there *are* other chess pieces?" Adam asked. "Another set? Or more?" Uilleam's stare was so flat, it could have passed for insolence. "You know where they are? But you won't…show them?"

"I will not," Uilleam snapped. "Even if the knowledge dies with me, at least they will remain here, and safe. And now you know there is nothing for you. You have no right to the queen piece. It's been passed down my family as the symbol of their task. Which *Crown* can claim what has been our purpose for eight hundred years? They've stolen enough."

"This is pointless," Calum said to Adam. Then with cold, official politeness, "Thank you for your time, Mr. Macaulay." He didn't know who he felt more furious with—that baleful old man, or himself.

He didn't wait for a reply he didn't want to hear. He turned and made his way out of the house, letting the sharp, sane, sea wind cool the heat of his face. He put on his hat and pulled his phone from his pocket just as he heard movement behind him.

When he turned, Adam was standing just outside the open door, eyeing him as if he were a particularly obnoxious child. His hair blew wildly about his face in the Atlantic breeze. In the bright daylight, it had lighter streaks in it, the color of pale honey. Calum didn't want to notice.

Adam said, "This needs some diplomacy, not—"

"This needs some fucking honesty," Calum shot back. "Or have you really bought that bullshit? Whoever found that piece…him or his *forefather*…they've used it to feed this…family delusion. It makes them special. It keeps the eldest child tied here. Obedient."

Adam frowned. "There were certain factors in that story that render it plausible."

"*Plausible?* A magic chess set that saves the island from disaster?"

"That's not the part—"

"You want that *fairy tale* he spun to be true!"

"Of course I want it to be true! Well, a bit of it. And I'm *telling* you there are valid reasons to take it seriously. Why won't you listen?"

Calum paced and turned again. "I'm running a murder enquiry! This is a complete waste of time I *don't* have."

"And if I were someone else with expertise on the Uig chessmen, would you be sneering?"

Calum stilled. Would he?

Adam's voice dropped to dangerous softness. "Or is it that you just can't respect a poof?"

The word was like a bullet. Calum felt it hit home. He opened his mouth to utter an outraged denial, because it wasn't true. But he could understand why Adam believed it. Once upon a time, he'd *made* Adam believe it.

Calum's phone sounded in his hand like a half-time referee. There was a tight, furious knot of pain in his throat. But the name on the screen was a reminder of where he should be.

He choked out, "Inspector Macleod."

"There's been an incident, sir," Willie John said. The apprehension in his tone was enough, even without the sound of a police siren wailing behind it.

"For fuck's sake!" Calum spat. How many investigations had he run, and he'd never lost control of one like this. He closed his eyes and clawed back his temper. This *wasn't* him. It felt as if everything was conspiring to erode his sense of control.

When he opened his eyes again, he fixed them on the everyday order of the peat stack; its herringbone neatness. "Tell me."

"The sister and niece of the victim. Watch out, Alasdair!" Willie John yelled. "Sorry, sir. Joan and Julia Morrison. Their neighbor just called 999. We're on our way."

As if that wasn't evident.

Calum's chest was hollow.

This was *his* misjudgment. His stupidity. He should have been there instead of following this…glamorous fantasy, when the reality of the case was simple violence. But he'd known, hadn't he, that Tormod's death would pale, for his superiors or the press, next to the discovery of the chess piece.

And he'd allowed that to lead him away from murder.

CHAPTER SIX

The journey back to Stornoway was conducted in tense silence.

Angus more or less shut down when Calum told him about the attack, as if he couldn't take any more. Even Uilleam had the wind taken out of his sails. Adam climbed into the car without any further argument.

The road was single track most of the way, but the blue flashing light Calum stuck on the roof had oncoming drivers cowering into passing places to let them by. So they barely had to slow their headlong rush back to town.

Calum headed straight for the Western Isles Hospital, a sprawling, modern, two-story building set around a large car park. There were two police patrol cars idling outside the central reception area, and Willie John waited inside the glass doors. He was already moving as he began to speak to Calum.

"They're in a private room, sir, with a couple of men outside as ordered." They followed Willie through double doors into a generic corridor. "Mrs. Macdonald is in with them."

Angus made an urgent sound behind Calum. "Chrissie's awake!"

When Calum glanced around, he realized Adam had followed too, holding Angus's arm to steady him.

"This morning," Willie John said. "We took a statement from her first thing. They're in here."

He opened the door into a room containing two beds. One held Seonag. She'd already been extremely frail before this; now her face looked like a skull; her skin, the green-grey of a corpse. Her wheelchair sat by the window.

Chrissie lay in the other bed in a hospital gown, looking older than Calum had ever seen her. And in a chair by her mother's bed, Julia, fully dressed and battle worn.

She had a burgeoning black eye and a split lip, her chignon had collapsed, but she stood gamely to greet them.

"This is bloody ridiculous," she said, though her cut-glass voice trembled. "Like a Saturday night drama. Don't they know they're on Lewis?"

The tight ball of anxiety that had ground and scraped in Calum's stomach since he'd heard about the attack began to shrink.

"What happened?" he asked.

"The doorbell rang," she said. "And I opened the door without looking, like…" Like you did on Lewis. "Like an idiot. A man…a big man…pushed his way in. It was…" Her breathing shook. "He was wearing a black balaclava and…and surgical gloves. You don't know how terrifying that is till you see it in real life."

"What time?"

"About…half past nine."

"What did he want?"

"Money," Julia said. "Money we don't have. He said we have a month to pay Uncle Tormod's debt. And…" She touched her eye. "Mum was still in bed. He took me into her room and punched me a couple of times to show he meant business, and…I must have passed out. Mum couldn't get up on her own…I think she thought I was dead. When I came to, I got our neighbor."

Calum glanced at the bed. Seonag had her eyes closed, as if no one else was in the room. At the other bed, Angus huddled beside Chrissie, talking in whispered, urgent Gaelic.

"Is there anything else you remember about him?" Calum asked. "Anything he said?"

"He wasn't local. And he didn't care. There was nothing there to reach. Mum's... She's terrified. We can't pay them."

"Of course not," Calum said with disbelief.

But he realized he'd lost Julia's attention. Her surprised gaze had fixed instead on a point over his shoulder.

"Adam?" She sounded baffled. And it was only then that Calum remembered they couldn't explain Adam's presence to Julia without betraying Chrissie's secret right in front of her. He swung around quickly.

"I...thought I could, um..." Adam stuttered. Calum had never seen him at a loss for words before. "I wanted to see how you were."

"That was nice of you," she said. But the frowning glance she threw at Calum was puzzled.

Out in the corridor, Calum dispatched Willie John and his DCs to start procedures to monitor the airport and the two ferry terminals; one in Stornoway, the other in Harris, because if the attacker had any sense, he would prioritize getting off the island.

Finally, there remained only the two uniformed constables on guard, and Adam.

"I'll take you to your hotel," Calum said. He began to walk, and Adam followed without comment.

The car was back in traffic on the main road, when Adam spoke again. "I'm sorry, Cal." He gave a heavy sigh. "Of course the murder investigation has to be the priority."

It was an olive branch, the first thing Adam had said to Calum that didn't feel weighed down with old anger. And the first time Adam had used Calum's old pet name. Any name, really.

Calum took a treacherous, masochistic pleasure in the pain it gave him.

He said carefully, "You have your own priorities. I understand that." He hesitated and glanced sideways. "What are you going to do? About the chess piece? About Uilleam?"

Adam ran his hand back through his hair, an absent gesture that still somehow left the shorter locks on top of his head falling back in perfect, seductive order around the sides of his face.

Calum's eyes fixed front.

"I wish I knew," Adam said.

"It would be helpful...to the investigation..." *To me.* "If you could keep it confidential for a short while."

He glanced quickly at Adam again. The look Adam threw him made it clear the underlying plea had been understood.

"My boss'll want a report soon," Adam said. "But...I'll do my best to stall. Once he knows...he's a Twitter account in human form."

Calum snorted.

It felt like a truce.

"I need to go back to talk to Uilleam, though," Adam said. "He has to understand the queen *will* be forfeit if he doesn't put that story of long-term prior ownership to official channels. I mean... I suppose he can claim Lewis was under the Norwegian crown when his ancestor brought it in, but..."

The car pulled to a halt outside the front door of the hotel.

It had been an insignificant interlude. Maybe five minutes. But Calum didn't want the peace between them to end.

He needed to say it, though. "No one's going to believe they didn't find it recently. I have to put it into the evidence locker before the new SIO arrives, and then...it's fair game. Treasure trove, like you said."

Adam unbuckled his seat belt and opened the passenger door.

"Possibly. Though..." He shrugged. "Hard to believe, but *sometimes* I'm actually wrong." He climbed out of the car, then leaned inside again, hand propped on the roof. He met Calum's too eager eyes, and his expression slid from wry amusement to something that looked like pity. "And sometimes," he said softly, "you are."

* * * * *

The rest of Calum's day was an exercise in futility.

He called another briefing, listened to accounts of progress that hadn't been made, and gave out a new list of tasks. So far, only a handful of the hundreds of names checked on ferry and plane manifests for the previous four days, cross-checked with past, serious criminal activity. They unearthed a few convictions for possession, a convicted burglar from Watford, and someone who'd served time for assault in Dundee. But no convenient flags for a hard man from Glasgow.

With his limited manpower, Calum organized a watch on both ferry terminals and the airport, in case a name came through, though he knew the likelihood was vanishingly small.

Chrissie's interview had given them nothing. She'd found Tormod dead on the floor and seen no one else. They closed off Seonag and Julia's flat in Stornoway as a crime scene until the Inverness forensic team could get at it, after dusting what they could for fingerprints. But it was a formality. From what Julia had said, the man had been wearing what amounted to a pro's uniform to avoid leaving DNA traces.

Calum called one of his old mates in the Glasgow force, a DS called Jimmy Leary, to ask him to nose around any word of a hit on a bad debt on Lewis. But Jimmy's surprise underlined his own nagging unease…because it was extreme even for the thugs they'd customarily dealt with. Bad debts usually led to broken legs or no kneecaps. Not a cut throat. It was bad business. Dead men couldn't pay you back.

So he had to ask himself—what else had Tormod been up to?

At four thirty they heard that the IP address used to send the threatening emails to Tormod had been traced to a public computer in an Internet café on Woodlands Road in Glasgow.

Every line of inquiry was collapsing around them. But these kinds of people weren't accustomed to leaving loose ends.

Chief Inspector Martin, when he called in, was sympathetic but unsurprised. "You've covered all the angles. The only one expecting miracles was you. The Inverness lot'll stand a better chance."

Which did nothing for Calum's mood. By ten o'clock that evening, cross-checking yet another list of passenger names, Calum was ready to swing for someone.

He leaned back in his office chair and squeezed his eyes shut until sparks appeared behind his lids.

He used to be good at this. At thinking things through rationally, while knowing too, when to listen to his gut. But this time…

Maybe it was being here. Back at home…

He had to stop reacting and start reasoning.

Focus!

A murder committed over a bad debt. The murderer staying behind on the island to rub the message in, even though he must have known the risk. An island was easily closed off.

What was he missing?

The extraneous factor? The chess piece?

Perhaps he needed to look at it from another angle. He'd been so focused on indications of a professional hit that he'd sidelined the piece as an active factor.

Well, yes, Calum, because that's where all the evidence points.

But what were actually the odds of a priceless antique turning up at a murder scene and having nothing to do with it?

Calum hadn't thought of a rational reason why it would be left behind by the murderers if they knew what it was, but that didn't mean a reason didn't exist.

Maybe he'd been too logical, closing off his instincts. Maybe he'd been so preoccupied with staying away from Adam, he'd failed to examine all the avenues.

He lifted his phone and looked at it for a second or two, then deliberately pressed the mail app. It felt like defiance. His personal email account. "For Calum 5." He tapped it open without second-guessing himself.

Mairi told me today that my indifference has broken her heart. She said she loved me since we were children and marrying me was her greatest dream. And I understood that she is me. I loved you from childhood, and my love broke my heart. Sometimes I wish I had never known you, and then perhaps I could have told myself that my strange feelings were nothing. Imagination. In innocence, perhaps I could have lived something like a normal life. But I bit the apple. I cannot un-know. She deserved someone to love her as she loved them. But this is the world of the living. Each day behind my mask, I think that of the two of us, you and I, you were by far the more fortunate.

Calum read it twice before storing it in the locked folder he'd created. Then he called the number for the Suilven Hotel.

* * * * *

When Calum arrived, Adam was sitting at the hotel bar, dressed in a thin black V-neck jumper and black jeans. The outfit was casual and unassuming, while most of the other patrons were dressed up for a Saturday night out, but Adam looked to Calum, effortlessly, the most glamorous person in the seriously dated room. A couple of young women standing at the perpendicular leg of the bar seemed to agree, because they were eyeing Adam like starstruck lions sizing up a gazelle.

Calum pulled up the red velour stool beside him and sat down. Before leaving the station, he'd changed out of his uniform into a pair of blue jeans, a casual collared pale-green shirt, and a light leather jacket he kept in his office for emergencies. Emergencies like going to meet someone in a bar.

"Hey," he said. Adam looked up from his contemplation of his glass. His drink was half gone. "Thanks for meeting me."

"No problem." There was still distance there, of course. Calum had cemented it in a long time ago. "You want a drink? The bar'll be closing soon. Or…are you still on duty?"

Calum thought about it. "Yes and no," he said. "But on the whole, no."

"Well." Adam smiled, though he didn't show his teeth. "This is Isle of Harris gin. It's good. Have you tried it?"

"Too expensive on a policeman's salary. I'll have a pint."

Adam opened his mouth as if to argue the point, but he didn't. He attracted the barman's attention, ordered a pint of lager, and despite Calum's protestations, put the drink on his room tab. Calum took a sip and considered his approach.

"What you said in Uig," he began. Adam raised an eyebrow. He was almost ridiculously attractive, as if the universe had created him and dropped him back into Calum's life just to sneer at him. "You said there were reasons you didn't discount Uilleam's story." Adam's focus on him was unnerving. "Can you tell me what they were?"

He waited for Adam to claim his pound of flesh, but he merely frowned and pursed his mouth into a thoughtful pout. Calum looked away, only to find the two women down the bar avidly studying both of them now. Gearing up, he realized, to make a move.

"Let's find somewhere we can talk." He slid off his stool and led the way to a small rectangular table tucked into a corner of the room.

They each took a chair on either side, facing each other.

"Okay," Adam said. "The Macaulays. Genetic research suggests the mainland clan is most likely descended from Vikings. The name comes from a derivative of Óláfr. But, with Macaulay males on Lewis, concentrated in Uig, the analysis of Y-DNA's different. It shows genetic origins in Southwest Ireland. That specific DNA marker's very rare in Scotland, and there's a theory it may come from Irish slaves, taken by Vikings to the islands. They called them thralls."

Calum rubbed his mouth with the tips of his fingers. "So...I suppose... that bit might fit."

"You may not remember local legends of a convent in Mealista. It was called *Tigh nan Cailleachan Dubha*." His Gaelic accent was creditable. "No evidence has been found it actually existed, but..."

"But Uilleam Sgàire backs it up," Calum said.

Adam's eyes glowed with enthusiasm. "And that's another thing. I've been doing some work on that name. It's only used in the Macaulay family in Uig. And Uilleam's right. The proper English translation isn't Zachariah, it's Iskair. In Old Norse, *írskr* means Irish."

Calum rubbed his forehead.

"And," Adam barreled on, "Uilleam said the pieces went to Ireland from Iceland. I didn't mention that's the second main theory of origin—that they were carved *in* Iceland by a famous female artisan called Margret the Adroit. *Plus,* the Lewis chess set was the first we know of to have bishops as pieces. And *those* carvings—along with a coincidental easing of some epidemic of illness—could be why the nuns thought they were sent by God."

He sat back, waiting.

Calum chewed his lip. He was unnervingly reluctant to piss all over Adam's enthusiasm, but his role was devil's advocate.

"None of that's new, though. Uilleam could have found all of it by reading around, if he's as obsessed with the chessmen and his family as he seems. He could have just…incorporated it to create this legend to protect their queen piece."

Adam frowned. "From Treasure Trove laws you mean?"

Calum shrugged. "Maybe. Though…I admit, he's shown no sign of wanting to benefit. He could have sold the queen alone a thousand times over to a private collector."

"If he doesn't believe that stuff about the pieces protecting the island," Adam said, "he's a bloody good actor."

Calum sighed. "Maybe his own father fed him the story. Who knows how far this goes back."

"To the twelfth century?"

"Adam…" It took a moment to understand Adam's flinch of surprise, the same reaction Calum'd had to "Cal." Calum hadn't called Adam by his name for a very long time. "I was just going to say," Calum went on stiffly, flushed with self-consciousness, "that it's far more likely to be a legend than anything like the truth."

"And I agree," Adam said. "But it's my job to follow the threads to wherever they lead. You know legends often turn out to have a basis in reality. If the successive eldest sons really have been aware of the location of more pieces through the generations, superstition and family tradition could have prevented them from trying to profit from them. Well, until Tormod."

They both took a sip of their drinks and mulled it over.

"So, why are you listening now?" Adam asked at last. "You thought the chess piece was irrelevant."

"Because…it feels like too much of a coincidence."

Adam said slowly, "So you think someone else may have found out about it?"

"Perhaps. But the problem with that is, the murderer left it behind," Calum pointed out, but as he spoke something tightened in his chest. "But *maybe* that's because the piece wasn't where he expected to find it, and he didn't have time to search after Tormod disturbed him. Maybe, he didn't know it was in that bag, ready for Tormod's meeting with you. I mean… who'd treat a priceless object like that?"

"But the man who attacked Julia and her mum said he was after what Tormod owed," Adam reminded him. "He didn't mention the piece."

"I suppose it's possible *their* attacker was here to get Tormod to pay up, but…someone else got to Tormod first and killed him. I mean, if Tormod told the people he owed that he had a priceless object to sell, why would they dispose of him before they got their hands on it? Or at *least* got repaid from it? But…Uilleam's a very old man. If he's been talking too much…it's possible Tormod's murder had nothing to do with his debt…"

An electronic bell began to shrill with hideous insistence.

"The bar's closing," Adam said.

"Kevin," Calum said. They both stood in obedience to the sound. "Kevin's with him every day."

In the corridor outside the bar, Calum called the station and asked the duty DC to check for Kevin Reid on the PNC.

"Wouldn't he need background checks to work with vulnerable people, though?" Adam asked doubtfully when he finished the call.

"*If* he disclosed any convictions, it's not unusual to overlook them in favor of rehabilitation. But…" Calum sighed. "Let's face it, he doesn't have to be a convicted criminal to be tempted by stories of a priceless treasure. That's just me…hoping for a big cosmic arrow pointing his way."

The corners of Adam's mouth twitched up. "It'd be a hell of a coincidence, though...if the people Tormod owed were on Lewis when he was murdered, but they had nothing to do with it."

"Coincidences happen," Calum said. "More often in this job than you'd believe. What the guy did to Julia and Seonag... *That's* what I'd have expected for Tormod. It makes no sense that they'd kill him."

"I suppose...I see that," Adam said slowly. "But in any case, Kevin couldn't have attacked them at nine thirty in Stornoway. He was in Uig when we arrived at nine forty-five. Uilleam said he was a little late, but..."

"But Uilleam was up and dressed," Calum agreed. "So Kevin had been there a while. We can conclude *that* attacker wasn't him. And...Julia'd have known him anyway, balaclava or not. Doesn't rule him out for Tormod, though."

"It suits you," Adam said suddenly. "Being a policeman."

Calum stilled.

"Does it?" he asked warily.

Adam grinned. "Yeah. It's not what I pictured you doing, but...I should have. That righteous urge."

Calum huffed in unwilling amusement. Then he sobered.

He cleared his throat loudly. "Adam. I...wanted to say..." Adam's smile fell away. His eyes glowed like mercury in the flat, dim light of the hotel corridor. Calum forced himself not to look away, to do this like a man. "I wanted to...to apologize. For the things I said when we... At uni. Last time we...um...we met. I was just..." He groped for some form of words that might begin to explain the complexity of all he'd felt, but all he could find was, "It had to end."

Adam studied him for guarded beats of silence. Then he sighed. "And I put up a fight. I should have known better. I should have known *you* better, after four years."

Familiar emotion balled in Calum's throat. He swallowed hard, trying to dislodge it. "Then...you knew I didn't really..."

"That you didn't really believe I took advantage of our friendship to try to pervert your sexuality? That I didn't try to make you believe you were gay?"

Calum drew a shivering breath. "I know you didn't. But…you refused to accept I'd realized I'm straight. So I…lashed out."

Adam's expression slid again to pity.

"I'm not gay!" Calum looked away and dug for defensive anger. Scrabbled for it. "I'm at *most* bisexual. I've had lots of girlfriends." As if Adam didn't know. Those last months at uni after they'd split, he'd made sure Adam saw him with them.

"I'm sorry too, Cal," Adam said, unexpectedly. "I shouldn't have tried to interfere with your choices. Maybe I should have been a better friend."

Calum's gaze shot back to his. "I'm…" He was appalled to realize that tears were gathering in his eyes, though he hadn't cried for a very long time. Not since the day he'd destroyed his relationship with Adam.

He swallowed again, but his emotions wouldn't obey him.

"Do you want to come upstairs?" Adam asked, frowning. "Maybe have some tea? Talk some more about the case? Though maybe you should go home. You look exhausted."

The genuine concern in his expression defeated any apprehension Calum would have felt just that morning.

It seemed ridiculous now. Adam had let go of him long ago.

So Calum said, "I'd like to talk some more," and followed Adam to the lift, and up to his third-floor room.

Twin lamps were glowing on either side of the double divan bed when they entered. The curtains, orange and flowery to match the chronic bedspread, were closed against the night.

Adam went at once to a tray with a kettle on it, set on a long shelf fixed to the wall. He flipped the kettle switch, and it began a familiar *hum*.

Calum sat on the end of the bed.

"Have you eaten?" Adam asked. "I can get room service." He opened a large leather-bound book of hotel information and began to flip through it. "Maybe a sandwich or something?"

Calum shook his head.

He was eighteen again. Overwhelmed by his first sight of Adam strolling into his History lecture. The first time they'd talked...Calum tongue-tied, starstruck by Adam and his English accent and his easy, friendly charm; not understanding what he was feeling or why. Or how the need to see him could become more intense with time, the need for his company submerging every other relationship. He'd hidden from himself for almost two years before Adam had finally forced his eyes open. And then, after their stay on Lewis, he'd deliberately closed them again.

"I'm not hungry," he managed. This was something he'd made himself forget first. How kind Adam was.

Adam looked up from the leather book. Something in Calum's tone seemed to sharpen his gaze. His tone was cautious. "You used to say you wouldn't come back here unless you had to. Not until you'd lived a life and your parents couldn't do without you anymore."

When Calum had said that, he'd imagined Adam eventually coming back here with him. Like a child would.

He wanted to tell Adam he'd come back because a romance with a girl had gone wrong—like he'd told his parents. Or maybe he wanted to tell Adam about the pregnancy scare that had at first thrilled him, because he'd have no escape left after that, and he'd be what his parents needed him to be. And then, how it had terrified and appalled him so much that he'd gone to the first gay bar he could find, and got himself ecstatically sucked off by an anonymous man in the toilets. Not that he hadn't had the odd slip before that.

He wanted to tell Adam how he'd finally accepted, when the pregnancy had proved a false alarm, that he couldn't trust himself to kill this part of him if the possibilities were always there.

And that now it felt as if, when he'd finally made the decision to remove himself for good and seal himself into the life he was meant to live, his greatest temptation had been forcibly shoved in front of his nose again.

But he said, "They need me." And that was also true.

"You love them very much," Adam said.

Calum's throat worked around the stubborn lump of pain lodged there.

"I can't break their hearts." The simple truth at last. "They need me to be *their* Calum."

Adam's expression crumpled into sympathy. He moved a step closer and crouched in front of him, reaching up to touch his cheek in comfort. Calum closed his eyes, to feel it.

"You poor bastard," Adam said.

Calum's face twisted, and his eyes sprang open. "You don't get to pity me."

Adam shook his head and leaned forward until his forehead rested against Calum's.

Their eyes were open. It felt indescribably intimate—understanding and solidarity—and yet also the most sensual moment of Calum's life, feeling Adam's breath again.

His hand rose without thought and tangled in that glorious hair.

Adam's eyes closed.

It was Calum's decision what to do then. Except it never had been.

When Adam was near him, he was always the most important thing.

He leaned forward and pressed his mouth against Adam's, holding it there, still and breathless, as if he were touching something holy.

"It can only be this once," he whispered when he pulled back an inch or two. Not, he knew, that Adam would want more. It was a moment in time. Maybe, a chance to cauterize the open wound of their old love affair.

Adam's eyes remained closed. But he didn't move away. So Calum leaned forward again.

Their kiss flashed to hunger. Six years of it, about to be satisfied; a brief moment of relief.

Adam took charge, as he always used to—as Calum wanted him to—and slid off Calum's jacket. Then he pushed both hands into Calum's hair to hold his head steady. Adam's tongue was hot, liquid velvet, juniper berries and citrus, and Calum moaned his pleasure into the ravenous kiss. He knew he'd been wanting it from the moment he'd seen Adam in the station reception. He'd been wanting it from the last time they kissed.

Maybe in his weakest moments over the years, he'd let himself remember how it felt, but none of his faded, muted memories had come close to doing it justice.

He let Adam strip him with deft efficiency, docile under his hands. His phone was taken from him, put on Silent, and dropped onto a bedside table.

Adam was far more adept now than he'd been as a student who'd only ever slept with one other man. Now he must have quite a scorecard. Like Calum had, except nearly all Calum's lovers had been female. His few men had been desperate, furtive, groping shame.

But it didn't feel shameful being with Adam. Despite everything, it felt pure.

Calum let himself be laid back, naked and hugely aroused, on the flowery coverlet, and allowed Adam to look at him. To take in the marks of adulthood; of a life driven by denial, to discipline.

Calum's body had been honed by extra hours in the gym and pointless runs to tire himself out. But as Adam stroked a reverent hand down his smooth, muscled chest, it felt almost as if he'd been working for this. For Adam's admiration.

"You look…" Adam's mouth twisted. "Beautiful. You always have been."

Calum shook his head restlessly against the pillow, because that was Adam.

"No. You wouldn't see it," Adam said. "But you are. The loveliest man I ever met. Those cheekbones. Those eyes. Those fucking eyelashes. God. Couldn't you have grown a big moustache? Got nose hair?"

The perfect echo of Calum's earlier thoughts, and it made him laugh out loud. Adam laughed back, eyes full of light, teeth showing this time, even and white.

Then slowly, their amusement faded. They regarded each other in growing melancholy, and Calum could feel the madness seeping away, though he tried so hard to cling to it. Reality was just outside those flowery curtains. What was the point of digging this open again?

His erection began to wilt.

"Don't," Adam said. He put the palm of one hand on the soft vulnerability of Calum's stomach. "Don't think. Let's just…" He grimaced and stood. "Watch me."

He pulled his black jumper up his body to reveal a taut, tanned stomach, and then up and over his head to drop on the floor. Then he began to tackle his belt, heeling off his boots at the same time.

There was nothing deliberately erotic about it; he was just stripping off. But Calum was hard again in seconds.

"You've been working out too," he managed, breathless, because grown-up Adam was just as well-muscled as Calum was now, and that was a surprise. They had the same basic build, tall, broad-shouldered and naturally slim, but Adam had never been a gym bunny.

"No option, past twenty-five on the scene," he said with a playful flex of a bicep. "It's kill or be killed."

Calum blinked and looked away. And thought about what that meant.

"What about your…partner? The actor?" How had he forgotten that? He felt more vulnerable than he could remember since his last times with Adam, stupidly close to tears again.

Adam gave a little sheepish grimace. "Well, I, uh…I might have overstated…" Then he sighed. "He won't mind."

Calum looked back at him, uncomprehending, and he felt suddenly the full gulf of the years between them. The understanding that this Adam wasn't his. He was a stranger. And his life was alien to Calum.

"*I* would mind," he said.

Adam sighed. "I know." He pushed down his jeans and underpants together in one movement, freeing his big, bobbing erection. Then he climbed, naked, onto the bottom of the bed, and crawled up until he crouched over Calum's still form, studying his upturned face as if he were mapping it. "If it were you…" he said, "I would too."

He leaned down carefully and brushed his lips over Calum's. Their cocks touched too. Calum hissed and arched, as if he'd taken a burn.

Excitement churned nauseously with uncertainty and jealousy. Trying not to imagine Adam with other men. Looking at them like this, as if he couldn't wait to have them. But part of him couldn't help it.

Adam bent down again, but tentatively, as if he expected to be pushed away at any moment; then he stretched out fully, until Calum bore his weight. And they were touching everywhere. Hot skin on hot skin, indescribably wonderful.

They lay still for a second or two before Adam leaned in and nuzzled below Calum's ear. He'd learned a long time ago which buttons to press. Calum moaned loudly on cue, and Adam licked the skin he'd kissed. Calum gave another helpless liquid groan.

"*Cal*," Adam whispered against his skin. "God, I missed this."

He held his mouth hot against Calum's neck and began a delicate circle of his hips, rubbing their tense abdominal muscles and swollen cocks against each other. An explosion of pleasure sparked up Calum's spine, so intensely good it almost felt like pain. He pushed helplessly into it, head thrown back, pressing the crown into the pillow. His toes curled in the extremity of the sensation, his fingers digging into Adam's rock-hard biceps, and all the time Adam licked and sucked, scalding at his neck, leaving marks probably. But Calum couldn't care. He writhed underneath Adam's muscular weight and he felt...perfect.

"Can I fuck you?" Adam's voice was barely audible, breathed into Calum's ear, as if he were afraid for him to hear.

It had been a thing between them once, how much Adam loved it, how much Calum fought it, because that one act had always felt too real for the illusion he'd been living. As if, every time he took Adam's sex into his body, every time he surrendered to that raw, unmanning pleasure, it exposed him to the truth of who he was.

But this would be the last time he'd ever be fucked.

The realization burst in his mind like ripe, messy fruit hitting the ground.

Never again.

He'd made that choice already. And he'd held to it. But it had seemed reasonable when he'd believed Adam would never again be the one to do it. When the last time had been far in the past; a pale, unreal sense-memory. Not this blaze of need in his guts.

The thought came from nowhere—what would the man in his unwanted emails have given for this choice?

One last time.

"Yes," he said. "Yes."

Adam pulled back and frowned down at him, searching his face. His tanned skin looked flushed, his eyes feverish. But he must have seen what he needed.

He peeled himself off Calum's body, rolling off the bed to stride to the room's ensuite bathroom. The light flipped on, there was a sound of rummaging beneath the *hum* of the electric fan, and then the light and the fan went off and Adam was back, walking toward the bed in all his aroused masculine glory.

He smiled down at Calum, and the soft happiness in it evaporated Calum's last tenuous grip on his emotions. He reached up, grabbed Adam's forearm, and yanked him back down on top of him; then he wrapped both arms around him in a tight, desperate hug.

All that feeling he'd buried, and none of it had died obediently in the dark.

"Do it," he muttered. "Fuck me, Adam." The words sounded alien coming from his mouth. Like lines written for someone else.

Adam gave Calum one soft pecking kiss, then slid to his side and urged him over onto his belly, all practiced eagerness, stroking down Calum's spine and into the small of his back, up the steep curve of his arse to take hold of the meaty part of one buttock, and spread him just enough to expose him. His long, teasing fingers, never too rough, never too tentative, slid inside Calum's body with an exquisite burn—one, two, three—to stroke and cajole and press, seducing him to relax and let his body do this.

The sensations were terrifyingly good when Calum gave himself permission to enjoy them—*last time, no harm*—the slippery push of someone else's flesh inside him, where no one should go. First those expert fingers, before a thick, hard, latex-covered cock, pressing at his tender, nerve-rich anus, then sliding inside, inch by glorious inch.

"*Adam*," he panted, too full and not full enough. Why did it feel so good and right when it shouldn't?

"God, Cal," Adam groaned. His hands felt ridiculously big on Calum's back, stroking his sleek skin, grasping his narrow waist. "You feel fucking incredible."

He started to move, slow and smooth, then to thrust in earnest, and Calum knelt and took it, speechless with erotic sensation. His legs and arms trembled as they held him upright, compromised by the molten pleasure at his centre. And he acknowledged he had never felt anything that came close to it—to being fucked by Adam. A part of his mind remained clear even so, the part that would not allow him to forget what he was doing, kneeling in submission and letting a man mount him and have him. Yet somehow, this time, after so long, it just turned him on more.

The act couldn't last long, because it was just too much...too much joy. Calum was desperate to grab his own swollen, bouncing cock, but he knew that would finish him at once. So he remained on his hands and knees and surrendered totally to Adam's control. Each punishing stroke of Adam's cock rubbed the tight, neglected bundle of nerves inside, and when he finally took mercy and reached down to cup Calum's dangling, desperate balls, to stroke his aching prick, it was too much. Calum groaned, "Adam!" and began to come copiously all over the twee hotel bedspread. Somehow that image made his orgasm feel all the more gloriously erotic as he spurted and spurted, pushed higher still by the helpless clench of his body around Adam's rigid, buried cock. And he was still coming when Adam muttered something garbled in his ear and with a juddering push, began to come too, hard, into the condom, moaning his name.

When they finished, they collapsed together, quaking, onto the bed, Adam's weight smearing Calum's belly into the mess he'd made. But Calum couldn't care. He hadn't felt so physically relaxed for years, all his unacknowledged, repressed stress dissipating like fine mist in a breeze.

But inevitably, the seconds ticked past and his mind jogged back into action.

It's done. Go. Leave now.

"Don't," Adam slurred in his ear, as if he were inside his head. He sounded almost asleep. "Not yet. Stay the night with me."

Calum tensed, ready to refuse, because that was what he did. But he wanted to stay. Perhaps he was vulnerable in the aftermath of making love. The only time in his life he'd ever made love was with Adam. Perhaps he wasn't quite ready to climb back inside his armor. Perhaps he wanted to give himself this, for a little longer.

His muscles relaxed, and he let out a tired breath. Adam's hand found his and entwined their fingers. They didn't need to say the words.

CHAPTER SEVEN

Daylight woke Calum, shining garishly orange through the unlined curtains.

It took a moment to orientate himself. He still felt exhausted, and when he stretched, the bruised ache in his muscles brought it all back to him.

He turned his head quickly on the pillow.

Adam lay sleeping beside him. Well, he was hardly going to have left, given this was his hotel room. But still, Calum was aware of some irrational panic subsiding in his chest.

They'd barely slept. They'd talked about all they'd done since Calum had finished them. How Adam got his prime placement at the British Museum. How difficult his boss could be. Why Calum had been drawn to the self-discipline and public service of a police career. How sexy he looked in the uniform. Why he was still called 'Orlando Bloom' when Adam agreed that he didn't really look like him. "You're *so* much prettier," Adam teased.

And they'd made love again. This time Calum took Adam, and as before, it was mysteriously, inexplicably better than with any woman he'd fucked. Then, after they dozed for a while, they'd woken in the early hours, showered together, and sucked each other off.

Calum lay on his back and looked blindly at the ceiling, scrabbling for anything to divert him from the realization of the emotional price he'd have to pay for what they'd done. How had he ever thought this could close a wound so deep? Panic fluttered under his breastbone.

He groped for his phone and turned it on. There were a lot of missed calls and texts, as he'd expect after going incommunicado, but he went straight to his email. It was there, as reliable as sunrise. "For Calum 6."

I have a grandson. They called him after his father of course, which means they called him after me, and my father. All these years, and nothing changes. I tried suggesting your name again, but my son would never challenge tradition. He's very upright and proper. A bit of a prig, they'd have called him in the army. Perhaps it's inevitable, being brought up in a house like this. I have not been a good father. Too stern. Too distant. Too angry. And Mairi is angry too. Seething with resentment. But...I'm a grandfather. I just truly understood I'm an old man now. All those empty days have passed without notice, and my skin is wrinkled, my hair is silver, my bones ache. Do you remember that last, first letter I wrote to you? How I mocked the public-school poets. I was very wrong. I read them now because they're the only ones who understand what we were and what we are. 'They shall grow not old, as we that are left grow old.' In my mind you are still young and beautiful, my darling. I hope if you're watching me, you'll forgive me my age, my ugliness. It brings me closer to you, every day.

Calum closed the message wearily. He didn't know why he kept reading them other than self-punishment, before the punchline finally came. Except... maybe he wanted to know what happened to the main character in this cautionary tale. The thing was, the sender didn't seem to understand that Calum couldn't go for the happy ending either.

He studied Adam's sleeping face again; drank in every aspect. Saving it up for when he needed it. Except he was going to have to try again to forget.

He should go. But he couldn't bear to just creep away. He couldn't bear to leave at all.

He raised his phone again to check the rest of his messages when a word in the list of emails skimmed the edge of his attention.

Chessmen.

He looked closer. It was one of the multiple newspaper notifications he'd set up to make sure he was on top of events. A tabloid. The *Sun*.

A gap of apprehension opened in his chest.

He clicked on the email.

NEW LEWIS CHESSMAN FOUND AT ISLAND MURDER SCENE

He stared at the screen as if a snake had appeared in his hand.

He would suspect a leak at the station, except no one knew he'd found the chess piece at the scene other than Adam, Calum's mum and dad, and Tormod's parents and grandfather, none of whom were likely to call a tabloid. *No one* else knew. Not the rest of Calum's team. Not his boss.

He was totally fucked.

His hand shook slightly as he clicked on to the newspaper website, and it got worse.

Tormod was named as the murder victim, even though, until his post-mortem confirmed it, the police were still publicly classing him as a "sudden death." The story played up the fact that it was only the third murder on the island in fifty years, and the discovery of a new Lewis chess piece at the scene. Even worse, it reported rumors that the family of the victim had possession of many more chess pieces of unknown value. And then Calum finally registered something else: the article was illustrated with photographs of the new piece.

He sat upright in bed as if someone had shoved a knife into his back.

It was exactly what he'd joked about wanting for Kevin—a finger pointing at the culprit. A smoking gun.

They were the same photographs Tormod had sent to Adam. No one else but Adam had them except, perhaps, Adam's PR-savvy boss. But he wouldn't know the piece was genuine, or its place in the murder.

Unless Adam had told him after all, no matter what it meant for Calum. The pain of betrayal was stupidly agonizing.

"Cal?" Adam murmured. "Is something wrong?"

"For me…yeah. You could say." He threw back the bedclothes and scrambled upright. His arse ached. He felt utterly disgusted with himself, and his heart was ready to break. "For you…well, maybe you and your boss have managed to force Uilleam's hand."

"What?" Adam looked commendably bewildered.

But what the fuck else should Calum have expected, with stakes like this? Why would Adam risk holding back on a find that could transform his own and his boss's careers, especially if they could get Uilleam to surrender a whole new collection of chessmen? Calum had blindly trusted the word of the boy he'd known at uni. But he didn't know the man he'd just given his body to, bared his soul to.

"You can stop," he snapped. "It's in the fucking *Sun*." He pulled on his clothes, crumpled from lying on the floor after their removal the night before. Adam was tapping at his phone, looking perplexed, until he fixed on the screen and read. He looked up as Calum was tying his shoelaces.

"This wasn't me."

"Then you told your boss." *Though you knew what he'd do.*

"I didn't tell anyone!" Adam shouted.

Calum's phone began to ring as he pulled on his jacket.

"Fuck," he muttered. It would be Martin, ready to cut off his balls.

"Cal!"

Calum paused at the door, his back to Adam, but he shook his head and slammed out of the room before he answered the call.

It was Willie John. A reprieve of sorts. But he'd let him down as well.

The case had stripped Calum of every good copper's instinct he had.

"I don't know if you got my messages, sir," Willie John said. And, heroically, he didn't launch into the story in the *Sun*, or the chess piece, or Calum's decision not to tell his own team about it. "Kevin Reid has form. He served twenty months for assault and demanding money with menaces. I got the Council's human resources woman out of bed." On a Sunday too. Willie John was unstoppable. Calum kept walking until he reached the stairs, trotted down them fast, listening. "She said he declared his convictions and he's been an exemplary employee."

Until, perhaps, unprecedented temptation was placed right under his nose.

"We've also had, uh…a few calls from the press," Willie said at last, with classic understatement. "I declined to comment. Or confirm anything other than a sudden death."

Calum sighed. The hotel reception was thankfully empty as he passed the desk. "Thanks, Willie John." He hesitated, but what could he say in mitigation? He had evidence from a murder scene in his desk drawer rather than the evidence locker. "I've been trying to explore a…delicate line of inquiry."

"Yes, sir," Willie John said staunchly. "That's understandable. Something like that would overwhelm every other avenue we could look at. Um…Chief Inspector Martin's been trying to get hold of you, sir," he finished with unusual delicacy. "Just to let you know."

Calum closed his eyes briefly, but Willie John's loyalty was steadying him. Willie John, at least, still had faith.

The phone rang again immediately as Calum was pushing out through the hotel's revolving glass door, into Sunday daylight.

It was shaping up to be a beautiful day.

Well, fuck that.

There was no reprieve this time.

Chief Inspector Martin, all the way from Seattle.

"Is it true?" No preamble.

Calum didn't even try to play dumb. "Yes, sir."

There was a short pause before detonation.

"What in all hell do you think you're up to, Macleod?" Martin howled. "I've had Craig Campbell on to me for half an hour. Do you know who he is? He's a *bastard*, that's who he is! The bastard who's arriving from Inverness tomorrow, as SIO on our case. I worked with him in Edinburgh, and by God, he loved getting the chance to accuse *my* officers of unprofessionalism! Destroying his case! Boxing above their weight! For God's *sake*, man, why didn't you say anything? A new Lewis chessman at the scene, and you don't even *mention* it?"

"Sir," Calum said. At least he'd always had the ability to remain calm when cornered. "With respect, I found a chess piece in a plastic shopping bag at the scene. A relative of the victim claimed it was a new piece, but that was obviously hard to believe. I had to get it verified before the circus came to town and swamped the investigation for nothing."

He could hear Martin trying to calm down on the other end of the line.

"And?" he sounded as if he half wanted, and was half unwilling, to be mollified. "Please tell me it's a copy."

"An expert on the chessmen from the British Museum is in Stornoway, and I'm afraid he thinks it's genuine."

"An expert?" Martin exploded again. "And that's a coincidence, is it?"

"No, sir. We have reason to believe the victim, Norman Macdonald, contacted him with a view to selling the piece. His grandfather in Uig claims the location of more hidden pieces has been known to particular family members for generations." Martin groaned in despair. "But the queen piece is the only one not hidden. He says they've been passing it down. Since, um...he says since the twelfth century."

"Dear *God.*" Martin was a religious man, not usually prone to taking the Lord's name in vain. But Calum had driven him to it.

"At the moment I have two lines of inquiry," Calum slogged on. "One is the threats from whoever lent the victim money and possibly sent muscle to attack the victim's sister and niece. The other is the grandfather's care assistant. He has a record involving violence and theft. If the old man started to ramble and said anything to him about having those pieces, he could have decided to try to get ahold of the queen for a start. Except, Tormod...the victim walked in on him. The killer can't have known the piece was in the carrier bag."

There was a long, long pause. "All right," Martin said at last. "That sounds...plausible. I was told when you came that you're a lone wolf, Macleod. But I do *not* appreciate being kept in the dark. I'm your superior officer."

"Yes, sir," Calum said meekly.

"I even agree with your call on the chess piece. I suppose. Except, *I* should have been the one to make it. Did you think I was going to call a press conference, man?"

"No, sir." But clearly, deep down, he had. "I...apologize. I should have told you immediately."

Martin made a harrumphing sound. "Twenty minutes of Campbell gloating and accusing is enough to strain anyone's powers of forgiveness. You leave it here, Calum."

At least he was *Calum* again, he thought, before the sense hit home.

"*Sir?*"

"You leave it to *him* from this point. DCI Campbell's arriving on tomorrow morning's ferry with his team and the pathologist. *And* probably half the world's press, but that's his problem."

"But I still have a day—"

"*Leave* it, Calum. We do *not* want to wade any deeper into this fiasco. Anything that arises from your existing lines of inquiry goes to Campbell from this point. That's what he's demanded, and much as I hate to say it, he's right. You've done exceptionally well with the limited resources you had, so Campbell has live lines to pick up. That saves our face. But now you back away. This is too big even for Campbell, he just doesn't realize it yet. Take the day off. It's Sunday. Go to church. Go for a bloody walk, man. But let it *go.*"

Calum walked to the station, picked up his car, and then drove home, all in a haze of frustrated, furious disbelief.

He was relieved beyond measure to see that his parents were out when he got there—at church, of course, and Shep greeted him as always, as if he'd been away to war, but that unconditional adoration did nothing to lift his mood.

Loss. Anger. Humiliation. Despair. Pain.

He took a shower and changed into jeans and a thick jumper, then, on furious impulse checked his emails.

There it was. "For Calum 7."

...I think what I feel is something like relief, but it's been so...

Calum archived it without reading any more.

* * * * *

The sun blazed in a hot blue sky all the way to Uig. Calum drove fast along the Atlantic coast, up toward Mealista, passing bays that looked turquoise and then malachite in the sunlight, with pale sand setting them off like some scene from the Caribbean. And scattered over the sands, spectacular striated boulders of Lewisian gneiss, one of the oldest rocks in the world. In the right weather, Uig beaches were matchless, unless you tried to go into the water.

Maybe Uilleam didn't know what had happened yet.

That was why Calum had come.

He still stood a chance of getting there first.

Once, he'd have been safe until tomorrow. As it was, almost every shop on the island was shut because of Sunday observance. Ferries and planes on Sundays were relatively recent developments. In fact, Calum had been eighteen, in Glasgow, when he first read a Sunday newspaper on a Sunday, rather than on Monday when they arrived in the newsagents shops in town.

But there were now a scattering of tiny outlets which managed to get ahold of the few copies flown in. And there was radio and TV and the Internet. The story may be slowed down because it broke on Sunday, but it would be seeping out already. Calum couldn't see Uilleam as someone who got his news online, but he had to try to reach him before anyone else did. To explain. Not that he really could. It wasn't going to be an easy interview.

His hopes plummeted when he drove up the narrow road toward Uilleam's house. There were three cars outside. The same black Fiesta he assumed was Kevin's; a Mini that looked like Julia's, and another he didn't know. He could only hope the press hadn't found Uilleam already.

Kevin opened the door to his knock. He looked less than pleased to see him.

"You people…" he muttered darkly, though he stepped aside to let Calum into the back porch. "You tell the bloody *Sun* before you tell the community that Norman was murdered."

"We didn't tell the press," Calum gritted. He sure as hell wasn't going to be talked down to by a suspected murderer. "And it's still an *unexplained* sudden death."

"Well, Julia's just arrived, and she's furious," Kevin said with satisfaction. "Your partner in crime's been here more than half an hour." Another police officer was here? *Fuck!* "Much good it's done him. William hasn't said a word to anyone since I told him. It's just as well I got here first."

"Isn't it just?" Calum said coldly.

Kevin narrowed his eyes. "They're in the living room. I'm making tea."

He stomped off along the corridor and disappeared into a room on the left. Calum followed the sound of muffled shouting to the closed door of the room in which he'd last talked with Uilleam.

"And you think you can browbeat an old man into just *handing* everything he values over? After doing *that*?" Julia.

"…do anything." A much quieter male voice, trying to calm things down.

Calum opened the door.

The first person he saw was Adam, sitting at the wooden table.

Calum froze for a beat, then walked inside and closed the door behind him.

He should be relieved it wasn't one of his colleagues and he hadn't been caught in what might look like meddling in a case from which he'd been officially removed.

But he didn't feel relief. Adam had come here, unrepentant, hustling in to position himself, whatever might have happened to Calum as a result of the article.

Adam stared at him, startled. Calum looked away.

Uilleam sat in the same chair as before, still sternly upright, looking into the glowing peat fire—exactly the same, and yet, an entirely different man.

His defiance, his sharp purpose were gone. He looked unaware…as if he'd left his body behind, sitting there in that chair.

Beside him, Julia stood like an avenging harpy, defying all comers. She had dressed, haphazardly for her, in a navy-blue fleece and ripped jeans, and her bruised face was twisted with emotion. Calum could easily identify it as outrage.

"And what the hell are *you* doing here?" she shouted at Calum. "Both of you—get out and leave us alone! You lie to me! You throw my family to the wolves! And then you turn up to pick at the carcass? *Leave!*"

"We didn't talk to the press!" Adam snapped before Calum could open his mouth.

"Then how did they have the photos Tormod sent *you*? You did it to try to force Seanair Uilleam into the open, to give *you* what you want."

Calum held his impassive mask in place.

Rationally, now that the first shock of betrayal was past, he couldn't even blame Adam, really. He'd been sent on a mission by his boss to find out about the chess piece. And there were those laws of treasure trove he'd repeatedly warned Calum and Uilleam about, laws that Calum shouldn't have expected a professional in Adam's position to ignore.

Calum was Adam's distant past. How could Calum have expected him to put his career on the line for an ex-lover, and one who'd wounded him badly? Even when that ex-lover had become a one-night stand.

The truth was, Calum had no one to blame but himself for letting his resolve soften. And now, remembering all the vulnerability he'd revealed, humiliation was a lash that shriveled his stomach and scattered his thoughts.

He forced his focus back to Julia. He'd have more than enough time to take out his regret and smear it over himself later. First, he needed to sort this out. And something had started to nag at him, like incipient toothache.

"I came to try to talk to William about his options now," Adam said. "That's all."

"Oh, really?" Julia sneered. Strands of shining dark hair had come loose from her chignon, and along with her bruised mouth and blackened eye, it added to the impression of violent rage. "And what's your advice, Adam, now you've forced his hand? Just...*give you* my family's whole purpose? *What?*" she barked at Calum.

Calum blinked. Her righteous fury was actually unnerving, because they'd never fallen out before. He'd never seen Julia angry.

"You know what your great-grandfather is claiming, then?" he tried.

"You mean my family's *eight-century history* with the chessmen? Yes! I do! If Tormod hadn't died, I'd never have been the wiser, of course, but Granny *finally* told Mum and me. Just in time to stop you rolling over all of us."

Adam said, "I told Uilleam that he can negotiate to—"

"*Negotiate?* Look at him! You think he can *negotiate* with snakes like you? You'd do what you're planning to do with the queen piece. If he ever showed you the rest, you'd take them away."

And Calum thought, *She's right.* But at least the family now had a serious defender against the forces they were about to face.

"I'm the last of the Macaulays," Julia said. "You've broken my great-grandfather, but you won't break me."

Calum glanced at the figure in the chair, vacant and apart, like his grandmother when she'd finally gone to senility. And he felt an unexpected surge of regret for the difficult, implacable old man he'd met.

"Eight hundred years," Julia repeated furiously. "I'm not going to let you just take it away from us."

Calum sighed. "Jools, you're going to have to—"

"Don't bother!" Julia hissed. "*You* were meant to be my friend, and you didn't tell me. And let's face it...if *he* didn't give it to the press, *you* did. You— I want *both* of you to get out!"

"I didn't give..."

"Shen said *no one* knew. Just the family and both of *you!*"

"And, possibly the killer," Calum pointed out.

"Oh, the *killer* called the press?" Julia sneered. "After leaving a priceless object behind in a Tesco bag?"

Calum's face heated under her mockery. He opened his mouth to defend himself again, but instinct had already stolen the breath from his lungs seconds before he understood why.

His blank eyes met Julia's. She turned and stalked impatiently toward the back of the room.

"How did you know Tormod put the piece in a Tesco bag?" he asked.

"Shen told me," Julia snapped. She didn't turn around.

And the jarring *something* that had been worrying at his subconscious resolved into perfect, unwanted clarity.

"How did you know Tormod sent the newspaper pictures to Adam? Or what they looked like? No one saw them but me and Adam."

His eyes had fixed on Julia's straight, slim back, her disarranged chignon, as she bent to tidy something. He felt numb. There was an easy explanation. He just had to wait for it.

In his peripheral vision, he registered Adam's head jerking round to look at him in shock, but Calum couldn't drag his eyes away from Julia's back.

When she turned around, though, he saw that she hadn't been tidying.

One of Uilleam's shotguns was held straight and level in her arms, the twin black holes of the barrel trained between him and Adam, the gun-cabinet door wide open behind her.

And he thought...how the fuck could he have forgotten that cabinet?

He'd blundered into this as everything else; off-balance from the start, everything too close to home.

"You used to be a hotshot policeman in Glasgow..."

He'd gone soft here. Trusting and complacent, too involved in his own misery, his instincts blunted by familiarity.

He dragged his eyes up from the twin black holes of the barrel.

He was still lying in that hotel bed, fast asleep and dreaming. He was going to wake up and laugh about all this with Adam.

In the dream, Julia's face was twisted with an emotion that looked like grief, but how could he believe anything about her? She was a brilliant actor. How could he have forgotten that too?

Except he hadn't. He'd just trusted her, like his own family.

"It's loaded," she said. "Three shots, as usual. You were meant to be taken off the case, Orly." Her voice trembled. "After that story, you had to be."

"I was," Calum said. He sounded stunned even to his own ears. "I came to see if Uilleam was all right."

Julia's laugh sounded desperate. "Fuck, of course you did. You always do the right *bloody* thing."

"Cal..." Adam's chair scraped on the lino floor as he shoved it back from the table, making to stand. The gun swung fast to point at him, and the expression on Julia's face was feral. No tears for Adam.

"Don't!" Calum lurched forward at once, a deliberate movement to drag her attention back to him. "Stay still, Adam."

Adam looked ashen, but he subsided back into his chair. "Cal, for fuck's sake..."

"I know," Calum said. His eyes fixed on Julia and the gun, a mouse in front of a cobra.

He'd gone to a seminar once on hostage negotiation. Just...they were the hostages.

Stage one. Listen actively.

"Tell me what you want, Julia."

She eyed him wildly. "*Want?* I want you not to have come! I want *both* of you to have left before..."

"You know who killed Tormod?"

At some point, Kevin was going to come in with the tea, and she couldn't cover three people. Just so long as she didn't shoot when the door opened.

She made a sound of desperate amusement. "What d'you think?"

"Who killed him, Jools?"

"Don't *call* me that!"

"Did you kill him?"

Julia's breath shook, but she didn't deny it.

"*Why?* You loved him."

"Because it was my life or his!" she burst out. "*God*, you wouldn't understand! You *chose* this. I went from the brink of everything to…*nothing*. I had a *major* agent, did you know that? Even as a student, he was getting me calls for TV, theatre…he'd contacted people in LA. They said I was going to be huge! A huge star. And *look* at me. I'm cleaning up piss and shit and drool and watching *other* people *living* through a fucking screen. And that's meant to be *it*, every day until I die? Forever and ever *amen*?"

"Fuck, Julia! *You* chose as well, to come home for your mum."

"I had no way to stay on! No money to pay someone to look after her or get me through my course. And my family just expected me to give up my 'silly ideas' and do my *duty*. And then, after years of this *bullshit*, I find out they're as rich as *fucking* Croesus, and they're sitting there, letting me and Mum live in misery because they're too *primitive* to know superstition from reality."

"How did you find out?" Adam asked, as if he understood they had to keep her talking. "Only the son who succeeds was supposed to know."

She scowled. "And the son told me. Tormod. The day after Granny told *him*. He was distraught. It *should* have been Mum. She was the eldest child by five years, but *they* had to wait for the *boy*."

"But Tormod was going to sell it," Calum said. "And he'd have shared the money with you. Why would you kill him when he was trying to get out too?"

"Because he *wasn't*," Julia snapped. "He gave in. Just like you did."

Calum said, "So…all the stuff about LA…"

"God! He was too afraid of life to do anything *brave*. Seanair Uilleam had been badgering him since he was eighteen to get married. Have a *son*. But he'd held out, the only time he ever stood up for himself. Then Granny told him about the pieces and showed him the queen, and the pathetic bastard thought he had to. Like a sacred charge. I couldn't talk him out of it, never mind convince him to sell." She glared venomously at Calum. "He really *was* like you. In every way."

Something about the way she said it made Calum ask, "What do you mean?"

Her face contorted into a sneer. "I *mean*, *he* was gay and spineless too!"

Calum's breathing stopped. He should probably have been appalled that he felt more stunned by that, than Julia pulling out the shotgun in the first place.

And then it made sense.

"*You* contacted Adam. And you used an email address that would point the finger at Tormod." Her silence was a reply. "You chose Adam specifically to throw me. Because…you knew I'd lead any inquiry for the first couple of days, and I'd fuck the investigation up for good if you could distract me."

And those insinuating emails, throwing him more off-balance… God, she'd planned it all; used all she knew against him.

She sniffed hard. "Why are you so surprised? Anyone who saw the two of you together could tell." Despite himself, Calum shot a glance at Adam, but Adam was staring at Julia as if he couldn't believe his eyes. "I knew your reputation as a *detective*. So yeah, I knew I had to get past you first. But I should have known better than to think love would slow *you* down." Her voice rang with spite. "Self-sacrifice is what gets you off."

"You're not really in a position to lecture anyone about love," Adam said. "Are you?"

Julia swung the gun toward him.

"Tormod didn't borrow money," Calum blurted. "Or gamble."

Ask questions that move the discussion forward, his mind parroted. He was sure that had been the next point on the PowerPoint slide at the seminar. *Establish trust so that you can work on a solution together.*

But in the real world, all he could do was play for time.

Where the *fuck* was Kevin?

Maybe they'd laugh about it afterward, he and Kevin. How Calum had got it so disastrously wrong, he'd had to rely on his prime suspect to save him.

But then Julia glanced at the door, and Calum realized with a sinking heart that she was waiting for Kevin to come in too. To pick them all off together in the same room.

Three shots.

"A friend in Glasgow sent the emails about the debt," Julia said. "I told Tormod they were money scams. To ignore them."

"God, Julia." Calum was only just beginning to understand how intricate it had been. "Premeditation isn't even in it. You planned everything to the last detail."

Without warning, the living-room door pushed open, and Kevin shouldered his way in, bearing the same flowery, heavily laden tray.

"Tea," he announced.

"Run!" Calum yelled. "*Run!*"

But instead, Kevin froze in the doorway as the gun moved in a smooth arc, covering him, then Adam, then Calum, and back.

Kevin gaped at it. "What are you *doing*?"

"It's the only way," Julia said.

"You can't be serious," he pleaded.

"I have a plan." Julia swung the shotgun back to its place between Calum and Adam.

Kevin said wearily, "You always do."

And Calum's last hope extinguished. He hadn't been wrong about everything, after all.

"He was your intruder," he breathed. It was all suddenly so clear. "You lied about the timing to give him an alibi. To confirm the murderer was your imaginary loan shark."

Julia gave a tired laugh. "And there's the smart detective I heard so much about," she said. "We just…staged it an hour before I said, to give Kev time to get here. I changed the clocks in Mum's room and pretended to be unconscious for as long as it took, after Kev hit me. Mum didn't even register much of it. And *you* came here and cemented Kev's alibi." She sighed. "Kev's all that's kept me going for the last year, you know. And you, Orly."

Kevin moved to the table and set down the tray carefully before reaching down into his boot and, with an air of casual habit, pulling out a closed knife. He pressed it, and a long, wicked blade shot out. A flick knife. Illegal. Lethally sharp.

Julia gestured at Adam, then at the corner of the room by the door. "Hold him over there."

Kevin nodded and moved behind and to the side of Adam's seated figure to press the tip of the blade to his throat.

Calum jerked forward, but the gun now fixed on him alone. No more hope of distraction. His senses felt elevated, sight and hearing and smell.

It was two against two. Armed against unarmed.

Calum watched in agony as Adam eased to his feet, taller than Kevin by a few inches, the knife point held expertly against his lower jaw. And it made still more sense.

"*He* cut Tormod's throat," Calum accused.

"No," Julia countered. "It had to be me. My DNA's already everywhere in the house. I used Granny's Marigold gloves."

And somehow that was the most disgusting thing Calum had yet heard from her. Julia interpreted his expression well. Her mouth tightened. She didn't seem to enjoy his repulsion.

"You're so shocked," she sneered. "After all *you've* seen? I acted cutting a throat in a play once. It didn't feel that different in real life. He sat down in his chair, talking. I was at the sink, behind him, washing up. I grabbed his hair and did it. It was quick." Calum could see her defensiveness was translating into bravado. Perversely, trying to shock him. "I'd borrowed his car so anyone who saw it, would think it was him when I arrived at the house. Then after, I walked down the side of the croft where Shen couldn't see, and Kevin picked me up. No one noticed. Even in that gossip pit. I could have talked my way out if they had, but we got all the luck."

And Tormod—*Lucky*—got none.

"Why didn't you just steal the queen and sell it?" Calum asked in despair. "You'd have been rich enough on that. No one had to die."

"But Tormod would have known it was me," she said, as if it was obvious. "And he'd have told Granny and Seanair Uilleam. I didn't want them to hate me."

Calum stared at her in disbelief, then at Uilleam, long gone inside his own head.

"And I'd never be told where to find the other pieces," Julia went on reasonably. "I had to force their hand. So, I set it up to look like Tormod had been ready to sell, and I left the queen for you as bait. I got Adam in"—she shrugged—"then called the paper with Adam in place to take the blame. Tormod was the roadblock. He'd never sell the pieces, even if the whole world knew about them. But without him, the secret would pass to Mum and then me, like it should have anyway. And if the government won't play ball with us, I have people willing to pay almost anything if the pieces are authenticated by the British Museum. And that'll happen when the queen's officially examined. There are places all along the coast where we can get things out when the fuss dies down. I'll look after all the family, though. They'll never have to worry about anything again."

And then there was nothing more to say. No more revelations or distractions.

The last stage in hostage negotiation: *influence and change behaviour.* But Calum had no cards to play. Just an appeal to reality.

"You know you can't shoot us. One murder's bad enough."

Julia's face twisted. "Oh, Orly. What would anyone sane choose? Pay the price for one, or get away with three?"

Calum's gut turned over.

He raised his chin. "But you won't get away with it. People know we're here," he lied. "And believe me, when you kill a police officer, they don't go easy."

"But Seanair Uilleam's going to do it," Julia said. "He shouldn't have these guns. He's far too old and irrational, and he thought you told the papers about the chess piece. That you'd come to take them. Kevin and I were in the kitchen. We couldn't stop him in time. And then he slipped into…this state. They won't punish him. He's far too old. And I'll take care of him."

And Calum understood then that he and Adam really were out of luck. Julia had a strategist's mind, taking all her opportunities, turning them to her advantage. And she *could* get away with it. He could see how she would.

"Let Adam go," he said, though he knew it was hopeless.

He felt icy-cold suddenly. Everything had slowed. The scent of peat burning on the fire was more powerful and pungent than he'd ever smelled it before. The sun, struggling through the two small windows, was blinding, like twin floodlights. A bird was cheeping directly outside. It must be on the windowsill, to sound so loud.

"Turn round," Julia said softly.

Calum didn't move.

"Turn. Round!"

"Cal!" Adam screamed, and lunged away from Kevin.

Calum stared into Julia's eyes. In his peripheral vision, he could see Adam being yanked back by Kevin's hugely muscled arm and forced to his knees, the knife at his neck. A line of blood was forming on his throat.

Well, that'll fuck up forensics, Calum thought with distant satisfaction.

"I want you to remember my face," Calum said, but his own voice sounded far away to him, echoey and strange. He thought the bird was louder.

His lungs felt too heavy to breathe.

These were the last few seconds of his life.

Julia's expression contorted, but she raised the gun a few inches to make sure of her aim.

"I did this in a play too," she said distantly.

Despite himself, Calum looked away at the last instant, because given a choice, his final sight on earth had to be Adam.

The shotgun roared.

Adam's face twisted in a scream of horror and grief, drowned by the deafening blast. Calum flinched and braced.

But instead of agony, there was a fall of brown snow.

It took him a stunned second to look upward, ears ringing. Tobacco-stained plaster dust was sprinkling down from the gouged ceiling, and

Uilleam, discounted in his chair, had twisted around, half risen, and he was wrestling with the barrel of the gun, trying to keep it pointed upward.

Julia had both her hands on it, trying to pull it from Uilleam's grasp, but somehow he clung on, indomitable, even as Calum leaped forward and grabbed the barrel too.

The smell of gunpowder and old plaster was sharp in his nostrils. His ears buzzed and rang.

It took seconds of struggle to yank the gun away from both of them, the old man and his great-granddaughter.

Then Calum swung around, dragging Julia with him with one hand, pushing her where he could see her.

Adam still knelt on the floor, but both his hands were locked on Kevin's wrist and muscular forearm, trying to force the blade away from his throat as Kevin strained to hold it there.

Calum pointed the gun at Kevin's chest. He yelled, "Armed police! Drop your weapon!"

Kevin's eyes were wild with panic. But Julia screamed suddenly, "Don't! He won't shoot!" and darted toward Kevin, toward the door, right into the line of fire.

Calum aimed for the floor inches in front of her and pulled the trigger.

The shocking violence of the blast, the explosion of splinters, froze everyone in place.

"I have one more shot," Calum said, "and I'm going to take out one of your legs or his shoulder if you don't *both* raise your hands and stand down. I'm not fussy which one of you I blow bits off."

His eyes were on Julia, though, all the way through her slow, panting understanding that he meant it, and then her reluctant obedience as she raised her arms, her face contorted with distress.

Kevin followed her lead, as he'd done, apparently, all the way. The knife dropped to the floor with a dull *thump*, and Adam was on it in a second.

"Tormod was a man of honor," Uilleam said shakily behind them. "But you, girl…" He spat on the floor. "You should never have been born."

Calum watched the words hit home. And incredibly, despite everything, after all Julia had done and planned to do, he saw something in her buckle. A part of her actually loved the old man, a part of her had wanted to be loved back.

Her face crumpled, and like a scolded child, she began to cry.

CHAPTER EIGHT

They sat and waited for the police for almost an hour, but Calum had two sets of handcuffs in his car, so he was able to keep Kevin and Julia contained, if not docile, while he called Chief Inspector Martin to explain. He thought by the end, that Martin would never go on holiday again.

When two police cars finally roared up, lights flashing, with an ambulance for good measure, it became a weird mix for Calum of taking charge and giving evidence. He wasn't sure it was in the rulebook, but Willie John had gone along with it.

While they'd waited, Uilleam had listened, glowering, as Adam advised him to play as tough as Julia'd intended: to demand an agreement to keep the pieces on the island, if that was what was important to him; or to demand money, if that's what he wanted. Or, Uilleam could say it had all been a hoax and never let the pieces be seen again.

When they all left for Stornoway, Uilleam hadn't told them which he was going to choose.

Two officers drove Calum's and Adam's cars back to Stornoway, and they and Uilleam had to agree to get into Willie John's car, because they were deemed unsafe to drive. The way Calum was shaking by then, Willie John was right.

They'd been driving for half an hour of exhausted silence when Adam said, "You're covered in plaster dust." Calum blinked at him stupidly. Adam's expression softened. "Your hair. Maybe try ruffling it?"

Calum obeyed, watching pale dust fall onto his jeans and the pristine carpet of the car.

"Better," Adam said solemnly. "Less Hamlet's ghost."

"I'm sorry," Calum said. "For not believing you." He kept his voice low, though in the front, Willie John was conversing with Uilleam in Gaelic.

Adam looked down at his hands. "Yeah. Well. She set it up that way."

But Calum should have known instinctively that Adam wouldn't break trust—whatever the evidence against him.

He blurted, "It's just…we weren't friends anymore, and I thought, why would you risk the biggest break of your career and maybe get into trouble, to indulge my stupidity?"

"Except I did," Adam said.

Calum grimaced. "I'm sorry."

"You really believed…last night…that I'd just…" Adam threw a frustrated glance at the front of the car. They were speaking more or less in whispers. But Calum understood without Adam spelling it out. He'd believed Adam had slept with him, knowing he'd already betrayed the secret.

"I suppose I thought it… That maybe it wasn't that important anymore." Calum cleared his throat. "To you."

Adam shook his head. All of his body language conveyed amazement and disgust. "You're a bloody moron, Cal." His jaw tightened. "*But.*" He blew out a long breath. "You being such a badass in there sort of…serves in mitigation."

Calum gave a startled snort. "I wasn't. But *you* were great. You didn't freeze."

"You know what's disappointing?" Adam asked. "I do Muay Thai—Thai kickboxing—every week. It's supposed to be good against knives. But…it turns out you don't necessarily understand someone's going to attack you until the knife's already at your throat."

"You couldn't have seen that coming," Calum protested. "I'd just been planning how to apologize to Kevin for suspecting him."

Adam's eyes lit with amusement. "So what's going to happen at the station?"

"Willie John'll take formal statements from the three of us. Julia and Kevin go to the cells. The forensic postmortem on Tormod and the scene-of-crime examination still have to happen. I'd guess the Inverness SIO'll want to do the interviews tomorrow too, if only to save face."

Adam frowned. "Well, that's not fair."

"It's politics, and…" Calum moved restlessly in the seat. "I don't think I could do it anyway." He met Adam's eyes. "I've known her all my life. I thought we were friends."

Adam moved as if to touch Calum's hand in empathy, but he drew back at once.

Thank you, Calum thought, and wished he meant it.

Adam sighed. "You've been a murder detective, Cal. You've seen the underbelly before this. What people do when they're desperate."

Calum considered for a moment. How he'd felt when he realized how badly he'd failed as a policeman.

"But I expected it there," he said. "Here…I let down my guard, because I thought *here* was different. That the people were different."

"They are," Adam said. "On the whole. And you did brilliantly. You found the killers, and you brought them in."

Calum looked at him gravely. "I stumbled on the killers by accident, I almost got both of us shot, and we got saved by a ninety-six-year-old man."

Adam nodded. "That too."

They both began to snigger, high on the hysteria of relief.

The car was on the outskirts of Stornoway now. Only a few more minutes to the station.

"I have to catch a plane at twenty past five," Adam remarked.

It felt a bit like Calum had expected the shotgun bullet to feel. He fixed his eyes on the back of Willie John's head.

"Will you be back? For the chessmen?" He hoped it sounded equally casual.

"I don't know. It'll probably be my boss. Though…" Calum felt Adam's eyes on him, studying his profile. "Would anything… Would anything be different?"

Calum swallowed miserably.

"I see," Adam said.

"There was a pride march here this year." Calum's voice was barely audible. "The first one. My mother held one of the placards at the side: 'Marriage is honorable. Therefore shall a man leave his father and his mother and shall cleave unto his wife.'"

He heard Adam give a shaky sigh, but he said nothing else.

Calum laid his head back on the headrest and closed his eyes.

* * * * *

The house was empty when Calum arrived home that afternoon. Wherever his parents were, they'd be doing something church-related, because it was Sunday.

Calum stood looking out the big window at the too-familiar view, and he wanted to scream. To weep.

He and Adam had said a polite goodbye in reception at the station. A car had been organized to take Adam to his hotel and then to the airport. And it had felt final, as somehow the last, brutal ending hadn't felt final. As if this time Adam too understood there could be no fairy-tale ending.

Calum slumped down at the iMac and clicked open his mail. He found he wasn't surprised to see there had been a last manipulative message from Julia. "For Calum 8."

...I think I have a friend...

Calum couldn't stand it.

He jerked to his feet, hands on his head, clawing for calm. He closed his eyes and took a shuddering gulp of air. Held it. Let it out carefully.

He could do it the way he did it before. Breath by breath. Minute by minute. Let time eat away at the leaden weight of misery in his chest, pressing down on his glass heart.

He forced open his eyes again and, only then, he noticed a large, unfamiliar manila envelope lying on his desk beside his keyboard. The words "For Calum" were written across it.

His guts lurched sickeningly to his boots.

The top of the envelope was open, and there were papers poking out of it. No stamp. No address. It had to have been hand-delivered.

He picked it up and pulled out the papers, flicking quickly through the whole big sheaf of them. He registered that some were yellowed and old, that the writing was in faded blue ink. Neat, old-school handwriting. Gaelic. Not like the script on the outside of the envelope.

His heart galloped, fast and hard.

Each letter had a typewritten text in English attached to it by a paper clip.

...I can't believe it's over because...

Julia hadn't fabricated them?

Then...where had she found them?

The envelope had been delivered open, for anyone to read. Calum's mum or dad must have put it on the desk, and of course they would respect his privacy, but...

Julia had wanted him to feel like this—panicked, threatened, afraid. Or...perhaps giving him the originals had been her idea of mercy, of telling him it was over, since she'd known the case would be taken from him. Once she'd neutralized him, she could afford to be generous.

Fuck! It didn't matter what she'd bloody intended.

He needed it to go away now, for good.

He walked to the fire and pulled away the guard, using a poker to break through the crust of coal slack and stoke the flames he'd freed. Then he sank to his knees on the hearth rug and pulled out a first handful of letters and translations from the envelope, crumpling them up, ready to burn.

"Calum."

Shock dropped the papers from Calum's hand. He swung around toward the door, still on his knees, eyes huge with alarm.

Calum's father hadn't been out after all.

Calum gestured weakly at the hearth. "I was just getting the fire going."

"Don't destroy them."

Calum's breath stuttered. "You *read* them?" A few minutes before, he'd almost wanted it, but now… The most stable and loving structure in his life teetered on the brink of destruction. And he couldn't bear it. "I don't know why they were sent to *me*. Or…I mean, I know it was Julia, but…"

"Julia?" his father repeated. And of course, he wouldn't have heard anything yet.

"Yes," Calum said quickly. "She was the—"

"They belong to me," Donnie said. "Not Julia."

Calum sank back on his heels and stared up at his father as if he'd struck him. He thought it was as well he was already on his knees.

"To you?" he breathed. Then, "*Why?*"

"Because I needed you to see."

To see? Calum wanted to howl his hurt, his abject humiliation.

His father. Of all people to play this game with him. His own father.

"I already *see*," Calum spat. And it was as if Shep had turned on him and savaged him. Unnecessary proof of how conditional love really was.

He was used to his father's silent presence backing up his mother, allowing her to speak for them both; always giving way when she challenged him. But he was also used to his father's quiet affection.

Donnie worked the croft, and his loom, he was a church elder like his own father and grandfather had been, he had his Bible and his books and his computer, and his dry, unassuming sense of humor, and that was what he was. As uncomplicated as that.

But…he'd known? And he'd decided to teach Calum this…lesson.

"I'm back *here* because I see," Calum said. His voice trembled with grief. "You didn't have to do this."

"The letters were written by your great-grandfather, Calum."

Calum's betrayed gaze froze on his father, then dropped, stupidly, to the envelope still in his hand.

That wasn't possible.

But his father wouldn't lie.

"Do you remember him?"

Calum nodded slowly at the envelope, dazed. The straight, shriveled old man in the chair, who'd once stroked his hair.

All that passion and devotion and misery…?

"Donnie Maiseach," his father said. "That was the name they gave him because he was a beautiful man. Like you. My dad and I had that name too. But you were named for his lover."

Calum hauled in a huge, stunned breath and looked up at his father again. Fragments of the letters were sliding back to his blithering mind. The son who wouldn't call *his* son anything other than his own name.

"*Donnie,*" he breathed. His father's birth had been wearily recorded in those pages and then…

"When I was a young man," Donnie said, "he started to talk to me. I don't know why. I'd always been afraid of him, and my grandmother. They were cold and strict and…bitter. And they never spoke to each other unless they had to. Perhaps…I said something that interested him—we both read a lot. But, bit by bit, as we came to know each other, he confided in me. And I…listened. I asked your mam if we could call you Calum, and the day I told him, he wept."

Calum tried to comprehend it: the old man who'd once been beautiful, and Calum's father who'd once been his lifeline.

…I think I have a friend…

"God, Dad," he choked.

His father frowned. "I'm going to tell you a secret now that no one else alive knows. We planned something together, Seanair and me, and I think… he lived his last years with hope. He asked to be cremated when he died, and you know how it is here…no one was happy about that, but…he got his way, so long as they interred his casket beside his wife and put his name on her stone, even though we all knew she hated him. But…the night before that happened, I got up when everyone else was asleep, and I transferred his ashes into another box, with a last letter from him. And I crept out of the house and drove to Aignish cemetery, and I stumbled around in the dark with a little torch until I found it. Calum Matheson. Aged twenty-two. And I buried him there, as deep and close to his Calum as I could."

Calum never took his eyes from his father as he spoke, but his vision had blurred with the tears coursing silently down his cheeks. It felt like catharsis. Like years of pain vomiting out of him.

"I see you, Calum. I see the mistake you're making. I don't want you to become that old man in a stiff chair, angry and bitter and hating. I don't want some woman to end up poisoned with resentment like my grandmother. I thought maybe I'd been wrong when you came home. But since you've been here, I saw I wasn't wrong. You're ready to sacrifice yourself for us, and I don't want it. I don't believe the Lord wants it. But I'm not...good with things like this. I thought I should try to *show* you first, what you mustn't become."

Calum rose to his feet and stepped into his father's open arms. He hugged him with all the love he felt, and he was hugged back the same way. He was a child again; secure, loved just for being himself.

Nothing like the man readying himself to take care of his parents; nothing like the hardened policeman he'd thought he'd become.

"But Mum won't..." He stopped and gulped back tears.

"You know it's not a fairy tale, Calum." Donnie's voice shook too. "Your mam will find it hard. But she loves you...very much, and she'll come to see that you are as the Lord wills, and wonderful, as are all His creations. She'll come around eventually. I'll make sure of it."

Calum hiccuped a wet laugh against his father's neck. He felt weird. Light and free.

"Besides," his father went on seriously, "I think she likes Adam better than she likes either of us."

Calum hitched in a telling breath.

"You're in love with him." Donnie said.

Calum nodded against his neck like a little boy. He didn't even have to think about it, though it was the first time he'd ever admitted it, even to himself.

"Did you know he was on Lewis?" Calum asked. "When you sent me the first email?"

"I had no idea," Donnie said serenely. "But it seemed like God's will."

Calum sighed. "He's leaving. His plane'll be boarding now."

Donnie thrust him back to arm's length. "Leaving?"

"I told him I can't be with him."

"Well then," Donnie said. "Go and tell him you can."

Calum looked at him with wonder, then down at the sheaf of letters he held, another man's lifeline. He handed them to his father, then lunged forward and hugged him again with all his strength.

It was Donnie who disentangled them and hustled him out to the kitchen and then to the back door, pushing his car keys into his hand.

"Siuthad! Go on! You're going to miss it!"

Calum was halfway down the path when a thought struck him. He turned. "Dad, why was Tormod called Lucky?"

"What has…?" His father blinked with perplexed impatience. "Because he followed me onto a roof when he was eight and fell off. He dropped seven feet without breaking a bone."

Calum shook his head and turned front again. He'd only had to ask.

* * * * *

He broke the speed limit all the way. The airport was a fifteen-minute drive at normal speed; ten when driving like a maniac. The thought came that it was like one of those romantic last-minute dashes in the movies, but the hero in those always made it. He was almost certainly too late.

He tore past the Braighe, past the cemetery where Donnie Maiseach and his Calum were buried, finally together. In the distance he could see the Beasts of Holm, where the *Iolaire*, and that other Calum, had both met their end.

He was going to find the grave one day soon; find it and put flowers on it.

He still couldn't reconcile his memories of that rigid, frightening old man with the man in the letters, eternally and wildly in love. But, he realized, the young stripped the old of passion.

He turned the steering wheel violently right, into the turning to Melbost village and the airport, and shot up the road with screeching tires until he had to ease over the speed bump at the airport gate. Then he accelerated toward the small one-story terminal, parked illegally on the tarmac outside the main door, and ran inside.

The startled woman behind the check-in desk told him that the Glasgow plane had already boarded and was closing its doors, but he flashed his warrant card and demanded one of the ground staff took him across the tarmac.

They reached the plane just as the steps were being taken away. So the staff dutifully rolled them back into position, allowing Calum to race up and inside the still-open door.

The cabin was almost full, so there were plenty of startled, agog faces to witness his entrance. But he waved his card anyway and told the steward he needed to talk to a passenger. Adam was already half out of his seat, frowning with concern.

"I need ten minutes," Calum told the steward. "He's a witness in a case."

The steward nodded eagerly, thrilled by the drama.

"What's happened?" Adam asked at once.

"If you'd come with me, Mr. Patterson," Calum said in his official voice. "We won't delay your journey for long."

He led Adam out and down the steps, away from the plane and anyone who could listen, not that the roar of the engines made that easy even a few feet away.

They were still airside, and Calum was seriously abusing his authority. But fuck it. He'd just been held at gunpoint. He could say he had PTSD, if it came to it. In fact, he probably did.

When he thought they were far enough away, he stopped and turned around. Adam stopped too, hair whipping wildly in the engine downdraft.

Twenty yards away, the ground crewman who'd taken Calum to the plane watched them avidly, waiting for Adam's arrest.

"Cal?" Adam shouted over the engines. "What is it? If she's tried to out you, I'll deny it."

"I changed my mind," Calum yelled back.

"What?" Adam blinked the hair out of his eyes. "About what?"

Calum swallowed. "Things *can* be different," he shouted. Adam's mouth fell open slightly. Calum hurried on. "In London. Or...*here* if you want to be with the bloody chessmen."

Adam's bewilderment wasn't promising. "I don't understand."

"I got it wrong! Partly. God! It's a long story."

Behind Adam's shoulder, the ground crewman began to sidle closer, while the steward monitored them from the top of the plane steps. Desperation clawed at Calum's throat.

"I want to try," he shouted.

Adam's bafflement began to melt into suspicion. "Cal?"

"I want to try...properly," Calum yelled. "If you give me a chance." He stopped, disgusted by his own incoherence, his inability to vocalize emotion.

Adam's expression was unreadable, but he didn't pretend to misunderstand. "What about your parents?"

Calum pushed his hair out of his eyes. "I got taught a lesson," he shouted. "About wasting a life."

Adam frowned, and for the first time Calum saw something other than caution. "You're serious?"

"Yes." Calum gave a mad grin.

Adam produced a startled, tentative smile in return. "Well..." He shook his head, but the smile widened relentlessly. "In that case..."

Calum laughed, wild with disbelieving relief. It was too much for the ground crewman, who began to walk toward them.

Adam moved a step closer, but checked and moved back again.

"Do I leave now? Or stay?" Adam asked. He laughed too. "This is insane. My luggage is in the hold."

"I have a warrant card," Calum said recklessly.

Adam shook his head, still grinning. "We can't hold them up anymore. You'd lose your job. Will I call you when I land?"

Calum nodded vigorously. His own happiness frightened him.

Adam said, "Maybe I'll just turn right around when I get to Glasgow and come back."

But the ground crewman was almost upon them.

"That's entirely at your own discretion, sir," Calum shouted.

Adam had his smile under control, but his eyes blazed with feeling.

"I'll get in touch then, Inspector. As you requested."

"That'd be much appreciated. Thank you for all your help, Mr. Patterson."

But instead of walking away from each other, their gazes locked helplessly. The ground crewman looked from one to the other, narrow-eyed.

At last, Calum began to back away. "Have a good flight, sir."

Adam nodded, grinning again. Then, still bellowing to be heard over the roaring engines, "I just want to know who to thank."

The answer came without thought. "Old men," Calum shouted, still walking backward, fighting his own exultant smile. "Thank old men."

THE END

GLOSSARY: SCOTTISH GAELIC WORDS/PHRASES

Aonghas — *Angus*

an talamh trom — the heavy earth

Bha me a chreid gu robh — I thought it was

bhalach — boy

bodach — old man

bhròinean — poor soul

Chan eil e air a bhith air a h-innse a-riamh roimhe ann am Beurla — It has never been told before in English

cianalas — homesickness/melancholy

co dhiù — anyway

Cò tha seo? — Who is this?

feannagan — lazy beds for crops

goirt — sore

gràidh — love

m'eudail — my darling, my treasure

maiseach — beautiful/lovely/handsome

mhic — son (of)

mo — my

mo chreach-sa a thàinig — good heavens, my God!

Niseach — a person from Ness, at the far north of the island

obair an diabhail — the work of the devil

poileas — police

seanair — grandfather

shen — short for *seanair* (grandfather)

siuthad — go on

strupag — cuppa

Tha fios agam air a phàrantan — I know his parents

Tha me cho duilich — I'm so sorry

Tha thu ceart gu leòr — You're all right

Tha u glè snog — You're very pretty/good-looking

Thighearna — Lord

Tigh nan Cailleachan Dubha — House of the Old Black Women (i.e., nuns)

tìoraidh — cheerio

PEPPER THE CRIME LAB

BY Z.A. MAXFIELD

*When Lonnie Boudreaux's neighbor is murdered, he must foster the man's
dog, befriend a mysterious former cop, and stop the killer—or else!*

CHAPTER ONE

Oh, why did I touch the knife? Everyone knows better. If you find a dead guy
with a knife in his chest, you *don't touch the knife.*

But that Shun Premier knife was so familiar. Withdrawing it from flesh,
second nature. Shock or instinct must have taken over, because before I
knew it, I'd wrapped my fingers around the handle and pulled the blade all
the way out.

Maybe I did it out of detached curiosity. Or maybe I did it because I
couldn't get my mind around what I saw.

It came away from my new neighbor's body with a wet *slurp.* The sound
made my skin crawl with horror, so I dropped it on his chest.

Then the blonde girl from 3F started screaming.

Since I'd only moved in that day, I didn't know her yet. We'd bonded over not being able to sleep because the dead guy's dog had been barking for hours.

Other neighbors entered the apartment behind us, and even though we probably all spent half our lives watching cop shows on television, by the time the police arrived, we had tromped all over the scene of the crime.

No one more than me, obviously.

The guy who lived in the apartment on the other side of…er…the *deceased's* was smart enough to herd us all to the hallway, where he did a quick check on the dead guy's injured Labrador retriever. The black Lab's furry head was matted with blood from a gash over her eye, and she had a lamp cord wrapped several times around her neck. He spoke gently and petted her to soothe her while he bundled her in a towel. That was cool and all, except he'd left me sitting in the stairwell—jeans bloody from where I'd wiped my hands on my legs—with a vicious warning not to move or else. Did the blood come from the dead guy or the dog? Things were really fuzzy for me just then.

I told him, "I didn't do anything."

"I don't know if you did or you didn't." Under his gaze, I wanted to appear smaller. "But that was an idiot move, touching the body."

"I didn't." I wanted to tell him I'd touched the knife, not the body, but that was probably irrelevant. Why did I do such a thing? *Wait.* I'd recognized the knife. The type of knife. The handle. "I was just—"

"Save it." In that moment, I thought he might be someone I knew. His face seemed familiar. Restaurant reviewer, maybe? Disgruntled patron? Definitely someone I'd disappointed in the past. But that could be practically anyone.

"Have we met?" Like a lot of the tenants, he had the actor-model vibe—a gym bunny with chiseled cheeks and bedhead. We'd seen each other in the stairwell a couple of times that day. There was something off about him. I had the feeling he noticed every little thing about me, even when he appeared to pay little attention.

"Doubt it." The quick grin didn't carry to his unexpectedly dreamy brown eyes.

"I didn't do anything." That time, I felt like I sold it. "Except find the body."

"The police will want to ask you about that. Wait here." He left to circulate among the growing crowd, murmuring things like, "Stay calm. The police are on the way. There's nothing to worry about."

Some of the nosier second and fourth floor tenants came to see what all the commotion was about, and he turned them away. 3F spent her time fussing over the dead guy's dog.

Eventually Bossy Guy returned to me.

"You all right?" I looked up the long length of his body. He wore cargo shorts and a tight T-shirt that said: *World's okayest brother.* Brown hair, brown eyes. Distracted, sour expression.

I said, "Shouldn't we take the dog somewhere to get her checked out?"

"In a bit." He focused on my hands. "I'm Enrique Garcia. 3C. Was Stephani with you when you found Jeff?"

"That his name?" *Jeff must be Mr. Body.* Stephani had to be the girl from 3F. "No. She stayed with the dog when I went into the bedroom."

He looked me over again. "Sure you're all right?"

"I could use a glass of water."

He went into his apartment and returned with a bottle.

"Thank you." I drank gratefully. "I'm getting over the flu."

In point of fact, I'd recently had a bad-to-worse cascade of health issues that left me looking pretty ragged—a virus that turned into pneumonia, and a bad reaction to an antibiotic, which damn near led to organ failure. All told, it would set me back about six months if my doctor was to be believed.

"Think that's why you lost your mind in there?" He crinkled his nose. "That was some next-level dumbassery, bro."

"So? It's my first dead body. I mean, you watch cop shows and reality medical shit. I didn't expect it to be so gruesome." I had no excuses. "Anyway, the knife looked familiar."

"Did it? How so?"

"It's a Shun." To stay out of stairway traffic, I scooted over to the side. "I own them."

"It's a cooking knife? Expensive?"

"Good knives are key." In case he misunderstood, I added, "I'm a chef."

"You don't look like you're any good at it." His gaze traveled from my face down my too thin body. Despite the cool air, I started to sweat.

"Looks can be deceiving." I'd lost nearly forty pounds from my over-six-foot frame, and there had been days where I couldn't make it up a single flight of stairs without stopping to rest. I was aware of how frail I looked. "Like I said—"

"You're getting over the flu. What I want to know is why you broke into Jeff's apartment in the first place."

His words shocked me. "We didn't break in. We tried the knob. The door was unlocked."

"You and Steph?" I nodded. "Go on."

"I heard someone on the other side." Did he think I went around trying people's doors all the time? "I don't just—"

"What, exactly, did you hear?"

"The dog has been barking all night. I met Steph in the hall while I was trying to get the manager to do something about it."

"Yeah, good luck with that."

"I know. I called Dave, and he basically said, 'I'm sorry. I can't do anything,' because he took an Ambien or something. He was too groggy. He said he called and got no answer. That the tenant was probably out."

His lips quirked. "Go on."

"But we heard footsteps and then a loud *thud* and a sharp *yelp*. It got quiet for a few seconds. That's when we heard the dog crying."

"Crying?"

"Dog-crying. Whining in pain."

"So you heard a *thud*, then the dog, and that's why you tried the door?"

"I thought someone hit the dog. The door was unlocked. The dog was lying just inside. She had the lamp cord wrapped around her neck, and a gash over her eye. There was blood everywhere."

"But there was no one there."

"No one but the...um...deceased, obviously. Steph said we must have imagined the footsteps—that Pepper had gotten tangled up in the cord and pulled the lamp down on her head. I said no way. I know what I heard."

"You thought you heard human footsteps?"

"I did hear them."

"And then what?" he asked.

"Steph sat with Pepper, and I went to see if someone was in the bedroom."

"Why?"

"I don't know. It was late. I couldn't sleep. I was pissed."

"Then what?"

"I found the—" I couldn't decide what to call it. Him.

"Jeff." He offered the dead guy's name again.

"He was lying on the bed with a knife in his chest." I focused on my memory of the scene. "There was no spatter like in the movies. Just this... glistening pool that soaked his clothes and bedding."

"And you managed to get it on your hands."

"I guess." Enrique's feet were bare. They lent a certain vulnerability to his powerful body. Made him seem approachable. Just a dude. Someone I could confide in.

"I must have lost my mind, because without even giving it a thought, I pulled the knife out to look at it."

He tsked. "You knew he was dead?"

Did I? I believed he was. But what if he wasn't dead *yet* and I could have done something?

What if pulling the knife out actually *killed* him?

"Oh Christ." My spleen tried to exit via my throat. "You don't think I accidentally—"

"No." Garcia shook his head decisively. "Jeff's been dead for a while, Mr...."

"Boudreaux. Lonnie. 3A." I remembered my manners and held out my hand. He didn't take it.

"Don't touch anything until the police get here."

"You sound like a cop yourself." I laughed. "You gonna bag up—" I broke off because he didn't laugh with me. His eyes stayed on mine, his expression guarded, laced with something focused, and in a way, ruthless.

"Oh Jesus." I sighed the words.

He laughed. "Not exactly."

"You're a cop, then?"

"Not exactly that either." He asked again, "Why didn't you knock on Jeff's door before trying the knob?"

I had only moved in that day. I'd gotten no sleep. I'd found a corpse, for God's sake.

Had it been my idea to try the knob, or Steph's?

I couldn't remember anymore.

I let my head fall back against the wall. This was supposed to be the start of my new, less stressful life. Get a place that takes dogs. Get a dog. Spend less time at work and more on my actual life.

The police arrived. I stood to let them pass and then followed them into the hall. *Right. This isn't going to be stressful at all.*

CHAPTER TWO

After a quick look around, an officer with the name Chandler on his uniform addressed my new pal Enrique, "Rick. You kill one of your neighbors?"

"Not today." He glanced at me. "Not yet, anyway. This is Lonnie—" He tapped my arm and lifted his eyebrow.

"Boudreaux," I reminded him.

Chandler got out a little notebook and asked me to spell it. I did. He asked, "That your legal name?"

"It's the name my mother gave me." I didn't know if Boudreaux was her legal name.

Chandler pulled me into a corner while the rest of the responding officers talked to other residents. Rick hovered nearby long after it was necessary. He made me nervous. Was he trying to see if I kept my story straight?

"I found the body." I confessed. "Stephani came in right behind me, along with half the people who live here."

"She corroborated his story. They heard the dog. Called the manager." Chandler tried to ignore him. "They wanted the manager to come up and handle things, and when he wouldn't, they tried the door. Stephani agreed it was unlocked."

"Thanks, but I've got this." Chandler gave a weary eye roll. "Which one is she?"

"Me." Stephani had dressed in leggings and a tank with a lightweight running jacket in a shade of neon green that suited her. She came toward us, clutching a handful of tissues. "I saw Jeff just this morning. When Pepper started barking, I thought he'd left her all alone again. Jesus."

"He do that a lot?" Chandler frowned through a fresh wash of Stephani's tears. "Leave the dog locked in there?"

"All the damn time," Rick said grimly.

Chandler asked her, "What did you see?"

She nodded, sobbing softly. "Pepper had a cord wrapped around her neck and a gash over her eye."

"While she saw to the dog, I checked the bedroom." I picked up the story to give her some time to get hold of herself. "He was lying in bed with a Gokujo sticking out of his chest."

"A what now?" Chandler narrowed his eyes.

"It's a blade for boning and filleting fish. I have the exact same knife." His unwavering gaze made me so uncomfortable, I added, "For boning and filleting fish."

Rick and Stephani exchanged glances. Chandler said, "Mind showing me?"

"Mine? Or—"

"Yours," he said wryly. "Yeah. Can I see it?"

I blinked. "Sure. Come with me."

Officer Chandler followed me to my apartment. Despite the way Chandler had treated him, Rick trailed after us.

"You got no business here, Garcia."

"What's up your ass, Chandler?"

"I'll be out to take your statement when I'm done here, *sir*." Chandler's hostility bordered on the aggressive. Rick appeared used to such treatment. The pain he tried to hide caught me by surprise.

There was a whole herd of armed and intimidating men and women roaming around the building, knocking on doors. From watching television, I assumed they'd be followed quickly by crime-scene investigators and detectives. For reasons I couldn't articulate, I felt better having Rick there.

"I want Rick to stay," I said firmly. Chandler relented, and we entered my place.

Most of my boxes were stacked neatly in the rooms where their contents belonged, so I led them into the kitchen. Any chef will tell you they only use two or three types of knives in the course of their daily work, but most of us collect them. I took excellent care of my knives, and I found them immediately, as I'd packed them on the top of a midsized box marked "knives."

Let it be known I am an imaginative, creative chef, but a pedantic packer.

"What's that?" Chandler asked about my knife roll.

I glanced up. "It's where I keep my knives."

"No block?" Rick looked around as if he had to memorize the space and take a test after.

"You can't throw a block into your backpack when you need to take your knives somewhere."

"You carry your knives with you? Why's that?" The suspicion in Officer Chandler's voice made me glance up, but I couldn't tell if he was serious. Did he really believe I carried my knives around so I could stab people?

"I cook at other peoples' houses a lot."

"Don't they have knives?"

I met his gaze sternly. "Do you leave your weapon at home in the hope that someone has a nice one you can borrow at a dangerous traffic stop?"

"You win." That got me a smile with a bonus dimple from Rick. "Show us this gojo-whatever."

"Go-ku-jo. It's like…all-in-one." I untied the laces and unrolled the simple waxed canvas tote. It had ten pockets for knives and another for a meat cleaver. "It's almost like a Western boning knife, but the blade's not as flexible. I use a thinner, flexible blade sometimes when I need one. I just like this one more for most— *Wait*."

Though we could all see the single empty spot in the roll, Rick gave me the benefit of the doubt.

"Which one is it?"

"It's not here." Light-headed, I braced against the counter. Already my heart thudded with a kind of guilty shock. "Why isn't it here?"

"When did you last use it?" Chandler's expression remained amiable, but behind his warmth I guessed he was estimating my size for an orange jumpsuit.

"Before I moved." The way the two of them eyed me made all the hairs on my skin ripple.

"I think you should come with me." Chandler led me back to the hall. "Stay put."

Technicians were now trudging into Jeff's place with toolboxes. They wore protective coveralls and nitrile gloves and put shoe protectors on at the door, just like on TV.

"I'm going to take Pepper to the vet." Stephani had bundled up for the cooler weather outside. The dead guy's leashed dog clung to her morosely. "Do you think she understands what happened?"

"How would one tell?"

"She's usually so happy." The dog looked as dazed and uncertain as I felt. "Do you suppose she saw the murder? Or tried to protect Jeff and that's how she got hurt?"

"They'll probably figure that out from the evidence inside." I hoped they'd figure everything out, and without me in the picture as the prime suspect.

A mousy woman with dark hair in a style that covered her face carried Steph's yappy shih tzu in one arm and a disappointed-looking pug in the other. They hugged. I'd seen the woman come and go from 3E, and now I assumed they were friends. Stephani took a deep breath and squared her shoulders.

"I hope this doesn't cost a lot. I don't have much headroom on my cards."

"Let me know how much, and I'll help." No one was more surprised by the offer than I was, but the damn dog was a puppy, practically. It wasn't her fault some human killed her owner. I had money. Steph was young and probably struggled.

"Oh gosh." She beamed at me. "Thanks."

I felt momentarily heroic, but then I remembered I'd probably also have to call Dillon Kimble, a successful criminal-defense lawyer, who would not hesitate to charge me top dollar after our forgettable one-night stand.

"I can give you some cash. Let me get my wallet."

"Don't go back inside, Mr. Boudreaux," Chandler warned.

Rick tightened his grip on my arm. "Uh-oh."

"Am I allowed to ask why?" I thought I knew, but I wanted him to spell it out.

Rick winced. "They're going to want to get a closer look at your place. See if anything's been disturbed. If you give permission, it will save them having to get a search warrant. If you have anything to hide—"

"I don't!" I was suspect number one. Why didn't he just come out and say it? "I didn't do anything but try to get some sleep despite a frantic dog in the next apartment."

"I'm sure they'll get to the bottom of this."

And I was equally sure that was something the police said to make suspects feel better, on a par with doctors who claim, "This won't hurt a bit," and boyfriends who swear, "I'll never even look at another guy."

Liars, the lot.

Although for someone with Rick Garcia's good looks and charm, I might have taken my chances. Except, no. I only had two hard and fast rules: never mix sex with business, and never fuck the neighbors. So far, I had avoided about three-fourths of the drama my staff got into because I kept those rules religiously.

Chandler came back. "Would it be okay if the technicians go inside your place?"

After flicking a glance toward Rick, who didn't indicate whether I should or shouldn't, I nodded. "Sure."

Chandler went to speak with them, leaving me and Rick alone.

"Can you think how your knife disappeared from its holder?" Rick's tone was mild.

"It had to have happened while I brought things up from the moving van." I'd been quite proud of myself, even using the stairs to the third floor a couple of times. It meant I was recovering. Slowly, but making progress. "I didn't bother locking the door after each trip. There wasn't that much, and I barely saw anyone else around."

He narrowed his eyes. "Were the boxes open or sealed?"

"I cut the kitchen boxes open with a box cutter as I brought them up to make them easier to unpack. But like I said, I get tired easily. I didn't get too far before I opened a bottle of red wine, had a glass, and called it a night."

"But you didn't sleep."

"I *couldn't* sleep because the dog was going crazy next door." I thought back to the drowsy feeling I'd had. The contentment as I'd slipped between fresh, clean sheets on my newly delivered bed and tried to doze off. "I drifted for about an hour, I think."

"So after that, how long was it before you got up and went to the hall?"

"Why are you asking me all these questions?"

"I *live* here. It's normal to be curious when your neighbor gets killed."

"Guess so." He was right about that. Everyone was coming out of the woodwork with curiosity.

"I'm probably going to get in trouble for talking to you like this."

"Will you?"

"Yeah. And for telling you you're gonna need a lawyer. Do you have one? You should call them." He pulled out his phone, and when I reached for it, I noticed my bloody hands again.

I stared at them. "Fuck me."

"Mm. Not really a good time."

I took a fresh look at him. He had the aforementioned dreamy brown eyes, but he was nothing like the men I normally dated. He was burly, with a sleeve of colorful tattoos that disappeared beneath the fabric of his shirt. He looked like he could throw me around or hoist me up and carry me over his shoulder.

He also had tan skin. A full, soft mouth and a thick brush of hair, buzz cut on the sides and longer on the top. That smile... It teased a memory.

I gasped. "Dine-and-dash."

"What?" I'd clearly shocked him.

"You're that dine-and-dash kid. At Hugo's on Santa Monica. I worked there as a server when I first came to LA."

He flushed. "You're crazy."

"Nuh-uh." I remembered *everything*. That face. The cheeky grin. The serious eyes that crackled with challenge but held so much promise.

He'd been with a party of raggedy hooligans who'd ordered everything from appetizers to desserts and then took off without paying. Last out the door, Rick had glanced back. Our gazes locked. The look we shared lasted an instant before his pals dragged him away, but it stuck in my mind. I thought at the time he regretted what he and his friends had done. He obviously did regret it, because later I found him waiting for me in the moonlight, after I got off work.

"Sorry," he'd said as he shoved a wad of folded-up twenties at me.

"You need better friends." I counted the bills. The cash didn't come close to covering the cost of their meals. "And math skills."

He winced. "That's all I've got right now. I'll bring the rest soon."

I was angry, but I believed him. He didn't seem to want any part of his friends' little game. He couldn't know that was my last night at Hugo's. I was moving to a different restaurant and a new job as a line cook, and I wasn't going to be there when he returned.

"You probably shouldn't bother," I told him. "Whoever you give it to won't remember what you did."

"I will." His hot gaze burned my skin.

That was it. Just, *I will.*

Proud little monster. And determined. We stared at each other for a long time.

I had a feeling he was thinking about punching me. Or kissing me. Back then I would have enjoyed either one from Rick—a fight or a fuck. I was young, and he was a gorgeous kid, tough and angry, just like now. Powerful in a way that made my belly quiver.

Unfortunately, back then he sighed and glanced away.

I should have called one of the busboys to kick his ass. It's what my mother would have done. Instead, I kept my mouth shut and let him go.

That kid was Rick. It was *definitely* Rick.

"Nah," he lied to my face. "Wasn't me."

The warmth I'd been feeling dissipated like smoke. "I found the body. I had nothing to do with Jeff's death."

"Except"—a smile kicked up on one side of that smart mouth—"he probably had your boning knife in his chest. Who should I call, Lonnie? You need a lawyer."

The shock of seeing him again like this was eclipsed by my fear he'd already made up his mind about me.

He was right. I needed a lawyer. But I wasn't going to give Rick the satisfaction of thinking he was doing me any favors.

"No worries. I know a guy."

CHAPTER THREE

It killed me to ask Dillon Kimble for help. When we talked, he didn't hesitate to remind me of our sad little one-off. He held it over me like blackmail until I was polite enough, desperate enough, to agree that maybe I'd cook him a private dinner sometime to make things up to him.

He arrived at the police station an hour after I did, dressed in a fancy gray Italian suit, blue shirt, and repp stripe tie. I still couldn't understand how someone who had such great style and a first-rate education, someone who'd traveled all over the world, could drive me batshit crazy.

He smelled of too-sweet aftershave and the pomade he used on his hair. I still resented that hair stuff. I'd had to throw out a bamboo pillowcase because of Dillon Kimble, and I was not over the loss.

We spent all morning in the interview room together. I stuck to the truth and didn't let the detectives rattle me. Whatever the police thought they had, they were no closer to finding the killer than they'd been before talking to me.

I figured my chances were fifty-fifty I'd spend the night in jail. Dillon didn't seem too worried, but I compensated for his lack.

I was anxious about my new place and how I'd live there if everyone thought I was a murderer. I fretted about my mother, because finding out her only son was in jail would probably amuse her but also drive her to homicidal rage on my behalf.

Mostly, I worried that since I looked so good for Jeff's murder, they wouldn't look for the real killer. That being the owner of the knife, they might fit the case around me.

After they left us, Dillon turned to me.

"So, you finally killed someone?" He probably hoped it was true. Most of his clients were guilty sons of bitches, and it gave him a big rush to defend them successfully.

"Of course I didn't."

"Fine. Right." He waved a beringed hand. "But hypothetically speaking, if you did stab your neighbor, why on earth would you use your own knife?"

"I *didn't*." I couldn't believe I'd slept with this guy. His sense of humor could be unkind at times, plus he had a fetish for people with names like mine.

"Aw. You're still stubborn as a tick on a fat man. My big ole ragin' Cajun."

For the record, I was born in Las Vegas, Nevada, the only son of Calliope Boudreaux, burlesque throwback, pole dancer, and sometimes porn actress. I didn't have a Cajun accent, I rarely cooked Cajun food, and Dillon's fetish creeped me out. It forced me into a boudin casing that didn't fit.

"I did *not* kill him."

"Of course you didn't." He winked.

This was getting us nowhere. "What will happen now?"

"They're deciding whether to charge you, which means you might be in real deep doo-doo, babycakes." Dillon was enjoying this way too much.

The police had searched my apartment, taken my clothes, and looked me over for signs I'd been in a struggle. They photographed my hands and gathered trace evidence.

Dillon continued, "They're looking for any connection they can find between you and the victim. Are you sure he didn't leave you a bad Yelp review?"

"Like I read those. I swear, I don't remember seeing his face before tonight."

"In which case, he could be any one of your lovers because you don't seem to remember those either."

"I don't have lovers. Do I need to call someone else to represent me?" I spoke between gritted teeth. "I'm not asking for any favors here."

"Of course not. I'm a professional. I just like getting your goat." He stood, stretched, and whispered close to my ear. "Say it."

"No." Up close, his cologne was gross. "Nah-uh."

"I'll need to hear you say it, Lonnie."

"I'm not even from—"

"C'mon, Lonnie *Boo-droh*," he drawled my name. "Say it for me. I'm not taking your case unless you do."

"Fine." I sighed. His eyebrows rose in anticipation. "*Laissez les bon temps rouler, cher.*"

He gave a discreet, delighted wiggle. "You might want to think about who you're gonna call for bail money."

God, I should have used a public defender.

* * * * *

At two in the afternoon, the detectives let me go. Since I expected to end up in jail, the feeling of freedom I got was like that experiment where you tense the muscles in your arms for so long they feel all floaty when you're done—only all over my body.

I wanted to dance my way down the street. I wanted to fly. Instead, I went home with some idea of changing into my own clothes and going to Factory to check in on my employees. Maybe have a decent meal.

As I huffed up the stairs, I heard an argument coming from my floor. I slowed my steps because I didn't want to seem like I was listening, but I totally was.

I'm a curious guy. And why have neighbors if you can't spy on them?

"Don't get me involved. It's nothing to do with me."

"But you talked to the police before, right?" I knew Rick's voice. I couldn't tell who he was talking to. A woman, though.

"They were no help." She sounded angry. "They said they'd *talk to him*. Of course, that made everything worse. I got threats from him, his lawyer, and his parents. And they didn't even ask about it last night."

"The detectives must know someone took a call here that involved the victim." I flattened myself against the wall in the stairwell. Were they talking about Dead Jeff?

"What happened to me has *nothing* to do with Jeff's murder. Don't you dare cloud the issue, or they'll put me in the frame for his murder."

"But that's just it. It could have something to do with what happened, couldn't it?" The silence stretched out between them. "You're not the only woman he tried that shit with."

"I'm the only one who called the police, thanks to you."

"I'm sorry if you felt pressured." His voice softened. "I thought you wanted to make a report. I thought I was supporting you, not..."

"Look, when something like that happens, the cops don't believe you. They'll say you asked for it, or—"

"Hey there." That was it; I showed myself. It was one thing to hear who parked in whose space or who left their dog's poop lying around, but this had the sound of something truly personal, and I hated myself for listening in.

I found Rick with 3E. There were six apartments on each floor, *A* through *F*. My place, *A*, was next to the stairs, then came Jeff's place *B*, then Rick's apartment, *C*. On the opposite side, Rick's apartment was across from *D*, whose occupant I hadn't met yet. I was across from Stephani, in F.

3E still had both her dog and Stephani's shih tzu. They frolicked on glitzy little leashes, tangling themselves around her ankles as she talked. With her head tilted down, I couldn't tell if she was looking at me or not, but I said hello to her too.

Rick turned to me. "Hey, they sprang you."

"Disappointed?"

He ignored that. "This is Carla."

"We met last night. Nice to put a name to the apartment number." I would have held my hand out to shake Carla's, but instinct told me she'd leave me hanging.

"I should go now." She turned to go back inside her place.

I glanced down at the dogs. "Stephani not back yet?"

"She called." Carla untangled their leashes. "She'll be back soon. They want to make sure Pepper's okay."

"Good. I hope she is. Nice meeting you." She closed the door between us.

Rick and I stared after her. He said, "I was going to leave this for you."

He stuck a Post-it on my borrowed T-shirt that read: *Stop by after you get back? 3C.*

Did he know they wouldn't charge me? Or had he written the note just in case?

"I need to get a shower and change first."

"Take your time." He stopped at his door. "I'll be here."

When I entered my place, the mess shocked me. Greasy splotches covered the walls and kitchen counters. My stuff had been flung all over. I got it. The cops wanted a nice, neat solution to their case, and so far I was looking good for the role of "mystery killer."

But did they have to trash my place?

With a sigh, I put my problems aside in favor of a steaming-hot shower and a change of clothes.

I should have let the curiosity in a certain pair of shrewd brown eyes go. I should have avoided Rick altogether. That didn't stop me from putting on my softest man-trap jeans and a gray V-neck sweater that showed my stockpot-hoisting shoulders and meat-cleaving arms to advantage.

Rick might be straight as an arrow, and his concern of the protect-and-serve variety, but I doubted it. I didn't get looks like that from straight guys.

Plus, no matter what he said, I thought he remembered me. There hadn't been much light the night he tried to pay me back what his cohorts owed the restaurant, but I'd seen him clearly enough to remember the moment all these years later.

I was young then, and he was even younger. I'd wanted him, thought about pulling him into the shadows and kissing the smug smirk off his face. It appeared nothing had changed with time.

I was new in the building, and I needed friends.

Whatever drove his invitation was fine by me.

* * * * *

I knocked on Rick's door at around four. He opened almost immediately.

"Hey."

A huge, alarming snout poked between his knee and the doorjamb. Belgian Malinois, the *other* German shepherd.

Belgians were loyal, intelligent dogs. I'd read they were less likely to have hip problems than GSDs, but equally useful in combat and law-enforcement situations.

"Hey you." I admit I kind of froze with terror when Rick's dog growled. I didn't know if it was trained for personal security, and I didn't want to enter without its permission. "What's its name?"

"His name is Chancho." Rick opened the door the rest of the way and invited me in.

I stayed where I was. "Is he friendly?"

"He'll get used to you. No sudden moves."

"No problem at all." I took slow steps into his apartment and kept my hands at my sides, letting Chancho sniff me all over. He appeared to find me satisfactory because he lost interest after what seemed like a very long few seconds.

Rick kicked a Kong toy Chancho's way. The dog plopped on the kitchen floor to gnaw at it. I smelled peanut butter.

"How'd they treat you?"

"Fine." I hoped my gaze wasn't as thunderstruck as Chancho's, but honestly. It was hard to look at Rick without noticing the heroic proportions of his body. He had grown up. Filled out. I had too, though you couldn't tell from looking at me now. After that bout in the hospital, my clothes pretty much hung on me.

"Fine? That doesn't sound like—"

"They treated me carefully." Momentarily softened by the concern in his eyes, I sighed. "I've been in worse places."

In fact, the building was much nicer than the one where I'd waited, several times, with my mother's friends to bail her out of jail.

He chuckled. "You aren't from around here?"

"Not originally."

"Why'd you move here?"

"Here to this building specifically? Or to LA?"

"Both."

Another round of quick-fire questions caused me to rub my hands together nervously. "I went to cooking school in Pasadena and never left the area. I moved to this apartment because they accept large dogs."

"You don't own a dog." His eyes sparkled. Oh, he liked being in control of things, didn't he?

"I'm getting one."

He invited me to take a seat at the kitchen counter. "I'm about to fix lunch. Beer?"

"Sure." He went to the refrigerator and pulled a couple of bottles out. "But if you think alcohol will make me confess, you're wrong."

"Shut up. You didn't eat?"

I shook my head. "I came straight back from the station."

He gave a funny tilt of his head. "I'm going to have performance anxiety."

"'Bout what?"

"Cooking for you." He waved a grill pan at me before putting it on the burner.

"Are you that bad?"

"No, I'm good." He sneaked a look at me. "I just don't know how good you are."

"I'm fucking awesome, but I'm not a jerk. Anyway, no one is worse than my mother, and I still love her."

"She's a bad cook?"

"She's the worst." I pictured Mom in the kitchen, frilly apron on, trying her best. God alone knew why I hadn't died of malnutrition or food poisoning. "My mom was built for display only."

He said, "If I didn't cook, my aunts and cousins would marry me off so fast, my head would spin."

"Ah." I nodded. "So it's self-defense."

"Rick, you're so skinny," he mimicked. *"Rick, you need someone to feed you. Rick, when you gonna settle down and let a good man take care of you."*

And there it was. He'd spilled the beans, and now I knew for sure that the spark I'd sensed between us all those years ago wasn't my imagination.

But although he'd evaded the question, I still thought he was some kind of cop. And I was a murder suspect. He was pumping me for information. He was also trying to charm me. I had seriously conflicted feelings about him. My brain said "red alert" while my body went into overdrive.

I cleared my throat while he turned chicken strips with tongs. Had he brined or marinated them? If not, they were going to be hella dry.

"Tell me about Dead Jeff?"

He sent a glance over his shoulder. "What do you want to know?"

"Who killed him? Because it wasn't me, no matter what you guys think."

"*I* don't think anything."

"I find that hard to believe, considering you and the rest of the cops last night—"

He turned. "I'm not a cop, Lonnie."

"What are you? Because you've grilled me like those chicken breasts."

He shrugged. "I used to be a cop, but I'm not anymore."

"I could tell that Chandler guy knew you." I relaxed fractionally. "He didn't like you very much. You still ping every one of my law-enforcement tripwires."

"Maybe you shouldn't stereotype. And why do you have tripwires?"

"What do you do?"

He hesitated before answering. "Private security."

"Like...driving around neighborhoods in a marked car at night? That kind of private security?"

"Hell no." He frowned. "I'm the kind you're not supposed to know is there until I'm needed."

"I— Oh."

Before I could ask more about that, he said, "If you want to know about Jeff? I'm surprised no one popped him sooner."

"Why?"

"You overheard me and Carla talking about him." Guilt flooded me while he took the meat off the heat and tented it with foil. "Why do you think?"

"Sorry for eavesdropping."

"Are you?"

"I guess...not really."

He took his time heating small tortillas over the open flame. "I'm not saying anything the rest of the tenants won't tell you. He lived here for free because his parents own the building. He acted like the place was his."

"Popular guy, then?"

He shook his head. "Crashed everyone's parties whether he was invited or not. Several of the women complained."

"Complained about what, exactly?"

"He hit on them." His eyes narrowed. "Sometimes he didn't want to take no for an answer. Sometimes he didn't worry too much if someone was clearheaded enough to consent."

"Are you saying he actually raped someone? In this apartment building?" Was that what Carla was talking about? That was certainly what I imagined when I overheard them, but wouldn't the police have done more than talk to him if that were the case?

"Sexual assault doesn't necessarily have to be rape the way you think of it. But yeah. I thought so. Carla wouldn't let me get involved, but she agreed to call the local PD. I don't know how many women he tried his shit out on, but I know he was bad news. And because of family money and bogus alibis, there were never any consequences."

"Bad news," I repeated.

"We all wanted to get rid of him."

"And someone did." I flattened my hands on his counter. "But it wasn't me. You should remind the detectives about Carla and the other women Jeff was messing with."

"Just throw them under the bus?"

"Well, yeah. Maybe I'd like some company down here." I figured now was a good time to ask again. "Admit it, Rick. You're the dine-and-dash kid."

"Okay, yeah," he said unhappily. "Just so you know, I'm sorry I didn't admit it when you first asked."

"You *lied* to me."

"We'd just met." He pushed his empty bottle away. "I didn't want to admit I'd been a part of something so...douchey. And I did go back a week later with the rest of what I owed, plus a tip, but you were gone. The server I talked to told me he'd get it to you. Did he?"

"Hell no." I wasn't surprised. "Who was it? Tonio? Black hair, tiny mustache like John Waters?"

"That's the fucker." He flushed. "Sorry."

"Tonio probably pocketed it."

"Lemme give you the money now." He started to take out his wallet, but I stopped his hands. "No. C'mon. I don't want this on my conscience anymore."

"I'll take a beer and we'll call it done." He went to the fridge and got us both another. "Tell me about the little bastards you were with that night. Were you in some kind of gang?"

"Hardly." He smiled ruefully. "That was my older brother and his merry band of asshole friends. They used to call me Mr. Clean."

"Oh yeah?" I leaned in, drawn by his obvious chagrin. "Because...?"

"My brother was ultra cool and he loved to push boundaries. I was younger, and more like my mom, so I constantly lectured him about right and wrong. I drove him batshit crazy."

"You were his self-appointed conscience? I can see where he'd hate that."

"Yeah, anyway, my family lost its collective shit when I went into the police academy. Mom didn't want me in danger, Dad thought I'd forget where I came from. That night at the restaurant was Nico's idea of a hilarious prank."

"He wanted a partner in crime, and you were Mr. Clean."

"He isn't a bad guy. Just liked to play tough. You kind of needed to where I grew up. He was scared for me, I think."

"Because you're a decent guy and he didn't want you to stand out and be different."

"Truth is, back then…" He worried his luscious bottom lip.

"What?"

He shrugged. "I wanted to be Batman, I guess. I thought I was going to protect people and right all the wrongs in the world." Color and passion imbued his words, turning him from a complex adult to the untarnished boy he must have been back then.

"That's…adorable."

"I was a kid. Now I know better. People suck."

"Thanks for clearing that up." I scratched at the label on my beer. "You did make something of an impression on me. I guess I felt cheated when you lied about it."

"I'm truly sorry I lied." He used a single finger to trace the veins on the back of my hand. "I knew who you were. After, I felt bad for not admitting it, but I think I was in shock. Never in a million years did I expect to run into you again."

I believed that. "Okay, your secret life of crime is safe with me."

"Hope so." He covered my hand with his. "We had a moment that night. Remember?"

"I remember. You tried to charm me with your bad-boy ways."

"Tried? Try succeeded. I thought you were so hot. You weren't much older than me, but you had this…attitude, like you were light years ahead. Still do."

"Yeah?" I thought for sure he wanted to kiss me then. I wished he'd kiss me now.

He quirked a smile. "Doesn't it seem like we always meet each other in the worst possible way?"

"Yes." He was so close, his breath warmed my lips. When he finally pressed his lips to mine, they were lush—and much softer than I imagined.

He tilted his head and teased my lips apart. I let him in, and he did not disappoint. Not one little bit. He was every bit as sexy, as tender, as wonderful as I was afraid he'd be. Then he pulled back.

"And I didn't throw you under the bus." Rick's cheeks darkened. "You got there by playing grabby hands with a murder weapon."

I gasped. "Maybe I did. But I had the excuse of shock. It's not every day you find a dead guy."

"All right." He glanced away. "It is weird when you find a dead guy."

"Right. So let's figure out who else wanted him dead? You said yourself—"

"The police will figure it out." Rick had a lot more faith in them than I did. "They don't need us involving ourselves in this."

"But—"

"No buts, Lonnie. The smartest thing you can do is lie low and let the police do their job."

"All right." I still resented the implication that I had involved myself somehow.

Also, I wasn't so sure the police were doing their job, especially if Rick was shielding his neighbors.

But the aroma coming off Rick's street tacos made my mouth water. At least I think it was only the food. It could have been Rick, who looked delicious too.

I had no choice but to follow up—on the food. I'm a curious guy at the best of times. How well Rick could cook was just one of many things here to be curious about.

CHAPTER FOUR

Rick could definitely cook. The marinated breast meat was juicy and full of flavor, and he topped it with pickled onions, avocado, and Cotija cheese. His phone buzzed while we were eating. While he took the call on the balcony, I stared at Chancho nervously and he stared back.

Rick came in and went back to his food without a word. Chancho put his muzzle on his knee, lifting one eyebrow and then the other with each bite Rick took.

"Was that about the murder? Did I pass the interrogation?"

"No and no. They're not gonna confide in me. That was about work."

"What do you do when you're on the job?"

He glanced away. "I mostly stand around, trying to look like a wall."

I grinned. "So, typecasting?"

He gave me an eye roll. "Sure."

His dog thought he was a pushover. "Every time you lift your taco, he thinks that's the bite you'll give him."

"I don't feed him human food."

"I will." Human food? That was the same stuff they made dog food out of as far as I could tell. Good dog food. "I'll do meal prep for mine when I get him."

Rick lifted his napkin to his lips. "All the time?"

"It's no trouble. I can cook chicken in the pressure cooker and then add brown rice and vegetables. My dog won't be eating the dyes, preservatives, and antibiotics in regular dog food."

Rick smothered a smile. "What kind of dog do you have in mind?"

"I'm getting an Afghan hound."

An eyebrow rose. "The really hairy noodle dogs?"

"Yup." I got out my phone to show him a picture. "Afghans are aloof, highly intelligent, independent, and strong willed. Here. I'm waiting for this dog's litter. If I want, I get first pick of the puppies."

"You want an *aloof* dog?"

"I work long hours." I defended my choice. "I need a dog that can take me or leave me, not some dog boyfriend, hanging on my every move."

After a prolonged silence, I glanced down at Chancho. He gazed up at Rick with visible adoration while drooling all over his jeans.

I coughed. "Not that there's anything wrong with that."

"Dogs are individuals." Rick stroked Chancho's velvety ears. "You can't bank on dog stereotypes."

"It's just that I'm not looking for more than I can handle right now. I've spent the last several years working sixty-hour weeks, but then I got so sick. I don't have time for pets or relationships, but I'm trying to make a little space in my work life for the trappings of an actual life. Doctor's orders, really. I don't even know where to start."

Some idea seemed to flicker to life in his eyes but died there. "I hope you get what you're looking for."

That sounded like a curse.

No. I'd read about dogs, and I knew what I wanted. A purebred male. Classy and stylish. Not a dog you saw every day. One who would attract the pretty gay boys whenever I took him to the dog park. While Afghans might be grooming nightmares, you certainly didn't see them everywhere. They were aristocrats. Plus, they had great personalities for a guy like me. I hoped so, anyway.

"Why is it you want a dog again?" Rick asked.

"For company." I heard what he wasn't saying. Dogs need company too. "But it doesn't seem fair to get a dog who might become dependent on having me around."

"So why not get a cat? Or a parakeet," he asked. "It's not just about you. You gotta think about what the dog needs."

"That's why I'm trying to pick a dog that won't care." Although I liked him more for his concern over my someday dog, I knew what I was doing.

"See, when I was growing up, I could never have a dog. My mother's the goddess of chaos. I went to school and spent my free time wherever she worked. We moved constantly."

"What does she do?"

"She's…" I hesitated, not because I was embarrassed by my mother, but I'd learned that people could be awfully judgmental, and I didn't feel like dealing with questions. "She's in entertainment."

He eyed me. "Cool."

"So, after my recent health situation, I think it's high time I tried some things I've been meaning to get around to." I'd wanted a dog the way any kid does. After my brush with death, I wasn't about to wait for the things I wanted anymore. Not if they were possible. "I moved here because the Fillmore Arms is the only place in Pasadena that takes large-breed dogs."

Lucky for me, when I called they had a vacancy.

Lunch itself got serious when Rick offered me chips with a choice of hot sauces. He had both my favorites, Yellowbird Habanero and El Yucateco. The fruity, smokey habanero heat forced us to open some more of his ice-cold beers. I couldn't say when I'd had a better home-cooked meal. Not recently, and none cooked by an amateur.

Suddenly, Chancho sprang to his feet and bounded toward the door. The knock came a few seconds later. Rick backed Chancho away from the door and told him to sit. Even though every muscle beneath his fur shook with the desire to leap forward, he stayed put while Rick opened it.

Stephani entered with Pepper, who walked clumsily but with great care. A plastic cone made her look like an old-fashioned Victrola. I noticed they'd stitched the cut over her eye. Poor thing.

Chancho gave Pepper an interested sniff, but she stiffened and her hackles rose. Rick told him to leave her alone, and he dutifully backed away some more.

"She's okay." Stephani looked much more relaxed than she had the night before.

"That's good." Relief for the dog, and Stephani, filled me.

"No, it's not." Stephani sank onto one of Rick's barstools with a gusty sigh. "When I came in, Dave said there's no one to take her."

"What about Jeff's family?" Rick offered Stephani one of the tacos. She shook her head.

"They don't want her." While she unwrapped her scarf, Pepper lunged at us. "Wait. No!"

Despite how slowly Pepper moved on the way in, she fired up the afterburners and snatched a taco right off the platter Rick held.

"Whoa." I met Rick's surprised gaze. "Jesus. Did you see that?"

"She's a bit of a handful." Stephani flushed as she gave the dog a gentle rebuke. "Bad dog. Aren't you, sweetie? Aren't you a handful?"

Rick ignored the schmoopy dog talk. "Why won't his family take her?"

"They have white carpets or something. They travel a lot. Idiots. She's a doll." She put her face right into Pepper's cone. "Aren't you, Pepper? Aren't you?"

"She's a good-looking dog." Rick knelt and called her forward. She trotted over, eager for cuddles or probably more tacos. "Someone will want her."

Chancho yipped and gave a warning growl before butting his head against Rick's shoulder.

"All right," Rick reassured his dog. "Easy there."

Chancho's possessive behavior seemed meant to remind Pepper whose human Rick was. It was easy to forget the sheer power of a dog like Chancho when he was being an affable cuddly guy. Now, for the first time since I'd arrived, the air tightened with menace.

"Hush," Rick commanded, but the dog continued with the narrowed eyes and subtle growling. Rick looked pained as he rose and started clearing our lunch dishes. "As you can see, I can't foster her."

"Chancho gets jealous," Stephani informed me.

"No kidding."

"Mm-hmm." Rick's gaze drifted over me. "He only gets jealous of other dogs, though."

"Good to know." He held his hand out, and I gave him my plate.

"I can't take her." Stephani complained, "She's still growing. I can't afford to feed her, and she needs more training, and I have Lulu, and I don't know how they'll get along."

"Even to foster her for now?" Rick asked. "I can help with the cost of food."

She shook her head. "Pepper isn't very socialized with other dogs. I'm afraid she might hurt Lulu without meaning to. Lu's so small compared to her."

"She seems to be okay with Chancho here."

"She's still dopey. Believe me, I had to leave the vet's place through the back. She lost her mind near the cages."

"It won't be easy to find someone to take her on. Everyone here already has a dog." I felt Rick's eyes on me. "Almost everyone."

My neck tingled. "Oh, no."

"It's only going to be for a few days." Stephani pleaded, "And you said you'd help."

"Yeah, but I meant I'd splash the cash. I can't take care of her. I go to the doctor, like...every other day." This was an exaggeration, but not very far off. "When they sign off on me, I'll go back to work. Plus, she's a Lab."

"And?" A wicked smile played over Rick's lips.

"And that means she'll chew everything I own to bits."

"Not if you keep her with you."

"How can I do that? I work twelve-to-sixteen-hour days."

"All the more reason," she said. "Humans need balance. Get some."

"You sound like my mother."

"You could take her until you go back," Rick said reasonably. "You're home now, right? She'll keep while you're at the doctor's. Jeff left her alone all the time. And what did you plan to do with your Afghan while you're at work?"

"I have a day-care place lined up. I—" They stared at me, waiting. "I suppose I could see if they'll take Pepper."

"You mean you'd *board* her?" She said the word like it meant *take her out back and shoot her.*

"If they can watch her when I can't, I *might* be able to foster her." I cautioned, "I'd want to think about it for a while first."

"Yay. I knew you'd do it." Stephani threw her arms around me, pulled me close, and kissed my cheek. "I'm sure we can find people who will help."

"Wait just a minute, Stephani," I said. "You said yourself she's not socialized. They'll test her to see if she's okay with the other dogs. If they can't make it work, she can't go to day care. And if she can't go to day care—"

"I'm sure it will work. And you'll love her. You really will. She's such a sweet dog. Jeff kept her cooped up in his place alone all the time. She just has to spend some time with other dogs to see that it's not so scary, and then she'll be fine."

"I'll probably be in jail, anyway." Would I even be at liberty to take the dog? Rick's thoughtful expression said he knew something I didn't. "What?"

"The investigation is ongoing. Will be for a while yet."

"That's not very reassuring."

"Look at her." Pepper leaned drunkenly against Stephani's leg. "None of this is her fault. She's practically still a puppy—a crime victim, for God's sake. She needs someone to take care of her."

"Oh, all right." I was going to adopt a dog of my own soon, so it might be valuable experience for me.

Anyway, how hard could it be to take care of an already housebroken dog?

CHAPTER FIVE

Housebroken, my ass.

The only way I could take care of my new "foster dog" was to wrap the eight-foot leash Rick gave me around my waist and keep her physically with me at all times. First, she figured if I could pee in the bathroom, she should be able to as well. And then I couldn't stop her from nosing into every single box as I unpacked, disturbing my carefully laid plans, chewing my shoes, and generally making a total pest of herself.

Therefore, I had to unpack and get rid of the moving boxes and wrapping paper on hyperdrive, which made it necessary for me to rest every two hours. But did Pepper rest? Nope.

I thoroughly exhausted myself dog-proofing the house, and after every dust-up, Pepper turned to me with a smug doggy smile, which I refused to believe was simply the way she looked with her mouth open like Stephani said it was.

But then Pepper would push her nose into my leg, and I'd dig my fingers into her glossy black fur, and we'd achieve détente for a few minutes.

Nothing that ever happened to me compared with witnessing a murder and being beaten over the head with a lamp. Her plight *forced* me to practice empathy.

Still. How was I going to clean, shop, cook, run errands, do laundry, etcetera, with Pepper actively working against me?

I texted my mother to commiserate, and she sent me an entire phone screen full of LOLs and laughing emoticons.

Welcome to motherhood, Bubba.

Thanks a lot. For the record, I've never been, nor will I ever be, a *Bubba*.

You're welcome. She texted that she was working and didn't have time to chat. I appreciated making contact. I did feel isolated since my illness. I tried calling Factory, but my sous chef told me she'd have the staff throw me out if she saw me before the doctor released me to work.

So at dusk, I took Pepper outside, where she tried to put her nose to the ground and sniff around. But with every other step, her cone banged flat against the concrete like a suction cup. Even with my newly acquired empathy, I found this hilarious.

I tried not to laugh. I really did. I may have taken some pictures. Okay, I took lots of pictures. Her dozy frustration was my first #dogsofinstagram post.

That night, at the trash bins, we found Dave with a young woman I'd never met. They waved. I went over to say hello.

Pepper went crazy, struggling against the leash, barking madly, wrapping herself around my ankles clumsily until we both nearly got killed.

"Hey, Lonnie," Dave greeted me while I got unwound. "You took Jeff's dog? That's so nice. I would have—"

"Right." The young woman laughed lightly. "You'd take the only dog in the world that doesn't like you?"

"All right. It's not funny. Yeah." He flushed. "I get along with the other dogs fine, but Pepper has hated me since day one."

"It's funny if you know Uncle Dave," she said. "He's such a pushover for the dogs in the complex. Every one of them adores him, except Pepper."

"I'm taking her for now." I had to drag her away to get her to settle down. "Honestly, we're feeling our way."

"Have you met my niece Sharona yet?" He pointed to five overstuffed garbage bags. "Look what she's making me do."

"Recycle?" I asked. "What a monster."

"She's helping me clean out my place." He presented her with a slight bow. "Sharona's going to be a professional organizer, like Marie Kondo. We love that show."

"Call me Shar." She thrust out her hand and gave mine a firm shake. She couldn't have been more than eighteen. Razor thin, pretty, and dressed in a twinset and short floppy skirt like her idol. She sparkled in the way of girls-next-door, if those girls had fairy blood. "Nobody is making you do anything, Uncle Dave."

Pepper started barking at him again. I had to haul back on her leash.

"Aw… Hey, girl. Knock it off." Shar got between Pepper and Dave. "Remember me? How're you doing? Unhappy this evening, huh? Poor baby. Must have been so traumatic seeing Jeff like that."

"She's still a little dopey," I said. Pepper plopped down and rolled over with a *thunk* of her cone.

"I would have taken her"—Shar stood and whipped her dark hair away from her face—"but I can't have dogs in my building. With the new organizing business, I don't have a lot of time anyway, but—"

"Speaking of which." I took out my phone and scrolled through images until I found one of my sock drawer. It was unforgivably weird, but I showed her anyway. "I fold everything, just like Marie says."

"Good for you!" She clapped her hands. Pepper thought that meant it was time to stand and flop her weight against Shar's leg. "Do you like it?"

"I just started, since I had to take some time off work. Before Pepper came along, I was bored out of my mind."

"Well, the upside of putting things neatly in drawers is keeping them away from this one." She smoothed her hand down Pepper's back. "You don't want her swallowing a sock."

"God no. We've already had a couple skirmishes in what I gather will be ongoing sock wars. I learned quickly that I can't leave anything lying around."

"If you're having any trouble related to organization, I can help."

"She's a miracle worker," said Dave. "She's got me tidying all my crap up."

"Uncle Dave," she chided, whether for his language or his habits, I didn't know.

"Don't let her eat that!" Dave shoved Pepper away from something on the ground near the Dumpster. He scooped up whatever it was and threw it into the Dumpster. "Don't let her eat anything she finds on the street. There have been several dog poisonings in the area."

"Intentional poisonings?"

"They were." A muscle ticked in his jaw. "Over the last three months, pet owners have been finding scraps or bags of poisoned meat. Two dogs died before their owners realized something was wrong. A few others have been treated for poisoning and survived. Seems like someone's deliberately attacking the local dogs, so please, please keep a sharp eye out."

I tightened Pepper's leash. She jerked and sneezed unhappily but finally subsided next to my leg. "What kind of person poisons a dog?"

"Dunno. Police came by to warn the residents, though, so it must be serious. People are assholes."

Shar said, "Uncle."

"I'm just saying."

"Jesus." Pepper couldn't get her mouth on much of anything due to her cone collar, but I moved her away from the offending trash area altogether.

"She's a great dog, despite hating me." Dave eyed her fondly. "Does she still get into everything?"

"Yeah."

"Well, watch out. Nothing has happened to the Fillmore dogs yet, but you can't be too careful."

"Thanks for the heads-up."

He nodded. "Gonna be quieter around here now that you're looking after her. I got a lot of complaints, before."

"Because of the dearly departed?"

"I don't know about dearly. Jeff left Pepper alone a lot, so she'd bark and scratch at the door. He had a way of ruffling the other tenants' feathers too."

Was that what the kids were calling assault these days? "Seems to me people aren't surprised somebody killed him."

"Well, I'm just sick about it." Shar tightened her hands into fists. "And you shouldn't listen to gossip. Jeff could be really nice, and I hate that everyone's trashing him now that he can't defend himself."

Dave winced. "Now, honey, there's a reason people talk about him like that. I told you, he—"

"He was spoiled. He was rich, and he liked to rub it in. So what?" She set her jaw. "Not to make excuses, but it's his building. His family has owned the Fillmore Arms for the last hundred years. Maybe he just wanted people to take care of things?"

Her words got me thinking the obvious: *Like he took care of Pepper?*

"Did you ever go out with him?" I asked.

"Me? No. To him, I was a bothersome kid." She laughed ruefully. "He barely noticed me until I started my business."

"Speaking of which, we'd better get this finished up and go back inside. There's so much more to do." Dave picked up a mammoth trash bag and threw it into the Dumpster.

Despite his words, she stayed where she was, eyes downcast. "Jeff was going to hire me to organize his place. That would have been so awesome."

"I'm so sorry, honey." Dave met my gaze as he put his arm around her. "I'm sure there will be other clients."

He knew Shar had dodged a bullet. If Carla and Rick were to be believed, Jeff was worse than bad news with the female population of the Fillmore Arms.

"Maybe you could give me some suggestions?" I asked, feeling rather avuncular myself. "I'm pretty organized, but I suppose I could always use some new tricks."

"Thank you!" She dug around in her skirt pocket. "That would be great. I'm trying to build up my business, so if you know anyone else, can you pass my cards along?"

I took a few, sure some of the staff at Factory would be interested. Then I helped the two of them load up the rest of the garbage bags.

Footsteps slapped our way from behind us, causing Pepper's ears to perk adorably. She turned and tried to run toward the sound, but my feet got tangled with hers again. Neither one of us knew how to walk on a leash. Mom would say we both needed obedience training.

Pepper nearly pulled my weak ass over, but Dave steadied me. We definitely needed one of those face halters when Pepper healed.

Or whoever took her would. Not me.

"Whoa, Pep." I stopped her from charging Dave again. "Wow. Knock it off, dog."

"Hey, Pepper. Hi, baby." The newcomer's intensely blue eyes and flawless face turned my way. "Do you remember me? I'm Caleb."

My heart did an embarrassing little shimmy. "Of course."

I met Caleb in the laundry room, where he'd started a load, removed his clothes to add to it, and then returned to his apartment wearing only a thong. Now I considered his six-pack abs and tight derriere a perk of living in the building.

Pepper was more smitten than me. She wagged her tail, rolled over, and banged down to collect more tummy rubs. Shameless.

I considered doing the same but stopped myself in time.

"Pleased to see you again, Caleb." Another one of the many undiscovered actors/models who dwelled among us mere mortals, Caleb was pleasing to the eye and quite sweet. Today he wore a skinny black tank top and abbreviated red running shorts. "You wouldn't happen to need a dog?"

"Can't." His grin blinded me. "I got a job today."

"What's that got to do with it? We probably all have jobs."

"Mine's a location shoot in Canada." He lifted his pretty hands helplessly. "As it is, I have to leave my dog at a friend's place. Otherwise, for sure I'd take Pepper. For a while, anyway. She's an awesome dog."

"You got the part?" Dave asked. "You celebrating tonight?"

"Yeah, no thanks to you-know-who."

Dave toed some sticky mess on the ground. "Sorry I couldn't help more."

Caleb turned to me. "Jeff blocked my car in deliberately last week. He knew I had a callback and I was really nervous. I had to take an Uber. It was a miracle I got there in time."

"Guess it all worked out," said Dave.

"You and Jeff get into it a lot?"

Caleb gave a growl. "Every single time I saw him."

"How come, if you don't mind my asking."

"I'm about to pop a cork and get the party started. Come and ask your questions at my place." Caleb shot me a sly glance. "Bring Pepper. You're my hero if what they're saying is true."

Curious, I asked, "What are they saying?"

"That Jeffrey Dearborn, of the old-money Pasadena Dearborns, looked better wearing your butcher knife than all those fancy suits he—"

"Hey, now," Dave warned.

Shar gasped.

"All right. I know." Caleb sighed. "I'm speaking ill of the dead."

"It wasn't a butcher knife, anyway," I corrected, stupidly.

"Whatever." Caleb's fingers drifted through Pepper's sleek, seal-like coat. "He treated people horribly, and dogs worse, and I'm glad he's dead."

"No one should be *glad* anyone is dead." Shar—all eighty pounds of her—stepped forward to do battle.

Dave put his hand on her shoulder. "Now, honey, Jeff just wasn't good at making friends, is all. He wasn't nice."

Understatement.

"You're all horrid." Shar's face darkened. "The man is dead."

"Ding, *dong*," Caleb sang out. "Dave, you come up later, if you want. I'm celebrating."

His new job or Jeff's demise? Maybe both, I thought.

"I'm sorry, sweetheart." When addressing Shar, Caleb wore his million-kilowatt smile. I doubted it softened his next words. "You're way too precious for my crowd. They'd consume you like a bonbon, and we can't have that."

He stretched, showing the tan strip of skin between his shirt and his shorts. When he turned, the back of his thong was visible above the elastic waistband.

Despite being a neighbor, despite my rules, he made my mouth water.

"You coming?" His eyes stayed on my mine a little too long.

"What time?" I wasn't fooled. Caleb was simply one of those guys with charisma to burn. The heat melted my spine, but it wasn't personal. He turned those same high-beams on everyone.

"I'm starting now." One perfect brow lifted. "C'mon up."

"Okay. Sure." I didn't look to see what Dave made of Caleb's behavior. Champagne sounded good. In fact, I could guarantee it would be.

"I'm in 4B." He pointed toward the stairs.

We said goodbye to Shar and Dave, he picked up his mail, and together we walked Pepper toward the stairs. She seemed bent on tripping us, and not in any romantic, *101 Dalmatians* way.

"Let's go by my place. I've got some chilled champagne in the fridge."

"Really?" He glanced over. "Sure. Only for a minute, though."

"Afraid I'm a serial killer?" His surprised expression made me regret my words immediately. "Was that too soon?"

"No, silly." He booped my nose. "You're funny."

I hadn't been *booped* in about twenty years, so shock held me silent.

"It's just that I've got to take Mac out." He swept the hair off his forehead with a jerk of his head. "He has a really small bladder."

For a lot of reasons, I hoped Mac wasn't his boyfriend. "So, you don't really think I murdered Jeff?"

"Of course not. Wait." He blinked at me guilelessly. "Did you?"

"Nah. Just in the wrong place at the wrong time." God, they made them pretty in this town. I was nowhere good enough to live here. "I thought someone was hurting the dog."

"Aw." He folded his hands over his heart as we started up. "You are my hero."

"Ask Stephani. She was with me. She heard it too. Someone was inside."

"Of course there was. Jeff was an asshole anyway. My sister stopped coming over because he'd try to catch her in the hall. Kept offering her drinks. You know. She told him she doesn't drink, but that was like waving a red flag at a bull. He wouldn't quit hitting on her. I didn't trust the bastard one little bit."

"I'm so sorry." Jeff hadn't endeared himself to any of his neighbors, it seemed. "Just a minute."

I went into my place and grabbed a bottle of Dom Pérignon from the refrigerator. I always kept a couple of bottles on hand for hot dates. Caleb wasn't going to be one, but he deserved a celebration anyway. It wasn't Cristal, but it was damn good.

"Oh boy." Behind me, Caleb laughed at the state of my place. Signs of a mischievous dog were everywhere. "You don't need a sign Pepper was here."

"It's just temporary." I detangled Pepper again before handing the bottle to Caleb with a flourish. "For you. Congratulations."

"Awesome. Thank you!"

"You're entirely welcome."

He held the bottle to his chest. "So what are your plans for Pepper?"

I shrugged. "Once I go back to work, I'm going to have to put Pepper in doggy day care until we can find someone to take her in."

"Oh no. She'll hate that." He lowered his voice. "I think she's intimidated by all the other dogs. They probably bullied her when she was little."

"Really?" To my mind, that said more about him than her.

"I hate bullies." We headed back to the hall. "You have no idea."

Since we weren't coming back for a while, I locked the deadbolt behind me.

"If you're going to put her in day care, you're gonna need her vaccination record. Do you have it?"

"No, I don't," I confessed.

"Do you know which vet Jeff used?"

"Er... I—"

"I'll bet we can find out." He stepped across the hall and banged on Carla's door. "Carla, honey?"

A lock clicked. Then another, and another.

"It's Caleb. I'm here with Lonnie."

The door opened a crack, and she peeked out from behind the chain. "Hi, babe. Ooh, champagne. You got it?"

"Yes!" They air-kissed. "Wanna come up? I'm celebrating."

"So happy for you! Sure, I'll be up in a bit."

"Thanks, hon." He leaned against the doorframe. "Lonnie needs to know who Pepper's regular vet is. Do you know?"

"How would I?" Her eyes widened. "Ask Dave. He might know."

"Okay," I agreed.

"Text Steph and tell her to come up when she gets back from work." Caleb turned to me, somewhat chagrined. "The show is a series. My agent thinks it's going to be a big deal, and..."

"Hey, you have a right to have fun. You have food? I'll see what I can do for your guests, if you want."

"That's so nice." Again, he did that little clutch at his heart.

"You've reached a career milestone. You should have a wonderful celebration to remember this day forever."

He told me about his new role in a paranormal prime-time drama for teens while we headed up the last flight of stairs together.

I remembered every one of my milestones. Looking at the extremely youthful Caleb, they all seemed so long ago. Maybe my plans needed refreshing?

Pepper coughed twice, then horked up a foamy mess of packing paper and yellow bile.

I sighed heavily.

Caleb didn't seem fazed by dog sick. "Dogs can be gross, huh? That always happens at the worst possible time too."

"I guess." In stupefied fascination, I watched Pepper try to lick the stuff off her cone.

Caleb whipped his shirt off and wiped the plastic contraption down. "No, honey. Don't do that."

I eyed his torso with a kind of cosmic shock.

Caleb was stunning. A product of time spent in tanning booths and the gym.

And my dog had cleverly caused him to strip for me.

Pepper and I exchanged a look while he wiped up the floor. I gave her that I-have-my-eyes-on-you sign. Two fingers, pointing from my eyes to hers.

After Caleb cleaned Pepper's mess, I followed him into his place.

"Let me just throw this away." He tossed the shirt, washed his hands, and went to the cabinet to find champagne glasses. "Can you open the wine?"

"Of course." I popped the cork. The bottle gave a perfectly satisfying sigh.

Pepper sat, tongue lolling.

I got the feeling she waited for me to say or do...something, but I didn't know what.

"Good girl." I tried scratching her behind the ear. "Aren't you a good, good girl."

She barked, *ruff*, as if to say, *"Damn right I am."*

CHAPTER SIX

Minimalist and gorgeous, Caleb's apartment contained charcoal couches and black Ikea occasional tables against a backdrop of dove-gray walls. Even his dog was black, a Scottish terrier named Mac. Short, I learned, for "The Macallan."

Artsy black-and-white photographs of Caleb's face hung everywhere. His gorgeous blue eyes seduced bystanders to buy cologne, or underwear, or in one case, an expensive watch. If ever a man was born to grace *GQ* magazine covers and underwear ads, it was Caleb. The result was like Mac's namesake: it went straight to my head.

Caleb's friends, nearly all beautiful, tan twentysomethings, made me feel weak and old, but it wasn't their fault. They were simply young. Oblivious. Frolicking around his apartment in varying stages of minimal dress, striking poses against the bland backdrop like colorful tropical birds.

Set apart from the rest of Caleb's guests by my lack of perfection and beauty and youth, my flaws were all the more glaring because of my recent illness.

So I did what I always do in these situations, even though I had to do it with a skittish, too-curious dog circling a scant five-foot radius around my person—I looked in the refrigerator and pantry and made myself useful for as long as my energy held out.

It took a couple of elevator trips to my apartment and some asking around, but soon I had a pretty good spread of simple appetizers going. Despite the poached chicken I fed her, Pepper tried to eat everyone's shoelaces. She dug through the trash and went after throw pillows and cabinet knobs.

Pepper didn't like taking no for an answer, and despite her neat ploy with Caleb, I'd begun to fear she wasn't that bright. Plus, Stephani's words proved correct. She didn't want anything to do with the other dogs. We were forced to stay in the kitchen to avoid any conflict of the canine variety.

At first, most of the guests refused food, but once the champagne started flowing, no one worried about their calorie intake. After a while, I watched my new neighbors—and several of their dogs—enjoy Caleb's success, and told myself: this is what you came for.

Dead Jeff notwithstanding, I'd made an awesome choice moving here.

At around ten Stephani took Pepper outside, thank God. She gave me a yearning backward glance—that is, Pepper did, not Stephani. I assumed her look had more to do with the food than me. I didn't feel relieved. In truth, Pepper had simply become an extension of me, even though she was needy and submissive and lay down for tummy rubs if you gave her so much as a sideways glance. Not at all like my imaginary Afghan, whom I expected to snub people—even me—most days.

While I moved around introducing myself, more than one of Caleb's guests made sly references to Jeff's death. The general consensus seemed to be that I must have done the murder, either because of Pepper's barking, or because I had some vendetta against Jeff before I moved in.

Caleb's guests acted flustered in my presence. Or titillated, which was far worse. Reality television made crime into a parlor game, and I was the new *it* boy, for bringing murder to the Fillmore Arms, which made me look at everyone else and wonder...

Because I knew I hadn't done it.

A quick walk with Stephani finally tuckered Pepper out. We tied her leash to Caleb's kitchen table base, where she snoozed contentedly near my feet. She woke up once or twice to look around, found me with that sleepy doggy gaze—as if to reassure herself I was still there—and put her head back down.

I found her behavior uncomfortable as hell.

What would I do if she started depending on me? I wasn't planning to keep her. I didn't do relationships. Not with people, and not with dogs, which was why I wanted a dog who treated me like staff, who behaved like a member of the aristocracy, whom I could leave in a pet spa without giving it a second thought, while I worked.

Pepper was not that dog.

Though my muscles screamed with exhaustion, I didn't feel like going home.

Instead, I watched Caleb interact with his friends and tried to imagine which of them used my knife to kill Jeff. When that proved fruitless, I grabbed a six-pack and took Pepper onto the balcony to get some relief from the noise. One beer turned into two and then three. By then I discovered my recent illness made me a lightweight. Carla, who'd pulled her hair back enough that I might recognize her the next time we met, stepped out onto the balcony with me.

"Oh, hi. God, Caleb's parties are always such a crush. I was gasping. I hoped nobody'd be out here." She seemed the type to want to escape from parties, whereas I normally wasn't. Except for tonight, when everything was too much for me.

"Sorry. I'll leave you to it." I started to go in, but she stopped me.

"No, don't go. It's fine."

"Are you sure?"

She perused me a while. "You're not like them." She jerked her head in the direction of the party. "The shallow talkers. All they do is gossip."

"I gossip. I just don't know anyone yet. You'll probably want to escape from me someday too."

She gave a surprised grin. "I think I like you."

"Well, you have my permission to tell me to fuck off, anytime."

She nodded. "That takes the pressure off, thanks."

"My pleasure."

We sat for a while, isolated from the rest of the world. Music and chatter and traffic sounds floated past us into the night. Dogs barked in the distance. Eventually, she stood and looked out at the horizon.

"I want to thank you, but I don't know how."

"Thank me?" I asked.

"For Jeff."

I shook my head. "I didn't—"

"It was your knife." She went to the sliding door. "If his death weighs on your conscience, don't let it. Whoever killed Jeff saved the world a lot of heartache."

"It wasn't me, Carla."

"I know." She glanced back before she slipped inside.

She knew? What did she know?

Who had access to my knives while I was moving my boxes up?

Stephani could have taken it, but I didn't see her stabbing Jeff and then leaving Pepper alone and frantic.

Carla was a much more likely suspect because she had real reason to hate Jeff. But I'd think it would take strength and rage to stick my knife into another man's chest with a single stroke. Carla had the rage, but she was small, almost skeletally thin.

Rick could have done it, although I hated the idea. Rick had the strength, and opportunity, and a background in law enforcement. He would know how to cover his tracks.

So while I'd been sighing over his bulging biceps, he could very well have been setting me up for a crime he committed.

I went to the railing and looked down at the building.

Odd. I hadn't noticed how close the balconies were to each other. Caleb's neighbor's balcony was only a few feet away from his, and I wondered if that was the case with Jeff's and mine. If so, it'd be entirely possible for someone to jump from one to the other if they had the nerve.

I glanced behind me to make sure no one was watching. There was barely any wind. Maybe the building blocked it?

I leaned over and checked, and sure enough, I could see my balcony and Jeff's, and they had a similar setup.

I contemplated this fact for a full minute.

In my current state of inebriation, it seemed like a good idea to test my theory out.

I'd spent half my childhood playing on the catwalks over a stage while my mother performed below. I must have seemed pretty fearless even then, because one day Mom brought a Czech acrobat by our house. He taught me juggling, tumbling, gymnastics, and how to walk a tightrope.

While other eight-year-olds played video games, Mom dressed me in a French clown jumpsuit and had me balance on a wire with a pole, while she upstaged me in a giant champagne glass, singing "La Vie En Rose."

As a bonus, I no longer had any fear of heights.

Any person familiar with parkour could make the jump from one balcony to the next.

Any second-story guy, anyone with some nerve, or like me, just enough liquid courage on board to make this seem like a good idea.

I could do it, although I was well out of practice. I stepped onto a patio chair to study the distance and the level of danger. Then I climbed onto the wooden railing to get a feel for its stability. Maybe I should have gotten a feel for *my* stability before I got up there, but once I was, that balance came back to me—just like making hors d'oeuvres.

The construction felt solid beneath my feet. Walking along the wide boards to the side nearest the neighbor's balcony was effortless. If I wanted to jump, the neighbor's balcony was close enough and uncluttered, so landing would be no problem.

I could do it.

I could definitely do it.

I wasn't planning to do it because I didn't know who lived there, and also, *I'm not an idiot.*

I was in that special place in my head where everything else disappears. So deeply focused, I felt the board beneath my feet and the one I needed to jump to simultaneously—as if I was simply moving between dimensions— and it would have been so easy.

"Jesus. Get the fuck off there!" Rick's authoritarian voice shredded my composure. Pepper barked like a mad thing, startling me double. I lost my balance and sprang, helplessly, for the other balcony's railing. To my horror, I missed. Shit, shit, *shit.*

Forced to scrabble in midair, I made a grab for the iron balusters. I caught hold of one out of sheer desperation. Relief brought icy sweat, a racing heart, and instant, bitter sobriety. For several long seconds, I simply hung there, forearms burning like fire, hands throbbing from the impact. *Ow.*

I nearly jerked my arms out of their sockets from trying to hold my weight, and came to the inescapable conclusion I was not strong enough to hold on for long.

Dangling four stories off the ground, I held on while waiting for my heart to restart. *God*, I was gonna bruise. Were people watching? I rested my forehead against my upper arm and tried to disappear while Rick continued shouting curses at my stupid, stupid ass.

"Hang on, sit tight, I'm getting help."

I was too busy getting purchase with my feet and climbing into my neighbor's balcony to answer with more than an angry grunt.

He waited until I was safe to move. "Oh my God, you dumb fuck! Wait there."

Where did he think I'd go? I'd managed to *survive*, barely. I wasn't going to jump back the way I'd come.

He opened the slider and shouted into Caleb's place, "Ramone, go next door and let Lonnie in. He's on your balcony."

That got a chorus of disbelieving voices.

I plopped down with my back to the wall, burning with shame and resentment while I relived the experience over and over.

I'd been a little loopy before, but adrenaline had jolted me into a state of high anxiety. I couldn't catch my breath at all. I didn't know how long I had before the crash came, but when it did, I wanted to be in my place, alone.

Actually, I wanted to be alone right then, but several people—and dogs—spilled onto the balcony with me. Before I could begin to worry we'd have one of those disasters where a whole balcony falls off the side of a building, Rick muscled them back through the slider.

Stephani pushed Pepper through to me. She curled into a big ball in my lap as if she sensed I'd nearly had a fatal tête-à-tête with gravity. She covered my face with licks I didn't deserve. My God. What if she'd tried to follow and fallen?

I got rid of her cone for the moment, holding her soft furry body close to my chest for comfort until my heart rate slowed. Her ears felt like velvet beneath my fingertips as she snuggled in, offering warmth and softness and more little dog kisses until I felt grounded and whole. Safe again.

No doubt about it, I'd made a name for myself with the neighbors. And shoot. I'd *proven* I could have murdered Dead Jeff without anyone seeing me enter or leave his apartment.

Rick studied me like a new species of parasite—probably trying to decide whether to call the guys with backward jackets or sic the cops on me for being a nuisance.

I spoke first. "Before you say anything—"

"Don't talk yet," he snapped.

"All right."

"Don't. Talk. Yet." Those fierce brown eyes burned holes in my forehead. "I need a minute. Is that okay with you?"

"Sure." I looked over his shoulder while I waited for him to do whatever. He looked as shaken as I felt.

I *wanted* to explain that I would have been perfectly fine, if not for his silent footsteps and bossy shouting. Maybe I shouldn't stand on railings, but maybe he shouldn't *sneak up on people.*

"I take it you learned what you wanted to learn?" His question surprised me.

"I didn't want to learn anything." I shot him an unhappy glare. "Anyone could jump that."

"You barely survived."

"Because you *startled* me." I drew in a deep breath. "I wasn't planning to jump. I *fell* when you came up behind me and yelled. After that I had to figure things out, midair, thank you very much."

"That's why *normal people* don't stand on railings four stories up."

What did I say to that, I was once a teenage tightrope titan? I didn't have to explain myself. "Maybe I'm not a normal person?"

"You think?"

Still, he stared at me. Far from making me uncomfortable, his attention made me want things. He smelled so fucking good. A mix of bourbon and bacon cheese straws and pure male sweat. The way he looked at me, like when we first met and he saw something he wanted... He glanced away.

"Don't." My heart fell a little, as if his hungry expression was all that was bracing it.

He huffed impatiently. "Don't what?"

"Don't judge me by what just happened."

"I don't even know what that"—he pointed toward Caleb's balcony—"was. What did you hope to prove?"

"Prove? Nothing. Only I saw how close together the balconies were, and realized—" Uh-oh. He'd apparently come to the same conclusion. His narrowed eyes and harsh breathing weren't due to relief or anything sexier. He was pissed as hell.

"You realized your little stunt implicates you further? Your balcony is the one next to Jeff's."

I swallowed. "So's yours."

His face darkened with anger. "Yes it is, brainiac. And how angry do you think I'd be right now if I were the killer? If I can jump one balcony, then I can jump *two*."

"So?" I jutted my chin. "Same goes for you."

Anxiety took desire's place, for the moment. Nobody actually hypothesizes about being a killer, right? Not if they actually did it. Chilled, sweaty, and unsettled, I lifted Pepper off me and stood. She shoved into my leg and stayed there, no leash required.

"I've gotta go." I needed to go home and regroup. Two times in as many months, I almost died.

I gathered up Pepper's cone collar and leash, and together we pushed through the crowd. This time, I left by the apartment's front door like a regular guy.

CHAPTER SEVEN

After Caleb's party, I was the talk of the Fillmore Arms. It's not every day I provide catering and a show. My neighbors were probably taking bets on whether I was the killer or not. All but Rick, whom I didn't see much of for the next few days, unless I counted meeting him out walking his dog.

Sometimes, we'd walk together stiffly, barely exchanging a few words. Pepper and Chancho became tentative friends, but after my "stunt," as Rick called falling off the balcony, I could not say the same about him and me.

I guess what I wanted was the easy rapport we had when he invited me for lunch. Instead, he'd let things cool off considerably. It seemed I had to earn back his trust, which I had no clue how to do.

I didn't think he killed Jeff. Surely, he didn't believe I did. I wondered if I had to tackle the subject head-on, but I never found an easy opportunity, so the words remained unsaid.

Meanwhile, Pepper and I developed a routine. Every morning I grabbed a travel mug of coffee for our walk, and when we came back inside, we both ate a healthy breakfast.

Since Pepper's caloric needs were still on the puppy side of the equation, I fed her homemade chicken along with brown rice and vegetable patties, with a perfectly poached egg on top.

Probably, her routine with Jeff was similar and she was training me, and not the other way around. I doubted he was ever as consumed by perfecting a dog's meal plan as I obviously was.

Gossip at the party didn't reassure me he'd been a morning person either, but he must have taken her out early enough to keep her from doing her business on his carpet. Maybe he'd employed a dog walker?

From what I'd learned, Dead Jeff wasn't the most enthusiastic guy when it came to his dog. In fact, I wondered why he even had one.

I knew my emotional limitations, but he probably didn't.

Truth, the more I learned about Jeff, the less I liked him. I imagined their morning routine—he probably dragged her out on the leash, shouted at her to poop, and threw a cupful of generic kibble into a plain metal bowl because he wanted to go back to bed.

Even I could see she deserved better than a man like that.

After we ate our breakfast, she licked her eggy chops and joined me on the sofa.

If I was looking for a Pepper kind of dog—the cuddly, full of personality type—she would be my first choice.

But I didn't have any experience training dogs. I expected to leave that sort of thing to someone who had time for it. And I assumed they'd have to start on day one with a puppy, to do it right.

Her ears perked up, and a low growl rumbled in her throat. A knock at the door caused her to lose her mind. She leaped from the couch and charged it, barking like all the demons of hell were on the other side.

Except it was Rick standing there.

"Hi," he said.

"Hi." My breath gave a little hitch. He wore a dark charcoal suit, a white shirt, and a gray tie with polka dots. Had he dressed that way for work? "You look nice."

"Thanks." He glanced down, seemed to hesitate. "So. The techs are done with Jeff's apartment. Dave's supposed to box up his things. The owners are okay with me going in and looking for Pepper's papers and her vaccination record. I've got the key, so I thought I'd take a minute to look before work. You want to help?"

I would never forget the gory scene I'd found in Jeff's apartment last time. In the days that followed, the shock had worn off. Still, I hesitated before answering.

"I guess I could."

He laid his big hand on my shoulder. "It's okay if you don't want to. It might be hard after finding him. And it's been closed up for nearly a week. The smell—"

"It's not that." I wasn't sure I wanted to see Jeff's place again, but it wasn't the smell or the mess; it was my recent acquaintance with my own mortality that bugged me.

"It's okay, Lonnie," Rick said gently. "I'll find what you need."

"I'll go." I wasn't Jeff. Jeff wasn't me. And Pepper needed her vaccine record because we had an appointment at the Bark Right Inn to see if they'd let her stay with the day-care dogs when I went back to work. "Suppose she had a dog bed or anything?"

"If she did, you don't want it." He backed away so I could join him in the hall. "You'll never be able to forget where it came from."

"You're probably right." I turned to Pepper. "Sit."

She knew "sit," but she thought it was only for feeding time. Little did she know I'd use it to keep her from darting through the door after me.

"Stay. I'll be back soon." Her wide brown eyes promised retribution when I closed the door between us.

"You guys are doing great." Rick patted my back. "I never imagined you'd be so good with her."

I frowned. "Why not?"

"You know." He unlocked Jeff's door. "You seem like one of those guys who expects a dog to be something it isn't."

"Me? Like what?"

"I don't know. Dogs are animals. You seem like you want a polite roommate who won't get in your hair."

"Is it crazy to want a dog to behave? I'm going to hire a trainer for mine, and I won't bring him home until he's socialized. I'm going to start as I mean to go on."

"Right." He aimed a wry glance my way. "Good luck with that."

We stepped into Jeff's place, and all happy thoughts fled. Musty air reeked of dirty dishes and dog piss. A thick metallic sweetness hung in the air. The apartment gave off an awful vibe, and I was sure Rick and I were on the same page. Get in, get whatever, and get out.

He moved across the cluttered space quickly. "You look out here, I'll take the bedroom. They said we could have anything dog-related."

"Okay." I saw where Jeff kept Pepper's things, and I was right. Jeff fed Pepper some vile, off-brand kibble, the cheap bastard.

There were two leads, one leather and one retractable. I took one of the plastic grocery bags Jeff kept under the sink and gathered the things I thought we could use.

There were soft toys, but I didn't want them. Nor did I want her bedding or blankets. Just being there made me feel physically ill. I didn't want any reminders of Jeff or the night I found him. I made a mental note of what Pepper apparently liked and needed so I could take her to PetSmart and get her those things, brand new.

I did take a big red Frisbee and a Kong ball with holes for treats that looked sturdy and well loved. Maybe if she had them, she'd stop trying to chew my furniture.

Or wait... I'd be sure to give them to whoever adopted her.

Next, I looked for her vaccination records.

It felt all wrong shuffling through Jeff's drawers and going through his papers, but none of the people we'd asked knew which vet Jeff had used. I felt certain the answer would be in the kitchen, in a junk drawer where I found a bunch of bills shoved haphazardly along with scissors and tape and an ashtray full of used vape cartridges.

I thought going through Jeff's stack of unpaid bills for one from the vet might yield results. Then Rick returned.

"Nothing in there." He washed his hands and wiped them on a paper towel. "What'd you find?"

"Bills, some of which are way overdue. His filing system leaves me speechless." I shoved the pile I had toward him before pulling the drawer farther out to get the rest. "There's lots more where those came from."

The drawer caught on something. I leaned over and glanced inside to see what was blocking it. Rick waited while I shoved the drawer in and tried again.

No luck. I couldn't tell what was hanging it up.

"Is it stuck?" he asked.

"I don't know." I checked the cabinet beneath it and saw an envelope under the drawer. "There's something here. Looks like it's taped there."

"Bullshit. Crime-scene techs wouldn't miss something like that."

"I don't know what to tell you. There's an envelope"—I squatted and gave it a tug—"underneath the drawer."

"Wait. Don't—"

"Here." I handed the thing over to Rick as soon as I retrieved it. I was more interested in finding something that would help me convince the Bark Right Inn to accept Pepper into this year's obedience academy and day care.

After shuffling through another half stack, I found it.

"Bingo." I had a vet bill with a card stuffed inside. Rick was so quiet, I looked up. He'd opened the envelope I'd given him.

"Shit." His angry tone warned me it was nothing good.

"What?"

"Photographs." He didn't show me the contents, but from the look on his face, it was bad.

"Of what?"

"At least two of these women are our neighbors." He paled as he thumbed through them.

"No wonder they hated him. You suppose he's been holding these over their heads somehow?"

"Probably. Jesus. This changes things."

"What?"

"They're unconscious." He swallowed like he was going to be sick and closed the envelope. "They're all unconscious. I need to drop this off with the detectives working Jeff's case. You have what you need?"

"Yeah." I took the bag of dog toys and the vet bill with me. He slipped the new evidence into his jacket pocket.

When we went back to my place, he seemed preoccupied. I was too.

I had a sinking feeling the fact that I found those pictures would blow back on me somehow. Rick didn't meet my gaze. I guessed it occurred to him too.

"You know I didn't have anything to do with those pictures, right?"

"What? Oh. How could you?"

"I don't know. But you seem—"

"It's just really uncomfortable for me. I know some of these women. They're my friends."

"I'm sorry."

"I know. I have to go." I offered him coffee, but he declined. "No, thank you. I have work."

I couldn't help asking, "You work private security in a suit and tie?"

"Depends on where the client is going."

"So you're like…a bodyguard?"

He flushed. "I get a bodyguard detail occasionally. Sometimes I'm hired to assess someone's home or business security setup. Or I handle a client's digital security. Whatever they need, I'm there."

"For celebrities?"

He coughed. "I'm not at liberty to discuss my clients."

"So that's a yes. How awesome." I wanted private security, if it looked like Rick. "Where are you going today?"

He sent me a pointed look. "I'm not at liberty to—"

"You don't have to tell me who your client is. Just tell me where you'll wear the suit?"

His ran his fingers lightly over the lapels, and I wanted to do the same. "You like?"

"Mm-hmm. Wait." I straightened his tie needlessly and gave it a pat. "There."

He relented, a little. "I'm going to be in court today. That's all I can say."

"Should I look for you on the five o'clock news?" I asked for a lark, but his face fell, and I knew a high-profile client was involved. "Ooh. Anyone I might find interesting?"

"You're too nosy for your own good. You know that, right?" The way he said it, it didn't sound like a deal breaker. More of an annoyance. I could work with that.

"It's a feature, not a bug."

"Says you," he chided.

Before unlocking my door, I reached awkwardly for something else to say. "Have a nice day."

"You too." He held my gaze a moment longer before he stepped down the stairs.

My problem was that envelope.

Rick had been unhappy about finding it and upset by what it contained.

Why didn't the techs find it? Had they simply missed it? Because I could think of another reason—maybe it hadn't been there.

Much as I hated to do it, I called Dillon Kimble's cell.

"Hello, Lonnie. This is a nice surprise. What can I do for you?"

I swallowed, hard. "Guess who's cooking gumbo tonight, cher."

CHAPTER EIGHT

Dillon showed up at exactly eight p.m., wearing a bespoke suit and carrying a bottle of impressive wine.

He probably knew a lot about wine. It was obviously important to him that I acknowledge this fact, so I did.

Factory featured an impressive wine list, but the place wasn't called Factory for nothing. I built the entire menu around elevating the food of working men and women from all over the world—sandwiches, street foods, soups, and hearty stews—because I preferred them to haute cuisine. I liked to drink beer or whiskey, rather than even the finest of wines.

"Mmm… Smells fantastic in here." He grabbed my shoulders and air-kissed both my cheeks. I didn't stop him.

"Thank you. It's been a while since I made gumbo. I'd forgotten how much I like the aroma."

The holy trinity of celery, onions, and peppers perfumed the air, along with garlic, cayenne, and the rich, nut-brown aroma of a dark roux. I kept gumbo on the menu at Factory along with a lot of other deceptively humble dishes. I could have had someone on my staff send it over, but I'd decided an afternoon of cooking something low and slow would feed my spirit.

By the time I led Dillon to the table for two in the kitchen, I felt relaxed and happy. Pleasantly social.

"Sit here. I've got some work to finish up, and then I'll join you."

"Sure, babe. *Hey.*" He startled when Pepper clicked over to sniff at him. "When did you get a dog?"

"I didn't. I'm fostering Pepper for a bit. She belonged to the guy next door. The one that got—"

"Dead?" His eyes widened. "Is this a dead guy's dog?"

"Yeah. I don't think what he had is contagious, though."

"Can you put her somewhere while I'm here?" He wiped his hand on a monogrammed handkerchief. "I don't fancy cleaning drool off the suit."

"Nowhere she won't cause massive trouble." I wondered if he was afraid of dogs. "Love me, love the dog."

"I don't *love* either of you. I'm here for the food."

I had to commend his pragmatism. "Since this is a command performance, consider the dog part of the act."

He pursed his lips. "You called me."

"I promised you dinner." I smiled sweetly. "And dinner you shall have. You can live with a little dog drool."

He grimaced and turned away from her.

I opened the wine and let him do the wine-snob ballet. He swirled, and sipped, and oohed. I tasted it. The vintage was as good as I expected it to be. I got a Fat Tire beer for myself.

He didn't help me bring things to the table. He wasn't the kind of man who rolled up his sleeves to help chop and stir. Maybe that's why I didn't click with him.

Dillon wanted everything served up—drink, food, sex. He wanted to receive, not participate, and I liked people who dug into life with everything they had. People who cleaned fish and mixed meatloaf with their bare hands.

It was with a sense of irony and amusement that I set a bowl of rice before his majesty and spooned my richly flavored gumbo over the top. "There you go. Dig in."

"God, you're amazing." He audibly breathed in the aromas. "And fried okra? I'm going to have to take an extra spin class."

"I made hushpuppies too." I uncovered the basket with a flourish. "You're probably going to have to buy the gym."

"Not to worry. I have a Peloton."

"Of course you do," I murmured while I served myself.

He sat with his spoon in his hand, as if debating whether to say something or hold his peace.

I finally asked, "What?"

"I get that you think I'm a joke, Lonnie."

"I don't." Not a joke, precisely. He was too dangerous to be a joke.

"Yes you do. But if I'm useful to you, I don't see why I can't get a good meal out of it."

He wiped his mouth with a napkin. "And you cook amazing food."

"So maybe we've got something after all. Be nice, and I'll make Bananas Foster for dessert."

"You're on." He sat back in his chair with a smile. "Tell me why you invited me tonight."

I leaned against the kitchen counter, Pepper at my heels. Even though I no longer kept the leash around my waist, she glued herself to me without it, which was a blessing and a curse.

"Something weird happened today." I told him about finding the hidden envelope in Dead Jeff's kitchen drawer. "The thing is, it felt…orchestrated. Someone put the envelope there for us to find. I'm sure of it."

Dillon picked up his wineglass and absently swirled the ruby liquid inside it. "Don't you think you're being just a little paranoid?"

"Maybe."

He frowned. "What I'm hearing you say is you're worried someone planted evidence—"

"And I found it, so now my fingerprints are on it."

"While that could present a problem"—I waited for him to make one of his routine, cutting remarks—"no one will railroad you on my watch, Lonnie."

"That's…" I waited for him to say "just kidding," but he didn't. "Really nice of you?"

"Like you said, we didn't hit it off in the sack." He stopped me before I could say there was no maybe about it. "But that doesn't mean I'd abandon you if you needed my help."

"Thank you," I breathed the words with awe. "That's magnanimous."

"Still, you think I'm some sort of shallow idiot. I know." He folded his napkin, dropped it beside his plate, and waited for me to correct him.

"I don't think you're an idiot."

His face fell. Then he sighed deeply. "See, I actually like the way you did that. Not because it didn't hurt a little, but because you didn't mean for it to hurt. You were just being honest."

"Well, yeah," I admitted. "I don't want you to get the wrong idea."

"I know." His expression softened. "A man with money and power gets lied to every day. Some people like hearing only what they want to hear, whether it's true or not."

I understood that. Sometimes I wanted that too.

"I regret what happened between us"—his lips twisted wryly—"but never more than tonight. I wish I'd pursued you as a friend and not a lover."

"I wouldn't mind giving friendship a try." I scratched my jaw unhappily, wishing I hadn't let the stubble grow in. Damn dog got up to mischief when I turned my back, and shaving had become a luxury. "Just know one thing. It's never going to happen between us again."

"Okay." He held up both hands. "Nothing up my sleeves. As long as you never tell anyone you friend-zoned me. I gave you the slip. Got it?"

"Like I care what people think."

He gave a grin. "Maybe you don't. Whatever. It's the principle of the thing."

"Bananas Foster it is." I went around the island and took a shallow sauté pan down from the rack. I didn't have banana liqueur, but I did my best with what I had, caramelizing ripe bananas in butter, brown sugar, cinnamon, and dark rum. I dimmed the lights, tilted the pan, and ignited the liquor, giving Dillon the whole show. It was worth everything to see the childlike delight in his flame-lit eyes.

I wanted to be his friend. What had drawn me to him, the things I'd actually liked—his sophistication and his enjoyment of fine things—seemed tedious when he used them to get into my pants. But we enjoyed this moment together without any hidden agenda, and I relaxed. Showing off became a way to make him smile.

Dillon had an extraordinary smile.

When I plated the dessert and set it in front of him, he rubbed his hands together happily. "As for your worry about the new evidence, you say you found it when you were invited to look for the vet bill with your neighbor, this Rick?"

"Yeah."

"What do you know about him?"

I tasted the dessert. Heavenly. "He's in private security. Used to be a cop."

"Oh, did he?" Brows lowered, he asked, "And just how does he fit into this? How did he get along with the victim?"

"He didn't like the guy. Nobody did."

Dillon put his fork down. "Hm..."

"What does that mean—*hm*?"

"From what you've told me, the building is full of people who wanted this guy dead. And this Rick lives in the apartment on the other side of the victim. If he was around on the day of the murder…" He pursed his lips. "We can use that if they push on you. If they do bring you in again to question you about the new evidence, say nothing. Not one word. They'll try to tell you it makes you look guilty when you don't talk. That's bullshit. You call the office right away, and if I'm busy, I'll send someone to help."

"Thanks."

"And try not to worry." For a change, he was reassuring, not boasting. "Get some rest. You look awful."

"Gee, thanks." Oddly, the words warmed me up to him some more. I still didn't want to date him, but maybe he was okay with that.

"Want to take our drinks to the living room?" I asked. "Watch a game?"

"I'd rather watch something with a narrative. *Peaky Blinders* and *Penny Dreadful* are my two guilty pleasures right now."

"Okay. I could watch either of those." I gestured for him to go ahead. "Queue something up while I put the dishes into the washer."

Genuine happiness lit his features until he realized Pepper was going to follow him. He unbent enough to give her a scratch behind her ears.

"She seems remarkably chill."

"Remarkably chill." I laughed. "Right. Keep your shoes tied and your drink close, Dillon. That dog is a monster."

He laughed because he thought I was kidding.

Pepper watched our newfound camaraderie with an eye toward finding something to chew. When he dozed off, I chased her away from his hand-made Italian loafers, because if we were going to be friends now, I figured I ought to watch his back too. The good news was he was going to watch mine. I hoped that would be enough to keep me out of jail.

Something sinister was going on in this apartment building. There were things about Dead Jeff that no one would talk about.

Secret enmity. Vile behavior. Blackmail, maybe.

I was going to get to the bottom of it all. I had to, if I wanted to get my Afghan dog and start my new life.

CHAPTER NINE

At midnight Dillon put on his jacket and gave me a platonic hug good night. I didn't necessarily trust the change in his behavior, but he'd been pleasantly laid-back most of the evening, even drifting off a time or two.

I'd forgotten what it was like to socialize with someone unrelated to work. My staff were my friends and family. My customers were my social network. I spent so much time at the restaurant, I forgot what it was like to share my private space.

If anyone ever told me I'd enjoy spending time with Dillon Kimble, I'd have wondered about their sanity. But there he was, standing on my doorstep, drowsy and disheveled.

His smile was genuine. "Night, Lon. Don't hesitate to call if you need me."

"Thanks, Dillon. I really appreciate that." Maybe it was because we'd broken bread. Shared salt. I had a deep-seated need to nurture people with food, and when I did, things always changed for me. "Let's do this again sometime."

His naked pleasure shamed me. "Do I get to pick what you cook?"

"Maybe next time, you'll have to cook it with me."

He winced. "In the kitchen?"

"You can probably be trained."

"I doubt it." Heavy footsteps coming up the stairs drew my attention to the sight of Rick returning home from work. The man was mouthwatering. Dillon snorted. "Don't tell me. That's the famous neighbor, Rick?"

"Yep."

Rick's expression was unreadable. "Evening." His slow once-over made me shiver.

"Rick, this is Dillon Kimble. My lawyer."

Dillon extended a perfectly manicured hand. "How do you do, Rick?"

"Just fine, thank you." Rick held on too long, forcing Dillon to remove his hand.

"Well." Testosterone stung my nostrils as I rubbed my hands on my thighs. "Good night, Dillon."

"Night, Lon. Thanks for…everything." Dillon couldn't help himself, probably. He shot a grin of private satisfaction and dark humor my way and walked with fluid grace toward the stairwell. Rick and I watched him skip lightly down the stairs.

Now that I didn't have to worry about having sex with Dillon, his antics made me laugh. Rick was not amused. "That's a little cliché."

"What?"

"Getting fucked by your defense attorney."

Angry that he went there, I tensed. "Is it?"

"Seems like a douche move on his part." His tone as he backed me against the wall sounded irked.

"Which? Fucking me or representing murderers?" Fighting for control, I breathed in sweat and cologne and pure male ego. "He and I aren't like that."

"No?" Rick moved forward until his lips were inches from mine. Mm. He also smelled like night and earth.

"We hooked up once," I admitted. "Now we're just friends."

He lifted a brow. "He knows that?"

"I made it clear." What would happen if I moved just that speck forward? Would he kiss me? Or back off because I called his bluff?

Do it. My body sent me all kinds of heated messages. *Try it. You need it. When was the last time you felt fully alive?* How was it I could jump off a balcony four stories up, yet I choked over moving a few inches forward?

But he was a *neighbor.* Goddamn, my stupid rules.

I sighed, turning away. "Have a nice night, Rick."

"Don't go." His voice dropped low. "Look. I get that things between us went…sideways. What you did the other night? That was some stupid, reckless shit. Never mind if you fell, you could have hurt someone on the ground. Traumatized me and my friends forever. Frankly, I…didn't handle that well."

"I know. I'm sorry. I told you—"

"I meant to apologize for acting like a dick the last few days, but then I got preoccupied by what we found this morning." He pressed his lips together. "I wanted to say sorry then, but…"

I accepted the explanation. "You did seem upset by those pictures."

"Weren't you? They were fucking upsetting."

"I saw an envelope," I reminded him. "I only have your word for what was inside."

"You think I'd lie about that?"

"I don't know, would you?"

His eyes widened. "Let me get changed and come back. We can talk. I know I haven't been totally forthcoming."

"Sure." I wanted to believe he'd tell me the truth—about leaving the force, about those pictures, about everything. "I've got gumbo, if you're hungry."

"That sounds amazing." He stepped back. "I need a quick shower."

"Pepper could probably use a break before bedtime."

"Be back in a few." I watched him walk to his apartment and go inside.

Despite what Rick said, I was sure Dillon's innuendo influenced his desire to come clean, because he'd been making himself scarce for a couple of days. God save me from Alpha males. Amen.

Was breaking the ice with Rick a bad idea? My body didn't think so, but my brain said yeah, duh. I found him too attractive. I liked him too much.

I had my rules to consider.

But I also had leftovers, and I couldn't eat them all.

* * * * *

Pepper went berserk when I took her leash off the hook by the door. We took the stairs together, heading out the front of the building toward the street.

Since she no longer wore the hated cone collar, she sniffed her way carefully along the sidewalk. Every scent fascinated her. Every movement caught her attention, and she tried to drag me toward every sound.

We made our way around the block in a leisurely fashion. Sometimes I had to give the leash a pull. Sometimes she was the one tugging me.

The night was cool. Clouds had formed in the sky, promising rain by morning. Cars drove by, headlights illuminating the sidewalk around us every now and again, making Pepper's eyes glow an eerie green.

When she did her business, I dutifully bagged it.

A dog barked behind a fence, startling us both. Pepper wrapped herself around my ankle, tail between her legs.

"You chickenshit," I accused.

Her expression seemed to say, "What's your point?"

Dumbass dog. Contentment, almost happiness, filled me.

When we returned, Rick was waiting by the door with a six-pack of beer.

What did I want to happen?

I didn't know.

I fixed him a nice bowl of gumbo, with rice and some crusty bread.

His pretty brown eyes glazed over with appreciation while he ate. Like Chancho, Pepper rested her muzzle on his knee. Absently, he petted her soft ears.

"This is great, thank you."

"You're welcome, anytime."

He frowned. "You made this for him, though, didn't you? The lawyer."

"Yeah," I said warily. "Dillon's got a fetish for all things Louisiana. He loves my deceptively Cajun surname, so I made gumbo."

He tilted his head. "Are you from Louisiana?"

"Not even a little bit." I chuckled when Rick did. "But he likes me to playact sometimes."

"That sounds pretty skeevy to me. But this is delicious. My door is always open when you have extra food."

"I won't be around much after I go back to work, but feel free to come to Factory. I'll comp you dinner anytime."

"I pay my way," he said.

"I know you do. I've seen you in action."

"Not yet you haven't." His gaze shifted from my eyes to my lips. "But I think it's time, don't you?"

Despite his innuendo, I was surprised by the press of his lips to mine. Especially since he'd been so stiff with me for the last couple of days. His kiss tasted of gumbo, and beer, and something like relief—it was refreshingly honest, as if he were glad to lay his burden down, and I was his reward.

He wrapped his hand around the back of my neck and pulled me closer. I reacted, tasting the smile on his lips with my tongue. I'd have been content to spend all night prolonging such languid exploration, because where Caleb was made of physical perfection, and Dillon was brilliant and suave, there was just something about Rick that made it impossible for me to see anyone else when he was around.

Rick was good. He wanted to do right. He was the kind of guy who puts his shoulder to the wheel and makes things better for everyone. So there went my doubts. My rules. I let my heart be my guide. Rick seemed like he knew what he was doing, and I…I just wanted whatever he offered me.

If things got complicated, maybe I was ready for that too.

I heard a faint *thump*, first on the window and then on the balcony. Pepper shot up and barked, abruptly breaking the spell between Rick and me. I stood, almost dizzy, to see what it was.

"Something hit the window." I followed Pepper, who raced toward the balcony doors, stiff on her paws, circling and charging as though she wanted to kill whatever was out there.

I expected to find a bird, or a cat, or one of the squirrels that scampered up and down the trees across the drive winding around the building. Instead, when I opened the balcony door, Pepper charged outside and pounced on something I didn't recognize—a paper bag, which she instantly tore to shreds to get at whatever was inside.

Despite the shock that momentarily immobilized me, I grabbed her collar and yanked her off the thing, but not before she'd gobbled some of its contents.

I pulled her away from it just as Rick joined us.

"What happened?" he asked. "What did you see? Was someone out here?"

"That's not mine." I pointed to the bag, holding tightly to Pepper's collar while he went closer to examine it. She lunged, over and over, trying to get more of whatever it was. "What is it?"

"Shit." He knelt, taking out a pen to push back the paper and expose the contents. "Some kind of meat."

"What? Why would there be—"

"We need to get her to the vet. Now." He stood and pushed us inside.

"The vet?" I asked, unable to process what had happened. "You think it's poisoned?"

"Can you bag that up? Don't touch it with your hands." He took Pepper's collar from me and dragged her to the door for her leash. "We need to go."

"All right." I did as he ordered even though he was scaring the hell out of me.

"Chances are it's nothing," he tried to reassure me. "Chances are someone's just playing an asinine prank."

It didn't work. "You think it's the guy Dave talked about? The dog poisoner?"

"I don't think anything." His demeanor screamed *lie*.

"I thought you were going to tell me the truth from now on."

"All right. I'm sorry. I didn't want to seem…" He huffed a sigh. "Truth is, it's best if Pepper is seen by a vet right away."

"Should we induce vomiting?"

He shook his head. "That could backfire on us by causing a chemical reaction, or introduce something toxic into her lungs."

That was true in the case of human poisonings. You could do more harm than good if you didn't know what someone was poisoned with. There were appropriate steps to these things.

Rick attached Pepper's leash to her collar while I shoved the half-chewed bag into a plastic container.

He said, "Let's not chance home remedies. Keep her calm; we'll take my car."

"Where should we go? Her vet's not going to be open at this hour."

"Animal ER," he said. "They'll know what to do."

"You really think it's an emergency?" I wasn't hesitating so much as I was in shock. "It couldn't just be a—"

"I do, Lonnie." A muscle in his cheek flexed before he spoke again. "Someone threw that on the balcony, three floors up, knowing everyone in these apartments has dogs. We need to call Stephani and have her warn the other tenants."

"I'll call her on the way." I got a jacket out of the coat closet. "Let's go."

CHAPTER TEN

Pepper started drooling copiously on the ride to the animal hospital. Since the local poisonings had everyone on edge, the vet tech took one look at her and carried her to the on-call vet immediately. They told us they'd have more information for us later, after they'd had a chance to observe Pepper's behavior and get some blood work done.

Rick stayed by my side, offering his support.

"You okay?" The warmth of his hand on the small of my back steadied me. "Can I get you some coffee or anything?"

"I'm fine." I skimmed over the intake paperwork and asked him for a pen.

He handed one over. "I notified the local PD. If Pepper shows signs of being poisoned, they'll want the meat we bagged up."

"They're going to wait? Won't the vet need to know what she was poisoned with to counteract it?"

"*If* she was poisoned, the vet will know what she's looking for." He dropped his warm hand on my shoulder.

"What kind of sick fuck does something like this?"

"Who knows why sick fucks do anything?"

"You still have connections in the department, don't you? Can't you ask someone to expedite this?" I wrote the reason for Pepper's visit in the box provided on the form. *Possible poisoning.* A lengthy silence made me look over at Rick. "What?"

He swallowed, hard. "I— Remember when I said I wanted to be a superhero?"

"Yeah?"

"It didn't work out. That's the reader's digest version. One or two people in law enforcement wouldn't hang up on me if I called for help, but only to hear me beg."

"I don't understand."

He glanced at his hands. "I was a whistleblower, Lonnie." Suddenly Chandler's behavior toward Rick made some sense. "I did what I thought was right, but it cost me everything. It's unlikely we'd get anywhere, even if I hadn't left under a toxic cloud. There are backlogs filled with major crimes against humans."

Clearly, it had been difficult for him to share that. "I'm so sorry."

"It is what it is."

"Still—"

"Old news. But thank you." He flushed deeply. "I'm proud of what I did. I faced some backlash, but it was the right thing to do."

"If you ever want to tell me what happened, I'm here to listen. But Rick, if you did what you thought was right, you have every reason to be proud." I covered his hand with mine, then checked the time on my phone. Was time slowing down? "How has no one caught this pet poisoner in the act? Doesn't everyone have doorbells with video these days? Aren't there a million security cameras out there?"

"They leave poisoned meat on the street or throw it over a fence. They're picking properties with lots of foliage to hide what they're up to."

"Then why change things up and lob something onto someone's balcony? That doesn't make sense."

"Local PD doesn't even have a starting point on this guy yet. They'll catch him in the act, eventually, but until then…"

"This wasn't random. Think about it. I'm three floors up. Whoever did this was trying to kill one particular dog."

He leaned back. "C'mon, Lonnie. You don't know that."

"You don't think it's a little strange that someone murders Pepper's owner and then within a week, she's a target? Someone thinks she's a problem."

Rick laughed at me. "I understand why you're trying to figure this out, but—"

"Someone threw meat on my balcony. They targeted Pepper specifically."

"No, they didn't. The complex is full of dogs. It's a coincidence."

"Has this happened to anyone else in the building?"

"Not that I know of, but—" He raised a hand to stop me interrupting. "All right. I'll ask Dave. But honestly, this isn't some plot."

"That you know of."

He stood and stretched. "For all you know, someone's playing with you because you're doing so much poking around."

Stung, I frowned up at him. "What do you mean by that?"

"I've seen you asking your little questions about Jeff. Being a busybody."

"I am not a *busybody*. But even if I were, can you blame me? The police interviewed me for hours. They think *I* killed Jeff, and as far as I'm concerned, that's one hell of a reason to find out who did. Or do you think I should let them skip the formalities and put me in jail?"

"You're not helping yourself by digging around into everyone else's motives. It makes you look desperate. If you tell the police you think someone poisoned the dog on purpose, it's gonna backfire, because who has access, who has the best motive, and who is spouting screwy ideas about silencing a possible dog witness?"

"Rick, I—"

"Who *proved* he could hop from balcony to balcony like a fucking sparrow?"

My face heated. "Am I keeping you? Don't you have work tomorrow?"

He gave an unhappy grunt. "I'm taking the day off."

"Fine." I checked my phone again. It was two a.m. "But you heard them; it'll be hours before they know anything. Why don't you head back? I'll get an Uber later."

"Really?" His irritation was clear. "Just because I don't believe someone put a hit out on your dog—"

"I never said—" I took a calming breath. "You obviously think I'm a nutjob."

"I think you're recovering from an illness. Add a move and a murder and the new experience of fostering a rambunctious dog, and now you're tense and frightened. Don't make so much of something totally random. Let's just go home, okay? They're taking good care of Pepper. You should get some sleep so you'll be rested when they call."

"I..." It was irrational, but I didn't feel right leaving Pepper alone there. I *knew* how it felt to be sick and vulnerable and alone. She had no one. She didn't even understand. She was like a baby. *Wow.* When did I get maternal instincts? I certainly didn't come by them from Mom. Or... That wasn't fair. She had maternal instincts. They just played out differently in our world.

One thing she did prepare me for was to medal in the stubborn Olympics.

I said, "I'll wait."

"Oh, stop." He softened his tone. "You don't look so good."

"Thanks."

"I didn't mean it like that. You're pale as hell."

"I'm fine." I was cold, though, so I zipped my jacket. "You can go. Really."

He sighed heavily. "Be right back."

After he left, I read a dated *Animal Wellness* magazine. Every page challenged me to be a better pet owner about things I'd never given a thought to before.

Rick returned with coffee. "Here, drink this. I'll wait with you for a while."

"Thank you." The coffee was a horrible, bitter brew. It had too much sugar and some chalky powdered creamer, but I was so touched by his kindness, tears stung my eyes.

In fact, all my emotions seemed to have floated to the very surface of my spirit like sentient water lilies, rippling painfully with every *plink* of affection he gave me.

"Hey, what's that face?" He cupped my jaw, and I turned away.

"I'm just tired."

"Okay." He didn't let me evade his touch. "You've had a long day. It's easy to see how exhausted you are. Your doctor told you to rest, didn't he?"

"Yeah," I admitted.

"Maybe it was too much to ask you to take Pepper on this soon after." He rubbed his thumb over my unshaved jaw, my cheekbone, soothing and smoothing away the tension there.

"It's fine." I leaned into his big, calloused hand. "This has been eye-opening, if nothing else."

"You're pushing your limits, so I'm sorry we asked." He backed away and tapped my foot playfully. "Not what you expected, huh?"

"What?" Was he talking about Pepper, or himself? Because neither one was anything like what I expected.

"Dog ownership?" He rested his elbows on his knees and winked up at me. "Admit it. You had a picture in your head, and it hasn't gone like you planned."

He was right, damn him. "I admit nothing."

"Life is messy." He chuckled. "Especially when it involves kids or dogs. You can't expect everything to be perfect from the beginning."

"I know that."

"But do you? I think you kind of romanticize your Afghan hound."

"Maybe." I hid my irritation. "Doesn't mean I'm not ready to do what it takes."

"All right."

"Pepper might not be what I planned, but I'm taking good care of her."

"Of course you are." He frowned at me. "I never said—"

"And I'm not going to let anyone hurt her. You can take that to the bank. I'm not without resources, and if the police think they can slow-walk the results of the tests on that meat because she's only a dog, then they can expect to hear about it from every local animal lover I know."

"That's not how it works, Lonnie. Testing takes time—"

"It'll take more time if the police put Pepper last."

"That's not what they're doing. There are finite resources."

"Do you know how many pet lovers I serve on a daily basis? Do you know what Betty White, America's most ardent dog lover, enjoys eating? She's local, and—"

"Whoa, whoa, whoa." His wagging finger pissed me off. "Are you aware what would happen if you started threatening the local cops? Better put Kimble on Speed Dial."

"Oh, honey," I lied smoothly, "he's already on it."

That was nasty, even for me. In my defense...

I had no defense for being an asshat. Rick had been nothing but kind to me. He was a decent guy. But old habits died hard, and making things all about me might have been mine.

"I'm sorry."

His lips twisted. "I'm trying to help you here."

"I can't..." I shook my head. "Don't want you to get the wrong idea about me. I don't need *anyone's* help."

"That right?" Brown eyes burned into mine. "Fine."

He got up and left without a backward glance. The sliding doors chimed. His footsteps splashed audibly over puddles on the pavement outside before the doors closed behind him, shutting out the street noise.

I wanted to call him back. I wanted to sit with him, hold his hand, and rest my head on his shoulder. But leaning on him wasn't going to solve my problems. And he lived right next door. If things didn't work out, I'd have to see him every single day.

No coworkers.

No neighbors.

Those were my rules.

And already, I'd let things go way too far.

I didn't have an alibi. I could leap tall buildings at a single bound. It was my knife the killer used. The cops didn't need more than that to build a case.

They would eliminate all the people who wanted Jeff dead, one by one, and sooner or later, the detectives would circle back to me. Then the questions would begin again.

No matter what Rick said, I had to figure out who killed Jeff before that happened, and I thought finding out who poisoned Pepper was a damned good place to start.

"Mr. Boudreaux?" *Oh shit.* The vet tech didn't look happy. "There's been a development. Dr. Jones needs to see you right away."

CHAPTER ELEVEN

The vet tech led me to Dr. Jones's office, where two uniformed officers waited with her. They must have come in the back way. I froze with dread.

"Look, there's no easy way to say this"—Dr. Jones simply blurted the truth—"Pepper has ethylene-glycol poisoning."

"Antifreeze?" Ethylene glycol was the deadly ingredient in antifreeze. I don't know where I'd picked up that tidbit of information, but I'd heard it somewhere. Antifreeze poisoning was often fatal, causing kidney failure and long-term problems if not treated immediately. And Dave said the dog poisoner used it.

"I noticed a sweet odor on the meat you bagged," she continued. "I hoped I was wrong."

"Is she—"

"She's resting comfortably." She handed the poisoned meat over to the officers. "Within half an hour she started presenting with symptoms—drooling, acting uncoordinated, vomiting. We began treatment immediately, and though there aren't any guarantees, your prompt action in bringing her here means she's got a fighting chance."

"How…? Who would do this?" My hands tingled, which probably meant I wasn't pulling in enough air. I couldn't breathe. How was I making a sound?

I answered Dr. Jones's gentle questions about how the meat got onto my balcony, how the dog got it, why we decided to play it safe and come to the ER rather than wait for symptoms.

It was Dr. Jones who'd called the police. She had treated a couple of the other poisonings and was all too happy to put pressure on the department to find some answers. I liked her.

Like the men and women who oversaw the scene the night Jeff was killed, these officers were polite, efficient, and gave nothing away. They might have been on call that night for all I knew. Then, as now, I was blindsided by what happened.

They said they'd send the meat sample to the lab. I held back any questions about its connection to Jeff's murder because Rick was right. At best, no one would believe me, and at worst…

Given Rick's derision, I was better off not sharing without some kind of concrete evidence that what happened to Pepper was related to Jeff's murder.

Maybe I was crazy.

Maybe I did have too much time on my hands.

When I left, Dr. Jones showed me Pepper's cage. She'd been given IV fluids and meds. Dr. Jones said she'd keep watch. That was all I could ask for. I'd done the right thing. I held on to that on the way home.

"Is it true, Lonnie? The poisoner got Pepper?" Stephani stopped me on the third-floor landing. She had Lulu with her, preening in her sparkly collar. I guessed they'd just come from a morning walk.

"Yeah." I wasn't surprised to find her waiting for me after the texts I'd sent, but I was feeling a little too grim to pull my punches with perky

Stephani and her dog. "She found the poisoned meat on my balcony, so make sure everyone knows that's a possibility."

"My God." Tears glittered in her eyes. "I already made up flyers. Want to help me put them out?"

I looked longingly at my door. The new bed inside seemed to be calling my name.

"Sure." Despite my exhaustion, I pocketed my keys and followed her.

We started on the first floor, wedging flyers in the doorjamb of each apartment. Outside 1C, Dave was on a stepladder, changing a lightbulb in the sconce on the wall.

"Is it true?" he asked, turning. "Someone threw food on your balcony?"

"Poisoned meat." I nodded. "Are there any security cameras?"

"Sure, but we checked and didn't see a thing."

"We?" I asked.

"Rick and me. He stopped by first thing this morning. Told me about your...Pepper." So Rick was trying to get to the bottom of things, even if I'd blown him off. That made me feel worse.

"You want to see?" Dave offered. "I suppose we could have missed something."

"Rick wouldn't miss anything."

"Naw," he agreed. "He's a sharp one."

"Where are the cameras exactly?"

Dave took me and Stephani around to point them out. There were several different ways of getting that meat onto my balcony without being seen, but you had to know where the cameras were to do it. Someone deliberately avoided them.

"You ever see anyone wandering around here," I asked Dave, "checking the place out? People you don't know?"

"All the time." When I frowned at his words, he added, "The tenants all have guests, you know? People park out front or in back, then walk around looking for the closest entrance. Some take the elevator, some take the stairs.

Some folks around here look lost for a living, practically. I notice you always take the stairs these days."

I was surprised he'd paid attention. "I'm trying to get back my wind."

"Good for you." He nodded. "The cameras, they're mostly to prevent theft. They keep people from breaking into the apartments on the ground floor. They cover the cars in the tenant parking spaces. I'm not sure any cameras are aimed at the side of the building, much less the third-floor balconies. You kind of expect the height to protect people up there."

"And the dogs," I mused.

"Yeah." He grinned. "Even if folks could get up there, nobody could get past a dog like Chancho."

"What about Pepper?"

He shook his head sadly. "She's no watchdog. Except with me. She rolls over if you look at her sideways. Pepper's not the sharpest tool, you know?"

"She's smarter than everyone thinks." I bristled as if he was impugning my future Afghan hound. "It's a shame she can't talk, because if she could, I'd have the police off my back."

"Right?" We took a shortcut through the utility room, back to the first floor. "I saw that on *Columbo* once. Dog barks at the killer."

"There's an Agatha Christie like that too," said Stephani. "Poirot takes in this fluffy white dog—"

"Gotta love fiction. Dogs don't solve crime in real life. People do. And we have a chance to prevent one here." I held up my batch of flyers and started up the stairs. "Come on, Miss Marple. We've got flyers to deploy, and then I have to rest my little gray cells."

"See you later, Dave," Stephani said as he got back up his stepladder. "You're going to keep a sharp eye out, aren't you? With Jeff murdered and now the dog poisoner targeting our building? Be alert, yeah?"

"Don't you worry, Stephani." Dave took a cloth out and wiped a last spiderweb from the sconce. "I talked to the owners about hiring a private security guard. They've agreed it's best, at least for the foreseeable future. He'll be starting rounds tonight. Be smart, and don't let Lulu eat anything you're not sure about. Warn the other tenants, though I'm sure it was an isolated incident."

"Thanks, Dave!" She blew him a kiss.

He blushed furiously. "If I knew that's all it would take to get a kiss from a pretty girl…"

"You'd get one from me too," I said, "but I doubt it would have the same impact. I'll bake you some cookies later. Thanks for looking out for us."

He snorted. "Cookies are good too."

I followed Stephani up to the second floor, and we continued leaving flyers, all the way up to the sixth. We didn't bother putting a flyer on Caleb's door.

I missed Caleb. The laundry room just wasn't the same without him.

When we got to the last apartment, Stephani said, "I've got the makings for martinis. Come over at lunchtime and help me drink them?"

"I can't, babe. If I don't get some rest, I'll fall over." I was dead on my feet.

"Oh, honey. I am so selfish sometimes."

"Are not," I corrected. "I have awesome neighbors."

"Carla and I will be at my place all evening. We're going to drink, watch movies, and eat junk food. Come if you like."

"You had me at junk food." I unlocked my deadbolt, kissed her cheek, and let myself into my place. "Let me catch some *z*'s, and I'll take you up on it."

"Bye for now." There went that chipper little wave again. I wanted to live in a world where people were that nice—that smiley—all the time.

Of course if I did, they'd probably vote me into the first live volcano. I am not known for my cheerful disposition.

After closing the door behind me, I hung my jacket up in the coat closet, got myself a sparkling water, and twisted off the cap. Finally, I could let my guard down.

I took a look around and stilled, nerves prickling with unease.

Everything seemed fine. Everything was exactly as I'd left it the night before.

So what, exactly, was bothering me? Something was off with my place. *Oh.*

Things were too quiet.

I'd grown used to the sound of Pepper's doggy nails skidding across the kitchen tiles. To the sound of her tags jingling against the D-ring in her collar. I was accustomed to listening for destructive chewing. Now my apartment was so quiet, it unnerved me a little.

Pepper, Pepper, *Pepper.* She was a mess, but there I was, staring at her water bowl, heartsick, wondering if I'd ever need to fill it again.

Someone knocked. For a moment, I stood next to the counter, legitimately too tired to move another step. Whoever it was didn't give up, knocking a second time.

I hoped it was Rick. Not because I knew what to say to him, but a knock like that resounded with authority, and I didn't want it to be anyone else.

It took me longer to answer than I'd have liked. My body was simply slow, moving through space as if the air had suddenly turned into mashed potatoes. When I opened the door, I found Rick leaning against the doorframe.

"You heard?" I sagged against the frame on the inside.

"I saw." He waved the flyer. "I'm so sorry."

"Keep Chancho inside until they catch the guy?"

"He knows better than to eat something if I don't give the command."

I closed my eyes. "Of course he does."

"What's wrong?"

"I'm *tired.*" I said the words louder than I meant to. "I keep getting interrupted before I can—"

"Come with me." He let himself in, closed my door, and locked it behind him. Then he caught my hand and pulled me toward my bedroom.

"Er...no offense, but—"

"You need sleep. And I want to try out your new bed. Let's go."

In seconds, warm hands were lifting my shirt over my head. When it hit the floor, he pushed me down into the softness of my hybrid mattress and knelt to remove my shoes.

I couldn't remember the last time someone undressed me. The tug on my shoelaces as he loosened my trainers, the cold air hitting my feet when he pulled off my socks. Those were sensations I associated more with my mother than any lovers I'd ever had.

"Normally, I like to participate when I undress. I'm funny like that."

"Nah, I got you. You look too tired to think." He didn't stop until he had me down to my jock. "Well, would you look at that. Thong—th-th-th-thong, thong. Somebody's a freak."

"I find them comfortable." If he kept up with those delightful, teasing touches, he was gonna feel my piercing in three, two, one...

"Dios." He gasped. "S'that what I think it is?"

"Depends what you think it is."

He smoothed his fingers over the fabric but stopped short of removing my underwear. "You think you know a guy."

"Rick, look." I changed the subject deliberately. "About earlier."

He stopped to meet my gaze. "I know you didn't mean it."

Irritated by that, I said, "I did, though, actually. I'm just sorry it hurt your feelings."

He blinked at me, surprised, I had no doubt. "You want me to get lost?"

"I really want to sleep." That sounded pretty pitiful to my ears. "I can't argue with you. Don't want to—"

"Shh." He shoved me over and dug the covers out from under me. "Just relax, Lonnie. I'm not here for that. Go. To. Sleep."

"Jesus. Okay, already." I was so tired, I barely felt him climb into bed behind me. And I pretended I didn't reach for his hand and wrap his arm around me.

"I know you won't believe this." He tucked his nose right into my nape. Tickled the hairs there with each breath. "But I'm not the enemy."

The arm around me belonged to *Rick Garcia*. Neighbor. Friend. Smiler of wry smiles and bearer of brown eyes warm enough to melt me like butter. But he was also a *neighbor*. Didn't I need to keep him at arm's length? Maybe I didn't want to do that anymore.

I *wanted* to believe he cared about me, but I still had all those rules in my head. Inscribed on my heart.

In defiance, I let myself fall asleep before I could think about all the reasons I should make him leave.

I doubted I could come up with any, anyway.

CHAPTER TWELVE

It was dark outside when I woke to the aroma of seared meat, garlic, and fried potatoes. A kind of weakness had wormed its way deep into my bones, making even sitting up a prospect I had to consider before trying it.

"I'll tell him. Thank you." Rick came into the bedroom with a glass of red wine in one hand and my phone in the other. He ended the call. "That was Dr. Jones. Looks like Pepper's out of the woods for now. They want to keep an eye on her for another couple of days. I told them you'd call when you have your feet under you again."

"Thanks." I sighed with relief. Fell back against the pillows. He held out the wine, and I took a chance on it. I had to take some kind of pain reliever for my head, which had a whole symphony's worth of kettledrums beating inside it, but I didn't suppose a little wine would hurt.

He turned on the light, and I grimaced.

"Have you talked to your doctor about anemia?" he asked out of the blue. "Because I don't think I've ever seen anyone as pale as you are right now."

"I'm not anemic."

"Still," he argued. "It couldn't hurt to take some B vitamins or something, right? Are you taking vitamins at all?"

"I don't need vitamins. I eat food." But that wasn't entirely true. I hadn't been eating. Not like I did when I worked.

"Well, I made supper, so come out and eat, will you?"

"All right." Apparently, we'd settled into bickering like old men. "Keep your hair on."

He suppressed a smile while I sipped. Nice wine, since it was one of mine. I guessed it was the 2011 Malbec from Argentina. I put on a T-shirt and followed him into the kitchen. Checking the wine label, I discovered I'd been right about the vintage. I didn't give up the glass when he held his hand out.

"Get your own."

He got another glass and poured.

Matter-of-factly competent in the kitchen, he plated up a couple of hanger steaks and some potatoes and put them on the table with a spinach salad and bread.

"Someone's been busy."

"I figured if you can play detective, I can play chef."

"All right." I growled the words. In the cold light of reason, it did seem far-fetched to assume I could solve any crime at all, much less whatever was going on at the Fillmore Arms. "I was overwrought."

"And you don't trust the cops to get things right."

"You're half right."

He glanced up, fork halfway to his mouth. "What do you mean?"

"Mama Boudreaux didn't raise her boy to trust the cops at all."

He chuckled at that. "And you love your mother very much."

"I do," I muttered.

"I love mine too." He nodded. "After dinner, want to walk Chancho with me?"

"You think it's safe?"

"Who's gonna mess with me and Chancho?"

For the first time that day, I relaxed. "Not me."

* * * * *

We finished our food and did the dishes together. Then we picked up Chancho and let him lead us around to his favorite spots. Rick was right.

While Chancho probably liked marking every tree and fireplug and bush as much as the next dog, he never left Rick's side. Never pulled on the leash. Never barked at other dogs.

The attention he gave to Rick's every move was remarkable. Every part of him obeyed, from his rigid, swiveling ears to his big, softly padding feet.

A light breeze ruffled his dark fur as we walked. Chancho really was an amazing animal.

In the abundance of moonlight, he walked in Rick's shadow, slinking along close by his side. His ears perked up at every sound. He showed awareness of every animal, suspicion of each car that passed. He was perfectly, exquisitely trained. Exactly how I'd pictured my Afghan hound.

On the way back, I faced the very real possibility Pepper wasn't trained at all. "You think Pepper could heel like Chancho does?"

"Sure." He shot an amused glance my way. "If whoever adopts her is super consistent and works with her every single day."

"Yeah…" I pictured some drill-sergeant type putting her through her paces. Carrot-and-sticking her until she shivered with confusion. I jammed my hands into my pockets. "I guess."

"You want that for her, don't you?" he asked. "A forever home? Discipline. Maybe a job, even? We need to help her find that, don't you think?"

"A job? What do you suppose she could do? Write puff pieces for the *LA Times*?"

"Stop." He cuffed my arm lightly. "Dogs like jobs. Chancho protects my place. He runs with me, so I stay fit. He's my companion. That's his job. He takes it very seriously."

Whether it was the homey dishwashing, or the moonlight, or the lack of sleep, I gave my rules a hard pass. "You know, if he needs a little break every now and again, I'd consider applying for the job, on a temp basis." I bit my lip. "If you've got an opening you're looking to fill."

Rick stopped walking so abruptly, Chancho glanced up at him in dismay. "Did you really just say that?"

"I'm afraid I did." My cheeks caught fire, but of course I couldn't take the words back. "It was weird, huh?"

He coughed into his hand. "You're a riot, Lonnie."

God. Why didn't the ground just open up and swallow me? *Opening to fill?* Jesus. Last night I pushed him away like he had lice, and tonight I flirted like some idiot. *Make up your mind already.* One glass of wine, and I green-lighted him. No wonder he laughed it off.

The sight of one of our warning posters reminded me that Stephani invited me for drinks. "Hey, um, Stephani invited me to come by and get my swerve on. She's making martinis tonight. You want to come?"

"Yeah." He glanced at her door and then at mine. "Okay. Just let me put Chancho to bed."

"Aww." I wanted to clutch my heart the way Caleb did. "You're such a good dog dad."

He cupped my face and brought me in for a kiss. "The cold put roses on your cheeks."

I whispered, "Or something did."

"Either way. I like seeing some color there for a change."

He took Chancho inside his place. I let go of the breath I'd been holding.

Talk about mixed signals. I'd startled him there on the street with my unmaidenly ways. He acted interested in me. He'd cooked for me twice, and I—of all people—knew food was how serious wooers woo.

But *I* was the one with rules. He was uncertain. No wonder he'd evaded.

I shouldn't have made a move in the first place. But when had common sense ever stopped me?

CHAPTER THIRTEEN

"It's the boys. Come in, come in." Stephani let us inside her apartment with hugs and air-kissing.

Carla came over, leaned her chin on Steph's shoulder, and blinked slowly at us. She'd had a martini or three.

"How's Pepper?" she asked.

"Looks like she's gonna be okay."

"Oh, thank God." Stephani's relief was palpable. "I can't believe some bastard did that. None of our dogs are safe until he's caught."

"We need to go to the next city council meeting." Carla waved us into the living room. "This is ridiculous. They should have caught this guy months ago."

"They'll catch him. It's only a matter of time," Rick reassured.

Stephani held up her glass. "Get you guys a martini?"

"Lonnie shouldn't have the hard stuff right now. He's getting over an illness." I shot Rick an irritated frown. I didn't want to drink, but having him forbid it like that bugged me. *Nanny state. What. The. Fuck.* He shot me an evil grin.

"I brought my own, anyway." I showed her the wine bottle.

"Cool. Sit anywhere." Carla plopped herself on the love seat where Steph's shih tzu got busy attacking one of the decorative pillows. She pushed her to the floor. "Stop, Lulu."

Rick sat in an armchair. I took a spot on the floor in front of him, telling myself it was so I could play with Carla's pug. But who was I kidding? I wasn't a guy who sits on the floor, tickling dog paws. No, damn it. I'd done it so I could sit at Rick's feet while Chancho lay fast asleep in his wee little dog bed. The mutts who jumped into my lap were an excuse. A side gig.

Carla's pug was a cuddler. Steph's shih tzu seemed to be made entirely of tiny teeth and attempts at intimidation. I couldn't help but feel they'd each gotten the wrong dog.

The layout of Steph's place mirrored mine. Her living room was cozy, if a little too girly for my taste. She had floral print couches, a Flokati rug, and enough chintz throw pillows to make a really good nest during the end times.

Her paintings, mostly colorful, splashy graphics of high-heeled shoes, handbags, and lipstick were so *Sex and the City*, it surprised me they weren't serving cosmopolitans.

She couldn't be much of a cook, though. I saw just from looking at the pots in the dish drainer—they were pretty, but probably crappy heat conductors. I'd lay money she scorched more food than she put on the table.

Steph got Rick his martini and offered me a bowl of popcorn. When Rick laid his hand on my shoulder, it was the most natural thing in the world to lean back against his shins.

Steph and Carla seemed unsurprised to see us together like that. They exchanged knowing glances, but otherwise gave no outward sign what they thought about it.

"We're binge-watching *Riverdale*," Steph informed us. "In honor of Luke Perry, may he rest in peace."

"Oh goodie." Rick had not mastered the art of *subtle* sarcasm.

"No, you'll like it." Steph wrinkled her pert nose. "In the first season there's a murder, and—"

"Steph." Carla gave her an exaggerated eye roll. "Just because he used to be in law enforcement doesn't mean he likes murder."

"I never said that." She took her pink cocktail shaker to the love seat, where she refreshed her drink and Carla's. "Just that mysteries can be fun."

"I was never a detective, anyway." Rick took a sip of his drink and winced.

I reached for his glass and asked if I could have a sip. *Too sweet.* Flavored vodka, not gin. In my book, there was nothing wrong with any martini that top-shelf gin couldn't cure. I was glad to have my wine.

"I'll watch your show." Rick's glare brought the sudden fear I wasn't being manly enough. "Or grizzlies on Animal Planet. Whatever."

Steph turned on the big screen, and pretty people pretending to be high-school age spoke their lines with the kind of dramatic fervor you expect from shows like that.

"What's her name?" I asked after the pug currently snoring loudly in my lap.

"Mrs. Pugglesworth." Carla lifted her glass. "Call her Pug."

"Hello, Pug." I let my fingers drift over her wrinkly little body. Soon we were all engrossed in that ridiculously compelling show, but I was tired too. I hadn't finished drinking my wine, and holding the glass upright might have been the only thing keeping me from drifting off to sleep.

Rick took my glass and set it aside. I munched popcorn without a lot of enthusiasm.

Someday, I would make browned butter and mizithra cheese popcorn and bag it up for all my new neighbors. Or bake something. After all, I'd promised Dave cookies. Leaving bags of cookies on everyone's doorknobs was social, not weird, right?

Probably I should wait for the local poisoner to get caught first.

I rested my head against Rick's knees. His fingers tangled in my hair. He leaned forward to whisper, "You always wear your hair this long?"

I shook my head. "Been forever since I got to the stylist."

Those magical fingers stopped, then started again. "I like it."

"Okay." I hid a smile.

My thoughts drifted over my new life at the Fillmore Arms. On the one hand, I got a kick out of my new neighbors, despite the fact that one of them probably killed a guy and poisoned my dog. I felt safe here, but I wouldn't be happy until the police had Jeff's killer in custody and the dog poisoner went to jail. For me, Jeff's ghost sat in the room with us, between us, even.

Pug got up and sauntered to the door. Lulu followed. One of them gave the wood a scratch with her tiny paw, and Carla blinked herself awake. "I'll go."

Rick said, "I'll go with you."

You had to love that automatic chivalry. I mean, I didn't love it right then. I had his fingers in my hair, for God's sake. But I was awfully proud of him for not letting Carla face murderers and dog poisoners alone.

"I hate to move you, Rick." Carla stepped over my legs. "I'm just taking the girls for a pee. We'll be fine."

"No. I'll go. I could use a stretch." He stood. "I have no idea what's going on anyway. Did the redhead just light her house on fire?"

"Oh yeah." Steph grinned maliciously. "Spoiler: her mom too."

"That is every little girl's dream." Carla patted her jeans pockets. "I just need to get my jacket, and we can go."

Rick opened the door. "After you."

She picked up her jacket and felt through the pockets. "Oh, *shit.* I left my keys in my apartment."

"Again?" Stephani clucked at her.

"Shit, shit, shit." Carla fisted her hands.

"You seriously need to have a second key made for that doorknob lock. You can leave it with me. I promise I won't sneak in and clean when you're not there."

"For fuck's sake, you can clean my place anytime. Next time I go to Home Depot, I swear I'll have one cut."

Given the many locks on Carla's door, it seemed natural she'd be uncomfortable giving anyone a key. I asked, "Does Dave have a master?"

"Not to mine." Carla reddened. "I had my door rekeyed. He has no idea."

"A lot of us did," Steph said, "because of you-know-who being the owners' son. We didn't put it past him to take Dave's keys and have a look around our places while we were gone. He was such a sleaze."

"Hell yeah, he was," Carla agreed. "That's why I have the extra locks. But the doorknobs lock unless you untwist the little doohickey, and I always fuck up. I keep my keys in my purse, and I don't always bring it when I'm only going to the laundry or to walk Pug. Stephani and I lock ourselves out all the time. Guess I'll have to couch-surf here again. I'm so sorry. I'll call a locksmith in the morning."

"Too bad Caleb's not here," said Stephani. "He's a born housebreaker."

"Caleb?" I didn't see it. Heartbreaker, yes. Burglar? Caleb was too gorgeous for stealth.

"God yeah." Carla sighed. "He played a jewel thief on some show about a year and a half ago. The week before he auditioned, he did this method-acting thing with lockpicks. He practiced until he could do our doors in a heartbeat. Knob locks *and* deadbolts. He was so handy to have around."

Rick frowned. "How come I never saw him?"

"You're practically the fuzz, baby." Carla laughed as she clipped Pug and Lulu's leashes to their collars. "He probably didn't think you'd approve."

"I don't."

"Rick." I couldn't help meeting his gaze. He looked awfully surprised. I wondered if he was thinking the same thing I was. "Do any of you know Caleb's sister?"

Carla shook her head. "I met her. But I don't know her."

"I think she got a new job," Stephani said. "She hardly comes around here anymore. I wish she'd been at the party the other night."

Rick asked me, "Why?"

"Just thinking." I didn't want to say it in front of Carla. "Watch out for any food on the sidewalk."

"We will," Carla called back before shutting the door.

"Caleb's sister is gorgeous," Steph said into the silence after they left. "Like a female version of Caleb."

"Caleb said Jeff wouldn't quit hitting on her."

"So?"

"Steph, what if—"

"Wait. No." She held her hands out. "I know what you're thinking with the lock questions and the rest. Whoever killed Jeff, it was not Caleb."

"How do you know that?" My thoughts spun in circles. "Did Jeff assault Caleb's sister like he did Carla?"

"Oh God, how do you know about that?"

"I overheard something I shouldn't have. I didn't share the information with the police or anything." *Just my lawyer.* Guilt overwhelmed me.

"Caleb wouldn't hurt a fly. And his sister…that was a long time ago." She definitely knew more than she was saying.

"I need to talk to Dave."

"You're on the wrong track," she warned. "I'd believe Carla was a killer before I'd believe it of Caleb."

"Well, where was she that night? Do you know?"

"*None* of my friends are killers." She narrowed her eyes. "So just stop it."

"But Stephani, if Caleb could pick these locks—"

"Nothing you can say will make me believe he's a killer."

"I'm sorry, but that's not the point, is it? The police should know about this. Even if we both believe Caleb could never have done this awful thing, the police should know it's a possibility."

The problem was we both liked Caleb and everyone hated Jeff.

Maybe that was blinding the residents to an obvious connection between the two?

* * * * *

Later, I invited Rick in for coffee. What I meant by coffee was negotiable. If it meant discovering whether the thing I felt between Rick and me was for real, I could let the rules go for one night.

Even when he was a cheeky kid, even when he stole from me, I'd felt this exciting catch in my breath when I looked at him.

And sometimes, rules were made to be broken.

He opened his mouth. Closed it.

"It's all right, though." I turned so I couldn't see his face when I fumbled for my keys. "I'm tired anyway."

"Lonnie…"

"You don't have to explain." *I don't want you to explain.* "It's all good."

He caught my arm. "It's not that I don't want to be with you."

"It's fine, whatever the reason." I'd burst into flames if he said another word.

"But"—he let go of me—"you're my neighbor, you know? How awkward would that be if things got weird again?"

I did face him then. "Hoist with my own petard."

He blew out a shaky breath. "Plus, you haven't made any secret you're all about your job. I got that message loud and clear. You want your dog to be a part-time relationship. You don't want or need anybody else. I— I'm looking for a boyfriend."

"A boyfriend."

"You tick a lot of boxes for me, Lonnie. You're smart and funny and you can cook." As he talked, his gaze landed everywhere but on me. "You're just my type physically, even though half the time you look like death warmed over. I wish we could go out for dinner and drinks. Go dancing, see where things might lead, but…"

"But?"

"I want more than you seem willing to give. That's all. It's just"—he lifted his hands—"I already know what I want from you. And you don't seem to be in the same place. I want to cool my jets a bit."

Shocked, I said nothing.

Then he kissed me, and by kissed, I mean he placed the most chaste, tender peck on my lips before moving away and unlocking his door.

"I've still got your back, Lonnie. Don't go snooping around about Caleb. And if you ever do want more, just give me a shout."

"Um. If you're sure?"

"Absolutely." He shot a rueful look over his shoulder. "Take care of yourself. We'll see each other around."

He closed the door between us, and that was that.

My God. *My God!* I couldn't get my keys out fast enough.

I'd wanted to shout—to tell him, *Wait, I want that too.* I wanted to explore what was brewing between us, but the concept was too new for me. The warmth, the tender feelings, the fact that I would rather Netflix and chill with Rick than hook up with even the hottest guys in town were a *revelation* to me, and I didn't know how to admit that, much less do something about it. The door had closed between us before I could even begin…

Shocked, I went inside my place, and the next thing I noticed was how much I missed Pepper. Her happy, if drooly, welcome. The way she tried to knock me over, especially when I was carrying something fragile. The inevitable, chewed-up result of some petty revenge for being left alone, even though I rarely did it, and only for a few minutes at a time.

The second thing I noticed was the knob on my door. The knob locks were fairly easy to pick, so whenever I had a deadbolt, I always used that. In this case, rather than use two keys each time I entered and left my place, I *only* used the deadbolt.

But Steph said Caleb could unlock the deadbolts too.

If Caleb was everyone's go-to guy for breaking in, there might be more to learn about him. I didn't believe Caleb was the killer, any more than I'd believe it was Rick. But it was possible. It was reasonable doubt.

Despite screwing up so completely with Rick, despite the knot in my stomach that seemed to grow every time I thought about what I might miss out on with him, I had to make plans.

I set a reminder to call Dillon in the morning, as soon as I talked to Dave.

CHAPTER FOURTEEN

Rick said the detectives were no doubt working every angle on Jeff's case. He told me to stay out of things. But that was easy for Rick to say. I was the one they'd questioned. Were they even looking at anyone else?

I knocked on Dave's door the next morning with Rick's soft words and chaste kiss as fresh in my mind as his warning not to involve myself in any more snooping.

I couldn't seem to let either one go.

Proving someone else had means, motive, and maybe even opportunity could only help me. Once the police nailed down the timeline, they could ascertain where Caleb was on the day of Jeff's murder.

If they tried to pin Jeff's death on me, Dillon could use the information to cast doubt on their case.

I still hoped it wouldn't come to that.

The door of 1A had a little plaque that read "Manager" beneath the unit number. Dave answered in plaid sleep pants and a stained T-shirt. His bleary eyes and bedhead told me I woke him up, likely from another Ambien-induced night's sleep. I ignored that in favor of finding out what I wanted to know.

He was a big man. Taller than me, with broader shoulders and a slight paunch. He looked like a man who enjoyed good coffee. When he invited me in for a cup, I accepted.

I'd never been in his place before. The living room was packed with surprisingly nice furniture and some well-maintained antiques. There were bookshelves crammed with expensive tchotchkes, leather-bound classics, and modern crime novels. On one small table, he had a porcelain statue of a shepherdess feeding wolfhounds.

Instead of a balcony, Dave had a patio with substantial wicker chairs and a chiminea that looked like it got a lot of use.

If someone had given me a hundred guesses what I'd find in Dave's place, I would not have been right about one thing.

Turning to look around the place, I said, "This is amazing."

"Thanks." He smiled wryly. "This clutter is what you get when you've lived somewhere nearly fifteen years."

"That's called 'lived in,' not clutter."

"Thanks to Shar, it looks real good now, huh?" He motioned me to sit at the kitchen table. "She made me get rid of half my junk and helped me organize the rest. Don't tell her, but I took a storage unit. Some things you just can't let go, you know?"

"I do. But everything looks neat and cozy. I could definitely use Shar's help in my place, if this is the result."

"She's the neat. I'm the cozy."

"Well, maybe I'll pick your brain too, then."

"Anytime." He offered me cream and sugar, but I take my morning coffee black. And I was anxious to ask about Caleb.

"Look, there's no easy way to ask, but…" I hesitated, unsure how best to approach the subject of Caleb's sister. "You know more about Jeff than I do. When I was looking through his drawers for Pepper's vaccination records, we—Rick and I, that is—found an envelope full of photographs."

"Okay." His eyes narrowed. "Wait. What kind of photographs?"

"The, er, indecent kind?" Since I hadn't seen them, I couldn't describe them, precisely. "No doubt the police are following up on those. The thing is, I wondered if you knew Caleb's sister? He told me Jeff was all over her."

Cheeks red, Dave looked down at his hands.

I pressed. "Can you tell me what happened?"

"I don't want to get Caleb in trouble, or—"

"Caleb told me that Jeff made a nuisance of himself, and his sister had to stop coming over."

"It was a little more than that."

"Was it?" I couldn't let him leave it at that. "Tell me."

He glanced away. "Jeff was an asshole with the girls."

"Carla said she called the police on him. Did he physically assault her?"

Dave took his time replying. "There was never any proof of an assault. Jeff's parents gave him an alibi. How can it matter now?"

"Oh, it matters." Going by Rick's face when he saw the photographs, it mattered a lot. "The pictures we found might back up her claims."

"No shit?" He pushed his coffee away and leaned back. "You don't think Carla…"

"She certainly had a motive, but Caleb's the one who could break into any of the apartments."

He startled. "You heard about that?"

"Carla told me." I leaned forward. "How bad did things get between Jeff and Caleb's sister? Could Jeff have assaulted her too?"

He caught a fleshy lip between his teeth. "I couldn't say for certain if he did or didn't."

"But Caleb came to you for help, didn't he? He asked you to throw Jeff out of the apartments."

"He did, yes." Dave's fingers tightened on his mug. "But he didn't understand. I couldn't evict the owners' kid without a damn good reason. I told him if his sister was assaulted, she should go to the police. That I had no power to change things around here, but if the cops got involved, then maybe…"

"They didn't, though, did they? If Carla's right, Jeff—and his parents—made sure no one believed the girls. Carla bought extra locks. Caleb told his sister not to come around anymore. That's how they handled it."

"God, when you put it like that." He closed his eyes for a few seconds, opened them, and said angrily, "Yeah. I guess they handled it by avoiding him. And Jeff just set his sights on the next girl, because guys like that? They don't stop until someone stops them."

"Yeah, but who? I hate to believe it, but Caleb might have been that someone. Or Carla. Or maybe they worked together?"

"No," he whispered. "Not Carla. She's not the kind to…"

"How do you know? I'm not sure about either of them, but I *know* it wasn't me."

"Don't make trouble." His tone got frosty. "You don't know anything. You just *got* here."

"But this thing is going to hang over my head until the police find the real killer. Don't you see? I've got to turn over every rock until something crawls out."

"Look, I understand your anxiety." He reached over and gave my hand a fatherly pat. "But you're wrong about Caleb and Carla. I've known them a lot longer than you have."

"I *hope* I'm wrong." We sat there, sipping our coffee, lost to our own thoughts until he spoke again.

"Any news about the dog?"

"Pepper? Doc thinks she's going to be okay. I'm going over there to check on her this morning."

"Got any leads on someone to take her yet?"

I shrugged. "Not yet."

"Try putting an ad in the Nextdoor app. Someone will snap her up the minute you give them the chance."

"I'll think about it." Why was everyone so determined to move Pepper along? Couldn't they just let her get over losing her human to a grisly murder and then being poisoned? The poor thing had been traumatized enough.

"I notice you don't have a dog." I arched an eyebrow. "Why's that?"

"I had one." He pointed to a framed picture of a Jack Russell terrier. "Nipper. He passed away, and I haven't had the heart to replace him."

I was such a clod. "I'm sorry."

"Me too." He drummed his fingertips on the table. "About Caleb. You don't really think it's him, do you? You met him. He's no killer."

That was guilt talking. He probably didn't feel right, admitting Caleb had a motive.

"Just clutching at straws, I guess." I didn't want to upset Dave, so I left it at that. He obviously liked Caleb and Carla a lot. The phone on his kitchen wall rang, and I stood. "Thanks. You've been a lot of help."

"I should get that." He stood as well. "Probably a tenant with some disaster or other. Always is."

"I'll let myself out." As I was leaving, the phone on the wall stopped ringing and his cell vibrated. I turned. "Persistent bastard, huh?"

"Nah. My calls are forwarded, in case I'm on the grounds and I miss one."

I nodded. "Good to know. But no rest for the wicked."

He grinned. "It's always something around here."

I wanted to go back upstairs and ask Rick if Caleb's sister was in any of the photographs we'd found in Jeff's apartment. Rick might not know anyway, if he'd never met her. We could probably find an image of her on Facebook or Instagram so he could compare.

If there even was a *we* anymore.

He'd sounded oddly final, as if he'd made up his mind about questions I didn't know he'd asked. Like the coward I am, I decided to go check on Pepper instead.

On my way to the animal hospital, I made several voice notes about Carla, Caleb's sister, the locks, the photographs, and the timing of Jeff's death.

I called Dillon to tell him what I'd learned, but his assistant said he'd be in court all morning. He probably wouldn't get back to me until late afternoon.

I wished I could have asked Rick to come to the animal hospital with me. I felt bereft walking into the neat reception area without him. He was not only an ex-cop; he was my mentor with regard to pet ownership. Without Rick to talk to about either the dog or the murder, I felt more alone than I had in a long time.

I was no less determined to get answers because I still believed Pepper's poisonous misadventure had something to do with Jeff's murder, despite Rick's assumption to the contrary.

* * * * *

I arrived while the vet techs were feeding and walking their on-the-mend patients. Pepper seemed fairly lively for a dog who'd been poisoned the day before. As she curled around my ankles, I got a feel for why humans domesticated dogs in the first place. Pretty gratifying, being the center of all that doggy adoration.

Since I'd had a hard time sleeping all alone at my place the night before, I felt less conflicted about things in general and about Pepper, specifically.

She wasn't the dog I'd planned—the perfect, snooty Afghan hound who could take me or leave me.

Pepper was gangly, sloppy, clumsy, and ill-mannered.

She was destructive. Needy. She wore her little doggy heart on her furry doggy paw, and that wasn't want I wanted at all. Or was it?

Dr. Jones suggested I take her for a sedate walk on the grass path around their little parking lot, potty her, and bring her back.

While we ambled, I watched her experience every new thing with a kind of exuberant joy I'd never felt, and I started thinking about her in a new way.

She wasn't the perfect dog. But maybe she could be perfect for someone like me? Maybe I needed a little chaos in my tightly controlled life?

She made me wonder about Rick too.

Did I want him to see me as some hopeless perfectionist loner who didn't do relationships and didn't want more out of life than a convenient dog and a convenient fuck? *Criminy.*

Maybe I was that guy at one time. Probably, I'd had good reason when I was trying to make it in a business that ate baby chefs alive. But now? I'd earned my place among my peers, and Factory was *mine*. I didn't have to spend every waking hour at work because I had a great staff and we made an awesome team.

Being a workaholic was a habit, not a necessity.

It was a *habit* that had nearly killed me.

Why did I continue pushing away an emotional life when it was clear to me that in my heart, like Rick, I wanted more too?

I'd stopped walking at some point. At my heel, Pepper waited, watching me with solemn eyes. I stood there until she sat, panting heavily, patient with me as always.

Maybe she was a little confused. I certainly was.

One of us wasn't the brightest crayon in the box.

Now that I understood which one, I decided to do something about it.

* * * * *

I'd have liked to take Pepper home with me, but Dr. Jones wanted to observe and hydrate her further, if necessary. I felt a little sick, a little disloyal, leaving her behind again.

When I got to my car, I tried to text Rick about what I'd learned, and also, maybe, to apologize. But after holding my phone for several minutes without typing anything, I realized there was no reason to assume he'd want to hear from me.

He'd made himself pretty clear. He wanted more than he believed I could give him. He might be right about that. But that didn't mean I shouldn't try to talk to him. Instead of messaging him right then, I reverted to type and stopped by Factory.

My staff was both surprised and unhappy to see me.

I had to prevent Simone from calling my mother to tell on me, but then I got to spend a pleasant afternoon in the bar. My staff and I chatted, one and two at a time as they broke from work to eat. I caught up on their lives and shared what was happening in mine.

For the first time ever, I talked about my personal life—about the new place, Rick, Dead Jeff, and Pepper.

"For someone facing imminent arrest, you seem remarkably relaxed," Simone mused. "Did you have a personality transplant?"

"I did not." I flicked a straw paper at her. "I simply don't have the energy for drama right now."

"Well, watch out. Every word of this will go straight to your mother," she warned. "She's got spies everywhere."

"I know that. You're the most egregious of the lot."

"So I am. I like her." She laughed lightly. "This might prompt a visit."

"I wonder if she's ready for a furry grandkid."

I could not wait to find out.

I left Factory at dusk, after persuading the staff to package up potpies and salad for two. A great meal might give me a second chance with Rick. Maybe I could explain myself over dinner. But what should I say?

I was ready for the possibility of more. If I told him that, maybe Rick and I could find out what "more" meant, together. One meal at a time.

With that hope in mind, I grabbed the bags and the wine and started up three flights of stairs to my apartment. I broke a sweat, but hardly even had to rest on the way up.

Progress, not perfection. That's what they say.

No one else was around, but it wasn't even five yet. The girls were probably still at work.

I keyed my lock, entered my place, turned to close the door behind me, when *bam!* Someone hit the back of my head with something heavy. It was a glancing blow, but it staggered me.

What the fuck? Who was in my apartment?

Dizzy and disoriented, I tried to turn and look. It hurt like ever-loving fuck. Something oozed along my scalp, in my hair, down my neck.

I lifted my hands to protect myself, but they hit me again, and I sagged to the floor.

CHAPTER FIFTEEN

On sheer instinct, I began a wobbly crawl toward my door.

"Oh no you don't." Dave grabbed my hands and started hauling me backward, toward the living room.

"Dave?" I twisted, trying to turn over, struggling to yank my hands out of his grasp. I'm not a small guy. I fought him, but the blows to my head had me seeing double, and my attempts to get loose were no match for his leverage and strength.

"Just. Stop. Moving." He swore colorfully and gave my arms another yank.

"What the hell?" I blinked with confusion. "Why?"

"Because"—he grunted—"you just won't leave it *alone*."

"You used my knife." I grimaced when he got a better grip on my arms. I tried to scratch him, tried to get free. "You framed me."

"I didn't *plan* it." He delivered a punch to the side of my head, stunning me momentarily. "I needed you to sign off on the condition of the apartment, but then I saw the box marked *knives*. The hallway was empty."

"But—"

"I slipped inside Jeff's place, easy-peasy. Pepper reacted, snarling and barking, but she didn't go full-on apeshit, like later."

"And you stabbed a sleeping man?"

"I stabbed a monster. In and out. No one even saw me."

"But later?" Blood on the hardwood made it hard to get traction. My head throbbed. My arms ached. I twisted and thrashed, but nothing I did got me free. Then it all clicked into place. "It was you in Jeff's place. I was on the phone with you while you were inside and I heard Pepper, so loud—"

"That's right, dumbass." He punched me again, a glancing blow but still painful. "The second I told you my landline calls get forwarded, I knew I'd fucked up. I had to do something or—"

"You've sure got a lot of faith in me." I had been oblivious. "You killed Jeff earlier in the day. Why'd you even go back?"

"Because I heard Jeff brag about his photo collection. I knew he had pictures of Carla." He kept his steely grip on my arms. "I couldn't find them earlier, and I couldn't stay to look because Sharona was downstairs working on my place."

"You wanted to protect Carla?"

"There were a *dozen* girls." He grimaced. "A dozen reasons he should be dead, so I'm not sorry."

"But why kill Jeff *that day*? Why not before, when your tenants begged you for help?"

"Because *Sharona* was gonna be *next*." He punctuated the words by shaking me angrily. "She was falling for Jeff. She believed every lie he told her."

Oh God. "You killed Jeff to protect your niece?"

"Yes, goddamn it. I tried talking to his parents. Guess what? They got pissed! They said they were going to put him in my place."

"Your place?" I tried to free myself, but he gripped me tight. I gasped. "Jeff wanted your job?"

"Of course he didn't. They thought hard work would cure him. As if he could keep the tenants happy, take care of the building, handle security, and dog crap, and petty disagreements over parking. He wanted pussy and free rent. That's all Jeff ever cared about."

My stomach roiled. "Why plant the pictures for me and Rick to find?"

"I hoped Rick would think *you* planted them. You were no trouble until he started going along. Asking questions."

"He did?"

"Sure. And the local cops may not like him, but they'd listen to him…"

To open the slider, he had to put both my hands in one big paw.

He literally stepped on my chest while he worked the latch. Then he jerked me up and dragged me over the sharp frame and onto the balcony. Why was he taking me outside? What did he think he was gonna do out there?

Dave dropped my hands, and I tried to roll over. Before I could do it, meaty arms banded my chest, and he started to lift me up.

It happened so suddenly, it took me a second to realize he meant to throw me over the railing. I got a look down at the concrete path next to the parking lot below and weakly shoved back on the railing.

"Stop!" I cried out. "What—"

"Everyone saw your high-wire act, Lonnie. It's quite the little party trick."

I gave a choked sob. "Dave—"

"I couldn't believe you; all the way up on Caleb's balcony. You're an even bigger jackass than I am."

Privately, I agreed. "So the second time, you left through the balcony door?"

"Damn right I did. I went over the railing and onto the balcony below. The tenants are away on vacation."

I braced my feet against the railing and pushed back. "You don't have to do this."

"I don't have a choice!"

"You do!" I fought like a wild thing—limbs flailing, teeth gnashing, trying to bite him, anywhere I could get my teeth. "No one will believe I killed myself."

"Maybe it was an accident. You wanted to leave more 'evidence' in Jeff's place." He grunted with the effort of holding on to me. "Or maybe you like visiting the scene of the crime. It's a shame you didn't stick the landing."

"Rick won't buy it." I resisted with everything I had.

"The cops will." He slammed my chest onto the wooden railing and pinned me there with his body. "Over you go—"

"One more question!" Buying time was a gamble. I was getting weaker by the second. "Why poison my fucking dog?"

He gasped out loud. "I *didn't*. I would never hurt a dog."

"C'mon—"

"I. Did. Not. Poison. Pepper." He shouted. "What the hell kind of man do you think I am? I love dogs."

"You—" *Wait. What?* That was random? It really was random that someone threw meat on my balcony and poisoned my dog? Rick was gonna do some serious gloating about that.

"How could you even think I'd do something like that?" I tried to look at him, but he gripped my hair and held me tight. *Shit.* The parking lot seemed to boil beneath the balcony, blurred and swimmy. It was all-too-easy to imagine falling, crashing, and dying below.

"I look out for the dogs here, just like I look out for the tenants. It's my job. Nobody'd be better at it than I am."

Jesus Christ, I was going to die from the irony before I ever hit the goddamn ground.

Dave let go of my hair but kept me pinned in place while he took hold of my belt to hoist me over. I gripped the railing tightly and pushed back, terrified that any moment I'd be swept over. How many seconds would I flail before smashing onto the sidewalk? How would I fall? Legs first? Face first?

Dave gathered his strength to lift me. That gave me a single vulnerable second in which to act. I felt the give in his hold and snapped my head back as hard as I could. His nose made a horrible crunching sound, and he lurched away with a howl.

A quick glance showed him moving his hands toward his face, but his bulk was still between me and my slider.

Praying to a God I hardly believed in, I scrambled onto my balcony railing and started moving toward Jeff's.

Oh God, oh God, oh God. Please. Please help me.

I don't want to die.

Dizzy from a head injury, feet slippery with my own blood, and waving my arms wildly for balance, I nevertheless sloshed with adrenaline. Looked like my old chemical pal had come to walk the wire with me, hopefully, one last time.

Everyone should fear heights.

Everyone should learn to use that fear.

I listened to my instincts, trusted my body, and made the jump. Next thing I knew, I had landed sloppily on Jeff's balcony.

Then stupidly—because by that point I had no idea what I was doing—I climbed onto Jeff's balcony and jumped to Rick's, where I pounded on his slider with the flat of both hands.

Chancho went crazy, barking at me, but I kept on banging away at Rick's door.

The only thing holding me up was the idea of Rick and *more*.

I'd be *safe* with him. He'd know what to do, even in a world where my vision, my ability to reason, and quite possibly my sanity disintegrated around me.

After a few tense seconds, his face appeared in the glass between us. Relief blew up my heart. My body sagged the second he unlocked and opened the door.

"Lonnie." He caught me. "What the hell happened?"

"Dave," I managed to whisper. "It's Dave. Please—"

"Shh." As he pulled me inside one-armed, he yanked his phone out of his pocket and started dialing.

I rested my forehead on his shoulder. A voice said, "Nine-one-one, what is your emergency?"

Rick gave the address and a terse statement. After, he stayed on the line.

Chancho paced next to us, hackles still up, on high alert.

"What happened exactly?" I told him Dave attacked me and why. "Jesus. His niece? The organizer?"

I winced. "It was him I heard in the apartment. We were talking on his cell phone. I don't know why I didn't make the connection. I heard Pepper barking over the line."

He grabbed a clean kitchen towel and filled it with ice. "Press this to the back of your head."

"Are you going to go after Dave?"

"Hell no." He scowled. "Not my job anymore, remember?"

"Do you wish it was?"

"Sometimes." His gaze softened. "Not right now. Hold tighter."

"Watch it." I grimaced when he pressed the makeshift icepack to the back of my head. "That hurts."

"Gotta keep pressure on that wound." He let his fingers drift over my forehead. "I'm sorry."

"I'm sorry too." I bit my lip. "About a lot of things. I was coming to tell you. I had food from Factory. Wine and everything."

He smiled. "Oh yeah?"

"Yeah. Look." I gripped his hand. "I want more these days too. But…"

"What?" He tensed, as if bracing for another letdown.

"Maybe I just want to go slow, is all."

"Slow's okay." Rick pressed a delicate kiss to my lips. "Even glacially slow is still progress."

We were going to have to talk about all those extra-gentle kisses. Even though he was bigger, and I was a little frail right then, I intended to show him I was a lot tougher than I looked. Someday. When my head wasn't swimming.

He didn't let me go—even when the police arrived along with EMTs.

"Mr. Boudreaux." Officer Chandler, who got the original call to Jeff's murder, winced when he got a good look at me. "He tuned you up pretty good, huh?"

The police talked to Rick while paramedics bound my head and locked a contraption around my neck to stabilize me for transport. They started an IV—no pain meds because of a likely concussion. Except for Rick holding my hand—and Pepper holding her own at the animal ER—this had turned out to be an extra-shitty day.

The cops fanned out, but they didn't find Dave.

I wasn't surprised. Dave seemed like a runner, not a fighter. The slip he'd made about forwarding his calls caused him to panic. Without that mistake, he never would have come after me.

I didn't even realize what his words meant, but the thought that I *might*, made him desperate enough to try to get me off-balance and let gravity do the rest. Fighting back like that, being able to jump to Jeff's place and then Rick's—even after he bashed my brains in—was not part of his plan for me.

When things didn't go the way he wanted, I was sure he'd run.

"They'll find him," Rick murmured against my hair. "You'll see."

The only thing I cared about was getting rid of my headache. Well, I cared about how I'd left things with Rick. And that my restaurant wasn't going to chef itself forever. And I was worried about my dog...

I tried to sit up. "I should call the vet."

"Not a chance in hell." Rick's fingers tightened on mine as other, gloved hands kept me from getting up.

"But I need to take care of my dog."

"Your dog?" he echoed. "Despite your endless work hours? Despite the fact she's a swoony Lab who wants to be your dog girlfriend?"

"Must have got hit over the head."

"Are you sure you want that? There's no shame in—"

"I'm sure." I tightened my grip on his hand. "I guess I'm ready for a little chaos in my life. Maybe a lot."

He looked at our laced fingers. "How about we have dinner when they let you out of the hospital?"

"Sure. Now that I've caught Jeff's killer—"

"I hate to rain on your party"—he smothered a smile—"but wasn't Dave the one who caught you?"

"Whatever. Now that one mystery is solved, we need to stop a dog-poisoning asshole."

He frowned. "How are we supposed to do that?"

"Dunno, but you're an ex-cop, and I just caught a killer. We've got game."

"Like I said—"

"Hush." I pulled him into a kiss.

Kissing turned out to be a great way to stop Rick's sexy, sarcastic mouth.

He looked a little dazed when I let him go.

"Your place?" I gave him the ultra-hopeful smize. "You are a damn fine cook."

"Nuh-uh. How about we have dinner with my family? If you want chaos, you should try them. We can talk about maybe seeing where things lead after you pass muster with all my aunties."

"Oh, so that's how it's gonna be?"

"Mm-hmm." His lips curled into a saucy grin.

"Okay. I'll see your family, and raise you my mother."

"I'll call that bet. What have you got?"

"Not much," I admitted. "But for the first time ever, I want more."

"Even though we're neighbors?" That came with a coy lift of his eyebrow. "This is gonna get weird, isn't it?"

"Oh, I hope so." The gurney moved, bringing a fresh wave of dizziness to go with my pounding headache. "I really hope so."

THE END

LIGHTS.
CAMERA.
MURDER.

BY C.S. POE

Private investigator Rory Byrne has gained a reputation as someone the elite of New York City can trust to solve their problems quickly and quietly. So when a hotshot television producer hires him to recover a stolen script, Rory will have to go undercover on the set of a historical drama to complete the job. He has his hands full trying to investigate a skeptical crew while they work around the clock on The Bowery, *a new show that promises to shake up the television industry. To make a delicate situation more complicated, the production is led by out-and-proud actor Marion Roosevelt, and Rory is downright smitten.*

But every member of the cast and crew is a suspect in the theft. And the deeper Rory delves into their on-set personalities, the more suspicious Marion's behavior becomes. If Rory is to uncover the theft without sacrificing the fate of The Bowery, he will have to trust his identity and his heart to Marion.

INT. PROLOGUE – DAY

GET BENT, DIPSHIT

The love note was scrawled across my grocery list on the refrigerator door. Which was fine. I preferred keeping all my reminders in a central location. Now I knew I needed to pick up milk, sugar, bread, and a new boyfriend.

My cell rang as I splashed some cream into my coffee.

I pushed my tortoiseshell glasses up my nose and turned to pick up the phone from the counter behind me.

Caller ID: Nate.

Shocker.

I pressed Accept and put the phone to my ear. "Good morning, sunshine. I got your message."

"You're a sonofabitch, Rory!"

"I've been called worse things by better people."

Nate's audible gasp allowed me enough time to indulge in that first sip of morning coffee.

"Only an asshole breaks up over text message," he accused.

I winced at his shrill tone, pulled the phone away from my ear, set it to speaker, and put it back on the countertop. "I only have one rule, Nate."

"Screw your rule!"

"And you broke it," I continued without missing a beat.

"Maybe if you were a contributing member in our relationship, I wouldn't have had to find someone else to fuck me senseless."

I stared at the phone and messed my already disheveled hair with one hand. "I told you when we started dating just how much I worked."

"And?"

"And if you need it day and night, I'm probably not the most suitable candidate in the dating pool."

Nate let out a frustrated growl and then shouted loud enough to cause mic distortion, "Can you *pretend* like you give a damn right now?"

"It's not worth my energy. You swore to never lie, and I caught you in one." I took another sip of coffee while he sputtered and hissed. "Oh. I'd like my extra key back," I stated before casting a second glance at the fridge door.

"Burn in hell, Rory."

"Have a good life, Nate."

"Hey, while we're at it—I fucked your coworker too!" he screamed.

"Yeah, I know. Bye-bye." I hit End, promptly deleted Nate's contact information from my phone, and walked out of the kitchen.

LIGHTS. CAMERA. MURDER.
INT. CHAPTER ONE – DAY

FADE IN

The phone was ringing again.

I walked out of the steamy bathroom, wrapping a towel around my waist. I grabbed the cell from the kitchen counter. "Byrne."

"Rory."

I straightened instinctually. "Good morning, ma'am," I said to Violet Shelby, my supervisor at Dupin Private Investigations. She'd been working for the company since the '80s. And while Shelby no longer answered telephones for her boss, but instead *was* the boss, she'd never been able to shake the shoulder pads and power suits of those bygone days.

"It's a morning," she corrected. "What do you know about movies?"

I opened my mouth, paused, then gradually said, "I...took a film-appreciation course in college about a hundred years ago. I mostly recall the insides of my eyelids."

Shelby chuckled. "You talk like you're an old man."

Forty-five, but Shelby hadn't called to ask what year I graduated.

The brisk air of the apartment—a January chill that not even central heating could entirely dissipate—caused goose bumps to rise on my damp skin.

"Does the name John Anderson mean anything to you?" Shelby asked.

"Wes Anderson's less successful half-brother?"

"Funny," she replied, but her tone implied otherwise. "He's a hotshot television producer here in the city."

Hotshot. That was code for Royal Pain in the Ass.

"Uh-huh."

"I just finished a consultation call with him," she continued. "This will be an undercover case for you."

"As?"

"Well…" There was an uncharacteristically lengthy pause on her end. "It's a little outside the box for Dupin," Shelby warned. "I'm sending you onto a live set. A television show being filmed at Kaufman Astoria Studios out in Queens."

I put a hand on the doorframe and tapped the wall absently. "What *exactly* is the case, ma'am?"

"Theft. An inside job with a limited timeframe for investigation."

My towel started to slip, and I grabbed one corner, holding it against my hip. "Can you elaborate?"

"Unfortunately not. It'll be up to you to get further details from Anderson. *I know, I know*," she continued, almost as if she could sense my oncoming comment regarding my dislike of intentionally vague details. "But he came to us at the endorsement of *another* hotshot client. You know how they all are. He's looking to have this wrapped up quickly and quietly."

"Aren't they always?"

She snorted. "The suspect will be dealt with internally."

Always sounded a bit mob-ish when Shelby said that.

I started toward the bedroom. "All right. I'm getting ready now."

"I should warn you," Shelby said before I had the opportunity to end the conversation. "There are nearly a hundred people on set. They're all considered suspects."

* * * * *

Dress like a PA.

That was an easy enough instruction—if I knew what the hell a PA was. But Shelby hadn't elaborated on the matter. I suspected she wasn't certain herself and simply reiterated the undercover suggestion provided by Mr. Anderson.

So I googled it.

Physician's assistant.

I kept scrolling on my phone. Google seemed pretty convinced this was what I wanted—even went so far as to suggest courses for becoming a PA, salaries, and stats related to the industry.

I tapped the browser bar and redirected my search to include: what is a film PA?

And there it was at the top of the feed—*production assistant.* Although the title didn't suggest much by way of wardrobe. I stood in the middle of my bedroom, naked but for a pair of boxer briefs, perusing a few blogs on basic film industry etiquette before stumbling upon a recent article that fit the bill: "My First PA Gig. Now What?"

My thoughts exactly.

Not that I was looking to make a career change, but one of the traits of a successful PI was being able to blend into any environment like a chameleon. I'd been Shelby's top undercover man for nearly a decade. I sniffed out business fraud in action like a bloodhound, all while playing the role of some newly hired, clueless stooge. But performing for the benefit of the white-collar crowd around a water cooler was a lot easier than acting in front of *professional actors.* And if I had close to a hundred cast and crew members to sort through regarding this theft of...*something,* I needed to have a firm handle on the sort of environment I was walking into.

The article suggested closed-toed shoes, comfortable layers, and to expect being on my feet all day. All right. So not the correct industry to flaunt four-hundred-dollar, turquoise Fluevog Oxfords. And I definitely wouldn't need to waste time hemming and hawing over a matching tie.

I tossed the phone to the bed. Gary, my Siamese cat, raised his head from the pillows and made a sleepy pigeon sound in response.

"Sorry, baby," I said, looking over my shoulder. "Daddy's got to work."

Gary yawned and squeaked out another half-hearted *meow*.

"I know," I answered before opening the closet door. "But if you want to keep living this extravagant lifestyle, one of us has to bring home the bread. Right?"

No response.

I glanced at the cat again. He was asleep. Little shit.

I turned my attention back to the closet and began to sift through the contents. The clothes were mine, in the sense that I'd paid for them, but I considered my wardrobe that of a theater production's. A costume to suit every situation, every atmosphere, every sort of case a Dupin PI was entrusted with.

For the apparel oft proclaims the man, as Polonius said.

Sometimes, though, dressing for *me* was…a curious predicament. Such occasions were rare, however. I worked a lot. And that was fine. Investigating was what I did—what I *was*. I needn't be concerned with Rory Byrne because my skills were always in demand. Besides cleaning up Gary's hairballs off the kitchen floor and being some man's soon-to-be ex-boyfriend, dishonesty was the only consistency in this otherwise topsy-turvy world.

I tugged free a long-sleeve plaid shirt that must have been as old as the grunge movement itself, and a broken-in pair of Levi's from a shelf underneath. I put the clothes on, walked to the bathroom while buttoning the shirt, and took a look in the mirror. I'd definitely grown into my chest and shoulders since the last time I'd worn this homage to Pearl Jam, but it'd do in a pinch. I ran my fingers through my strawberry-blond hair a few times, letting it lie wherever and giving myself a less posh look to match the rest of the ensemble.

I went down the hall, fetched my peacoat from the closet near the front door, and looked back toward the kitchen as I adjusted the jacket collar.

Morning sun poured through the blinds onto the table piled with soldering equipment and half-finished projects that were my "de-stress hobby," and cast sharp rays of light across the stainless-steel fridge. Nate's addition to my grocery list shined like a beacon and reinforced my whole point about humans. I returned to the kitchen, gently plucked the note free from under a *Cat Dad* magnet, folded it, and slipped it into my coat pocket.

* * * * *

I didn't like Long Island City.

But I did like their parking fees.

Leaving my car in a garage for the day at a third of the price I'd have paid in Manhattan, I walked four blocks to Kaufman Studios. Despite the bright, sun-shining, blue-sky day, the mercury was flirting with zero. The Queens neighborhood wasn't the wind tunnel that my block on the west end of Midtown tended to be, but the sidewalk still leeched the life out of me with each step, until by the end of my brisk, twelve-minute walk, I felt as if I was walking on pebbles, not toes.

I crossed the street and took a right toward the security box outside the studio gates.

"Rory Byrne?"

I stopped midstride and turned, shoulders hunched against the cold. A short, round man in his fifties was picking his way along the slippery sidewalk. He had a cup of coffee in one hand, a cigarette in the other, wore spectacles too small for his face, and had on a pair of those wraparound earmuffs.

"Yes?" I asked.

He was huffing by the time he reached my side, little plumes of air briefly suspended in the cold. "Tall blond man with glasses, just like Ms. Shelby said. And on time too." He tilted his hand to confirm the hour on his watch and spilled coffee in the process. "Oops—shit." He hesitated a minute, stuck the cigarette back in his mouth, then offered a free hand. "John Anderson. I'm the client. *Your* client, that is."

"John," I repeated, shaking his hand. "How are you doing?"

"Not good. My nerves have gotten the best of me, I'm afraid," he muttered before removing the cigarette and blowing smoke to one side.

"I see that." I pointed to security. "Would you like to talk inside?"

"No! No, no, we can't do that. Someone might overhear," John hastily answered.

I tucked my hands back into my coat pockets and watched John tap ash from the cigarette almost a bit too aggressively. He shoved the stick back into his mouth and chewed on the filter.

"How about you bring me up to speed on this theft."

This was when a client (or ex-boyfriend) decided whether or not they liked me. And it was fine if they didn't. I could still see my investigation through to completion even if they had no interest in a round of beers afterward. Working on everything from cheating spouses to business fraud to missing persons makes for a lot of potential bullshit to sift through. The best method of approach was to look for deception right out of the gate.

I couldn't get caught up in whether John Anderson was a good person.

I actually didn't care.

All I wanted was the truth and nothing more.

"A script was stolen," John said. "*My* script."

"From this television show?" I studied his jittery movements.

Too much caffeine? Definitely.

Anxiety from being questioned? Probably.

Concealing information? Still uncertain.

"No." John shook his head and removed the cigarette from his mouth. "It has nothing to do with this." He waved his coffee cup at the studios behind me. "*The Bowery*, I mean. It's a script I wrote. Unpublished, but it's still protected by copyright law. This is a theft of my intellectual property. I'm a producer. I know all about—"

I held a hand up.

John frowned, sipped his coffee. "Sorry. I'm a little out of sorts. I haven't slept. I think I've developed an ulcer."

"Can you tell me why you believe the script has been stolen?"

He looked up at me, squinting behind his spectacles. "Because on Saturday night it was in my office, and yesterday it was gone. Are you new at this?"

"Twenty years this June. Who has access to your office besides yourself?"

John blanched a little. "I don't always lock it, if that's what you're asking. It's kind of an honor system, you know?"

What was that saying, the road to hell is paved with good intentions?

"Then who knows about this creative endeavor of yours?"

John shrugged dramatically and huffed a few times. "I haven't the faintest."

A lie.

"I can't do my job if you lie to me, John."

"I really don't know," he insisted. "Honest. I got a little, erm, drunk a few weeks back. I could have talked to anybody." He looked at his mangled cigarette, tossed it to the ground, and stomped on it. John wedged his coffee cup between his chest and arm, fished out a pack of cigarettes from his coat pocket, and lit a new stick. "But I'm here to tell you the script would have been stolen for the *idea*."

"Is this your belief, or do you have proof?"

"B-both," he stammered. "Mr. Byrne—"

"Rory is fine."

John licked his lips. "*Rory.* What do you know about *The Bowery*?"

"Nothing," I said simply.

"It's going to shake the very foundation of the television industry when it premiers," John said. "A historical drama, turn-of-the-century New York City. Thomas O'Sullivan is an Irish gang leader. He's also a gay man in a committed relationship. Throughout the entire show, mind you. None of this tragic, gay-character-dies-in-the-end garbage. And we don't shy away from *anything*. Violence—sure. Sex—of course. But it's the romance that makes this show what it is."

I waited for him to bridge the subject of his stolen script with the plot of this unrelated show being filmed.

Instead, John asked, "You aren't one of those 'I don't mind gay people, but do they have to be gay around me?' folks, are you? Because I'll tell you right now, there will be none—"

"Far from it," I answered calmly.

"Good," he concluded, although he didn't seem to entirely put two and two together on that one. He offered me his coffee cup. "Hold this for me."

I unhurriedly extended a hand, took the Starbucks beverage that weighed in at mostly foamed milk and zero coffee, and watched John remove his pack again. He started to put another stick to his mouth, realized he already had one lit and burning between his lips, and awkwardly put them back in his pocket. He snatched the coffee from my hand.

"My script," John said at length, "is *The Bowery* on steroids. All those things, but bigger. *Better*. We expect—*oh*." He looked up at me. "*Far from it.* You mean you're..."

"My sexuality isn't relevant."

John snorted and then coughed after inhaling wrong. He thumped on his chest a few times and wheezed, "Gay investigator on a gay drama helping a gay producer. It's relevant."

I absently stamped my feet a few times. "You were saying?"

"Er, right. Yes. We expect Emmy nods for *The Bowery*, maybe even an award or two, but my screenplay has more to offer. And the thief *knows* it!" John looked up at me again, fire in his beady eyes. "That script was my ticket to getting out of producing. It'd make my career as a writer. Not only in New York, but LA too."

Hotshot, indeed.

"I understand," I answered, keeping my tone neutral. "Tell me why you decided to hire a private investigator instead of reporting this incident to the police."

John's boisterous attitude deflated like a balloon. He took a drag off the cigarette and slammed back the final dregs of his coffee. "I don't want this going to court. I don't want to involve lawyers and unions. I just want to know who's willing to risk their career to claim my idea as their own, so I can squash them like a *bug*."

"You want to blacklist them from the industry?"

John smiled a *wicked* sort of smile. "It's far more satisfying. Besides, we've a lot of high-profile cast and crew on this production. If any of them got wind the police were involved, I could end up with contracts at stake and the thief may escape. And considering the show's content, we can't afford bad publicity before it airs. I mean, for God's sake, we've got Marion Roosevelt playing Tommy." He looked up again, squinting when I didn't offer an immediate response. "*Marion Roosevelt.*"

"I heard you."

"Do you know who that is?"

"I'm not a connoisseur of television."

"Good grief." John tossed his second cigarette to the ground. "And you call yourself a gay man."

I frowned at that.

He stepped past me and motioned to follow. "Come along, then. Let's get you set up with an ID badge."

INT. CHAPTER TWO – DAY

John wasn't lying. Of this, I was quite certain.

He was stressed. Violated and embarrassed. And angry. He wasn't angry at me, the questioner, but his situation. Listening to the way John had spoken outside, noting the lack of nonverbal indicators that would have had me leaning toward deception, I was convinced he was telling the truth. Where it mattered, at least. He had quite the grandiose ego, but I figured that came with the territory of the industry.

"The beauty of being a PA," John whispered as he led the way down a long hall, "is that it allows you to be *everywhere*." He waved his arms for emphasis. "The office, the set—and no one will be surprised a newbie PA is clueless about the ins and outs of the job." He stopped outside a doorway on the right that opened to a massive staging area with a ceiling nearly twenty feet tall. "We need some kind of cover story, right? Maybe I met you at a film festival, or—"

"No. That's too complex."

"Certainly not."

"Which festival?" I stared John down. "Who was there? What films did you watch?"

He held up both hands. "All right, all right. Point taken."

After a moment of thought, I said, "I'm a family friend looking for a career change. That's all."

John nodded, took a step through the threshold, then turned to me again. "A few suggestions: don't talk back, drink plenty of water, don't sit down, and *never* speak to talent." He walked into the huge room after sharing that tidbit, the *tip-tap* of his shoes bouncing off faraway walls and staged scenery to the right.

"John," I whispered loudly, catching up with him, "you do realize I'm not actually here to work on your show."

"Of course," he muttered, saying hello to passing crew members and not looking at me.

"Then you understand that everyone is a suspect in this theft and I *have* to talk to your cast."

John stopped and looked at me again. "It's not allowed."

"Do you want me to investigate this missing script or not?"

"Of course I do," he hissed, glancing from side to side. "But there are rules on a film set. You don't break them. And the most important is, outside of the director, no one talks to talent. You never know when they may be mentally prepping for a scene—and this show is *heavy* on emotion."

"That's not good enough."

John took off his spectacles and scrubbed his face vigorously with one hand. "Look. If talent approaches *you*, it's okay to chat. But they need to be seen initiating the conversation."

"I'll be sure to face-plant in front of your actors, then," I said dryly.

John patted my upper arm. "Attaboy."

I rolled my eyes to the ceiling once he turned his back.

This investigation was going to be...*a challenge.*

Laughter and radio-edited rap drifted out the open door of some sort of workshop to my left. Immediately ahead of us were two six-foot-long tables packed with an array of juices, coffees, teas, on-the-go breakfast foods, and various high-protein snacks. And at the end of the staging area farther ahead, a massive sliding door opened to the set beyond.

"Art department," John explained, pointing to the left. "And this is crafty. Help yourself when you've got a moment. No one is going to babysit you and make sure you're eating." He led the way onto the dimmed set. "Welcome to *The Bowery.* Specifically, the interior of Thomas O'Sullivan's home."

To my untrained eye, the layout, furniture, even color choices, seemed historically accurate. Definitely rendered as an apartment for someone with a fair amount of money and influence. Nothing out of Millionaire's Row, but also a far cry from some tenement in the Tenderloin District. Perfect for an Irish gangster, I supposed. A few crew members were moving about the area, minutely adjusting props, lights, and calling to each other in lingo sounding reminiscent of military jargon.

"Marion's been featured in *Out* magazine," John was saying, and I looked away from the set design to him. "'Fifty Up and Coming Out Actors.' He was ranked number four, *and* they wrote a snippet about his role as Tommy."

"So he has audience draw?"

"Oh, definitely. He's very charming. The camera loves him. And with this being his first leading role, his net worth is bound to go up a few mil."

Huh.

John touched my arm for a second time and not so discreetly lingered on my bicep. "Come over here." He led the way toward the back right corner of the stage, interrupting a Brooklyn hipster from his work. "Davey, can you spare me a second?"

Davey glanced up from a sheet of paper that looked like a script page, quickly set it aside, and smoothed his beard with one hand while tucking the other under his arm. Even at a foot or two away, I could smell an abundance of earthy, cedar-like cologne trying to mask the smell of too much tobacco. The edges of his fingernails looked discolored. He rolled his own cigarettes. Very edgy, Davey.

"Yes, sir, what can I get you?" he asked John.

"This is Rory Byrne." John brought me into the conversation with a small handwave. "A family friend and our newest PA. Rory, Davey here is Key PA. You'll report to him."

Davey immediately nodded and said, "Sounds good, sir." He still tugged on his beard.

John thanked him, gave me a thumbs-up, and left us.

Davey watched over my shoulder until the producer was suitably out of earshot. "Let me guess—first gig?"

"I'm a quick learner."

"Great," Davey muttered, sounding wholeheartedly unimpressed. Even his beard seemed to object to my presence on set. He grabbed a walkie-talkie from a large bay on a table. "Here you are. Don't forget to do a walkie check. I'm guessing you don't own a surveillance?"

I'd been officially undercover for no more than ten minutes and already found myself someone with a *Star Service* attitude. The man was lucky I wasn't armed.

I had at least a decade on this Brooklyn bro, but I was coming to realize that age probably meant little on a film set. Position is where the power was, not in life experience. So I was likely to be getting the college-kid treatment for the remainder of the investigation.

"Figures," Davey said when I hesitated over "surveillance." He grabbed an earpiece similar to those worn by Secret Service. "Put this on and stay out of the way."

I was certain Davey held his dick with five fingers and pissed on four of them.

* * * * *

Nearly one hundred suspects.

Not a workable number. I needed to narrow the scope to a handful of individuals almost immediately.

So the moment Davey sent me to the office to "make myself useful," I asked for a roster of the staff and crew. The production manager met the request with considerable side-eye, but I convinced her of my fledging PA status and talked up wanting to learn crew positions and names.

"You can't keep this," she said, reluctantly handing over a freshly printed sheet. "But go ahead and study it."

I accepted the list. "Thank you, ma'am."

"It's smart of you," she added after a pause. "A good PA should be familiar with all the departments."

I looked up over the rim of my glasses.

"*Including* the office. Most people forget we run the show."

The lines around her face were pronounced, as if she'd not smiled once in the last…oh…decade. She was stick-thin, with artfully curled brown hair, thick-lensed glasses, and she wore a shade of red lipstick that was particularly aggressive. There was also a touch of hostility in her tone as she spoke. A bit like, those who can't art, critique art.

Or in this case, those who can't work set jobs oversee from a cozy office chair. I mean, as far as I was aware, the general public was pretty interested in the behind-the-scenes of movie-making, but really, who cared about the phone calls made and emails sent throughout the day that kept the show chugging along?

Interesting.

I had no intention of broaching that bit of reality with—I scanned the list until I found Production Manager, Laura Turner—with Laura. She was especially salty for a Tuesday. But in order to weed out suspects quickly and efficiently, I needed to have key personnel cooperative.

"It's great to meet you, Laura," I said, offering a hand.

She narrowed her eyes skeptically but took my hand in a firm shake. "I don't have any jobs for you. Davey is trying to play a game of volleyball."

And I'm the ball.

"I'm not above stapling and collating," I said by way of suggestion.

"Eager beaver." She opened a few folders on her desk, pawed through some documents, then held up a few loose sheets. "Wow me with your photocopying skills, then we'll discuss stapling."

I accepted the documents, moved around the corner from her desk as Laura indicated, and walked down a short hall. Ahead was the copier, situated between two office doors, one of which read: PRODUCER, JOHN ANDERSON. A young man, who couldn't have been a day past his twentieth birthday, stood in front of the machine, leaning heavily on the top with both arms. He glanced sideways at me. "It's broken," he explained.

"Ah."

"Have to practically sit on it, or the copy comes out blurry."

Whirr-thck. Whirr-thck. Whirr-thck.

The tray was heavy with tree-pulp sacrifices shooting out at lightning speed, and it didn't look to be finishing up anytime soon.

The man inclined his head awkwardly. "There's another machine down the hall, past the Editing Suite. It's slow as hell, though."

"Thanks for the heads-up." I nodded and moved past him.

I took in my surroundings, memorizing several faces at desks in an open pocket of office space—admin assistants?—and walked by another closed office door, where someone inside was arguing animatedly with what I hoped was a phone on speaker. I came across a massive suite next, darkened and empty through the glass wall, with an impressive computer and digital display setup that *had* to belong to the editing team.

I checked my watch. Just after nine in the morning. And yet, everyone else appeared to have been manning their stations for some time. Did post-production work on a different schedule? I looked at the crew roster I still held on to. There were about a dozen names listed among editing, Foley, and post-audio. Considering John said the script went missing sometime between Saturday and Monday, depending on when these individuals came and went through the office area, it either eliminated them or narrowed my list of suspects to this Dirty Dozen.

I made a mental note to follow up with John about the post-production team in particular, and carried on until I found the lonely photocopier in a darkened, unused wing of the rented out office space. Curious setup. Abandoned desks that'd seen better days were haphazardly strewn around the area. Phones sat in piles on the floor beside wrangled office lines, and there was yet another hall to the left, tarped off for what looked like some minor building maintenance.

I peeled off the Post-it asking for fifty copies, set the papers on the feed, and hit Start. The copier groaned to life. I tugged my surveillance bud free and rubbed at my swollen ear. The tiny nub of plastic was already killing my inner ear, but there was a lot of communication going on between crew members—not that it all translated to plain English—and it was worth the discomfort to hear what was going on.

I slipped the piece back on in time to pick up Davey's voice saying, "Take it to two."

A second voice confirmed, and their conversation abruptly ended.

Take it to two?

I removed my phone from my back pocket, and as the copier sputtered along, did a quick Internet search.

Extend the conversation in private to channel two.

Did this work like John's unlocked-door honor system? When someone announced they were moving to the next channel, was it simply assumed no one would stick their nose into the chat? Seemed like a good way to hide in plain sight. And if it were this simple to stay in constant communication, it opened the possibility of more than one individual behind the theft.

I took the walkie off my belt and turned the knob on top to the next channel.

"No, sir, but—"

Davey quickly cut the other person off. "You answer to me, kid, *understand?*" he barked in a voice that suggested the only person he could possibly be speaking to in that way was a PA.

"Yes."

"If you go gallivanting off with the art department without reporting to me first—"

"They needed help quick," the PA answered. "I was just trying to lend a hand."

"They're not your boss. I am. And the minute I can't find your ass at any given second, consider yourself out of a job."

"Yes, sir."

"Report to set."

I twisted the knob back to the main channel and shook my head absently. No suspicious plotting, but for someone who was only one step above the rest of the PAs, Davey had an ego bigger than his beard.

Before leaving the isolated hall, I made a copy of the crew roster, carefully folded it, and tucked it into my sock. I then carried the stack of warm papers, slowing my walk to watch the same young guy still hanging over the finicky copier.

He turned his head, and his expression dropped. "*Jesus.* You finished before me?"

"I only needed fifty." I pointed at the massive stack he was working on. "So are you an administrative assistant or...?"

"I'm a PA," he corrected while leaning harder on top of the copier when one or two of the printouts came out blurry. "Davey sent me here my first day to make copies, and then I wasn't allowed to leave."

"What do you mean?"

He made a face and nodded in Laura's direction. "She won't let me work on set."

"Why's that?" I asked, lowering my voice a bit.

"She's a bitch."

I narrowed my eyes.

He swallowed. "Sorry. I mean—I don't know. Her and Davey don't like each other. One of the other PAs heard from a gaffer who worked on a Disney show with Laura years ago that she'd once been a set PA and got fired."

So there *was* a definite validity to that antagonism toward set jobs I'd picked up from her.

"Anyway," he said as the last page spit onto the tray, "don't make yourself too useful, or she might steal you from set. The office *sucks*."

"Thanks for the heads-up."

I went back to Laura at the front of the office. "Here you are." I handed over the stack of copies and the crew list. "Thanks for letting me look at the roster."

Laura took everything without even a half-hearted thanks. "Go find Davey if you want something else to do."

If there was a test I had to pass in order to be entrusted with her stapler, I guess I'd failed it.

Apparently it was for the best.

* * * * *

I spent my lunch break in the men's bathroom.

"*Shit.*" I studied my red, irritated ear in the mirror. I lowered my head, braced my hands on either side of the sink, and took a few deep breaths. Never having to wear that hard nub of plastic again was the biggest incentive I had for closing this case immediately.

"You okay?"

I jerked my head up, and in the mirror's reflection, I saw a man standing in the bathroom doorway. "Oh. Sure." I straightened and turned around.

The stranger was considerably shorter than me, maybe five-foot-five, with a lithe build. He had dark-brown hair, cut and styled in a decidedly outdated fashion, but hell if I could pinpoint the decade in question. He had a beautiful jawline, cheekbones sharp enough to cut glass with, and head-to-toe wore turn-of-the-century clothing.

"You must be one of the show's actors." *Fucking duh.* "Unless suspenders and waistcoats are proper set attire."

He cracked a smile. No teeth, but a cute, boyish smirk crossed his features.

"Grow a beard, and you'd fit right in with Davey at some purposefully divey bar in Williamsburg," I added.

His smile grew at that, and he looked away momentarily, giving his shoes his undivided attention while collecting himself. "I am talent," he agreed.

"A shame."

He brought his gaze up. "How so?"

I shrugged noncommittally. "I was hoping waistcoats were coming back."

"Nothing like a man in a three-piece suit."

"We all have our vices."

My handsome stranger let the door fall shut behind him as he strolled across the bathroom. "You must be new." He slid his hands into his trouser pockets.

Jesus. He looked so goddamn fine, it was practically criminal.

"What gave it away?" I asked, grinning broadly.

"I don't know your name," he answered.

"You make it a habit to learn everyone's name?"

"I try to."

I reached a hand out. "Rory Byrne."

He removed his hand and accepted the shake. "A pleasure."

"I suspect you have a name as well?"

The stranger flashed that lopsided smile again. "Sure."

I leaned back against the sink, crossed my arms, and gave him another once-over. "You must be...what, about thirty? The most popular name for boys back then was...Michael, I believe."

"I'm thirty-two," he corrected coyly.

"*Oh,*" I said, as if it mattered. "It was still Michael."

He laughed. "I'm afraid my parents used the census records from the 1880s to pick my name, not the 1980s."

"John?"

"Marion," he answered.

"Marion," I repeated, putting two and two together. "*Marion Roosevelt?*"

Shit. Playful conversation with a background extra was one thing, but the lead actor of the show? Although…he *did* initiate our dialogue, exactly as John had insisted. Keeping a line of communication open with Marion would help me feel out the rest of the cast, as well as crew members above me on the hierarchical ladder.

"Your surprise suggests we had a moment of authentic flirting in the men's bathroom," Marion stated.

"Ah. Yes, but I didn't—"

"Contrary to what the paparazzi would have you believe about film stars, we're just people who sometimes really hope to be treated normally." He leaned forward a bit. "That includes being flirted with."

"I'll remember that."

"Good." Marion moved to the next sink over, turned on the tap, and began washing his hands. "Because you're not half bad at it."

"I've got the beginning part down pat." I turned to watch him. "It's the part that happens *after* where my luck tends to run out."

"That's relatable." He shut off the water and grabbed a paper towel. Marion glanced at me, his brow furrowed a little, and he asked, "So how's your ear?"

I instinctively reached up and touched the tender skin. "Agitated."

"Some people have bad reactions to those surveillance pieces," he said, inclining his head at the tube hanging over my shoulder. "Most crew members buy their own."

"I'm still pretty green."

Marion tossed the towel in the trash and stepped closer to examine my ear. He had big, expressive eyes. The actual sort that poets must have in mind when referring to them as windows to the soul. Belatedly, I took in that one eye was a very light green, and the other was actually a dark brown.

Marion must have sensed my staring. "What?"

"Nothing."

"They're real."

"Excuse me?"

"My eyes."

"They're very pretty."

"They're responsible for the contracts," Marion said with a wink. "But luckily, I'm a package deal."

I snorted. "Funny."

"I am sometimes." He took a step back. "I might be able to help with your ear."

"I think I'm a bit too old for kisses on boo-boos."

Marion gave me a direct look, the corner of his mouth upturned again. "In that case...come with me." He walked to the door, opened it, and stepped into the corridor.

I took a breath and followed him out of the bathroom. He led the way down the same hall John had earlier that morning. Toward the end, the left branch led to the production offices. The right went to set. We took the right. Marion walked through the vast staging area, paused long enough at crafty to grab a miniature package of gummy bears, and then brought me through the open set door.

He picked his way around equipment and crew members returning from lunch break. "Paul," he called out to a man seated behind a cart loaded with a plethora of expensive-looking gear, including a multichannel mixing board. Sound recordist, I determined.

Paul looked up, headphones in his hands, ready to put them on. "Marion. What's up?"

"Do you have any extra earpieces?" Marion asked, tearing open the candy package. "The molded ones."

"Looking to become my apprentice?"

Marion smiled, but it was a different smile than what I'd experienced in the bathroom. Instinctual. Polite. A bit reserved, even. "My friend here is having issues with the cheapo ones they give PAs."

Paul only acknowledged my existence when Marion motioned to me with one hand. He leaned back in his chair and stared at the side of my head. "He sure is. You're what—about a medium?"

"Large where it counts," I joked, because I honestly had no idea what he was referring to. I glanced sideways at Marion. He'd crossed one arm over his midsection and placed a hand against his mouth, failing to hide his amusement. Nice to know my childish comment hadn't worked against me.

"Yeah, I bet," Paul said sardonically. He pushed his chair back, leaned down, and retrieved a leather pouch from the bottom shelf of the cart. He unzipped it, sifted through various oddities I'd never seen outside of the personal-care aisle in Duane Reade, then offered a pink earpiece still in its packaging. "Don't lose it. And you owe me twenty bucks."

"Thank you," I said graciously. "I really appreciate it." I tore it open, stuck the piece onto the end of the plastic tube, and fit it in my ear.

"Better?" Marion asked me as he stepped away from Paul.

I nodded, following him. "A lot better. How'd you know about these?"

"I try to be conscious of the crew."

I raised an eyebrow.

Marion simply shrugged. He popped a red bear into his mouth.

I started to speak, but someone called Marion's name from behind, interrupting the last chance I had to...well, do *what*, exactly? Flirt some more? Marion was undoubtably gorgeous, devastatingly sweet, and I was reluctantly enamored at first sight. But showing interest in a guy while working a case—where said heartthrob had not been ruled out as a suspect—was strictly against the policies of Dupin Private Investigations. I was merely rebounding after severing ties with Nate that morning.

And rebounds were fine.

Just not with Marion Roosevelt.

Nothing to see here. Move along, Rory.

A man easily my height and build, with black hair and a matching goatee peppered with silver, came toward us. He wrapped a large hand around Marion's arm and tugged him sideways. "I need to speak with you."

Marion's physical response would have likely gone unnoticed if I wasn't trained to read body language. The muscle to the right of Marion's mouth, which gave him such a pleasing, crooked smile, tightened. His heterochromatic eyes narrowed at the same moment. Maybe it was an over-the-top and unprofessional description, but the light in Marion's face seemed to...fade.

"Yes, of course," Marion answered, flashing a fake smile worthy of an Oscar. He followed Mr. Top-Ten-Beards-in-Hollywood-According-to-BuzzFeed back toward the set without so much as a second glance my way.

EXT. CHAPTER THREE – NIGHT

"So?" John asked impatiently.

We stood on the sidewalk outside the studios after dark. It was bitterly cold, and I pulled the collar of my coat up on the back of my neck before stuffing my hands deep into the pockets. Most of the crew had clocked out for the evening, giving John the opportunity to circle back with me for the first time since that morning to harass me for details I didn't have.

"Who did it? Who stole it?"

"John, please," I interrupted. "It's not that easy. These situations can take some time."

"I don't have time," he protested. "Once this show wraps on principal photography, that's it. The thief gets away. *Forever!*"

"I'd like you to clarify a few details for me," I said, reeling him back from the ledge he was about to fling himself from. "Tell me about the post-production team."

"What about them?"

"While I did some work in the office, I noticed their suite was empty."

"Yes. They arrive later in the day—after lunch. The schedule allows them to finish work from the previous day, and then by the time Ethan and I are done on set, we can sit with the editors and go over dailies and watch some rough cuts."

"And Ethan's the director, is that right?" I'd gathered that much after a sneak peek at the crew roster when work resumed after lunch and Mr. Goatee was the one calling *action!*

"Ethan Lefkowitz," John said with a nod.

I grunted. "And on Sunday, was the editing team working?"

"No. None of us were. Double time on Sunday. We avoid it at all costs."

"And you are *absolutely* certain your script was in the office Friday and Saturday, but gone by Monday?" I pressed.

"Yes, and I'll tell you—we had a pick-up scene to shoot Saturday. A character that only appears in one episode had a scheduling conflict. We *had* to shoot Saturday. So I was here. I went to my office afterward, did some minor editing on the script, but I was so tired, I didn't stay late."

"But production had for sure wrapped by then?" I asked, using the term I'd heard the assistant director call out earlier on set to indicate our job was done for the day.

John nodded vigorously. "*And* we had no post-production crew on Saturday."

"What about the office staff?"

"I recall a few," he confirmed.

I ran my fingertips through my hair a few times. "What about the possibility of someone coming in to work on an unscheduled—"

John shook his head dramatically. "No, no, no. Union rules, Rory. That doesn't happen without the assistant director or production coordinator knowing. News would travel like a wildfire in California."

"Fine. Tell me what time you arrived yesterday morning."

"Seven."

"And the script was already gone?"

"I, er—" John hesitated. He started patting his jacket, searching for his cigarettes, no doubt. "I'm not...certain. *Probably.* But I didn't take notice until I'd gone back to my desk around ten to make a phone call."

Based on this timeline—unreliable though it was—I could rule out the entire post-production team simply because they hadn't been in the building over the weekend, nor did they arrive on Monday early enough to abscond with the script. I couldn't clear all those admins in the bullpen, though. Either before John's early arrival yesterday, or in between his back-and-forth to the set, any one of those staffers could have been presented the opportunity to slip inside his room nestled between the production manager around the corner and show accountant in the next office over.

I also couldn't rule out Ethan Lefkowitz, the director. It seemed ridiculous that a director would have a reason or desire to steal a script. As far as my understanding went, he was near the top of the food chain on a film set. He held a lot of power over the content, gained prestige for overseeing the performances, and was likely being compensated quite well. On the other hand, if there was a crew member John would have casually spoken to about his personal writing, or mentioned it to in a moment of bragging, it'd be someone he considered his equal.

Plus, I hadn't been able to silence the warning bells in my head after witnessing the domineering way Ethan touched Marion, and said actor's *almost* flawless performance to cover his discomfort.

Something was wrong there.

Something that merited further inquiry.

So where'd that leave me? Twelve suspects down, only about eighty to go?

"I'd like a list of all the cast members who worked Friday, Saturday, and Monday," I said.

"Sure." John tugged a cigarette free from a crushed pack and lit it. He stuck the stick in his mouth and then immediately took it out when the request sank in. "You think the thief is talent?"

"I think nothing. I want the names in order to do cross-referencing."

John's face was pinched, his spectacles lifting up with the movement of his muscles. He took a few puffs, then whipped out his phone. "What's your email?"

I recited my Dupin address, retrieved my cell from a pocket, and less than a minute later it dinged with an incoming email. I swiped, opened the message, and several PDFs with the cast schedule loaded. "Great," I murmured, studying the times and names.

Marion Roosevelt.

Marion Roosevelt.

Marion Roosevelt.

So there was no crossing my—*their* heterochromatic actor off the suspect list yet.

"Does Mr. Roosevelt work every day?" I asked.

John turned his head and blew smoke into the darkness. "Most. Marion is a true gem. No complaints, no egotistical, star-studded temper tantrums, and he doesn't use a stand-in."

I turned off the phone's screen and stared at John.

He shook his head like, *Oh, right, this man has no idea what I'm talking about.* "Some actors have a double stand in for them when shooting the lines and reactions of the other talent. Marion is vehemently against that. He'll be on set twelve, sometimes fifteen hours just to respect the process of his fellow actors."

"He seems like a decent person," I agreed.

"To say the least." John tapped the end of his cigarette. "Do your cross-referencing-what-have-yous with those names, but Marion is *not* a suspect. In fact, I'm asking you as the client, don't investigate him."

"John, that's not how—"

"I can hire someone else," John threatened.

That'd piss off Shelby.

"No one is above suspicion."

"If I lose Marion, the whole show falls apart. There's no appeal without him. No audience draw. The man is just *this side* of perfect," John babbled.

Picture perfect.

"He's not a thief," John continued. "If there's one person I'm certain is innocent, it's Marion. So I'm telling you, I do not want him investigated."

I took a deep breath and let the air briefly freeze my lungs. After a slow release, I avoided a response by motioning to the pack John still held in one hand, and asked, "Can I bum one of those?"

He looked surprised but offered a cigarette. "You shouldn't smoke."

"Yeah," I agreed, accepting his lighter next and setting the flame to the tip. "How much is your script worth?"

John wiped his forehead with the sleeve of his coat. "It's a *really* good idea," he said by way of answering.

"If the thief isn't caught now," I continued, before taking a brief drag, "you could still easily prove the project is yours."

"True. It's not like I don't have copies. But…if *I* stole it, I'd rework it, you know?"

"Hmm."

"Harder to prove it's stolen when it's not outright plagiarism," John murmured, looking at the ground. "But the idea would be tainted after that." He sounded almost…*melancholy.*

"Do you know of anyone on set having issues? Finances, things like that?" I tried.

"I'm not their damn mother."

I raised an eyebrow.

"Sorry," John said quickly. "Oh boy. Too much nicotine." He flicked the cigarette. "Not enough sleep."

I checked my watch. "Why don't you go home? I'll see you tomorrow?"

"Tomorrow," John echoed, but he headed back in the direction of the studio.

I turned to Thirty-Fifth Avenue and walked toward the end of the block. Potted plants lining the Kaufman entrance were buried in freshly fallen snow, and my shoes crunched loudly on the salted sidewalk.

"Rory Byrne, are you following me?"

I looked over my shoulder while taking another drag from the cigarette. Marion emerged from the darkness, as if he'd detached from the night itself and taken human form. "I think you're following me," I countered.

I caught his smile as he walked under a lamppost before coming to a stop beside me on the street corner. "Think I can steal one of those?" he asked, pointing discreetly at the cigarette hanging between my lips.

I removed it and said, "I actually bummed this one." I twisted my hand around and offered the filtered end.

"Are you sure?" Marion asked.

I nodded. "It's a bad habit."

"Don't I know it," he said before accepting. "I've been trying to quit. One of those New Year's resolutions."

"Not working out?"

"January came in like a freight train," he said with a melodic chuckle and careless wave of his hand.

I allowed myself a brief, unabashed moment to study Marion. The way the orange glow of the nearby tungsten bulb cut sharp shadows across his face. The way his cheeks hollowed a little when he inhaled. The way he licked his bottom lip after blowing smoke.

"What?" he asked.

Marion's voice was deep, but he didn't speak with the strength of his diaphragm. So his tone was lighter, gentler. A careful and practiced sort of speech.

"May I ask you a question?"

"Okay." He smiled. Like he knew what was coming—was expecting it.

So I threw him a curveball. "Do you enjoy working with Mr. Lefkowitz?"

Marion's facial expressions flickered like an old television. Charm gave way to confusion, to disappointment. Then he squared his shoulders, cleared his throat, and inhaled another breath of smoke. "Why do you ask?"

I shook my head a little.

A black car pulled up to the curb. The driver got out, called a greeting to Marion, and walked around the trunk to the back passenger door. He opened it and waited.

Marion held out the cigarette. "Thank you for the nicotine."

I accepted the stick. "Sure."

"That's my ride."

"I figured."

Marion looked up at me, considered something to himself, but ultimately said, "Have a good night."

"You too."

My cell rang as I watched him walk to the hired car. I reached into my pocket, took out my phone again, and looked at the screen. It was the Big Boss.

"Rory," Marion called.

I glanced up, thumb hovering over the Accept button.

"If you're around tomorrow," he started, blunt fingertips tapping the top of the car door in a hesitant manner. "After lunch—I'll be washing my hands again."

Hell. What a bad week to end it with Nate. I felt stripped and naked. Defenseless against the subtle charms of an unconventionally handsome man who absolutely *knew* I was goddamn smitten.

No.

Do not pass go.

Do not collect two hundred dollars.

I smiled apologetically and did the only thing I could to break the moment. I answered the call. "Byrne."

"Rory. Have a moment?"

"Yes, ma'am." I kept my gaze on Marion as he climbed into the car, shut the door, and the vehicle sped off into the night. I flicked my cigarette, crossed the street, and went in the opposite direction, toward the parking garage.

"How's TV life?"

"About as hectic and ego-driven as you'd expect it to be."

Shelby's laugh was warm. "So I won't be losing you to the limelight?"

"Afraid not, ma'am."

"Good."

"The theft was of a script. An unpublished piece Anderson wrote. It was taken from his office," I explained without prompting.

"I see. Were you able to narrow the scope of the investigation from that ridiculous initial suspect count?"

"A bit," I said, switching the phone to my other side and putting my cold hand in my pocket. "The post-production department can be omitted on account of their scheduling. But there's still a lot of coming and going to take into consideration. Some crew members, electricians and such, are more restricted in duties, I've noticed. I'm fairly confident in disregarding them as suspects on the grounds that there's little if no way for them to step into the production office without it being questioned."

"But?" she prompted.

"But there is a pecking order on film sets unlike anything I've seen before. From a sociological standpoint, it's fascinating. From an investigative one, it's extremely frustrating."

Shelby made a humming sound. Her thinking-out-loud noise.

I continued. "On the one hand, it narrows the scope considerably, as the only individuals who have immediate access to John are those in positions of power themselves. But not all these department heads have an obvious motive. There are some low-ranking crew members I'm having to consider as well."

"How would they know about the script if they don't speak with the producer like you say?" Shelby questioned.

"Besides the fact that Anderson can't remember who he may have spoken to about it?" I said with a *touch* of annoyance. "Everyone on set has a walkie." I dug out my parking receipt as I reached the garage. An attendant stepped out of a booth, took the paper from my outstretched hand, and went to fetch my car. "There's a process for having a private discussion, but everyone has access to the channel in question. It's possible any number of conversations could have been overheard and used to an individual's advantage."

"What do you think about Anderson?" Shelby asked at length. "Is this script of his worth a lot?"

"It may be worth nothing."

"Oh?" I could hear the wry smile in that single word.

I glanced toward the ramp leading from the underground garage as my car's headlights lit up the street. "I've noticed a considerable amount of hostility and abuse of power among certain individuals. I don't believe the script itself is worth money. It's the idea. And if the idea *is* a moneymaker, it could be a reasonable assumption that someone was willing to steal it in order to get out from under someone else's thumb."

* * * * *

Gary was sitting on the table when I entered the apartment. My soldering iron was dangling over the edge by its cable, the floor was littered with strips of PVC shrink tube, a partially unspun roll of alloy wire for soldering, and a pair of wire strippers were under a chair. He meowed loudly as I shut the door and hung up my coat.

"Hi, baby." I walked toward him, leaned over, and kissed his head. "Is this some sort of social protest?"

I bent to collect the fallen hobby items, and the cat jumped onto my shoulders. He meowed a second time before digging his claws into my shirt and holding on as I straightened and set everything back on the tabletop. I scratched Gary's chin while I walked into the kitchen. I didn't bother with the light. I grabbed a beer from the fridge, then went to the couch on the other side of the room from the table and sat down. The cat climbed onto my chest, butt directly in my face before he turned, got comfortable on my lap, and continued to voice his disapproval over my tardiness.

"Sounds like you had a rough afternoon." I leaned over awkwardly, pulled free the crew roster from where it'd been wedged in my sock all day, and tossed it onto the cushion beside me. I untwisted the top from the beer bottle and took a sip. "Did you want to hear about my—no? Okay. Keep going."

Gary talked while I kicked off my sneakers, grabbed the remote from the coffee table, turned on the television, and took another drink. He was still vocalizing as I went into the TV guide and did a search of programs by actor.

MARIO...

Marion Roosevelt popped up as a suggested name, and I tapped Search. One movie was available for immediate viewing. *Bastard Boyfriend.* A new release too, although I considered anything post *Star Trek: The Next Generation* to be a relatively new release. Film-related entertainment had simply never held my interest or imagination. And once I'd finished college and was hired with Dupin, every minute of my life had been dedicated to my profession.

Followed by Gary.

And then men.

In that order. That's how I liked it. Zero drama, maximum efficiency.

I tapped Play on *Bastard Boyfriend.*

I found Marion to be extremely attractive. I wouldn't have bothered watching his movie if I didn't enjoy staring. Physically, he was everything I liked in a man—slender, toned, shorter than me, and pretty in a decidedly masculine way. He wore a suit like it'd be a sin to undress him. And those eyes. Thirty seconds into this movie and Marion already conveyed more emotion with those heterochromatic eyes than his costars did with their lines.

But he didn't get a free pass in this investigation simply because his ass looked fine in tweed.

And that was all there was to it.

Gary meowed loudly in my face, crossed blue eyes giving me a level look.

"Sorry." I continued petting him, and his eyes fluttered shut in contentment.

I leaned over once again, set my beer on the coffee table, picked up a pen, then snatched the crew roster. I unfolded the printout and diligently crossed off each post-production name. I wrote Marion's name in the margin, crossed it out, then wrote it again. Outwardly, there seemed very little reason for him to betray John and bite the hand feeding him. He'd landed what sounded like a dream job for most actors, and his millions were expected to continue multiplying. Marion's motive may have been more unconventional, of course, although my gut was saying no. But I wasn't paid for instinct. I was paid to produce facts and hard evidence.

For certain, there were a few folks raising red flags that I needed to do a background check on and shadow tomorrow. Some of the key personnel on *The Bowery* represented a number of humanity's greatest sins to such a *T*, Dante himself couldn't have done better.

Envy—Production Manager, Laura Turner.

Wrath—Director, Ethan Lefkowitz.

Pride—Key PA and my good pal, Davey.

INT. CHAPTER FOUR – DAY

My reports on the three musketeers came back surprisingly bland the next morning. No criminal records, no serious debt beyond an unruly credit card, consistent employment for the last five years. There was nothing to suggest financial constraints were a factor in the theft, if indeed Laura, Ethan, or Davey were guilty beyond being Grade A assholes with excellent credit scores.

But I wasn't able to easily shake off their abrasive personalities and consider them clean like post-production. A major factor in this case was the environment itself. This wasn't some high-rise office in Midtown caught performing underhanded accounting, because in that setting, it was *always* about the money. Ego, popularity, and fame came with the territory of the film industry. And if a crime was committed in order to rise in the ranks of power, well, there wasn't any sort of background check I could run on that.

I was further cockblocked that morning by Davey's unrelenting attitude toward me. I was certain he didn't suspect I was anything but an inexperienced PA, but that didn't stop him from taking every afforded opportunity to kick me off set in order to complete some menial task for another department. I understood that PAs were, by their very nature, assistants to any part of production, but it seemed counterproductive to send them away from the very location where they needed hands-on experience the most.

Or in my case, where I needed to be in order to oversee Davey's movements. Specifically because his job *also* allowed for a great deal of flexibility, and I wanted to confirm for myself *exactly* what he did with his time on and off set. I'd noticed, upon arriving at the same time as the crew, that there were several set PAs who answered to Davey. And like me, he sent them elsewhere.

Why?

Less eyes on his movements?

If it were only me being punted about, I'd say it was because he resented the way in which John had dropped me into his lap yesterday. But all of us?

"The only job lower than a PA is an intern," said the wardrobe assistant.

I'd been sent upstairs, to where the costume department stored all their clothing, to aid Elizabeth Something-or-Other, who could have been Bettie Page's contemporary sister, in a "double-check" of all the attires organized by episode and character.

"Some people in the industry get shit on when they first enter," she continued while reading the labels on hanging garments and cross-checking each with her clipboard. "So once they get to a position of power, they return the favor and claim newbies gotta earn their keep like they did." She stared at me over the rack. "Davey's swell. *If* he likes you. If not, I hear you end up making photocopies all day for Laura."

"I did that yesterday."

She shook her head, took a hanger, and moved it to a different rack. "Want a piece of unsolicited advice?"

"Sure."

Elizabeth paused and looked at me again. "Make yourself useful to someone other than Davey. But be subtle. No one likes a know-it-all PA. If you can be That Guy, though, departments will request you by name. Davey won't be in a position to say no to someone over his head."

"Won't that piss him off?"

"You want to get a call back for a job in the future or not?"

"Point taken."

Elizabeth nodded and returned her attention to the clipboard. "Do you have Tommy O'Sullivan's episode three suit on that side? Gray tweed."

I looked down at the line of clothes in front of me and quickly pawed through them. "Right here." I removed Marion's costume and passed it to her.

Elizabeth muttered something about interns under her breath as she relocated the outfit.

"So how do you suggest I make friends with the crew?" I gently prodded.

"You have any gum?"

I frowned and patted my jeans pockets. "I have Altoids." I held up a miniature tin of breath mints.

"That'll work. Everyone wants fresh breath after lunch."

"Ah. Bribery." I laughed a little.

"Davey for Rory," said the static voice in my earpiece.

I reached for the mic button of the surveillance. "This is—er—go for Rory."

Goddamn set talk.

"What's your 20?"

I resisted rolling my eyes. As if he didn't already know where I was. "I'm still upstairs in wardrobe storage."

"Report to set."

"All right."

"*Copy,*" Elizabeth whispered loudly. "Say you copy."

"Copy," I hastily added into the mic. "Thanks," I told her before stepping out of the maze of clothes. "I've got to run."

"Hope it's not for coffee," she called after me, tone sympathetic.

I left the stuffy storage room, hurried down the back staircase, and ran along a practically hidden hallway lined with dressing rooms. I stopped at the side entrance to the stage. The red light, which indicated recording-in-session, was off, and the door had been propped open. I stepped inside. Crew was busily adjusting set pieces and relocating the camera when I heard Davey shout my name.

I turned to my left, wove around equipment, and found him standing beside Paul, the sound recordist who'd provided me with the new earpiece yesterday.

"We need you to make a run," Davey stated.

"Where to?"

Paul, still sitting, dropped a frayed cable into my hand. "An audio rental house a few blocks from here. Camera ripped my timecode cable, and there isn't time for me to make one."

I held up either end, studied the connectors, and realized the perfect opportunity to get in with a different department had just presented itself to me. This case could be wrapped more quickly than anticipated if I could hang out around Paul. I'd have a vantage point from which to study the inter-actions of Ethan, Davey, and—whether or not John liked it—the talent. "If you have the supplies," I began, looking back at him, "I can make this for you right now."

"We'll buy one," Davey quickly interjected.

Paul held up a hand at Davey. "These cables are like eighty bucks, cowboy. I don't want to get in a tiff with Laura." He gave me a concentrated stare. "You know how to solder? Because LEMO connectors aren't a joke."

"I'm certified. Give me the schematics, and I can do it in fifteen minutes."

Paul made a gruff sound under his breath. He tore a piece of paper from a small notebook, hastily drew a wiring diagram, and held it out. "Make sense?"

"Yes."

"Good." He stood, went to a hard-shell case covered in logo stickers propped up against the back wall, then returned a moment later with a Ziploc bag full of unassembled connector parts and lengths of cable. "There's a sol-dering iron in the art workshop."

* * * * *

I was back in sixteen minutes, but I did have to allow the soldering iron to heat first, so the discrepancy seemed a reasonable excuse. And the cable worked, much to my relief, Paul's gratitude, and Davey's annoyance—so all was right with the world.

"Take a listen," Paul said, handing me his big headphones. "What do you hear?"

After proving myself useful, Paul kept me at his side and dismissed Davey, like I'd hoped. And hell, unlike most of the crew, he was more than happy to talk about the ins and outs of his job. Should I have actually been a PA, Paul would have been the saving grace of my career thus far.

But I wasn't a PA. I was a PI.

Big difference.

So every little detail he taught me about mics or timecode or whatnot was simply one more opportunity to glean information regarding his interactions with individuals on set. It gave me a chance to present myself as someone he could trust. Someone to complain to. To confide in.

I put the headphones on my ears, and after a moment, said, "Sounds like clothes rustling."

"That's right. It's Marion's tie mic. No one notices good sound until it's bad."

I set the headphones down and looked toward the set. Marion was standing in the middle of the scene, arms crossed, shifting absently from foot to foot as someone from makeup touched up his face. Ethan was talking animatedly with a second actor who, I think, portrayed Tommy's lover in the show. John sat in one of those folding director's chairs several feet away, texting a mile a minute and seemingly oblivious to the nonsense Ethan was spouting.

The assistant director yelled a warning that camera was almost ready to roll on the new angle.

Paul stood and motioned for me to follow. The set was bright and uncomfortably warm under the thousands of watts of light, but I guess it was something one simply got accustomed to. Marion lowered his hands to his sides as Paul replaced the woman who'd been brushing his jawline. He silently lifted his chin when Paul indicated what he meant to do. The sound recordist hastily loosened the knot on Marion's tie and deftly adjusted a hidden microphone in the clothing.

Marion must have seen me. It would be impossible to miss my towering presence directly behind Paul. But his gaze was focused on some distant point over my shoulder. His expression was hard. *Dangerous.* So unlike the sweet man with the boyish charm from yesterday. It'd taken a moment for it to sink in that Marion was on the clock. This was his work. Not only was he an actor, and quite a good one if *Bastard Boyfriend* was anything to go by, but in *The Bowery*, he portrayed a high-class, violent criminal. He must have been in some…dark character zone.

The second actor detached himself from Ethan at that point, stepped behind Marion, put a hand on his shoulder, and whispered, "That entire tirade can be summed up as: be more sad."

Still staring at that faraway point, Marion made a quiet shushing sound under his breath.

"I'm sick of it," the other actor continued. "Was I hired to parrot back Ethan's bullshit acting or do the role myself?"

"All set," Paul declared, taking a step away from Marion. "Let's go," he said to me as he moved out of the glow of lights and headed for his sound cart.

I heard Marion say, "Do the scene as we discussed. I'll handle Ethan."

I dared one glimpse over my shoulder. Marion put a hand on his costar's chest, gave him an affirming little pat, and walked out of the scenery and surrounding props.

"Out of the shot, PA!" someone near camera shouted.

I hauled ass back to the mess of sound equipment.

"Always take a listen after making a mic adjustment," Paul said without skipping a beat, as if we'd been talking the entire time. He handed me his headphones again before busying himself with buttons and levels on his mixing board.

Not that this multimillion-dollar production should be trusting *my* untrained ears, but I obediently put the headphones on and took a listen. I heard nothing but the set ambience—faraway voices, the sound of equipment and tools—then Marion's sudden voice gave me a start.

"I think James did wonderful during rehearsal."

"*You* think?"

I raised my head, scanned the massive room, and found Marion in a secluded corner, speaking with Ethan.

"Yes," Marion said, quiet but insistent. "And telling him *how* to do this scene instead of helping him find it—"

"He's not finding shit, Marion," Ethan spat, voice farther away but still heard through the tie mic. "I was hired to make this show a triumph, and James is an albatross."

"Ethan."

I picked up a fluttering, almost thumping reverberation from Marion's microphone. Quick but constant.

Like—a heartbeat.

Marion's heart was pounding so hard, the microphone was actually picking up the sound.

"Are you the goddamn director?" Ethan retorted.

"No," Marion whispered, the courage in his tone waning considerably. As if this was a battle he knew from the start he'd lose.

Even from where I stood, I could see Ethan step closer and point a finger in Marion's face that in turn caused Marion to visibly bend away from the invasion.

"Remember who made you."

"We are *not* a package deal," Marion replied.

"We'll see about that," Ethan answered. "Get back to one."

* * * * *

I didn't like Ethan.

Although the reason I detested the man was admittedly a bit unrelated to the actual reason for my being at Kaufman Studios. I'd had hours on set in which to study him, and Ethan's treatment of the talent was subtle but reprehensible. With John however, he was completely cooperative, communicative, and polite. I could imagine their rapport flourishing into something collaborative—like maybe directing John's script. Ethan had moments with him that seemed a bit too...ass-kissy, but it was clear he knew not to shit where he ate. And either John enjoyed the attention, or didn't notice he was being sucked up to. The producer's slightly oblivious personality made me think the latter.

John had already established that he and the director left set together in the evenings in order to watch edits in the office. So despite Ethan's behavior suggesting he'd never double-cross John, the fact that he'd been in the vicinity of the script countless times couldn't be disregarded. However, it was worth noting that Ethan hadn't once left set during production hours. So while I had no hard evidence that proved him highly suspect *or* innocent, should Ethan had been the one to steal the script, it likely would have been in the evening.

There'd been no editing done over the weekend.

And John said his script was still safe in his office Saturday night.

But still. Ethan was an egotistical prick to the nth degree.

He wasn't a director.

He wasn't even an *artiste*.

He was a manipulator and a bully.

I needed to speak with John to clarify what time Ethan had arrived on set Monday morning. But I also needed to bring his treatment of talent to John's attention. If he was so protective of Marion and of keeping him on *The Bowery*, John needed to be aware of the fact that actors were uncomfortable on set with the one man allowed to interact with them. Upset and frustrated, even.

I simply couldn't in good conscience look the other way when Marion visibly recoiled around Ethan Lefkowitz. No success was worth it—not my case, and not a groundbreaking television show—if it came at the expense of another's emotional safety.

I rose from the lunch table as that revelation reared its ugly head. I was willing to compromise—*no*. It wasn't compromising anything if I simply asked John to be more cognizant. I moved with the intention of making a quick dash to his office, when a few seats down, Davey stood as well. I watched him pick up his jacket from the back of the chair, pull his arms through the sleeves, pat the pockets, and walk out of the room.

Cigarette break.

Shit.

Davey had been doing a good job at keeping real low-key that day. Even being granted set access all morning, I'd found it difficult to keep eyes on him and had been unable to confirm where he occasionally disappeared to. Now that I had a hot second in which to corner him, I wanted to go the opposite direction and spend the last few minutes of my break with John. I hesitated on my feet, mentally flip-flopping over which angle was more important. I'd even reacquainted myself with nicotine last night, after years of being smoke-free, because of the tobacco stains I'd noticed on Davey's fingernails. A cigarette break was the closest thing to water-cooler chitchat with these folks, and I couldn't afford to miss those opportunities.

After all, people love to talk.

People love to *gossip.*

It didn't matter if it was a high-rise, corporate accounting office, or the back lot of a film set. Universally, humans craved knowledge of one another. Gossip was a tool—a currency—in which individuals bonded or excluded those who didn't support a group mentality. Statistically speaking, Davey would spill something interesting to me sooner or later. There was no denying human hardwiring. Also, taking into consideration his antipathy toward me, it would likely result in boasting to belittle me. And that was fine. Because when men *shoot the breeze,* it's usually in regard to status or position.

In other words, a perfect cocktail for an admission of guilt without their knowledge.

"How's the weather up there?" a woman beside me asked, looking up. "Breezy?"

I laughed politely. Automatically. "I'd love to have a quick smoke. Where should I go for that?"

She pointed in the direction Davey slipped out. "Take the elevator to the ground floor, but then go out the door on your immediate left. It's the loading dock. Everyone smokes back there."

"Thanks."

She finger-gunned me and continued eating lunch.

I grabbed my peacoat and put it on while walking out of the room and down the long hall. I buttoned the front before slowing outside the bathroom door where I'd met Marion.

I almost stopped.

Almost poked my head inside.

"After lunch—I'll be washing my hands again."

The rebound of a lifetime.

But I had a job to do.

I reached the elevator and pressed the button with my thumb. The doors opened with a *ping*, I stepped inside, chose the first floor, and rode it down. The ground-floor hallways were decorated with framed movie and television posters of productions filmed at the studios—*Sesame Street, Nurse Jackie, Orange is the New Black*. Granted, I was only familiar with the big yellow bird…

I went out the door marked LOADING DOCK and feigned surprise when Davey turned at the intrusion. "Sorry. Ah, do you mind if I smoke out here too?"

Davey raised his cigarette, licked the paper, and carefully rolled it shut. "I don't own the place." He put it in his mouth, fetched a Zippo lighter from his pocket, and lit the end.

I took a few cautious steps forward, the door falling shut behind me. I tapped a cigarette out of a pack I'd bought that morning, turned away from the wind, and lit it. I took a few drags and watched as Davey ignored me in favor of scrolling through a Facebook feed on his phone. "How long have you been in the industry?" I asked at length.

"Five years," he replied absently.

"Wow."

He grunted.

"Did you go to school for film?"

He laughed at that and looked up. "I earned my career by getting on set and *doing the job.*" He started to put the cigarette to his mouth before pausing long enough to say, "And a family friend didn't help."

Oh, touché, you little dick.

I shrugged and leaned out the open dock to tap ash onto the pavement below. "John's a decent guy." I gauged how much of Davey's cigarette was left and took a deep drag from mine. The rush of nicotine made my head swim. "The PA gig is tough," I said after blowing the smoke into the biting-cold afternoon air.

Davey finally smiled, wide and sharkish. "Giving up already?"

"No, no. But I don't think I could make it my career."

"It's a stepping-stone," Davey answered, his tone inflecting upward in a curious, knee-jerk response to some perceived criticism in my comment. He reached up and combed his fingers through his Gimli beard.

I kept my face neutral but carefully prodded at that exposed insecurity. "What's that?"

"No one wants to be a PA until the job cripples them."

"I see."

"I've got a way out, in fact," Davey continued. He nodded to himself, took a final drag, then squashed the leftover bit of cigarette into an overflowing ashtray some other previous crew member had left behind. "I recently took on a project. Working on lining up investors too. I won't be organizing lemmings for a paycheck forever."

I smiled and licked my lower lip.

INT. CHAPTER FIVE – NIGHT

John was walking toward the elevator.

Another day of production had wrapped on *The Bowery*. I'd just stepped out of staging and into the long corridor when I recognized the shorter man from the back, dressed for going outside.

I quietly moved down the hall, easily catching up to his slower pace. "John—"

He jumped, gave a surprised shout, and practically tripped into me as he spun around.

"Easy," I said, putting my hands out to steady him. "I didn't mean to startle you."

"Rory...sorry...I didn't hear you." He cleared his throat and squared his round shoulders.

"You're leaving early," I observed, making it a point to check my watch.

"Am I?" John started walking again.

I followed him. "Can we talk for a moment?"

"Not really. I've got to see a man about a horse." He turned to the elevator panel on the wall.

I reached over John's shoulder and covered the buttons with the palm of my hand. "I am not the person to do that with."

John huffed. He leaned back to look around me, confirmed the hall was empty, and then said, "I have a standing date every Wednesday."

"With who?"

"Irrelevant. They're not in the industry." John made a shooing motion at my hand.

I didn't budge.

"Mr. Byrne," he said in an authoritative tone oddly reminiscent of the one every high-school teacher seemed to possess. "I see a lovely young man Wednesdays at eight p.m. And he charges whether or not I show up on time. Now, do you mind?" John asked with growing frustration.

First Nate. Now John. Am I the only one—

The unbridled and unfinished thought felt as startling as being doused in ice water. Quite suddenly I was—what? Offended? Disappointed? Not exactly. Because I could literally not care any less how John conducted himself in private.

The realization had nothing to do with John.

Nothing to do with Nate, even.

And everything to do with me.

The stark truth was, I was a good—*damn good*—investigator. But I'd never once been able to stop looking for deception, even in my own love life.

I sabotaged myself. Went out of my way to isolate myself. To lose myself in the job.

Zero drama. Maximum efficiency.

My life was fulfilled.

But was it...*happy*?

I physically jerked at the notion, as if it were the painful sting of some venomous creature.

John was staring hard, brow furrowed. "Are you okay?"

"Yes," I lied. I moved my hand and pressed the elevator button.

The doors opened, but John was still giving me a doubtful expression.

"I'm fine," I insisted. I reached my arm out over John's head so the doors wouldn't close. "You're going to be late."

"Shit. Right." And just like that, John was done worrying about me. He quickly boarded the elevator.

I stepped in beside him, chose the ground floor, and said as the doors slid shut, "I have some concerns regarding a crew member."

"You found the thief?" John exclaimed.

"No." I looked sideways. "It's about Mr. Lefkowitz."

"Ethan? What about him?"

"What time did he arrive on set Monday morning?"

"Eight o'clock."

"Positive?"

John looked annoyed. "Yes, of course. I met him at the elevator, in fact. We walked onto set together."

So Ethan hadn't arrived before John to grab the script that morning.

"I witnessed some disconcerting behavior today," I said next. "I know this is unrelated to my investigation, but—" I took a moment to collect my thoughts. John already seemed upset. *Tread carefully.* "Ethan appeared to have caused a fair amount of discomfort to your talent while on set today."

"What? No! He's a little intense, I do agree with you there," John babbled, waving a hand. "But he's the real deal. Raw. Powerful. He's got a vision for—"

"I'm only asking that you keep an eye on him."

The doors opened.

John stepped out first, shaking his head and pulling out those silly wraparound earmuffs from his coat pocket. "I will, but believe you me, he's one of the good guys."

"I can't *not* investigate certain people, simply because you insist," I replied, stepping out after him. "The investigation loses integrity that way."

John started for the front doors while saying, "I'll worry about Ethan. You worry about— Marion!"

Said man appeared as we turned the corner. He stood in front of the glass doors, bundled in his winter coat. He raised his mouth from the folds of his scarf, politely greeting John. And unlike earlier, when I might as well have been invisible on set, Marion's gaze zeroed in on me like a gunshot to the chest.

"Get home safe, honey," John told Marion as he brushed past and opened the doors.

"Yes, you too, John," Marion called. He never took his eyes off me.

This man was not making my job easy.

The cold air from outside ruffled Marion's hair before the doors fell shut. He smiled and said, "I washed my hands earlier. Must have missed you."

"Sorry about that. I was bonding with the Key PA."

"Davey. Did you braid his beard?"

I laughed. "Had a smoke."

"Are you two BFFs now?"

"No. He still hates me."

Marion clucked his tongue. His eyes glimmered, and I *knew* I was being laughed at.

"What're you doing?" I asked him.

Marion jutted a thumb over his shoulder at the doors. "Waiting for my ride." He added after a brief pause, "You weren't outside. I didn't think you'd left yet, so I waited here."

Fuck. This wasn't fair. And *that*, in and of itself, was a childish thought, fueled by nothing but primal desire and frustrating, professional limitations. I'd never been so keenly attracted to someone as I was to Marion. Every man I'd been with, from the onset, I knew—hell, *expected*—to be an ex. But I didn't feel that inevitable finale when I stared at Marion's sweet, charming face.

And that I was thinking about a tomorrow with him when there wasn't even a now was…absurd.

When had I become this? A man brought to his knees by a bit of harmless flirting from someone a decade younger. It had to be some instinctual, rebellious action because my brain knew I couldn't have Marion. Because there was a case. Boundaries between us. And after I wrapped everything up, the only place I'd see Marion would be on television reruns.

Except…that hurt.

Hurt like hell to think about.

"Don't stop flirting." Marion's voice broke through the cascade of self-deprecating thoughts. "I was having fun."

I could lose my job—my career—by screwing around with him.

And yet, the foundation of the wall between us was eroding as if having been battered by relentless tides for a century. Right now, *right here*, I could so easily convince myself to have fun tonight.

John had made it clear he didn't want me treating Marion Roosevelt as a suspect. And did I even believe him to be one?

No.

Not really.

Not at all, actually.

Marion was an actor. He gave no hints that he desired to be anything else. He appeared to love what he did. And Marion was a darling to John, to the rest of the cast, to all of the crew. Even some lowly, nobody PA on his first day. And to top it all off, he clearly had unresolved issues with Ethan, who'd made my lifelong shit list.

He deserved to have his kindness returned.

I stepped closer and carefully leaned into his space. He didn't move away. So I kissed his smooth cheek.

Marion studied the linoleum floor. "That was the sweetest letdown I've ever had."

"I'm sorry," I whispered.

He looked up. "I thought for sure I had a chance to figure out who Rory Byrne was."

"It's not you."

"Ah." Marion shrugged a little. Smiled a little. Broke my heart a little. "They always say that."

I touched his chin. Just a fingertip. But he looked at me again. "It's *not* you," I reiterated. I kissed his mouth. Soft full lips worked in contrast to the hard lines of Marion's jawline and cheekbones.

I backed away.

And left.

* * * * *

I recycled empty Altoids tins.

They could be turned into basically anything.

I sat at the table, Optivisor pulled down over my glasses as I stripped the ends of two cables to solder onto a panel small enough to fit into the box. This was the third solar-powered USB charger I'd built since getting home.

The television murmured on the other side of the room. Some show called *New York, New York*. I didn't know anything about it beyond: canned laughter sitcom and Marion Roosevelt's first big break. According to IMDb, anyway. He'd come out in real life after the second season aired, à la Ellen DeGeneres, so said one comment. Marion was several years younger, practically baby-faced. But he still knew how to steal the camera in every scene.

"Jack's gay?" a woman asked, question delivered in over-the-top comedic acting.

I glanced up, raised the visor, and watched Jack—Marion's character—sink into a couch as two friends argued on either side of him.

"*Did you not just see the man attached to Jack's face? It was like something out of* Alien," the second actor countered.

Insert audience laughter.

She looked down at Jack. "*Is this true?*"

Jack stared up at her. "*You know how you hate my dad jokes?*"

"*Yeah.*"

"*When I have a family, my kids will hate them twice as much.*"

More laughter.

Marion was a good comedian, even when he had a shitty script to work with.

I heard the *schiiik* of a key being inserted into the front-door lock, and turned in time to see the apartment door open and my most recently acquired ex step inside. I took off the visor as I quickly stood. "Nate?"

"Hi, honey." He shut the door.

I held my hand out. "Key."

Nate ignored the demand, unbuttoned his coat, and walked to the couch while watching the flickering TV screen. "Are you really watching this show?" He picked up the remote from one of the cushions and turned the television off. "It's awful."

"It's not bad," I countered.

Nate turned toward me, rolling his eyes. "And if I'd said it was great, you'd have said it was shit."

"Why are you here?" I asked sternly.

He approached, drew close, and placed his hands low on my hips. "We broke up."

"Right."

"So—"

"I'm not interested."

Nate blindly reached down to grope me through my jeans. "You feel interested."

I grabbed his wrist and pulled his hand away. "Not with you."

He huffed and stepped back. "You have something more pressing to do than getting some no-strings-attached sex?" Nate laughed and held his hands up to interrupt anything I may have tried to say. "*Sorry.* I forgot. You're too busy working. What's the investigation this week? Undercover work as a drummer for some punk band that meets in mom's basement?" He motioned to the worn-out clothes I was still wearing from all day on set. "And what about next week? CPA? Stock trader on Wall Street? Living out of your car while you track—"

"*Nate.*"

"You need to get a fucking life," he shouted.

"Did you come here to fight with me?" I asked calmly.

He might as well have not heard me. "I think it's disconcerting," Nate began, "that in the three months we dated I never knew what in your closet was actually something *Rory Byrne* would wear to the grocery store."

I crossed my arms over my chest, keenly aware of the defensive posture I was taking with him. "I have my groceries delivered."

Nate raised his hands like he wanted to wrap them around my throat. "Your only friend is a cat. Your one hobby is studying wiring diagrams. Every scenario that doesn't play out according to the Dupin Decree, you say fuck it. You only live once and *this is it?*" He looked around the room—a bachelor pad in every sense—and snorted.

I pointed at Nate and said in a collected tone, "I have one rule I live by."

"That's bullshit and you know it. Your life is defined by a rulebook, Rory. You enforce *no lying*, which is pretty fucking ironic considering that's all you do for a living. I mean—who are you? *Really?* So I screwed around. But in our three months, were you ever once *yourself* with me?" Nate reached into his coat pocket and threw the house key at me.

I caught it against my chest and watched him storm to the door. "Hey—"

"Get bent." He slammed the door behind him.

INT. CHAPTER SIX – DAY

I didn't sleep Wednesday night because of Talking Heads.

The band, that is.

"This Must Be the Place" was running on a nonstop loop in my mind, which considering I'd probably last heard that song in 1988... I don't know. I couldn't even remember the lyrics properly.

Something about no money. Always for love.

La, la, la...find me or you?

No.

Did I find you?

Something like that.

But it wasn't a coincidence—being stuck wide-awake in bed, humming the tune to an uncertain and uncomfortable love song while I mentally tended to the wounds Nate burned into my heart. In the solitude and darkness of night, I couldn't dispute his accusations. I used my profession as a yardstick, keeping at bay anything and everything that threatened to make me lose control.

To such an extreme, that I had instead lost my *life*.

Nate was right.

I didn't have friends. I didn't take in the sights of the city. I didn't take a chance on the guy flashing enough signals that he could have landed a jumbo jet, because...why? I'd seen enough shitty human behavior over the last twenty years and wanted to protect myself? At the cost of not experiencing love at all?

I guess, in a sense, I *was* a professional liar. And it was fucking screwed up that I could spin an untrue story to Marion as quickly and easily as breathing, but I couldn't have a drink with the man because my job said no—*he* might be *lying*.

It was barely after seven in the morning, but I was already stalking through staging. Past crafty, I turned down the back corridor and walked along the hall of dressing rooms. I stopped outside the closed door marked with Marion's name and knocked loudly before I could stop myself.

Before I could doubt myself.

"Come in," came a muffled response.

I grabbed the knob and opened the door.

Feeble, wintry sunlight was peeking in through partially closed blinds. An early morning talk show whispered from the television mounted on the wall. Marion stood in front of a full-length mirror, tugging suspenders over his shoulders.

He turned, looked surprised. "Rory—"

I shut the door, walked across the room, took Marion's face into my hands, and leaned down to kiss him. He opened to it without question, without coaxing. He tasted of coffee and something sweet—like pancakes and syrup. Marion drew his hands up my biceps, squeezed, and then settled them around my neck.

He fit against my body as if he were made for no man but me.

I broke the kiss, drew back enough to touch my nose against his, then pressed our foreheads together. "I made a mistake."

"Did you?"

"Last night. I shouldn't have…" I leaned back a little, stared at his mismatched eyes. "Think we could do another take?"

Marion's mouth quirked, then broke into a wide smile. "Lights."

"Camera."

"*Action.*"

"Can I take you out for drinks tonight?" I asked.

"I'd love that."

I kissed his mouth again, sealing the deal.

There was a loud knock at the door, followed by Ethan calling Marion's name.

Marion dropped his hands from me and took a quick look around the tiny room. "Shit." He moved to the standing shower, pulled the curtain back, and motioned me inside. "Get in. You're fired if he finds you in here."

I wanted to say, screw Ethan. Wanted to tell Marion then and there I wasn't a PA and not to worry about me. But even if I was going to throw caution to the wind and take him out tonight, I'd still been hired to do a job. It was one thing to blow my cover with Marion, and another entirely with a hothead I couldn't trust like Ethan. I obediently climbed into the shower and pulled the curtain.

I listened to Marion open the door, quickly followed by the scuff of steps and someone backing into a chair, wooden legs dragging across the linoleum.

"I don't have it," Marion said without prompting.

"Then what the fuck are you doing?"

"I'm getting ready for my job, Ethan," Marion said firmly.

The sound of bodily wrestling nearly undid me—the thought of Ethan trying to manhandle Marion against his will making me see red. My heart pounded in my throat as I debated for a split second whether to jump out of the stall and smash his face in with my fist.

"I made you," Ethan hissed. "And I can ruin you. Don't forget that."

Another shove, and this time it sounded as if Marion hit the floor. Steps drew close to the shower, continued past, and retreated out of the dressing room. The door slammed shut.

I left the stall in a rush to find Marion sitting on the floor. His knees were partially drawn to his chest. "Did he hurt you?" I bent down, took his hands, and pulled Marion to his feet in one quick, fluid motion.

"I'm fine."

I barely heard him over the roar of blood pumping in my ears. I took his face into my hands, inspecting him for any visible damage. "What did he want?" I asked, tone severe and clipped as I struggled with unexpected anger.

"Nothing," Marion insisted. "Please—don't worry about it." He put his hands over mine, pulled them away, and stood on his toes to kiss me. "He's an arrogant asshole. I can handle Ethan."

Marion was lying.

I didn't need deception training to know that.

* * * * *

I'd left Marion alone at his insistence that he was quite fine and needed to get into makeup. But I wasn't happy. At all. Which is why when I came around the corner and saw John at crafty, I made a beeline for him at the expense of the actual task I was being paid to do.

"John. We need to talk," I said when I reached his side.

John looked sideways as he filled a cup with coffee from the airpot. "Oh. You've got an update?"

"No." I shook my head.

"You've got to give me something," he murmured, grabbing a handful of Sweet'N Low packets. "I'm going stir-crazy."

He was not getting any names. Not until I had my Hercule Poirot moment. Because the second John knew about any suspicions I might have, he'd act differently around those individuals. It wouldn't be his fault—human nature and all. But if the thief was smart, the change in John's behavior would be the warning bell to get the hell out of Dodge before I was able to pin them to the wall.

"I'm considering several individuals," I answered. "And that's all I can say at this moment."

"I don't like being told no," John remarked, dumping the artificial sweetener into the black coffee. He stirred the concoction with a plastic spoon before giving me another look.

"You'll like a compromised investigation even less."

"Then what did you want to talk about?" His voice dropped to an almost inaudible whisper when a few crew members entered the staging area from behind us before retreating to the art department's workshop. John took a sip of coffee, made a disgusted face, and started walking away.

I caught up with him in a few easy strides. "Ethan," I said.

"Didn't we discuss him last night?"

"We did," I agreed, following John into the hall and on toward the production office.

"Then why are we revisiting an old conversation?"

"I'm sorry you don't want to hear this, but the reality is, he's a caustic—"

"Randy," Laura exclaimed as we approached her desk. She looked to have just arrived herself, taking off her coat and shoving her purse into a drawer. Her lips were an almost neon pink today.

I paused midstep. *"Rory,"* I corrected.

She waved a hand, picked up a sheet of paper with the other, and held it out. "Close enough. I need a hundred copies of tomorrow's sides. Distro when you're done."

"What?"

"I've got to make a phone call," John said as a means of excusing himself.

"Hold on— John!" I said after him.

"I need these right away," Laura interrupted.

Fuck.

I took the sheet from her with a snap of my wrist and walked past her desk as John shut his office door. The same young man—the fellow PA who'd been forever relegated to office duties—glanced my way from where he was once again leaning against the top of the copier. He took note of the paperwork I held, then pointed down the long, dim hall.

"The other—"

"Slow as hell, I know," I muttered, marching by.

I passed the closed office doors, the darkened editing suite, and went to the lone photocopier in the unused portion of office space. It was especially eerie in the morning, with hardly a sliver of weak sunlight reaching between the tightly drawn blinds on windows. I opened the top of the machine, put the sheet down on the glass, tapped buttons more forcefully than necessary, and took a step away as the copier coughed to life.

I hadn't even made it to the tenth copy when a prickle of discomfort began to make itself known, tip-tapping along my spine and causing the hair on my neck stand on end. I glanced to the right. Lights and the voices of staffers seemed so far away, encased safely in a bubble I was given no access to. I looked to my left, studying the dark expanse, the nothingness broken only by the shapes of haphazardly placed furniture.

I wasn't alone.

Taking another step back from the copier, I walked farther into the shadows, to the very end of the room, and took a peek around the corner where construction tarps blocked access.

Nothing and no one.

But the distinct edge of uneasiness was still there. Like a dull blade digging between my shoulder blades. I took a few careful steps through the office space before the loud crackle of an open walkie shattered the eerie silence.

"Anyone got eyes on Davey?" the voice of a crew member came through.

I followed the tinny sound into the farthest corner of the room.

Davey was dead on the floor, unwrangled phone cable wrapped around his neck.

INT. CHAPTER SEVEN – DAY

"Rory Byrne," a plainclothes officer said as he was shown into a conference room inside *The Bowery*'s office. He reached a hand out. "It's been a hot minute."

"A few years," I agreed, quickly shaking Detective Grey's hand. A lifetime ago, we'd been briefly...acquainted. But like all my relationships, it'd gone the way of the dodo.

"What the hell mess you get involved with now?" Grey asked. He turned and watched through the glass wall as a medical examiner, flanked by uniformed officers, wheeled a gurney down the hall. John and Laura were hot on their heels before the producer gave an instruction that sent Laura to make phone calls at her desk, directly across from us. Damage control for the production, no doubt. John disappeared out of view as he rushed after the ME. Grey looked at me again.

"Theft," I stated. "John Anderson is my client."

Grey put a hand on the back of a chair. "So is this an unfortunate coincidence or relevant to your case?"

"The victim was actually my number-one person of interest," I answered, keeping one eye on Laura over Grey's shoulder. "So I'd say it's pretty relevant."

"Sorry."

I crossed my arms and leaned back against the far wall. "It obviously wasn't him."

"Hmm. What's this do for your pool of suspects?"

"I've still got a few."

Two, really. Ethan Lefkowitz was going to remain a suspect until I could piece together his hostility toward talent—Marion especially. And Laura Turner, based on the fact that she flanked John's office, that I'd not been able to prove her innocence via the current timetables, and that she harbored an intense dislike for set crew in particular, which was decidedly strange.

Grey took out a notepad from his coat. "Mind if we play Twenty Questions?"

"Please do. I'm still undercover and may be able to salvage this case."

He shot me an amused smile. "You'd have made a better cop, you know."

I shrugged and adjusted my glasses. "I don't like guns."

Grey set his pen to paper. "What time did you get in?"

"Around 7:15 a.m."

"And you found the victim when?"

I pulled back the sleeve of my shirt and checked the time. "Around 7:30 a.m.; Davey—the deceased—has a 7:00 a.m. call-time. I didn't check in with him when I arrived, so I'm not sure what his movements were prior to death."

Grey took a folded sheet out of his pocket and waved it idly. "Mr. Anderson has already provided me with this."

I pushed off the wall and snatched the paper. It was cast and crew call-times for that Thursday. "Can I borrow your pen?" I took the offering, leaned over the table, and began to cross off names. "John is not a suspect. Mr. Roosevelt was in his dressing room—"

"Marion Roosevelt," Grey agreed, watching me mark up the list. "He looks hot as hell in the promos for this show. Is he really as short as they say he is?"

I glanced at Grey over the rim of my glasses. "Yes," I answered brusquely, returning to the call-times. "Mr. Lefkowitz... I had, well, ears on him." *Unfortunately.* I circled a few more names and handed back the paper. "These ones with circles—you've got a few PAs who may have seen Davey come through the office. And he was certainly with someone, unless he strangled himself." I said that last part dryly.

"He might have," Grey stated.

I shook my head. "No. This was a murder."

"When folks have a mind to end it...they find a way."

"This isn't a suicide," I insisted.

Grey stared at me for a beat, offered a sympathetic expression, then said, "The ME will decide that. In the meantime, I'm going to have to shut down production, at least for today. I've got to get CSU down here to comb over the scene."

"That's highly problematic for me."

"A death trumps robbery, Byrne."

* * * * *

I could hear John speaking, his voice bouncing off the walls of staging as the remaining office staff and I were escorted from the area by the police. I poked my head into the doorway to see him addressing the entire cast and crew from set. Every single person listened in utter silence. I stepped quietly into the massive room, moved closer, and identified a few fellow PAs among the crowd. Grief-stricken, confused, one was even crying.

The reactions of those immediately under Davey's power-tripping little fingers all appeared sincere in their upset. Good for them—they weren't suspects in the murder as far as I was concerned. Bad for me—because they weren't suspects in the murder.

"Rory," someone whispered.

I quickly turned to my left and looked down at Marion. His expression was disorganized heartache and a failing attempt at remaining stoic. "You okay?" I murmured.

He nodded, indicated toward John, and stepped closer to me.

John was saying, "The police have informed me that we will be closed down for the day." The crew finally began to mutter among one another. "People—*people*! Please. I know this is unprecedented. There's a deadline for the show, folks are working under contracts, and we all need our paychecks. But we are obligated to accommodate the needs of New York's finest as they investigate what happened to one of our own."

"How'd he die?" someone asked.

"I heard he hanged himself," another called.

John put both hands up. Even from the back of the throng, I could see his round face breaking out in a sweat. "We all want answers," he insisted loudly over the raised voices. "But it can't come from us. We must let the police do their job so we can come back and do ours and make Davey proud with a complete season of *The Bowery*."

"This is like that *Supernatural* episode," someone in front of me muttered.

"The what?" a coworker whispered back.

"Where on-set deaths finally shut down production, but really no one cares, they just want to do their job. It was a funny one."

"Dude. Davey is dead."

"*I know...*"

I felt Marion take my hand into his own, squeezing tightly.

John continued, "Don't call us, we'll call you." He reached into a pocket for his handkerchief. "And we will all get back to work as soon as humanly possible."

Marion let go of my hand as cast and crew began to turn around and head toward the door immediately behind us. He took a deep breath and ran his fingers through his hair. "A hell of a day, and it's hardly ten," he said, eyes cast down. His face had a decidedly gray shade to it. "I guess this puts a damper on our drinks."

I started to agree. Because that would have been following the rules.

"*No,*" I abruptly answered.

Marion looked up. "No?" he repeated, confused.

"No," I said again. "We—we should still go out."

He raised one finely shaped eyebrow.

"You only live once."

Marion cracked a smile. "That's true, I suppose." He looked at the folks shuffling around us to the doorway to go home, then nodded. "All right. Let me change out of costume."

"Sure. I'll be here." I watched Marion head in the opposite direction of the crowd, pass crafty, and disappear down the side hall. I retrieved my phone from my pocket, walked to the far corner for a bit of privacy, and dialed Violet Shelby.

"Morning, Rory," she answered. Never *good morning*. Shelby was a realist.

"Ma'am, there's been a situation."

"Report."

"Murder. Well, I'm certain it will be a murder once the ME files the paperwork." I glanced over my shoulder at the handful of folks left standing around John. "Davey—Key PA. He was my first boss in the film hierarchy."

"Was he a suspect?"

"My most likely candidate."

Shelby muffled a curse. "What happened?"

"It's unclear. There's a branch off the production office that's unused due to partial renovation. I found him in the corner on the floor, a bunch of phone cords wrapped around his neck."

"Jesus. How're *you*?"

"Fine, ma'am."

"Yeah?"

"It's not my first dead body. I'm okay, really. But it throws a hell of a wrench into the works. Davey had motive, means, and he even talked about a recently acquired project that was going to get him into the big leagues."

"Guilty innocence," Shelby said thoughtfully, almost to herself.

"The police are shutting down production for the day," I continued. "Someone killed him. I know it. And that person works for the show. There's a chance it's unrelated to the theft, but given my own belief that Davey possessed the missing script, I don't put much stock into these being two distinct events."

"I'm inclined to agree. Listen, Rory...you be careful. Someone at Kaufman is so desperate for their fifteen minutes, they're willing to lie, steal, and kill. If your cover is blown—"

"It won't be," I said with absolute certainty. "Twenty years, ma'am. Have some faith in me."

"I've never doubted you."

I looked toward John again. He was mopping his face with the handkerchief while talking with Ethan and two other department heads. The director's body language was interesting. He was rigid. Taut, like a rubber band about to snap. Ethan spoke with his hands, gesturing with concentrated intensity.

I took a few steps to the side to change my angle.

Ethan's pant leg was discolored over his right knee, and a dusty white clung to the material.

"Rory?" Shelby's voice in my ear jerked me back to the conversation.

"Sorry. What was that?" I turned away, saw Marion returning in street clothes.

"I want you to keep me updated. I'll phone Anderson, but let me—"

"I will," I said hastily. "I need to go, ma'am."

"Good luck," she said and ended the call without another word.

I put my phone in my pocket, fetched my coat from the crew lockers nearby, and pulled my arms through as Marion shot me a smile while walking past me. I discreetly followed him out of staging, down the hall, and to the elevator. We rode to the first floor in silence, stepped out the front doors and into the now-bright, crisp-cold morning.

"Do you like beer?" Marion asked.

"For breakfast?"

He laughed a little, looked up at me, and squinted one eye as the sun hit him just right. "Steinway Bierhaus is only two blocks from here. They serve a mean pint-and-pretzel combo."

"This is a film neighborhood," I started. "You don't mind being seen out with a guy?"

"I think the industry as a whole would be more shocked if I was out with a woman."

I stopped at the end of the block. "You know what I mean."

"Not if you don't care."

It felt liberating to say, "I don't."

We walked the rest of the way in a comfortable, companionable silence. Marion kept his hands tucked into his pockets, shoulder bumping into me now and again. I took a deep breath of cold air scented with exhaust, garbage, and road salt, then draped my arm across his shoulders. Marion tucked into my side. Warm and perfect.

A feeling of respite came over me. A calmness and gentleness that in all my forty-plus years I couldn't ever recall experiencing quite like this moment. That it was okay to need this—human touch and tenderness—even in the midst of a job. *Despite* the job. I could uncover a thief, stop a killer, and still take a moment to love a man.

I could take a moment to live.

We entered Steinway Bierhaus, and a *whoosh* of warm air hit my face. I followed Marion up the steps from the front door. He gave a friendly hello to a man putting away glasses at a bar well stocked with high-end spirits, then led the way into a large communal drinking hall. Multiple big-screen televisions were turned on, each playing a different sports channel. A scattering of customers sat on benches at the long tables, mostly eating, but a few shared pitchers of beer while glued to a hockey game.

Marion stopped at a counter on one end of the room, ordered for us both, and insisted on paying. I took the glasses of beer and followed him to a table near the back windows that was completely empty. He set the basket of hot pretzels and mustard down, unbuttoned his coat, and piled the winter garments beside him on the seat. I sat next to him and slid a beer over.

Marion accepted the drink, considered for a moment, then raised it. "To Davey."

I nodded and tapped my glass against his.

Marion took a sip and said, "It isn't selfish to not want to think about it, is it?"

"No," I quickly answered. "Dwelling on death never helped anyone."

He reached for a pretzel. "I never would have guessed you were a PA when I first saw you." Marion dunked one end into the container of mustard and took a bite. "I noticed you on set, when you first arrived."

"Did you?"

"You carry a lot of confidence." He sucked the salt off his thumb and then motioned to his shoulders. "Here. But you weren't dressed like a producer. I thought, perhaps a stand-in gaffer for an episode."

"Why's that?"

"They're usually big guys like you." Marion reached for my hand, turned it palm up, and stroked my fingers. "But when I shook your hand—too soft."

"You *are* observant," I answered, my heart thudding hard.

"I told you," Marion said with that cute grin. "I've been racking my brain, trying to figure out what you did before deciding to toss your hat into the film industry." He tore off another bite-size piece of pretzel, coated it liberally in mustard, and ate it. "It wasn't a physical-labor job."

I shook my head. "No."

"But not paper-pushing like an accountant either."

"No."

"So what?"

I turned my hand over to cover his. "Promise me it remains between us?"

The delight in Marion's face waned a little, but he tried for a casual tone. "Was it porn?"

I laughed. "Definitely not."

"All right. I'm officially stumped."

"I don't work in the film industry. I'm not really a PA."

Marion cocked his head. "I'm confused."

"I'm a private investigator. I'm working undercover on set." I removed my wallet before Marion could ask another question, and showed him my PI license. "I work for Dupin Private Investigations."

The blood had all but drained from Marion's face. "Why—I mean—what are you investigating?"

I snapped my wallet shut. "A theft."

"Theft?" he echoed in a whisper.

"Of a script."

"The— *John's* script?"

My heart missed a beat. "You know about that?"

Marion stared at his beer. He rubbed his hands up and down his thighs. "He's talked about it."

"To who?"

But Marion shook his head. "It was at our Christmas party. John was drunk—first time I'd ever seen him have more than one glass. He doesn't hold his drink very well." Marion glanced at me. "John told me about it. He might have said something to James, my costar. I...I mentioned it in passing to Ethan. I don't know if John told anyone else at the party."

I shifted on the bench, put a leg on either side, and took Marion's hand in mine. I gave it a firm squeeze. "I need to know who'd steal that script."

"I don't know."

"Marion—"

"I don't!" he insisted. His hand was clammy. "Why would I?"

"Because you're perceptive," I answered quietly.

"It wasn't me," he said hastily. "I would never."

"I know it wasn't you." After a pause, I asked, "But did Ethan?"

Marion's head jerked, and he looked at me. "No."

"Why are you lying about Ethan? You've been covering his behavior and protecting others since I met you."

"Don't worry about—"

"I have to," I replied. "He's a suspect."

Marion pulled his hand free, shifted to mimic my sitting position so that our knees bumped together, and said, "Ethan is an asshole. But I'm telling you, if that script is already missing, it's not because of him."

That was the truth.

A truth stuck in the middle of lies, but a truth nonetheless.

Marion reached up, scrubbed his face with both hands, and blinked his pretty eyes a few times. "I need this show," he said, voice low. "I can't give up Tommy's character. Being able to lose myself in him. He—he loves with a love that is more than love."

"Poe."

Marion flashed a weak smile. "There's a dichotomy to Tommy's character. He can be violent. Cruel, even. It's a cathartic experience...I need."

"Why?" I dared to question.

"Because I'm angry," Marion said, as if it were an admission of guilt. "And Tommy O'Sullivan gives me a constructive outlet to work through some shit."

"We all get angry."

Marion snorted. "We didn't all date Ethan Lefkowitz." He stared at me, and the grim line of his kissable mouth said a lot about what my facial reaction must have been. "So even if it means running interference and taking the brunt of his anger, fine. But I won't have this show taken away from me. I'm doing my best to keep James on for another season as it is. He's been thinking of quitting the industry altogether. It's important, you know?"

"What is?"

"That viewers see Tommy and Hugh together forever. It matters. To people like us. Doesn't it?"

My shoulders dropped a bit. I slipped my hands around Marion's wrists, petting his forearms. "It matters," I agreed.

"I understand you've been hired to do a job," he continued. "But please—don't do anything that would jeopardize this show."

"My ex," I murmured.

Marion glanced up. "What about him?"

"He made me angry too."

"Why? I mean, besides being an ex."

I slid my hands free, reached behind me for my peacoat, and removed the folded grocery list I'd been carrying for three days. I offered it to Marion.

He unfolded the note and laughed a little. "Oh...*Rory.*"

"I broke up with him in a text."

"Did he run over your mother?" Marion asked, his chuckle growing a bit stronger, more authentic.

"He broke my one rule."

"Which is?"

"Don't lie."

Marion sobered again. "Even a white lie?"

"If I fuck up the pancakes but you don't want to discourage my culinary interests, that's one thing. But if you lie and I catch you, I can't forgive that."

"I'd never deter a man from pursuing the perfect pancake." He folded the note, still staring at me. "Are you over your ex?"

"Oh yeah." I reached out, touched Marion's smooth cheek, traced an eyebrow. "Are you over yours?"

He tore the dipshit note into several pieces and tossed the confetti onto the tabletop. "I'm onto bigger and blonder things."

"Have you ever been to the Observation Deck of the Empire State Building?"

Marion looked particularly confused at the sudden subject shift. "*No...*" he drew out, almost as if it were a question.

"Me neither," I said. "I've lived here my entire life, and I've never gone to the top."

"So?"

I looked at the table, picked up my beer, and took a sip. "So let's do it."

INT. CHAPTER EIGHT – NIGHT

Wind in our hair on the eighty-sixth floor.

Bags of honey-roasted Nuts 4 Nuts.

Shopping at Macy's.

Too many Manhattans at dinner.

Caresses and kisses in the taxi to my apartment.

By nightfall, I was at the mercy of my own uninhibited desire. An animalistic lust so visceral, so *ancient*, it seemed to vibrate outward from the marrow of my bones. My entire body thrummed like a musical instrument. And every chord, every note, played only for Marion.

Coats lay scattered down the hallway in our wake.

Marion bumped into the bedroom doorframe, then the door. His arms were wrapped around my neck, mouth hard and insistent on my own. I shoved the door open with one hand and used my body to push Marion into the room. He hit the foot of the bed with the back of his legs and went down with a drunken laugh, taking me with him. I pressed my thigh against his crotch, threaded our fingers together to hold his hands above his head, and sucked hard on Marion's neck.

He gasped, writhed, thrust up against my thigh. "*Rory.*"

I let up on his neck, moved my hands to the hem of his long-sleeve shirt, and yanked it to his chest. Marion sat up so I could finish pulling it over his head. I wrenched myself free from my own shirt, and then pulled Marion up and against my chest. Flesh-to-flesh.

Soft skin, flexing muscles, and the unmistakable hardness of a man's body pressed so intimately against my own turned the flame inside me into a wildfire.

There was no stopping this.

Not until it burned me whole.

Marion shoved his hand between us, fondled me through my worn jeans, and whispered against my lips, "I want you to take me."

I moved my hands under Marion's ass and flipped him onto his back again. He let out another boyish laugh, and then it was a race to see who could unbutton their jeans the quickest. I leaned over to the nightstand, knocked off my alarm clock, hit the switch to the custom LED installation I'd built, and accidently set the room alight in muted, shifting-color palettes.

"Shit." I finally grabbed the handle on the drawer, opened it, and took out a box of condoms.

"Are we fucking inside a rainbow?" Marion laughed.

"Sorry, I—"

"Keep it on."

I found the lube and turned to look at him. The room was still dark, but the colored lights mounted to the corners of the walls and along the ceiling bathed Marion's naked body in soft, glowing hues of alternating reds, blues, purples, and greens. He met my look, grinned, and rolled onto his stomach in blatant invitation.

I got behind Marion, leaned over him, and we passed several drunken moments probing and stretching and caressing until he was a supple, quivering mess underneath me.

"R-Rory," he pleaded, sounding next to tears. "Not yet. Not like this."

I removed my fingers and smoothed his ass cheek with one hand. I shushed him, murmured sweet words against his neck as I kissed and sucked his skin. Marion's voice cracked and hitched. He arched his back and rubbed his ass against my pelvis.

I pushed back to meet him. "Think you're ready?"

"Please," he begged. "Be rough. I like it."

I could do that.

Sitting up, I opened a condom and rolled it over myself. With one hand holding the base of my cock and the other firmly planted between Marion's shoulder blades, I rocked my hips back and forth until I breached muscles and sank into his gorgeous ass.

"*Jesus.*" I leaned over Marion, got an arm under his chest to hold him flush against me, then shoved hard into the tight heat.

Marion cried loudly. He scrambled for purchase, grabbing at a pillow with one hand and the other reaching back, fingers digging into my hip hard enough to leave marks. "Oh God! Like that!"

I bit Marion's earlobe and murmured, "This what you wanted?"

It's what I've wanted.

"You're so big—don't—don't stop."

I grunted. "You gonna think about my cock tomorrow?"

I'll be thinking of you.

"Yes! Holy shit. Make me feel it." He turned his head, arched his neck, awkwardly kissed my mouth.

I sped up. The bed squeaked, and Marion's voice was hoarse with screams. "Don't forget who gave you this ride."

I can't not see you again. Please let there be a tomorrow for us.

My muscles burned. My breathing came out in harsh pants. I paused for a brief moment to collect myself.

"Wh-what're you doing?" Marion protested. He ground his hips roughly against the mattress. "I'm almost there!"

I tilted my head close and kissed him again. "Say my name," I demanded.

Marion looked utterly wild in the psychedelic lighting. His hair was in complete disarray, and his two-toned eyes black, pupils blown wide with hunger and want. "Rory," he said obediently. "*Rory*, please. Let me be the best you've had."

Then he flexed his muscles around my dick, and I groaned. I let go of him, pushed up onto my fists, and used the bed as leverage to screw Marion into next week. Orgasm hit me like a horse kick to the chest.

Powerfully.

Violently.

A release so good, so euphoric, it fucking hurt. An experience like nothing I'd ever had with a partner in all my life. I slid out, lifted up Marion's ass, and reached under to help him finish.

But the bed was already wet with his cum.

* * * * *

Beep. Beep. Beep.

I opened my eyes and regretted the decision nearly immediately.

The room was still awash in neon colors.

My mouth tasted like I'd been licking a wet dog.

And my head was thudding, each pound a reminder that I was too old to abuse whiskey the way we had last night.

Beep. Beep. Beep.

I rolled over to smack the clock, then remembered it was on the floor. I leaned down, blindly hit a few buttons—which, after I turned the radio on and adjusted the volume to a morning talk show, managed to turn the alarm off.

"Marilyn Monroes are delicious," Marion murmured, his voice slurred as he spoke into a pillow.

"How many did you have?" I asked, gingerly putting a hand to my forehead.

"One bottle of champagne's worth," he answered, still unmoving. "Four ounces per cocktail...so six Monroes. And a dozen maraschino cherries."

"Hedonist."

Marion laughed a little. He rolled onto his back and looked at me. "You look like you got rode hard and put away wet."

"I had several Manhattans."

"I drank more than you."

"I'm a dozen maraschino cherries older too." I slowly sat up, swung my legs over the edge of the bed, and took a moment to gather my balance before I fell off the side of the world. "I can't believe I remembered what apartment I lived in."

"I'm glad this one is yours. Otherwise, whoever owns this bed would be pissed."

I grunted and got to my feet. I felt around the floor a moment, tugged on my jeans from last night, found my glasses, and stumbled out of the room. I made a quick stop in the bathroom, relieved myself, brushed my teeth, and splashed several handfuls of cold water on my face before continuing to the kitchen. My bare chest pimpled from the coolness in the air, and I stopped long enough to adjust the thermostat on the wall.

Gary stood on the kitchen counter, looking harassed, despite the crossed eyes. He meowed loudly and paced back and forth.

"Morning, baby." I kissed his head. "I'm sorry. Daddy had—a night out." I fetched Gary's food, refilled his bowl, and set it beside the water dish.

While the cat ate, coffee brewed and I blundered my way through cooking an entire frying pan full of bacon and eggs. Anything to sop up the last of the alcohol in my system, especially if John ended up calling the crew back to Kaufman today. As the food popped and sizzled, I finally heard Marion leave the bedroom, pad down the hall, and come to a stop at the kitchen doorway in nothing but boxer briefs and my T-shirt from last night, a few sizes too large for him.

"I can't find my shirt," he stated, running his hand through his dated and currently disheveled haircut.

It wasn't until that moment that I understood the whole straight-guy thing—why they loved their girlfriends wearing their too-big-for-them shirts and how their ladies straddled the adorable yet positively fuckable line. Because Marion might have looked as if he was wearing a bag, but it was definitely waking certain bodily responses in me.

"You look better in that."

He gave me a lopsided smile before glancing at the coffee pot. "Mugs?" He pointed to the cupboard above, and I nodded. Marion retrieved two, set them on the counter, then helped himself to the fridge for cream. "John hasn't called, has he?"

I took one of the cups he offered and had a sip before saying, "I don't think so. But if you couldn't find your shirt, I don't have high hopes for my phone."

Marion chuckled. He studied the decal on his coffee mug for a beat, looked back at the magnets covering the stainless-steel fridge, then said, "You really like cats."

"I really like cats," I agreed. "Gary's around here somewhere. He doesn't like new people."

Marion poked his head back out of the kitchen doorway. "Oh. That would be the sweet, blue-eyed baby giving me stink-eye."

"That's him." I grabbed two plates from the nearby cupboard and started shoveling fried food onto them. I gave Marion one, looked over his shoulder at the table covered in my techy supplies, and cursed.

Marion set the plate on the counter. "Don't worry about it." He hoisted himself up, put his plate in his lap, and took a bite of crispy bacon.

"Sorry," I said. "I'm really not used to guys spending the night and staying for a breakfast that should be eaten at a table the next morning."

"Should I have left already?"

I shook my head and put a hand on his bare thigh. "No." I kissed his lips and licked off a flake of bacon.

Marion was staring intensely as I pulled back. "Can I ask you something? Get the serious shit out of the way before it gives me anxiety?"

"All right…"

"Do you regret last night?"

"No," I said again. "Do you?"

Marion quickly shook his head. "But I…like you. I think a lot more than I've let on." He set the plate aside, licked his lips nervously, and put his hands on my chest.

I stared at Marion's bright, mismatched eyes. His expression was…so human. Not acting human. It wasn't that perfect. It wasn't choreographed or *in the moment*. He didn't know the lines of this scene unfolding before us.

His expression faltered, hesitated, but more than anything, there was a vulnerable hopefulness twinkling in those green and brown eyes.

"Go ahead," I prodded.

Marion's fingers tensed a little against my muscles. "Could we do it again? I don't only mean the sex, but yeah, that was good. I mean—all of it. I think yesterday was the best date I've ever had."

I put my hands over Marion's and realized he could feel my heart pounding against my rib cage. I released a breath, and simultaneously, his fingers relaxed. He petted instead of digging his fingers into my flesh.

"It was the best I've had too," I whispered.

INT. CHAPTER NINE – DAY

"Don't you speak that way to me, Tommy O'Sullivan! You might blaspheme in front of the lads, but I ain't one of them," Marion's costar ordered, in character as Hugh.

The entire set was silent. Engrossed. Mesmerized by Marion and James lost in a moment of intensity as longtime lovers. I stood near the back, behind the sound cart with Paul, holding my breath as I watched *Tommy* pace like a caged animal. His agitation and anger were palpable, and the focused conflict between the two men spread outward until every crew member on set seemed to be scratching at some unpleasant itch on their bodies.

As expected, John had been given a conditional all-clear by the NYPD that morning. Department heads phoned crew and cast in for a ten o'clock call-time, which set the production behind schedule about thirteen hours since the day before, but it was better than nothing, I figured. Marion took a taxi from my place to his for a shower and change of clothes, and I, having left my car at the garage in Queens the day before, took the subway into Astoria. The next time I saw Marion since closing the apartment door behind him was in this scene, literally vibrating with negative energy he released through Tommy.

It was one thing to watch such masterful acting on a screen, removed from the moment. But experienced firsthand…frankly, it was overwhelming.

Tommy pushed his suit coat back and settled his hands on his hips as he came to an abrupt stop. He stared at the floor.

Hugh stepped forward, took Tommy by the chin, and had to grab his shoulder when the gang leader physically recoiled. "Stop fightin' me," he whispered.

Tommy's Adam's apple bobbed painfully. He looked up, eyes glossy with unfallen tears of rage. "Some days I hate you," he said in an Irish accent intentionally bastardized to convey years of living in America.

"Aye," Hugh answered with a small nod. "But you love me in the night." He kissed Tommy, hard and aggressive.

"Cut!" Ethan shouted. "Print that!" He stood from his chair.

Paul whistled to himself while removing his headphones. *"Jesus Christ, can Marion act."*

The entire crew seemed to let out a collective breath when the two actors stepped away from one another. The assistant director announced twenty minutes for lights and camera to prep for the next angle. The technicians had a job to do, so no one questioned the directions as they descended onto the scenery. But there was most assuredly a somberness to their moods, and the complexity and seriousness of this scene weren't helping to lighten hearts any. Orders being barked in film-set lingo had a heaviness to them. I hadn't seen many, if any, people smiling or joking so far that day.

"The crew is taking Davey's passing pretty hard," I said, glancing down at Paul.

He leaned back in his chair to stare up at me. "Ah, well, a crew is like a family. Sort of like Thanksgiving. You've got all these competing personalities forced together, and everyone needs to get along and not upset Grandma. You've got that one uncle who has been drinking since noon, and there's also the cousin who brags about everything, and sooner or later you're going to reach over the table and sucker-punch them... But you're still a family. Everyone's saying Davey hanged himself in that back office."

Not true.

But Paul thought it was gospel.

Detective Grey had felt it was a likely scenario too.

It wasn't. I was *certain*. But for now, having near a hundred folks think it was self-inflicted was better than them realizing a murderer worked alongside them.

"Who's saying that?" I asked.

Paul shrugged. "I dunno. Everyone."

"I see."

"It's a hell of a way to call it quits," Paul said sadly.

"Rory!" I looked ahead and toward the left. John was sitting in his chair, phone to one ear, waving for me to come hither.

"I'll be right back," I said, patting Paul's shoulder. I sidestepped a few crew members and frowned as I approached John. "What's wrong?"

He put a hand over the phone's mouthpiece and whisper-spoke, "I need you to do me a quick favor."

"John."

"I know, I know. You're an *I* not an *A*," he said. "But we're really scrambling today."

I crossed my arms and begrudgingly asked, "What do you need?"

"*What?*" John returned his focus to his phone call, leaving me hanging. "No, no. Meredith… When the NYPD storms the house and shuts production down… Hopes and dreams aren't a practical insurance."

While waiting for John to tear himself away from the argument he was getting into over money, time, contracts, and whatever other problems producers got paid big bucks to untangle, I shot the actors a quick look. Costar James had taken a seat and accepted a water bottle from someone nearby. A makeup artist joined him to do light touch-ups after the hot and heavy kissing between him and—

I spun around where I stood, looking for Marion. He wasn't standing in Tommy O'Sullivan's parlor, and he wasn't seated with James, who was clearly waiting on the technical setup. I uncrossed my arms, took a few steps backward, and caught Marion speaking with Ethan farther away on the stage. He looked upset—pleading, even. Ethan dug his phone out of a pocket, turned the screen toward Marion, and the younger man sobered considerably at whatever he was staring at. He straightened his shoulders, nodded minutely, and started walking toward the side door.

"Striking!" a big guy's voice bellowed from nearby, and then a massive light turned on and completely blinded me. "PA! Don't look at the light when we call that."

"Yeah," I answered gruffly, blinking away the spots.

John grabbed my arm, another one of those not so subtle bicep appreciation squeezes. "My planner," he murmured, pulling the phone away from his ear very briefly. "On my desk."

With that dismissal from John, I picked my way around people and equipment and left the set. I made a quick detour, turned right, and slipped down the dressing-rooms hallway. I stopped outside Marion's door and knocked gently.

No response.

"Marion?" I called.

Nothing.

I tried the knob, found it unlocked, and the door swung open.

Empty.

Strange. I couldn't imagine he'd go anywhere else when taking the side exit, but maybe he was in the bathroom down the main corridor. Or even sneaked down to the loading dock for a smoke. Either seemed likely, considering the emotional high he'd been on, followed by yet another spat with Herr Director, so I shut the door and continued toward the production office.

"Randy," Laura stated as I entered.

"Rory," I corrected again, not stopping for any handout this time.

"Can I send you on a run?"

"I'm actually doing one for John at the moment, but I'll swing back in a bit," I replied.

Davey's death had really gotten me thinking. The lack of any real crossover between set and office—and what did exist with PAs, Davey and Laura had dissolved by relegating them to one location or the other—suggested to me that his killer worked with him.

That it'd be someone from set.

And that if his death and the missing script were indeed related, the killer could very likely *be* the thief.

Laura was one of my first suspects. She was higher up than Davey. She hadn't liked him. And her petty jealousy of even his lowly set position had been brought to my attention. But she wasn't a cold-blooded killer. That was simply not in her makeup as a human being. And yesterday morning she had only just arrived for the workday when we crossed paths. Her cheeks had still been flushed from the cold, for God's sake. There hadn't been time to overpower a bigger man and strangle him to death.

No. It wasn't her.

Both events originated with someone on set. I'd stake my reputation on it.

"How many people does John need doing errands for him?" she asked with a shake of her head.

I started to consider that muttered question, but as I stopped outside of John's office and opened the door, the words crumbled like ash from the tip of a cigarette.

Marion jerked his head up. He shut the bottom drawer of John's desk and quickly stood. "R-Rory."

Had he—?

Was he—?

"Wh-what are you doing here?" he stuttered.

I let go of the doorknob.

"*Wait.* It's not what you think." Marion moved around the desk to stop me from leaving.

I took a step back.

"Rory, please." Marion was following me out of the office.

I glanced over my shoulder, and a few of the staffers were looking up from their desks at us. Taking Marion by the arm, I quickly led him away from the open area, past Laura and the conference room, down the hall, and back to staging.

"Would you let go of me?" Marion protested.

"*No.*" My voice shook with even that one word as I tried to tamp down the rage boiling inside me. I could barely breathe the rest of the walk to his dressing room, which upon reaching, I shoved Marion inside and slammed the door shut behind us. "It was you this entire time?"

Marion swallowed hard and vehemently shook his head. "It wasn't. I swear to God."

"Where's the script, Marion?"

"I don't know!" he cried.

"Then why the hell were you in John's office?" I retorted. I'd been hurt in the past, but this betrayal was akin to my heart being torn from my chest. I was shaking with a mixture of fury and anguish and adrenaline. How could I be so *stupid.*

"It— I was— Because of Ethan," he said, voice trembling and lip quivering. Marion looked as if he were about to pass out. "I let him take…pictures. When we were dating."

"What kind of pictures?" I demanded.

Marion looked up. "The kind you blackmail someone over." He wiped angrily at his eyes. "He's refused to delete them, and now he's threatening to give them to tabloids if I don't steal John's script for him."

"You're lying."

"No!"

"I have one rule," I started, and my voice caught again. "I *told* you that."

"I never lied. I didn't tell you about… Those pictures are humiliating and embarrassing, and I'm trying to deal with the fallout of a bad breakup while working with my ex on a project that means more to me than the air in my lungs. I can't be faulted for that."

"If Ethan has the script—"

"He *doesn't*, Rory," Marion shouted. "You said the script was already stolen. And I told you last night, if it's gone, Ethan doesn't have it. And I know that because he's forcing *me* to do his bidding. He doesn't know it's already gone."

I stared at Marion for an intensely long, unnerving moment. "But you know it's gone."

He nodded weakly.

"Why are you bothering to raid John's private office?"

"For a copy," he admitted. "Or—or anything I could give Ethan to get him to *back off.* I'm desperate to save my career." Tears slipped down his face. "I want to be a man that younger people can look up to. And I can't do that while being plastered on grocery-store tabloids. I can't bear being the face of homophobic jokes and stereotypes." He wiped at his face again with the sleeve of his suit coat. "I'm worth a lot in the industry right now. Ethan wants to be attached to whatever project I take next. I kept telling him no. I wasn't going to abuse John's trust. I wasn't going to be Ethan's ticket to the top. But…"

I took a deep breath, distancing myself from Marion's grief. "Who has the script?"

"*I don't know,*" he said again. "I'm telling you the truth. Until you told me yesterday, I assumed John was still fiddling away at it." Marion reached out, but I stepped back. "Rory—*please.*"

"You've got to do better than that," I answered. "What about Davey?"

Marion's brows knitted together. "What about him?"

"Who killed him?"

"*Killed?* But I heard…people…they're saying he hanged—"

I shook my head.

Marion put a hand over his mouth. He turned quickly, knelt in front of a small desk overlooking the window, and was sick into the trash bin. Instinct took over hurt, and my need to ease Marion's discomfort forced my deadened feet to step forward. I crouched and put a hand on his back, soothing up and down. He wiped his mouth with a shaking hand before gripping the bin again like he feared there'd be a round two.

You couldn't fake this sort of response.

"Would Ethan kill someone?" I asked in a quiet tone. "Even if by accident?" Not that Davey's death was anything but intentional.

Marion didn't immediately respond, his silence speaking volumes more than his eventual words. "I don't…" He spit into the trash. "I'm not sure."

"Babe."

Marion looked at me again.

"What about James?"

"He'd be the last to steal a script. I'm serious. He's done with the industry. He wants to go into *construction*. Work for his brother's company."

"Then could someone else have overheard your conversations with Ethan? When he's been pressuring you to take the script?"

"No. We spoke in private."

"On set?" I clarified.

"Well, yes, I don't see him anywhere else. But no one would have heard—"

And it was like both of us came to the same startling conclusion at once.

I held my breath.

Marion snapped his mouth shut. He reached to his chest and very delicately touched his tie.

The microphone.

He reached around his back to unclasp the transmitter worn under his coat, which sent the audio wirelessly to Paul's receivers on the sound cart. Marion stared at the buttons for a moment, but I guess after having been wearing the gear for so many years, he knew how to turn them on and off.

"Could Paul have picked up our conversation this far from set?" I asked.

"Yeah, maybe," Marion said with a grimace. He glanced up from the device. "Sound recordists are supposed to turn our mics down between takes—no eavesdropping."

"But?"

"Paul's forgotten in the past. People make mistakes. I thought nothing of it," Marion explained.

I recalled the intense disagreement between Marion and Ethan I'd overheard through headphones the other day, regarding his costar's performance. If what Marion said was true, Paul should have known better then.

He should have turned the mics off, especially if Marion had caught him previously doing no such thing. So how often did he listen in on conversations he shouldn't have been privy to?

Had he overheard Ethan's demands for the script? And while Marion was dragging his feet, refusing to act despite the threat to his future, had Paul made a move?

"What would Paul have to gain from stealing a script?" I asked Marion.

"The same thing Ethan wants, I guess," Marion said shakily. "Fame. It *is* a good concept. A really good one, in fact."

"Would Paul have any reason to blackmail or coerce you into taking on the project with him in some capacity?"

Marion's expression darkened. "I haven't slept with Paul."

"That's not what I mean."

Marion reached up and tugged at his hair. "I think John told me, even though he was drunk, because he wants me to seriously consider the script. Projects I want get well funded. They get noticed. I'm not being egotistical. That's the truth. I know that's Ethan's plan, at least—if he can rip that idea out from underneath John's feet—to ride my coattails to the top." He motioned with his hand. "Maybe Paul would do the same."

I stood, took Marion's hand, and hauled him to his feet. I reached into my pocket and handed him my tin of Altoids. "Here."

He smiled a little, almost like that simple gesture was going to undo him. "Thanks." He tapped a few mints out and popped them into his mouth.

"Come with me." I took his hand and led him out of the dressing room.

"Where are— Rory, where are we going now?"

"If Paul's overheard our conversation, he's going to pack up and hightail it out of here." I led the way through staging and toward the far corner where crew kept their belongings in assigned lockers. "I need some kind of tangible evidence that proves Paul stole the script, if not the script itself among his belongings."

"He wouldn't be stupid enough to keep it *here*, would he?" Marion asked, now willingly following instead of trying to pull away. His hand changed grip, moved to thread his fingers between mine.

"Sometimes hiding a hot item in plain sight is the smartest thing to do," I murmured as we passed the art department and kept walking.

Marion came to a halt outside the lockers. He was frowning deeply. "How would the evidence be viable if you obtained it without permission?"

"These aren't secured," I said, glancing at Marion briefly. "The lockers don't belong to any one individual. And John gave me all the permission I need." I popped open the first one and took a peek inside.

"I don't know which one is Paul's," Marion said. He crouched to check the lower level. "But he wears a green ski coat."

"That's good," I answered, moving from door to door as quickly as possible.

Marion opened another locker and swore as a pile of loose paperwork spilled out across the floor. He scrambled to collect all the sheets, then audibly gasped.

"What is it?" I bent down beside him.

Marion nodded his chin at the locker. "This is Ethan's. I'd know that stupid leather jacket anywhere. But look at this." He sifted through what were clearly disorganized script pages, before he found the title cover. "*Sunrise*," he read aloud. "By...hold on...Davey Heller?" Marion looked at me. "Why would Ethan have a script written by *Davey*?"

The broken photocopier.

Building construction—tarps and buckets.

A vacant and unlit hallway.

Drywall dust.

"Davey was making copies of his script," I said in a drawn-out, almost thoughtful tone. "But he used the copier in the vacant office space to hide the fact that he was using supplies for personal gain. Ethan saw him carrying this." I took the stack of loose paper from Marion and held it up. "A script. And Davey's acting squirrely. Ethan suspects Davey has somehow found out about John's script and is trying to sneak off with it. He surprises Davey in the empty hall, tries to forcefully take it. Davey fights him, protective of his own intellectual property. There was a struggle, and it escalated."

Marion's mismatched eyes were wide with horror and grief. "But—"

"Ethan had something on his pant leg yesterday morning. I didn't think much of it." I handed Marion back the papers. "But if he'd been crouched behind Davey, a knee on the floor as he wrapped a cord around his neck…" I demonstrated. "His pant leg would pick up what was on the floor."

"And what was that?"

"White dust—*drywall* dust. From the construction. Ethan must have run with the script, but by the time he got to staging, realized *this* script had nothing to do with John. He hid it in his locker, then went to your dressing room while I was with you."

Marion looked down at the crumpled pages, absently smoothing down creases. "Poor Davey… Now what?"

INT. CHAPTER TEN – DAY

Working until lunch break had been…troubling. Marion hadn't wanted to return to set, not after the likely truth of his murderous ex-boyfriend had come to light in the spilled pages of a script never destined for the camera. And I couldn't blame him. I didn't want Marion within a hundred feet of that rat bastard Ethan. I didn't want *anyone* around Ethan.

But I couldn't make my move yet. The minute I phoned Detective Grey, my cover would be blown. I had nothing on Paul but Marion's sureness that the sound recordist had been listening in on private conversations. And only wishy-washy, circumstantial evidence against Ethan, which might be *just* enough for Grey to receive a search warrant for the dust-coated jeans of yesterday. So if I was going to call the police to back me up after having reached the limits of my investigative license, I'd be damned if I'd settle for anything less than Ethan in handcuffs and Paul at John's mercy.

"Rory!"

I came to an abrupt stop outside the big, open door leading to the set. I looked over my shoulder and felt myself relax as Marion rushed across staging. His costume shoes *tap, tap tapped* the entire way. "Go back to lunch," I insisted. "Safety in numbers."

"Says the man wandering around production alone." Marion came to a stop beside me. "What are you doing?"

"I need to scope out the set for more evidence. There's a lot of equipment right in the open."

Marion blinked a few times as he caught on. "But because union guidelines don't allow departments to touch one another's gear…hiding in plain sight."

"Right."

"I'll help."

I quickly put a hand on his chest to stop him. "We can't allow Paul to see us both absent. It's too obvious."

"I rarely stay for the entire meal," he answered.

I moved my hand up and cupped Marion's jaw. "I've been doing this since you were in junior high. Trust me." I kissed his mouth lightly and took a step through the doorway.

I heard Marion let out a held breath and say after me, "Has anyone told you how fine you look for your age?"

A grin crossed my face, but I didn't look back.

I heard his footsteps retreat after a moment, and I was left completely alone on the dimly lit, silent set. I carefully moved around light stands, piles of sandbags, and wrangled cables as I moved deeper into the room. Paul's sound cart was where it had been all week. There were no drawers, merely shelves housing a state-of-the-art mixing board and a few recording devices. The bottom part had a plethora of cases, small leather satchels I'd seen him pull various tools of the trade from—moleskin, Topstick, nail scissors, even a box of unlubricated condoms, the latter being something I'd not yet learned the importance of while on a film set.

But they weren't big enough to stuff a thick stack of paper into.

Another bag of suitable size was empty but for a few pairs of unused headphones.

I stood, rubbed my lightly bristled chin, then turned on my heel. The hard shell equipment boxes were still stacked against the far wall. Stickers of competing companies adorned the outsides, fighting for limited advertising space. They were Paul's. I'd first seen him go into one the day we met when he needed a cable made. I walked forward, unsnapped the top case, and looked inside.

Nothing.

I closed the lid, pushed it aside, and crouched to open a bigger one. There was some kind of mixer-looking gadget safely tucked into the foam specially shaped for the gear. I started to close the box as the convoluted foam fell. I muttered a swear and pushed it back into the top of the lid, then paused to stare at it.

Removable.

I leaned the lid against the wall, carefully took out the equipment, then hoisted out the middle section of foam. Underneath was a stack of white printer paper, held together by a binder clip. I picked it up, angled it toward a nearby security light, and read, *John Anderson*, across the title page.

I let out a quiet *whoosh* of air. All right. I'd have to put this back. Assemble everything just the way I found it, and give my evidence against Paul to John. The producer would have the authority to search—

"Son of a bitch!"

I was hit in the face and went sprawling sideways across the floor, script tossed somewhere in the dark. My tortoiseshell glasses dug into the side of my nose and snapped in two, leaving me at a distinct disadvantage. I slowly raised myself up on one arm and spit blood from my mouth.

"Who the fuck are you?"

I turned my neck with considerable difficulty, to see Ethan holding one of those foldable, high-legged director's seats. The asshole had hit me with a goddamn chair. "Rory Byrne," I answered.

"I don't care what your name is," he said. "I asked who you *were*. A cop?"

"No."

"You're sure as shit not a PA."

"No," I said before spitting again.

"*No,*" he agreed. "Because a PA would never be so stupid as to suck face with Marion Roosevelt out in the open for anyone to see." He walked toward me, holding the collapsed chair like he was ready to beat my ass with it. "Do you have any idea who *I* am, Rory Byrne?"

"I know exactly who you are. A murderer."

That gave Ethan pause. He wasn't expecting that sort of response. Wasn't expecting some nobody to be aware of his crime.

It was enough for me to scramble to my feet and lunge for the script. But the chair came down on my back with a deafening *smash*, and I collapsed. The wind was knocked from my lungs, and I gasped like a fish out of water. I tilted my head where I lay, watched Ethan toss the mangled furniture to the floor and walk to the script.

He bent down, retrieved it, and stared at the title page for a moment. "How did you find this?" Ethan looked down at me.

I winced, managed to swallow a shallow breath of air, and started to get up on my knees, when a suppressed shot rang out from behind me. Ethan screamed as he crumpled to the floor. It happened so quickly, I literally couldn't react accordingly.

Not to my own pain.

Not to the sound of a gun using an illegal silencer.

Or the fact that Ethan had just been shot.

My adrenaline went into overdrive, and I scrambled the rest of the way to my knees.

"Don't move," Paul ordered, his voice too close for comfort.

I froze, hands up in surrender. "Paul," I said, my voice almost steady. "I'm unarmed."

"I know."

I dared a quick look toward Ethan. He was alive, curled in the fetal position, and whimpering. The script had fallen nearby and was soaked in blood. "Can I stand?"

"No," Paul answered without hesitation. "You move, and I swear to God, I'll pull the trigger."

"All right," I said slowly. "But listen, we need to get help for Ethan—"

"*Shut. Up,*" Paul hissed.

I struggled for a plan, but I'd been dealt a dud hand in this round of poker.

We were alone. My phone was in my pocket. Ethan was of no help. Paul was in flight–or-fight mode. And while silencers didn't work like movies portrayed them, no way would folks all the way in the lunch room have heard the *pop.*

All I had on my side was a bluff.

"Paul," I said again, keeping my voice low so as not to startle him.

"*What?*" he snapped. The rubber of his sneakers squeaked against the floor as he moved to the equipment cases and closed the lids.

"I have backup coming."

"I heard you," Paul answered in between the snapping of the locks. "You aren't a cop."

"No, you're right, I'm not." Sweat prickled under my arms. "I'm a private investigator."

"Who'd you call, then?"

"Detective Grey," I lied. "He's a homicide detective with the 105th Precinct. He was here yesterday when I found Davey."

"Let him come," Paul answered. He moved past, gun trained on me with one shaking hand as he bent to retrieve the script. "If Ethan killed Davey, he deserves to rot in a cell."

I watched Paul's blurry shape walk to my right and then disappear from my line of sight as he moved behind me again. "And what do you deserve if you shoot me?"

Paul didn't have an answer to that.

"You can't use John's script as your own. You can't even take the idea now. You've been caught."

"I said shut the hell up," Paul warned again. "*Damn it.* If you'd just kept your fucking nose out of it, Rory—"

"I couldn't do that."

"No, of course not," he spat. "I knew you'd come here to sniff around after I heard you talking with Marion." Paul laughed, full of vitriol. "That overpaid prima-donna actor living off the laurels of us nobodies instead of accepting he's a commodity—"

Paul was interrupted by a sudden scream. There was a *thwack*, a *crack*, and then the unmistakable sound of a pistol sliding across the floor. I jumped to my feet and turned to see Marion's outline in the poor lighting. He was breathing hard, visibly shaking, and holding a graphite boom pole in his hands like a bat. Paul had crumpled to the floor like a ragdoll after a knock to the back of the head.

"He—he was going to *shoot you*," Marion protested.

I nodded in agreement as I reached for the fallen weapon. I got down on one knee beside Paul, put two fingers to his neck, and felt his pulse. "He's alive. Going to have a hell of a headache when he comes around, though." I went to Marion, pried the pole out of his hands, and took him into my arms. "Thanks," I whispered as he wrapped himself tight around me.

EXT. CHAPTER ELEVEN – DAY

I stood outside of Kaufman Astoria Studios with a few dozen other cast and crew members of *The Bowery*, watching the ambulance crews pack up Ethan and Paul into their own buses.

"You sure you want to refuse medical treatment?" Grey asked.

I briefly removed the ice pack from my jaw. "I've still got all my teeth."

"He hit you with a chair."

Like I needed to be reminded.

"Paul will be okay, right?" Marion asked. He'd been all but glued to my side since we'd phoned 911 and effectively shut down another day of production. "I *had* to hit him," he insisted for probably the dozenth time. "He was going to shoot Rory."

Grey held up a hand. "He's going to be fine, Mr. Roosevelt. Had you not acted, Byrne might have ended up with more than simply a bruised jaw."

"You saved Rory's life," John agreed as he turned away from the ambulances. "But why were you even on set, honey?"

"That's a good question," I said while looking down at Marion. "Not that I'm upset, but I'm pretty certain I told you to *go away*."

"I did," Marion answered. "I'd barely reached crafty when Ethan stopped me. He saw you kiss me before going on set."

Grey gave me a you-dog look.

I ignored it.

Marion swallowed, pinched the bridge of his nose, and shook his head. "We've been broken up for six months, but he's so... He still tries to control what I do. Who I see. He said he was going to beat the shit out of you."

"He did a fairly decent job," I remarked.

"Because I was afraid to stop him," Marion murmured, finally looking up. "But he's...he's a *killer*. I couldn't leave you alone with him."

I put an arm around Marion's slender shoulders and gave him a sideways hug.

"And when you went after Mr. Lefkowitz?" Grey pressed.

"Paul was already in there," Marion answered. "Maybe he'd been in there the entire time, or came through the side entrance, I don't know. But I saw the gun—saw Rory with his hands up—so I grabbed the first thing I could find. When I was pretty certain I had a half-second's chance of stopping him..." Marion motioned swinging a bat.

The ambulances turned their sirens on and pulled out of the studio driveway.

Grey motioned John aside to speak semi-privately.

I dropped my arm from Marion's shoulders and pressed the ice pack to my jaw again. "I'm sorry."

He moved to stand in front of me. "For?"

"For my accusations earlier."

Marion squinted a little as the sun peeked out from behind winter clouds. "Did you really believe I'd lied to you? That I could have stolen the script?"

I considered the question for a long while. Cold air puffed around my face as I breathed. "No...but...I'm a rational, work-obsessed person. I follow the rules. *The facts.*"

"And the facts were stacked against me?"

"I felt like I *had* to believe them. Even though I didn't want to." I lowered the ice pack. "I wasn't joking, Marion. I'm no good at the stuff that happens afterward. That's why I have an extensive ex-boyfriends list."

He chewed his lower lip for a moment as he stared at the road. "Maybe you need more rehearsals."

"Come again?"

Marion looked up, and his mouth quirked into that smile I loved so much. "And if we need to go off script to figure it out, that's fine. It doesn't matter."

"I thought movie-making took teamwork."

"Two makes a team." He removed the ice pack from my hand and gently pressed it to my face. "The MET is having a special exhibit on Kuniyoshi and his woodblock art of cats. There's a really great Indian restaurant nearby too. If you're free later."

My jaw was throbbing, but it didn't stop the smile from breaking out across my face.

FADE OUT

STRANGER IN THE HOUSE

BY JOSH LANYON

Miles Tuesday's memories of Montreal are happy ones, but now that he has inherited the mansion at 13 Place Braeside, everything feels different. Was Madame Martel's fatal fall really an accident? And who is stealing her treasures?

One thing has not changed: Miles still wants handsome and sophisticated art dealer Linley Palmer to have a place in his life.

CHAPTER ONE

The gate was locked.

Which was not a surprise. Miles had told himself that if he couldn't get in, it would be fine. He could wait until Monday when Monsieur Thibault was back in his office and could supply the keys. It would be enough just to see the house from the outside.

But of course, when the moment came, when he was gazing through the ornate wrought-iron fence at the red ivy-covered Jacobean stone mansion with its distinctive turquoise-green oxidized copper roof, it was not enough to be stuck gawking on the outside like a tourist.

Because he was not a tourist. Not this time. This was not a visit. The house at 13 Place Braeside in Westmount was his.

He had arrived at his hotel in Montreal only two hours earlier on this rainy Friday evening. He had not even waited to unpack. The shock that had driven him since learning of "Aunt" Capucine's will had made it impossible to relax and wait like a—well, grown-up. Encouraged by dim memories of the first season of *Downton Abbey*, he had assured himself that someone was bound to be there to let him in.

But no. As the grand old house, half-hidden in the surrounding gold and red foliage, faded into the twilight, every single window remained dark.

No one was home.

So Miles did what any red-blooded American male would do. Praying that he would not begin his tenure as a Canadian immigrant by getting busted for trespassing, he scaled the gate.

At twenty-six, he was a little old for climbing over fences, but this one was not that tall, and he was in good shape. He grabbed the top rail, swung himself up, and scrabbled for a foothold in the inner curves of the black curlicues. He found a toehold—barely—and climbed clumsily over the top, then dropped to the damp bricks of the exterior courtyard.

He wiped the wet from the gate on his jeans and gazed around himself. The evening shadows deepened, the natural wood doors of the long garage to his left and the white balustrades lining flower beds to his right blurring, becoming increasingly indistinguishable in the gloom.

Hopefully, he had not just tripped an alarm.

He did not see any security cameras. There had not been any in the old days, but the old days were a *long* time ago. A decade ago. He had been sixteen the last time he had visited the house.

It was so *quiet*.

He closed his eyes and breathed in the scent of a rainy autumn evening. The fragrance of wet stone and woodsmoke and dripping leaves. The more distant city smells. This was how home would smell from now on.

He smiled, but then a feeling of unease crept over him. He opened his eyes.

Quiet was one thing. This was an almost deathly stillness. So weird. The garden and surrounding trees seemed to swallow all sounds of the nearby city. There were houses all around, but the size of the grounds and the dense trees created the illusion of being on a country estate in the middle of nowhere.

Back in the day, one of the boys had always been coming or going—Miles recalled the purr of sport cars zipping in and out through the gates at all hours of day and night. He could hear the ghostly echo of voices: Oliver's deep and measured tones, Linley's lighter, more sarcastic commentary, Capucine's affected but charming Grand Dame accents. Oh, and music. Music had always been playing. Capucine had been a great fan of musicals of the '50s. The grand halls had echoed with the strains of kooky retro tunes like "I Love Paris" and "Que Sera, Sera."

Capucine claimed to have given up her career as a showgirl to marry Gordon Beauleigh, but Miles's mother had told him that the closest Capucine had come to being a showgirl was her unsuccessful audition for *South Pacific* in college.

Miles shook off the memories. This was not the time for looking back. This was a new beginning. This was a chance to have the life he had dreamed of—hell, this was *way* beyond anything he had dreamed of.

He crossed the wide, watery courtyard, passing the benignly smiling stone lions, sooty-colored with the recent rain, and a bronze lamppost, slightly forlorn with its five round white dripping globes—as though a balloon man had recently wandered away. The bricks gave way to squares of black slate. He waded through the sodden, multicolored leaves, went up the narrow, curved steps, past the stone urns overflowing with teary ivy, and stepped under the carved stone archway. The whisper of his rubber-soled Converses sounded like thunderclaps in that profound and watchful hush.

He stopped before the massive double set of carved wood and smoked glass doors. He drew a deep breath, let it slowly out, and pressed the doorbell.

He heard the deep and sonorous chime roll through the house…and fade into silence.

No one came.

Of course not. Because no one was home.

Capucine was dead, and her sons had moved out years before.

He waited, hesitantly rang the bell again—impatient with himself for that hesitation. Who did he think he was disturbing? Anyway, for all he knew, there *were* servants in the house. He couldn't see from here if there were lights in the back of the house. He was just assuming—

But no.

As before, the bell tolled, dwindled, then died.

No one answered.

He sighed.

Okay, he would have to wait until Monday. After all, it wasn't like the house was going anywhere. It was still his, whether he could get inside or not. Every inch of the 43,000 square feet of land the building sat on belonged to him now. Every sliver of artisan-carved wood, every pane of leaded glass, every gritty bit of brick and paver and marble. His. All his. No strings attached.

Five days after finding out, he was still trying to absorb it.

The house alone was worth over nine million dollars. Nine. *Million.* When Miles had first received M. Thibault's letter, he had read that as nine hundred *thousand* dollars—and been thrilled to pieces. A million-dollar inheritance was a dream come true for a high-school art teacher earning just over sixty grand a year.

It was his friend Robin who, over lunch, had pointed out those three extra zeroes. In the space of a grilled-cheese special, Miles had gone from delightedly planning to build a home art studio and invest heavily in his 401K, to planning out the rest of his life.

Frankly, that amount of money was a little frightening. A million dollars was not out of reach with luck and the right investments and a hearty economic wind to fill the sails of his retirement strategy. He had fully planned on having a million dollars in his retirement fund by the time he quit teaching. *Nine* million dollars was beyond his imagination. People had committed murder for less.

But once he got over the shock, once he understood what this inheritance could mean—not just a comfortable retirement in the far distant future, but the ability to pursue his old, abandoned dream of becoming a painter—a *real* painter—

Okay, it was Canadian dollars. But still. No inheritance tax. For the love of God. No death duties. Nothing like that.

Oh, and that nine million was just the house! According to M. Thibault, the contents of the mansion had not yet been appraised. If the inside of 13 Place Braeside looked anything like it had when Miles and his mother used to visit Capucine, it would be stuffed to the rooftop with old furniture and objets d'art.

That was different, though. He was uncomfortable with the idea of taking possession of Capucine's belongings. He had to consider the feelings of Oliver and Linley. Losing the house was enough of a blow. He wouldn't want to deny them anything of sentimental or personal value. What could have happened that Capucine had made such a decision? She had always doted on both boys. Especially Lin.

Miles frowned. He did not want to remember Linley. He could imagine what Linley would think of his plans.

Anyway, that was one of the things to be sorted out. And sorting out was why he had dropped everything to rush to Canada. To Quebec, Montreal... and finally to this old and exclusive enclave of Westmount.

He tipped his head back, studying the carved stone frieze above the massive double carved wood entrance doors. In between the symmetrical triglyphs were metopes featuring a raven, a thorny rose, and an upraised sword. As a kid he'd loved trying to figure out the significance of those emblems.

"Just decor, darling," Capucine had told him.

In her own way, Capucine had been a realist.

Or maybe not. *Seven* bedrooms. Five-point-five bathrooms. A four-car garage. A swimming pool. A wine cellar that wasn't a repurposed coat closet. It was *crazy* that all this was now his.

"You'll want everything put on the market as soon as possible, no doubt," M. Thibault had said during their single phone conversation. Capucine's lawyer had been kind but had quickly tired of Miles's babbling amazement— and anxious concern that there had perhaps been a mistake.

"There is no mistake, Mr. Tuesday. It was the clearly expressed wish of Madame Martel that the house and all its contents go to you, her godson."

Who was he to argue with Capucine's wishes?

"Hold off on listing the house," Miles had said. *"Hold off on appraising the furnishings. I haven't made up my mind yet. I might want to live there."*

He had surprised himself popping out with those words, and he had certainly surprised M. Thibault, but the lawyer had assured him nothing would be done until Miles had a chance to survey the property for himself.

Which…was going to have to wait until Monday.

Miles reluctantly turned from the grand entrance and went down the steps and the slate walkway. As he headed to the gated entrance, he caught motion in one of the windows on the second floor. He glanced upward at the rectangular window behind the narrow, wrought-iron balcony, and for an instance he thought he saw the pale blur of a face looking down at him.

He stopped in surprise.

The face disappeared—if it had ever even been there—the window now filled only with the blank of colorless draperies… Were those drapes *moving*?

He stared, unable to be sure. It was nearly dark by then. The drizzling twilight had skipped over dusk and gone straight to indigo-edged night. The first faint stars, like moth holes in blue velvet, were dotted over the black silhouette of the roof and chimneys. He sucked in a breath at the outline of a figure sitting on the highest rooftop, then relaxed, recognizing the bronze statue—or more correctly, grotesque—of a satyr playing a pan flute.

He expelled a shaky laugh. His nerves were getting the better of him.

He looked back at the window where he'd imagined he saw the face, but it was too dark to see anything now, even if there had been anything to see.

If someone were home, they would have answered the door. If someone were home, it would be a caretaker, and if they weren't answering the door, they were probably on the phone right now summoning the police to deal with a trespasser.

That thought spurred Miles to action. He jogged to the gate, clambered over it, and headed to the main drive. He turned his collar up against the wet October breeze and began the walk back to his hotel.

* * * * *

Montreal in autumn was quite a bit different from Montreal in summer—or even Chatsworth in autumn. Miles had not planned on wind and rain and temperatures in the low fifties. He had not packed properly. In fact, he had barely packed at all.

By the time he reached his hotel he was drenched, chilled through. He was staying at Chateau Versailles on Sherbrooke Street. M. Thibault had suggested Hotel Gault in Old Montreal, but not only did the price per night make Miles feel queasy, it was too far to easily walk to Braeside Place.

A hot shower and a pot of tea delivered by room service sped up the defrosting process, and by nine thirty he was sitting in his comfortably appointed hotel room, thumbing through the tattered address book that had once been his mother's. Sure enough, there was a listing for Capucine.

He thumbed the number into his cell and waited as the phone—someone's phone at least—rang on the other end. He had no idea whether Capucine's phone would already have been disconnected and the number recycled, but it was worth a try. He'd had time on his trek to the hotel to realize that if there was a caretaker at the house on Braeside, he or she might be more likely to pick up the phone than answer the door to a stranger who had jumped the fence.

He listened hopefully as the phone rang a second time.

If he was right, he might get inside the house as early as tomorrow.

"Come on, pick up," he muttered.

To his surprise, someone did. The phone came alive in his hand, and a male voice cautiously inquired, "Hello?"

"Hi," Miles said. "Who am I speaking to?"

"This is Miles Tuesday," the voice clipped. "May I ask who's calling?"

CHAPTER TWO

"Wait. *What?*" Miles said. "*Who* did you say?"

In reply, the phone slammed down.

Miles stared in disbelief at the black screen of his cell phone.

Loud and buzzy dial tone filled his ears.

Had he misunderstood? Had— Hell, no. He had misunderstood nothing. The guy on the other end of the call had identified himself as *him*.

Miles Tuesday, he had said, and the craziest thing of all was he had kind of sounded like Miles. Or at least about the right age and with a similar low, slightly husky voice. No discernable accent, although in fairness, how much accent would he show in two sentences? He hadn't said *eh?* And he hadn't said *allô?* So...

"What the..." Miles murmured and hit Redial.

The phone rang again—and continued to ring.

This time no one answered.

After ten rings, Miles gave up. He stared at the ghostly reflection of himself in the dark flat screen of the TV on the dresser across from the bed. He wasn't dreaming, right? He was awake? He was really here, sitting in a hotel room in Montreal and not sleeping on the plane? This was either the weirdest manifestation of jet lag he'd ever heard of or...

He rose and took a turn around his hotel room, eyeing his still unopened suitcases uneasily.

He should do something. Call someone.

He should call the police.

He tried to imagine explaining what had just happened.

I called my dead godmother's house, and a man answered and identified himself as me.

They would assume he had somehow gotten mixed up—that the guy in Capucine's house had simply repeated what Miles said or something like that. They would think he had reached a wrong number or that someone was pranking him. Or he was pranking them.

Or they would think he was crazy.

Even if they took him seriously, it was going to get awkward quickly if he admitted he did not actually, officially have possession of the house, and he did not want to confess he had climbed over the fence and wandered around the property. Not that he had done anything illegal—he hoped—but he also hadn't done things properly.

The proper way would have been to wait until Monday when he'd have met with the lawyer, and the keys and whatnot had been handed over.

Wait. He could phone M. Thibault.

Except…same problem. In their brief conversation, M. Thibault had not sounded like the kind of lawyer who liked clients who did not follow protocol. Besides which, it was now after ten o'clock. M. Thibault would surely have left his office, and Miles did not have his home number.

It was just the weirdest damn thing.

He returned to the bed and stared at his suitcases.

He could go back to the house.

Hey, that was a great…

He remembered the dark and listening silence of the garden. The steady *drip, drip, drip* of rain on sodden leaves, the wavery lamplight on wet bricks. The damp and chilly breeze whispering down his neck.

Yeeeah... Maybe not. In fact, definitely not.

A wave of tiredness swamped him at the idea of that uphill slog to Braeside and all those quiet, tree-lined, and not well-lit streets.

He had been traveling since nine o'clock that morning, and it was ten o'clock now. Somewhere in the middle of that was a time change that should be working to his advantage, but didn't seem to. He hadn't eaten since leaving LAX, and he would not be getting any dinner now since the hotel did not have a restaurant.

Whatever the hell was going on, he was too tired to figure it out tonight. He'd get a good night's sleep and tackle this problem in the morning when he wasn't fogged with exhaustion and low blood sugar.

He flipped shut the address book, set his phone on the nightstand, and went to bed.

* * * * *

He woke starving.

Timid sunshine peeked through the filmy sheers and tiptoed across the yellow and blue squares of the pseudo-Matisse over the fireplace. It took him a moment to remember where he was—and confusion was followed by a jolt of excitement. *Montreal!* A hasty glance at his phone informed him that it was after ten, and he sat upright.

Ten o'clock? He *never* slept late—proof of how beat he'd been last night.

He remembered exploring the grounds of the Braeside house the evening before and the bizarre phone call to Capucine's old number, but it all seemed distant and dreamlike.

Could he have made a mistake about what the man who answered had actually said?

No. He distinctly remembered asking who he was speaking to. The man on the other end had answered *Miles Tuesday*. There had not been any hesitation either.

What the hell could it mean?

There was probably a perfectly reasonable explanation, but he couldn't think of one off the top of his head.

Anyway, first things first. Breakfast and then maybe he'd return to the house and have another look around. Someone had certainly been there the night before. Maybe in the daylight that someone would be more comfortable opening the door.

If that failed, he could do a little sightseeing. Since he was planning on moving to this city, he should probably start familiarizing himself with it.

He listened to a gust of wind rattle the tall bay windows and shuddered at the memory of rain down the back of his neck. It wouldn't hurt to buy a heavier jacket.

Throwing off the striped sheets and cashmere-soft blankets, he started for the bathroom, but the hotel phone rang. He picked it up.

"Miles Tuesday." He was reminded once again of the phone call the previous night.

A cheerful, vaguely familiar male voice said, "It *is* you."

"Um, yes. Who am I speaking to?"

"Miles, this is Oliver. Capucine's son. I don't know if you remember me. It's been ten years."

Miles was surprised—not least at how glad he was to hear a friendly and familiar voice. "Of course I remember you."

Oliver had been a tall, serious, dark-haired young man with long-lashed hazel eyes and glasses. He had been the "nice" brother. Not that Linley hadn't been nice, but eight years made a big difference when you were in your teens and early twenties. Though Oliver had been the elder brother—or maybe *because* he had been the elder—he had found time for things like showing Miles a litter of kittens, sharing his *Hardy Boys* mystery books collection, and taking Miles for a "test drive" in his new Mazda MX-5.

"Mother's lawyer told me you were here—although he thought you were staying at the Gault. It took me a few phone calls to find you."

"Right. This was closer." Miles abruptly recalled what it was closer to—and that Oliver, despite his cheery tone, might have serious problems with his mother's will. "I'm so sorry about everything." He added, "Your mother, I mean."

Well, that was awkward.

But Oliver said gravely, "Thank you. It was a shock. If she hadn't fallen, she'd have been good for another twenty years, I think." His tone grew brisk. "Anyway, you should have let me know you were coming. What are you doing this morning? Can I take you to brunch?"

"I…well, yes. That would be great."

"See you in thirty minutes."

* * * * *

Brunch was at Olive & Gourmando, a cute and cozy place near Old Montreal, famed for its pastries, which were indeed mouthwatering. The interior was rustic, crimson and wood, with colorful chalk messages scrawled on huge blackboards behind displays of cinnamon buns, turtle bars, Bretons sanded with lemon, and fruit tarts on crowded counters. Jaunty Quebecois music played overhead, and every seat in the house was taken. Conversations ebbed and flowed about them, people changing effortlessly from English to French mid-sentence. Miles gazed about the packed restaurant and thought, *This. This is why I want to live here. I want every day to be an adventure.*

"Old Thibault said you're thinking of moving here," Oliver said around a bite of Cuban panini.

Oliver had changed quite a bit. But then in ten years, he would have. He had been twenty-nine the last time Miles had seen him. He had filled out, and the glasses had given way to contacts. His dark hair was thinning, but attractively so. He now wore a precisely trimmed Vandyke beard that gave him a sharper, more sophisticated look.

Miles hastily chewed his Oeuf Coquette—poached eggs, tomato, chickpeas, fennel, potatoes, homemade Toulouse sausage, avocado, feta, and yogurt all piled onto garlic-rubbed flatbread—swallowed, and said, "I've loved Montreal since the first time Mom and I visited. It was like...Paris-lite. Beautiful and historical and cultured, but...accessible."

Oliver grinned. "You mean people speak English."

"Yes." Miles grinned too. "That helps."

Oliver's smile faded. He said seriously, "I'm sorry you weren't invited to the funeral. It was...overlooked in the shock of things."

"That's all right," Miles said quickly. He knew what Oliver did not want to say. He and Linley probably had not given him a thought in years. It wasn't as though Miles had been in close contact with Capucine. In fairness, *he* had barely given *her* a thought in years.

"And I was sorry to hear about your mother. I liked her very much."

"Thanks." Five years had passed since his mother had died. Miles still missed her. He did not have much extended family, and his father had lost interest in him after his divorce and remarriage.

Oliver looked sympathetic, but said briskly, "You should be able to get a very good price for the house."

That was kind of a relief, because Miles had no idea how to approach the subject which he couldn't help feeling loomed in the background all the time.

"True. Yes. But...I might not sell."

Oliver's brows rose. "No?"

"No. I love Braeside. I always have. It seemed so magical when I was a kid. The stone lions and the lamps in the courtyard. The Japanese mural next to the library. The suits of armor and grotesques. The marble fireplaces and doors with inlaid paintings..." He stopped gabbling at Oliver's wry smile, and sucked in a sharp breath. "But I wanted to tell you that you and Linley can have anything you want. Of course. From the house, I mean. If there's anything—furniture, art, Capucine's personal things—*of course* you can have them."

Oliver looked taken aback. "That's...very generous."

"No. I mean, I'm not sure why the house was left to me. It means more than I can ever— But that doesn't change the fact that I wasn't—am not—family, and I'm not sure why..."

He was not putting it at all well, but his confusion was genuine. He wanted the house, was abjectly grateful for the opportunity it presented, but he was guilty about it too. How could he not be? Maybe it was childish, but he did not want Oliver or Linley to hate him.

Not that Oliver showed any sign of resentment, let alone hatred.

After a moment, Oliver admitted, "Mother said she planned on leaving the house to you. I guess Lin and I both thought she was kidding. But there was no reason she shouldn't have done so. It's not as though the house had been in our family forever. My father bought it for her after they were married."

"It was your home. I know—" Well, he didn't know. Couldn't imagine being cut out of his mother's will, not that his mom had had much to leave in the way of worldly goods.

Oliver shrugged. "It was. But we don't live there now. Haven't lived there for years. Mother was generous with us. Plus, Lin inherited a pile from his father. I don't think we can either of us complain." His tone turned wry again. "But since you've offered, I do still have some things there from when I was a kid. School stuff mostly. Books and sports equipment. That kind of thing. Nothing valuable except from a sentimental standpoint. There was never any rush on clearing things out. We all thought she'd live forever."

"Anything," Miles said, relieved that there appeared to be no hard feelings. "Whatever you want."

Oliver gave a short laugh. "You always were too eager to please. But I wouldn't repeat that to Lin, if I were you."

The too-eager-to-please comment smarted a little, though there was probably truth to it. Miles had wanted Oliver and Linley—particularly Linley—to like him. But he kept his expression neutral and said, "No? Why not?"

"You know Lin. Give him an inch, and he'll have a mile-long moving van parked in the front drive."

"Ah." Miles smiled doubtfully. He had never thought of Linley as particularly materialistic, but then ten years ago he had not been much of a judge of character. "How is Lin?"

"Same as always."

"Sure. Right." Miles had no idea what that meant.

The brothers had always seemed more like amicable neighbors than kith and kin. Granted, not having any siblings had given Miles a probably unrealistic idea of what that relationship should be like.

Oliver's smile was quizzical. "You used to be afraid of him, didn't you?"

"*Lin?*" Miles was startled. "No."

Oliver continued to smile.

"Intimidated maybe." The truth was, he'd had a ferocious crush on Linley, which had made him shy and self-conscious. And Lin, sharp-tongued and casually brusque, *had* been more intimidating than Oliver. Even as a teenager there had been something avuncular about Oliver.

Whereas Lin...

Suffice it to say, his instinctive reaction to Linley Palmer had been part of what helped nine-year-old Miles figure out he might be gay.

"Okay," Oliver said, clearly unconvinced.

The lighthearted notes of the music playing in the background caught his attention. It sounded Irish, though the words were in French.

"That's nice. What is it?" Miles asked.

Oliver listened for a moment, made a face. "'*Et l'on n'y peut rien.*'"

"Ah." Miles's French was not up to much.

"It means: *and there's nothing one can do about it.* It's kind of a love song, I guess."

Eager to change the subject, Miles cast around in his brain for a new topic and remembered the strange events of the previous evening. Now that he knew Oliver was okay—or at least had come to terms with the idea of his inheriting Capucine's house, he didn't mind admitting that he'd climbed over the fence to prowl around the courtyard.

He told Oliver the whole story, and when he got to the part about thinking he saw a face in the upstairs window, Oliver started to laugh.

"My God. That had to be Agathe."

"Who?"

"Agathe Dube. She's since your time. She was Mother's housekeeper. In theory. According to the will, she goes with the house, though I believe you have the option of buying her out. Old Thibault will explain everything in exhaustive detail on Monday, I have no doubt."

"Well, but why wouldn't she answer the door, then?"

"She lives in fear of being raped and murdered." Oliver seemed to find this amusing too. "She spends all her free time watching gruesome true-crime shows, so she won't answer the door after the sun goes down."

"That's…"

"I know." Oliver shook his head. "The irony is the only real criminal she's ever met is her son, Erwan. He's been in and out of prison his entire life."

"Is he in or out now?"

"No idea."

"Because that wasn't the only weird thing." Miles told Oliver about phoning the house after his return to his hotel and hearing the stranger on the other end claim to be Miles Tuesday.

Oliver looked taken aback. "You can't have heard right."

"I know it sounds nuts, but that's what happened."

"You must have automatically given your name, and you just don't remember."

"I'm sure I didn't."

He must have sounded sure, because Oliver looked thoughtful.

"And if it did happen that way, why would the guy have hung up on me?" Miles pressed.

"Good question." Oliver frowned, and then his expression cleared. "Why don't we go find out?"

"Go—? What do you mean?"

"Let's get this cleared up now. Let's go to the house and see who's there with Agathe. If it's Erwan—" Oliver looked grim.

Was it possible it could be this easy? "I don't have a key," Miles reminded him. "I don't officially take possession until Monday."

"I have a key. So does Lin, for that matter. Anyway, Agathe will let me in. I can introduce you to her. In fact, you could move out of your hotel and into the house tonight, if you like."

Miles's heart seemed to rise like an air balloon slipping its moorings. "Really? Are you sure? Isn't that liable to violate some legal clause?"

"What legal clause?" Oliver seemed amused. "The house is yours. Lin and I aren't going to contest Mother's will. Even if we wanted to, the will is perfectly valid. Mother was of sound mind. Everything was signed, dated, and witnessed." He shrugged.

It sounded like Oliver and Lin had done some double-checking on that score, and Miles's pleasure faded. But after all, it was reasonable they might have questioned the validity of Capucine's will. No matter how good a sport someone was, they were bound to feel a twinge or two at handing over nine million dollars to a stranger.

"If you're sure it's no trouble," Miles said.

"No trouble at all," Oliver assured him. He winked. "Besides, you've got me curious. I still like a good mystery."

CHAPTER THREE

The sun had at last boldly ventured forth by the time Miles and Oliver arrived at the gate of 13 Place Braeside. The brass tips of the black gate gleamed like spear points in the autumn sunshine.

Oliver hit a button on his key fob, the gate glided smoothly open, and they zipped through to the grand exterior courtyard, parking in front of the natural wood doors of the garage.

"Home sweet home." Oliver turned off the engine of his black Mercedes and smiled at Miles.

Miles smiled back. He felt a little awkward again, remembering that this had previously been Oliver's home sweet home.

They got out, looked around. Sunlight through the trees cast lacy shadows across the warm stone walls and windows. The drying puddles reflected glints of pink and green light as they walked across the bricks to the blue-black paving slabs leading to the massive custom-made double wood doors beyond.

Overhead, drapes were still drawn, no lights shone, no smoke drifted from the chimneys; in daylight the quiet seemed ordinary, expected.

"The roof's still in good shape," Oliver observed. "You're lucky there."

"It all feels lucky to me," Miles said.

Oliver's laugh was brief. "We'll see if you still feel the same at tax time."

They reached the arched entrance. Oliver rang the bell. And, like the evening before, nothing happened.

Oliver rang again, sighed. "That's what I thought. Agathe is almost completely deaf." He took out his keys, hesitated. "Would you like to do the honors?"

"No, go ahead," Miles said quickly.

Oliver inserted his key in the lock, pushed the door open, and stood back for Miles to enter.

Miles gulped. It was like gazing into the past—or a dream. He could see through the vestibule to the foyer with its ten-foot ceiling, Harrogate black-and-cream marble floor, and the white fireplace with its long, ornately carved mantel.

Nothing had changed.

Two Empire style chairs in black and white stripes sat before the fireplace on a red and blue Persian Heriz rug, a round giltwood table with ball and claw feet positioned between. Over the fireplace hung a large gilt-framed painting of red roses in a blue vase. The painting was flanked on either side by ormolu and crystal twin-branch wall appliqués.

No, actually something *had* changed. In the old days a pair of blue and white ginger jars with a phoenix motif had rested on either end of the fireplace mantel. They were gone now.

No doubt many things were gone now—including Capucine.

"Is it like you remember?" Oliver asked.

"It's *exactly* like I remember."

Oliver smiled faintly. "Agathe's quarters are this way. Come on."

Miles followed him down the gleaming hallway, past the graceful, curving Spanish style marble staircase—trying not to stare when he remembered this was where Capucine had fallen to her death—past inlaid doors and ordinary doors, and many, many paintings. Some by famous painters and some by nobodies like Miles.

Capucine had considered herself an art connoisseur. The house was filled with her acquisitions. Linley had held a different view of her "expert eye," but then, as Miles knew firsthand, teenagers were naturally sarcastic smart-asses.

They went through the conservatory with its shining black-and-white check marble floor and delicately arched ceiling to the enormous old-fashioned kitchen, passed the tall frosted glass doors of the pantry and reached the servants' hall, where they could hear a TV blasting from several doors down.

"*Hikers discovered the nude body of a young woman lying on the rocks below the cliff...*" shouted the program announcer.

"Yikes," said Miles.

"Agathe?" called Oliver. "Are you here? You've got company! Agathe?"

The TV volume cut off sharply. A door at the end of the hall creaked opened, and a stout middle-aged woman with tortoiseshell-framed glasses and hennaed hair warily poked her head out.

"Mr. Oliver? Is that you?"

"It's me," Oliver said. "With your new lord and master."

"Don't say that," Miles protested.

Agathe took a cautious step out of her room, peering down the hall at them. She wore a shapeless gray skirt, a white blouse beneath a baggy gray sweater, black low-heeled shoes, and a long rope of pearls. "What's that you say?"

"This is Miles Tuesday," Oliver told her. "Mother left him the house."

Agathe didn't exactly hiss, but she was clearly not overwhelmed with joy at the sight of Miles. She scowled, still peering nearsightedly at them. "From America?"

"That's right. All the way from California. That was Miles here last night. You should have answered the doorbell."

"No one rang last night."

By then they had reached Agathe. Miles took note of her hearing aid. He offered his hand, raising his voice, "It's very nice to meet you, Agathe."

Agathe looked at Miles, looked at Oliver, and finally, reluctantly, shook hands.

"You'll have to get the girls back," she announced. "I'm too old to manage this house on my own. I'm a housekeeper, not a maid."

"Oh. Uh, right." Miles gave Oliver a doubtful look.

"Now, there's no need to go into all that this minute," Oliver said. "Miles is—"

"He can't get rid of me. It's in Madame's will. I can live here as long as I like." Agathe glared at Miles.

"No one's trying to get rid of you."

"What?"

Miles called, "I promise I don't have any plan to get rid of you." He was sort of sorry for her—and sort of alarmed by her.

"Not yet you don't."

Oliver laughed. "You didn't make a very good impression last night, that's for sure."

Agathe looked genuinely baffled. She returned to her point of grievance. "Dusting and vacuuming. Light housework. I don't cook for anyone but Madame. I don't—"

"That's all right. I'm used to cooking and cleaning up after myself," Miles said.

"What?"

He said loudly, "You don't have to worry about—"

"So you think you don't need me!"

This lady was a real character. He couldn't wait to tell Robin about her.

"Okay, Agathe," Oliver intervened. "Settle down. Miles is familiar with the terms of the will."

Well, not really. And he couldn't say that the news he'd be sharing the house with Agathe Dube was great to hear. But one thing at a time.

Miles said, "Not at all. I only mean I'll try not to add to your workload."

Agathe's expression was skeptical.

"Do you have someone staying with you?" Oliver asked.

Agathe's skepticism gave way to instant defensiveness. "Who? Who do I know with time to waste visiting?"

"What about Erwan? Is he around much?"

"No." Behind the thick glasses, her pale eyes were hostile. "Mr. Linley said he wasn't allowed here anymore."

Oliver looked unimpressed. "Miles says he phoned the house last night and a man answered."

"No one phoned this house." The look she threw Miles said plainly that this was all his fault.

"Are you sure you would have heard with the television on?" Oliver asked.

"Of course I'm sure."

"You didn't hear the doorbell."

Miles was starting to wish Oliver would drop it. He knew he was not mistaken about phoning the house, but it was equally clear that this line of questioning was not winning him brownie points with Agathe.

Agathe said sullenly, "There must be something wrong with the doorbell."

Oliver glanced at Miles, and Miles gave a slight shake of his head. *Let it go.*

"All right," Oliver said. "Miles is going to move his things from his hotel and stay here tonight. So don't be alarmed if—"

"*Tonight?*"

"Is there some reason he shouldn't stay here tonight?"

She shook her head reluctantly. Said again to Miles, "I don't cook. You'll have to get your own meals."

"Yes, I understand. I don't expect you to cook for me."

"There's nothing ready. I wasn't expecting you until Monday."

"That's all right. I can fend for myself."

Oliver said in the tone of one fast losing patience, "We're just letting you know what's happening, Agathe. This is Miles's home now. He can come and go as he pleases. The smart thing for you to do is try to make yourself useful."

Miles winced. Oliver had always seemed so tactful, but maybe that had just been in comparison to Linley and Capucine. Or maybe Agathe was enough to aggravate even the most patient person. He was definitely getting that impression.

Agathe looked both angry and frightened. She said haughtily, "That may be, but I'm not on the clock until Monday." She turned and stomped her way down the hall to her room, went inside, and slammed shut the door. From inside her quarters, the volume of the TV instantly rose to wall-shaking levels.

"...*of a woman, and a block of cement. The body was examined by the coroner...*"

Oliver's smile was wry. "So that's Agathe. Don't ask why Mother was so fond of her. It's a mystery to me. Mother always loved to swoop in and rescue people, whether they needed rescuing or not."

Interesting. Did Oliver see Miles as fitting into the needed-rescuing category? That was certainly not how Miles saw himself. Just because he wasn't rich didn't mean he was circling the drain.

"I will say Agathe was devoted to her. Anyway, I believe her when she says she didn't hear the phone or the doorbell. I'm not so sure that Erwan hasn't been lurking around the place, but if he is, that will stop once you're on the premises. He's a sneak and a thief, but he's not dangerous. Shall we go get your things? Or has Agathe scared you off?"

Agathe was definitely a fly in the ointment, but nothing could dim Miles's joy. The house was even more beautiful than he remembered, and this was the first day of the rest of his life.

"Let's go get my stuff," he said.

* * * * *

It took very little time to throw a few scattered items into his mostly still packed suitcases and pay his hotel bill. At Oliver's suggestion they stopped to pick up a few groceries at Metro Westmount, and then they returned to Braeside.

"I feel like I'm taking up your whole day," Miles apologized as they wound back up the tree-lined drive to Braeside.

"Not at all. I'm enjoying myself. It's nice knowing the house is going to someone who'll love it as Mother did. When those front doors opened and I saw your face…" Oliver's smile was wry. "She'd be very happy to know her gift was so well received."

"Well received? She changed my life," Miles said simply.

"Were you so unhappy at home?"

"No, not at all. I was happy enough." Miles considered that. "I mean, I wasn't *dissatisfied*, because it never occurred to me I had other options, but I always felt like there should be more, that it wasn't how I had pictured my life, that maybe I shouldn't have given up so easily."

"Given what up?"

"Just…dreams."

Oliver made a sound of amusement. "I forget how young you are."

Now there was a bucket of cold water. Miles changed the subject.

"How did Capucine's accident happen? Monsieur Thibault only told me she fell down the stairs."

Oliver's smile faded. "That's all we know. She was in perfectly good health. No problems with her heart. She didn't have a stroke. It seems she just lost her balance and fell. Those marble steps…" He shook his head.

Yes, iron railings and fifty marble steps meant a tumble down that staircase was not going to end well for anyone.

"Was it at night? Was anyone around?"

"It was a Friday night. Lin found her. He had planned to stay over. He does—did—occasionally just to keep her company. He had dinner with friends and then arrived at the house after midnight and found her."

"That's awful."

Oliver nodded absently. "Yes. They always fought like hell, but I think he was very fond of her."

That seemed weirdly detached, but Oliver was a restrained sort of guy. He'd always treated his brother and mother with disinterested affection. In fact, it was hard to imagine him getting passionately worked up about anything.

"Agathe didn't hear her fall?"

Oliver snorted in answer.

When they reached the house, Miles once again invited Oliver to take anything he believed had been promised to him or that he simply wanted for sentimental reasons.

Oliver considered, but shrugged off the idea. "I got a lot of my father's things after his death. The rest of this isn't really my style even if I had room in my apartment."

"Maybe a painting? Or one of the statues? A lamp? Or…you used to play piano. Would you like the piano from the conservatory?" Miles asked.

"Next you'll ask if I want a suit of armor."

"Would you—?"

Oliver laughed. "No. I would not. And I don't have room for a piano either. Besides, I quit playing years ago. That was Mother's idea, not mine. Piano lessons for me and clarinet for Lin. I think she wanted us to be able to play accompaniment any time she happened to burst into song."

Miles grinned. That did sound kind of like Capucine.

Oliver said, "According to Lin, most of the artwork isn't worth anything. If there is any good stuff, you could donate it to a museum. The rest should probably be on a junk heap; frankly, I don't know the difference between either."

"You know what you like."

Oliver gave him a quizzical look. "True. And I can't think of anything here I really like enough to cart home."

That was clear enough, though surprising. The house was a treasure trove of beautiful and interesting things. It was hard to believe there was nothing Oliver wanted. But he was very precise in his dress, and his car, though not new, was expensive and immaculate. Maybe he was one of those people who knew exactly what they wanted and didn't clutter their lives with anything extraneous. Maybe growing up with a rich pack rat for a mother had convinced him living simply was the way to go.

"If you change your mind…" Miles said.

Oliver thanked him, and then they went to his old room, and Miles helped—which really amounted to watching—Oliver pack the few things that were left. There wasn't much.

"Ha. Look familiar?" Oliver held up a copy of *The Tower Treasure*.

Miles grinned. "Yes. You had different versions from my copies at home."

"Yes, so you kept saying." Oliver considered. "These are first editions. Maybe I'll hang on to them." He stacked the books on his old desk and knocked out another cardboard box.

"You know, Mother had quite a lot of jewelry. I think that goes to you as well, although I'm not sure how…" He changed what he'd started to say. "Thibault will know. I assume most of it will be in Mother's safe-deposit box."

"Oh. Right." Miles said awkwardly, "Would there be something in there that you wanted?"

Oliver looked surprised and then thoughtful. "I don't know. I hadn't thought— I wouldn't mind having a look before you dispose of everything."

"Of course!"

"If you do move here," Oliver began a short time later as he was taping up the cardboard boxes, "would that be on your own? Are you— Do you have a partner, perhaps?"

It was asked cautiously, which for some reason amused Miles. Oliver didn't want to presume anything, which was tactful, but Miles had recognized his own sexual inclinations early on.

Though they were the same generation, thirteen years made a big difference.

"No. I'm on my own."

"Of course," Oliver said in a bracing, big brother kind of tone. "You don't want to rush into things at your age. Especially now."

Right. Because now he was worth nine million dollars, and conceivably there were people who would want to take advantage of that—and him.

"What about you?" Miles asked. Oliver was not wearing a wedding ring and had not mentioned a wife, but that didn't necessarily mean anything.

"Confirmed bachelor," Oliver said.

In the old days, confirmed bachelor was code for gay, but Miles was pretty sure in Oliver's case it meant middle-aged-heterosexual-used-to-having-his-own-way.

He asked—casually, he hoped, "Is Lin married now?"

Oliver made a disapproving *nnnn* sound. "He and Giles broke up a year or so ago. I think Lin is still bitter."

"Oh, I'm sorry to hear it." Miles didn't remember Giles, whoever that was, but it did confirm his understanding of Lin. Which was to say, he'd always assumed Lin was gay, but no one had ever come right out and said so. Capucine had always seemed to regard her sons as amusing characters in an off-Broadway production that she happened to be financing.

Oliver said easily, "I think Lin finally got tired of making allowances for the artistic temperament. Not that I blame Giles. Lin would be hell to live with."

"Do you see much of him? Lin, I mean."

"No," Oliver said. "He has a house up in Gore now."

"Right," said Miles, who had no idea where Gore was. He did not know much about Canada as a whole. That would have to be remedied. He was also going to have to brush up on his French. He didn't want to be one of those people who always thought of themselves as ex-pats and didn't fully embrace their new homeland.

"He's always been a ski nut, and it's only about an hour's drive to Mont-Tremblant."

Miles told himself he was relieved he wouldn't be running into Linley, but the funny thing was it felt more like disappointment. Surely, after everything, he had outgrown that old crush?

"I feel like all we've done is talk about me," he said. "What is it you do, Oliver?"

"I'm an enterprise architect for BEC Financial."

"Enterprise architect. Is that something to do with IT?"

"It's everything to do with IT," Oliver said cheerfully.

It sounded *really* dull, but Oliver seemed happy about it.

Oliver finished boxing up the last of his books and model planes. He and Miles went into the English-style library with huge bay windows offering panoramic views of Montreal and beyond, walnut floor-to-ceiling bookcases, fireplace, and a neatly concealed wet bar.

"What would you like to drink?" Miles asked. It felt surreal to be standing in this dreamily familiar room with all its paintings and old books, fixing drinks as though he owned the place. Which, apparently, he did, but it did not feel like his house.

He was not sure it would ever feel like his house—but it was still amazing.

"There should still be a bottle of Yukon Jack in the cabinet," Oliver threw over his shoulder. He stood at the bay windows, gazing out at the trees, toward the city and beyond, at the blue haze of the St. Lawrence River.

Miles searched and found the bottle of Yukon Jack pushed to the back. He located a set of crystal tumblers and looked for a shot glass. Memories of afternoons and evenings in this room, Capucine and his mother drinking cocktails and laughing about the "old days," came to him. Funny that those memories were now *his* old days.

"Remember that funny silver shot glass? It was shaped like a hunting horn with a fox head on the end."

"What a memory you have," Oliver said. And then, "It was a pewter jigger. It belonged to my grandfather. It should still be there somewhere."

That casual *it belonged to my grandfather* landed heavily on Miles.

"If it's still here, why don't you take it?" He began to hunt through the barware in earnest, but couldn't see the fox-head jigger anywhere.

"Miles."

Miles glanced up at the unexpected edge in Oliver's voice.

"Stop feeling guilty. Pour us a drink, and we'll toast to your future. I've got a dinner engagement."

Miles abandoned the hunt for the fox-head jigger and hurriedly poured them each a Yukon Jack. Oliver came to join him at the bar. Miles handed one short tumbler to Oliver. They clinked glasses.

"May the best of the past be the worst of the future." Oliver swallowed the liqueur in a single, neat gulp and then hurled the empty glass into the fireplace, where it smashed into a million glittering pieces.

He took the house key off his ring and set it on the polished bar top. Meeting Miles's astonished gaze, Oliver said crisply, "Good luck, Miles. Come see me anytime."

With that, he was gone.

CHAPTER FOUR

When Miles had turned twenty-two, he had done something completely out of character. Something that still made him burn with embarrassment to remember.

It was one year after his mother had passed away. He had just got his teaching degree and had dutifully applied to a bunch of Southland high schools. In fact, he had one firm offer to teach art at Canoga Park. The school was less than half an hour drive from home, the student-to-teacher ratio was better than average, and he liked the staff and administration members he'd met so far.

It was an ideal position in a lot of ways, and he knew that accepting that job offer was the right thing to do. Or at least, the responsible thing to do.

But at twenty-two he had still been young enough, idealistic enough, or maybe just dumb enough to agonize over giving up his dream of doing art for a living. His mother had been a teacher, and he knew firsthand that teaching was not something you did on the side. Teaching was not a job—it was a vocation.

He understood with painful clarity that if he took the job at Canoga Park, he would be relegating his art to hobby status—maybe forever, but certainly for the foreseeable future—and he had not been able to *bear* the idea. At that time, art had been the single most important thing in his life.

His mother had teased that he ate, drank, and slept oil paints, and that was not far from the truth. Art was his passion, and while he enjoyed sharing that passion with students—in fact, he had been more surprised than anyone by his aptitude for teaching—he did not want to spend his life in the classroom. He wanted to spend it *doing.*

So, in desperation, he had done the thing that still made him feel hot and sick at night when he remembered. He had phoned *éclatant,* the trendy Montreal gallery where Linley Palmer was making a name for himself as a hotshot art dealer with an unerring eye for the exceptional. In other words, he had called in a favor from someone who did not owe him any favors. Who barely remembered him.

To his credit, Linley had heard out Miles's largely incoherent plea for help and guidance, and then instructed him to bring three of his best works to Montreal. Maybe Linley had been trying to discourage him by making things so complicated and expensive, but Miles had not been discouraged. He had been elated. He had selected three of his best canvases, packed them carefully, and caught the first flight he could get to Montreal.

It was excruciating to recall the excitement and hope that had accompanied him on that journey. He had been so sure he would receive the validation he desperately craved—that Linley would not only tell him to keep painting and never again consider taking a day job, but that he, Linley himself, would want to represent him.

God.

He had dreamed— Well, honestly, better not to think of any of that. He had been so young and inexperienced and…and *gauche,* to use a French word. To use the word Linley had probably used.

In short—and it should have been unsurprising—things hadn't gone at all as Miles had fantasized.

Linley had been startled to see him—first clue right there—but he had examined each of Miles's paintings with serious, almost stern concentration. He had asked Miles about his work and about his life, and he had let Miles talk himself to a standstill, and then he had told him to take the teaching job.

"I'm sorry, Miles. I don't see the necessary spark," Linley had said in his cool, crisp voice. *"Color, focal point, movement, yes, you're more than*

competent, but there's already enough of that to go around. Too much, really. What I would need to see... Well, I'm looking for that special..." He had made one of his characteristic graceful, restive hand gestures. *"I'm not sure how to phrase it, but when I see it—"*

"Je ne sais quoi," Miles had said woodenly.

Linley had flicked him a glance, their eyes had locked—Linley's eyes were almost shockingly blue in his thin, dark face—and Miles saw Linley absorb exactly what this rejection had meant to him. He saw Linley's instant discomfort, his wish to unsee what Miles's expression had revealed, even a flash of something like dismay.

So that was that.

One part of Miles's dream did come true. Linley had asked him to dinner. He was dining with friends that night, and he'd told Miles he should come along.

Miles, standing in the blasted rubble of his dreams, had thanked Linley for his time and his advice, regretted his inability to join him and his friends for dinner, and walked out of the gallery. He had tossed his three canvases in the first dumpster he passed.

As soon as he arrived home, he had taken the teaching job.

He did not paint for almost an entire year.

But then the old fever sprang back to life. Maybe he didn't have The Necessary Spark, whatever the hell that was, but he still wanted to paint. *Needed* to paint.

So he did. He painted solely for himself, for his own pleasure, for his own satisfaction. He grimaced when friends and students told him he should go pro. He had it on the best authority he should not. He had learned the hard way that *passion* was the most overused word—and sentiment—in art.

If he'd had to continue to earn his daily bread teaching, painting would have remained a hobby forever, passion notwithstanding. But Capucine's bequest had changed all that. He could spend the rest of his life painting. He could organize his own art shows and exhibitions if he wanted.

It was an exhilarating thought.

Maybe a little frightening too.

Be careful what you wish for, right?

He had made difficult choices, charted out his life, and now everything had been turned upside down. Once again, everything was possible. The difference being that this time it wasn't youthful naivete propelling that notion. This time everything *was* possible.

Money really did change everything.

* * * * *

After Oliver left, the house was eerily quiet.

Miles wandered through the rooms, reacquainting himself with old friends like the twin suits of armor guarding the staircase, meeting new acquisitions like the bronze replica of Botero's fat-horse sculpture at the top of the landing.

So. Much. Stuff. Without Oliver's comfortable presence, the house felt more like a museum than a potential home.

But that was on Miles. It was up to him to separate the fondly remembered past from the future he hoped to build here.

Ten years was a long time, and despite Oliver's comment on his memory, many of the rooms were quite different—larger or smaller, wider or narrower—than he recalled. He had never been inside most of the bedrooms. Wandering through the master suite Capucine had shared with three husbands definitely felt like trespassing. It was a beautiful room: gorgeous light pouring through bay windows, cathedral ceiling, glossy hardwood floor. But—taking in the blue and silver peignoir draped across the foot of the bed, the little gold-topped bottles and jars on the dressing table—no way could Miles picture himself sleeping in there.

Was it strange that no one had cleared out Capucine's belongings? Maybe not. Maybe it was a matter of legalities. But it certainly was unsettling that everything was laid out as though in wait for her return.

Was it now his responsibility to dispose of her clothes and personal effects? It seemed like a job for loving family members. Or at the very least Agathe Dube.

It reinforced his feeling that Capucine's relationship with her sons had been seriously strained.

For the first time it hit him what a huge endeavor this was—to leave his job, his friends, his home. To leave everything and everyone he knew for...a dream.

A well-financed dream, but still a dream.

Was he really going to live in this giant house all by himself?

Maybe it did make more sense to sell everything and use the money to build his "new" life in familiar surroundings.

As Miles considered that option, his heart sank, so perhaps *that* was his answer. Yes, this move was in some ways a daunting prospect, but it was thrilling too. He didn't want the safe and sensible. His entire life had been safe and sensible. He wanted adventure.

Shouldn't he take into consideration that Capucine had wanted that *for* him?

He had been given the chance of a lifetime. Surely the right thing to do was seize that opportunity with both hands?

From her gold-framed portrait across the room, Capucine smiled enigmatically.

* * * * *

His decision to investigate the grounds that evening was a good one. Not only did he feel refreshed and invigorated walking in the cool evening air, he discovered Oliver had left the main gate unlocked.

He locked the gate, then strolled around the courtyard and gardens. The autumn air was sweet, the fading light luminous. There was something particularly magical about autumn light, and he began to itch to get out his paints. He could smell woodsmoke and see the lights starting to twinkle to life in the city below. He walked along the brick paths winding through the gardens—flowers fading with the approach of winter—climbed up and down stone steps leading to small private terraces, tested the iron chairs on the colonnaded terrace behind the house.

Yes, the house was too big for one person, but he didn't plan on always being alone. In the summer he would invite Robin and her husband and kids to stay for a few weeks. He would invite other friends to visit. Maybe Canada— Montreal—would be good for his personal life too. Maybe he would settle down with a nice guy and they could raise a bunch of kids. That was one of the unexpected things he'd learned teaching. He did actually like kids. He hoped to be a father one day.

Back home—rather, in California—he had dated a few guys, but it had never really gone anywhere.

One guy—Larry...something—had even told him he was *too* nice. *"You're just a really* nice *guy,"* Larry had said in parting. Which everyone knew was dating code for *You are* way *too* dull *for me.*

Fair enough. Larry had not exactly set off any fire alarms for Miles either.

And really, what was wrong with being a nice guy? With being responsible and playing fair and trying to keep a positive attitude and looking at things from the other person's point of view? What was wrong with being the guy everyone could count on?

Nothing. Except maybe everyone got in the habit of counting on him too much. Of expecting him to always be the one to pick up the extra project or cover a class or sponsor or coach or babysit or guide or volunteer or be there in a pinch.

Not that he minded any of those things, but maybe he'd be a better fit in Canada, where people had a reputation for being nicer.

Did that include Montreal? Montreal seemed a little edgier, a little buzzier than the rest of Canada. Not that he was familiar with the rest of Canada, but so he'd heard.

Well, either way, maybe he would meet the man of his dreams while following this other dream? Capucine had arranged everything else for him; why not this?

* * * * *

"The naked, mutilated body was discovered partially submerged by a troop of Venturer Scouts..."

Miles sighed, slid the cheese omelet from the frying pan onto his plate, grabbed his wine glass, and departed the kitchen and the gruesome soundtrack supplied by Agathe's television.

It had taken him a while to find his way around the multitude of cupboards and cabinets—he did not dare disturb Agathe—but he was pleased with himself for not only managing to cook his first meal in his new house, but having the nerve to brave the wine cellar and select a bottle of Sauvignon Blanc to toast his accomplishment.

He ate dinner alone plenty of nights, so there was no reason dinner on his own at Braeside should feel any different than at home. But…it did. He ate his solitary meal in the library, watching the shadows deepen, the sunset change colors, the lights in the courtyard blink on, and he made a list of things he wanted to do the following day. Buy a warmer coat, for one. Buy more groceries. Or—how about this?—buy some new art supplies.

When a floorboard creaked behind him, he jumped half out of his chair, whirling to see who was behind him.

CHAPTER FIVE

No one was behind him.

No one stood in the doorway. No one hovered in the hallway.

It was an old house, and of course it had *creaks* and *cracks* and all the normal old-house sounds.

He had not recognized until that moment that he was uneasy—and was instantly impatient with himself. For God's sake. Was he twelve or twenty-six? Then he realized that it would soon be dark inside the house and he did not know where the light switches were. He felt a flare of near panic.

Now *that* was ridiculous—he had never been afraid of the dark, not even as a little kid—but somehow his fear didn't feel ridiculous. He rose and began to turn on lamps in the library, then went to look for the switch controlling the lighting in the hall. His suitcases still sat at the bottom of the staircase. He had not decided yet what room he would use in the interim, nor had Oliver offered any suggestions. He moved past them and went up the staircase, reached the open, airy second level, and began switching on lights there as well.

He couldn't keep this up or he'd have one hell of an electric bill, but until he was more comfortable with the house, he preferred to have the lights on.

All the lights on.

Of course, it wasn't just about illuminating the house. It was also a way of checking without admitting he was checking that no one was there.

And, of course, no one was there.

He was being a complete and total doofus.

He went to the head of the staircase, gazed down the deadly curve of gleaming marble steps, and listened intently.

Nothing.

Okay, if he really focused, he could probably pick out the distant stentorian notes of the narrator of another true-crime show and the occasional dismaying word: "*...strangled...tortured...secret...corpse...*"

No wonder Agathe was afraid to open the front door at night.

No wonder if she was afraid to open it at all ever.

Maybe it would be a good idea to figure out where he was sleeping and get settled for the night. Sitting around listening to the floorboards pop was not good for his nerves.

If he was not ready to take over the master suite, then where?

He had spent a fair bit of the day in Oliver's room, but Miles was not comfortable choosing that room. Not after Oliver's flash of whatever it was that had made him smash that crystal glass in the library fireplace.

He began to prowl through the remaining bedrooms and discovered the beds were not made up. Nor did he have any idea where the linens were kept.

In the end he settled for a large bedroom looking out over the trees behind the house. The view was great, but what sold him was the neatly folded stack of laundered sheets on the foot of the bed—and a couple of brand-new art books still lying in their Indigo bag on the window seat. That almost felt like a sign.

Plus, the art books convinced him the room had once been Linley's, and was still occasionally used by him. Maybe it was a little voyeuristic choosing the former bedroom of his boyhood crush, but since Linley would not be using it in the future, what was the harm in sleeping there?

Miles went downstairs, grabbed his suitcases, and carried them up. For some reason, finding Linley's room had given him a little confidence, and he even switched off a couple of lights as he went.

Once he had made up the bed and unpacked the articles he'd need for the night, he gave in to his curiosity and checked the closet. It was empty but for a tuxedo jacket draped haphazardly over a hanger. Who went to so many formal occasions he needed to *own* a tuxedo? It seemed Linley did. A crumpled silk bow tie lay discarded on the floor of the closet.

It was probably his imagination, but he thought he could smell the ghostly hint of aftershave, a cool scent vaguely reminiscent of green tea and eucalyptus, which he traced back to a nearly empty bottle of Proraso in the adjoining bathroom. There was a single red toothbrush in a juice glass and an orange tube of something called Buly 1803. Toothpaste? It smelled like oranges.

You could probably tell a lot about someone from their grooming products. Miles wore Nautica Voyage and brushed his teeth with Crest 3D Whitening. He liked Captain lace-up boots by the Thursday Boot Company, Levi's, art T-shirts, and clothes that didn't matter if you splashed paint on them. He had only worn a tuxedo a couple of times in his life.

And this was starting to feel a little stalkery.

He returned to the bedroom, settled in the undeniably comfortable bed with *Endless Enigma: Eight Centuries of Fantastic Art*, and began to read.

After about five minutes he realized he was reading the same paragraph over and over.

The book was interesting, but he had trouble concentrating—because he was too busy listening.

Listening for *what*?

He had no idea. Once more he tried to focus on the book.

A floorboard squeaked down the hall. His heart jumped into his throat, and Miles jumped from the bed. He threw open the bedroom door—and of course the hall was empty.

Of course it was.

This was truly exasperating because he really was not prone to nerves. He taught high school, for God's sake. What was more nerve-racking than that?

He climbed back into bed, picked up the book again, but his curiosity got the better of him, and he opened the drawer of the bed stand. He found a nearly empty box of very stale Nicorette gum and a black-and-white photo in a silver frame.

The Nicorette hinted at an unsuspected vulnerability in the always impervious-seeming Linley. Even he was not immune to addiction to nicotine.

The framed photo was of Linley—older than the last time he'd seen him, but Miles would recognize his lean, intense features anywhere—and a good-humored-looking man with shaggy blond hair and a broad toothy grin.

Perhaps this was Giles, the ex with the artistic temperament. He didn't look prone to temperament or like the kind of guy Linley Palmer would partner up with, but people's romantic choices were even more puzzling than their grooming-products selections.

Anyway, they looked happy enough in the photo.

But then it was easier to hide in a photograph. It took a painting to show the underlying truth.

And he was once again snooping into things that were not his business.

Miles firmly closed the drawer and determinedly picked up the book.

* * * * *

He dreamed of footsteps in the dark.

The surreptitious whisper of soles drawing steadily closer…

His heart began to pound in dread.

His eyes popped open. He woke, confused and alarmed—a feeling that was becoming all too familiar—to blinding light and noise.

The chandelier—*chandelier?*—over the bed—where the hell *was* he?— was ablaze, and from across the room, a man's startled voice exclaimed, *"Jesus! Who the hell are—"*

Miles was out of the bed in a single bound, blinking at the tall, dark figure in the doorway.

"*Lin?*"

"*Miles?*" Linley sounded as bewildered as Miles felt. He recovered faster, though, saying accusingly, "My God, it *is* you. What are you doing here? I thought you weren't coming until Monday."

"Oliver had a key."

Linley repeated blankly, "Oliver had a key…"

He would be thirty-four now, but he had the kind of bony, elegant looks that didn't change much over time. His hair was black and straight, his eyes were a blue that seemed to pierce you through the heart like a pin through a butterfly. His brows were straight and formidable, but the line of his mouth was sensitive, almost pretty.

When Miles had been a kid, he had thought Linley Palmer was the most handsome, confident, stylish man he'd ever known. Which was especially funny, given that when they'd first met, Linley had been a teenager, not a man, and had presumably suffered from all the insecurities and uncertainties inherent in puberty. Not to mention acne.

In fact, he *wasn't* classically good-looking. His features were too sharp, too fierce for handsomeness. He did have something, though. Even in the middle of the night, looking weary and rumpled in jeans and a gray fisherman's sweater, he had a certain polish. No, *savoir faire*. That was the word.

He had always seemed more French than Oliver, although both were Anglos. Only Capucine's final and briefest marriage had been to a French-Canadian.

"What are *you* doing here?" Miles shot back, because he wasn't a kid anymore and he wasn't so easily impressed, savoir faire or no savoir faire.

To his surprise, Linley pushed his hair off his forehead and laughed. "I'm sorry. I didn't mean to frighten you. I came to move my stuff out before you took possession of the, er, baronial manor."

Baronial manor. That was vintage Linley. Always a little flippant, a little sarcastic.

"I arrived last night," Miles said.

"*Ah.* I see. If I'd realized you'd already moved in—"

The smile made him look younger, less formidable, much more attractive.

"Not officially," Miles admitted. "Oliver thought it would be all right if I stayed here." He added uncomfortably, "Sorry for taking your bedroom. Most of the other rooms aren't made up. I didn't feel comfortable in your m—in Capucine's room."

Linley considered this, tilting his head, cocking an eyebrow—all at once very French. "Your bedroom now, isn't it?"

"Yes. Well," Miles said. It had been awkward covering this same ground with Oliver, and at least he felt he knew Oliver a little. It was worse with Linley, whom he really did not know at all.

But Linley's thoughts seemed to be running on different lines, because he gave another of those funny, surprisingly charming smiles and said, "I almost didn't recognize you. You've grown up, Miles."

"I should hope." He knew exactly what Linley meant, and it wasn't a compliment. Yeah, he'd changed, all right. He was no longer the gawky, painfully shy, and desperate-for-approval boy he'd been. Thank God.

Linley's thin mouth quirked at Miles's tone as though he too understood the unspoken message. The sudden appraisal in his gaze made Miles self-conscious.

He glanced down at himself. He was wearing red-and-black check boxers and a black T-shirt—not enough of either, given the chilly autumn night. "I wasn't expecting company." He reached for his sweatshirt, dragged it on.

"Don't get dressed on my account," Linley said. "I can take one of the other rooms—if that's okay. I wasn't planning to pack tonight."

Miles picked his jeans up from a chair and stepped into them. He couldn't imagine falling asleep now. "Of course it's okay. You can stay here whenever you like."

Maybe that was too generous. Linley arched an inquiring eyebrow, started to say something, but apparently thought better of it.

Miles said, "Anyway, I'm awake. I'll make coffee. Did you want some?"

"Thank you. That would be great." Linley moved aside, politely waiting for Miles to lead the way.

Definitely a different reunion than his meeting with Oliver. Oliver had shaken hands warmly and pulled Miles into a rough half-hug. He'd said, *"Well, well. So you finally grew into those paws!"*

Miles couldn't imagine trying to hug Linley, nor did Linley show any inclination to bridge the gap.

"I guess Agathe didn't hear the door either," Miles said, heading for the kitchen.

"She wouldn't hear a tank rolling past her bedroom," Linley said. "I'm sure Thibault told me you were arriving Monday."

"That was the original plan. I was able to catch an earlier flight."

"I see."

All the way down the grand staircase, Miles rattled on about his trip, and meeting Oliver for brunch, and Oliver handing over his key.

"The rat never said a word to me," Linley remarked when they reached the kitchen, and Miles finally came to a stop.

Linley waited politely while Miles fumbled around, trying to find the light switch, and then finally reached over and flicked on the overhead copper pendant lights. "Voilà."

So people did actually for real say that.

"Thank you." Every time Miles met Linley's blue gaze, he felt compelled to start talking again. "It wasn't a plan or anything. I thought it would be nice to have a couple of days to see the city. Oliver didn't think I had arrived yet either. He was just trying to verify where I was staying. But then here I was, so he took me out to brunch, and then we drove over to the house."

Linley sorted through that jumble of information and excuses easily. He said, "Of course. Why not?"

"I thought if I stayed here, it would be easier to think things over."

Linley's expressive brows rose. "Think what things over?"

Here was the awkward part.

"Just…whether it made sense to sell or…live here."

After a moment, Linley said, "Ah."

Miles threw him a quick, uncertain look. "Lin, I told Oliver, and it's the same for you; if there's anything you want—any of the furniture, or art, or your mother's belongings—it's yours. Honestly, I'm not sure why she left me the house—"

Lin said coolly, "Presumably because she wanted you to have it."

Miles didn't know what to say to that.

Linley studied him and seemed to relent. "You don't have to feel guilty, Miles. I know Mother thought of your mother as a sister, so I think it makes sense she'd want to know you were looked after."

Over and above her own sons? It still seemed odd.

Miles found the coffee machine, located a bag of Van Houtte, and scooped the ground beans into the basket. He filled the machine with water and switched it on.

"Since you're kind enough to offer, there are some things I'd like." Linley's abrupt voice broke the silence between them. "My father's signet ring. That should be in the will. But there are two or three other small items that Mother always said would be mine, though it turns out no official arrangement was made."

"Name them."

"The red and blue Persian Heriz rug in front of the fireplace in the vestibule." It was thrown out like a challenge.

Miles said, "All right."

"And the two framed oils sketches of Algonquin Park in the dining room. An anniversary gift from my father to my mother."

"Okay."

Linley was watching him curiously. "You should know the sketches were painted by Tom Thomson."

"Nice." Miles knew a bit about Thomson; knew at least that his work was enormously influential on the legendary Group of Seven and that it went for a pretty penny these days. He had looked Thomson up because that was something else Linley had told him that fateful day at *éclatant*: if he was going to riff on other artists' work, he should find someone more contemporary. Or something to that effect. By then, Miles had been numb.

"They're quite valuable."

Miles shrugged. "They're yours. Is there anything else you want?"

Linley continued to regard Miles with that indecipherable expression. "No."

"What?" Miles asked unwillingly, defensive.

Linley shook his head. "Nothing."

Miles thought he knew. "The house is more than enough."

"Perhaps. I don't think most people in your position would think so."

"I doubt you've ever met someone in my position."

Linley gave a curt little laugh. "True. So that's the plan? You'll emigrate to Canada and live in this mausoleum?"

"Maybe."

"By yourself?"

"For now."

Linley nodded thoughtfully. "Well, the house is paid for anyway. What is it you do?"

"I teach," Miles said. "That was the idea, right?"

He hadn't meant it to come out sounding so sharpish. Linley's eyes narrowed as though he didn't quite understand the note of hostility.

"You don't enjoy it?"

"I enjoy it all right. I think I'm a decent teacher. It wasn't my life's dream."

He saw the light go on behind Linley's bright blue gaze. Had the bastard really *forgotten* until now? Did he not understand how devastating their last encounter had been for Miles? What a complete self-centered *asshole*.

"Right. Of course," Linley said. It was the only time Miles had ever heard him sound uncomfortable. "You wanted to be a painter."

"Oh, I *am* a painter," Miles said. "I just couldn't earn a living at it. But now, thanks to Aunt Capucine, I don't have to. I can spend the rest of my life doing art, and that's exactly what I intend."

It seemed he was angrier and more hurt than he'd ever acknowledged, because the words smacked down between them, flat and hard.

"Uh, okay," Lin said politely after a moment. "May it be a long and happy one."

CHAPTER SIX

It was not in Miles's character to hold a grudge.

By the time the coffee was ready, he regretted his outburst. After all, he had asked Linley for his honest opinion. How fair was it to blame him for giving it? And it was all such a *long* time ago.

He turned off the machine, poured two cups of coffee, and asked Linley how he liked his.

"Black. Two sugars." Linley had been studying—in fact, had it been anyone but Linley, Miles would have said *pretending* to study—the cover of the latest issue of *Chatelaine* lying atop the pile of unopened mail on the long wooden table.

Miles doctored the coffee, handed Linley his cup. Linley took a swallow. His eyes widened. He said admiringly, "That is *truly* terrible coffee, Miles."

"I know," Miles admitted.

"Possibly the worst cup of coffee I've ever had."

"Thank you." Miles made a face. "I prefer tea."

Linley laughed. "I'll fix us a pot of tea, shall I?"

"*Please*," Miles said, and Linley laughed again.

He prepared the tea in short order. When he opened the fridge to look for milk, he found the half-empty bottle of wine Miles had had for dinner. His brows shot up.

"Clos la Neore. Good choice."

"Is it expensive?" Miles asked uneasily.

Linley seemed amused. He repeated, "It's a good choice."

He found an unopened box of Petit Beurre biscuits hidden in the rear of the pantry, and they sat down at the farm table. It felt surprisingly companionable.

Miles opened the biscuits and dunked one in his tea.

"How old are you now?" Linley asked.

"Twenty-six."

Linley nodded. Following his own thoughts, he said, "You should sell off the cars first thing. The Daimler would fetch eighty grand or so, at a guess."

Miles managed not to gasp. He'd entirely forgotten about the small fleet of classic cars garaged on the estate.

"You'll want to keep something to drive around in, of course."

"Of course. But I don't need a vintage car to run my errands."

"No. The Austin-Healey would probably suit you."

The Austin-Healey? Miles managed not to choke on his biscuit. He was thinking more along the lines of shipping his own Kia Rio to Montreal, although it would probably cost as much as the car was worth.

Linley was still thinking aloud. "There's a lot of rubbish here, but there are valuable pieces as well. If you were to unload an heirloom or two each month, you could probably stay afloat for a few years."

He was perfectly serious—also, it seemed, a born organizer. Who would have guessed?

"I can take care of myself. You don't have to worry about me," Miles said.

"No," agreed Linley. "And yet, that's the very thing I find myself doing. This is not a small thing you're planning."

Miles snorted. "You never struck me as the type to worry about other people."

Linley's expression changed imperceptibly. "But then you don't actually know me."

His tone was chilly, and Miles realized he had managed to offend him.

"True."

"The occasional summer visit decades ago hardly makes you an expert on me or this family."

Yes, he was definitely pissed off.

Miles said, "You're right. I apologize."

Some of the hauteur faded from Linley's face. He made a sound of exasperation. "And now I feel I'm being unfair. You know, it wasn't my intention to hurt you all those years ago. I didn't—"

When it was clear he wasn't going to continue, Miles said, "It's all right. Your opinion shouldn't have meant so much to me."

Linley opened his mouth, closed it, said at last, "That's true, but I find myself reluctant to admit it." His smile was unexpected and rueful. "I'm sure I could have been kinder."

Miles shrugged.

After a moment, Linley said seemingly at random, "And you don't... There's no... You're really going to make this move all on your own?"

Might as well get this out of the way. "Yes. I don't have a partner or even a boyfriend."

Linley's alert blue gaze rested on him. He nodded slowly. "I see."

As Miles stared into Linley's eyes—it seemed suddenly impossible to look anywhere else—his heart picked up tempo. His face warmed, his body felt flushed.

He had to be misreading that look, right? Because another time, another place...

His thoughts—confusion was probably more accurate—were interrupted by a horrendous scream, followed by a crash from down the hall.

"Jesus *Christ*," Linley exclaimed.

They were both instantly on their feet.

"What *was* that?" Miles demanded, though obviously Linley had no more idea than himself. It sounded as though part of the roof had fallen in.

Linley was already moving toward where the sound emanated from. The dining room? The foyer? Miles followed on shaking legs.

They burst out of the doorway and into the hall. Miles could hear Agathe calling out in fright behind them.

The silence that followed the crash had a terrifying quality.

Linley glanced toward the foyer, started across to the dining room, and did a double take. "Oh, *fuck*." He started back to the front doors—no, not the front doors.

Miles, on Linley's heels, saw what had stopped Linley in his tracks. It took willpower to keep his own feet moving forward.

A man lay sprawled at the foot of the marble staircase. The heavy bronze replica of Botero's fat-horse sculpture lay half on top of him.

How? Where the hell had he come from? Who was he?

Impossible that the sculpture could have fallen over the iron railing.

Which meant...what? Miles was having trouble processing.

Beneath the fallen man's lolling head, a pool of sticky bright red began to spread. Miles's stomach lurched. He couldn't seem to look away as those wet red rivulets seemed to stretch into fingers crawling across the white tiles. He felt a little light-headed.

That was a *lot* of blood.

He wasn't sure he'd ever seen so much blood.

Still swearing with quiet ferocity, Linley dropped on his knees beside the intruder and checked for a pulse. Miles watched, feeling rooted in place. Though Linley mostly blocked his view, he could see that the man was about forty, tall and spindly—or maybe that was the way he had fallen, like a broken stork—with gaunt, sharp-hewn features and a tuft of gingery-gray hair.

"Is he dead?" Miles asked. He was afraid to hear the answer, but Linley didn't reply.

Miles said, "Was he trying to carry that sculpture from the landing?"

Again, Linley did not seem to have an answer.

Though not as large as the original, the replica sculpture probably weighed nearly two hundred pounds. One man trying to hurriedly carry it on his own down those slippery steps was pretty much a suicide mission.

"*Que s'est-il passé?* What has happened? *Quelqu'un me répond?*"

Agathe's frightened shrieks grew louder as she rushed down the hall toward them. She wore a quilted pink and green flowered bathrobe, a full head of curlers, and an expression of utter dread. Linley said urgently, "Miles, don't let her see this."

Miles moved to intercept Agathe, who tried to push past him.

"Erwan? *Mon Dieu! Est-ce lui?*"

It had not occurred to Miles that she was French-Canadian. It also had not occurred to him that this intruder or burglar or whatever he was might not be a stranger.

"Stop. Don't look. It's better if you wait—"

She swung a punch, but years of teaching Southland high school stood Miles in good stead. He blocked her, grabbed her arms, and said, "*Hey.* Don't try that again!"

Agathe unleashed a stream of invective the likes of which he'd never heard, especially out of a dignified middle-aged lady who favored cardigans and pearls.

"Erwan? *Erwan?*"

Miles remembered Oliver saying that Erwan was Agathe's ne'er-do-well son. The ex–con, who Linley had forbidden access to the house. Was this his intruder?

Linley rose. His face was pale. He joined Miles and Agathe, and spoke gravely to her in French. The one word Miles caught was *mort.*

Oh hell.

Agathe let out a blood-curdling scream and put her hands over her face. She began to sob.

Miles met Linley's gaze, and Linley shook his head.

Miles swallowed. That expression was the same in any language.

"We have to call the Emergency Centre," Linley said.

"Yes." God. He didn't even know what that number was. "Was he…? What was he doing?" Now Miles's uncomfortable feeling of not being alone in the house made sense. Someone *had* been there, lurking just out of sight, watching and waiting for him to go to bed.

"It seems pretty obvious." Linley took charge of Agathe with brisk but not unkind efficiency, guiding her back down the hall. They disappeared into the kitchen.

Miles hesitated. He turned to study the dead man, ignoring the queasy dip of his stomach as he took in Dube's gray complexion and sunken cheeks.

The long face of the bronze horse was flattened against the marble floor, indicating the force with which they had landed.

Even if Dube hadn't had that heavy sculpture crash down on his chest, the fall could easily have killed him. It had killed Capucine.

Two deaths on that staircase within the space of a month?

It seemed like a lot.

* * * * *

Constable MacGrath of PDQ12 or *Service de Police Ville de Westmount* appeared to think it was a lot as well.

An ambulance and three police cars—sirens wailing, lights flashing—pulled into the grand courtyard within five minutes of Linley's phoning emergency services. MacGrath seemed to be the officer in charge. He was a short, squat, grizzled black man, his stature and demeanor reminding Miles of a suspicious Scottie dog.

"Two deaths on that staircase, and you here visiting both times, Mr. Palmer," MacGrath said to Linley once the preliminaries were out of the way.

"If you'll recall, I wasn't home when my mother had her accident, Constable. I arrived at the house some hours later." Linley's tone was flat, unemotional.

"I believe you gave a statement to that effect."

Was MacGrath intimating that Capucine's death was *not* an accident? It sure sounded that way to Miles.

Miles said, "We were talking in the kitchen when we heard Dube scream. There's no way Mr. Palmer could have had anything to do with the man's death, if that's what you're suggesting."

Linley shot him a quick, surprised look.

Constable MacGrath's broom-handle mustache seemed to bristle. "Only stating the facts, sir."

"Well, this is another fact. We were together when Dube fell."

"*If* he did fall," MacGrath said.

After that, Miles and Linley were separated and interviewed on their own.

Miles told MacGrath about finding the front gate open after Oliver left and his disquieted feeling all evening that someone was in the house.

"Dube wouldn't need the gate unlocked," MacGrath pointed out. "He's a professional criminal and his mother works here."

"True."

"Granted, your suspicion was probably correct. He probably was here the whole time."

That reminded Miles of his weird experience Friday night—he had almost forgotten about the face in the upstairs window and the phone call where someone in the house had identified themselves as Miles Tuesday.

He told MacGrath all of it. The constable, predictably, took a dim view of Miles's semi-trespassing, but acknowledged that it had probably been Dube in the window and on the phone.

"He'd have to conceal his presence. Mr. Palmer had forbidden him access to the house after the last time."

"After the last time what?" Miles asked.

"After the last time he beat his mother up."

Okay, so not a nice man, Erwan Dube. And MacGrath's theory made sense, although the voice that had answered the phone on Friday had sounded younger than forty.

But then what did forty sound like?

MacGrath said, "I'm guessing Dube was trying to get away with whatever he could before you took possession of the house on Monday. One last score." He gave a humorless laugh. "It ended up that, all right."

"I suppose so," Miles said.

"That statue must be worth a few thousand dollars."

"Yes. I'm sure it is."

"You'll want to go over the inventory list of the house's contents with Mrs. Martel's lawyer. Who knows how long Dube has been helping himself to the family valuables."

"How long has he been out of prison?" Miles asked.

"Just over a month, according to his mother." MacGrath added, "She swears she had no idea he was on the premises."

Well, maybe not. But Agathe had certainly jumped to the right conclusion when she'd heard the crash. She had been screaming for Erwan before she ever saw him lying at the foot of the stairs.

By the end of Miles's interview with Constable MacGrath, it was clear that the police did not really believe Dube's death was anything but an accident or that there was any real connection to Capucine's death. It was equally clear that something about Linley put MacGrath's back up. It wasn't hard to figure what. Linley came across as aloof and slightly supercilious. And he probably was both those things, but there had been a few moments in the kitchen when Miles felt he was seeing the real Linley.

"You know, it wasn't my intention to hurt you all those years ago."

Linley had seemed sincere, and his sincerity had assuaged some of the old hurt. Plus, there had been the way he looked at Miles—as though seeing him for the first time—that had started Miles wondering if maybe...just maybe...

If they *had* been about to have a moment, the moment had passed. When MacGrath finished interviewing them, he regretfully—more sorry not sorry—informed them they would have to find other accommodations for what was left of the night. Though preliminary findings indicated accidental death, the official ruling would not come for a day or two. At that time, the case would be transferred to the Coroner's Office.

Miles wasn't sure what that meant. He only had two weeks of vacation before he had to return home to finish out the school year, and he did not want to waste that time waiting for the house to be cleared as a possible crime scene.

Linley received a curt reminder that 13 Place Braeside was no longer his home—he kept silent, but clearly *that* did not go over well—and Miles got a little lecture on waiting to speak to M. Thibault on Monday.

"Thank you for your help," Miles said to MacGrath before they were ushered out of the house, and Linley threw him a look of disbelief.

"He's just doing his job," Miles told him as they walked across the strobe-lit courtyard.

"Not very well," Linley snapped.

Linley would have been perfect as Lord Whatshisface on *Downton Abbey* or maybe one of those Masterpiece Theatre dramas Larry had been so fond of.

Miles didn't say that, of course, but Linley still directed a narrow glance his way. "Are you *laughing* at me, Miles?" He sounded astonished and slightly offended, which nearly made Miles laugh aloud.

"Sort of."

"I'm glad you find our situation amusing."

"Not the part about having nowhere to go," Miles admitted. Being turfed out of Braeside was disappointing for a number of reasons, not least being he would probably not get another chance to spend so much time with Linley.

Linley digested that and apparently decided not to be offended. He sighed. "I just made the drive from Gore. I don't feel like doing it again. Let's go knock on Oliver's door."

Miles hesitated. "I have a feeling Oliver probably had enough of me for one day."

"*Ce n'est pas possible*," Linley exclaimed, and that time Miles didn't bother to hide his laugh.

Linley's mouth quirked in faint response.

"I think I'll try my hotel," Miles said. "Chateau Versailles on Sherbrooke Street. Technically I still have my room until Monday. I paid for it, anyway."

"I see. All right."

If he hadn't known better, Miles would have sworn that Linley was maybe just a little disappointed.

For the second time in his life—and for the second time with Linley—Miles did something completely out of character.

"We could spend the night together," he suggested.

Linley stopped walking; his expression was guarded. "Together?"

It was tempting to qualify, give himself an out if the answer was no, clarify that he simply meant they could share the room. But Miles did *not* mean that, and he did not want to modify his invitation. He had made it on impulse, but he did want to spend the night with Linley. In fact, the thought of it made his mouth dry with longing and his knees weak.

"Yes," Miles said. "I'd like to."

CHAPTER SEVEN

He really just did *not* learn when it came to Linley.

Linley hesitated for an excruciating moment. "That's a very tempting offer," he said finally, courteously. "But I don't think it would be a very good idea."

Miles's heart plummeted from the highest hopeful peak and crashed all the way down, hitting rocks and cacti as it went until it landed in bits at the bottom of a gully.

What had he expected, after all? A couple of kind words didn't mean Linley was ready to jump in the sack with him.

God.

He summoned a smile and a shrug. "Oh, well. You don't know till you ask."

Linley looked...taken aback. That was the only way to describe it. One moment he was looking all unreadable and distant, and the next he looked almost...*Wait. What?*

Funny in other circumstances. Kind of. Surely, he wasn't expecting to be *begged*? No, it was something else. What?

Did it matter?

No. Not really. The answer was still the same. *Thanks but no thanks.*

Linley recovered, said briskly, "I'll give you a lift."

Probably not, judging by past events.

But Miles said, "That would be great. Thank you."

* * * * *

The drive to Chateau Versailles was very short and very silent.

The adrenaline that had energized Miles ever since waking to Linley's shouts of alarm drained away, and he just wanted the peace and quiet of his hotel room. He wanted to go to bed and forget all about the huge, empty house on Braeside, and Erwan Dube's dead, staring eyes, and getting turned down unequivocally by Linley for the second goddamned time in his life.

At last Linley's Jaguar XJ glided to a stop in front of the hotel's entrance.

Miles reached for the door handle, saying, "Thanks again. I'll let you know what M. Thibault says about getting into the house to grab your things."

Linley said, "You're...a very nice guy, Miles."

Miles groaned. "Oh my *God*. The kiss of death." He laughed.

"I'm sorry?" Linley had that taken-aback look again.

Miles shook his head. He was still laughing—sort of. It *was* kind of funny. One day it would be funny. "Nothing. Good night, Lin."

"Wait," Linley said quickly.

Miles waited.

Linley drew a breath—as though taking a risk?—and said, "Miles, would you like to have dinner tomorrow? Rather, this evening?"

Yes. Oh yes. And no. Hell no.

Miles said, "Um...the thing is, I'm not sure what I'll be doing later..."

"Having dinner at some point. Yes?"

"Yes. But..."

Linley was suddenly smooth, almost teasing, back on solid ground. "You let Oliver buy you lunch. It's only fair to let me buy you dinner."

What did fairness have to do with it?

But despite everything, he did want to have dinner with Linley. It might be one of the last times he saw him, so why not? Besides, if he said no, it would look like his ego couldn't take being turned down.

"Why not," Miles said.

"I'll pick you up at seven."

Miles got out of the car and went up the steps, past the bronze lions— so much smaller and tamer-looking than the Braeside lions—and under the orange awning. Linley waited, Jaguar purring smugly in the frosty night, until Miles pushed through the ornate glass and bronze doors.

Miles heard the Jaguar accelerate away from the curb. He did not look back.

* * * * *

Sunday was a great day, and that wasn't just Miles trying to stay optimistic.

He woke early, enjoyed the hotel's relatively lavish continental breakfast buffet, and, despite the cold and drizzly weather, sauntered out to spend the day sightseeing and shopping.

He bought a new and warmer coat—okay, a parka—on sale at The Bay, and then splurged and purchased a pearl-gray, slim-fit dress shirt for dinner.

He stocked up on paints and brushes at Avenue des Arts in Westmount and then treated himself to obscenely delicious butternut-squash soup for lunch at a tiny little place called Café Bazin.

He returned to his hotel and dropped off his purchases, checked to make sure there were no messages from the police or anyone else—warning himself not to be too disappointed if Linley canceled—and then spent a few hours wandering the cobbled Saint-Paul Street, enjoying a glimpse of the last few *calèches*—horse-drawn carriages—and admiring the beautiful architecture of old buildings and secret alleyways. He passed a multitude of quirky galleries, quaint gift and overstocked souvenir shops, promising himself there would be plenty of time to explore all these and more.

He spent time in a little side park sketching. No question, this city was going to be good for his art. No question, it was going to be less good for his waistline. He sampled bagels, maple-flavored coffee, maple ice cream, and spruce beer.

A couple of times he got lost wandering down side streets, but even that was sort of fun. It was on one of those small side streets that he came across the pawn shop.

An old-school easel in the corner of the crowded front window first caught his attention. The oak tripod was about five feet tall with two pegs to support the canvas. It probably weighed a ton compared to Miles's light and flexible aluminum tripod at home. On the other hand, the wood, polished from years of use and handling, had a kind of beauty his easel did not. It looked very well made. It looked like it had helped produce good art.

Was there a demand for such items? How much did an old wooden easel go for nowadays?

His gaze idly traveled—and then sharpened as he noticed a familiar-looking pair of blue and white porcelain chinoiserie ginger jars.

That was odd. They looked almost exactly like the pair that had once sat atop the fireplace mantel in the foyer at Braeside.

He peered more closely through the dingy glass window.

Like the Braeside jars, these were about fourteen inches tall and featured Chinese phoenixes. Both jars had their lids and appeared to be in good shape.

Of course, there was no shortage of ginger jars, and it was over a decade since he'd seen the Braeside jars. He could easily be mistaken. He probably *was* mistaken. But he couldn't help wondering what had happened to those ginger jars. Had they been sold? Moved to a different part of the house? Or had Erwan Dube perhaps cashed them in?

Miles took a step back to read the unlit neon sign across the front of the small brick shop.

Monsieur Comptant.

What was "comptant"? Cash? Money? Compensation?

Well, it wouldn't hurt to ask about the jars' provenance. Just to satisfy his own curiosity. He went to the front door, only then noticing that the sign hanging in the window read *Fermé.*

That word he did know. CLOSED.

* * * * *

"I don't remember," Linley said when Miles asked him about the ginger jars later that evening.

They were dining at Le Fantôme on William Street in the heart of Griffintown's Montreal Art Centre. It was the kind of place Miles loved. Or would have loved if there was anything like it in Los Angeles.

The restaurant was small and crowded—a single narrow room of white walls, concrete floor, and dark, distressed, none-too-comfortable wooden furniture, softly lit by candlelight. A series of gorgeous collages in swirls of earthy golds, browns, and reds decorated the walls. Despite the piped-in music and volume of voices, the atmosphere was hushed and surprisingly intimate.

Linley had asked permission to order for Miles, which Miles found amusing but sort of charmingly old-world, so they were dining off the very pricy but delectable eight-course tasting menu and drinking some of the best wine Miles had had in his life.

"You don't remember the last time you saw them?"

"No."

"Is it possible Capucine might have sold them?"

"Of course. She wouldn't pawn them, however." Linley's light gaze was curious. "What is it you're thinking? Dube stole the jars and pawned them?"

"It's possible, right?"

"I suppose so. Thibault should give you a list of the house's contents tomorrow." His smile was wry. "Trying to play match-up should keep you busy for the rest of your stay."

Every time Miles looked directly at Linley, their gazes seemed to tangle, and his face warmed.

All the while he had dressed for dinner, Miles had warned himself not to view this meal as anything but a casual and kindly gesture on Linley's part, like Oliver taking him to lunch the day before. But this sensible attitude melted away every time he caught that warm gleam in Linley's eyes.

With anyone else… But Linley was not anyone else, and he had unequiv-ocally turned Miles down the night before.

So…?

Even the way Linley had greeted him at the hotel, kissing him lightly on both cheeks, looking Miles up and down with flattering appreciation and complimenting Miles's new shirt, *"That color suits you. Your eyes are the same shade."*

No, Miles's eyes were not pearl-gray. They were gray-blue. Furthermore, he needed a haircut and new blades for his razor. But he appreciated a compliment as much as the next guy.

Linley wore what appeared to be a black cashmere turtleneck and ass-hugging indigo jeans. He looked suave and cosmopolitan, which of course he was, and Miles would not have been surprised if people wondered what on earth they were doing together.

In fact, every so often their meal was interrupted as someone stopped by their table to speak to Linley, and each time Linley courteously introduced Miles as a very old friend visiting from the States. This was greeted with a variety of wise looks or knowing smiles.

The jaunty notes of a song playing in the background caught Miles's attention. "There's that song again."

"What song?" Linley listened. Smiled. "Oh." He quoted, "'That's the way of love, and there's nothing one can do about it.' Are you a romantic, Miles?"

"I don't know. I do like the song."

"Try this." Linley held out his fork, and Miles, heart beating so hard he thought he'd suffocate, delicately nibbled a bite of…what the hell was it?

"Lobster grilled over charcoal, paired with a crémant d'Alsace," Linley supplied.

Miles chewed, swallowed, said faintly, "Wow."

It was almost orgasmically good.

Linley smiled faintly, reached across, and brushed his thumb against the corner of Miles's mouth. Miles went rigid because there was no way that gesture was anything but— His thoughts flatlined as Linley licked the bit of crémant d'Alsace off his thumb.

Whatever Linley read in Miles's face made him smile. "Enjoying yourself?"

"The condemned man ate a hearty meal," Miles said.

Linley laughed, but said, "I'm not sure I get the joke."

"Can I ask you something?"

"Of course."

"Why did Capucine leave me the house? And please don't say *presumably she wanted you to have it.*"

Linley's expressive brows shot up. "Presumably she did."

"Yes, but why? We weren't that close. I don't feel like I ever really knew her. And"—this one still hurt because it had hurt his mother—"she never came to see Mom once she was diagnosed."

Linley's gaze flickered and fell. He said after a moment, "No. My mother was not good at…reality."

"What's that mean?"

"Just that Alex getting sick and dying did not fit Mother's script. Only happy endings allowed in that production."

Miles had no response. He wasn't even sure he knew what Linley meant.

"Afterward, when it was too late, she felt terrible. That was Mother." Linley's mouth curved, but there wasn't much humor there. "So she decided to play fairy godmother. She always preferred grand gestures to the day-to-day grind."

That was a pretty cold-blooded assessment, although frankly, it confirmed Miles's impression.

"Don't misunderstand," Linley said. "I loved her. She was my mother. But I was never under any illusions regarding her." He added sardonically, "Also, bequeathing the house to you saved her from having to decide what would go to Oliver and what would go to me. I'm not sure if her fear was that we would fall out over divvying up her treasures, or we wouldn't care at all and would simply put the house and all its contents on the market. Either way, I'm sure she viewed it as a salutary lesson for us."

"Are you angry about the house?"

Linley seemed to consider. "At first, perhaps. Oliver more so than me. But the house was hers. It was her right to do as she wished."

"You've both been amazingly gracious about everything."

There was a hint of mockery in Linley's smile. "I didn't plan to be. But there's something about you, Miles—"

"Speak of the devil!"

Miles glanced up and found Oliver and a tall, elegant young woman with long caramel-colored hair standing beside their table.

"Hey," Miles said in greeting and rose.

Linley groaned, but maybe that was in fun because the girl laughed. Linley stood, kissed her on both cheeks, and said, "Can't you do any better than this, Juliette?"

"I could ask Miles the same," Oliver said.

Introductions were made. The girl was Juliette Simard. Oliver introduced her as his girlfriend, and Juliette drew back and gave him a *seriously?* look.

Oliver appeared flustered. "Actually, we just got engaged. We're celebrating."

Juliette held up her bare left hand. "The truth is, I asked him. And he was kind enough to consent. Under duress." She and Linley seemed to find that very funny. Oliver less so.

Miles said, "Congratulations. Join us for a drink."

"Under no circumstances," Linley said.

"In that case, gladly." Oliver pulled out the chair next to Linley for Juliette. He sat down beside Miles.

Linley sighed heavily and raised his hand for the waitress. While he was ordering champagne, Oliver said quietly to Miles, "If you're still agreeable, I *would* like to go through Mother's jewelry."

"Sure. Of course."

They chatted about people and events Miles did not know. Juliette wrinkled her nose. "I saw Giles last week. He's got a show coming up at Galerie NuEdge."

Linley made a disinterested noise and finished his wine. He smiled at Miles.

Miles smiled back automatically.

The champagne came, a toast was made to Oliver and Juliette's future happiness, and the talk moved to the shocking events of the evening before.

"How terrible for you," Juliette said to Miles. "I hope it hasn't put you off us."

"Not at all."

Oliver said, "I always knew Dube would come to a bad end. He's probably been pilfering things from the house since he got out of prison."

That reminded Miles of the chinoiserie ginger jars. He asked Oliver if he remembered the last time he'd seen them.

Oliver admitted he couldn't recall. He said to Linley, "Miles has a mind like a museum curator. I think he remembers every painting, every objet d'art at Braeside. Mother would be thrilled."

Linley smiled, but had seemed distracted since Juliette mentioned Giles.

They finished the champagne, Oliver and Juliette moved to their own table, and Linley asked for and paid the bill.

The silence on the drive back to Chateau Versailles was smoothed over by classical music eddying from the state-of-the-art stereo system.

"I liked Juliette," Miles said finally.

"Juliette is adorable," Linley said. "Oliver better not fuck that up again."

His tone was a little cool, his expression distant. Miles didn't breach the silence again until they reached the hotel.

"Well, thank you for a really terrific evening," he began as Linley pulled up in front of the bellman.

Linley, already starting to climb out of the car, looked startled. "You're not going to ask me up?"

Confused, doubtful, Miles said, "Would I get a different answer than last night?"

Linley smiled, said lightly, "You won't know until you ask."

It seemed a good time for honesty. Miles said, "Yeah, but it does hurt getting turned down. And I'd prefer not to make a fool of myself."

Linley's smile faded. He said gently, "You're not a fool, Miles. I'm not going to turn you down."

CHAPTER EIGHT

When Miles stepped out of the bathroom, Linley was sitting on the foot of the king-size bed, slowly flipping through Miles's sketch pad. He glanced at the quick portrait of an old woman playing a squeeze-box, a child feeding pigeons, soft pencil drawings of fountain details, and a geometric jumble of road signs and lights.

Miles resisted the temptation to snatch it away and say, *Don't look!*

He knew his work was good. Not up to Linley's standards, but so what? He wasn't looking for Linley's approval. Not in that arena. Not in any arena, really. Sure, they had different backgrounds, different life experiences, but they were equals now. Equals in any way that counted.

So he said, "Would you like something from the minibar?"

Linley glanced up, set Miles's sketch pad aside, and came to join him. He studied the contents of the minibar. "I'll have a water, thank you."

Miles took out two bottles of Canada Geese sparkling water.

Maybe it was a strategic error, but he preferred to know exactly where things stood. "Oliver said you recently broke up with your partner."

Linley screwed off the bottle cap. He made an unamused sound. "Oliver should mind his own business."

"I asked him."

Linley's blue eyes flashed to Miles. "Did you?"

"Yes. I asked if you were married or anything. I had a horrible crush on you when I was a kid."

"On *me*?" Linley looked astonished. Then, "Why horrible?"

Miles shrugged. "Crushes are always horrible. Because they're unreturned."

After a moment, Linley said, "You're a very surprising person, Miles."

Miles laughed.

"I'm serious. You have no idea how refreshing it is to—" He seemed to change his mind mid-sentence. "I thought I terrified you. We all did. You used to turn around and go in the opposite direction if you saw me down the hall."

Miles shook his head. He could joke about it now. "I was just shy in your godlike presence."

Linley's eyes widened, he inhaled sparkling water, and began to cough. A lot. It was not a graceful or sophisticated procedure.

"My God, I'm sorry," Miles said, though he was laughing. There was definitely something disarming about seeing Linley shoot sparkling water out his elegant nostrils. "You should put your arms above your head."

Linley, struggling not to drown, shot him a look of outrage and spluttered and choked some more. When he finally had recovered enough to speak, he said hoarsely, "You should come with a warning label."

"Contents may explode under pressure," Miles agreed.

Linley laughed, set the bottle aside, and drew Miles into his arms. His face was still wet, eyelashes dripping, but his mouth was warm and sweet. His lips pressed against Miles's. He was still smiling, and Miles could feel the smile in his heart. He had waited twenty years for that kiss.

When Linley drew back, he said, "It was over with Giles a long time ago. A long time before we actually split up."

"Oh."

"Afterward, I swore I would never do that again—let something obviously wrong drag on and on because I was too busy or too tired to deal with the drama."

"Was there a lot of drama?"

"Yes. There was a lot of drama." Linley's smile was derisive, but meeting Miles's gaze, his expression softened. "The other thing I never want to do again is drag my feet when something is so obviously right."

Miles studied Linley's face. He was talking about sex, of course. Nothing serious. Nothing life-changing. Well, considering that kiss, maybe life-changing. For Miles. But that was all right. He was not a kid. He knew how it worked. He wanted this night too—even if it was only going to be this night.

"I agree," Miles said softly. "Life is too short."

* * * * *

More kisses. Soft kisses, hard kisses. Hungry kisses, cherishing kisses. Warm as sunlight, tender as something newborn. Kissing had never felt so… intimate. So important.

"How did you get this?" Linley dropped a tiny kiss on the small curved scar on Miles's chin.

"I crashed my bike into a cement wall when I was fourteen."

"Ouch," Linley murmured. He dropped another nuzzling kiss on Miles's chin. "Montreal is a very bike-friendly city."

"That's good." Miles had never had anyone spend so much time on the preliminaries of sex. Had never had anyone focus so much attention on him. It made him a little shy. He knew how to have sex. He wasn't sure he knew how to do *this*.

"It's unusual to have such blond hair with so black eyebrows and eye-lashes." Linley grinned. "Do you tint your hair, Miles?"

"*Me?*" Miles shook his head.

Linley's mouth curved, he bumped his nose against Miles's, brushed his eyelashes against Miles's flickering ones. "You taste like peanut butter foie gras."

"I forgot to brush my teeth."

Linley chuckled. "Such an American reaction. I *like* the way you taste, Miles. I want to taste every inch of you."

And he kind of sort of did, while Miles gasped and blinked, gulped and tried to reciprocate in kind.

He was surprised—and maybe this was unfair on his part—to find that Linley was an attentive, even sort of courtly, sexual partner. Miles was not used to receiving so much attention—or having to pay so much attention. Linley offered compliments and asked questions. Not the necessary safety-related questions, but low, husky inquiries.

"Do you like this, Miles?" or "Are you sensitive here?" or "Will you tell me what you want?"

Not that Miles had ever had a *bad* sexual encounter. A few awkward ones, maybe. But he'd never had anyone who tried to charm and seduce him once he was already in bed. It felt sort of decadent. Like peanut butter foie gras sandwiches.

He would definitely have to up his game if this was how sex was played in Montreal.

Linley's naked body was lithe and strong, golden as a California summer. He had the powerful legs and shoulders of a skier—not to mention the taut abdomen and ass—bracing himself on his arms, blue eyes glinting as he gazed down at Miles.

"Since we have all night, who goes first? Hm?"

"*F-first?*" Miles had been thinking—assumed—Linley would probably bang the bell and run, but wrong again. *We have all night.*

Linley laughed softly. "Are you still a little shy, Miles?"

Miles laughed too because no, not really, but Linley was full of surprises, and he was enjoying discovering each and every one.

He reached out, taking hold of Linley's cock, feeling hot blood beating beneath silky skin, and Linley sucked in a sharp breath and threw his head back. "That's lovely. I like that."

Miles liked it too, sliding his palm farther down to cup and caress the twin fragile sacs. Linley made a sound like a purr and pushed into Miles's touch.

"Mmm. What would you like, Miles?"

"You can fuck me," Miles said.

Linley's nose wrinkled. "So romantic!"

"Is there a French word for it?"

"There are words and phrases. Some better, some worse. *Faire des galipettes*. Making somersaults. *Tremper le biscuit*. Dip the bis—"

Miles burst out laughing. "You're totally making this up."

Linley chuckled. "No. So you want to fuck?"

"I want to fuck and be fucked," Miles said.

"Your wish is my command…"

Linley was off the bed in one agile jump. He rifled through his jeans pocket, pulled out a foil-wrapped condom, and tossed it to Miles. "Hold that thought." He stepped into Miles's bathroom and switched on the light. He returned a moment later with a small tube of Crabtree & Evelyn.

"Verbena and Lavender de Provence."

"Lavender? I hope it doesn't put me to sleep," Miles said.

Linley grinned. "I'll try my humble best to keep you awake."

He joined Miles on the bed, and they shoved the comforter and blankets out of the way and settled themselves in the pillows and sheets.

Miles stretched out, shivering, as Linley kissed and sucked his way down his spine, nuzzling the small of Miles's back, his fingers lightly tracing the crevice between Miles's cheeks.

Miles gulped, but that was pleasure, not alarm.

The earthy perfume of lavender, verbena, and precome warmed the air as Linley's finger inserted itself delicately, deliberately into Miles's body. The cream was warm from Linley's fingers and stung ever so slightly.

"You're so quiet," Linley whispered. "Are you all right?"

"Yes, don't stop," Miles whispered in return.

Linley did not stop, and when he had Miles sighing and squirming pleasurably in the sheets, he maneuvered him onto his knees and elbows and guided his cock slowly, sweetly into Miles's body.

"Oh God," Miles breathed. Linley was not extraordinarily large, but the moment was.

Linley paused, courteous and concerned, and Miles pushed back until his ass pressed up against the soft, furry warmth of Linley's groin.

Linley began to move, slow, steady thrusts, the labor of love. Miles shoved into his strokes, and they slipped into an easy rhythm that picked up speed and then grew urgent.

The mattress bounced beneath them. Linley's breath was hot against Miles's ear. He was quiet now, focused, intense... Miles too, concentrating, reaching out for that dancing, elusive light sparking behind his eyes and flickering up and down his spinal cord until at last it ignited.

Release came rolling up out of that deep profound silence, a hot, wet, sticky, joyous eruption.

They collapsed, wet and shaking in each other's arms, like storm-tossed survivors on an uncharted beach.

* * * * *

Sometime later, Linley asked lazily, "How can it be you're making this move on your own?"

Miles kept his eyes shut, savoring the light touch of Linley's hand stroking his hip. "What do you mean?"

"Just... How is it no one snapped you up before now?"

Miles snorted. *Snapped you up* sounded like he was a handful of nuts and pumpkin seeds.

"You don't have a boyfriend or a partner?"

"If I had a boyfriend, we would not be here now."

"Apologies," Linley said. He sounded more satisfied than apologetic. "One likes to be sure."

"Probably one should be sure *before* hopping into bed?"

He must have sounded tart because Linley gave a quiet laugh. "True. But sometimes the little head thinks for the big head."

Fair enough. Who hadn't made that mistake? Hopefully Miles hadn't made it that very night.

No, whatever happened or didn't happen, he was not going to regret this night.

Miles sighed. "I'm the guy whose friends are always saying *I have the perfect match for you*, but it's always a disaster."

Linley made a little *tut-tut* sound. It made Miles smile. "A disaster?"

"Maybe not a disaster, but never the perfect match."

"Are you so hard to please?"

Until that moment Miles had taken it for granted everyone else was the hard-to-please one. It dawned on him that maybe he had been the problem all along. And maybe problem wasn't the right word. Maybe in this part of his life too, he had just been waiting for something else, holding out for something more.

"I wouldn't think so." He said thoughtfully, "Selective?"

"Discerning," Linley offered.

"Persnickety."

Linley gave another of those low chuckles and captured his mouth again.

* * * * *

In the morning they had breakfast at Café Joe on Rue Saint-Antoine, Linley declining the bounty of Chateau Versailles's breakfast spread in preference of the eight-minute drive to one of his favorite eateries.

"I'm afraid I don't do buffets," he informed Miles as they dressed.

"Wow."

"You think I'm a snob."

"Absolutely."

"Is that a problem?"

Was it? Miles considered. He already knew several things about Linley, besides the fact that he was a snob: he was arrogant, he was used to having his own way, he liked to fix things whether they were broken or not. He was also surprisingly tender, occasionally self-effacing, and generally considerate. Also really good at sex. Miles did not see any deal breakers. "Is it a problem I'm not?"

"No. Not at all."

Miles shrugged. "There you have it."

As Linley was heading straight for the gallery after breakfast, Miles grabbed his backpack and sketch pad. His appointment with M. Thibault was not until after lunch, so he planned to spend the day exploring.

Linley observed him, started to speak, seemed to change his mind.

But of course, being someone who liked to fix things, he could not let it rest there, and over the ham and eggs Benedict, Linley said, "I'd like to see your work one day."

Miles chuckled. "No, you wouldn't."

Linley said, "I'm serious."

"So am I," Miles said. "No."

Linley stirred his coffee, frowning.

"When you came to the gallery—before you began teaching—"

"That's all right," Miles said quickly. He did not want to hear about The Necessary Spark again. Did not want his confidence or his joy in his work destroyed, did not want this bright and promising day spoiled by the reminder that Linley could be an asshole.

But Linley forged on. "I was still very new in my position at the gallery. New enough—young enough—that I didn't always trust my instincts. I feared being wrong."

"Mm-hm."

"I had received a lot of attention, and it went to my head. Not in the way you might think. More...I feared discovery. I feared my reputation was built on a few lucky guesses."

"Imposter syndrome," Miles said. He found it hard to believe Linley had an insecure bone in his body.

"I suppose so. So when you showed up—"

"Really, we don't need to go over this. I kind of wish we wouldn't."

Linley was silent.

Miles drank his tea, uncomfortably aware that Linley was studying him. He did not want to argue over this, but why couldn't Linley leave it alone?

After a moment, Linley said with unusual diffidence, "I think in order to clear the way for the future, it would be best to deal with the past."

"Is there going to be a future?" Miles asked cautiously.

"Yes. I hope so." He made a face. "This is probably too fast for you?"

"Well, I mean, I'd definitely like to see where things go." Miles was proud of himself for managing to sound so calm when his heart was hopping and skipping like a tap dancer in one of Capucine's beloved musicals.

Linley nodded gravely. "So. When you showed up with your paintings, I was predisposed to..."

"Not like them."

"No, as I recall, I did like them. But I was inclined to believe they couldn't be anything more than competent, workmanlike. You were the son of my mother's best friend, a shy little boy—"

"I was sixteen the last time we visited Capucine."

"And later a shy teenager who left the room whenever I entered. I'd known you for years and never even knew you painted. It seemed impossible that there would be—"

"The Necessary Spark."

"What?"

"That's what you said my work was missing."

Linley groaned. "Oh my God. What an ass I can be."

It was so heartfelt, Miles laughed.

"I don't remember much about your work. That's the truth. I believe I thought it had promise, but it lacked... It felt young."

Miles shrugged. "I *was* young."

"Yes. Also, it felt to me that you were asking me to make a major decision for you. A decision that might affect the rest of your life. It's not easy to make a living as a painter. In fact, it's damned difficult."

Miles had not considered any of these things.

Linley said, "When I looked into your eyes and saw how much my opinion meant..." He shook his head. "But I also thought, if he's serious, if he has what it takes, he won't give up based on what I tell him. If he does give up..."

Miles had not given up, but it had been close.

But wasn't that really on him?

"There's no crying in art," Miles said.

"Actually, there's a lot of crying in art," Linley admitted.

CHAPTER NINE

"I'll call you," Linley said as they were saying goodbye in front of the Metro stop. "Maybe we can have dinner again?" His smile was confident, but there was something tentative in his eyes.

Miles's heart leaped like a fish on a hook. "Sure!"

"Maybe tonight?"

Miles just managed not to say, *Really?* He didn't want to appear thunderstruck that Linley would ask him out again so soon, but he was surprised and delighted.

More so when Linley leaned in to give him a quick kiss on his mouth.

* * * * *

Only one Thibault of Thibault, Thibault & Thibault remained.

The current M. Thibault was a small, elderly French-Canadian with shrewd black eyes and a mouth that looked permanently pursed in withheld judgment.

He was clearly reserving opinion on Miles as he ran briskly through the details of Capucine Martel's will.

When they came again to the subject of Miles living in the house on Braeside, the lawyer informed Miles he was not an immigration lawyer, and then could not help pointing out a few additional realities.

"Yes, the house itself is paid for, Mr. Tuesday, but there are other expenses to consider. There are property taxes. There is home insurance. There are repair and maintenance bills. A house that old requires a great deal of upkeep. If you plan to keep staff on—and the property is far too large to try to maintain on your own—those salaries will need to be paid. There are utility bills. And you will need to eat."

"I realize that," Miles said. And he did, though it all sounded more daunting when spelled out by M. Thibault.

M. Thibault permitted himself a small, pained smile. "Forgive me, but do you have additional financial resources?"

"No." Unless he counted his 401K, and even then, that $31,000 was not going to last long. It sounded like it would not even cover a single year of property taxes. "I thought I could sell some things," Miles said.

"You can. The most obvious thing to sell is the house," M. Thibault said acerbically. "Were you to sell the residence, you could buy a much more reasonable property and live in comfort for the rest of your days. Alternatively, you could sell the contents within the house and keep the property going for a few years, but eventually you will be forced to put the house on the market anyway."

"I could rent out the carriage house."

M. Thibault looked surprised. "You could, yes."

"There may be other possibilities."

M. Thibault sighed. "There are always possibilities, Mr. Tuesday." He pressed the intercom. "Mr. Wesley, bring me the Martel file, *s'il vous plaît.*"

While they waited, Miles asked M. Thibault if the police had been in touch, and then proceeded to tell him about Erwan Dube's doomed attempt to steal the fat-horse sculpture.

It turned out that, yes, M. Thibault had already been informed by the police of the events on Saturday night. He listened grimly to Miles's version of the incident and then offered the opinion that Erwan Dube's criminal actions should not come as a surprise to anyone.

"I tried to warn Madame Martel. She was very fond of Agathe."

"Is it true that Agathe is allowed to stay in the house permanently?"

M. Thibault started to speak, but the door opened and a slim, blond, twentysomething in a brown herringbone tweed suit entered the room. He deposited a thick folder on Thibault's desk and departed, throwing Miles a curious look before pulling the door quietly shut after him. Capucine Martel's bizarre will was no doubt the talk of Thibault, Thibault & Thibault.

"Would you have any idea in a case like this how soon I might be able to get back into the house?" Miles asked.

"Not before midweek. I will contact the police for you and verify when it's permitted for you to return." M. Thibault thoughtfully flipped the folder. "Hm. Everything appears to be in order."

"Oliver mentioned Capucine had a few pieces of jewelry that might be valuable."

The lawyer looked pained, though whether at Oliver's lack of taste or Miles's was unclear. "Yes. I believe there are one or two very good pieces. Those will be in Madame Martel's safe-deposit box."

"I could probably sell those." Miles added quickly, "Anything that Oliver and Linley don't want, I mean. Linley mentioned there was a signet ring that had belonged to his father."

M. Thibault raised his eyebrows. He said dryly, "Did he indeed? I think you can assume that if Madame Martel had wished to give such a ring to Linley, she would have done so."

That provided a natural opening to the question Miles had been wanting to ask of the one person who was most likely to be completely objective on the matter.

"Monsieur Thibault, do you know why Capucine didn't leave the house to her sons?"

"You needn't concern yourself on that score. Madame was beyond generous with Oliver and Linley. Both were pampered and indulged from the moment of birth. Both received ample provision upon attaining their majority. Additionally, Linley received a sizeable inheritance from his father."

"Oliver's father—?"

"Oliver's father spent much of his fortune purchasing Braeside for Oliver's mother. Nonetheless, to my knowledge, both Oliver and Linley have prospered financially."

That sounded straight out of Dickens, but it was also reassuring.

"I see."

"After the death of your mother, Madame wished to ensure your financial future as she believed your mother would have done had she the means."

He shrugged. Something about the way French people shrugged seemed to convey so much more than a shrug in any other language.

"It's an amazing thing to have done—leaving me the house and her belongings."

"She was an amazing woman."

"Is there a copy of the list of the house's contents?"

"*Mais certainement.*" M. Thibault removed a sheaf of papers from the folder in front of him and slid it across the desk to Miles. "This is not up-to-date. Nothing has been recently appraised. For the sale of any of the better articles, may I suggest Sotheby's or Christie's?"

* * * * *

Miles left the lawyer's office with a very long inventory list, several letters of authorization, and a key to Capucine's safety-deposit box.

At the bank he went through the safety-deposit box and found the usual papers—marriage certificates, insurance papers, real estate deeds—as well as several pieces of jewelry. With the exception of a man's platinum signet ring with a green-blue stone and diamonds, the jewelry was all women's things: rings with blingy, outsize stones, clunky, glittery bracelets, and heavy, showy necklaces.

According to the insurance papers, some of the sparkling pile was costume, some the real thing. He would have to get it appraised to know which was which. But before he bothered with that, he would let Oliver take a look. He suspected Oliver was hoping to find a potential engagement ring for Juliette. And of course, he would give Linley the ring he had requested, regardless of it not showing up in Capucine's will.

He snapped a bunch of photos with his phone, slipped the heavy signet ring on his finger, and returned the safe deposit box to its shelf.

* * * * *

Since it did not sound like he'd be able to return to the house for a few days, Miles decided to return to the pawn shop to find out what he could about the ginger jars.

He was happy to find Monsieur Comptant's open. An elderly woman was showing wristwatches to a much younger woman.

The older woman smiled and greeted Miles in French.

He smiled back. "Just looking."

For a fleeting instant, she looked surprised. "Take your time," she called.

Miles went to the window display. The ginger jars were still there, priced at a staggering $555 for the set.

Were they the same ones? His gut told him yes, but he had no real grounds for thinking so.

The shop proprietress was still busy, so he began to browse the cases of jewelry and silver. In one such case was a small, silver, funnel-shaped object topped with what appeared to be a grinning dog—no, a fox. A midcentury English fox-head cocktail jigger.

The midcentury English fox-head cocktail jigger currently missing from the barware collection at Braeside. He'd bet on it.

He took a photo with his cell phone, and the old woman looked up. She said sharply, "*Pas de photos, s'il vous plaît.*"

"*Excusez-moi,*" Miles said. He put his phone away.

She harrumphed but returned to speaking with the girl.

Miles waited, hovering, until at last the girl purchased a watch and departed. Miles stepped up to the counter.

"I was curious about the jars in the window."

The old woman brightened. "Monsieur has an excellent eye. The jars are vintage 1880s. The phoenix of Chinese legend is a symbol of heaven's favor, virtue and grace, luck and happiness. It is worshipped as one of four sacred creatures presiding over China's destinies."

"Cool. Would these be unique?"

"Unique? No. But at the same time, they do not grow on trees."

"Do you remember where you got this pair?"

She continued to smile, but her dark eyes grew wary. "*Je regrette, je ne me rappelle pas.*"

Miles held his hand above his head. "Tall guy—er, *garçon*—about forty? Reddish-grayish hair?" In his excitement, he was forgetting the little French he knew. Was *garçon* right? Or was that *waiter*?

She stared blankly at him, not bothering to answer.

"What about the pewter jigger with the fox head? Do you know where that came from?"

Her gaze automatically slid in the direction of the case with the jigger. "*Je ne sais pas de quoi vous parlez.*"

Yeah, right. Or as they said in California, *Me no comprende.*

But she comprended, all right. Not that he would get anything more out of her. That was obvious.

His suspicion hardened into certainty. "Well, thank you for your help."

She nodded politely, motionless and staring as he left the shop.

Miles hesitated on the sidewalk outside, then opened the door and ducked back in. The old woman was on the phone, which she promptly hung up when she spotted him.

It was such a guilty, revealing action that Miles couldn't remember why he'd returned—oh, to give her his cell number in case she decided to remember anything. He saw now that was liable to be a bad idea.

The woman glared at him.

"Sorry," Miles said and hastily ducked out of the shop again.

CHAPTER TEN

It turned out M. Thibault was wrong about Miles not being able to get into Braeside, because when Miles checked his phone on the Metro, he had a message from a sergeant at PDQ12 informing him Dube's death had been ruled an accident and the house was cleared as a potential crime scene.

This was unexpected good news. Miles could return to Braeside whenever he liked—and he liked as soon as possible.

He phoned Linley's cell but got his voice message. He left a message saying he was returning to the house, and would Linley like to have dinner there.

He got a reply shortly after.

Linley was regretful. "It looks like I'm going to have to pass on dinner. We have a buyer flying in from Japan."

"Damn," Miles said. "Are you driving back to Gore afterward, then?"

"I was planning to." Linley hesitated. "But if you don't mind my showing up late, I could swing by after dinner and spend the night."

"I'd like that," Miles said.

There was a smile in Linley's voice as he replied, "So would I. Are you always this easy-going, Miles?"

What did that mean? "Is there something *not* to be easy-going about?"

Linley gave a funny laugh. "I'll see you around midnight or so."

"See you then."

* * * * *

After picking up a few additional groceries at the Atwater Market, Miles lugged his suitcases and an ungodly amount of cheese, bread, and chocolate to 13 Place Braeside, letting himself in the tall gates and walking across the wide, leaf-strewn courtyard.

The sunny promise of the morning had faded into a cool, moist afternoon. Behind the long black silhouettes of the trees, the sky looked bleached of all color...the gray-white of old bones and storm-tossed seashores.

When he unlocked the front door it felt...maybe not like coming home, but familiar. He was glad to be back.

"Hello?" he called.

Which was kind of silly since no one was there to hear him.

Or maybe Agathe was there?

He walked past the Spanish staircase, staring at the polished perfection of the marble tiles—no indication that a man had died at the bottom of those steps just two days ago—carrying his bag of groceries to the kitchen. He set the sack on the counter and went to listen at the head of the narrow corridor leading to the servants' quarters.

Silence.

Either Agathe had not yet received word they could come back, or she did not want—was not ready—to return to the house where her son had died.

Miles poured himself a glass of the leftover Clos la Neore. He put the cheese and bread and chocolate away, finding his way around the kitchen, remembering he had not clarified with M. Thibault what arrangements could be made regarding Agathe. There had to be some mutually agreeable arrangement they could come to.

Maybe Linley would have an idea.

When he had finished in the kitchen, he went upstairs—the staircase had to be faced eventually—and unpacked his suitcases in Linley's old room.

In time he settled in the library with its amazing view of the red-gold treetops and the silver-blue city beyond, and began to unfold the list of papers M. Thibault had given him. He slowly read through the pages.

A lot of pages. A *lot* of stuff.

Aynsley oak leaf bone china, antique sterling and enamel silver, embroidered linens, assorted ivory carvings—*uh-oh, what were the laws in Canada regarding ivory?*—Waterford crystal... *Ah, two Tom Thomson paintings...* Yes, Linley had been telling the truth; those were valuable, all right. Chippendale furniture, Persian rugs... Miles's eyes began to glaze.

There was no mention of the fox-head jigger, but maybe that was too small and insignificant an item to make the inventory list. It didn't matter; he knew he wasn't mistaken. He vividly remembered the jigger. Remembered Capucine mixing drinks, shaking back the sparkling bracelets on her tanned arms as she reached for this bottle and that, talking animatedly all the while.

And remembered his mother's easy laughter, her endless tolerance for the theatrics—stagecraft?—that defined Capucine's life, her amused affection for her dearest and oldest friend.

"Not so much of that oldest *business, darling!"* Capucine's ghostly voice reminded him.

Miles smiled faintly, returned to Thibault's inventory list. Blue and White Porcelain Chinoiserie Ginger Jars, Pair. There they were. At the top of the fourth page.

So the jars had been in the house until a few weeks ago.

Not sold by Capucine.

Stolen.

The question was, what to do about it? Was there any chance of recovering them? With Erwan Dube dead, how could he prove the jars at Monsieur Comptant's were the jars from Braeside? How did the laws of stolen property work in Canada? Probably M. Thibault would know.

Preoccupied with his thoughts, he barely registered the distant closing of a door.

When Miles realized what he'd heard, he jumped up, heart pounding, and went to investigate.

The front door was still locked.

He went through to the kitchen and found that door locked too.

There were other doors. French doors leading off bedroom balconies. Side doors opening onto private terraces, small staircases winding down to the garden. There were lots of ways in and out of this house, but as Miles checked them, one by one, they all seemed to be locked securely.

He returned to the kitchen and nearly jumped out of his skin at the sight of Agathe standing motionless—almost spectral—in the corridor leading to the servants' quarters.

"It's you," she said. She looked dreadful. Haggard, white-faced, red-eyed, as though she had aged a hundred years over the weekend.

"Yes. Did I startle you?" No question she had startled him; his heart was still pounding.

She didn't seem to hear the question.

Miles said, "Agathe, I'm sorry about…Erwan."

She glared. "My son was not a thief."

Miles had no answer to that. Erwan had literally been caught red-handed.

"Circumstances are to blame," she insisted, as though he was arguing with her.

"Uh...I'm not a police officer. I don't—"

Weren't circumstances always to blame? For everything? What did that have to do with it?

"Erwan was driven to do the things he did. He had to survive. No one would hire him when they discovered his record."

She was freaking him out. That glazed stare, that furious, trembling voice. He was very sorry for her, and with every word she spoke, he was more determined to buy her out and remove her from Braeside once and for all.

"I'm sorry," Miles said. "I know it must be very difficult."

Her gaze seemed to focus. "You don't know *anything*. You don't belong here. You're not part of this family."

"Okay, well, I'm not going to argue with you about it," Miles said. "You've been through something terrible, and I'm very sorry for your loss. That's all for now."

That's all for now? Was he signing off for the evening?

No, apparently he was dismissing her—those episodes of *Downton Abbey* coming in useful at last—because Agathe turned without a word and vanished down the dark hallway.

The door to her room opened and closed with an eerie softness.

"Ohh-kaaay." Miles resisted the impulse to close the door leading off the kitchen to the servants' quarters and bar it after her.

Had she been here the whole time? Hiding out from the police and the emergency services? He wouldn't be entirely surprised. She needed to be with friends and family, but maybe she didn't have anyone. At the very least, she needed to speak to a grief counselor. For the second time the thought came to him: *maybe Linley will know.*

He needed to watch that. He should not be relying on Linley for everything. In fact, he should not be relying on Linley for anything.

He washed his hands and fixed a light supper of bread and cheese and fruit and wine—a meal that would have seemed sort of frivolous at home, but that somehow seemed exactly right in Montreal—and carried his plate and glass back toward the library.

He was passing the large pen-and-ink Japanese mural in the hall outside the library when something caught his eye. He stopped, scrutinizing the edge of the mural, and saw tiny lacerations in the painting as well as chips in the doorframe next to it.

It looked like someone—not realizing the painting was executed directly onto the wall—had attempted, or at least explored, the possibility of removing the mural.

Surprising to think Miles had stood in that alcove, being interviewed by Constable MacGrath for how many minutes, and never even noticed the gouges at the edge of the mural.

Thank God Dube had stopped before he destroyed it. That had been a close call. But who knew how many other of Braeside's treasures he might have destroyed or disposed of before his fatal overreach?

* * * * *

Miles had his supper watching the sunset from the library. He hoped Linley might call, but he did not. No one called, and the evening stretched endlessly while Miles dutifully finished reading through the list of house inventory.

The good news was there were a lot of things he could sell over the next few months to finance his stay at Braeside. The less good news was he did not really want to become a curator for Capucine's collection. He wanted to paint, he wanted to explore where this thing with Linley might go. Maybe, ironically, the house and all its contents were liable to get in the way of that.

He was still thinking that over when he went upstairs.

He showered, undressed, once again uncomfortably aware of a certain listening unease—how long before he was truly relaxed in this house?—and climbed into bed to read Linley's art books while he waited.

But his lack of sleep from the night before caught up with him, and before long he was asleep.

* * * * *

He dreamed he heard someone scratching at the front door.

Miles climbed slowly out of bed and walked down the hall, across the landing, down the deadly curve of marble stairs, only to discover the noise was coming from the library.

He followed the cutting sounds until he came upon Erwan Dube using a penknife to dig the Japanese mural out of the wall.

"Hey, you can't do that," Miles objected. "You'll destroy it."

In answer, Dube gave a wide, weird grin, snatched the mural from the wall, and rolled it up in a single *snap*, like a piece of wallpaper.

Miles put his hand out to stop Dube, and Dube sliced him across his palm with the now very large butcher's knife. Dube began to laugh.

Miles gasped, staring down at the blood streaming from his hand. He raised his head to look at Dube, and Dube, eyes blazing with a maniacal light, sprang at him.

* * * * *

Miles jerked awake.

For a second or two he lay blinking at the celling, feeling his breathing slow, his heartbeat calm as horror faded in recognition that he had been dreaming.

He gave a shaky laugh and felt for his phone. A bleary glance at the screen told him it was after one.

Good. Linley should be driving in any second, hopefully.

His thoughts froze.

Linley.

The signet ring.

A tourmaline and diamond ring worth—according to the insurance papers—ten grand. Which Miles had left sitting in a spoon rest next to the sink when he'd washed his hands before preparing his dinner that evening.

Shit.

He climbed out of bed—this time for real—and stumbled barefoot into the hall.

A few downstairs lights were on—he had missed them when he'd turned everything off before going up to bed—and the empty, shining halls of the house looked golden in the mellow, muted light.

He headed straight for the kitchen and flipped the overhead light switch on. To his relief, the ring was sitting right where he'd left it. He slipped it on his finger and noticed that the door to the servants' quarters was closed. He tried the handle. Locked.

Was Agathe afraid of him, or was she attempting to send some other message?

Or had the door swung accidentally shut? Maybe it had an automatic lock.

If that was the case, and Agathe discovered the locked door, she would probably flip out.

Still half-asleep and not really processing, Miles unlocked the door to the servants' quarters.

He looked around the kitchen, yawning, absently scratching his head. Should he fix coffee for Linley? Would Linley want something to eat? Did *he* want something to eat?

He was considering this when he heard footsteps, quick and light, approaching the kitchen.

Linley had arrived at last.

Miles turned, smiling. His smile faded.

The man checked on the threshold. He was not Linley. Did not look remotely like Linley.

He did look vaguely familiar: tall, slim, very fair. He was about Miles's age.

"What the hell are you doing here?" the man demanded. He sounded legitimately outraged.

At the exact same moment, Miles said, "Who are you?"

"*Fuck.*"

Miles finally placed him—the dark clothes had thrown him. Last time, he'd been stylishly dressed in a herringbone suit.

He said slowly, wonderingly, "Wait a minute. I know you. You're him. You're Monsieur Thibault's clerk. You're Mr. Wesley."

It was so surreal; he hadn't even had time to feel afraid.

Wesley's face twisted. "Fuck. Fuck. Fuck. You *weren't* supposed to be here." He looked around the kitchen, then looked down at the thing he held in his hand—a black steel utility knife.

His gaze met Miles's. Though his eyes looked sick, his expression was set.

Miles felt a flash of fear. "Don't be ridiculous."

Wesley shook his head and took a step forward. Miles immediately moved to put the large farm table between them. Probably he should have grabbed a knife from one of the drawers—assuming he could find the right drawer—but what was he going to do? Have a knife fight with Mr. Wesley? The whole situation felt impossible, preposterous.

Miles automatically slipped back into teacher-breaking-up-a-fight mode. "Look, you're just making it worse for yourself. Don't compound the error."

Wesley—the expanse of table between them—looked exasperated. "You know you're not going anywhere."

Miles thought maybe he was. If he could get over to the door and unlock it before Wesley reached him, he could probably make it out to the garden and watch for a chance to slip through the gate and go for help.

A utility knife, though potentially lethal, was not the wieldiest of weapons.

"You were here on Friday night," Miles said. "You answered the phone, pretending to be me."

Wesley looked pained. "That should be obvious."

"Were you working with Erwan?"

Wesley made a sound that fell somewhere between snort and hoot. "Working with—? You're insane!"

"*I'm* insane?"

"Work with that cretin?" Wesley seemed indignant at the idea.

"Did you kill him?"

"Of course not. It was completely an accident. The fool was trying to carry the Botero sculpture down the stairs. He looked up, saw me, and slipped. How is that anyone's fault but his own? Greedy bastard." Wesley shrugged in a no-harm-no-foul sort of gesture.

Now or never. Miles started for the door. His plan was to drag the table with him and keep it between them while he got the heavy locks undone, but the table weighed a ton—maybe literally—and did not budge. In fact, he almost lost his balance. Wesley sprang at him, nearly caught him, and Miles just managed to leap back behind the table.

Wesley gave a breathless laugh. "Nice try."

The one good thing was Miles did now have the advantage of being on the opposite side of the table, giving him access to the doorway leading onto the main hall.

Wesley saw it the same moment Miles did and charged around the end of the table, swinging the utility knife like he thought he was in the last act of *West Side Story.*

Miles bounded for the doorway, Wesley right on his heels. He made it through, grabbing and throwing a small decorative table in Wesley's path. He heard Wesley go down, heard the clatter of the utility knife bouncing across marble, and sprinted for the front door.

A few steps from the door, he heard a key being inserted in the lock, saw the door handle turn, saw the door swing silently open.

"*Lin,*" Miles gasped.

Wrong again. It was not Linley standing in the foyer, and Miles skidded to a halt. Wesley, only a few steps behind him, also stopped in his tracks.

Miles stared in astonishment at the diminutive figure in black overcoat and black gloves.

"What in the name of God is going on here?" Monsieur Thibault demanded.

CHAPTER ELEVEN

"He knows everything," Wesley gasped.

Monsieur Thibault looked heavenward. "Yes, *imbécile*, because you've just told him all he did not know." He drew a black snub-nose revolver from his pocket and shook his head regretfully. "Why, Mr. Tuesday, will you never follow instructions?"

Too late all the pieces fell into place. Little things, like M. Thibault trying to convince Miles to stay someplace not within walking distance of Braeside. And bigger things, like the proprietress of Monsieur Comptant's thinking she recognized Miles.

Because yes, while he and Wesley were not twins, they were roughly the same height, same age, same coloring.

Who better than M. Thibault would know which pieces at Braeside would be simple to liquidate: easy to remove, unlikely to be missed, and sure to fetch a good price. M. Thibault would never make the mistake of trying to remove a wall mural, although maybe Wesley might.

And, of course, M. Thibault had tried to prevent Miles from coming back to the house until midweek.

"You've been robbing this house since Capucine died," Miles said.

"Eh bien," M. Thibault said. "After all." He shrugged.

"After all *what*?" Miles demanded.

"There's plenty here. More than enough for you. What did you ever do to deserve nine million dollars? What have any of these rich, spoiled parasites done?"

"What should we do with *him*?" Wesley asked.

"What can we do?" M. Thibault looked apologetic.

"Wait," Miles said. "There's a big difference between stealing and murder."

"Unfortunately, yes."

"So how do we..." Wesley let that trail.

Into that pause came the unmistakable sound of a key biting into a lock. M. Thibault jumped and swung the revolver.

No. He could not let Linley walk into this. Here was as good a chance as he would get. Miles grabbed at M. Thibault's gun hand—and Wesley grabbed for him.

From down the hall behind them echoed an unholy shriek, and Agathe appeared in her flowered pink robe. She came hurtling toward them, screaming at the top of her lungs and swinging a frying pan.

"*Fucking hell,*" Wesley gasped, raising his utility knife.

Everything happened at once. Miles slammed M. Thibault's arm into the opening door, which slammed shut again. Thibault dropped the revolver, which bounced and went off with a deafening and terrifying *bang*. The bullet hit the staircase, ricocheted and shattered the window opposite. Agathe reached them, swinging her frying pan like a tennis racket, and smashed the utility knife out of Wesley's hand. He howled in pain, which cut off abruptly as Agathe swung again, backhanding him in the face with the frying pan.

Wesley went down like falling timber, out cold as he hit the marble tiles. M. Thibault landed on his knees, gasping in pain as Miles wrenched his arm backward. Linley shouted his alarm from outside and gave the door a ferocious shove, knocking M. Thibault flat.

The door burst open. "Jesus Christ, what's happening in here?" Linley demanded.

"Hey, you're home!" Miles panted, and fell into his arms.

* * * * *

"Only ten more days before you have to leave," Linley said. His smile was rueful. "Given the first four, are you sure you're coming back?"

It was Tuesday afternoon, and they were walking along Sherbrooke Street on their way to visit *éclatant*, the gallery where Linley worked. They had spent much of the night and all of the morning giving their statements to the police. Thibault and Wesley were currently in jail on an assortment of charges including theft over $5000, culpable homicide, and attempted homicide.

"Hey, I wanted adventure. Of course I'm coming back. And I'll be flying in as often as I can until I make the final move this summer."

Linley nodded. He did not seem entirely convinced.

Miles said, "Do you believe Thibault's claim that they had nothing to do with your mother's death?"

Linley seemed to weigh it. "Yes. They weren't in the business of murder. They were in the business of robbing the estates of Thibault's deceased clients."

True. And a very nice supplemental income they had earned from it. After the police had departed with Thibault and Wesley in custody, Miles had discovered the two Tom Thomson prints cut from their frames and lying on the dining table.

"They sure seemed willing to expand their business model when they were cornered."

"Yes," Linley said.

"But something's worrying you."

Linley said slowly, "I can't help wondering… Erwan was released from prison only a few days before Mother's fall."

"You think he might have had something to do with it?"

Linley shrugged. "We'll never know. If she came across him creeping around inside the house? If he startled her?"

Miles winced inwardly. "I hope not." If Erwan was responsible, directly or indirectly, for Capucine's death, there was a poetic justice to his own fate.

"So do I."

"One thing for sure, I'll never again even consider trying to get rid of Agathe."

Linley smiled faintly. "She's not so bad when you get to know her. And she makes a really wonderful chocolate soufflé."

"I'll win her over," Miles said.

"I'm sure you will." Linley sighed. "Two months is a long time."

"Not that long. And we do still have ten days."

"Did you want to have lunch before or after we visit *éclatant*?"

They were passing a small gallery. Miles glanced in the window—and did a double take. He stopped walking.

"What's wrong?" Linley asked.

"I just— Can we step inside here?"

"Of course."

Puzzled but patient, Linley followed him into the shop. Miles went straight to the counter at the rear of the gallery and stared up at the large rectangular oil on canvas hanging there. He felt...almost light-headed, like he was moving through a dream.

"*Bonjour*," the woman behind the counter said. She studied him, smiled. "*C'est charmant, n'est-ce pas?*"

He didn't answer her. He was not dreaming. He *knew* those quick, keen brushstrokes—knew the desperate need to get it all out, the emotion, the hunger, the excitement—maybe those strokes were not as sure, as decisive as they could have been—and that ardent, unpredictable rush of color: alizarin crimson, vermilion, cadmium yellows, cobalt yellow, viridian, and ultramarine. A little emotional, Linley would have said. Linley *had* said.

"That's Lake Tahoe," Miles said.

The woman smiled at him. "Is it? I never knew before."

"It's wonderful," Linley said. He rested his hands on Miles's shoulders as though he felt Miles needed support, even if he didn't know why. "Shall I buy it for you?"

The woman said quickly, "Oh! It's not for sale."

"Where did you find it?" Miles asked.

Her face lit up. "You won't believe it. I found it many years ago in a dumpster."

"There were three of them," Miles said.

Her eyes widened. "Oui! There were three. I sold the other two. This one I kept for myself. Sometimes I need to remember why I'm in this business." She hesitated. "Is it possible you are the artist?"

"There should be an MT in the right bottom corner."

He wasn't sure why his throat closed and his voice sounded all choky, but it did. That had been the worst day of his life. But this woman with the wonderful smile had come along after him and found his art, and it had moved her—she had kept it close ever since. And wasn't that the way it was supposed to work?

"There is." She didn't bother to check the painting. She was beaming at him. "And what does the MT stand for?"

"Miles Tuesday."

She offered her hand. "It is an honor to meet you at last, Miles Tuesday. I am Zoe Grenier, and this is my gallery."

* * * * *

Linley raised his glass. "To your first show."

They clinked glasses, and Miles sipped the champagne. The bubbles went up his nose and straight into his heart. He could not remember ever feeling so happy.

He was not even sure where they were. A little café within walking distance of Zoe's gallery. But the sun was shining, music was playing, and there were no more mysteries.

He smiled at Linley, and Linley said softly, "If even some of that smile is for me, I'll be content."

"Oh, a lot of that smile is for you," Miles said. "I think I'm falling in love with you."

Twice he had gone out on very shaky limbs for Linley, so he would not have been surprised if Linley had made a little joke to diffuse the moment.

But Linley said quite seriously, "Good. I think I fell in love with you the night I said you were a nice guy and you said, 'The kiss of death!'" His smile was lopsided.

Miles laughed.

Linley added, "Thank you for giving me another chance."

"Thank you for giving *me* another chance," Miles returned.

Linley wrinkled his brow. "I want to ask, though. I've been wondering ever since you told me you took the teaching job after my appraisal of your paintings. Why didn't you ever get another opinion?"

Miles stared at him. Now there was an obvious question. As he met Linley's smiling blue gaze, the answer suddenly seemed so obvious—and this journey of his, inevitable.

He said softly, "Well, you know. *Et l'on n'y peut rien.*"

THE END

A sincere thank you from all the authors to
Keren Reed and Dianne Thies
for their work on this project.

ABOUT THE AUTHORS

NICOLE KIMBERLING

Nicole Kimberling is a novelist and the senior editor at Blind Eye Books. Her first novel, *Turnskin*, won the Lambda Literary Award. Other works include the Bellingham Mystery Series, set in the Washington town where she resides with her wife of thirty years, and an ongoing cooking column for *Lady Churchill's Rosebud Wristlet*. She is also the creator and writer of "Lauren Proves Magic is Real!" a serial fiction podcast, which explores the day-to-day case files of Special Agent Keith Curry, supernatural food inspector.

http://www.nicolekimberling.com/

MEG PERRY

Meg Perry is the author of the popular *Jamie Brodie Mysteries* series. She lives by the beach in East Central Florida, from where she can easily see rocket launches from Cape Canaveral. After twenty-eight years in the Sunshine State, she feels enough like a native to take #FloridaMan and alligator encounters in stride.

https://megperrybooks.wordpress.com/

S.C. WYNNE

S.C. Wynne has been writing MM romance and mystery since 2013. She's a Lambda Literary Award finalist, and lives in California with her wonderful husband, two quirky kids, and a loony rescue pup named Ditto.

www.scwynne.com

L.B. GREGG

L.B. Gregg loves to run, bike, hike, eat, drink wine, listen to The Front Bottoms, and visit far-flung places. She lives most of the time in New England, and part of the time in Asia. Though readers best know her for *Men of Smithfield* and the *Romano & Albright* series, at home she's simply Nanna Banana, grandma extraordinaire.

www.lbgregg.com

DAL MACLEAN

Dal Maclean comes from Scotland and is a Lambda Literary Award finalist for Gay Mystery. She loves imperfect characters, unreliable narrators, and genuine emotional conflict in fiction. Her background is in journalism, and though she's lived in Asia and worked all over the world, home is now the UK.

www.dalmaclean.com

Z.A. MAXFIELD

These days Z.A. Maxfield is getting her kicks writing on Route 66 in Rancho Cucamonga. She lives with her husband, three of her grown children, and a dog of indeterminable variety named Dr. Watson. Despite the world we live in, she still believes in first love, second chances, and kissing in the rain.

http://www.zamaxfield.com/

C.S. POE

C.S. Poe is a Lambda Literary and EPIC awards finalist author of gay mystery, romance, and paranormal books. She is an avid fan of coffee, reading, and cats. C.S. is a member of the International Thriller Writers organization.

cspoe.com

JOSH LANYON

Josh Lanyon is an Eppie Award winner, a four-time Lambda Literary Award finalist (twice for Gay Mystery), an Edgar nominee, and the first ever recipient of the Goodreads All Time Favorite M/M Author award. She is married and lives in Southern California.

http://www.joshlanyon.com

CPSIA information can be obtained
at www.ICGtesting.com
Printed in the USA
BVHW061350010719
552379BV00021B/1717/P

9 781945 802843